Arianne Richmonde's full-le
Shades of Pearl, Shadows of Pearl, S
Pearl follow the tumultuous and heart-rending love story
between Pearl Robinson and Alexandre Chevalier. All five
books are bestsellers in erotic romance. The first three books
are also available in an e-box set as *The Pearl Trilogy.*

What people are saying about the Pearl Series:

"There is one regret I have about reading this series—that I
waited so long to read it."
—*New York Times bestselling author Nelle L'Amour*

**"Just when I didn't think there would ever been room in
my life for anyone but Christian Grey, along came
Alexandre Chevalier! Christian who?"**
—Cindy at *The Book Enthusiast*

"The best erotic romance series I have read to date."
—*Megan Cain Loera*

**"If you like 50 shades of Grey and the Bared to You
series, you are ABSOLUTELY going to LOVE The
Pearl Series."**
—*Books, Babes and Cheap Cabernet*

"CALL THE FIRE BRIGADE my house is burning down
from Alexandre's sexpertise!!"
—*Island Lovelies Book Club*

"This is a MUST READ!!!!"
—*Sugar and Spice Book Reviews*

"Before I knew it, I was completely entrenched in this story. The descriptions. The emotions. I loved these characters. I hated these characters. I loved these characters again. I didn't know who to trust and who was lying. Between the mystery, the lies, and the hot sex… my head was literally spinning and going to explode."
—*Love N. Books*

"If you haven't read this series yet, put it on your Must Read list!! I look forward to more from Arianne Richmonde!!"
—*Sassy and Sultry Books*

"I loved the older woman/younger man dynamic of this series. The love scenes are passionate and raw. A complete love story from beginning to sweet end and I enjoyed every single word…"
—*Martini Times*

"I couldn't turn the pages fast enough. This book was HOT and sexy. Ms. Richmonde gave the reader a little of everything."
—*Wine Relaxation And My Kindle*

"Alexandre is one of my original Book Boyfriends right up there with Fifty."
—*Mommy's A Book Whore*

"Awesome; full of heart, tears and much laughter. It flows together and feels so real and true I forgot I was actually reading a story. I love these characters. If you want to read something great, get these books."
—*Dawn M. Earley*

The Pearl Trilogy:

Shades of Pearl
Shadows of Pearl
&
Shimmers of Pearl

by

Arianne Richmonde

About the Author

Arianne Richmonde is an American writer and artist who was raised in both the US and Europe. She lives in France with her husband and coterie of animals.

As well as **The Pearl Series** she has written an erotic short story, *Glass*. She is currently working on her next novel, a suspense story.

The Pearl series:

The Pearl Trilogy bundle (the first three books in one e-box set)

Shades of Pearl
Shadows of Pearl
Shimmers of Pearl
Pearl
Belle Pearl

To be advised of upcoming releases, sign up:
ariannerichmonde.com/email-signup

For more information on the author visit her website:

www.ariannerichmonde.com

Acknowledgements

To every one of my amazing readers who demanded more of Pearl and Alexandre. Thanks for all your love and feedback. *The Pearl Series* would not have been possible without you. Thank you to all the bloggers and readers who recommended my books to their friends and followers. Your tireless support and enthusiasm have me in awe. Thank you so much.

Shades
of
Pearl
(Book 1)

1

Park Avenue is broken into a patchwork of glimmering colors, the streets a slick, shining wet as rain makes mirrors of the red and green of the traffic lights. I am mesmerized by the windscreen wipers of the taxi cab washing away the deluge of a sudden summer downpour that has taken the city by surprise.

I love New York City in the summer rain, a relief from the muggy air. But today it threatens to make me late for my appointment. I always aim to arrive early because, by nature I'm disorganized, so I need time on my side. I ask the driver if he can go any faster, if he can pull a miraculous short-cut out of the bag, but no, he and I are both aware that that's impossible. The traffic is lugging, straining; all we can do is be patient, all I can do is calm myself, take a breath and remember that work is not the be-all and end-all of my existence. So what if I'm late? Does it really matter in the big scheme of things, in the giant picture of life?

Life – that's something to mull over. I wish work wasn't so important to me, but I cling on to it like a piece of driftwood in a stormy ocean. Work is all I seem to have right now. I've just turned forty, I'm divorced, single - I live alone and don't have a child. Work is my lifeboat.

I sit back into the scuffed seat of the cab and look through the notes on my iPad.

The conference will be packed, my boss has assured me. Replete with an international crowd from all corners of the globe. It's the biggest I.T convention of the year and I know I won't fit in. Nerdsville here I come. I know very little about this world, and the only reason I have been summoned to go is to see if I can connect with two of the people who will be speaking today. They are a brother and sister from France who have made a small fortune, seemingly overnight, not unlike Facebook computer programmer and Internet entre-preneur, Mark Zuckerberg. This duo is young, too. She's the business and he's the brains, apparently. They started a social network company, HookedUp, a sort of Twitter cum social dating interaction which, although not so popular in France, went pandemic here in the U.S. Everyone has joined, even married couples, even me - which is really saying something as dating is a game I play badly; I've had no luck and I've all but given up.

My company, Haslit Films, wants to do a documentary about this pair of siblings. Not so easy. They are very private and rarely do interviews. They don't go to openings or parties. They don't do Red Carpet. There was a big piece about them in the New York Times, but other than that they are a bit of a mystery. He, Alexandre Chevalier, is twenty-four and she, Sophie Dumas, is ten years older, his half sister from a previous marriage. They share the same father. This much I know. But I can find only one photo of him on the internet and he's wearing a hoodie, his face practically masked - he looks like a typical college student. His sister stands beside him, her hair in a neat chignon – looking formidable, poised. HookedUp is going from strength to strength. Rumor has it they are looking to sell or go public but nobody can be sure. All this, I need to find out.

I stare out the cab window and sigh with relief as the traffic speeds up. I think about all the millions out there trying to find a mate, trying to get 'hooked up' - and smile to myself. When was the last time? Two years ago? It was a rebound disaster waiting to happen, or rather, I was the rebound waiting…hoping to find love again. I hadn't expected my divorce to knock me sideways the way it did. I didn't even love him anymore. It was mutual. There was nobody else involved, we just drifted apart. We had gotten to the point where we couldn't even watch each other eat. Yet when those papers came through, the ink hardly dry, I cried myself to sleep for weeks. If Saul and I had had a child, at least that would have given me some sort of purpose, a perspective - but there I was, a two-time miscarriage vessel, empty, null and void - my sell-by date looming.

It's funny how others see you, though. So many of my friends were envious of my life. They still are. 'So glamor-ous,' they purr. 'So free'. No homework to deal with, no snotty nose to wipe, no husband's dirty socks to pick off the floor. Instead, a fabulous, well paid job with a fabulous, successful film company making top-notch documentaries, meeting fascinating people…and yet. Yet what? What excuse did I have, *do* I have to feel unfulfilled?

Perhaps everyone feels this way, no matter what cards

they hold. Always looking for something richer - something or someone more satisfying to fill an empty hole. Turning forty didn't scare me until after it happened. 'But you look amazing,' said friends after I'd blown out forty candles on my birthday cake. The 'but' spoke volumes. Tick-tock. Tick-tock.

That last date I went on, just after my divorce - what a fiasco. I thought it might give me confidence – make me feel stronger but I found myself tumbling into bed with a man I hardly knew, after he'd taken me out to an oh-so-expensive dinner. I think he felt I was dessert, and I can only blame myself as I offered myself up as such, accepting a 'night cap' at his apartment. Just thinking about it now makes my mouth pucker, as if I had a lemon in my mouth. Bad sex. Grappling, groping, sweaty hands on my breasts, the poking and panting. Ugh, just the thought of it. He sent me flowers the next day, saying what a wonderful evening he'd had. He was so keen. So well-meaning. So clueless.

Not that I'm any expert. No. Sex has rarely been good for me. My ex-husband was very attractive but his idea of foreplay was rubbing my groin as if I were a horse needing a good rub-down. Rhythmic efficiency.

It seems that men have read about the clitoris (the Big C), the nerve-rich locus of women's sexual pleasure, and think it's a target to be zoomed in on *immediately*. All those women's magazines don't help, either, that go on endlessly about multiple orgasms - something that has eluded me like a fugitive on the run...forever out of my range. Perhaps it's all a conspiracy and the big M O, or rather, Multiple 007 doesn't actually exist...just a fantasy that we all believe in.

It reminds me of my old Al-Anon meetings – a place for family members of alcoholics to find solace and talk to one another. That was before my eldest brother died, when my family was struggling to understand his alcoholism - his personal demons which were ripping us apart. I was searching for help, for answers. The meetings, for some odd reason, were ninety-eight percent women. Once we'd all gained each other's trust, we started to explore other problems and to really open up with one another - problems not related to our families, but our own deep secrets, which turned out to be collective insecurities. Sex came up. Of course, doesn't it always? We had all sworn honesty, not to judge each other, not to share our experiences with anyone outside the room. It turned out that many of the women there - in fact, *most* of the women there - had unsatisfactory sex lives, if any at all. Several bowed their heads in shame when they admitted they'd never reached orgasm through penetrative sex. Others, that they couldn't bear to have their clitoris touched (manhandled), or they felt too self-conscious to have their partner go down on them. We all laughed about *that* scene in *When Harry Met Sally*. So true. Women faking orgasms so they can get to sleep, take the kids to school, or just get it over and done with. But you still soldier on, still hoping for that magical person who can wave a wand and make it all happen - hoping that same person will be your soul mate, or at least, that you'll have a good deal in common. *Or* that your present partner, or husband, will wake up one day and find you gloriously sexy, and that his top priority in the world is to give you carnal pleasure and become a veritable god in bed.

As for me? Right now my confidence is wobbling and wavering with desperate insecurity like a child learning to ride a bicycle way too big for her. Sex, or any kind of a relationship, is the last thing I feel equipped to navigate my way around. On paper, I look good. Had a great education, a degree from Brown in Comparative Literature. I worked my way up from research and I am now a producer with Haslit Films, a job I love. I own my own apartment, a one bedroom co-op on the Upper East Side. I travel to a different place in the U.S every year for a ten day vacation, usually in September when the crowds have died down. My life is wonderful.

But I'm single.

And, just to add salt to the wound, I haven't reached that exclusive O during sex with a partner of any kind, for nearly eighteen years.

The conference center is all a-buzz. There are placards filled with names and seminars. *Deep Dive: Best Practices for Wireless and Mobile Management, Operations and Security.*
Selecting the Right Platform Solution.
Cloud-based Convergence of Desktop, Communications & Social Apps: Microsoft Office 365 vs. Google Gmail/Docs.
Social Media as the Top Malware Delivery Vehicle - How to Protect Your Network.

I scan the list to find out what I am looking for, but cannot see the French sibling duo anywhere. I make my way to the ladies' room and check myself in the mirror. I see a blonde woman staring back at me with her flecked blue-gray eyes, wearing a tight gray pencil skirt and fitted white T-shirt, her bra making her breasts seem larger than they are in reality. Cheating. That's what we females do whenever we can. The woman is familiar yet, every time I see her, it shocks me that she is *me*, a person who only yesterday was climbing trees and asking her mother for more ice-cream. It sounds like a cliché, but where did all that time go? Who is this woman looking back at me? This seemingly self-assured lady with marshmallow insides who hides her insecurity with designer clothes and a bright smile – who is she? I open my old, oversized, leather bag and take out some high, nude platform pumps, slip off my sneakers and put on the shoes, one foot at a time, leaning against the wall to balance myself, swapping comfort for extra height. My five foot seven frame is now several inches taller.

I wish I had a sweater now; the air conditioning is up high, my hair is soaked from the rain – no wonder we get summer colds in New York City. I inspect my face in the mirror and wish I could magic away these crow's feet that have nestled themselves so comfortably on my face. I put on another layer of mascara which brightens me and makes me feel younger. I never wear foundation; the beauty of getting older is the absence of pimples. Reading novels on my co-op's shared roof terrace has given me a golden, sun-kissed glow – no need for blusher at this time of year. I dab on a touch of pinky-red lip gloss, let down my damp, wavy blond hair from its pony tail, and consider myself ready to enter the world of I.T.

I move back to the lobby and stand in line, waiting to collect my name tag. "Ms. Pearl Robinson," I say to the man behind the desk.

He hands me my badge and I pin it on my T-shirt. I read a banner which says: 'THE #1 meeting place for the global business technology community,' and for some odd reason, I feel nervous.

I clear my throat. "Um, excuse me but I've never been to one of these business technology conferences. I'm trying to find one of the speakers today. Two of the speakers, actually."

"Yes, ma'am, how can I help?"

"Can you direct me to Alexandre Chevalier and Sophie Dumas?" I'm aware of my voice. I feel ridiculous trying to make the Alexandre come out with a French accent. My French is limited, to say the least. Restaurant French. Directions French. It occurs to me that if I take the Alexandre and the Dumas and put them together I have Alexandre Dumas, the French author who wrote the swash-buckling adventure, *The Three Musketeers*. But this Alexandre is a recently graduated college kid - a geek who wears a hoodie and probably keeps pet rats in his bedroom.

"One moment," the man replies, "let me see...the HookedUp guys? I believe that-"

All I can hear is a booming voice behind me, chatting excitedly. "Everybody was talking about Data Center last year. This year, did you notice that hardly a word was spoken? Did you not notice that? I mean, dude, the buzz instead is about software-defined networks, decoupling the network control plane from the data plane and using the OpenFlow protocol to give servers, which inherit network control, access to devices such as switches and routers."

I turn around and glare at the bearded guy behind me speaking double-dutch. Then I say to the man at the desk, "I'm sorry, I couldn't hear you, what were you saying?"

"That the seminar is over ma'am. The HookedUp guys? It finished, like, twenty minutes ago."

"But my schedule said 11am."

"It was brought forward by an hour. You should have been informed if you'd booked ahead."

Booked ahead? What is this, Broadway? "Are they speaking

again? At a different time?" I ask, knowing I've blown my chance of ever seeing this elusive duo.

"No, ma'am. That's it. It was quite a coup getting them here. The audience was the biggest we've ever had. Sorry you missed out."

"Me too," I mutter.

I think how disappointed my boss will be whose idea it was to do this documentary. I feel so unprofessional. I should have double-checked the hour. The duo wouldn't submit themselves to an interview just, 'Come and see us speak at the InterWorld show on the 12th – we'll talk then.' I secretly wonder if I subconsciously willed this to happen - messing it all up. Surely my own project can now take preference? I've been hatching and researching an idea for a year now, a venture that really interests me, something that deserves worldwide attention. *The Aftermath of World Aid* is its working title. What happens to the billions of dollars that never reach the victims after a natural disaster? Everyone digging into their pockets to unwittingly fund corrupt governments - siphoned-off aid – money in the wrong hands. It's a political hotbed. Nobody wants to tread on toes.

My other ambition is to run a special on arms dealing. People talk about world peace but how will that ever happen as long as dealing in arms is legal? As long as its trade is used as world currency by governments? If the profit were taken out of war, if war was no longer business, surely then wars would end? At least, on such a terrifying scale.

My reverie is broken as I hear my cell phone vibrate in my bag. I fumble about for it, my hand wading through my sneakers, hairbrush, iPad and a thousand other things which make my handbag feel like a training tool for women's welterweight boxing.

I look at my cell, holding it out at arm's length. Another annoying thing about getting older - my eyesight is not what it was - yet it's not bad enough (yet) for me to have to wear glasses. Uh oh - my boss calling via Skype. Her picture comes up on my iPhone screen, her smooth caramel-colored face poised with questions, her large hazel-brown eyes expectant.

"Hi Natalie," I say with a hint of a sigh that I can't manage to keep to myself.

"So it's been cancelled," she says in more of a statement than a question.

As usual she's one step ahead of me.

"No, not cancelled, it was moved forward. I've just missed them."

"Darn."

"I'm so sorry, Natalie. It's all my fault, I should have checked. Look, I'll track them down somehow. I'll get onto it. I promise."

"You know what? Forget the whole idea. These guys are obviously not up for it. They're too hard to get hold of. We don't have time to be messing about with subjects that are not interested in collaborating with us."

"Really? You mean that?" I ask, relieved.

"Really. Get your butt back into gear on one of your other topics, we'll figure out something else."

My lips curve into a subtle smirk. I'm thinking about the tsunamis….Japan, Sumatra, Thailand. The earthquake in Haiti. Maybe she'll green-light my *Aftermath of World Aid* project after all.

"Okay, I'm going to grab a coffee and we can talk," I suggest. "I have a few ideas in the making."

"Oh yeah, I know you do," she replies, laughing. "But,

honey, I'm out the door now. I need to pack and I have a ton of stuff to take care of first. And just to be clear, please don't disturb me while I'm in Kauai, I really need this break."

"Okay, I promise."

"You'll be okay for two weeks without me to guide your skinny ass?" Natalie is being ironic – she knows I can hold my own at work. *I hope.*

"Not so skinny," I joke. "Have a ball, Natalie."

Natalie was single until I introduced her to my father – but that's another story. She has two teenage daughters and, luckily, her sister is coming to stay to look after them while Natalie takes a deserved break in Hawaii. By the time she returns, I'll have a nice package to offer – I'll work hard on my presentation and come up with a choice of projects.

I head across the road for a coffee.

It's both a comforting and disconcerting fact that there's a franchise coffee shop on practically every corner of NYC. You don't have to go far to feed your addiction. I shuffle through the door, now back in my sneakers – New York City sidewalks do not favor high heels for any period of time. You can tell how long someone has been living in New York by their footwear. Comfort first. Heels are for visitors. Or women from New Jersey.

I stand in line and ponder over the rich choice I am presented with. A wave of guilt washes over me as I mentally tot up the money I've spent on superfluous coffee breaks over the years – money needed by charities, for water wells somewhere, for a child's education. Stop! Life isn't fair. Yum, *Mocha Cookie Delight…coffee blended with mocha sauce, vanilla syrup, chocolaty chips, milk and ice.* Or a *Vanilla Cappuccino - coffee flavored with vanilla and blended with milk and ice – and fewer calories.*

A man's voice interrupts my chocolaty train of thought.

"So how did you enjoy the conference?" His accent is foreign, his voice deep and melodic.

I look up, feeling now dwarfed in my flat sneakers, petite against his tall, solid frame. The first thing I notice, at eye level, is the definition of his pec muscles underneath his sun-faded, pale blue T-shirt. He's tanned; I see he has a name tag just like mine from the InterWorld conference, which reads: *Alexandre Chevalier.* My gaze rises higher and I observe a pair of penetrating peridot-green eyes rimmed with dark lashes, friendly yet intense, looking down at me. His hair is dark, his face unmistakably European - yes, dare I say it, he even looks French, the profile of his nose strong, the jaw defined. He's so handsome I feel a frisson shoot up my spine. He's smiling at me. My stomach flips. I'm speechless with surprise.

"Your name tag," he clarifies. "Were you at that conference around the corner?"

"Yes, I was." I can't say any more. I feel like a teenager. My mind is doing acrobatics, trying to figure out why his presence makes no sense at all. This man must have borrowed the tag of the real Alexandre Chevalier. Why?

He's at the front of the line, now, talking in French to another woman. She looks familiar. I feel an inexplicable pang of jealousy. Absurd! I don't even know him. *Get a grip!* But then realize—

"I'll pay for whatever this lady's having too," he tells the woman serving behind the counter, and he pulls out a wad of notes. I notice a stash of hundred dollar bills which he is trying to surreptitiously stuff back into his jeans' pocket, without drawing attention to himself.

He turns back to me and looks at my name tag. "For

Pearl," he adds, rolling his tongue around the R of Pearl.

My name suddenly sounds beautiful, not like a pseudonym a hooker might use, which is what I was relentlessly teased for in high school.

"Pearl," he says again. "What a beautiful name. I've never heard that before. As a name, I mean."

"Well, my parents were kind of hippies. Thanks for the compliment, though. I'll have a….a…um, I'll have a *vanilla cappuccino,* please. You really don't have to do that - buy me my drink, I mean."

I fumble about in my 'handbag' - although it seems more like an *overnight* bag - and try to locate my wallet. I'm not used to strangers buying me drinks. My fingers can't seem to find my wallet, anyway. I often fantasize about inventing an inside handbag light that switches on automatically whenever you open it – I'd make millions – they'd be sold at supermarket checkouts nationwide. My bag is pitch dark inside, I can see nothing.

"And what's your name?" I ask, still not believing that this man before me is Alexandre Chevalier, the twenty-four year-old nerd in the hoodie, as he appeared in the online photo. This Alexandre is sophisticated – looks way older than that. Even though he's just in T-shirt and jeans, he's stylish. Very Alpha Male - yet oozing *je ne sais quoi.* I could describe him as 'beautiful' but he is so much more than that. There is an aura surrounding him of power and sexuality yet blended with an unassuming sort of friendliness as if his good looks are accidental somehow.

He laughs. His teeth flash white and are almost, but not quite - perfect. An almost perfect, ever so slightly, crooked smile - disconcertingly sexy. "Very funny," he replies tapping his long fingers on his ***Alexandre Chevalier*** name tag. "Oh, this is my sister, Sophie."

The Sophie sounds like Soffy. His accent is disarming me. I think of those classic, 1960's French films - Alain Delon movies - yes, he does have that air about him - a young Alain Delon - mixed with the raw, untamed sex-appeal of Jean Paul Belmondo in his prime — What was that film? Ah yes, *À Bout de Souffle* - *Breathless* was its translation. That's how I feel now...

Breathless.

Sophie locks her eyes with mine and smiles at me. She's smartly dressed, elegant. We move forward to shake hands. My fingers brush across Alexandre's T-shirt for a second and I feel the hardness of his stomach. I catch my breath. I want to blurt out about our company, Haslit Films, who I am, why I have a name tag for that conference, but I find myself behaving like a character from a TV sitcom - Rachel from *Friends*, or Lucy from *I Love Lucy* - compelled to tell fibs, invent some cover-up. I feel as if my hand has been caught in the cookie jar, and then wonder at my own absurdity. *What cookie jar?* I haven't done anything wrong! I can feel my face flush hot and know that if I were the type of person to blush red - these two strangers would be able to detect the embarrassment glowing in my cheeks.

"What a coincidence," I say, tossing a coin in my head about whether to explain everything.

"Really why?" Sophie asks.

But I go all *Rachel* again and find nonsense spurting from my lips.

"Well, just that you were at the conference and so was I."

I suddenly think that if I tell them about my film company and why I was at InterWorld, they'll think I've been stalking them. Trailing behind them, pursuing them into the coffee shop like some low-grade paparazzi reporter for a cheap newspaper. The fact that Alexandre Chevalier is no longer a rat-loving geek locked in a dark room programming codes, unnerves me. He looks like a movie star. He's as rich as one - maybe more so. For some reason I can't come clean.

They are chatting away in French to each other. Good, eyes are off me. *Damn, why did I take off my heels?* I feel so insignificant - so low down. My jittery hand gropes about in my monster bag again, and my fingers feel the sharp points of my shoes. The fingers wander about some more. Ah, the wallet, *phew*, I can feel it. But my heart jumps a beat when, for all my fumbling, I can't locate the keys to my apartment! *Why is this man making me so nervous?*

The alarm on my face must be obvious, as he asks, "Is everything alright?"

"Well, for just a second, I thought I'd lost the keys to my apartment. Ha ha. I mean, that second is still ticking," I tell him, my voice rising higher. "The keys don't seem to be there."

"One iced vanilla cappuccino, one iced coffee and one black shaken iced tea," the server announces.

Before I've even lifted my eyes from my bag, Sophie has grabbed her drink-to-go, and says, "Nice to meet you, Pearl. Maybe see you around sometime." And she adds in French to her brother, "*À plus*," and she's off, out the door and onto the street.

"I had got the drinks to go but do you want to sit down?" he asks. "Have a better look for your house keys? A man's life is so much simpler – we carry everything in our pockets."

We find a couple of free armchairs and sit down. His cell phone buzzes. I slip on my high pumps, just for good measure - no pun intended.

He smiles at me. "Excuse me, do you mind? I need to get this call."

So polite. I don't even know him and he's already bought me a drink and asking me if I mind him taking a call. He looks embarrassed as he speaks in hushed tones into the phone.

"What's it like? Is it worth that inflated price?" he murmurs.

I'm looking through my bag, but curious about his conversation, so keep an ear inquisitively cocked – if I were a dog, my ear would be raised. Ah, here they are, those elusive apartment keys, always giving my heart a run for its money. I swear - that pumping, lost-my-keys-lost-my-phone-lost-my-wallet adrenaline is going to give me a literal heart attack one day.

"Okay," I hear Alexandre say, "I'll buy it. Yes, even at that price - it's a one-off - I might not get this chance again. Yes, wire the money. Okay, bye Jim. Thanks."

I want to ask him what he was talking about, but don't dare to be so snooping.

The look on my face, however, must give away my curiosity, as he reveals to me, "A vice of mine. My sister's sure to disapprove."

"Oh? Why?" I ask innocently.

"She thinks cars are for getting from A to B, and one's enough."

"Buying another car, huh? How many do you already have?"

He looks almost ashamed. "More than I need."

"A collection?"

"You could say that. But they are all works of art in their

white cravat on his chest. One of the advantages of France is that you can take your dog anywhere. To restaurants, even. Especially, black Labs. President Mitterrand had a black Labrador and ever since then, they've been very respected creatures in my country."

My eyes widen. "Seriously? You can even go to smart restaurants with your dog?"

"I usually call ahead to be polite. I book the table and then add, 'Oh yes, just one thing, do you mind if I bring my dog along, you know, he's just a typical *Black Labrador.*' They always say yes. But I'll tell you a secret-"

He leans forward and, oh so slightly, rests his hand on my knee. It starts to quiver, goose bumps shimmer along my thighs, my arms.

"What's the secret?" I ask, my voice sounding like a small child's.

"He's not pure Labrador. I think he's got a little Pit-Bull in him. He has a wide face and compact thigh muscles that feel as if they're made of rock. He's the sweetest dog that ever lived. The sweetest, the gentlest. You know Pit-Bulls were originally bred to be nannies? To be guardians to babies and young children – to watch over them?"

"No, really? You're kidding me."

"I'm serious. A whole lot of vintage photographs have been discovered from the Victorian age. American Pit-Bull Terriers were used as baby-sitters. Unfair they've been given a bad rap and their loving natures abused. In France, they were forced to be sterilized some years back, but my Rex has some Pit-Bull genes in his blood, I'm sure. They were never considered dangerous in the olden days."

Don Gaire Oose….dangerous…his accent is so alluring. "That's fascinating," I say. "I never knew that. I'm crazy about dogs.

I had one as a little girl. She was a Husky."

"Huskies are beautiful."

"Mine - she was called Zelda, she had one blue eye and one golden eye. She was a real stunner. But she'd run off whenever she could. They're real escape artists, Huskies. She was okay for the first year, but as soon as she turned thirteen months she started doing her own thing, escaping, getting into mischief. She killed chickens, unfortunately. One day she ran off and didn't come back. We never knew what happened. It broke my heart. Since then I haven't had the courage to get another dog."

Alexandre brings his palms up to his face and covers his mouth with genuine empathy. "That's a very sad story. I'm so sorry. You'll have to meet Rex. I'm organizing his move – should be in the next couple of months."

An invitation? Is this for real? "I'd adore to meet Rex – he sounds lovely. So why did you choose to live in New York?" I ask, not wanting this conversation to finish. Ever.

"France is one of the most beautiful countries in the world. Fine wine, great cuisine, incredible landscape - we have a rich culture. But when it comes to opportunity, especially for small businesses, it's not so easy there."

Small businesses? His company is worth millions! No - billions, even.

My sitcom alter-ego is rearing her naughty, lying head again. "You own a small company? What do you do?"

He narrows his penetrating eyes. Every time he does that, it sends shivers coursing through my body. "That's why I was at that conference," he explains. "I was answering a few questions, giving people some tips, you know, advice from my own personal experience. It's done nicely my company."

screenplay."

"Really? I love theatre. I don't know much about screenplays or movies, but I adore going to the theatre. Actually, I prefer a good play to a novel. Molière, Voltaire, Jean-Paul Sartre, Camus. We have pretty bad translations of Shakespeare into French – they just don't do him justice – another incentive to perfect my English. I've seen some great plays in Paris and London. My sister used to be an actress. She got me into plays. Theatre is her passion."

"It sounds as if you two are really close," I remark, amazed at how sophisticated he is, and how well read. He seems so much older than his years.

"I guess we are."

"So when you're not going to the theatre, or working, or zipping about in your beautiful classic cars, what do you do to relax?"

"Let's see. I love rock-climbing."

"Not so relaxing, though."

"Not physically, but for your mental state of mind, it's great. You have to concentrate so hard on what you're doing - it cleanses the mind from all the clutter. A bit like meditation. Not that I meditate, but you know, I can imagine. It's not a team sport, it's boring for any spectator – it's about personal satisfaction, personal goals."

"You sound as if you're very accomplished at it."

"I've climbed a bit. Rock climbing involves strength, control and finesse. Using the muscles in your arms and legs to pull yourself up a sheer rock-face takes strength and control. Using your brain to place your hands and feet so that your muscles can do their job - that's finesse."

I study the *finesse* of his chest, his lithe, tanned arms, and see where he gets his worked-out physique from. But he's not overly muscley, not exaggerated. There's no bull-neck there, no bulging, bulky biceps. He's long and lean but not too slim, either - he has definite substance.

"I tried rock-climbing once," I tell him. "I was terrified but I could see the attraction to the sport. It was fun, I'd love to try it again someday." I'm aware that I'm fishing and he takes the bait.

"Really? Would you like to come with me? My sister hates it. I can never get anyone to go with me."

"Your girlfriend doesn't like rock-climbing?" I hear myself spurt out and wish I had a mouth-plug.

"My girlfriend?"

Oh no, he does have a girlfriend, after all.

"I'm unattached," he lets me know.

I sigh with relief and hope he hasn't heard my body heave gratitude. I sip a long, long mouthful of cappuccino through my straw. "I'd just *love* to come rock-climbing with you."

I notice he's watching my mouth clamped around the straw, and I feel self-conscious. I wipe my mouth – fearful that I have foam on my upper lip and it looks like a moustache.

"Great," he says, not taking his eyes off me. "How about the weekend?"

"You mean this weekend, or next?"

"That's right, today's Friday. It's all a bit last minute and I have something on tonight so it might–"

"What?" I ask, panicked he'll change his mind.

"It's too hot to climb midday in summer, so I usually set out very early. I mean, I often spend the night there – makes it easier. But it's already Friday so–"

I am waiting; my breath uneven. The cappuccino is gur-

"Actually, it's usually men who are attracted to my collection. I'm a man-trap, unfortunately."

"What's your Lamborghini like?" I ask, clueless.

"It's the *Murciélago*."

"That means bat in Spanish."

"Exactly. It looks like Batman's car. It's outrageous. It's a stunning design. But it was actually named after a brave bull called Murciélago which fought with such spirit that the *matador* chose to spare its life, a virtually unheard of honor."

I grimace. "I hate bull-fighting."

"Me too. There are two things I can't understand in this world – cruelty to animals and cruelty to children. Oh, and women too – I don't understand how anybody could physically hurt a woman."

"Even if the woman agrees?"

Alexandre furrows his brow and stares at me hard for a second. "Why would any woman agree to being hurt by somebody?"

Uh, oh, where's my mouth plug? I find myself stuttering and wish I hadn't said that but then I dig myself in deeper and blurt out, "Whips and handcuffs are all the rage right now – rope is flying off the shelves at the hardware stores."

He narrows his eyes at me but I blabber on, "Well....a friend of mine......there are a bunch of books....so many erotic romances these days with a BDSM and bondage theme to them – they've gotten everyone curious...I mean women seem to be intrigued by the whole thing." *Shut up, Pearl, what made you come out with all that?*

"France has a tradition of literary erotic writing," Alexandre tells me. "The Marquis de Sade, Anaïs Nin, Pauline Réage - you know, the one who wrote *The Story of O*? But any sort of sexual slavery is a real turn-off for me."

"But what if it's consensual? You know, the dominant role-play with the submissive female – if it's an agreement between both parties?"

"It depends how young the girl is. Any woman under twenty-five is underage for that sort of role-play, in my opinion."

"But *you're* under twenty-five!" I exclaim, alarmed, and immediately wish I hadn't come out with that. *My God! He considers himself underage.*

"How d'you know how old I am?" he asks, and I can feel my face go hot.

"Just a guess," I lie. *Please don't ask me how old I am.*

"Almost right. I had my twenty-fifth birthday several months ago, actually. But I'm old for my age. I'm different, Pearl, I grew up way before my time – I was wise in all manner of things before the age of fourteen. Also, I'm a man. Young women are still vulnerable, still discovering the world and in my opinion it's not right for a girl to get involved with that sort of kinky stuff. It could be damaging psychologically as well as physically."

"Wow, you have very old-fashioned morals," I remark, surprised at his conservatism.

"Each to their own, but for me that sort of practice is so *not* erotic."

"What if it's the other way round? With some–" I am about to say, 'some Mrs. Robinson type,' but stop myself. *I am Mrs. Robinson in many people's eyes.... being forty, hanging out with a younger guy – having designs on him sexually. Pearl Robinson - Robinson is the last name I need right now.* My lips curl up at my silly pun.

"Well, being male that's hard for me to imagine because as a teenager, I happened to love more mature women and always had older girlfriends but I suppose a boy, in certain instances, could also be vulnerable."

"Well, millions of people might disagree with your attitude. Most people believe anyone is a fully-fledged adult at eighteen."

"You see?" he exclaims. "That's what's so strange about this country. You can whip and tie a girl up at that age with her consent but not offer her a glass of wine, or you'd be breaking the law."

"You're right, I hadn't thought of that. Most states you have to be twenty-one to drink."

"Anyway, wielding a whip is not my cup of tea, I can assure you, Pearl. Even if it is consensual. I can't imagine wanting to hurt a woman. Females are the gentler sex and should be treated with respect. Wanting to tie up a person and spank or whip her is something I could never do. I can't imagine how anyone could seriously get off on that."

I catch a glimpse of Alexandre's face and he looks angry as if I've touched a nerve. *Mama Mia, what made me steer the conversation in that direction? He must think I'm a pervert! Now I've really blown my chances.*

But then he adds with a wry smile, "A little harmless dress-up, maybe. A little food-play, but nothing that could *hurt* anyone."

Food play? Dress-up? My only contribution to dress-up was when I put on some heels and asked my ex-husband to do it to me with my shoes on. He didn't get it at all, told me to take them straight off. Seriously, is this what turns Alexandre on? Dress-up? Food? What kind of food? Mick Jagger and his legendary Mars Bar, shoved up you-know-where, type of food? (My brother told me that – is it true, I wonder)?

"Speaking of food, Pearl, you must be starving, I bet you

didn't have time for any breakfast. I picked up some fruit and croissants and a couple of bottles of freshly squeezed orange juice." He leans behind him and produces a bag of goodies. "We can stop off for a coffee if you like or just wait until we get there."

"I can wait."

"Really? *Can* you?" The way he looks at me when he says it makes me wonder if there's a *double-entendre* somewhere. His eyes seem to be undressing me and he runs his tongue along his bottom lip ever so slightly. Perhaps the *double-entendre* is my imagination, and maybe he's just innocently licking his lips. Whatever, I'm feeling the heat between us.

Then he says, "As well as literature there are lots of erotic French films, too. Here, I'll play you the soundtrack to this famous one from the 70's – *Emmanuelle* – maybe you know it."

He puts on the music and I do recognize it – beautiful and very sensual. There's something about a man singing in French which is a real turn-on. Alexandre hums along to the tune and winks at me again. I sense a tingling in my groin which takes me by surprise. Our conversation about sex, the erotic music, the deep vibration of the Corvette's heavy engine makes me throb with desire. I wriggle in my seat just looking at him - his defined arm muscles flexed at the steering wheel, and he looking so handsome, driving this sexy femme-fatale of a car with such control - all this is excitingly new to me, truly unexpected.

I feel a pulse between my legs.

It's amazing how just ninety miles away from New York City you feel as if you're on a different planet. When we arrive at Shawangunk Mountains - pronounced Shon-gum and known simply as 'The Gunks' - Alexandre informs me that this is one of the best places for rock-climbing in North America and has a steady stream of eclectic visitors from all over the world. It is also home to several conservation groups. The scenery is breathtaking. Lush green stretches as far as the eyes can see, topped by imposing white and gray quartz cliff-bands, several miles wide, shooting up from the earth like proud monuments.

Alexandre has thought of and organized everything – packed water bottles, sunscreen, bug-repellent, even a spare camera in case I forgot mine (which I had) and, of course, his own gear. The guide will bring mine. I see Alexandre is a man quietly in control of situations – organized, methodical, leaving nothing to chance. He behaves way older than his years and has a cool sophistication about him, too. No wonder he's been so successful at such a young age.

"That's where we're going to climb along the Shawangunk Ridge. Up there where you see that tower?" he says, pointing. "That's Sky Top."

There's a stone tower perched on top of a mountain with a craggy rock-face below of pale golden stripes, creating from afar a series of patterns like old men's distorted faces etched into the rock formations. It looks terrifyingly vertical. Each horizontal stripe adding age to this natural masterpiece of nature. It's awesome in the real sense of the word.

"Sky Top is home to about three hundred rock climbs like Strawberry Yoghurt, Petie's Spare Rib and Jekyll and Hyde. Don't you just love the wacky names? It's private property and has been off-limits to climbers for more than ten years but we'll be having lunch at Mohonk Mountain Lodge so we're all set up. You look nervous, Pearl. Don't be, our guide knows these climbs like the back of his hand so you'll feel quite safe. I've been here several times - I know them too."

Our guide, Chris, is young and enthusiastic and looks like a surfer. He has a hard tan and deep crow's feet around his sun-weathered eyes. He claps his arms around Alexandre and says, "Hey, man, you made it. My favorite frog in the world."

"Very funny. This is my friend, Pearl. What have you got planned for us today, Chris? As I told you on the phone, Pearl's just a beginner, so we don't want to scare her with any overhangs - go easy on her today."

"Frog?" I ask.

"Don't mind me, just teasing," Chris cackles.

"As you probably know, we French get called Frogs by half the world – can't think why. Don't worry, when you come for dinner I won't serve you frogs or snails."

"You cook?" I ask Alexandre.

"A little."

Chris squints at the mountains before us. "I thought Pearl could start with Finger Licking Good this morning and see how we go."

We make our way along the trail until we come to a clearing beneath a massive rock-face. Chris goes through endless instructions, teaches me knots, commands, names of bits of equipment and safety checks. There is so much to learn and I kick myself. *Why did I agree to this?* The truth is, I lied to Alexandre. I have never been rock-climbing. Well, I once went with a group of friends in Idyllwild, California, so technically I did *go*. I even put on the gear but the rock-face was so daunting, I was too chicken to go through with it. I am a novice and I'm too ashamed to tell him. I've never, ever climbed more than several flights of stairs. It's too late now to come clean without humiliating myself further.

Alexandre helps me step into the leg loops of my harness and tightens the straps around me, hitching me up so it's snug against my pelvis and hips. When he touches me I sense my heart race. The shoes feel as if they are four sizes too small but they both assure me they are the perfect fit for good grip. I'm also given a helmet – uh, oh, not such a sexy look, but at this point, peering up at the rocky wall in front of me, I need all the help I can just to stay alive.

"You said this was for beginners," I grumble.

Alexandre looks amused. "It is."

"But I can't climb that!"

"Yes you can. Rock climbing is about faith, Pearl. Faith in yourself. Believe that you can overcome anything and you will. Trust me."

"I'll try," I say, not completely convinced.

"Good girl," he says tapping me on my behind. "Now climb up that rock-face and remember, don't look down any further than your feet. Keep going higher and higher. Take your time, don't rush, don't panic. Just believe in yourself. Now, I'll go up first, I'll be leading. There will be this rope connecting us. If you fall I'll have you – the rope will catch you, hooked into pre-placed bolts in the rock, so don't worry. Chris is down here with you. He'll be coaching you all the way. Trust him. He's been doing this for years, he's a pro."

I watch Alexandre as he climbs without hesitation up the sheer rock-face, clipping the rope into nooks and crannies. Easy for some. Meanwhile, Chris is explaining more technical stuff to me, how the ropes work, the carabiners.

He explains, "Now, whenever possible, Pearl, you should try to do most of the work of climbing using your *legs*. In the ideal case, climbers try to keep their centers of gravity over their feet and then push upwards with their legs. Only use your arms and hands just for balance and positioning."

"But where do I put my feet?" I squeal, looking up at what seems to be an almost smooth surface.

"You'll feel your way as you go and I'll guide you. Little itty-bitty notches and indentations – that's what you need to feel for with your hands which will, in turn, guide your feet into the right positions. Those shoes you're wearing have a lot of grip. Imagine you're climbing a ladder, it's that simple. But keep your weight down on your toes, not your heels."

"I *wish* it was that simple." My palms are sweating with trepidation.

"Here, dip your hands in this," Chris says, and I put the tips of my fingers into a little bag he offers me, filled with what seems like white chalk.

Alexandre is way up high, lodged on a small ledge, waiting for me. "Ready?" he shouts down.

I nod and take a sip of water to ease my nerves. Trembling, and I haven't even started.

"How much experience do you need to have to lead a climb?" I ask Chris, double-checking Alexandre's prowess – *can I trust him?*

"There's no set answer to that. Leading is an art form, make no mistake, and it requires an incredible amount of climbing experience - stress management, decision making, route finding, rope management, gear placement, anchor systems, climbing technique and God knows what else, to be brought together all at once. You need to have a good head on your shoulders, and it helps to be mechanically inclined. I

"Grab that bit that's jutting out to your right, above your head."

"I can't, it's too high."

"Yes you can. Just do it."

I reach up but feel myself slipping. Oh no! Mother of Mercy, what's happening? I can feel my body lose balance, I'm going to fall, I'm going to kill myself. I yelp. I slip. But at the last second my right foot finds a hold and I'm re-balanced, hugging the rock-face once more.

"That's a tricky bastard that tiny crack, isn't it?"

"I almost fell," I pant.

"But you didn't. I knew you'd find that hold – you were positioned right," he says. "Well done, chérie, well done."

I'm in reach of him now. Just one more push and I'm there on the ledge with him. Did he just call me chérie? Or was I imagining it? I make one final heave, my leg quivering with exhaustion and I'm there, hurling myself onto him.

He catches me and hugs me tight in his arms. "I'm so proud of you, you did great. Good girl." His skin smells of sun and open air, and something else wonderful – a happy memory I can't quite place. He takes my hand and kisses it with a flourish, then raises my other and kisses it too, but more slowly this time, his lips soft against my fingers. I can feel the breath of his nostrils, gentle like an imperceptibly warm breeze, and I go limp in his strong arms, my legs buckling under me with fatigue.

We're in Alexandre's beautiful LeMans Blue Corvette heading back to New York City. I'm stretched out in the front seat going over all the sweet details of the day in my mind. It was arduous but probably one of the most satisfying days of my life. While I was getting my breath back after the first climb, mentally gearing-up for another assault on my limbs, I watched Alexandre and Chris scale a rock-face with overhangs, called *Sound and Fury*. Alexandre maneuvered his body with grace and precision – I was in awe, especially knowing how hard it is to cling on almost vertically, let alone upside down horizontally! They discussed it afterwards, describing their 'free-swinging ape-man moves' and it was true, they looked like agile monkeys – it was nail-bitingly tense to watch. Then I did another climb after lunch, harder than the first, and felt as if I'd conquered the world. It was exhilarating. We took lunch at the luxury resort hotel, The Mohonk Mountain House, situated right on Mohonk Lake. It looked like a Victorian castle, with balconies and tall windows and replete with period decor. I guess this must have been where we would have stayed had my face not registered such alarm yesterday. Shame.

I am wary of my desire to please this man. I have never felt this way before. At least, not since my early years when I wanted to please my father while learning to ride a bicycle. The determination to get it right and earn approval from Alexandre is shocking.

I'm mulling all this over, enjoying the car ride, when he turns his head and says with a little smile:

"You've passed the second test."

"Second? What was the first?" I ask bemused.

"You can't guess?"

"No."

"You have no idea?"

"No, not a clue."

He smiles, says nothing, and I'm racking my brains wondering what the first test was.

"Give me a hint," I plead.

"You'll find out, soon enough."

I picture myself wearing the helmet today, my ungainly positions, my elbows and knees scratched all over, and wonder if he's teasing me. The music is loud - a soulful, dusky voice surrounds us, singing about giving over your heart. I feel vulnerable and know that if I did give Alexandre my heart he could break it.

I ask him, "What's this great song? I don't think I've heard it before."

"By an artist called Rumer. Doesn't she have a lovely voice? The song's called *Come to Me High.*"

The lyrics speak my mind. I *am* on a high. A high from the feeling of staring death in the eye. Of course it wasn't really that way, the ropes could have caught my fall, and did at one point on the second climb – but still, every nerve in my body has been awakened by the thrill of today. The buzz of fear, the fear of failure, and the thrill of the way Alexandre makes me feel inside.

"You should feel proud of yourself, Ms. Robinson." *That R again. That sexy accent.* "You've really piqued my interest," he purrs in a soft voice.

He puts his hand on my bare thigh and I feel a shiver run up my spine. I'm wearing a thin cotton skirt which he pushes a couple of inches higher up my leg. His fingers linger on my flesh and I'm too stunned to stir. He starts to move them softly, one hand edging towards my crotch, but oh so subtly – so much so I wonder if I'm imagining it. His other hand is on the wheel. I can feel that pulse deep in my groin again. I look at him. So gorgeous! His chest muscles are ripped from today's action. I saw him change out of his T-shirt and put on a linen shirt before lunch, and I nearly passed out. His skin was smooth, tanned and flawless with just a small amount of body hair in between his pecs. Just thinking about his body now makes me throb with desire - his elegant fingers imperceptibly still resting on my upper thigh – I feel as if my heart-beat is between my legs. But then, he takes his hand away, back to the steering wheel. I let out a sigh of frustration. He's tormenting me with this tease.

"Tell me about yourself, Pearl. You're a mystery to me. I know you're brave and up for a challenge. I know you like dogs, and I can sense you're smart. What else?"

I feel as if he's asking, what else do you have to offer me? I can't seem to answer him. I rack my brains for something clever to tell him about myself, something impressive. I'm still wondering what the first test I've passed is. Rock-climbing being the second – but the first? "I don't know what to say, really," I begin. "My life is pretty hum-drum compared to yours."

"I doubt that very much. Tell me about your family."

"Well, my mom died three years ago. Of cancer."

"I'm so sorry."

"Yeah, it changed my life, we were very close. I'm only just getting over it. I mean, you can *never* really get over it but I'm finally accepting what happened. My dad lives in Hawaii and owns a surf shop."

"Another passion of mine. So you surf, then?"

"No. No, not at all. I've never even tried. He left us when I was six years old to go 'find' himself. He did. He found himself. Found himself a new wife, too. I guess I always associated surfing with abandonment. I went to see him last year – see if I could lay a few ghosts to rest. I

43

wanted to tell him what I thought of him, unleash all my anger."

"And?"

"And....well, it didn't work out that way. The second I laid eyes on him I burst into tears and all I could think about were all those wasted years between us. We hugged like two long-lost bears. He had such a kind face. I fell in love with his little-boy-lost look, just the way my mom had done all those years ago, and I couldn't help but forgive him. He was lonely - his second wife had died several years previously. All my anger melted away. We talked every night watching the moonlit waves, drinking cocktails under the stars. Then he came to Manhattan to visit me. We keep in touch by e-mail - Skype every week. You know, I'm so glad to have him in my life, even after all the heartache he caused."

"And what about brothers and sisters, you have them, too?"

"I have a brother who lives in San Francisco. Anthony. We see each other once in a while." I want to tell him about my late brother, John, who died of an overdose ten years ago but I can't seem to bring myself to mention his name.

"Does Anthony have children, a wife?"

"No, he's gay. He lives with his boyfriend, Bruce. What about your parents?" I ask.

"Well, I had a similar upbringing to you. My mother was a single parent. It was just the three of us. 'The Three Musketeers,' she called us. All for one, and one for all. We were very close. Still are."

"Oh, I thought when you said that your dog, Rex, lived with your parents, your dad was—"

"My step-father. She re-married when I was sixteen."

"Ah. Is he nice?"

"He helped me and my sister set up our business. He's a good man. And most importantly, he's a great husband to my mother."

"What about your dad?"

"I don't talk about him. Ever."

"Oh, I'm sorry."

I want to ask him why. But I can see his eyes alight with fury, his mouth shut tight as if a floodgate has just been opened and streams of polluted water are flowing uncontrollably and it needs to be locked shut again. His look scares me. The charming Frenchman has turned. His face is dark with resentment. Is it resentment? Or am I reading him wrong? Perhaps he misses his father. I wonder if he is still alive and what the story is, but I'm too nervous to ask. I quickly change the subject.

"So, tell me about—" we both burst out simultaneously, our voices in unison. We laugh.

"You first," I say.

"No, you. What were you going to ask me?"

"Just about your work."

"Me, too," he says laughing. "I was going to ask you about what *you* do." *Phew, his furious scowl has dissipated.*

"I was just going to ask you about the way your company is linked to charities," I venture.

He narrows his eyes. "How do you know that?"

"I read a piece in *The New York Times*. How all the advertising for HookedUp automatically gives a percentage to charity."

"That's right. People like giving to charity but they *don't* like giving to charity, if you see what I mean. People want to, and often do, but when they have their hard-earned pay check in front of them, bills take priority, especially in these

"Are you making fun of my accent, Ms. Robinson?" Alexandre's half-cocked smile lets me know he's enjoying being teased. "My turn," he continues, more seriously now. "I was about to ask you about *your* work. You said you write. Tell me more."

"Actually, I make films. Documentaries."

There, I said it. He'll probably realize now, why I was at the conference.

"An activist, then."

Good, he's not put two and two together.

"I have my ideas. And yes, often they are quite controversial. Topics for discussion and thought."

"Like what, for instance?" he asks.

"We did something on pharmaceutical companies. The hold they have over the world. The exorbitant sums of money they earn, often at the expense of poor nations."

"So you like to kick up a storm?"

"I like to reveal the truth."

I say this but it has struck me that there are all sorts of truths I am masking from him. Not to mention my age. Thank God he hasn't asked me that. Yet.

"You have your own company?" he wants to know.

"No, I work for someone. Her name's Natalie. She's actually visiting my father in Hawaii. She left today on vacation. Ironic, that - that my boss should hook up with my dad. Didn't see that coming when I introduced them." The hook-up word, again. Clever name for a social media site.

"Keep it in the family. What's she like, your boss?"

"Smart. Beautiful. Opinionated. Tough to please."

Sounds like I'm describing Alexandre himself.

"From New York?"

"Yes. From Queens. But she lives in Manhattan now."

"French origin?"

"No, why do you ask that?"

"Because Natalie is a really common name in France."

"I don't think she has French roots – she's African-American."

"Seems like your dad lucked out. She sounds interesting."

"She is. It complicates things a little having two such close people to me, together in a relationship but I'm getting used to it now."

We've been talking so much I hardly realize that we've already arrived outside my building. It's now dark. Alexandre parks the car by the curb next to my apartment block.

"Well, here we are. Thank you, Pearl for a wonderful day." *Wonder Fool.*

"Thank *you.* You've awakened my senses."

"Oh, that's just the beginning, believe me," he says enigmatically.

I catch my breath and feel my mouth part. *The beginning? Please say he's not just kidding.* I'm hoping he's going to kiss me. But abruptly, he gets out of his side, walks around and opens the car door for me. I scramble out of this low Corvette, trying to look composed, but my legs are momentarily splayed apart, showing off a flash of my white panties.

He undresses me for a second, his eyes in a half-closed bedroom, *come hither-and-fuck-me* look, noticing the color of underwear I have on - I'm sure of it. He bites his lower lip and I feel those butterflies again.

"Would you like to come in? Have a bite to eat, a glass of wine?" I offer.

"No, Pearl. Thank you, but I have an early meeting tomorrow."

"But tomorrow's Sunday," I protest, having somehow whipped up a dinner à deux for tonight, a romantic interlude and at least a long kiss between us.

But it's clear to me now that our 'date' has ended. He's been toying with me. Amused to see me all flustered, turned-on and worked up. He's a professional charmer. Of course he doesn't want any romance with me. *He's twenty-five years old!* He's probably going off to dinner somewhere else, *with* someone else, and then on to a trendy club to dance the night away with her - some nubile sex-pot, before fucking her senseless and then taking her out to a fabulous Sunday brunch somewhere tomorrow. *Stop!* I say to myself. *Enough! He's taken you rock-climbing - you've had a great time. Leave it at that.*

"I had a fabulous day," I say.

"Me too."

"Really?" I ask with an unwanted tinge of disbelief in my voice.

"Really. It's been fun. Night-night. You'll be tired and will sleep like a baby. Get some rest, your body needs it."

If only, I mull, he knew what my body *really* needed. It has been awoken, and now awake, it is *pining* for attention.

He walks me up to my door and then presses a light kiss on my lips. No tongue, no exploration, just a gentle, soft kiss. "Night Pearl, take care."

"Night," I murmur, my voice small.

I turn to go inside and the doorman lets me into the lobby. "Good evening Mrs. Robinson, did you have a good day?"

"Marvelous thanks, Dervis."

"Oh, Mrs. Robinson. One thing - I'll be on vacation this week. There'll be the new boy here taking my place. Luke."

"The skinny one with dark hair?"

"Yes. That's right."

"Okay, thanks."

I turn my head and look through the glass of the wrought-iron door to see Alexandre's expression but he's already revving up his car and driving off. He didn't even say he'd call. Who knows? I guess I'll never see him again.

3

The following day is slow torment. All yesterday's fun is being marred by my own insecurity and post-mortem blues. I almost wish I hadn't met him, my senses being stirred, like hearing a beautiful piece of music for the first time. Or a poem. And then having it snatched away from you forever. *How can this whippersnapper of a man have this effect on me?* I think of my last name, Robinson, and feel a wave of clichéd embarrassment surge through my veins. *The Graduate* - Mrs. Robinson. How apt. Except I am *Ms.* Robinson now. At least *Mrs.* Robinson got to see it through. At least *she* had guts. There I was, last night, like some simpering fool as I said goodbye. I should have taken the reins. Pounced on him. Okay, it would have only been one night probably, but one night of bliss, surely? Now I have nothing.

No, that's not true, he's done me a favor – he's made me

realize that there *are* fish in the sea. There is life after divorce. And I can, literally, climb a mountain.

As if reading my thoughts telepathically, my brother calls. His usual Sunday call. Comforting.

"Hi Anthony."

"So where are you having brunch today?" he asks.

"I don't know," I answer despondently.

"Hey girl, you sound happy. What's up?"

"No, I am happy. Really. Just—"

"What?"

"Just a guy."

"Hallelujah! I never thought the day would come. Tell me more, girlfriend."

"Stop that 'hey girlfriend' talk, Anthony."

"Seriously. Who is he?"

"A young guy."

"How young?"

"Twenty-five."

He hoots with laughter. "Cradle-snatcher."

"Shut up."

"So, how was it?"

"That's just the problem. It wasn't. Nothing happened."

"Oh, I see. So you're just *friends?*"

"Maybe not even that."

I tell him about our day, all the details about Alexandre, re-hash our conversations. Anthony is silent for a beat. He is never silent.

"Speak. Say something," I plead.

"Just forget him. I don't want to see you get hurt."

"You mean, I'm past my sell-by date and this man is way too young and gorgeous for me?"

"I didn't say that."

tractive. Maybe you can bolster me up."

She chortles with laughter. "*You?* Unattractive? You make me sick. Wish I had your beautiful blonde hair, your perfect body."

"I'm old."

"Oh pl−*ease*."

"I feel old."

"You *so* don't look your age. You could pass for thirty."

"Still too old."

"Too old for what?"

"I'll tell you at brunch."

We are downtown in The Village on the outside terrace of the restaurant where we've chosen to eat, blessed with another sunny day. The young and beautiful are wandering by in polka-dot dresses and designer shades, some with designer dogs. I'm people-watching and glugging down a Bloody Mary with extra horse-radish sauce, for kick and punch. I've wolfed down my Eggs Benedict and I'm ready for my third drink. This is unusual for me – I don't usually have more than a glass or two of wine.

I can hear my words slurring, morose pessimism thick in my voice. "Why do you think I haven't dated all this time? It's too raw, too painful, that's why."

Daisy is married with a child. She has forgotten what it's like *out there*. She's looking fresh-faced and jolly; her husband has taken her daughter, Amy, to the park for the day and Daisy has a few hours free. Her dimpled cheeks and curly red hair make her look like a grown-up *Annie*.

"Bollocks!" she exclaims. "You've been locked away at work and have not even given dating a chance. Anyway, it sounds like this Alexandre guy is into you."

"That wasn't my brother's opinion."

"Yeah, well, this happens every week. After you've spoken to Anthony you always seem to want to slit your wrists."

I say sarcastically, "I haven't noticed that."

"Families – often they do more harm than good. Take what he says with a pinch of salt. Look, Alexandre fondled your thigh, kissed your hand like some romantic, courtly knight from the Medieval Age. Come to think of it, isn't that his last name? Knight?"

"Alexandre Chevalier."

"Exactly. Chevalier means knight in French."

"That's right, I'd completely forgotten that. My French is pretty poor. I can speak some Spanish, though."

"Listen, he took you away for the whole day, treated you to everything, including a beautiful lunch at that fancy resort."

"But that doesn't mean he finds me sexy."

"If you looked like the back end of a bus, believe me, Pearl, he wouldn't have bothered. He must be interested to have invested a whole day with you. Men are basic. They don't do favors, they do what they *feel* like doing."

"I'll tell you something interezz - ting," I slur, the Bloody Marys making me bold. "When he had his hand on my thigh, I thought I saw a big rock in his jeans. I assumed it must be his wallet but later, when I looked again, after he'd taken his hand away, it had gone down. Could be my imagination—"

"You see? He had—" - she lowers her voice and looks about to check nobody is listening - "-a *hard-on* when he touched you."

sheepish look on his face. "I'm so sorry, Mrs. Robinson. There's a package for you. The new boy put it in the store room and I've just discovered it."

"When did it arrive?"

"It had Mrs. Meyer's dry-cleaning with it which was delivered last Tuesday so it looks as if it has been there for a few days. It came by hand delivery."

"But it's Friday today."

"I apologize. Luke has made several other mistakes and has already been dismissed. He won't be working with us anymore." Dervis goes to retrieve a large, gray box wrapped in a white, velvet ribbon, and hands it to me.

"Thank you, Dervis. Oh, and by the way it's Ms. - not Mrs."

"Pardon?"

Poor Dervis can't get his head around feminist American culture.

"I'm not married anymore, Dervis," I explain. "Mzz is better for me than Mrs." I smile at him sweetly.

I ride up in the elevator and race to my front door, but typically, I can't find my keys. In a panic, I empty the entire contents of my handbag on the floor. I discover them. They were hiding themselves, lodged in my address book. Why I still have an address book when all my numbers are in my iPhone, I do not know, perhaps the weight of paper reassures me. Or the infallibility. I fumble with my keys and unlock the door. This package is making me nervous.

I walk into my messy bedroom, place the box on the bed and stare at it. It is not my birthday. My heart is racing. *Is it possible that….?* No, surely not.

I open the box. Inside is another one, also donning a ribbon, the box much smaller. I lift off its lid and again, another box, oblong in shape. Also, tied with a ribbon, but one made of silk.

My hands are trembling. Another box now – in pale blue leather edged in gold, but it isn't new. It is slightly tattered. I open it. It's velvet-lined and has the name of a Parisian jeweler of *La Place Vendôme* inside - the most expensive jewelry quarter in Paris. The box is antique. I can't believe what I'm seeing. *Did the young doorman make a mistake? Surely this must belong to Mrs. Meyer on the eleventh floor?* I check the name on the first box again, **Ms. Pearl Robinson**, written in large, black letters. No mistake.

I gaze at the stunning piece of jewelry nestled in the leather box: an exquisite double strand of pearls with a diamond and platinum, Art Deco clasp. This definitely looks vintage – they don't make designs like this anymore. There is no way this is a copy. And the worn blue box – unquestionably antique.

I lift the necklace out of the box, delicately. It's a choker; the pearls perfectly round, graduating very subtly in size - fine lustrous pearls with overtones of cream, rose and hints of pale honey and bronzy gold. I hold them up to the light – the myriad colors shimmer with unfathomable depth. I cannot count the different shades; if I were an artist and had to paint them I'd need to mix at least forty hues of subtle colors to do them justice. I think of their origin, each pearl starting its life off as a grain of sand locked in an oyster shell – how each one turns into a perfect, complete jewel. Naturally iridescent, polished by nature, not man.

I unhook the intricate clasp of the necklace and walk to the large mirror in my bathroom, terrified my fingers will fumble – *please don't let me drop this work of art on the floor!* I lay the choker around my neck, the clasp at the front so I can see what I'm doing. A perfect fit. Its beauty is breathtaking. I gasp. My namesake - Pearl. My nose starts to prickle as tears well in my eyes, now glistening like pools of water – like the pearls. I stare into the mirror in disbelief. Nobody has ever given me a gift this special. *But no note? Nothing?* I go back and search amongst the boxes on my bed and inside one of them I find a small envelope. I open it. A handwritten card reads:

Pearl,

These Pearls belonged to a unique Parisian lady called Delphine Aimée. This necklace was a wedding present from her husband, designed especially for her. She was a happy woman, a shining star ...one of the greats. This choker will bring you good luck. There are precisely 88 pearls. Eight is a lucky number.

Eighty-eight is an untouchable number. It is the symbol of infinity – the double directions of the infinity of the universe. It is the period of revolution, in number of days, of the planet Mercury around the sun. It is the number of constellations in the sky. It is the number of keys on a piano.
It is your number, Pearl.

Alexandre.

I am suddenly aware of how embarrassing this situation is. Days have passed since the gift was delivered. Not knowing, I haven't called to say, thank you. He must think me the rudest, most ungrateful woman that exists. I can't believe he hasn't called me to check I'd received the package. Surely he must be worried. How valuable is this piece of exquisite jewelry? It doesn't bear thinking about. Where, now, did I leave his business card?

I find it in the kitchen and call. No answer. His voice-mail picks up. I leave a message, my speech garbled, my apologies profuse with jumbled explanations as to why I haven't called.

I go into the bathroom, quivering from the surprise and excitement of the last fifteen minutes. I need to relax. Friday evening is my weekly personal hygiene, me-time. I check my roots. They're fine. My pedicure still looks perfect but I need to do my legs and double-check my underarms. I strip off my work clothes, brush my teeth until they squeak, and run the bath. I need a good long soak to ease away the stress of the week and the tension of worrying if Alexandre will return my call. Perhaps he has given up on me by now, wishing he'd never given me such an extravagant gift. Maybe he'll even demand the pearls back. Punishment for being so ill-mannered. Can I accept such an expensive gift? Perhaps he got them in a foolish moment, a hasty decision which he now regrets. I must be prepared for that, prepared to let them go.

My beauty regime begins. I take out the cold wax strips – I can't be bothered with salons, it takes too long, so I always do this myself in the privacy of my own home. It's quick, painless, like ripping off a Band-Aid – I've been doing this since I was fifteen and proud that I've never let a razor near my skin. This way, the hair grows back sparse and soft, not stubbly as it does with shaving. I had my bikini line dealt with years ago – electrolysis did the trick, but I regularly give my pubic hair a neat, close trim with a round-ended pair of small scissors. No gray down there, thank goodness. When that day comes it'll be a full Brazilian, all the way.

I look at myself in the long mirror – I'm naked, except for the pearl choker; I look like a vintage hand-tinted photograph of a 1920's glamour girl, my make-up still on but my body nude. I clip my hair up and try to take off the necklace. It won't come off. I don't want to force it, God forbid something should happen. Can you wear pearls in hot water? Suddenly, I fear they could melt. *No, that's absurd, of course they wouldn't.* I climb into my nice, warm, bubble bath, laced with aromatherapy oils, lie back and pick up the book I've been reading but haven't been able to concentrate on. As usual, I start thinking about Alexandre Chevalier but now my reflections are tempered with sweet hope. He bought me a gift! And not just a box of chocolates (which in itself would have been enough of a thrill) - but an out-of-this-world, one of a kind necklace.

Unique. Precious. Personal. With a beautiful message - the number eighty-eight with all those meanings.

How *Romantic*.

I let my hands explore my body, massaging the oily water around my knees, my elbows. I take care of my skin in this way - it keeps me soft. I rub the heels of my feet and in between my toes and soon my fingers wander northwards. I have Alexandre's buffed-up torso in my mind's eye, the sexy glint in his expression, his prowess as he climbed that rock, the texture of his messy dark hair, the smell of his skin and the huge, hard bulge I could see in his pants when he touched my thigh. I sense a throbbing tingle in my groin and slip my middle finger inside myself and rub the sweet-smelling water around me, gently on my clitoris and up around my mound of Venus. I think about my anatomy and suddenly coin a new V word inspired by the number eight: the number of infinity, and eighty-eight, double infinity. V for vagina. V for Vajayjay. And now V for V - Eight.

She is my V-8. Like a powerful car engine, she needs to be fine-tuned.

Or just plain "V," vagina sounds so clinical.

I can hear the house phone ring but I ignore it, I'm not getting out of this heavenly bath. But then my cell starts buzzing. I reach for it on the edge of the tub.

"Hello?"

"I'm downstairs," a familiar voice says.

My heart misses a beat. It's Alexandre. It must have been Dervis calling on the land line to let me know I have a visitor. Alexandre is here in the building!

"I'm in the bathtub," I say.

"Good," Alexandre replies, "I'll join you."

"Pass me onto Dervis," I say.

I can hear Dervis's breathing on Alexandre's cell. "Dervis, you can let him come up," I tell him.

"Okay Mrs. Robinson."

I scramble out of the tub and quickly dry myself. The pearl necklace is glistening, even more now, with drops of oily water. I wrap a huge white towel about me and glance into the mirror which is all steamed-up. I wipe a corner away and see my mascara is smudged, my eye-make-up dark, like coal. I swab a little away with a Q tip and let my hair down. My doorbell is buzzing. I feel my heart thud and I go to answer it.

I open the door. He's more striking than I remembered. He looks disheveled, his dark hair unkempt, his shirt half unbuttoned. He's wearing flip-flops and his feet are elegant and clean. He has a huge bunch of the palest pink roses in his grip, and a bottle of chilled champagne.

"I've missed you Pearl," he says, taking a step towards me.

I feel myself go weak.

"You're wearing the necklace," he observes, running his fingers on the nape of my neck. I tingle all over.

"It's the most stunning thing I've ever seen. I can't thank you enough."

"It's normal," he replies, which I think translated directly from the French means, 'you're welcome'.

No, it's not normal! I want to shout out. But I say, "Are you sure? I mean, I shouldn't accept such a generous gift."

"You *have* accepted this gift, Pearl. You're wearing it and it couldn't suit you more. So stop protesting and come closer." He puts the flowers and champagne on the hall table and takes me in his arms, pulling me tight to him. "You look beautiful," he whispers, staring into my eyes. "How perfect those pearls look on you."

He pushes me against the wall and plants a gentle kiss on my mouth. I gasp. Then his tongue opens my lips apart and he begins to explore slowly around my mouth, licking me softly. My jaw is slack, my breath fast, hungry to be as close to him as possible, greedy for more. The points of our tongues touch and I feel a spasm of desire shoot through my body. Then our mouths are full of each other, tongues probing, locking together.

He pulls off my towel, stands back from me as if to take in the image. "Beautiful," he says with approval. His mouth traces itself around my throat and shoulders - then my nipples which his tongue licks deftly, flicking around each areola until both are erect. He simultaneously strokes the small of my back and buttocks with the tips of his fingers, running them lightly along the crack of my butt. I moan with pleasure. I feel how moist I am between my legs, my V-8 swelling hot. I lower my eyes and notice the huge bulge in his jeans and I gasp in anticipation.

He sucks one nipple and then takes it gently in his teeth but without hurting me. "I'm going to have to do things to you, Pearl. I want you so much. But you know that, already, don't you?"

"I wasn't sure," I say in a thin voice.

I reach for his crotch but he stops me. "Not yet - ladies first," and then he moves his tongue around my breasts again. "I love your tits, they're perfect - your skin's so soft."

His hands are now firmly around my waist. He licks one nipple and lets his fingers walk down one of my thighs. His large hand cups my mound of Venus and I feel one finger slip inside me.

"So, so wet," he murmurs, biting his lower lip. "You're making me rock-hard, chérie. I'm going to have to do something about that. You're really asking for it, aren't you, Pearl? So soon? And I haven't even started yet."

He adjusts his position so he is standing behind me, my back pressed up against his torso – I can feel his hard-on. His thumb is inside me now, his palm cupping the entirety of my vulva. He's holding me as if I were a six-pack! It feels incredible.

"So juicy," he breathes, grabbing the champagne and flowers in the other hand and pulling me close behind him, thumb still inside me, his palm pressing hard against my clitoris. "Come on, let's have a drink – you'll need to put these flowers in water."

I'm on tiptoes tottering in front of him, his hand maneuvering me, thumb still inside, slowly circling as if he is steering me. I feel him with every step I take - gently pushed ahead by him, his palm pressing my sweet spot. I lean back for a second and press my back against his torso. I feel his erection through his pants up against me - his hand still controlling me as if I were a glove puppet. So dominating! But it feels really erotic. Then he softly lets me go. I'm nude, panting, wet as an oil slick, not understanding what has just happened. I turn round to face him - he's smiling, amused.

"Let's have some champagne," he suggests.

"Let me put something on," I reply, confused.

He runs his finger up my spine and feels the choker around my neck, fondling the pearls with the tips of his fingers. "You've already got something on."

"Some clothes," I whimper. I feel vulnerable, exposed. It's as if he has control over me. No man has ever seen me this way. Nude with a choker of Art Deco pearls around my neck like an exotic dog collar. Yes, as if I were some expensive dog on a leash to be pulled and led this way and that! To be *manhandled*. I'm in my own apartment yet, for some reason, I feel helpless.

He holds me by the wrist and pulls me closer. "No clothes. Why would you want to put on clothes? You're so sexy as you are. So beautiful."

"I feel—"

"I forbid it."

He's French. Maybe the translation has come out wrong. The word 'forbid' sounds ridiculous. Like a command. So young, but evidently domineering. But then I see a humorous smirk on his face and I realize he's teasing me.

But before I can protest, he's on his knees, running his tongue around my navel and down towards my wet opening.

His head is underneath me now and his five o'clock shadow is brushing against my thighs and along my cleft. He starts licking me slowly, softly, as if I were an ice-cream on a sweltering day, under, over, around, up inside, running the tip of his tongue around to catch the melting bits. I'm groaning now, the pleasure is indescribable.

"So sweet," he murmurs. "You taste delicious. So, so ready for me. You have no idea how much I want to be inside you."

And then he stops.

"Come on," he takes my hand. "I think you need a glass of champagne."

I'm a wreck. I stand there, stupefied. Naked. Hot with longing. Desperate for him to lead me to the bed and fuck me. *What's he playing at?* I want him inside me. Right *now*. But he's talking about having a glass of champagne and putting the roses in water! Still holding my hand, he leads me to the kitchen. As if it's his own apartment, he starts opening cupboards and looking for a vase.

"Up there on the left, second cabinet," I say with disbelief - my groin on fire.

I watch him fill up the tall, glass vase with water and arrange the glorious bouquet of pink roses; pale, pale pink, like some of the highlights and shades of the pearls. Before he starts rummaging about for glasses, I climb onto a chair to locate my special, crystal, champagne glasses that I was given by my mother for a wedding present. Never used. How ironic, they, like the choker are also original Art Deco. They're shallow *coupe* glasses like saucers – the sort in 1930s Hollywood movies, when champagne flowed in fountains and *femme-fatales* smoked with silver cigarette holders.

Just as I've reached up for them, as I'm still standing on

the chair, I feel Alexandre's hand slip up between my thighs again. This yes-no tease is driving me to distraction. I nearly drop the glasses. I look down and see his head planted between my thighs, forcing them apart. I splay my legs a little. His soft hair is tickling me, brushing against my clit like silk. I close my eyes in bliss. He spins me around, his strong hands clamped on my hips. I can't move, I'm being manhandled again. He has my backside now in his face. I can't see him but I can feel him gently parting my buttocks with his fingers. His tongue starts licking between my crack. Up and down. Wow this feels incredible. *Thank God I had a bath and I smell of sweet oils,* I think to myself, as I whimper with pleasure. My hands cannot touch him, I'm still holding the champagne glasses and I don't want to drop them. He pushes my back down a touch so I am now leaning slightly forward, bending over, still standing above him on the chair.

"Relax, chérie," he cajoles, and I am too turned on to disobey.

His palm is cupping me, my clitoris throb-tingling as he slips his thumb inside and circles it, touching on my inner front walls. The base of his palm putting pressure against my clit – I'm flexing my hips back and forth. I'm really wet. This feels so....*oh my God!* His tongue is licking me up and down along the crack of my buttocks once more. Licking, flicking, darting, probing. He's still palming my clit. I think I'm going to come. That would be a first. All my sensations are deep and hot inside - my brain is like a marshmallow...

My mind is going into a tunnel of black and then flashing pink and red and ...*oh wow,* his thumb is pressing and circling rhythmically in a place at the front of my walls, in a place, oh....ah..., ah, *ah.* I feel every nerve inside me as I implode with pleasure in this deep, undiscovered zone, deep inside me. I cry out – this is the most intense, throbbing orgasm of my life.

He holds his grip firm as I writhe with ecstasy, letting the orgasm spasms of my pulsing, tingling nerves climax in waves, until slowly, very slowly it calms.

He takes his thumb and hand away and licks my juices from his fingers. "Hmm, tasty," he grins, looking up at me. He lifts me down from the chair and sets me on the floor, gently. He grabs the champagne bottle, takes the glasses from me and places them on the kitchen counter. He pops open the champagne and pours, as if what he has done is the most normal occurrence in the world.

I'm a quivering wreck.

"You like that, then?" he asks with a crooked smile.

My jaw hangs open. "That's never happened to me before. That was new. Where you had your thumb has opened up a completely new....a new–"

"I must have hit your G-spot."

I have read about this famous G-spot but was beginning to believe it was a myth. "It felt....how can I describe it? It felt *deep*. So intense."

He smiles knowingly and narrows his eyes as if to say 'that's just the beginning.' *Does this man realize what he has just done?* Oh yes, I think he does. He has a confident air about him as if he does this every day of the week.

"Well, I got to do a little exploration of your body so I had an idea," he says humbly.

I'm still in a state of wonder. Shivering with amazement. He seems to know my body better than I do and we hardly know each other.

"Are you cold, baby?" He looks concerned. A gentleman and a rogue rolled into one. I'm not cold, just shaking with post-orgasm ecstasy. He takes off his loose linen shirt and puts it around my shoulders. I drink in his torso. I close my eyes for a second and, like flash photography, or when you've been staring at something bright, the image makes an imprint on my brain. His stomach muscles ripple into segmented compartments – not a six-pack, no, that's far too crass a word to describe what I see. Nor the statue of David, whose penis is a sad let down and makes his body look like an excuse – no, I know what's beneath Alexandre's pants and I have a feeling it's beyond substantial. His body is superb; a work of art.

He catches me ogling at him and smiles, oh so subtly. He knows the effect he is having on me. Oh yes, he knows all right.

He leads me to my living room and places me on the chaise longue as if I'm his patient recovering from an operation. That's how I feel. Shaky, trembling with wonder at the skill of my doctor who has just discovered something about me, that I didn't even know myself.

I sip my champagne; we're christening my crystal glasses. A real celebration, I think. *That elusive G-spot was targeted!* The champagne is delicious - no wonder - it's Dom Pérignon - Marilyn Monroe's favorite. Music is playing softly on Alexandre's iPhone – I recognize it – Bach's *Air*...so beautiful and soothing. He is sitting beside me, wearing only his jeans. I notice his lovely feet bare – elegant, each toe pleasing to the eye. He's unbelievably handsome and I try not to stare too hard. I can't decide if he looks like a pirate or a gentleman – a mixture of both, I think. Like a pirate, he took me by surprise.

He has me transfixed, bewitched. I scrutinize his even features, his strong, straight nose, his defined jaw, his full mouth, and I wonder what it is that makes a person attractive. It isn't just the looks - no, it's a glint in the eye, the way a person laughs. Alexandre laughs a lot, his conversation interspersed with chuckles, which makes him seem carefree, light. But I saw that dark side last weekend, the flash of fury when he mentioned his father. And nobody as wealthy as Alexandre can be that sweet. He must have a ruthless edge when it comes to business, or some kind of killer instinct.

The Dom Pérignon has made me tipsy, not drunk, but gloriously relaxed. Alexandre is stroking my body, running his long fingers along its entirety, caressing me with a feather touch. Every once in a while he kisses me, soft kisses on the lips, before he lets his tongue dance with mine in a hungry embrace. I'm feeling needy; a longing is pulsing through my veins. How can that be? I have just been satiated. My legs keep opening wide with a will of their own. I want him to make love to me. For some reason, I want more. I feel less self-conscious now, half nude with nothing on but his shirt and the pearl choker, and he, still in his faded Levis, with a look of quiet contentment on his face.

It is dusk outside; the sky is turning orange and throwing a golden glow through the west-facing windows of my living room. I can feel the warmth on my face and an immeasurable sense of relaxation courses through my body as if I were a rag doll. He could do anything with me now. I am his.

He takes a swig of champagne and kneels at the far end of the chaise longue and pushes my legs akimbo. He blows softly between them and darts his tongue out touching my clitoris with the tip of his tongue, almost imperceptibly. I groan and wriggle on my back.

"You're so sensitive, aren't you Pearl? You like it soft, don't you?"

"Yes," I whisper.

"How do you like to come, chérie?"

But I already have come, I think. Doesn't he realize what a big deal for me that already is?

"Hum?" he asks.

I'm silent. What can I say? I can't tell him the truth. I can't tell him that I'm basically unable to orgasm with penetrative and oral sex.

"Tell me about your first time," he urges. "Not the first time you had sex but the first time your little pearlette exploded."

My pearlette. How dainty. What a beautiful way to describe it. Only a Frenchman could come up with that.

I don't have to think hard. I remember as clearly as if it happened yesterday.

"There was the very first time in the bathtub with the shower-head," I admit, almost shamefully. "The pressure of the water got me excited and I had a spontaneous orgasm. It was a huge surprise. I was ten when it happened. And then, soon after that when I was crossing my legs really tightly. I was taking an exam and the pressure, the fear and the panic gave me an orgasm – I didn't even touch myself."

He is still caressing me. I touch his arms and stroke the hair on his head. He's running his tongue along my thigh now and his pinkie finger is tapping my clitoris so gently like the delicate wings of a butterfly. I'm squirming, I raise my hips up, rotating them – this feels *so* good. All I can think of is him being inside me.

"And who was the first *person* to make you come, hmm? The first to give you extreme pleasure?"

I have never told anyone this. Ever. I lie there silent.

"Hmm? The first to give you that big, mind-blowing O?" he asks.

I say nothing.

"How old were you?"

"Fifteen," I whisper.

"Was she a girl?"

How did he know that? Is he psychic?

"How do you know that?" I ask.

"Because of the way your body is, Pearl. So responsive to the faintest, most delicate touch. Usually only girls know how to caress that way – young boys can be like bulldozers. Girls turn to girls; they explore each other as teenagers. What happened to you is more common than you realize."

How does he know all this?

He moves around to the side of the chaise longue and begins to fondle my breasts with a light touch of his fingers, flicking the nipple softly, and licking me on my navel, then under the arms, tracing his tongue to my nipple, now in his mouth. He sucks it and it hardens. I groan again. I start frantically unbuttoning his jeans and his penis springs up free, hard, erect and *enormous*. I cry out at just the thought of it inside me. But wonder if it's too big for me. *This is hot. He is hot.*

"Keep telling me your story," he entreats.

"We were just taking it in turns to tickle each other's arms and back with a bird's feather. You know how girls do? I felt so relaxed. The feather passed by my genitals a few times and I clenched my thighs tightly together and had an orgasm. It was shocking at the time - such an unexpected surprise. I felt embarrassed as she was my best friend. Soon, I started going steady with her brother. He was my first love, my childhood sweetheart. I trusted him so much. With him it happened – I used to climax. He always took his time. But after we split up when I was twenty-two–"

I can feel tears spilling from my eyes now, the champagne has made me open up, the music is so moving, and the truth, like an uninvited gatecrasher, barges its way through my mouth and into my living room. "I can't come anymore having penetrative sex," I weep. "I'm sorry, it's the way I am, there's nothing I can do about it. There, you know now, Alexandre. I'm sure you'd rather be spending time with another woman, someone young and more malleable - someone more receptive."

"But that's one of the things I love about you, Pearl. You're *very* receptive, and open to adventure. I don't want to spend time with another girl. I want to be with *you*, don't you see that?"

"I mean, I love this," I whisper. "I love everything you've been doing, I think you're gorgeous, you've turned me on more than anyone has for years. You've opened up a secret place that I never knew I had inside me. You're so sexy and everything but—"

"There are no buts, Pearl - it's all in the mind," he interrupts. "Without nerves sending impulses back to the brain, an orgasm wouldn't be possible. It's not just physical - it's a crescendo, an orchestra of emotions. The Big O is just an orchestra, chérie, that needs a conductor for guidance, nothing more. As I say, the biggest sex organ is your brain."

"But I don't want you to be disappointed. Please don't expect too much from me – don't take it personally, Alexandre."

"Oh, I'm going to take this *very* personally. You don't know me so well, Pearl Robinson, but one thing I love more than anything is a challenge."

5

It is the next morning and I'm going over the night before, analyzing every move, every word spoken.

Last night, after I told Alexandre about my inability to come from penetrative sex, he held back. I expected him to want to immediately prove himself, throw me on the bed there and then and hammer me senseless, but he didn't.

Instead, he took me out to an exquisite, outrageously expensive restaurant where all the waiters and staff appeared to be in harmonized sync - administering to your every need or whim without appearing to be there. Alexandre held my hand under the table as we languished over this sublime meal, then he walked me home and kissed me goodnight without coming up to my apartment. It all felt so natural in the moment, so romantic, but now Doubt with a capital D is creeping into my psyche and it has obviously decided to hang out with me like one of those 'friends' you've had for years and you don't have the gumption to tell them to take a walk.

The landline is ringing. Great. Just what I need, it's probably my brother and his Sunday call.

"Hi," he begins.

"Hi Anthony."

"Who are you having brunch with?"

"The usual."

"Your fat friend?"

"Daisy is not fat!"

"She is so."

"You saw her four years ago after she'd given birth, for Christ's sake. Not everyone can be like Madonna and Gwyneth Paltrow, and what's her name who—"

"So did you fuck him yet?"

"If you're going to talk to me please stop munching at the same time."

"It's just an apple."

"Well it's crunching down the receiver, Anthony, and it's very annoying. Anyway, why haven't you set up Skype yet? I'm trying to fold laundry and I have to squeeze the receiver to my ear with my shoulder. It's very irritating not having my hands free."

"Too much of a hassle to set up," he munches. *Crunch, crunch.*

"No, it's not. It's simple. Get Bruce to do it."

"Bruce is hopeless. You haven't answered my question."

"Well for your information, no, we didn't. But we did spend the evening together and we...look, I'm not going to go into details with *you,* Anthony, you're my *brother.*"

"Sounds like he's gay."

"Alexandre is so *not* gay. Why do you assume everyone is gay like you?"

"When was this?"

"Last night."

"And he didn't stay over?"

"No."

"And where is he today?"

"He had to fly to Mumbai," I answer.

"Mumbai like Mumbai as in Bombay, India?"

"Yes."

"On a Sunday?"

"Yes. He's an international business man. Very busy."

"You are so dumb, Pearl."

"What?"

"Do you not see a pattern here?"

"What do you mean?"

"Last Saturday you went rock climbing, right?"

"Yeah."

"And he didn't stay over. And, hello? Pearl? He had a 'business' meeting the next day which was a Sunday and today he's supposedly gone to Mumbai, also a Sunday. Duh! He has a girlfriend or a wife who he has to spend the weekend with. Maybe he can get away with 'hanging out with the guys' during the days every Saturday *day time* and *evening* but by night he's tucked up at home with wifey and hanging out with her and the kid on Sunday."

"He doesn't have a kid or a wife."

"How do you know?"

"Because Haslit Films was thinking about doing a documentary about him and his sister and the phenomenon of HookedUp, so we did some research."

"He has a girlfriend, Pearl."

My heart sinks. *Does Anthony know something I don't?*

"Otherwise a twenty-four year-old guy would have at

least fucked your brains out before going home."

"Actually he's twenty-five. He's twenty-five, not twenty-four."

"Ooh, big difference. Unless of course…"

"What?"

"Unless you've gotten all fat and he's turned off by you."

"I am not fat, Anthony! At least that's one area of my life that's in perfect shape. I swim almost every day. I do not eat junk food and slurp down endless sodas like you and Bruce. I take care of my body. Oh yes, Anthony, I forgot to tell you the most important thing of all? Apart from bringing a bottle of *Dom Pérignon* and a massive bunch of roses, he gave me a genuine Art Deco pearl necklace."

"You're kidding."

"So chew on *that*!"

"Pearly you sound real mad at me. I'm sorry, was I being bitchy?"

"Such a mega bitch. So negative."

"Pearleee."

"Listen, I have to go or I'll be late."

I feel as if I'm in *Groundhog Day*. The same conversation with my brother, the same brunch with Daisy. At least the restaurant is different. Today we're having sushi at a place near me on the Upper East Side. And today, Daisy announced at the last minute, she was bringing little Amy along. Sushi is not the best sort of food for a four year-old – I know our meal will be brief.

I have dipped my maki roll in too much wasabi sauce

and my nose is on fire. The restaurant has too many mirrors and my reflection is making me uneasy. *Do I have a double chin?*

"Stop inspecting yourself in the mirror - you look perfect," Daisy scolds.

"Do I have a double chin, Amy?"

"Now stop it! Don't answer her Amy, she's being absurd."

"What's absurd, Mommy?"

"When people say silly lies that aren't even *close* to being true, just to get attention."

"I feel so insecure," I grumble.

"He's crazy about you, it's so obvious. He bought you that freakin' necklace - what more do you want? Oh yes, and he lavished you with champagne and roses, too. How many guys do *that*?"

Amy is wriggling in her chair with excitement, swinging her legs back and forth. "Where's your necklace, Pearly? Can I see it?"

"It's at home, honey, but I promise that next time you come over, I'll show it to you."

"Can I play dress-up with it?"

Daisy laughs. "No, darling, it's not a dress-up necklace; it's a grown-up piece of jewelry. Seriously, Pearl, why are you looking so glum? Really, Anthony should be gagged and not allowed to speak. I'm sure Alexandre is telling the truth about his travels. It totally makes sense. He's out there earning money, not text messaging and calling every second. He must have to work bloody hard to keep his mini empire going."

"He told me he was basically a computer programmer."

"Yeah, right. He's being modest. Alexandre is obviously

I realize, now, that was an excuse. *He's a Latin Lover with a girl in every port*, my brother warned me. He doesn't want some sexually-problematic forty year-old. He's young. His ego would be too bruised by a woman not Orgasm-ing all over the place. Or, more likely - bored as hell by her. *Bored as hell by me.* He doesn't have time for my needs or someone like me. The world is his oyster. Literally. He needs a young woman his age, a twenty-two year-old with tight skin, zero crow's feet. Impressionable.

Damn! I should have kept my mouth shut. I should have dragged him to the bedroom and made love to him; done a *When Harry Met Sally* on him – so easy to do – all those men who think their girlfriends are having multiple orgasms at the drop of a hat – yeah right. I should have done that - not blurted out my sexual shortcomings as if I were sharing my innermost secrets with an agony aunt!

Perhaps a swim will do the trick, a swim at my club to cool off my fury. Fury at myself for getting into such deep water - no pun intended - *who was I kidding?*

I go to my gym. The pool is just what the doctor ordered. They use salt at my gym, not chlorine, so I don't get dry, bleachy skin or green hair. Swimming is what keeps me fit and washes away the tension. I can't run anymore at my age. Pounding the pavement is for women in their twenties. Gravity is not my friend. Swimming is the perfect exercise for me. I can push myself, but not damage tendons; the water holds me up, supports my muscles. I need to keep my bones moving, my spine flexible, my shoulders strong.

Ageing is no picnic.

I'll stay in tonight. I'll order in – maybe some Chinese. I love New York. I love the convenience of this city. Its vibrancy too – even with the endless police sirens, the crowded sidewalks. Paris? Who cares about Paris, I tell myself. New York has to be the best city in the world.

When I get home from the gym, I turn on the TV to distract my thoughts, but immediately switch it off again. How many wars can one planet take? How many more starving people, how many more orphans? I feel angry, depressed and, worst of all, helpless. Helpless to save the world, helpless to rescue just the speck of sand that is myself.

Helpless to get this elusive shit of a Frenchman out of my head.

Just then, my iPad rings. Someone is Skyping me. Has Anthony finally got it together? No, It's HIM! I pick it up. When his face comes on the screen my heart starts pounding – the orphans, the wars, the famine – all are momentarily wiped from my brain. I no longer feel sad but am jumping for joy.

"Hi Alexandre." I try to look calm, cool.

"Hello Pearl. How are you doing, beautiful?"

"Oh, I'm fine, just been swimming, Been really busy at work, seeing friends, you know."

I'm a busy, girl-about-town, have not thought about you at all, nooo way.

"You look lovely," he says.

"Thank you. Where are you?"

"In the back of a limo being driven to the airport, I'm on my way home to New York."

"How did the meeting go?"

"Meetings, plural. Lots of meetings. They went fine. We've sewn up an important deal."

"Great."

"Let's see you."

"What?"

"Stand back. Show me what you're wearing."

"Just my office clothes." I balance the iPad so it's standing high up on a chest of drawers so he can take in my whole body.

"Sexy. Open your shirt."

I unbutton my shirt. "Are you alone?" I ask, double-checking that I'm not sharing my image with a third party.

"Of course I am. Show me your tits."

I take off my shirt. I'm wearing a black lacy, push-up bra.

"You're making me hard." He bites his lip and squints his eyes. "Bring them out. Don't take off the bra, just lift them up."

I cup one hand around my left breast and free it from the bra. The nipple is poking over.

"Fuck you're sexy. Now the other one."

I do the same with my other breast.

"Now lick your fingers and fondle your tits."

I do as he says. I lick my fingers slowly, popping each one in my mouth and circle them around each nipple. They turn erect. I can feel a tingling inside me.

"Let me see *you*," I say.

"You want to see my hard cock? It's rock hard, baby, and it can't wait to fuck you. I'm on my way home to fuck you. That's all I've been thinking about. In between this big business deal, is your wet little pearlette. I want it impaled on my cock and to make you come all around it."

He holds his iPhone down by his crotch and I see his huge penis proud in his hand.

"I want to suck that," I tell him. "I want to lick it up and down, circle my lips around its huge head, lick it up and down and then I want to get on top of it and ride it. Ride it hard."

"Fuck you're sexy," he says in a low voice. He's moving his hand up and down, pleasuring himself. It's massive and it's driving me crazy. "Take off your skirt," he commands.

I unzip my skirt and let it drop to the floor. I'm wearing white cotton panties. I can see his face again now. His eyes are half closed – bedroom eyes, eyes of a man who thinks of nothing but sex.

"Wet your fingers," he whispers.

I'm really getting into this and feel like a porn star. I lick my fingers wiggling the tip of my tongue. Exaggerated. Dirty girl style.

"Now put them on your sweet little oyster. I want to see you bend over and press your pussy on the arm of that sofa. I want to see you fuck the sofa, Pearl. Move the iPad so I can see you."

I feel self-conscious but brave. I move the iPad into a better position. "But I won't be able to see *you*," I complain.

"You'll see me soon enough, chérie. Move over to the sofa arm. That's good. Bend over so I can see your sexy butt. Oh yeah, that's good, that's perfect. Keep those white schoolgirl panties on. Bend over. Oh yeah, that's good."

I'm bending over the arm of the sofa which is pressing on my clitoris. The vision of his huge erection is in my mind's eye. I'm feeling really horny now.

His voice continues over the speaker but I can't see him.

"Now fuck that as if you were fucking me, as if you were on top of me. I can see how wet you are. I can see that glistening little oyster and the wetness coming through your little white virgin panties."

I start to move my pelvis back and forth. The corner of the sofa is soft but presses beautifully up against me, pushing on my clitoris, pressing at my opening. I can feel my wetness. I'm moving back and forth and it feels great. *Why haven't I thought of this myself?*

"Keep moving, chérie. My cock is so fucking *hard*. All it wants to do is fuck you. Sleep next to you. Wake up. Fuck you again. Keep fucking you." I can hear his fast breathing and I imagine how colossal and stiff he is.

I keep my rhythm going and play with my breasts at the same time. I look down at them, the nipples hard as cherries, and I have a flash of a vision of making love to a woman with big breasts, then I have his thudding great erection in my mind again, then a threesome with him and this sexy, desirable woman. Me kissing her, Alexandre slamming me from behind and I can't hold it any longer. I can feel a rush of emotion gather in a crescendo hot between my legs and I'm coming - my orgasm, powerful like a tsunami wave.

"I'm coming," I moan. "I'm coming."

"Me too," he shouts. "Coming for you, chérie. You're so beautiful, so fucking hot - so sexy."

I lie forward for half a minute groaning with my release, my butt in the air, the throbbing of my orgasm calming itself to a lighter tingle. I collapse on the sofa, laughing with relief.

I can't believe what I've just done! I've had phone sex for the first time in my life.

7

I'm flying again. I'm back at school and soaring high above the room and it's effortless like a trapeze artist but without the trapeze. The freedom is liberating. The history teacher, Mr. Hand, who was hideous before with warts on his face, has morphed into a Greek god. He doesn't have a shirt on and his chest is buff and defined. Why is everyone so rude about him? He's gorgeous. The bell is going - loud in my ear. Time for class.

It's my cell.

I'm groggy. I was dreaming. Damn, so disappointing that I can't fly in real life – it seemed so true.

I pick up.

"I'm outside your apartment building on the street."

"Alexandre?"

"The doorman doesn't seem to be here."

"Sometimes he takes a nap and it's hard to wake him but

he's there. What time is it? Never mind, I'll buzz down. See you in a minute."

I call the doorman who is as surprised as I am. It must be before dawn. I frantically rush to the bathroom to brush my teeth, and give my private parts a quick wash. Just in case. Alexandre gets so *intimate*. I splash water on my face and around my eyes. I look at my phone, it's five am.

There's a light tap at my door. My stomach dips with nerves. All I've got on is my crimson silk robe.

I open the door and this vision is standing before me. He's even hotter than I remembered. He's unshaven and messy, his jeans not too loose, not too tight, but all I can see is his mammoth bulge inside as if just talking to me a second earlier has made him hard. Knowing he's lusting after me so much makes adrenaline surge through me - I can feel my juices start to gather – just looking at him makes me moist with desire.

He steps forward and kisses me hungrily. He tastes of apples and mint and smells deliciously of just Alexandre - a smell I wish I could bottle. He pulls off my robe and it shivers to the floor like a pool of red blood. His tongue explores my mouth, my lips – he's kissing my neck, my breasts and he palms my V with his large hand.

"I'm going to have to fuck you – so wet already," he purrs into my ear.

I grapple with the buttons on his Levis and go down on my knees. We are still in the doorway. His jeans fall about his ankles and his erection springs up, this huge arrogant thing, as if it had a life of its own. No underpants. Sexy. I start to lick him the way I described during our phone sex. I hold it in one hand and cup my other underneath his weighty balls. I lick them gently and take one, whole in my mouth, and suck tenderly. I don't want to hurt him or be too rough. I can hear him groaning quietly – his hands are rested gently on my head as he strokes me and runs his fingers through my hair. I lick his shaft slowly, deliberately, up and then down, up and down - then I stand up and bend over because he's tall and I need to position myself right. Still holding him in my hand firmly, I circle my tongue around the head, licking his juices from his one-eyed Jack – wow, he's just as turned on as I am.

"Fuck, Pearl, this is what I've been dreaming of. This is hot. This feels amazing."

My tongue finds its way up to his firm stomach, then back to his hard rod which I take in my mouth as if it were a giant lollipop. It reaches the back of my throat. I tense my lips about it and suck hard, up and down, up and down, up and down, stroking his balls with a feathery touch. I lick my fingers on my right hand, cover them with my spit and trace them slowly up behind in the crack of his buttocks. I press my wet middle finger inside his opening. He's groaning now and I feel powerful. I have this rich, controlling guy in the palm of my hand. Literally. I have him in my mouth. He's all mine and he's groaning with pleasure. I feel strong. Potent, like a queen with her empire. *He* is my empire.

My head is moving fast now, up and down – I'm trying not to gag with his size. Still with my left hand playing with his balls, I press my finger deeper into the crevice of his butt and that's it – a fountain of pleasure spurts hard at the back of my throat. He's calling out my name. He's all mine. I did this.

"Oh Pearl baby, oh Pearl," he rumbles. My eyes look up, my mouth still firmly in place, and observe his face grimacing as if in pain. His release is intense; his body judders.

A moment passes - he's coming down from his orgasm

now and I finally take my mouth away.

"That's maybe the best blow job I've ever had," he says, and then laughs.

I feel a wave of jealousy at the thought that other women have done this too. Other women have made him weak with pleasure. But he's *mine*. I don't want any other female laying her hands on him, her mouth. I want Alexandre all to myself.

Minutes later, my power is now diminished. He got what he wanted from me. His release. I am no longer the queen with her empire but a servant that can be tossed aside. Panic sets in as I fear he might leave now - might decide to go home.

But he says, "Come here you gorgeous creature and give me a kiss. It's your turn now, Ms. Robinson. I want to give you what you deserve."

"And what do I deserve?"

"I think you deserve to be made love to, don't you?"

"Yes," I murmur with gratitude. I want him inside me. I notice he's still as hard as he was, still as erect.

"Now bend over and touch your toes," he commands.

My moment of power is over, my reign as empress brief. He holds all the cards now. I bend over. Is he going to spank me? No, he starts licking me delicately around my core. Licking, then sucking. This feels hotly erotic.

"Always so wet, always ready to get fucked by me, aren't you?"

"Yes," I whimper.

"Is it only me? Is it only me you want inside you?" His voice is almost a roar.

"Yes. I don't want anyone else! I can't even look at anyone else." Except in my dream, I think. *What was my old History teacher, Mr. Hand, doing in my goddam dream??*

"Do you want to kiss anyone else?" he mumbles, now only touching my entrance with the very tip of his tongue. He's teasing me again. My hips start gyrating, trying to push myself closer to his mouth. "Do you want to kiss anyone else?" he asks again savagely.

"I had a little fantasy. When we were Skyping together, I imagined I was kissing another woman while you were fucking me from behind."

"And what was she like? Was she pretty?"

"Stunning. With big, perfectly shaped breasts."

He lifts me up by my shoulders so I'm standing straight and then spins me around; I'm now facing him. He kisses me hard, our mouths hungry for each other.

"You're making me fucking horny," he says. But then his face goes suddenly dark, his eyes fiery. "Who else has been fucking you? Before me?"

"Nobody. I practically feel like a virgin, it's been so long."

He steps away from his jeans which are still pooled about his ankles. "I don't believe that. You're too good. Too expert. Where did you learn all this? Where did you learn to do that?"

"Instinct," I bleat out. "I've never done this before in that way. It's *you*, Alexandre. You make me this way. You make me want to do these things."

"Who else has been making love to my Pearl and her juicy little oyster?" he demands, flicking his tongue on my nipple and then nipping it. A spasm of pleasure shoots directly between my legs.

"Nobody, I swear. I haven't had sex for two years. I haven't had sex since my divorce." *Okay, there was that one terrible time but I keep quiet about that.*

My answer seems to placate him but he stares at me for a second as if to read my face for lies. "Good girl," he whispers in my ear. "I don't want you involved with anyone else, is that clear? I want to keep you for myself. I'm not a jealous man but I am possessive of my treasures."

I'm a treasure?

"This beautiful Pearl and her pearlette are mine, is that clear?"

"Yes." I smile, and feel as if I've won something. Jealous men have always irritated me but this is making me hot. I have made a young, twenty-five year-old possessive of me, and I'm loving it. "What about you? Are you seeing anyone else?" I ask with trepidation. What if he says 'yes' – I'll fall apart.

"I already told you I was unattached."

"Unattached means no girlfriend, no relationship. Are you fucking anyone else?"

"Not now, I won't be. Why go out for hamburger when I have steak at home?"

"Paul Newman said that."

He laughs. "I know - it's a good line. Seriously, Pearl, I really don't want to waste my time with anyone else, now I've found you. You passed both tests one and two, remember?"

I had almost forgotten about that. "Remind me what they were?" I say.

"Test one – you're a dog lover and you care about animals. Test two – you're brave and adventurous; you came rock climbing with me, even though it was obvious you'd never done it before."

"I told a white lie," I admit. "I was worried you wouldn't invite me otherwise. Dogs..." I smile. "Is that the only reason you like me?"

He laughs and adds, "You're the whole package. You're beautiful, smart, sexy, independent, mature, and I still have that little 'challenge' in mind. We still have work to do. Now stop doubting me and get on the bed where you belong."

Did I just hear that right? Where I belong!! Who is this guy with his old-fashioned values? But then I see a glint of humor in his eye and I know he's just kidding.

"When you say 'mature' what do you mean exactly?" I ask. *Is mature a code word for old?*

"Mature. A woman who is mature knows what she wants. Like you. You have a past, you've experienced life. You've borne some knocks and bruises, perhaps. Suffered, had your heart broken maybe. You're a whole person, Pearl. You have a good career. I'm not interested in some young, naive girl hanging on to my every word, my every movement - I'd find that unappealing. I want someone who's my equal. I'm not perfect but I feel comfortable in my own skin and although I'm young I have everything, and I want a woman with substance like *you*," he says, moving close.

I hold him back. "You say mature. How old *am* I?" I ask apprehensively.

Brave move. *What if he thinks I'm older than I am?*

"I don't know and I don't care. I would never ask. But you're beautiful and you have my attention. Now get on the bed."

I lie nude on my four poster bed, lapping up all his compliments and bathing in honeyed words like 'beautiful' and 'you're the whole package.' Pack Age, his accent says – uh, oh, that *age* word again drumming in my ears. But it's my hang-up, not his. I've got to move on from that.

He straddles me and kisses me softly on my nose, my

eyelashes, my lips, my shoulders. I've been waiting for this – waiting to be fucked by him. Whether I have an orgasm or not, I don't care – I want him inside me. My breath is shallow – butterflies are circling my stomach.

His fingers are draped against the full expanse of my vulva like a velvet curtain, cupping me like a glove. What a great fit it is, too. I'm pushing my pelvis against his palm, and his index fingers are making rhythmic upside-down 'come hither' movements along my hot wet entrance, probing into my glistening doorway. He's reaching in and upwards with his smooth finger against my ceiling and hoists me up several inches off the bed. So dominating, so in control – instinctively he knows what my body wants. It feels incredible – my G-spot is hungry for him, hungry for his magic wand.

Still with his fingers inside me, he pulls my groin up towards his face - my back arches off the bed and he presses his still tongue against my vulva. He holds it flat against my clitoris without movement. I'm squirming up against it, gyrating my hips, arching my back more to get closer to him, moaning with pleasure. I'm pushing and grinding and suddenly his tongue, from being quite still, strokes me vertically and diagonally in sudden flashing lashes. He's whipping me with his tongue. I'm tingling with desire, throbbing with longing.

Then he stops. His tongue is still again. My V-8 is humming like the fiery little engine it is. I can feel my juices oozing. I'm so revved-up.

"Please," I beg. "Please fuck me."

"Not yet. All good things come to little girls who wait. Especially neo-virgins – I need to take it slowly with you."

His tongue starts probing deep inside me, in and then out. He stops again. I'm squirming on my back, his head is between my thighs and I grab his hair and try to pull his head up towards my face. I need him inside me. I *need* that huge beast of his phallus deep inside. His tongue starts fucking me, in, out, in out. It feels amazing but I want more, I yearn for all of him to go deep. I miss him so far away from me. I want the intimacy of his entire being, his face on mine, his torso on my breasts. I need him whole. I'm longing for that erection to probe deep inside against my walls.

He gets up and I hear him rummaging about in his jeans pocket. I open my eyes which have been closed in ecstatic reverie and see the condom packet which he is ripping open with his teeth. *Yes, yes, at last!* It's a brand I haven't seen before - XL lambskin. I didn't know they made them extra large but I guess it makes sense for him. He rolls it on to his erection - my V-8 humming away in preparation, throbbing with the thought of him inside me.

He straddles me again – then moves down the bed and circles my clitoris with his tongue, careful not to touch it directly, which makes it more desperate to be fondled. But, he leaves it be. He slowly moves his way higher, his chest now on top of me, my nipples hard beneath his strong torso. I can feel his whopping great cock pressing up against me, about to enter me. I moan with anticipation. I grab it – it is rock hard inside the condom which feels soft, not the usual rubbery texture. I guide it towards my wet opening but he pulls back.

"You cannot have it all, little Pearl. Not yet. Greedy girls have to watch their appetites."

He lets the tip probe my hot entrance but just the tip.

"*Please.*" I am pleading now, whining like a child for candy.

He starts with shallow thrusts, barely penetrating me, his

arms enclosing me tightly, his mouth on mine. Then he pauses and lets his erection rest just an inch inside me. He's lingering close but not moving. I'm flexing my hips, desperate to get closer, my hands are like claws on his tight ass, pulling him toward me. *Fuck me all the way. Please,* I beg silently. But he's holding back, his strength and willpower overcoming me.

"So wet, I'm going to have to suck that little oyster later. I'd like that little oyster and its Pearl to come with my mouth around it," he whispers in my ear as he nibbles the lobe.

I groan and tense my buttocks, thrusting myself at him. Only the tip of his huge erection is inside me, then he makes tiny thrusts – and pulls out, each time its soft, huge head pressing up and brushing past my clit. The shaft of it is rubbing against me and he's gently thrusting between my labia without entering me. I'm screaming now. This feels incredible.

"Shush, quiet now. So juicy," he murmurs. "I love your hair, your body, your soft skin, your blue eyes, I love the way you smell. I love the way you're so desperate for me to fuck you." As he says this he plunges his erection deep into me, the whole of him inside, simultaneously pressing his pelvic bone against my clit, holding himself firmly in place before withdrawing again. The tease is driving me crazy. My body is begging for each plunge, the taut fullness of him. I can feel the nerve endings on my clitoris swelling with heat. He pulls out. He's guiding his penis now with his hand – he's slapping it against my clit and I'm moaning.

"I'm going to really fuck you now like you deserve, you greedy little girl. You want my cock? All of it?"

"Please," I cry. "It's so big it scares me, though."

"Too big for you? Too big for your tight little pearlette?

It's so tight. Like a virgin. I think it needs to be ripped open by my big cock. I think it needs that."

"Yes," I groan, my buttocks clenched, my pelvis rising higher so I'm pressing deep up against him, his erection poised at my soaked entrance.

"Are you sure you're ready?"

"Yes," I cry. "Please, *please*."

But he starts teasing me with the tip again and, just as I can't take any more, when I think I'm going to come from the rhythmic brushing on my clit, he suddenly slams himself hard into me; his erection swelling inside me, his immense size filling me whole, his pelvic bone pressing hard down on my clitoris. I'm shouting out, my brain concentrated on nothing but my center - my entire universe at this moment. All I care about, all I desire. He takes his cock out again tantalizing me at the entrance, circling me and then slaps my clit with it again. The sensation is so intense. He plunges into me once more, I can feel his pubic bone pressing against that sweet spot and I start coming in a rush of heaven, all my nerve endings in that one area sending my whole body into a quivering spasm. My contractions are tight about his erection, squeezing him as he's holding it there. He pulls away then thrusts it in hard and then goes still. He's moaning quietly now and I can feel his hardness inside me as he explodes. My hands are clawed about his ass, holding him close. My pulse is pounding between my legs...ah...ah...I'm still climaxing and so is he. He's kissing me, his tongue ravenous for mine. My pelvis starts to move up and down. I could keep going with this all day.

"I came with penetrative sex," I gasp.

"I hardly even fucked you, if you noticed. I didn't need to. This is just getting you warmed up, Pearl. Just getting you used to me inside you. We'll get there. This isn't a race, time is on our side." He pulls out of me slowly and I suddenly feel bereft. His face is inches away, his lips on my cheek but I feel lonely already. I can't get enough of him. This is crazy.

"I want more," I breathe, still feeling tingles from my intense orgasm, craving him inside me again, the intimacy, the deep connection.

"I know you do."

"I want more *now*."

"Well you'll have to wait," he says with a trace of a smirk. "I have work to do. And you do, too." He looks at his watch. "It's seven a.m."

"*Please.*"

He starts laughing. I suspect he loves being in control. He is in command of my body as if I were a marionette. I'm writhing on the bed, the sheets deliciously rubbing between my thighs, extending my post orgasm thrill. I swear, if he were to enter me again, I could come once more. But he's standing up putting on his jeans.

"Breakfast time," he barks. "Up, up, lazy girl, get that sweet butt off the bed, move that little Pearlette into action."

"More action - exactly. Give my Pearlette more action. *Please.*"

He laughs again. "Let's just say things are going as I hoped they would. I like seeing you hungry for me."

I'm on my stomach, still lying on the bed. I press a cushion in between my thighs and start moving up and down, my buttocks high in the air - trying to tempt him.

"Careful, little girl, or I'll have to fuck you from behind. But really fuck you hard. Till you're ravaged inside."

I start moaning. Begging. "Yes *Please.*" I have no shame. No composure. No dignity.

He approaches the bed and I feel victorious. *He's going to give it to me. Ram it up me. Fill me up. Yes!*

But instead, he lifts me off the mattress and carries me like a baby in his arms to the bathroom. He sets me down. He opens the glass doors of the shower and turns on the faucet. He claps his hands loudly and there's a ringing in the air. He says, "Shower time! In you get, Pearl."

I do as he says. He eyes my naked body up and down and takes his jeans back off. He's stiff again. *Yes!*

We are both in the shower together and I'm still feeling stimulated. I want my power back. I take the shower gel, put some on my fingers and lather it across his back, shoulders and his athletic torso, and I move down his thighs. He's hard as a diamond. I crouch down, feeling the warm water splashing on top of me and take him in my mouth again. I'm hungry - desperate for him, shameless with my voracious appetite. I concentrate hard on making him groan, clinging to his leg as I suck on him.

"You just can't stop, can you?" he says. But I know he likes it, as he flexes his hips towards my mouth.

"No, I can't get enough of you," I pant, and then start licking his shaft as if my life depended on it.

My nipples are erect without him even touching them. The water is splashing on them, arousing me. I stand up and kiss him on his mouth, holding his erection tightly in the grip of my hand. He shoves his thigh between my legs and I gasp. His wet flesh is pushing against my clitoris; he rams it hard against me as I start to writhe on his leg. My hand is moving up and down on his hard-on, faster now to the same rhythm that my pelvis is pushing up and down, pressing against his firm thigh. My hard nipples are smacking against his chest. I keep this up for several minutes until I feel the blood rush along his phallus, and creamy liquid ooze in a gush in between and over my fingers. I push harder on his thigh and hit that divine spot. My orgasm is rising hot between my legs. I'm groaning, kissing his chest, taking his nipples between my teeth. He growls out my name. It's a simultaneous orgasm - both of us pleasuring each other in the same moment.

"Pearl/Alexandre," we cry out at once.

I collapse in his strong arms, the water beating on my head.

Finally, I feel satiated.

Now I can go to work.

8

I have never been this obsessed by sex. Ever. I am akin to a thirteen year-old boy reaching puberty, with sex constantly on the brain. All day, I walk about with fire between my legs. I am like a zombie at work, an automaton. After this morning's love-making I can't think of anything but Alexandre and his body parts and all the things he has done to me, and will do to me.

I am playing *Under My Thumb* by The Rolling Stones on my iPod – how apt. I have been, literally, under his thumb.

My cell phone wakes me up from my shallow-breathed daydream.

The voice says, "Are you thinking what I'm thinking?" It's HIM.

"What are you thinking?" I ask guardedly, my stomach dipping with excitement and nerves. I've already humiliated myself enough this morning, already demonstrated that I'm like an addict who needs a fix, and that I have no control over myself whatsoever. Not when it comes to him, anyway.

"I'm thinking about you," he tells me, his voice deep and seductive. *Thank God he still wants me.* "And you? Are you thinking the same?"

"No," I reply.

"Oh." I can hear the disappointment in his tone.

"Why would I be thinking about *me*?" I say. "It's *you* my mind is focused on."

He laughs at my silly joke. "I've been planning what I'm going to do to you. Have you thought about that, Pearl? The things I'm going to do?"

"Yes," I whisper. There is someone else in the editing room. "And little else," I add quietly.

"Dinner tonight?"

"I'd love to. Where?"

"At my place. I'll be cooking. Anything you don't eat?"

We both burst out laughing, realizing how apt his question is.

"No red meat. Only free range chicken."

"I'll send a car to pick you up at eight o'clock."

"I'll be ready."

"Oh yes, I know you will."

So arrogant! This man is sure he has me just where he wants me. *Under his thumb.* And what a thumb it is too, zeroing in on my G-spot the way it did the other day. Just thinking about it has me feeling all melty again.

Eight O'clock is going to feel like an eternity.

The exterior of Alexandre's corner-lot, pre-war apartment building is particularly elegant. It is entered on Sixty Second Street under a very high fixed marquee, rather than the ubiquitous green awning seen everywhere else in Manhattan. The doorman lets me in with a flourish. It seems he is expecting me. The lobby is grand and makes my place look humble. This is how the other half live, or rather, not the other half (I am the other half – I have food on the table, right?) This is how the 0.75% lives - the ridiculously wealthy. The old black and white marble floors are polished to a high sheen, set off by large arches. Antique sofas upholstered in silk damask are placed strategically by a vast, marble fireplace overhung with a Louis XIV mirror. I doubt people sit on those sofas very often, as they are pristine. The flower arrangements look as if they were prepared for a wedding or for some charity benefit, towering in old-fashioned copper vases, which gleam so brightly they reflect the room. All this, for just the lobby.

The doorman buzzes open the elevator for me and says, "The Penthouse, Ms. Robinson."

"Thank you."

I walk inside the roomy elevator that smells of roses. Just as the doors are about to close, an elderly lady shuffles forward, shouting, 'wait' but the doors magically reopen, controlled at the entrance by the doorman. The elderly lady steps in. She is draped in jewels, dons oversized dark shades and carries a host of shopping bags from Tiffany and Neiman Marcus.

"Hello," I say and smile.

"Hello dear," she croaks.

The lit-up buttons display our floors, although neither of us has pressed anything.

"You're visiting Alexandre?" she enquires.

"Yes. For dinner."

"How exciting. He's a marvelous cook. I wonder what he'll serve you."

"You've had dinner with him?" I ask, trying not to sound too surprised – I don't want to seem rude.

"Dinner, lunch. He's a lovely boy - everybody in the building just *adores* him. Such a talent at everything he does. He's arranged some soirées for charity with musical quartets and just the best food ever. He's so kind and has time for everyone - even an old lady like myself. Such a honey."

Her door opens at the third floor. "Have a lovely evening, dear."

"Thank you. You too," I call after her.

The elevator is lined in mirrors and has a small bench to sit on, also upholstered in silk damask. I inspect myself. I'm wearing a black dress, a beautiful, vintage Jean Muir which I picked up for a song somewhere in The Village. It is silk knit and hangs like a dream. Simple, elegant, understated. It fits like a glove, perfect around my bust and breasts, demanding no bra. I have a small back which means a lot of tops and dresses swim about me, but it's also a blessing as it means I can pick up things from the sixties and seventies that don't fit today's modern woman.

I left my apartment looking as if vandals had ripped my bedroom apart. Every single item of my wardrobe is lying in chaotic piles on the bed, strewn over chairs, on the floor. They have even found their way into the bathroom. Decisions, decisions. I was going to wear a slinky, long, red dress but thought it was too 'sex siren' - not the message I want to advertise. I think Alexandre has got the point. I don't want overkill. I tried on a beautiful cream dress with rosebuds but

I looked too 'little girl'. Then I decided that I *must* wear the pearls. Not something I can put on for work, and where else can I wear them if not for dinner with Alexandre? So then the dress became all about, 'what will go with the pearls?' Thank goodness I left work early and gave myself time. I finally settled on this old favorite, the Jean Muir. Classic. Timeless. It reaches just below my knees, is tight about the bust but flares in two layers so if I spin about it almost makes a circle around me. I put on some simple pearl studs but would you know it? The pearls of the earrings did not match – did not pick up even one of the forty shades of the choker. So I tried some diamond studs which my mother gave me for my twenty-first birthday, which match the clasp of the necklace - just about. The faithful, high, nude pumps complete the outfit. Nude pumps with a black dress? Yes, they lengthen the legs. A tip I picked up from Vogue.

Hair loose, mascara, a little eyeliner and some lip gloss. My eyes don't look good with a lot of make-up, and I'm so bad at blending foundation that I pass on that.

My bag is a simple black clutch (that's a first) and I just have a pale blue cashmere wrap, in case I get chilly, but right now it's pretty hot outside.

The elevator doors open directly at the Penthouse on the thirteenth floor (lucky for some) and I walk inside the apartment. There is no corridor. It seems that there are no other apartments on this floor – Alexandre has it all to himself.

He welcomes me. He looks even more informal than usual in just his Levis and a T-shirt. He's barefoot and I catch a glimpse of those elegant toes.

"Good evening, Pearl, you look quite beautiful." More *Beauty Full* than *Beauty Fool,* his accent says. Let's hope I can keep going with the Beauty Full and not slip into the Fool which I fear I did this morning with my needy begging for sex. He said himself he likes me because I am 'mature' – I need to act like a grown-up, not a spoiled brat screaming for more candy.

He kisses me softly but not passionately, as if to say, *let's try not jumping each other's bones in the first few seconds.*

I keep my shoulders back (thanks for that tip, Mom, it has served me well) to try to give the gliding, poised look. It seems to work. I feel tall in my heels.

"You look so elegant in the necklace," he says. "I appreciate that you're wearing it for me."

"Not as much as I appreciate the gift. Every time I look at it, I'm bowled over."

"I have another gift for you."

"Oh no! Alexandre, please. You're cooking me dinner, that's already special. And this choker was beyond generous. You really don't have to give me anything else."

"Don't worry, it's very simple. I'll show you in a minute. Now what can I offer you to drink? Champagne? A cocktail?"

"A cocktail sounds tempting but I think I'll go with champagne, please."

"As lovely as you look in those shoes why don't you kick them off - you'll be way more comfortable – I'll show you around my abode."

His *abode?* His palace, more like.

He's right. I'm tottering about and feel self-conscious with Alexandre being so informal. I sit on a chair and slip my shoes off my newly buffed and pedicured feet. My toenail polish is ice blue. I look in awe about me. Like the main lobby, the floors are marble, not black and white but a pale gray. Up here the feeling is more Bohemian chic than in the lobby. Nothing is too polished, nothing flashy or overdone. It gives the air of an eighteenth century Parisian house that you might read about in a novel or see in a period movie. Everywhere there is wood paneling, even hiding the elevator when it closes. There are paintings on the walls, mostly figurative - an eclectic mix of modern and old, and a worn priceless-looking tapestry – a medieval scene of unicorns and ladies picking apples from trees.

Just this hallway is practically the size of my whole apartment.

Alexandre takes my hand. "Come, I'll give you a tour."

He leads me into the first room. The floors are now parquet, the wood buffed to a warm glow. The room is also completely paneled.

He stands there, his legs astride, and tells me, "This walnut *boiserie* is original 1930s when the building was constructed. None of the other apartments have this paneling. See how the era's ribbon-edge wood motifs are intact?"

I notice how it adds a kind of rococo accent to the place, adorning the doorframes, and the cabinetry and bookshelves which are integrated within the paneling. They run along one side, and on the other are picture windows looking across Central Park to the West side, letting in beams of evening light. The massive room has two fireplaces and a double-aspect - from the south windows there are views to the Plaza and Fifth Avenue. In the middle of the room are two enormous sofas facing each other with a coffee table in between, and at one end of this striking living room cum library is a black, grand piano.

"Do you play?" I ask.

"No, but my sister does."

"Where is she now?"

"In Paris. But she always stays here when she's in New York."

"How often does she come?"

"Once a month, or so."

"What's it like having a business partnership with a member of family?" I pry.

"Put it this way, I couldn't have done it without her. We're a team. She's savvy, smart and has a good head on her shoulders when it comes to deals. She's a tough negotiator."

"Did she go to Mumbai, too?"

"Oh yes. I don't make deals without her present. She got a scholarship to Harvard Business School – she's very well versed when it comes to corporate, multinational stuff."

I lean against the Steinway and run my fingers along its smooth lines. "I used to play," I say. "If only we'd had room for a piano like this in our small apartment, maybe I would have continued more seriously."

"Really? Be my guest. Play something now."

"Oh, I'm very rusty."

"No, you're not," he replies with a wry smile, and I roll my eyes at his innuendo. "Go on, play something," he entreats.

I sit at the piano stool and shake out my fingers and wrists. "It's been a while."

He leans languidly against the grand, waiting. I take a deep breath and begin one of my favorite tunes.

"Erik Satie," he says with a knowing smile. "*Gymnopedie number 1* – so haunting. You play beautifully, Pearl."

When I finish he claps and I feel pleased that I didn't make any mistakes. It makes me remember why I chose the instrument in the first place. I would give anything to have a piano like this.

"Some champagne," he remembers, opening a hidden bar, camouflaged by the walnut paneling. He looks into a small refrigerator. "For some reason there doesn't seem to be any in here. Let's go to the kitchen."

We make our way down a wide corridor and I find myself in - not a normal kitchen - but a sort of show-room. The ice-box alone would fit a regular-sized bathroom inside it. There is an island in the middle of the room, a big round table at one side, and wall to wall cabinets reaching to the high ceiling. All is white, the counter-tops marble, the floor marble. Light is pouring into the room as the windows are massive. There is a gas-burning stove, wider than an elephant, from which is emanating a delicious aroma of something roasting quietly in the oven.

"That smells wonderful," I comment.

"Well, let's hope it tastes as good as it smells." He walks over to the refrigerator and takes out a bottle of Dom Pérignon rosé champagne and pops open the cork.

"The lady from the third floor was raving about your cooking," I tell him.

"My grandfather was a chef – I picked up a few tricks."

"I guess you have the best food in the world in France."

"Oh, I don't know, lots of other countries have caught up with us in many ways. I had the most exquisite dish near San Sebastian in Spain a couple of weeks ago, and some of the pizzas here in America rival Italy."

"Pizza doesn't count," I exclaim, "as world-class cooking."

"Never underestimate the culinary importance of pizza, Pearl," he tells me with a sardonic smile. "If you were on Death Row you probably wouldn't ask for *haute cuisine*."

"I'd ask for my mother's macaroni and cheese."

"Exactly, there you go. It's the Italians that have us all hooked on their food." He pours us both some chilled champagne. It's crisp and aromatic. Champagne, an unbeatable French export.

I raise my eyebrows. "Do you sometimes think about that? Imagine being on Death Row?"

"We don't have the death penalty in France but since I've lived here in The States I do question the possibility sometimes." He says this with a serious look on his face. Is he kidding? I can never quite tell with him.

"Do you think you'd be capable of murder, then?" I ask, half teasing.

But his answer is serious. "We're all capable of murder, aren't we, Pearl? Given the right - or rather the wrong - circumstances."

I stare at him. I can't read his expression. He's a dark horse - an enigma, that's for sure. I return to the more comfortable topic of food. "You're probably the only European I've met who hasn't touted his country's cuisine as the best in the world."

He laughs. "Oh, I never said we weren't the best. We take our cooking very seriously. The lunch hour in France is sacrosanct. Everybody sits down for a three-course meal. The point is, we *want* to be the best – our reputation matters to us. We want to create gastronomic fantasies – so that our guests beg for a second helping."

The way he says this speaks volumes. That *double entendre* again. He's got me begging for a second helping, that's for sure.

"Follow me." He leads me by the hand to another room with a flat screen TV splayed across one wall – the room peppered with opulent sofas and chairs. There's a wrought-iron, spiral staircase and he leads me to it, guiding me as I climb the steps in front of him. At the top, we arrive in a Victorian-style conservatory, spilling over with tropical plants and trees. "I have several species of rare plants here. My sister could be arrested by Customs. She transports cuttings from all over the world in her suitcase."

"Don't the plants die in transit?"

"The secret is to wrap the cuttings in kitchen paper towel first, and then plastic. The paper towel is important or the cuttings sweat to death with too much moisture. This way they can survive a good twenty-four hours."

"Your sister sounds like quite a character."

"Yes, Sophie can be formidable. Not someone to have on the wrong side of you."

The more I hear about his sister, the more wary I am, although she seemed perfectly friendly when we met in the coffee shop.

I look about this conservatory which is full of small orange trees, purple bougainvillea and towering palms. It has a sweet aroma of jasmine which I notice climbing on trellises, wild and free.

There is a table in the middle, and elegant garden furniture composed of wrought iron, topped with sumptuous cushions, and double French doors which lead out on to a garden.

"You have a *garden* on the roof? In New York City?" I squeal in delight, running outside.

"I told you I was organizing my life around my dog. Rex should be quite content here, don't you think?" His lips curve into a mischievous grin.

The garden has real grass running across the length of

the roof and small trees which are swaying in the evening breeze. The view across Central Park is spectacular – a sea of green reaching across the park to the Dakota on the Upper West Side, and I can even spot the Empire State.

"Now, where would you like to eat? Up here in the conservatory or in the dining room downstairs?"

"I don't know, I haven't seen the dining room yet."

"Well, I'll show you."

The dining room is perfectly round and a work of art. *Tromp l'Oeil* murals adorn the walls, making everything look three dimensional. Looking up, there is a painted blue sky around a dome with puffy wisps of clouds and a hawk flying through the air. It looks so real! There are double-doors opening onto a lake with swans, the view reaching to a far away horizon. The effect is extraordinary. I feel as if I am in an Italian palace centuries ago.

I catch my breath. "I'm in awe"

"So which is it to be, the fake view or the real, rooftop view?"

"I don't know which to choose. Both are unique. Which one would you suggest?"

"Let's toss for it." He reaches into his jeans' pocket and pulls out an odd silver coin.

"That doesn't look like a quarter," I remark.

"It's my lucky coin. I carry it with me everywhere. It's a silver stater from ancient Greece." He shows me a wonky coin, almost the shape of a small pebble – more oval than round with an image of a sea turtle. On the other side are triangular notches.

"Heads for upstairs, tails for down here, okay?"

"Okay, which side is heads?"

"The turtle side."

He throws the old coin in the air and catches it between his palms. *Those palms that cupped me and pressed against my sweet spot only this morning.* A shiver rushes through me. He slaps the coin on the back of his hand.

"How d'you know that stater is real?" I ask, foolishly forgetting for a minute that Alexandre is so wealthy he can buy anything he wishes, even museum relics.

"Because I had it checked out by an expert at the Met. She said one of the earliest and busiest Greek mints was on the island of Aegina, off the north-eastern coast of the Peloponnese. It's probably from around 550 BC. It comes everywhere with me. Nice to have a slice of history traveling about in my pocket wherever I go. Tails it is."

Before I can ask him where he got the coin from, he takes his cell from his other pocket and says something to somebody in French. He then turns to me. "Let's go back on the terrace, Pearl, and watch the sunset."

After we spend a good twenty minutes watching the sky turn from hues of deep oranges and shades of purple to spotting the first star (which happens to be Venus), we go back down to the round dining room. I do not see or hear a person anywhere. It is as if invisible fairies have swept about and organized everything: the table is set for two with a white damask tablecloth, crystal glasses and silver candlestick holders. There are just the candles lighting the room – those on the table and others in sconces on the walls.

The mood is romantic; a warm, golden glow flickers about the room. Etta James is singing *At Last* softly in the background – mirroring my frame of mind exactly – that's how I feel right now...*at last*. At last I have met someone I feel so strongly for. At last I feel passion again.

I look about the room. "Where did those magic hands

come from? The noiseless ones that laid the table?"

"You'll soon see. You sit and I'll bring you a little *amuse bouche.*"

"What's that?"

"Literal translation: something to titillate your taste buds. A bite-sized *hors d'oeuvre.*"

I sit in a daze studying the room, letting my eyes stray to landscapes of lakes and trees. I can hear low mumblings in the kitchen. He has help but obviously likes to keep that low-key. Soon, he comes in carrying two small glass dishes and sets one before me.

"This is a little Carpaccio de Dorade - sea bream - with Gelée de Poivrons – peppers. Sorbet Poivron et Piment d'Espelette. Special peppers from the French Pays Basque region right next to the Spanish border."

He pours me a glass of chilled white wine and I notice three glasses in front of me – this is sure to be quite a culinary experience to be paired with different wines.

He sits down and we begin. I pop the little roulade into my mouth and feel it melt. The chilled creaminess melds beautifully with the delicate flavor of lightly spiced fish. Sublime.

"So do you ever get tired of traveling so much?"

"You know, Pearl, even if I had the budget of a student, I think I'd be getting away whenever I could, maybe back-packing about the globe. You learn so much by visiting other parts of the world, immersing yourself in other cultures - the music, the language and customs. And it makes me grateful for what I have in life when I return home. I work hard but still, I'm not unaware of my luck. Every time I come home I think, look, look at everything I have."

"And where do you consider your home is? Here or Paris?"

"Good question. More and more I feel rooted to New York but I suppose there'll always be a place in my heart for Paris. Rex is there, of course. When he gets here, I'll find it harder to leave."

"When's he coming?" I ask with too much eagerness in my voice. Selfishly speaking, I want that dog to arrive ASAP.

"Soon. I have some more business meetings overseas and when a few more deals are tied up, I'll go and pick him up by private jet." He is not smiling when he says this.

"Really?"

"It was your suggestion, Pearl, and what a good one it was, too."

"I never said—"

"You sowed the seed in my mind - asked me the other day if I flew about by private jet. Why should poor Rex be subjected to a travel crate in the hold of a commercial plane – the air conditioning blasted up too high, or worse, none at all?"

A young girl in a shift dress appears from nowhere. She looks no more than eighteen. The smile on my face drops with consternation because she's extremely pretty with long dark hair, a neat little figure and rosebud lips. She silently clears away our plates. He takes her by the wrist. *A sexy little maid he sleeps with on the side?* My heart races with envy and suspicion.

"Elodie, meet Pearl. Pearl, this is Elodie, my niece from Paris - Sophie's daughter. She's working for me this summer. Learning a few tricks of the trade."

"How do you do?" I say, wanting to shake her hand but she's holding the plates.

She smiles awkwardly. "Bonsoir," and slips away, faster

117

than a stream of water - back to the kitchen.

"She's very shy. She comes with me to the office every day – she's quite a wiz at programming but she's a loner, she keeps to herself. Her English is appalling so I'm trying to get her to go out and about more to meet people. She refuses. I thought I'd make use of her this evening so she's been working as my sous chef and helper."

Elodie brings in two more plates and exits as quickly as she entered.

"This is my version of one of Paris's great chefs, Guy Savoy's signature dishes. It's Artichoke and Black Truffle Velouté. You are meant to dunk the brioche into it. Usually the soup is served hot but as it's summer, I thought it would be good chilled. I baked the brioche – everything here is made by me from scratch."

The soup is rich, silky and earthy, and the accompanying toasted brioche flaky, with a smear of black truffle butter on top. I dip it into the creamy soup, garnished with fresh black truffle and shaved Parmesan. It's mouth-watering. "This is delicious," I gush.

"Thank you."

The whole evening has a surreal quality to it. It feels formal and now I know his sister's daughter is milling about the apartment, I feel uneasy and self-conscious. I expected Alexandre to have a sleek, modern home full of leather and chrome and Italian furniture, but I see he lives in a wacky sort of museum. He drives classic cars, one of which looks like the Bat Mobile, and he plans to travel, not by private jet himself for business, no, but to accommodate his dog. Are all French men like him?

We have two more dishes, both served to us by the bashful Elodie. Razor Clams from Galicia, garnished with

Seaweed Butter and Ginger, and then, for a second course, Roasted Pigeon with Tomato Chutney and Tiny New Potatoes. That was what I smelled wafting from the oven earlier. All this Alexandre has concocted himself. It rivals the best restaurants I have ever been to.

Last comes home-made vanilla ice-cream (made with real Cornish cream from England, no less) topped with his own Rose Jelly made by him.

"I collected the rose petals from my garden," he says, his eyes bright.

"In Paris?"

"Didn't I tell you? I have a place in Provence?"

My stomach churns. I went to Provence when I was a child and remember fields of lavender, vineyards and clear blue skies, but not much else, except a yearning to return one day to a place that captured a young girl's heart.

"You have a house there, *too?*" I ask him.

"Yes. I believe in putting my money in bricks and mortar in preference to the stock market. If things go wrong, at least I'll have a roof over my head – that's how I see it. You must think me very greedy owning all these properties."

"Not greedy, just lucky."

"I told you I was lucky. The house in Provence was a ruin when I bought it. It's an old stone farmhouse, a *mas*. It's very rustic and I never go in winter so it doesn't even have central heating. I have a few vineyards and some lavender fields."

Every word that comes out of Alexandre's mouth makes me want to weep. With joy. With fear. Fear that he won't want to be with me anymore – that all this could be over. That I'll never be invited to Provence. My dream is to run through lavender fields, taste the sun on my skin, be loved forever and ever by this man's side; this man who has seduced me with his quirky sense of humor, with sex, and now his home-made food, and hints of what could be in the future. I find myself speechless. Lavender fields. Vineyards. *A man who makes his own Rose Jelly? Really?* Am I in a dream? A fantasy in some romance novel? I pinch myself because I seriously wonder if I am. Surely this is all a figment of my overactive imagination?

To make matters worse, he adds, "If you play your cards right, I'll take you there."

That has done it. My cards? *What are my cards?* My hand is shaky, at best. If I only knew the secret ingredient to capture Alexandre forever, I'd bottle it and sprinkle it on his food when he wasn't looking.

I laugh uneasily. "I went to Provence once when I was about five. With my parents before they split. It was magical. I remember the scent of lavender."

"I have something to show you," he says, taking me by the hand, "that might invoke those sweet memories."

He leads me to a large bathroom tiled with white mosaic. At one end is an Art Deco bathtub, and at the other a shower, also covered in mosaic. There is a floor to ceiling Italian-looking gilt mirror - antique, of course. On a table are two bottles filled with clear liquid. He pops off the top of one and presses it to my nose. The sweet odor hits the back of my throat as I breathe the delectable scent into my lungs and fill them as wide as they will go. I'm in a trance of memory, of desire. Now I think about it, is that what has hooked me? *That is what his skin smells of.... Lavender!!*

"That smells out of this world," I say.

"I bring vats of it back. If I ever feel down or stressed I breathe in the lavender oil and all my troubles melt away in seconds." He starts to run the bath pouring the liquid in. "It makes your skin really soft, too, and has great healing properties, gets the circulation going." He gives me a mischievous smile.

Circulation. I think of the blood pumping through his veins, of his rock-hard erections. It causes a pool of nerves to gather deep in my solar plexus.

"So that was the smell I couldn't quite fathom," I reply, remembering reading somewhere that lavender oil is an aphrodisiac.

"They say people are attracted to each other mainly by scent-based chemistry. Now you know my secret," he tells me with a grin.

"It's true. I've read that some researchers think scent could be the astrophysical secret in the sexual universe, the key factor that explains who we end up with."

"So if I didn't happen to have a few drops of this lavender up my proverbial sleeve, perhaps you would have ignored me when we met in the coffee shop," he jokes.

"Maybe - who knows?" I tease. "But more likely, it was those subtle olfactory messages operating below the level of conscious awareness emanating from your pheromones, or whatever they're called."

I know this is true. The faint fragrance of Alexandre's sweat when we made love sent me into a frenzy. He smells delicious, never mind the lavender. I'd marry that smell.

We strip naked and lower our bodies into the water. Alexandre takes off my pearl choker - perhaps it would melt, after all. The bath is big and he positions himself at one end and I, in between his legs, my back pressed up against his chest.

"What about Elodie?" I ask suddenly, feeling as if she

could burst in on us any moment, even though the size of his apartment means we can't hear her at all.

"Don't worry, she's going on a date tonight. Someone from work is taking her to a club. I made her say yes. She's in New York City, for God's sake, she has to learn to be more social."

"I didn't know your sister had a daughter."

"Elodie's her step-daughter. Same thing."

Feeling more at ease now, I relax back into his arms. He kisses my hair. "You smell great," he remarks.

"It's the lavender."

"No, it's you."

He starts to massage my shoulders and I feel myself unwind and my body slacken. "That feels wonderful."

"You have such beautiful shoulders."

"It's all the swimming I do."

"Some women's shoulders slope - not yours. But they're not broad, either, they're elegant, poised, you have a great posture. And your waist - so pretty, so hourglass."

His hands slip around my hips, massaging the oil into my skin. He kisses the nape of my neck and a quiver shimmies along my spine. All of a sudden, I hear some pages flicker and his voice, deep and melodic, begins to read to me in French. I don't understand, but it's beautiful. No man has ever read poetry to me before, let alone in French.

"Who's the poet?" I ask when he pauses for breath.

"Baudelaire." He continues reading and I close my eyes, listening to the pleasing rhythm, the cadence of the lines, but just as he is saying:

Avec ses vêtements ondoyants et nacrés,
Même quand elle marche on croirait qu'elle danse —

my backside slips beneath me and I go sliding under the water, my head knocking the book into the bath, splashing lavender-scented water all over the floor. When I come up - my hair soaked, water up my nose, I see the sinking poetry book and I gasp. It's an old leather edition. *What have I done?*

But Alexandre bursts out laughing, takes the sodden book and puts it aside. "What am I doing? I'm being absurd – reading you poetry when I have poetry right here in my arms, poetry in your lips, in between your thighs."

He guides my body around so I am facing him. He runs his finger across my Cupid's bow, holds my chin in one hand and then kisses me, first by letting the tip of his tongue part my lips, pushing it into my ready mouth, longing for him, waiting. I've been controlling myself all evening and now I let myself go, responding with heat and aching desire. I can hear myself moan which makes him react with increased ardor. He's kissing me hard now, his tongue probing deep – he's growling like an animal, forcing me closer to him by cupping his hands under my ass and grabbing me tight, holding me up with the strength of his muscular arms. He's licking me all over, my chin is in his mouth - he's moving down to my throat, my shoulders, and in a circular motion around my breasts, grazing just the edge of his teeth gently against each nipple until they harden. He catches one in his mouth, sucking lightly. It's as if a golden thread links them directly to my groin - I can feel that deep tingle inside me. His rigid erection is above the water, pressing up against my stomach. I feel myself wetting up, even though I am already in a bath I can feel myself oozing with excitement. His fingers are exploring in between my thighs and his index finger slips its way inside me.

"So welcoming, Pearl."

I take his erection in my hands and massage him with the oily water. Ooh, he's big. How did I forget that? It was only this morning and yet it's as if I'm feeling him fresh for the first time again. I can't get enough of him. He's making soft little nips around my shoulders now and I shiver even though the water is still warm.

"It's too small in here, let's move to the bedroom," he suggests.

Like a true gentleman, he lifts me up from the tub so I don't slip, takes a warm towel from a heated rail above, and pats it about my body. We get out, and my legs still dripping, he scoops me up and carries me in his arms, the towel still wrapped about me. I can smell the lavender oil sweet on my skin and in my hair. When we get to the bedroom he throws me onto the bed, literally, I land on the soft mattress with a bounce. I open up my towel, my nipples still erect, my body shiny with droplets of oily water.

"Spread your legs," he demands.

I do as he bids. He doesn't have to speak, I can see his huge erection flex so I know how much he wants me and all I can think is how much I want to covet that organ – the centerpiece of his beautiful body.

He's standing there above me naked, running his eyes over me. "Look at you," he says, "you're beautiful. All I could think about all through dinner was fucking you. Making you come, making you cry out my name. What have you done to me, Pearl Robinson?"

I smile, feeling triumphant inside but not wanting to gush.

"Oh yes, I almost forgot - the gift I have for you. Wait there, don't disappear on me now," he jokes.

He leaves the room and what he said gives me an idea.

I'll hide! I look about and wonder where. The room is huge, grand. It could be at the Ritz in Paris or anywhere opulent. There is even a mini-bar next to the bed. There are sweeping silk drapes pooling on the floors in front of enormous windows. I could hide there. No - too obvious. Under the big brass bed? Too uncomfortable. I make a dash for his walk-in closet. So childish - but why not? I hide behind rows and rows of laundry-fresh shirts. Behind them are suits. Suits? I've never seen him wear one. I ease my naked body behind a row of jackets. My breathing is heavy and I hear him bluster into the room.

"Pearl? Pearl? Where are you?"

He walks out again, probably thinking I've gone to the bathroom, or something. This goes on. I almost come out but decide to stay put. His footsteps fade as he walks about the vast labyrinth of his home. I hear doors opening and closing and then he's gone. Has he gone up to the roof terrace? This game is silly, I realize, and am about to come out, when he enters the room again. For some reason my heart is pounding, the way it does when you play Hide and Seek as a child. I hear the closet door open and light floods in. There are neat rows of shoes and trilby hats on shelves above. I see silk ties and color-coordinated sweaters and T-shirts.

"I think a naughty little girl is playing games with me and she could be in here. I think there's a naked creature in here who's asking to be punished for her naughtiness."

I feel genuinely frightened now. What if he's some crazy that wants to beat me up? His tone is serious. I push my way back further but the movement makes a shirt fall on the floor.

"Caught you, you minx. I can smell you in here. I can smell lavender and little girl, and I think she needs a good beating."

I swallow a glug of air and see his hands come through the suits and land on my wrists. He pulls me out of the closet his face harsh - no smile.

"I'm not kidding, Pearl, you've been disrespectful and I'm going to have to teach you a lesson you'll never forget." I notice his jeans are back on but he's topless. He grabs a couple of silk ties from his closet. He lifts me up again and carries me like a child and dumps me on the bed. "Lie on your back."

"What are you going to do to me?"

"You've been a bad girl."

"I was just kidding."

"I'm French, I don't share your sense of humor." He binds each leg so I am straddled on the bed on my back, legs wide open, each ankle attached securely with an ice blue silk tie to the brass bedstead. I want to thrash myself out of this position but curiosity is impelling me to stay. A little voice flashes through my brain saying, *Idiot, what if he's like that American Psycho character? All charming, at first, but who'll stab you in a hundred places and chop you up – too rich to be caught, so clever he gets away with it all. He said himself he was capable of murder.*

Please help me God, I hardly know this man.

He's scanning my body with his eyes. "Okay that will work. Now, these pearls will do nicely for your wrists." He takes the pearl choker from his pocket. "I'm going to tie your wrists together with this. Now, you know how valuable this is, don't you?"

I nod. God knows what he paid.

"Any struggling, and you'll break it, and we wouldn't want that now, would we?" He fiddles about with it, his expression severe. No kissing – his look is tough. I sense he is genuinely annoyed with me. He wraps the pearl choker around my wrists and guides my tied hands above my head. "I was going," he continues, "to let you open the box with your gift inside, but now you've spoilt things. Now you won't get to see it, only feel it - because I'm going to blind-fold you."

"Please don't hurt me, Alexandre."

"But you've been bad, and as I said, you need to be pun-ished, Pearl. Haven't you ever heard about a Frenchman's pride? I'm going to have to teach you a lesson in good manners."

From his other pocket he produces a blindfold. It's big, somewhat padded or something.

I feel so vulnerable lying on my back, my hands tied to-gether above my head with the pearl choker, my legs wide open, each ankle bound.

"Please don't hurt me," I repeat. I think back to our con-versation in the Corvette on our way to rock climbing, and remember how horrified he seemed to be by bondage, and yet here he is about to do something cruel. Will he bring out a whip?

He leaves my side for a moment and is doing something - putting on a record – it's an old-fashioned record player. Music begins. I recognize it - Chopin – I used to play it on the piano – *Prelude in E minor.* He puts the eye mask around my head. It's heavy on my eyes as if it's been weighted down with something and it smells of heavenly lavender.

His voice is low. "I had this eye mask made for me. It's stuffed with lavender from my fields in Provence, together with grain to make it weighty. I've put on a record as the sound is always crisper than a CD – I love Chopin - isn't this beautiful?"

I feel more relaxed with the soft music and fragrance of lavender all about me, heavy in my nose, but I'm still nervous

- thinking about what he's going to do to me as I can't see a thing. *Why did I stupidly hide in his closet? It was all going so well!*

"I'm going to open up your gift now. If you hadn't been so disobedient, Pearl, you could have done it yourself."

"What is it?" I ask with trepidation.

"You'll soon find out."

I hear the ribbons being untied and the lid of the box being pushed off, as it lands on the sheets beside me.

"I'm going to start now, okay, Pearl? Your punishment will begin after I count to three. Are you ready?"

I brace myself for something horrible. Tense my legs and stomach and scrunch up my face in preparation.

"One."

His voice is low, forbidding. My heart is pounding with dread.

"Two."

I can hear his heavy breathing – he's really concentrating, and adrenaline is pulsing through my veins.

"Two and a half."

I'm really scared now.

"Three."

Yet….Nothing.

Then I feel something so light I know he can't have started the punishment. There's a tickling on my toes and then above my ankles. It is brushing me weightlessly along my calf. It is not his finger, what is it? A paintbrush?

"Can you feel what it is?" he asks in a soft voice.

"It feels good. Really good."

"Remember that little story you told me? About your first time?"

I'm focusing now. It's on my other leg, trailing up my thigh. It is indescribably erotic. Not being able to see or move, I still feel fearful, but the sensation is radiant, wispy. I am aware of my pelvis moving, wanting whatever it is to move higher between my legs.

"You still can't guess, Pearl?"

"It's a feather."

"A Kingfisher feather. It's blue and orange at the tip. Can you imagine how pretty?"

He's tracing it up my body, onto my belly and circling it around my breasts. It's barely credible how such a light, helpless object can have this sensual effect. It's under my arm now and it tickles. Now on my throat, my lips, and now back on my throat, my shoulders, flicking with such delicacy on my nipples. I'm tingling all over.

"It's glistening like a little pearl."

"What is?" I ask.

"A part of you I want to put my lips around and then fuck."

I groan with anticipation. I'm feeling ready.

"It's wet and shiny and inside it's like a velvet glove, welcoming me, encompassing me whole - pulling me in, grabbing me all around in a tight embrace."

"What does it feel like?" I ask. "Making love to a woman? To me, I mean?"

"Oh, Jesus, you have no idea how good. It's warm and wet and delicious. It tastes sweet and salty and it wants me so much. It's greedy for me like a comforting house inviting me in where I belong and offering me comfort - but with hot, hot sex at the same time. Do you want me inside you, Pearl? Deep inside?"

"Oh yes," I say, wriggling beneath the touch of the kingfisher feather. "I can't think of anything else. All day long I get moist and throb with desire, just imagining that huge great erection of yours - your sexy lips kissing me, your eyes - that tongue darting in and out of my secret places."

I'm trusting him now, my fear has left me and I'm opening up. *This feels amazing.* The feather is now brushing past my clitoris and I sense his thumb enter inside me as he makes slow circles with it, engulfed by my juices. Then he takes it out and I can hear him pop it into his mouth and suck it.

"So tasty, but I think we need a few extras to sweeten you up even more."

It's dark behind my blindfold. I hear him open the mini-bar door beside the bed. *What's he doing? Having a drink?*

After much rustling about, I feel something cold oozing onto my navel. It shocks me for a second. What is it? It's thick and gooey, not too runny. It smells sweet. So sweet but the lavender is making me confused.

"What is it?" I ask.

But he doesn't respond. Then I feel something cold being pressed inside me. Maybe round. Something fruity. One, two - three of them. *Wait a minute! All this was already in the mini-bar – did he plan this?*

"I smell fruit," I say.

"And what else?"

"Honey?"

"Big, black cherries and honey. But Pearl, I'm going to untie your ankles now – I think your punishment has gone far enough."

"No! *Please*, Alexandre. Please punish me some more."

"More punishment? Really? Don't you think you already paid the price for your disobedience?"

"No, I was a bad girl and I need to be disciplined."

"Okay then. I'm going to add another ingredient. Something very French. Something I used to eat for breakfast as a boy."

I'm waiting. Eager. I can feel the cherries inside me like little balls – so sensual - and suddenly he smears something creamy on my breasts. There is a whiff of chocolate. Do I smell Nutella?

My hands are still above me, clasped into the Art Deco choker, which I'm scared of breaking, so I hold still. He starts licking my stomach, his tongue lapping up the honey. His mouth heads up to my breasts and he sucks each one greedily, flipping his tongue back and forth on my nipples. I'm moaning and writhing about like a snake. The large cherries feel so good inside me. The pleasure is intense.

"Your breasts are like fruits. They fit perfectly in my mouth, not too big, not too small. I'm going to have to fuck those tits."

His hard penis laps against my stomach and then in between my breasts. His hands are cupping them, clamping his erection between them. When he moves up I try to catch it with my tongue.

"I want it in my mouth," I beg.

"I thought those avaricious lips might want my cock."

"*Please.*"

It's in my mouth now, dripping with honey and Nutella. I'm licking him, ringing my tongue around the head of his shank, sucking. He rises higher and I catch his balls and I suck each one individually, each one whole inside like enormous balls of candy, as he guides his penis over my face stroking my nose, my forehead with it. He moves away now, his tongue trailing south down my body, parting my lips, holding my inner thighs with his thumbs as he starts to suck out the cherries inside me – vacuuming them out. His tongue is wild, slapping against my entrance – then he lets just the very tip touch my throbbing clitoris and then holds his tongue down still on it, pressing hard. I start thrusting myself up and down on his flat, motionless tongue, pressing against it and I start coming. It's in hot waves rushing through me. I still can't see, can hardly move, my body a vessel of pure pleasure. Behind my blindfolded eyes I see flashes of color and I go into a tunnel of black and red and gold, still climaxing, still pressing myself against his tongue as my body ripples and tremors.

"Ahh…ah…ah…aaaaa."

Then he starts licking again, sucking out all my tastes from my opening but careful not to touch my tender clit. It makes the climax all the more intense.

Then slowly, slowly, I come down, the spasms gentler now, the tingling in tiny bursts but still on a plateau. Such a surprise, this has never happened before. The myth has come true – *I'm having an orgasm from oral sex!*

He begins to remove the ties on my ankles and then unclasps the choker around my wrists. He kisses me softly on the lips and I taste the mélange of flavors; honey, cherries, my salty turned-on self and Nutella. He lies beside me on the bed. I shake my hands free and bring them about his arms and shoulders. Finally, I can touch him. I unravel my fingers, stretch out my palms and stroke his smooth back. I'm still wearing the blindfold and don't take it off. I can hear him fiddling about with something and more music comes on.

"This is for you, chérie. The song's called *Black Cherry.*"

I grin. "Very apt. That was amazing but what about you?"

"You think I haven't enjoyed this? I nearly came just giving you so much pleasure. I had to count to ten to stop myself. And another ten to stop myself from plunging into you."

"Why didn't you?"

"This isn't about me, Pearl, it's about you."

"It's about us both, isn't it?"

"I want you coming," he says in a low voice, "all around

me when I'm deep, deep inside you."

"But you've already hit the jackpot."

"I want to make sure it wasn't just luck, though. I was just skimming the surface. The most important erotic muscle you have is your mind. I have to get to know your mind better, get inside you, metaphorically as well as physically."

The way he says that frightens me. He's already got me free and clear, can't he see that? *Is he trying to give me pleasure or control me?* I want to say something, put up a fight but my body lies there exhausted, and the only expression on my face is a contented, I've-had-the-first-and-best-oral-sex-orgasm-of-my-life smile.

He strokes my head. "Sleep now, princess. At least for a while."

The chill-out music is making me relaxed, heavy-eyed. I run my hands over my body, assuming I must be a sticky mess, but find myself quite clean. Licked new. He did a good job.

A very good job indeed.

9

I don't know how long I've been sleeping, but when I awake he's sitting on the bed next to me, watching - his eyes resting on me, transfixed.

"I wasn't snoring, was I?"

He laughs. "No."

"Not dribbling or anything horrible, or talking in my sleep?"

"No, not at all. You look beautiful and serene. You had a sort of Mona Lisa smile set on your lips, so you must have been dreaming about something very pleasant."

"How long have I been asleep?"

"All night. It's time to rise and shine."

I sit up and see faint light coming through gaps in the heavy drapes. "You're kidding? It felt like I was asleep for ten minutes."

I can't believe I wasted that precious time with him

merely sleeping. *What a fool!*

"Sorry, I must have really taken it out of you," he apologizes.

"You took cherries out of me," I joke. "And there I was, terrified, thinking you were going to thrash me with a whip or something." *Even kill me.*

"I'm sorry, Pearl. Did I really frighten you that much?"

"I was nervous when you tied my ankles."

"But you could have escaped any time – the knots were very loose, the necklace you could have snapped open at the clasp."

"At the peril of destroying an original Art Deco piece of jewelry? Never."

"I'm sorry, seriously, if I scared you. I would never, ever, hurt a woman. Not even kidding around." After he says this his lips are tight, pressed together, all humor wiped from his usually open face.

"Whenever you mention women and beating you look as if you're talking from past experience. Did something happen once?" I ask. "Are you trying to chase away personal demons?"

"Unfortunately, you can't chase away something that lives inside you."

"You have a violent past?"

"Yes."

Uh oh. I look at his face and wonder what he did that was so violent – he's fighting against his dark side. "Can I ask what happened?"

"I'm not so keen to discuss it."

"Surely you need to talk about it with someone?"

"I hardly know you, Pearl."

"You know me well enough to have tied me up, to have

135

bought me an outrageously expensive gift, to have delved, literally, into my private places. You think I've ever let anyone that close to me before?" I bark. "You think I go round opening my legs up with abandon like that, opening my heart up like that to any man?"

"I'm sorry, I didn't mean to sound dismissive."

I start to get out of bed, hurt that he is choosing to close himself off from me, and fearful I am falling for a man who has a violent side. I've heard that men like him do that; ply you with gifts, win your confidence, make you fall in love, and then, when it's too late, they show their true colors.

"My father used to beat the shit out of my mother," he suddenly says, his eyes on the floor as if he were ashamed.

I observe the grim expression on his usually happy face. "How awful. Are you violent, too?" I ask nervously.

"I have been."

"With women?"

"Christ no."

"When?"

"In certain situations. I have triggers that set me off which I try to keep under control."

"What happened with your father, then?"

"We nearly killed him."

"We?"

"My sister and I wanted him dead."

"Well, it must have been your sister more than you, she being so much older." *So much older? She's still five years younger than I am. Wish I hadn't said that.* I look at him hard, trying to read his face but he's staring into the distance as if not focusing – a memory stirred up of something better forgotten.

"Because I assumed you were young," I continue, "when

your father left. I mean, how could a little boy have hurt a grown man?"

"I was seven."

"Only seven." I don't comment more but cannot imagine what a seven year-old could have done.

"My sister was seventeen. But it was my idea, not hers. I was mixing rat poison with his food. Amongst other things."

"Wow, that was imaginative."

"My sister stabbed him in the groin when he was sleeping."

I try to picture the scene. Worse than any movie. "What had he done..." I inquire tentatively, "to deserve that?"

"He was a monster. The shit really hit the fan when that happened. The stabbing. He threatened to put Sophie in a juvenile delinquent home for offenders – we had to get away from him at any cost. The only reason Sophie stuck around was because of me, otherwise she would have left home a lot sooner. By the way, this is private information, Pearl. I have never told a soul any of this."

"You can trust me. I would never say a word to anyone. I swear. So you all left?"

"Sophie and I packed and told our mother we were leaving. Told her that if she ever wanted to see us again, she'd better come with us."

"And?"

"She stayed behind with him."

"You're kidding. Why? She was your *mother*? You were so young."

"She wasn't Sophie's mother. Her mother died when she was ten – our father remarried my mother."

"But she was *your* mother. Mom to a seven year-old boy! I'm sorry, but I find that outrageous that she stayed with him after everything."

"She was terrified. That's what can happen in abusive relationships. One partner gets worn down so much, they lose all self-confidence. It can happen in subtle ways at first, until the dominant one has all the power. It defies common sense, transcends reason. She was too weak – we tried to protect her, but failed."

"You did not fail! You were only children. *She* failed," I exclaim, as I angrily run my fingers through my hair.

"Anyway, we left home. She joined us a year later."

"One whole year later? She chose her violent husband over her seven year-old *son*? Ouch."

"My sister was like a mother to me."

I let out a heavy sigh. "I find this really hard to comprehend. I thought you said you called yourselves The Three Musketeers."

"Sophie and I were The *Two* Musketeers for ages. My mother couldn't contact us. We didn't trust her not to tell him where we were, so we remained invisible. My sister got cash jobs, waitressing and other things, and we had alias names. Sophie pretended to everyone that she was my mother – lied about her age, said she was older."

He is staring into space now, locked in this memory. The way he is spilling all this out to me makes me feel as if he hasn't shared this with anyone for a long time. Maybe never.

"Later," he continues, now glancing at me, "Sophie called my mother and met up with her, but kept me hidden just in case. But my mother had learnt her lesson by that point and swore she'd leave him. She did, and never looked back."

"How can you forgive your mom for not coming with you in the first place? For not denouncing your father?"

"You forgave your father, didn't you? For abandoning you?"

"Yes, but my brothers and I weren't in *danger.*"

"Brothers? I thought you only had *one* brother."

"Well, no. I had another brother," I admit. "John - who died of an overdose."

"Shit. I'm sorry."

"My life hasn't been such a picnic, either."

Looking at me, Alexandre asks, "What made your brother do that?"

"He was an alcoholic. I don't know, he was really messed-up about my father leaving, and was always disturbed as a young boy. He was a sensitive soul who took on too many burdens of the world. Then, one night, just over ten years ago, he had a lethal cocktail of drink, prescription medication and cocaine. He died."

Alexandre holds my hand and squeezes it a little. "Shit."

"Yeah, it was a shock. I still miss him."

"Yeah, I bet. People do strange things. Not a day goes by when my mother doesn't hate herself for what she did. Your brother, Pearl, was powerless against his addiction."

"Was your mother using drugs, too? Or drinking?"

"*He* was her drug. He was her poison."

I notice he can't bear to use the word *father.*

"Was he your step-father or your real father?" I ask.

"When you say, 'real,' do you mean biological?"

"Yes."

His normally sumptuous mouth sets into a thin line. "Good - because he was never a real father to us. His seed produced us, but he was not our father."

"I'm so sorry. I thought I had a sob story, but yours - well it must have been awful."

139

"You can't even begin to imagine."

"I could try."

"Pearl, what he did to us is *beyond* anyone's imagination."

"He abused you? Sexually?"

"Let's get something to eat. I'm hungry. They do a great breakfast at The Carlyle."

"Isn't it a bit early?"

"They know me there, it'll be fine."

I shower and put my Jean Muir dress back on. Alexandre offers to lend me something of Sophie's to wear but I decline. There's no way I'd feel comfortable dressed in anything of hers without her permission. Men don't get that - how women are about their clothing.

Alexandre puts on a dark gray suit, one of *the* ice blue silk ties, and shoes polished to a high shine. He looks so different, I'm stunned.

"You look highly sophisticated," I marvel, "very handsome indeed."

"Thank you, Pearl. I have a lunch meeting with an elderly gentleman, the type who wouldn't appreciate my usual attire."

I feel very 'morning after the night before' in my dress and heels, but when we arrive at The Carlyle by cab - I couldn't walk more than a block in those heels - I don't feel out of place. Plus, Alexandre looks so dapper in his suit; I'd feel ashamed to stand beside him in something more casual. I realize when we sit down for breakfast that I have left my gifts behind; the kingfisher feather and the pearl choker.

The hotel's dining room is elegant like an English country manor house, with plush chintz-covered banquettes, rugs adorning the floor, and mirrored alcoves set off by a towering floral arrangement of lilies in the center of the room.

This is a first – doing breakfast. I'm a grabber, a black coffee guzzler, running and eating at the same time. When I tell Alexandre this, he laughs.

"Food on the go," he exclaims. "Very American. In France, people are discussing what they'll be having for lunch while they're still eating breakfast, and while they're eating lunch, what they should make for dinner. People want a hot lunch, even in summer. Especially people who live outside big cities - everything closes at noon sharp until two o'clock."

"You can't go shopping during those hours?"

"No way! Everyone's having lunch. And on Sundays? Forget it. Sunday is family day. Walking in the park et cetera. You can shop on Sunday mornings for food - the supermarkets will be open - but little else. The afternoons are for relaxation only."

We sit down at a table with a white tablecloth and I feel as if I'm on a date, although it can't be more than seven a.m.

"What else is different about the French culture?" I want to know, smoothing out my dress.

"Let me see. Oh yes, your drinking laws. In France, teenagers are expected to try a little wine with their food."

"They must go wild."

"Not really. Because it's available, it's less of a big deal."

"What else?" I ask, fascinated.

"Well, I think I explained to you why Sophie and I have made our business more of a success here in the States than in France. Being an entrepreneur in the U.S is respected – something many people aspire to. Being an entrepreneur in France is what you do if you're unemployable or cannot get a 'real' job. Things are changing, but slowly. People have to stand on their own two feet more than before – 'jobs for life' are hard to get these days."

"Something you and Sophie had to do – fend for yourselves, stand on your own two feet."

"Exactly, we had training." He laughs – the somber look has been replaced again by his happy-go-lucky demeanor. Thank God. I see touching on his past can cause demons to re-visit. I would have liked to have delved more into who his father was, and what became of him, but the look on Alexandre's face, back at his apartment earlier, told me to shut right up.

The waiter comes over to ask for our order. I like to think that he imagines that Alexandre and I are married - a well-dressed couple at breakfast together. The fantasy of wedding this Frenchman is now taking hold of me like a child clutching a lollipop. *Pearl, get a grip,* I say to myself with wry humor. Clutching onto a dream, a fantasy – not wanting to let go of the lollipop.

"What would you like, Pearl?" Alexandre asks, putting his hand on mine. I feel all melty and warm. *We are together having breakfast. We have spent the night together.*

"I'll have poached eggs and smoked salmon with Hollandaise, please."

"Could you just bring me a big bowl of blueberries?" he asks the waiter. "I don't see it on the menu but—"

"Of course, sir, anything else? The waiter sounds deferential. The smart suit is working wonders.

"Shall we get coffee?" Alexandre turns to me.

"Sure," I reply. "And maybe some orange juice?"

"And some freshly squeezed juice, please," he says. "Oh yes, and a little yoghurt, perhaps."

"That's all you're eating?"

"I'm crazy about blueberries and stuff my face with them

whenever I can. You see that? How accommodating the waiter was? Blueberries not on the menu - but *no problem.* That's what I love about this country, people want to make you happy and there's no shame in the service industry – you guys go out of your way to smile. Americans have different values and one of those key values concerns the customer."

"Anything you don't like about us?" I ask.

Someone is leaving him a message on his cell. It buzzes on the table. He ignores it and also ignores my question.

"You Americans also value innovation," he carries on, back to his topic, "and individualism. Standing out is a good thing here, but in France, people can be suspicious if it's not done in the 'right' way. Don't get me wrong. At school I learned philosophy - and this wasn't a private school, even. We're educated very well in France - cheaply too. If you have a big family, the youngest get to go for free, even in a private school. But you aren't encouraged to think for yourself, nor operate by instinct or gut feeling, nor come up with original ideas – nor think too much 'outside the box.' It's drummed into you to only debate something if you have well, *thought out* opinions and arguments that can be backed up with a host of proven examples. And certain things are expected from us in society in France. The American dream still exists here. In France, people are discouraged to dream - it's not practical."

I'm in my element listening to him spout forth; his melodic voice spurting off opinions, his defined jaw raised, almost haughtily, with his beliefs. *Please, God, if you care about me, let Alexandre take me to Paris, to Provence.*

"And what," I press on, "about the positive side? The things you really *miss* about your country?"

"Well, leisure is a necessity in France, not a luxury," he

says, loosening his tie. "We live to eat not eat to live, and the same goes for relaxation. We spend time with family, have longer, paid vacations – we value our free time and don't feel guilty about it. In America, if you tell someone they're a workaholic, they take it as a compliment. In France, a person would be horrified if you said that to them. All these are sweeping generalizations, of course. There are exceptions to the rule in both countries. But this is what I've experienced with my limited understanding of this cross-culture."

"And what drives you nuts about France?" I ask, noticing his cell buzzing on the table yet again.

"Zero customer service. People can't get fired easily so they behave any way they feel like, especially with government paid jobs. The cockiness is something to be believed. In America, a company *earns* its clientele – in France the customer is not the king, that's for sure."

"Wow, it sounds both fascinating and frustrating."

"It is. It is."

"What about French women? Do you see a difference there?" *This is the question I have been longing to ask from the beginning – translation – are you and I serious? Or will you end up with a French woman because Americans just can't compete?*

He ponders this. "Not so much the women themselves, but people's attitudes towards them. In America, youth is worshipped. In France we love *women*. Girls are for boys. Women are for men. At least, I speak for myself. I am attracted to women, not girls." He looks hard at me and then smiles.

I know my days of being a girl are long since gone but I still find it hard to accept that I am 'mature' – I still hanker after being mistaken for a girl when I walk down the street. When you are a mature woman, the wolf-whistles from construction workers stop, and that's a scary thing.

The cell is vibrating, almost moving across the table of its own volition. Whoever is calling is desperate to speak to him. *At seven fifteen in the morning?*

"Excuse me, I obviously need to listen to these messages." He looks at his cell. "It's Sophie, it must be urgent."

Mess.... Ages, his accent says, as if in warning.

As he listens to his messages, I study the expression on his face which changes from animated and delighted to concerned, and then visibly upset. He makes a call. Calling Sophie back, no doubt. I watch him in as discreet a way as possible. I don't want to appear nosey. I pretend to look about the room. I fumble in my clutch bag, while all the time keeping my peripheral vision honed in on him. He is saying, "*oui, non, incroyable*" and words to that effect. At one point, he looks at me and then away. *Has somebody died?* He puts his cell on the table, sighs and brings his hand to his face, cupping his chin, half covering his mouth. Something is very, very wrong. His eyes are stony and just his expression is making me want to sink through the floor.

"Pearl. Oh, Pearl,"

I say nothing. He gives me a look that I can't quite fathom. He is not happy.

"Why didn't you tell me, Pearl?"

"What?" I ask innocently. I have a horrible feeling I know where this conversation is heading.

"Who you were?" he asks in a quiet, disbelieving voice.

Help! He thinks I'm a monster, I can see it now, written all over his face. His lips are tight - the way they were when he talked about his father. *I am now in the father category.*

"What do you mean?" I ask like a fool. I should just blurt out, 'I'm sorry' but I'm feeling defensive. *Really, I am not a bad person!*

"Is this what all this is to you?" he asks with disgust, waving his hand in the air. "This breakfast - spending time with me? Jesus - even making love to me. All this so you can glean information for your bloody *documentary*? Get me to open up to you, the way I did about my intimate *private* affairs? You asked me if there was something I didn't like about Americans – for all the good about your country, you lot would sell your souls, wouldn't you? Sell your own grandmothers if it meant advancing your careers in some way?"

A minute ago he loved America and Americans. Now, because of me, we are all slung like soiled underwear into the laundry bag.

"Alexandre, let me explain, let me−"

"Explain what? That you basically lied to me? Oh yes, very clever, not *lied*, exactly, no - just *omitted* to mention the fact that you were hunting me and my sister down. Why didn't you just come out with it? We're not ogres. Who knows? With some persuasion we might have even said, yes. Why weren't you honest and simply tell us that you wanted to do a documentary about us?"

"Because I−" I'm all tongue-twisted, I can't speak, my breathing is shallow and fast, my heart is racing and my eyes are welling up. "Because−"

"Don't fucking cry on me now. I'm not falling for that."

"I love you, Alexandre." It plops out of my mouth – I can't help myself.

"Yeah, right. That, I really believe."

The tears are flowing now – I'm mopping my face with my linen napkin and see the couple at the table next to us staring with curiosity. I don't care – I blabber on, "When I met you at that coffee shop - it was a mistake - I didn't even know you were there - I'd given up - I'd missed your talk." It's all coming out garbled, my lips stuttering as I swallow air in great gulps - "I don't care about the documentary. I want to do a film about arms dealing, *I don't care.*"

"That's clear. You don't care. Well you know what? I *did* care. I thought we had something special. I thought you were different, but all along, I see you wanted to get to know me for ulterior reasons! Not because you were having fun with me, not because you felt for me, but because you had a fucking film to make and I, along with my sister, were your targets. Why the hell didn't you just *say* that that was what you wanted? Be straightforward - not sneak about like some snake in the grass." He's standing now, not even looking at me anymore. He gets out a couple of hundred dollar bills from his suit pocket and slaps them on the table. "I don't know what the check will be," he snaps. "Please deal with it, keep any change."

Keep the change — what am I, a whore?

"Please Alexandre - my boss was away - I never even let her know I'd met you. I wasn't even going to tell her so she'd forget about that silly documentary—"

"There you go again, Pearl. Not being straight with people. Not telling your boss you met me? Hiding stuff. What are you - ten years old?"

"I'm sorry, Alexandre. I'm so sorry. I lo—" the rest of the sentence doesn't even get a chance to come out.

"Bye Pearl. I'll get your necklace delivered to your door. And that other ridiculous gift."

"I love that gift," I mumble pathetically.

I want to tell him he's the best thing that ever happened to me, that I'm besotted with him, but he's leaving now, not looking behind. I see the jacket of his sharp suit swish away as he walks with steely purpose out of the dining room. Mortification does not do justice to how I feel. I brought this upon myself. I dug my own grave. Nobody but my sorry-ass self can be blamed. There I was, fantasizing that I was like Rachel from *Friends, a* cute-charmer-character lost in a silly little sitcom predicament. But Rachel and I are worlds apart - I can't laugh over it with a mug of coffee. No. This is real.

I have blown everything.

10

"**D**on't you see how childish that sounds, Pearl?"

Like a real glutton for extra punishment, I have called Anthony. *Why, why did I do this?* I'm in my bedroom, throwing off the Jean Muir dress, while climbing into something more casual. If I don't hurry, I'll be late for work. Sinead O' Connor's *Nothing Compares 2U* is blaring on my music system, a reminder that Alexandre is irreplaceable. Unique. And I've lost him.

"Pearl? Are you there?"

"Yes, I'm here, I'm just battling with my dress."

"Rachel from *Friends*? Seriously? You're likening yourself to a ditzy TV character? I mean, maybe you are that way but you don't want others to perceive you so. Do you know how lame that sounds? Not to mention *dated*. So 1990s. It really shows your age, too."

"I happen to love Rachel. And you make it sound as if being forty is some sort of disease."

"It is when you're dating someone from kindergarten."

"Okay, I'm hanging up now."

"Don't hang up…did you mention that to Frenchie – that you are still hung up – excuse the pun – on Rachel from *Friends?*"

"His name is Alexandre. No, I did not mention Rachel from *Friends* to him. Maybe I did tell him I liked *I Love Lucy* and *Bewitched* and *I Dream of Jeannie.*"

"Forty years old going on seven. Honestly. Interesting how all those characters tell fibs. I guess you must identify with them."

"Well I love them all and I still laugh when I watch re-runs."

"Honey, you're not going to get a chance to re-run this little episode, don't you get that? And I don't hear you laughing now, sweet pea. Do you know anything about French men? Do you not realize they are the proudest people on the face of this earth? You messed with his pride, girlfriend, you ain't never gonna get another chance."

"Stop that 'girlfriend' lingo, Anthony."

I imagine Anthony swanning about San Francisco 'girl-friending' everyone and giving high fives, and for some reason it makes my blood boil. I yell, "Anthony, what is all this, 'French people do this and Americans do that?' We are human *beings*, not stereotypes from some 1960's Berlitz travel guide."

"Do you remember that Mexican travel guide of Mom's?" he cackles. "How we'd roar with laughter?"

"Listen, Anthony, I'll call you later, I'm running late. Thanks for listening to my woes. *And* being an ass."

"Laters, baby sis. Take care now, don't do anything rash, ya hear?"

When I arrive at work, I nearly have a heart attack. Natalie is sitting quietly at her desk.

"Natalie, why are you back so early?" I ask, dumping my monster handbag on the floor. It's back with full vengeance now – everything is packed inside – just in case. As in *suitcase*, it's so heavy.

"Good morning to you, too, Pearl."

"I'm sorry – just - I thought you were in Hawaii until Monday."

"I tossed up whether to stay and check into a hotel or come home early. In the end it made sense to get back."

"Hotel? What happened at Dad's?"

"Your dad didn't seem to want me there anymore."

"What? But he's crazy about you!"

"Was. Seems he got bored."

"No, Natalie, you just read him wrong. That's his style. He's a loner, a surfer dude – just been used to being independent."

"Selfish is what he is."

"Okay, you know what? You are my boss and I love and respect you but I spent my whole life hating my father and finally, finally we became friends. I know he's selfish, I know he is a terrible husband, boyfriend whatever, but I do not want to know all the details of what an asshole he is. Especially, not right now."

I find myself in tears again, and Natalie takes me in her

arms. I begin to howl like some sort of wolf. The fact that she says, 'there, there, let it all out,' makes it worse. I let it all flow freely. I am like a dam suddenly being unblocked. My whole life is being spilled into her bosom. In between sobs I tell her my Alexandre story, minus the mind-blowing sex. That is my precious secret - too beautiful to share with anyone.

"She listens carefully and then says, "Yes, I had his sister, Sophie Dumas, on the line this morning cross-questioning me."

"*What?*"

"I mean, it was pot-luck I was at my desk so early. I came here directly from the airport – took the Red-eye. I guess they're five or six hours ahead of us in France. She was pretty pissed."

"What did she say?" I ask - my heart on the floor.

"She wanted confirmation of your name. She had the e-mails in front of her, the ones I had sent her asking for a meeting and confirming your presence at the conference. She couldn't understand why you hadn't approached her honestly when you met them at that coffee shop after their talk at InterWorld. And, of course, she was aware that you've been dating her brother – he must have spoken to her about you."

Natalie is looking at me in a way that says, 'Yes Pearl, why *didn't* you just do things the way you were meant to? You have let us all down.' But no words come from her lips – just *that* look.

"I know. I know, Natalie. I screwed up. She and Alexandre were standing there in line. Very friendly. Very amenable. I just kind of froze with…I don't know…with what. Fear? Excitement? All I know is the second Alexandre spoke to me I turned to Jell-O. I thought he may think I was a stalker. I wanted to be the beautiful girl he met in a coffee shop, not someone…someone *wanting* something from him. I'm so sorry, Natalie."

"You would have still been that beautiful girl at the coffee shop, Pearl, no matter what."

"I'm sorry," I say again.

"They wouldn't have gone for it anyway," she says in a soothing tone. "At least, not Sophie. She sounded pretty fierce. It's just a shame it has all gone so horribly wrong with you and Alexandre."

So horribly wrong. Her words are like clanging cymbals, or nails on a blackboard.

"Were you planning on telling me?" Natalie asks, looking me in the eye.

"Of course. But you asked me not to disturb you on vacation," I stutter, telling a half-truth.

The day drags on. I can hardly concentrate. I do research, catch up with important calls and e-mails, but I can't picture anything but the shadow of disappointment on Alexandre's face. I don't mention the pearl necklace to Natalie. And hope he doesn't send it back to me, after all, as he promised. A reminder of what *could have been* if I wasn't such a dunce.

I reflect on all the dumb things I've said, the way I have behaved like a child when I'm almost a middle-aged woman. I loathe, loathe, loathe that word, 'middle-aged' and cannot bear to let it sneak its pushy way into my vocabulary, but as Anthony reminded me – 'how long, exactly, do you expect to *live*, Pearl? *Of course* you are heading into middle-age – you can't deny it.'

After hours of beating myself up, I start remembering the sex between Alexandre and me, and can actually hear low whimpers coming from my very being, the way when you have a fever and groan quietly. I think of his worked-out torso, his strong thighs pressed hard between my legs, how the water gushed down on us, swirling about our pleasured bodies. I think of his tongue meeting mine and how it licked me, pressed me on my sweet spot until I came, my body writhing in spasms of bliss. I think of him inside me - and my belly churns upside down.

I have to call him, or at least send a text – I can bear it no longer. Even if he thinks I'm a despicable human being who lies, surely he can at least have sex with me? I pick up my cell and begin to write him a message:

Dearest Alexandre - no, scrap the 'dearest,' that sounds ridiculous.

Alexandre, please forgive me. Can we meet up? Just to talk?

No, that gives him a chance to say no. I erase and start again.

Alexandre – I need to see you – please come over.

I can hear Anthony's voice, 'Helloooo, Pearl? *Desperate!*'

My cell rings and my heart practically pops out of my skin - it gives me such a jump. Alexandre? No, it's Daisy.

"Hi Daisy."

"You called me four times, is everything okay?"

"I've really screwed up, Daisy."

I tell her the whole drama in whispers. I don't want anyone in the office to think I'm a hopeless wreck (which, of course, I am).

"Okay, Pearl, listen to me. DO NOT send him a message or speak to him. Wait for me. How soon can you leave work?"

"In an hour," I murmur.

"Meet me in the park - no, better still, I'll pick you up from work and we can walk there together. I repeat, do not send any messages or call him, okay?"

I don't reply.

"Okay?" she repeats in a stern voice. "Promise me."

"Okay, I promise."

"What do you promise?"

"I promise not to send Alexandre any messages, nor call him."

I can hear her sigh with relief. "Good. See you in a jiffy."

Just knowing that Daisy's one-woman rescue team is on its way, I find myself (after a couple more black coffees) getting a ton of work done. I do more in an hour than I have all week. I need to get a grip. I listen to Julie London croon *Black Coffee* and identify with the lyrics as if the song were made just for me. I too, am feeling as low as the ground.

If I work really hard perhaps I can get Alexandre's smile, sex with Alexandre, and Alexandre's very being - which has bored its way into my very psyche - out of my one-track mind.

I am a successful documentary producer, not a teenager. I am a woman, not a girl.

I am in control of my life.

I thought Daisy would be bringing Amy along, as she suggested Central Park, but no, she is alone. I am delighted (selfish me) that I have her and her undivided attention all to myself. She is in her tough-love mode.

It's a relief to get away from the sounds of horns and the ebb and flow of traffic, from the hot dog vendors and the bustling streets, and enter Central Park. We sit down on a patch of lawn and Daisy lets out a stream of wise advice, enunciated slowly from her heart-shaped lips. Her red hair is wilder and curlier than usual today, which makes her particularly animated – the humidity has gotten to us both – curls for her - for me, hot and bothered between my legs, caused by a too-young Frenchman who is no longer interested in seeing me.

"Okay," Daisy begins, sounding more British than ever, the aay of the okay drawn out languidly like a yawn. "This is not a foregone conclusion. You still have hope."

"I do?" I shout out. "Really?" Music is playing in my ears. Operas, symphonies.

"IF you play your cards right. If you don't, you don't have a chance."

"What are my cards?" I ask desperately.

"To do nothing."

"But Daisy I need to apologize, I need–"

"You have already apologized. Worse, you blurted out to him that you loved him. Twice."

"One and a half times. The second sentence he cut short. And the first time, he didn't even believe me."

"He'll be clocking what you said, trust me. Men are not so far removed from us, you know. They *also* dissect conversations and do post-mortems, even if it's just privately in their own heads."

"Not to the extent we do, surely?" I ask.

"They do care. Remember, I'm married. I see their human side."

"Yes, but you've forgotten about the rest of it," I grumble, thinking about her sweet, kind husband who adores her - and knowing she could never truly understand.

"Pearl, you have no choice. You have to save your dignity. You cannot go running after him in guise of 'apologizing' or 'discussing' things. Firstly, men do not like to discuss. What's done is done. Men are more forgiving than we are, too. He'll forget what you've done soon enough and start remembering the good times he had with you."

"There's no way, Daisy. He was furious. He hates me now. He thinks I'm scheming and dishonest. And if I don't tell him that I'm sorry, he'll think I'm even worse."

"He'll think you're a bore. Let it go. Leave it be. If you do not, not, *not* contact him, he could call you, - he *could* want to see you again. He'll wonder why you haven't got in touch – it will pique his curiosity."

"But he was livid. Really angry—"

"Good, that means he likes you. You touched a nerve," Daisy expounds.

I say nothing and digest everything she has said. Then I come out with, "Daisy…the truth is I'm hooked on him. I want more sex."

"That's only because you hadn't had it for a couple of years so you're obsessed. Quite normal."

"No, really. He was like *a god* in bed."

"Even more reason, then, you need to listen to me. Even more reason you need to control yourself."

"What if I dress up really sexily, go somewhere I know he'll be, say hello so I don't seem rude, and then ignore him?"

"Pearl, how old are you?"

"That's what he said to me, that I was acting like a ten year-old."

"I can see you're not listening to a word I'm saying and you're going to do something really foolish, really humiliating that you'll regret later. And then don't come crying to me afterwards." She's standing up now, brushing down her dress and looking about the park. She's irritated by me, her pursed lips say it all.

"Daisy, where are you going?"

"To get an ice-cream, or something. I'm hot."

"I *am* listening to you, I swear." I stand up, too, and breathe in the smell of freshly mown grass. There's a baseball game in the distance and a dog chasing squirrels.

"Someone could get a ticket," I observe. "Aren't dogs meant to be on leashes at this hour?"

"As if you care, Pearl."

"I care for the owner and the dog. Of *course* dogs should be able to run free, as long as its owner picks up after it. Everything's gotten so regimented these days – so many rules." I can feel Daisy is bored by me so I try to win back a star. "What you're saying is really sound advice, Daisy. I'm going to try my hardest to follow it to the letter."

"Good!"

"I just need to keep busy."

"Normally, I can't even get you on the phone at all, Pearl. Your job has been everything to you. The fact that this Alexandre business is taking up all your energy just goes to show how you've lost the plot. This is not like you at all."

"I know."

"Remember when I went out with that Argentinean? Latin men like a chase. All men like to chase but that lot more than most. I have never dated a Frenchman but I'm sure if you come over as all keen, he'll run a mile."

"I guess you're right."

"Do you remember that little book that came out in the 90's? The one with rules for dating? That told you what and what not to do? How to get them to be crazy about you?"

"I'd forgotten about that – it was a bestseller."

"Do not ask a guy on a date. Do not accept a date at the last minute. Always end the conversation first–"

"Do not say 'I love you' until the guy has said it first," I interrupt. "I broke that one already."

"Well," Daisy says hopefully, "it isn't too late to repair the damage. Don't call. Don't get in touch. And if he rings you, don't go all gushy and pathetic. Stay cool, calm and collected. You are a busy woman. You have plans, places to go, people to see, deals to make. You are not some pathetic, whimpering, sex-craving fool."

"Do you think I can pull it off, Daisy?"

"I *know* you can pull it off."

11

A whole week of agony has passed. Work has consumed me – what choice do I have? I call Daisy when I'm feeling weak, when I need to be reminded to not humiliate myself, to keep my resolve.

I got my period and I cried. I had a fleeting fantasy that by some fluke the lambskin condom was faulty and I would magically be pregnant - carrying Alexandre's child. That when he met his baby, he'd fall in love with me, and we'd live happily ever after.

Dream on, Pearl.

I have a great new contact at the UN who is willing to talk covertly - things are looking up career-wise. But the second I let my mind wander, I re-live moments with Alexandre; the image of his body, the things he did to me - and a mixture of longing, lust and sadness surges through my body. I have had a few crying-on-the-bathroom-floor moments, but each day gets a little easier.

He hasn't called nor even left a message. I am being strong and have resisted the temptation. I even went out on a date with an old friend from college who used to have a crush on me. Yawn, yawn. We saw a movie and had dinner, and then I told him I had period pains in order to end the evening early. It was a half truth. The only pain I had was his pain-in-the-butt-you're-boring-me pain. Poor guy. I tried to disguise my feelings as well as I could. I smiled sweetly and told him I'd be so busy at work there was no way we could see each other for at least a month.

It will be hard to keep Alexandre off my mind as today is Friday and I won't have work to keep me distracted this weekend. But I have an idea....

When I arrive home I go online - I have to erase him from my brain. Perhaps it is a physical need that I've awoken and I can cure myself with a simple remedy.

My search online is for 'sex toys'. I have never in my life resorted to them, but hey, why not? Couples do it all the time. It's a good way to get to know your own body, apparently.

I had always thought using them was kind of like cheating. I have had a vague notion all this time - completely unfounded of course - that pleasure has to emanate from another person and anything else would be a sort of 'fraud.' *Ridiculous!*

I look at the range before me, the variety of colors and shapes. One is made from stainless steel. Ouch. Although it promises to heat up once inside - from your own body temperature. Others are neat things that look almost like cell phones and others, regular dildo shapes.

I read the reviews of one. '**YES, YES, YES! A great vibrator. Def worth the extra bucks. As soft or powerful as you want it to be.**' Hmm, sounds good.... I read on.... '**Not had solo use with it as it is so great with my partner.**' *Partner.* Good while it lasted with Alexandre, I think. Now I am partner-LESS. A dildo is a poor second choice, though, and could I even go through with it? All I want is *him* not some plastic substitute. As Alexandre said himself, the biggest sex organ is your brain. How much of a mental turn-on is a fake penis? I want to smell his skin on mine, taste his tongue.

No, Pearl. Stop! Don't torture yourself anymore.

I put some music on and start dancing to *Sex Machine* by James Brown. It happens to come up on random play. What are the odds of that? Not the most distracting thing to listen to while I'm trying to get my mind off Alexandre, but at least I get so into the song - I let loose, and forget for a while. I'm dancing wildly.....gyrating, grinding my hips.

I hear my landline go. Anthony calling to check up on me? Or the doorman? Maybe the pearl necklace has arrived, although surely Alexandre would have already sent it by now? If it is the necklace, I should really send it back - let him know, loud and clear, that I'm not somebody who is after *things*. There is also a pounding at the back door to the kitchen where the service elevator is. The trash. Did I forget to put it out? No, I did put the trash out. Why is the superintendent knocking at the back door? I go to answer.

My mouth hangs open when, what I see standing before me, is none other than HIM. As if my fantasies have materialized. Am I dreaming? He looks sexier than ever, beads of faint sweat on his brow, his dark hair ruffled.

"I came up the stairs," he pants.

"So I see."

"That'll be the doorman calling now to warn you that a rapist is trying to enter your apartment from the back door." He's not smiling. He's standing there, legs astride in *that* suit. No, it's a different suit, a shade darker – smart, elegant. I can feel my knees wanting to buckle beneath me but I take a deep breath and thrust my shoulders back. Daisy's words are echoing in my ear: *'Stay cool, calm and collected.'*

"Aren't you going to invite me in?" His foot is now planted firmly against the door so I can't close it on him, his tongue licks his upper lip for a split second. He's running his eyes up and down my body with a look of lust on his face. I can feel the familiar tingle in my groin.

"I don't know."

"Fuck it. I'll invite myself in," he says. Still no smile. He heaves himself forward, his body close to mine as I step backwards into the kitchen. His lips are centimeters from my face and he's breathing heavily. "I have to fuck you Pearl."

Before I have time to answer, he grabs me and pins me against the wall. He's kissing me hard, his hands in my hair. Gone is the sensitive man with the kingfisher feather. He's all animal and seems tremendously tall, like some sort of dark-haired Viking, but dressed in this chic, tailored suit. His tongue is licking my lips. He's hungry for me but seems full of anger. He cups my breasts and pulls my shirt off over my head. Forcing me. Forcing me to raise my arms, his fingers all over me, needy – stroking my navel, nibbling my nipples between his teeth. Then he's sucking my breasts greedily, and shoving his hands up my skirt pulling my thighs apart, palming me, pressing hard, then letting his middle finger slip inside me. I can hear myself moaning.

"You want to get fucked, Pearl? The way you fucked *me* over? Using me like some commodity to advance your career?" He's got his thumb inside me now and he's circling it. "Oh yes, Pearl, I can see you want to get fucked – really asking for it, aren't you? So wet. So tender."

Sex Machine is thumping loud. Alexandre has unzipped my skirt and I'm standing now in nothing but heels and panties, which happen to be red. I didn't put on a bra this morning; it was too hot. He grasps my hair and holds back my head, licking me on the tongue like a wolf preying on a bitch in heat. I want to push him off but I can feel the moisture between my hot, humming V-8 – it's beckoning – it wants only one thing. I fling back my head and groan, flex my pelvis forward. He's parting my panties now to one side. He hasn't even bothered to take them off. Then he goes down on his knees - peeling my panties aside with his teeth, licking me, shoving his tongue up inside my opening.

"You wanna fuck, Pearl? That's what you do in this country, isn't it? Fuck each other over, like the ambitious career whores you are."

He's still furious with me and the whole of the USA and something about his rage, coupled with his accent, wants to make me laugh and tell him to leave – take my control back. But the sweetness of his tongue, his soft hair brushing against my clit, his mouth making me wetter by the second, has me moaning in response.

He unbuttons the opening to his pants and his huge erection springs free like a beast. It's smooth, irresistible. I'm like a bitch in heat, a veritable she-wolf, and I grab it with both hands. He's fumbling now – putting on a condom.

"I shouldn't be using this," he growls. "I should just fuck you hard until my seed catapults its way inside you and makes you pregnant."

His words are Latin passion nonsense but they still turn me on, even though I know they can't be true. Yes, this man could make me pregnant – I'd welcome his baby. *Pearl, shut up!*

I'm still standing in my heels and can feel him slide into me and ram me hard, pressing my butt back against the wall. I cry out. This is hot. I shouldn't say it, but it is. He's pumping hard to the rhythm of *Sex Machine* and with every thrust I feel the muscles of my core clinging to him, not wanting to let him go.

"I. Love. Fucking. You." His voice is raspy. He's like a rock. It almost hurts but I can't resist. His tongue is on my neck, his hands clasping around each of my buttocks, pulling me close to him, sealing me against his groin. He's slamming me deep, his fingers clawed into the flesh of my ass.

"You like being used, Pearl? Or you just like using." The second statement is not a question.

"I'm sorry. I was just interested in *you,* not your company. I wanted to get to know you for *you.*"

"Is this what you wanted to get to know?" he says, slamming into me so hard it bruises me inside.

"Yes," I whimper. He sees me as a manipulative bitch and all I can do is moan with pleasure. I am being used by him and I love it.

"So tight!" he cries. "This. Tight. Velvet. Glove. Clenching. My. Hard. Cock….Your tight little pussy doesn't want to let me go. Don't tell me you don't want this." He's pounding hard, really cramming me full with his size, pounding into me with no mercy.

"I don't want it," I gasp. "Please release me, you're too big for me, it hurts." But my body is telling a different story - I'm driving my hips forward, meeting him with every thrust and I'm crying out with gratification. "I love you…fucking me," I pant. "I love you…. inside me."

"You love me Pearl? Is that what you're trying to say?"

I don't reply but moan even more. I tighten my fingers, like talons around his ass, and pull him closer. I can feel him thicken and harden even more, filling me up with his expansion and then burst inside me. He growls, literally - his release is like an animal in the wild. He's still fully dressed, jacket unfastened, only the opening in his pants from where his huge erection meets me, parting my panties to one side, his thick cock forcing my pussy lips wide open like the wake of a vast barge on a river.

I'm dreading the minutes ahead. He's got what he wanted and now he'll pull out and leave. Like a punishment. To teach me a lesson. This will be the last time I'll see him. I should have told him to go. Kept my dignity. I should have resisted but I dissolved, as I always do with him, like melting vanilla ice-cream.

All his. Wanton and lusty, letting sex rule my brain. Sensibility, not sense. Why does he have this hold over me?

He does pull out, but to my surprise, he isn't done yet. He's still stiff as if he hadn't had an orgasm at all. He spins me around, his hands forceful on my hips and shoves my ass against the corner of the kitchen table. He pushes me down, bends me over till my crotch is pinned against the corner.

"I'm not finished with you yet," he snarls, his body pressed flush behind me, holding me sandwiched between his crotch and the table. I can't move. I can hear no smile in his voice. No charm. He's pissed as hell.

I didn't climax, so I'm feeling hot and ready for another round even though I'm sore.

From my peripheral vision, I see him knot up the sperm-filled condom and put on another. Fast. I don't even need to suck or fondle him, he's ready all right, his huge member proud as the Washington Monument. I can feel it against my buttocks. He grabs a cushion from one of the kitchen chairs and wedges it between my groin and the table corner.

"Fuck the table," he commands.

I feel uneasy. Self-conscious. This is what he asked me to do with the arm of the sofa when we had phone sex. Furniture has a whole new meaning now.

He rips down my moist red panties with one hand and grabs my butt - I feel the soft hardness of his erection pressed up against my behind. I start gyrating in anticipation. I'm wet and I want him inside me.

"Good girl. Push harder against that cushion. That's right, just like that. Seeing that peachy ass moving, and pressing that hot little pussy against furniture gets my cock so fucking hard."

I'm moving my ass back and forth and sense the glorious head of his erection ease itself inside my rumbling V-8. He's taunting me with just the tip. I'm grinding back and forth, his tip teasing my opening and the cushion rubbing on my clit, which makes me wet and hot. Really hot. My nipples are erect. My skin is tingling all over.

"Gotta love this pussy," he murmurs in a rumbling voice. "It's warm and welcoming. So sweet and glistening."

I feel demeaned. He keeps using the word, *Pussy*. But something about feeling like a whore turns me on. I keep moving. I can feel my juices oozing, tempting the head of his thick shaft. I'm bent over almost double, my ass high in the air, as I press hard against the table corner, the cushion acting as a soft buffer. He's rimming the wet slits of my opening from behind, controlling his penis with his hand. Round and round – all my nerve-endings are alert and begging. Begging for him to thrust it all the way in. Every now and then he unexpectedly changes the rhythm and does plunge deep inside, pulls back, and then continues with the tease. I'm moaning, "Please Alexandre, *please.*"

My forearms are flat on the table, my body in an L shape, my panties around my ankles, my nipples like bullets. I can feel his suit pants rubbing against my thighs, his big balls are slapping slowly against my pulsating opening – it feels so sensual. Three places are being stimulated at once, all zoned like targets in between my legs. There is a whole empire going on there. Aah! I press backwards with each thrust to meet him - each and every time he eases into me and then nearly all the way out. Then he starts pumping hard, really fucking me, and I can feel an expansion of sensation building up, blood is rushing up inside me – one more thrust, any more friction on my clit against the pillow - one more thrust inside me and I know it's coming, it's coming….ah…AH!

My body is a convulsing, quivering nerve-mass. He's pumping rhythmically, but slower now, as I'm climaxing around him - I can feel his penis thickening even more. I'm still enjoying the intensity of my orgasm when he cries out my name and I feel a throbbing against my insides. He's coming too, simultaneously - he's emptying himself into my depths, expanding against my inner walls. My muscles contract and open, contract and open, clenching tightly around him. *I'm still coming – it hasn't finished - wow this is great. So intense.* I'm crying out.

"What am I going to do, baby?" His voice is almost a

whisper. "What can I do, I can't keep away from you. I have to fuck you. I just have to." He sounds anguished, almost tormented.

I feel mini after-waves undulating inside me, less like a tsunami now but the sensation of fluttering butterflies. I'm groaning softly. He's kissing my back, the nape of my neck and cupping my buttocks with his strong hands like he owns my ass. I collapse on the table, my chest flat down, my legs still splayed wide open on either side of the table corner, and I release a sigh. I want to tell him I'm crazy about him but I bite my tongue.

Cool calm and collected.

That's me.

12

"Pack your suitcase." He's doing up his pants.

"What?"

"It just occurred to me now. I'm taking you away for a long weekend."

"Well, I don't think I can go just like—" I click my fingers— "*that.*"

"Yes, you can. Don't argue, just get some stuff together."

I'm standing there, naked, in nothing but high heels. Who does he think he is? He barges through my back door unannounced, fucks me like I'm a whore, and is now demanding I go away for the weekend with him? Then my faux irritation relents. *Isn't this exactly what you fantasized about, Pearl?*

He looks at his watch. "We don't have time for procrastination. Hurry up, get your essentials and a change of clothes together. A friend of mine will be taking off soon – if we hurry we can get there in time, we can't miss the slot."

The slot? In a daze, I wander into my bedroom, find a suitcase at the back of my closet and start to throw a few things in. He follows me, watching to make sure I'm doing as I'm told - meanwhile speaking on his cell. He's talking to someone in French so I don't understand a word except 'jet' and 'passport'. Then he orders a cab.

"Passport?"

"It's in my handbag," I say.

"That giant ogre of a thing?"

"Yes."

"We'll have to do something about that." His eyes narrow, then he runs them up and down my body like he wants to fuck me once more. *Not again! How potent can his libido be?*

He claps his hands together. "Okay, done. Let's go."

"Wait, my toothbrush and stuff."

"We don't have time − I can buy you anything you need."

"That's a cute offer, but I usually buy my own things, thanks."

"Yes, of course you do. Hurry up," he orders, slapping my nude backside.

I scramble into the bathroom and run some water over a washcloth and wipe in between my legs, then race back into the bedroom and grab the first dress I see from my closet and toss it over my head. It's an old 1950's flowery thing with a dirndl skirt, cinched at the waist, full-skirted with a tight bodice and low neck. It's the last thing I want to wear but Alexandre is tapping his polished shoe on the floor with impatience.

"Perfect. You look like a little girl." He drags me from the room by my wrist and grabs my suitcase.

"Wait! I haven't put any underwear on."

"No time."

"Where are we going?"

For the first time today he smiles. "Surprise."

It was a race to get here, but now we are ensconced in the swanky private plane, luxuriating on beige leather seats, while each of us is being offered an *apéritif* by the hostess cum flight attendant.

His 'friend' turns out to be some high-ranking, government official, next in line, it seems, to the French president himself. The man is on his way back from a secret, unofficial meeting - in other words, he is using the jet for his own personal use.

He and Alexandre spoke to one another in their native tongue and it was translated to me that the politician didn't want to seem rude but he had a ton of work to do before we landed, so did we mind if he kept to himself during the flight? Thank goodness. My pidgin French would have been an embarrassment, coupled with the fact that, while we were walking up the ramp to embark, a breeze of air blew the skirt of my dress up above my thighs, and I was sure this high-ranking government man saw my bare, private parts. Alexandre laughed – the man he decided, was too ugly to pose a threat. "I don't know," I teased, "I could be the next Carla Bruni."

"Socialism in action for you!" Alexandre says now with a wry grin. "Our government is probably paying for his mistress somewhere, maybe a private apartment here or in Paris – don't you just love the double standards?"

"And what about us? Is this flight a freebie, courtesy of the poor French tax payers?" I ask.

"Let's just say the French government owes me a couple of big favors. I'm sorry to say, I have no control, whatsoever, with how they manage their budget. We're coming along for the ride, Pearl, that's all."

"We're taking advantage of a dishonest situation. That could be construed as immoral."

"I'm an opportunist, Pearl." His smile is bad-boy. "Just like you."

"I…" I stammer.

"You knew what you wanted and you came after it."

"What do you mean?"

"The way you sucked your iced cappuccino through that straw when we first met at the coffee shop. Flicking your tongue around your lips."

"It was *you! You* were doing that – licking your lips, staring into me with those startling eyes of yours, getting me all hot and bothered."

"I wanted to fuck you there and then."

"Well, why didn't you?" I demand. "What took you so long?"

"Because I was hoping you'd be - how can I say this?"

"Begging for it."

He laughs. "You said it, not me."

I stare out the window as we take off. I love that dip in my stomach the plane makes – it reminds me how I have felt these past few weeks. Alive. On the edge. I watch the twinkling city of New York gradually fade below - the lights of matchbox cars turn to tiny dots. Alexandre has one hand on my bare thigh and the other tapping on his iPad, writing notes.

"Sorry, just doing a list," he explains, "of things I need to get done."

"You're a list writer then?"

"That way, the problems are no longer swirling about in my head, but committed to paper, or these days, my iPad. That way they have less power over me, I don't have to think about them anymore – at least not until I look at my list and systematically knock each thing off when the time is right. It ensures a good night's sleep." He shoots me a sly glance. "One of my secrets of success."

"Like Madonna."

He knots his brow. "Madonna?"

"She also writes lists of things to get done."

"How do you know that?"

"Because my brother is obsessed by her. He also informed me that Beyoncé wears four pairs of pantyhose on stage to keep it all in place."

"She must get very hot."

"To use your expression - tricks of the trade. Secrets of success."

"And what's your secret of success?"

I raise my eyebrows. "Ah, that would be telling."

Alexandre nods over to the direction of his highfaluting friend. "So much for him getting important work done – he's already fast asleep. Look, he's snoring."

We are at one end of – I would like to say - 'room' - it's so spacious – and this man, wearing old-style spectacles, is at the other. He looks like a schoolteacher, not a politician. If I knew anything about French politics I suppose I'd be impressed but I do not have a clue who he is.

"Are you a member of the Mile High Club?" Alexandre suddenly asks.

I roll my eyes. "That is such a cliché."

Secretly, though, I have always wondered what it would be like to make love thousands of feet in the air. Probably uncomfortable – don't people always do it in the bathroom?

"In all seriousness, Pearl, are you a member of the Mile High Club?"

"No."

"Me neither. Should we join?"

"The membership comes at a price."

"I can afford it."

I give him a lopsided smile. "Maybe you can, but me? I'm not so sure."

"What kind of price are we talking about?"

"The price of discomfort."

He laughs. "Oh, you assume we'd have to do it in the toilet?"

"Well, yes, isn't that par for the course?"

"No, it certainly is not. There's no way I'm scrunching myself up double in some toilet," he exclaims with a look of mock outrage, smoothing his tailored suit pants with his hands.

"Well, where then?"

"Right here, baby. Right here, on these luxuriously comfortable seats. They've been very thoughtful – even made them of leather for us – easy to wipe down," and he mumbles in my ear, "because I know how wet you get." He slips his hand higher up my thigh.

"Shush, stop that dirty talk! The politician will wake up. Or the flight attendant will see us."

"No, he's out for the count – I doubt very much he'll stir for several hours. And the flight attendant – well I'm sure she'll make herself invisible. The staff isn't meant to hang about with the VIPs in private jets - unless they're needed."

"Are we Very Important People?"

He laughs. "Hell, yes."

"You're just kidding," I say, "about doing it in public."

"Don't be so sure. Haven't you ever had sex in public before?"

"No, I certainly have not. You?"

He temples his fingers and brings them up to his face as if in great thought. "Let's see. On a beach in the Bahamas once, on a yacht, in a swimming pool, on a ski slope just off *piste*, in the Bois de Vincennes, in a—"

"Okay, I think I've heard enough. I get the picture." I'm in a jealous sulk for a second, furious at the ex-girlfriend(s) who have dared to be so brave with him in all those places, but — then, I ask, "By the way, where's the Bois de Vincennes?"

"It's a huge park in Paris on the eastern side. The lungs of the city."

I say nothing. Back to my silent, jealous ravings.

"You're beautiful, Pearl, especially when you're green-eyed."

An unwanted smile steals itself across my face. *How did he know?* I pummel him, my mock angry fists coming up against his hard abs.

"I've never done it on a plane though," he tells me. "Promise."

"No. Forget it, Alexandre. I won't be part of one of your *lists*. Crossed off as something '*done.*' " I stick my tongue out at him like a seven year-old.

He's laughing again. "Touched a nerve, have I?"

"You've touched several nerves, actually. Did you know that" and I lower my voice to a murmur, "—the clitoris has over eight thousand nerve endings?" I squeeze my thighs tightly together so he can't get his hand any further. "Not here, Alexandre. Stop it."

"Well you *are* a mine of information - Madonna, Beyoncé, now this. No, I had no idea, but it does make sense. I'll remember," he whispers in my ear, "all those sensitive little nerve endings when I've got my tongue up there." He's trying to force my thighs apart and, although I desire his hands all over me, I cross my legs rigid and clench my thighs super-tight like closed scissors.

He's nibbling my lobe now and a frisson runs down my spine. "Careful now, we know what happens when you do that, little girl, when you cross your legs too tight. Especially with no panties on."

It's true. The pressure is turning me on and I start squirming in my seat, even though I have my seatbelt on. He eases his hands underneath me, cupping both his palms below my buttocks, lifting me a few inches off my seat. His fingers are slipping into me from behind, then tracing up the crack of my ass and back down. His thumb is inside me now – that magic thumb which seems to know where my G-spot is. I start moaning quietly. I have my eye on the flight attendant, still strapped into her seat. She's reading a magazine and the seats between us almost block her view. Almost.

"Haven't you had enough of me for one day?" I ask in a whisper, conscious that we could be seen.

"Don't forget, you're still being punished for being an ambitious little American brat." He punctuates the 'brat' with pressure from his thumb on that elusive spot. It feels amazing.

"What kind of punishment?" I ask softly - the throb more intense as his thumb circles inside me.

"I think a bit of slow torture, don't you? I think you need to be taught a real lesson."

"What kind of lesson?" I breathe.

"I'm sure I can think of something."

"Oh yeah? Like some more whipping me with your tongue? Or beating me again with the feather?" The idea of it makes me shudder with anticipation.

"No. Not that."

I can feel my breath quicken. "What?"

"You'll see."

My legs are still crossed tight. The full skirt of my pink flowery dress covers his hand, but the plane has leveled out now... oh no! The flight attendant is un-strapping herself from her seat and is making her way in this direction.

I wriggle in my seat, "Alexandre take your hand *away*," I hiss at him, but he's laughing and he won't move it. His thumb is pressing harder on that sweet spot now. Ah...panic - she's meandering towards us – smiling at us. This is the most embarrassing thing that has ever happened to me. Oh my God! I cross my legs tighter, my thighs acting as clamps to try and force his hand away out from in between my legs. She's upon us now. I can feel it building up. At the last second he takes his hand from out beneath me but it's too late because seconds before he releases it, he pushes hard with his thumb and I feel a volt surge through me and explode in a massive spasm...the fear of being caught, the excitement, the shame, all merge into one thundering orgasm, pounding like an adrenaline-rushed heartbeat shooting right up my V-8. My legs are still crossed. I keep the pressure up and squeeze my muscles together even tighter and a second rush is upon me. Boy oh boy, this is gloriously intense. But very embarrassing.

"Can I get anything for you both?" she asks sweetly.

My body is shuddering with delicious contractions. Every nerve is concentrated between my legs as if the rest of me was a rag doll. I'm coming in both places: Alexandre's thumb's final press on my G-spot, coupled with the clench of my thigh muscles putting pressure on my clit, has sent me over the edge.

Alexandre is laughing. My eyes are half closed, my mouth hanging open, my breath caught in what seems like a seizure. My stomach muscles are juddering. I'm shaking all over.

"Are you okay, *madame*?" she asks in a French accent with a look of great consternation. She is bending over me frowning - her eyes worried.

"She gets a little queasy," Alexandre replies, and then bursts out laughing again.

"Is she going to be sick?"

"No, she'll recover," he utters with an ironic smirk. "If you could bring us some champagne that would be great."

The hostess looks shocked. She must be thinking he's crazy to ask for champagne when I seem as if I'm about to barf, or worse, have a heart attack. "Are you sure?" she double-checks.

"Quite sure – champagne is good for her, eases up the muscles a bit. Don't worry, I know what her body needs."

Oh yes, I think, still shuddering. *You know my body better than I do.*

The flight attendant moves off. Thank God. I am aware that he could have said all this to her in French but he obviously wanted me to experience full humiliation. His punishment.

"Are you having fun, Pearl?" He chuckles again.

I can't speak – the mini aftershocks of that 9.1 earthquake on the Richter scale are still giving me ripples of intense pleasure – tremors like bells inside my body have every part of me shimmering and quivering.

"Such a disrespectful little hussy, aren't you? Have you no decorum at all?" He breaks into another grin.

I finally uncross my legs. "You bastard." Then a smile forces its way onto my lips.

"Well I did say we were '*coming* along for the ride.' But to be honest, I wasn't expecting it to happen so soon."

"*Coming* along for the ride. Really, Alexandre," and then I joke, "don't rub it in."

We both laugh. "Don't think you're off the hook yet, Ms. Robinson, we still have to fill in our membership form. I'd like to *come* along for the ride too, don't forget."

"Fill in – very funny. Forget it. I refuse to be a member of this silly Mile High Club. Won't do it. Just won't. You can put a giant tick against the 'Pearl - Public Humiliation' box on your goddam list and leave me alone in peace for the rest of the flight."

The chilled champagne arrives. I look up at the flight attendant from under my lashes and smile furtively, sheepishly - then keep my gaze down, mortified that she can guess what has just happened. Perhaps it's part of her job – to pretend she doesn't know what's going on.

Egged on by thirst and a sense of shame, I find myself glugging down my beverage like water, wondering what else could be on Alexandre's proverbial (or actual) list of things to 'encourage' me to do. He's clever – it all appears as if it is coming (no pun intended) from my own free will - and it is – yet-

Why do I feel I'm being controlled by him?

I curl up against his strong shoulders and the next thing I

know, my body collapses into an exhausted, profound sleep.

When I wake up all the lights are dimmed and it's pitch dark outside the plane windows. I find myself - not curled up next to him anymore - but stretched out, the seat down like a bed. He must have moved me when I was asleep. I glance over and he's working on something – charts or graphs – it looks extremely mathematical.

"Hey, baby, you're finally awake," he says, winking at me. I'm glad to see the gentle Alexandre has returned.

"How long have I been sleeping?"

"About four hours."

"You still haven't told me where we're going."

"Haven't I," he says distracted, still concentrated on his task.

"No."

"Hang on - I'll be all yours in a minute - just have to finish this."

I get up, grab my handbag and go to the bathroom. Even though it's a private jet, the toilet lights are disconcertingly bright. Yuk. It shows up every wrinkle, every blemish. I have to stop myself from launching into a full facial there and then. I pee, then wash my hands and face, underarms and private parts and brush my teeth. I notice panda rings about my eyes – how did that happen? I clean them up and re-apply my mascara, brush out my hair and dot myself with my perfume, which happens to be French, a heady but fresh scent of figs that always makes me feel invigorated. I dab some under my arms and a teensy bit on my mound of Venus. I look in the mirror. That's better, I'm ready. *Ready for what?* I ask myself.

Ready for anything.

When I get back to my seat, Alexandre has Bob Marley's

Is This Love? playing softly on his iPad. A good sign, I think. He welcomes me with a grin.

"Sexy woman," he comments, and he then unwittingly bites his lower lip. Uh, oh.

"Alexandre, we need to talk."

He looks me up and down. "I'm listening." But he's not listening - his eyes are roving all over me. I'm standing – a trick I learned about self-empowerment; when you have something important to say, take the high ground.

"We haven't had a chance to discuss what happened – the way I behaved, my reasons."

"It's in the past now," he answers, running his gaze to my cleavage.

"Well, it's not. You were so angry with me. You didn't call me for a week."

"You received your little punishment, it's over now."

"It's just - before I met you, I expected you to be some kind of geek. I'd only seen one photo of you–"

"I don't do photos or interviews, nor red carpet."

"I know - you took me by surprise. I didn't want you to think I only wanted to get to know you just because of what you did – your job. I wanted to–"

"You wanted," he clarifies, "to fuck me the second you saw me and you worried that if we were involved profession-ally it would spoil things. That you might blow your chance with me."

"You are so arrogant!"

"I'm French, what do you expect?" But he's laughing in a self-depreciating way, so I begin to laugh, too.

"What am I going to do with you?" I say, waving my fin-ger at him. I'm still standing.

He angles his seat into a flat bed and then grabs my legs. He's pulling me onto his knee. "You're going to ride me."

"No way, we've been through this. I won't."

"Oh yes, you will."

I look about the cabin. It's quiet and the politician is fast asleep. The flight attendant is nowhere to be seen. "No, Alexandre. And after your 'rape' earlier today in my apartment, to tell you the truth, I'm a little bit sore."

"You're right. I behaved like a thug. It was just that....all I could think about was you. All week. I was going crazy. Just picturing your ass in my mind made me hard. All I could think about was your ass, your tits, your face. Relax now, Pearl - sit on my knee for a bit and I'll tell you about where we're going."

I sit on his lap, feeling all warm with the knowledge that he was obsessing about me as much as I was about him. "I'm so excited about this trip. Paris?"

"No."

"Provence?"

"That's right, baby." He pulls out the kingfisher feather from his pants pocket and blows on it.

"I never got a chance to see this," I remark.

"Pretty, isn't it?" He brushes it lightly across my brow. "Close your eyes," he whispers.

I close them and feel the lightest touch. He strokes my nose with it, my lips. "Hold up your hair," he says in a soft voice. "And bend your neck down." I do, and he traces the feather along the nape of my neck. I purr with pleasure. "The lavender fields should be in bloom," he tells me. "There are wonderful markets everywhere with fresh produce sold directly by local farmers. Hundreds of cheeses to choose from - and olives and pastries. Pretty hats. Delicious treats to eat. Thousands of wines. Chilled rosé at lunch, pale as rainwater - *tapenade* on home-made bread."

His beautiful voice is distant as I'm in a zone all of my

own, enjoying the sensation of the feather on my neck. He draws it up behind my ears and I shiver. Then around to my front. It's on my cleavage now – my body with a mind of its own doing its tingling. I wanted to say no – I did say no, but I find myself silently willing him to unzip my dress at the back. He does. I wiggle on his thighs pushing my panty-free ass into his groin and feel that familiar hardness. I start throbbing. *Groundhog Day* all over again - but in the best possible way. I want to keep doing this forever. He's kissing the back of my neck so gently, and running the feather around my breasts, circling them, grazing the feather over my nipples.

"Oh Pearl," he whispers in my ear. "Sweet, delicious Pearl – so addictive." I can feel his hands pull his erection free from his pants and he lifts my skirt so it is flesh on flesh. His hardness against the soft pad of my butt. "I love you….so close. I love you….near me."

"Are you trying to tell me you love me, Alexandre?" I smile.

He lifts my leg over so I am in a straddling position facing him. He kisses me on the mouth. There's no turning back now. I simply don't have the willpower. He's pulled the top part of my dress down from my shoulders and his tongue is flipping and rolling over one nipple. He lies back flat, pulls me down and eases me on top of him by maneuvering my hips.

"So wet, baby," he coos as I slip right onto him. "Oh yeah, that's good. Soo good. Oh yeah. So ready. Now what I'm going to do is just lie here and you ride me as you see fit. You have the reins, okay?"

I nod. I'm loving this horse. This stud. Something about knowing we could be caught mid-act turns me on even more. He feels incredible. I straighten my legs so we are flush - flat body to flat body.

"Here," he says, popping a little cushion under his tight buns. This way I'm closer to you, you'll feel me more. Remember, go as slow or as fast as you want. You dictate the rhythm, chérie."

The cushion under him has his pubic bone pushing on my clitoris every time I come back down. I'm pulling out almost completely so that only his tip is at my entrance. My clit brushes against his taut stomach, the hard points of my nipples graze against the muscles on his pecs. I take another pillow and push it under his head so he's closer. He starts sucking my tits like they were fruits, rimming his tongue around them, nibbling them. I launch back down again so I'm all filled up, swollen and hot with his size. Then I pull up, slowly. Aah, this is bliss. I'm squirming about on him making little circles and then coming hard back down. It's making him groan and he grabs my hips so I can't move.

"I thought you said I was in charge," I scold, lightly biting his neck.

"Baby, if you do that one more time I'm going to come. Easy, you sexy rider."

I'm loving this; even more, knowing that it is just me and my movements that are turning him on so much.

"Suck my tits again," I whisper. He does.

I lie there languidly on top, his throbbing cock only an inch inside me. The pleasure from his nibbling and sucking is immense. I start moving now, just a little bit, and can feel myself building up to it. I circle some more and he's got his hands tight on my ass.

Now he's moving closer, lifting up his hips with each thrust and doing his mantra... "I.... Love...You....Fucking....Me."

His pubic bone is rising to meet my clit like a secret

weapon, his whopping great shaft inside pressing my sweet places, his abs, the sweat beading on his muscular chest, his lips, his hair mussed about his face, the biceps of his lean arms...it's all too much of an irresistible cocktail of pleasure and beauty....

A thunderous bolt pushes up through me, shudders roll over my body - I can feel the hot center of us united as one - I'm coming all around him – I start to moan, kissing his lips hard, then closing my eyes in concentration as I'm still fucking him. His penis is widening now - the spasms, his and mine together, are intense as I feel him spurting inside me, more than ever before.

"I'm coming Pearl – you sweet, sexy goddess."

"Me too," I gasp. I'm moving hard now. Slamming up and down on him - almost in tears with the power of my deep orgasm which I'm still savoring.

I feel like there's liquid honey down there. I keep moving, gently now, letting the tingles and ripples fade, until I collapse on his chest. I put my finger down below and feel a sticky pool leaking out everywhere. Then suddenly it clicks. Duh, he didn't put a condom on! He's come inside me!

I am not on the pill.

"Welcome to the Mile High Club." He grins. "We're fully-fledged members now."

13

Not even my childhood memories can compete with this. I look out the wide open French doors in my bedroom, which lead onto a Juliet balcony. I see rows and rows of deep blue lavender fields buzzing with activity - bees perhaps? Beyond, are pine trees, bright, deep green, and in the shape of giant parasols. The sky is like crystal, a pale morning blue which I know will brighten up as the sun gets higher. It's already hot but there's a small breeze shimmering through the doors, enough to blow a tendril of hair off my face. The smell of lavender is rich and heady; the faint air wafting the perfume towards me. It's so divine it knocks me back and I lie on the bed, looking up at the ceiling in a daze. I didn't see any of this last night in the dark, nor on the way here, as I fell asleep for most of the journey. The politician was also coming to his summer house. We landed in Avignon and his government limo picked us up and deposited us here, at Alexandre's house, en route. I still hardly know where I am - nor where the nearest village is. I guess I'll soon find out.

Alexandre must be downstairs, or even outside. I heard quiet activity earlier, voices chatting in French. I sit up amongst the fresh linen sheets and ease myself against the plumped-up pillows, thinking, *I am in Provence at Alexandre's beautiful house!* The bed is four-poster yet with no cloth, just the tall wooden posts reaching high. The room is like something out of Interiors Magazine – eclectic, yet somehow luxurious. The walls are white-washed and with dips and crevices – I could practically climb them if I had those rock climbing shoes. There is a vast fireplace of ancient stone with an antique gold mirror hanging over it. The floors are oak, I think, with different sized and shaped floorboards which creak as you step on them. Everything creaks here. Every-thing is crooked and topsy-turvy. There are paintings on the walls but the best painting of all, of course, is the view. There are massive wardrobes, the old-fashioned kind which you could walk inside and if you kept going you might end up in Narnia or some fabulous kingdom.

There is someone at the door. I sit up and fasten another button of a big white shirt I'm wearing which I found strewn across the end of the bed. The footsteps are not his, but light – a lady's footsteps.

"Bonjour?" I call out.

A slim woman enters, carrying a tray. She's wearing an apron and is petite the way only Europeans can be petite, with fragile bones like a bird. The tray swamps her and I immediately jump off the bed to help.

"Ah no, madame," she protests. "I put Break Fast on bed. You eat."

The way she says breakfast is split in two and reminds me about the origins of the word. She is smiling and gestures for me to get right back into bed. I do. She sets the tray before me, laying it carefully on the bedspread – it is replete with a variety of goodies that smell of oven baked freshness.

I breathe in. Heaven. Fresh-baked brioche and croissants, home-made jellies and jams of three or four different fruits, a mound of yellow butter, a pot of steaming coffee with hot milk in a jug. Melon dripping with honey and sprinkled with cinnamon, and some little mousse-like cakes which must be from the patisserie. All this combined with the view, the perfume of lavender blossom. Did somebody plunk me in Paradise?

She is shy and trots out of the room as soon as she is done. I begin to delve into the feast. Breakfast in bed. I can't remember the last time this happened – maybe only in some hotel when I've been on business. But the experience has never rivaled this. I spread the croissants with butter and it melts – naughty, I know. They probably don't need butter at all. You couldn't do this every day of the week. Or could you? I saw a book called, *French Women Don't Get Fat*, about dieting and food which says you can have it all, but in moderation. Is this moderation? I plunge the croissant into my mouth-watering jaws and feel the butter, the freshness of the pastry, mix with the home-made cherry jam, melting into one happy symphony on my tongue. The coffee is also delicious. French women might not get fat but this American sure as hell would - if she lived in this country!

As I'm chewing and savoring all the calories, I think of the possible consequences of what happened on the plane with Alexandre. I could get pregnant. The idea sends shivers of excitement through my body, but then my sensible, *don't be an idiot you hardly know him*, voice makes me stop chewing for a minute. When I pointed out what he'd done, he just laughed and said, "And what's so terrible about you getting pregnant? I think a baby would be a wonderful addition, don't you?" I was so stunned - I didn't know what to say except, "you're not HIV positive, are you?" He laughed again and said that no, he'd had a test only six months ago and that the last person he'd had relations with was a recently widowed woman who hadn't even done it with her husband for the two years previously, let alone anyone else. Then I told him that the chances of getting pregnant at my age were very slim and that even if I did manage, I'd probably have a miscarriage, as that is what happened to me before with my ex. He looked pensive when I said that, squinted his eyes as if he needed to find some sort of solution and then said, "no, we can't have that, a miscarriage won't do at all." Is this the Latin man-must-sow-his-seed thing, I wonder? Or does he seriously want my baby? I can't believe a man so young would consider getting tied in with a family. Certainly American men aren't keen for that at age twenty-five - most are commitment phobes.

Perhaps he doesn't want a family at all, but various replicas of himself running about the world – a woman, as my brother reminded me, in every port. Children in every port, too? He can afford child maintenance, so why ever not?

I'm so wrapped up in this train of thought and am beginning to feel furious at him when he enters the room. His charming smile soon makes all wrathful thoughts dissipate and, within seconds, I'm back to wanting his offspring again. Did I rush into the airplane toilet yesterday and frantically rinse off the sticky mess of the lovemaking aftermath inside me? No, I have to admit, I did not. Instead, I lay back on my beige leather seat with my legs up – a trick I read about when trying to conceive. I am as guilty as he is, if he is to be condemned for fantastical castle-in-the-air desires. Yet he started the ball rolling, not me.

Alexandre is standing before me now, his legs astride – a pose he often assumes. Very masculine. It's all Alain Delon again, and I'm melting all over just looking at his face and body. He's wearing loose black swim trunks and is all wet, his hair slicked back off his handsome face, his green eyes gleaming.

"Enjoying your breakfast?" he asks, kissing me and stroking my cheek.

"Dee-licious. Have you just been for a swim?"

"Yes, the pool's very inviting. Come down, I'll show you the garden."

The garden is more lavender, and paths meandering through secret entrances and archways, all divided naturally by hedges and plants. It is like a formal garden in a chateau, yet more rustic, matching this pretty stone house which he keeps referring to as a 'farmhouse' yet seems far too grand for that.

"You know why you can see the stone on my house and it isn't covered up?" he asks.

"Because it's so pretty? Why would anyone want to cover it?" I ask, my eyes distracted by white butterflies - like snowflakes everywhere.

"True, but in those days, the peasants who once owned houses like mine couldn't afford the *crepi*, the plaster rendering, so the stones remained bare. Each and every stone was collected by hand from the fields. Can you imagine the labor? They built their own houses in the past, maybe getting their friends and neighbors to help. Little by little, carrying sacks on their backs, or with mules and horses if they could afford them."

"And now it's some of the most expensive real estate in the world," I comment.

"I know. Sad in a way. A shame the billionaires have moved in and all the summer vacationers have pushed up the prices even more."

The billionaires…he's one of them, I think to myself. "I thought the English were the guilty ones. I read that book, *A Year in Provence*. Didn't that start it all?" I ask him.

"Well, it didn't help. But the British did us a favor, in a way. They went about restoring houses back to their original condition, ruins that were falling apart - things we French didn't even want at the time. Okay, they put in tennis courts sometimes, or pools, but they showed us how important our *patrimoine* was. They genuinely loved the land and all the quirkiness of the damp, crooked houses. But now, some people only want to live here to bolster up their status symbol. Still, I have an interesting bunch of friends around - some film directors, artists and such. It gets quite busy in summer."

"So who looks after everything when you're not here?"

"As you can see, even when I *am* here, I have people. You met Madame Menager this morning. She and her husband run the place, and a couple of others, too, who come and go. It may look quite rustic but a lot of care goes into this garden and house."

"Yes, I can see," I reply, looking around. The pool is now in view, the water rippling with a myriad of colors reflecting the blue of the lavender and the sky. It is bordered with real stone and has grass surrounding it, and trees shading one end. No Hollywood blue here. It's discreet. "I love the color of the water," I say.

"I had it rendered with a gun-metal gray – keeps the temperature up and gives off that natural, been-here-forever sort of impression. Come for a swim, the water's warm."

Like a schoolgirl desperate to impress her older brother and his friends, I do a back dive into the deep end, careful to keep my legs straight and my toes as pointed as a ballerina. I come up for air and then start the crawl – fingers out in a torpedo point, legs smacking the water with a fiery, rhythmical kick, and breathing only to one side. I clear a few lengths but realize my breakfast has hardly settled – my showing off has got the better of me. When I spring up with a splash, his eyes are fixed on me. Thank God. What if I'd done that show for nothing?

"Very impressive," he claps. "I can tell what country *you* come from. You really are a Star-Spangled girl, aren't you?"

I feel self-conscious. *Is that an insult or a compliment?*

"Most Europeans don't know how to swim like that," he explains.

"I swim a lot."

"I bet you were competitive at sports and games," he jibes.

I was. Ridiculously so. I always wanted to ace everything.

"What do you mean by that?" I ask. "Are you taunting me for being an American?"

"Being number one is important to you lot, isn't it? Winning?"

"What's wrong with winning?"

"It's partaking in the game that counts," he tut-tuts. "Not just the result."

"You can talk, Mr. Winner Takes All," I tease.

"Haven't taken all yet. Not quite. Still working on it." He

narrows his eyes.

"What more can you ask for?"

"You. I want you."

You've got me, buddy, I want to scream out. But I don't. Let him think I'm a challenge. Let him believe I'm special. I'll play along with that.

Cool, calm and collected. That's me.

We spend the day lolling about the house and garden and meandering through the lavender fields. Madame Menager prepares a delicious lunch outside, under a canopy of vines, which shades us from the hot sun. The crickets are chirping a high song, and there is a gentle crooning from a pair of doves in a pine tree. We drink a pale, pale pink rosé wine, so chilled, so refreshing, that I find myself flopping onto one of the living room sofas, unable to do anything.

Oh, this is the life.

The living room has a terracotta floor as old as the hills, and like hills, it undulates and buckles with a life of its own. The fireplace is at least eight feet wide and inside is a vast wrought iron fire-back of a dragon – iron to reflect the heat of the fire, I suspect. The room is lined with bookshelves and, amidst plays by Voltaire, Jean-Paul Sartre, Camus, I notice a lot of English titles of novels - smart sets printed by a publisher called The Folio Society. I inspect some. Several have stunning, color plate illustrations. He has The Wind in the Willows! I open it up and read an inscription: *Darling Alexandre, this was my childhood favourite, hope you enjoy. All my love, Laura.* Favorite spelled the British way. My heart starts pounding with an unfathomable jealousy. How dare she know about *The Wind in the Willows*? Who is this Laura? Laura, who must have been lining his shelves with classics in the English language! There is *Doctor Zhivago, The Greek Myths I and II, The Grapes of Wrath, Vanity Fair, Madame Bovary* - not in French but *Madame Bovary* in English!

Alexandre comes into the room. "Ah, there you are, I thought you'd done a runner."

"Where did you learn expressions like that?" I demand in a ridiculous way, my eyes turning from blue to emerald green.

He laughs. "Ah, I see, you've been having a look at my English books."

"Yes, I have. Who's Laura?"

"A friend."

"A friend?"

"She's a friend now. She was my girlfriend. From London. You'd like her."

I'd hate her, I think to myself, but say, "Oh yes? She has good taste in books. She must have been a great reader."

"Somewhat."

"Somewhat? There are piles of them here. Did she *live* here?"

"She comes in the summertime."

'She comes,' not 'she came,' Oh my God – he's still seeing her!

He says casually, "Why d'you think my English is so colloquial? It was Laura who taught me. She was ruthless - she'd correct all my mistakes."

"How long did you date her for?" I ask nonchalantly, trying not to show my envy.

"We didn't date, we lived together."

"Oh." *It gets worse!*

"We were engaged."

I feel as if I've been stabbed. "What happened?"

"She left me for someone else."

Was she nuts? "She dumped you?" I ask with disbelief.

"I don't like the sound of that word, but yes, I suppose she did 'dump' me."

"Are you still in love with her?"

"No, but I still care for her. A great deal."

I need to stop this conversation now. I feel whoozy. *Stay cool, calm and collected, Pearl. Don't be a bunny boiler.*

"That's nice that you're still friends," I say, and then smile sweetly at him.

"Hey, tonight there's a party and I said we'd go."

"Where?"

"A few kilometers away. At Ridley's house."

"Ridley?"

"He's a film director. You'll like him."

"I have a feeling I know exactly who you're talking about."

"All sorts will be there, it should be fun," he says with enthusiasm.

"Okay, great. Actually no - not great."

"Why?"

"Because I have nothing to wear. I was in such a rush I threw the worst outfits into my suitcase."

"Pearl, you could wear a potato sack and you'd look amazing."

"Thanks for the vote of confidence but I don't see myself in such a positive light."

"Alright then, let's go shopping."

"It's okay, Alexandre, I'll make something work." I say this because I don't want him buying me things. Ridiculous, but I'm not used to shopping with a man. "The truth is," I add, "it's so beautiful here, I'm loath to go anywhere."

"That's how I always feel when I'm here; it's hard to get away. But let's go for a drive and you can see some of the surrounding countryside. The party doesn't start till about eight – we have a few hours."

Alexandre's garage is a low stone building covered in pink, climbing roses. Perhaps they are the roses he uses for his homemade rose jelly. The garage blends in beautifully with his house. Madame and Monsieur live in a small guest house next door, and behind is a walled-in garden bursting with rows of organically-grown vegetables, dominated by tomatoes which are a dazzling sunny red – and other produce like cucumbers, onions and even strawberries. The garage houses a host of shiny vehicles, even a Deux Chevaux, the quintessential French car. Batman's car is there, too, in its full glory, the Murciélago, proud and intimidating but Alexandre opts for a royal blue, vintage Porsche.

"She's a 1964 356SC Coupé with an electric sunroof. I had to have her the moment I laid eyes on her," and he looks at me, his gaze roving from my toes up to my face where he fixes his stare. I catch my breath. I'm just wearing shorts, a thin cotton top, and flip-flops – nothing special, and am amazed how desirable Alexandre makes me feel. Each time he looks at me like that, his green eyes piercing me, my solar-plexus leaps and circles around itself. I feel like a teenager inside.

"She's adorable," I say, stroking her smooth lines. "So cute. I've always dreamed about having a car like this."

"Would you like to drive her, see how she feels beneath you?"

"You make it all sound so sensual, Alexandre, so naughty."

"She is naughty. She likes to be driven fast, likes to grip the road around corners. This baby likes to have fun."

"Speaking of babies," I say guardedly. "What you did on the plane? It's a slim chance but....I could get pregnant - a slim chance, as I say, but still possible. This isn't something you can treat cavalierly like it's all a game."

He takes my hand and holds it in his. "Pearl, you make me happy. I'm crazy for you - can't you see that? I want to be with you, and stay with you. I'm a monogamous type. Once I find someone special I don't play the field. Look," he emphasizes, locking his eyes with mine, "if you were twenty-something – which you wouldn't be because I'm not into young ingénues – but if you were, then you'd be on the pill or something. But we don't have time."

"You mean my biological clock?"

"I hate that expression - it sounds like some sort of time bomb, but yes. It's unfair for women and God was being pretty sexist when he designed that one, but there it is. Let's just see what happens, shall we?"

"You're acting as if I have no say in the matter. You're just assuming I want children. You never asked me. I have a demanding career - maybe I don't even want a family."

He looks shocked. "You're right - I never even brought the subject up with you. I did just assume—"

"But your instincts were spot on. I do want a baby. It's just....I'd given up. I didn't imagine I'd meet anyone special enough. You're the only person I've slept with since my divorce."

"I know. I was lucky to catch you before somebody else snapped you up."

I take a big intake of breath and ask him the question

that has been on the tip of my tongue all day. "Why did you split with Laura? Did you want to have her baby, too?"

"Laura…how can I explain Laura….I'll show you some photos of her when we get home and some letters she wrote me. When you see the pictures, you'll understand why she left me."

"Was she a supermodel, or something?"

"She was beautiful both inside and out. And yes, she did do some modeling."

I feel a painful stab at my heart. Obviously, I am the rebound and this Laura was some sort of goddess who I'll never match up to. I need to be more upbeat, not let jealousy consume me. He says he wants me and wants my baby – what more could I ask for? Marriage? I don't know if I believe in marriage, anyway. One divorce was enough - I couldn't risk that again. I need to change the conversation. I blurt out in a jolly voice:

"I always think cars have faces, don't you? This car has excited round eyes and the elongated Porsche badge looks like a funny nose. The way the hood is made looks like she's smiling."

He opens the driver door for me. "Slip inside. Doesn't she smell good?"

I ease myself behind the steering wheel onto the old black seats and breathe in the odor of vintage car. "She smells divine."

"Start her up."

Nervously, I do, and back the car out of the garage onto the driveway. It is a stick-shift and although I learned driving one, living in New York City doesn't give me the chance to practice very often, and I have certainly never been at the wheel of a car like this before. It is low, as he said, I can feel the ground beneath me – the idea of taking on something with so much personality and chutzpah is exciting. He jumps into the passenger seat – he's wearing a grin, thrilled, no doubt, that I'm taking an interest in his passion for cars.

We meander along country lanes, flanked by stunning views on either side of us. *What a Wonderful World* by Louis Armstrong is playing loudly and I think, yes, Alexandre couldn't have picked a better song – it really is a wonderful world. I mull over our baby conversation. It has been my secret fantasy, kept close to my heart; something I never share with anyone. Pearl, the career woman - the one who supports herself both financially, and in every other way. Pearl, who relies on nobody – that's what I have told myself for the past two years. There is no such thing as a knight in shining armor, I convinced myself – nobody is going to come along and wave a magic wand.

Then I met Alexandre. Is he waving a magic wand? Or is all this romance he is offering going to turn horribly pear-shaped?

I have been self-reliant and had even considered adoption but realized how tough it would be being a single parent and raising a child in New York City alone. Does Alexandre really *mean* what he says about starting a family? Or is he just so young he hasn't thought it through properly?

My thoughts now turn to the moving view – more of his magic, bringing me to this fairytale land. As well as lavender, there are vineyards and stretches of golden wheat every-where. Now and then, there is a tiny stone building plunked right in the middle of a field – so picturesque, it looks like a postcard.

"Don't be afraid, Pearl, to really give it to her. She likes to be pushed harder. You don't need to change gears so soon – keep her in third for longer. I know what she needs."

"You know a lot about what females need, don't you?" I tease. "You like to keep me in third for longer, don't you? And sometimes, when I'm begging you for fourth, or even fifth, you put me back into second. Sometimes even first."

He laughs joyously, his right arm relaxed against the sill, the wind whipping his hair from the wide open windows. "I love that analogy. Yes, women are like cars – they need to be controlled."

"You're so sexist!"

"They like to have their limits pushed - but not too much - and then be brought back on track. They like to be managed but at the same time experience freedom."

"You are quite something, Alexandre Chevalier. Quite a secret macho control freak, aren't you?"

He laughs. "Not so secret."

"And there I was, mistaking you for this humble gentleman!" I rev up and speed along a straighter road, gaining more confidence. I'm in my element driving this car!

"There, you see how happy she is? She likes to show you what she's capable of," he shouts above the vroom, vroom of the engine.

"She likes me?"

"She loves you, Pearl."

"Does that make her gay?" I joke, brushing my hand on his leg as I change gear.

"I think she's bi," he says, winking at me. "And if your sexual fantasies during phone sex are anything to go by, you'll get along together just fine."

"Shush, that's a secret."

I think about what Alexandre said earlier, "Pearl, you make me happy, I'm crazy for you..." and I hum Madonna's

Crazy For You to myself. Does he really mean those words?

Before long, we stop at his nearest village, Ménerbes, which is perched on top of a hill.

"You know, Ménerbes," Alexandre begins in a serious tour guide voice, "has been inhabited since prehistoric times. Archaeological excavations have uncovered the remains of villas and an ancient cemetery dating back to Roman times. These villages were built on hilltops to protect them from invasion," he informs me, "particularly during the religious wars. Picasso had a house here and Peter Mayle who wrote, *A Year in Provence.*"

"So this is where he lived," I murmur.

We enter through a large arch into the small central square, and potter about the tiny village which, from certain points, offers striking views of lush, rolling hills below, dotted with farmhouses and hamlets making a patchwork of colors like a quilt.

"This place is famous for its truffle market," Alexandre tells me. "They use dogs mostly, these days, for digging truffles, the pigs got a little greedy. Truffles are so expensive, they can't afford to lose even one."

Our next stop is Gordes, marked with a sign as one of the most beautiful villages in France, *Les Plus Beaux Villages de France.* It, like Ménerbes, is perched on a hill with breath-taking views below. We park the car and wind our way through the narrow cobbled streets where no vehicles are allowed, and look up at tall houses of honey-colored stone, many of them built right into the rock itself. Natural and man-made beauty rolled into one supreme medieval mélange. There is a castle in the middle of the village where we wander about watching tourists pass by, oohing and aahing at the history of the place. We sit in a café and relax our legs. I order an iced tea and Alexandre a Pastis, an aniseed drink that, when mixed with water and ice, turns milky - a drink favored by the people of Provence, he says.

On the way back, he drives. Way faster than I did, I may add. Even though it's past seven, the sun is creating a magical, golden dusk light and there's a cooler breeze now.

"So tell me, Pearl Robinson, did you grow up in New York City?"

"I still haven't grown up," I quip.

He laughs. "Alright, were you 'raised' in New York?"

"Yes, in Brooklyn. We moved to Manhattan when I was twelve because I got a scholarship to a private school on the Upper East Side."

"You must have been a good student."

"I worked hard. I was keen to prove myself, get top grades. I had to show them I earned the scholarship. I didn't want to let anybody down. What about you? Did you do well at school?"

"No, I was a disaster. I experimented with drugs, you know, smoked weed, dropped some acid. I was a bad boy. A high school dropout. But I did have a passion and that was IT - all self-taught, and bit by bit I cleaned up my act. I got into an excellent school in Paris for graphics and communication but only stayed a few weeks – the fees were too high. My sister tried to help, but when I realized the kind of work she was doing, there was no way I could accept, so I left to get a job."

"Why, what was she doing?"

"Just something that wasn't good for her soul."

"What?"

"Never mind."

He's whetted my curiosity, that's for sure. What could

Sophie have been working at that was so bad for her soul?

When we get back, I busy myself with getting ready for the party. I take a shower and put on a pair of high, platform sandals and a short, slinky dress that's red. Too much? Maybe. I look in the mirror and dissect myself. My hair is looking pretty good and I caught quite a tan today, just walking around and being in the pool. Those crow's feet though, they're a drag. I put on another layer of mascara to open my eyes up wider and I see the reflection of Alexandre standing behind me. He's back to his casual self, in a black T-shirt and jeans. His chest muscles are prominent, even though the T-shirt is quite loose. His hair is wet from the shower. His eyes rove over my body and I immediately feel self-conscious.

"Too much?" I ask. "The red?"

"No, not too much. Perfect. Sexy. You look stunning."

"Is it too skimpy, though? Too femme fatale?"

"Well if it is, I love it. You've got the body so flaunt it."

He comes behind me and cups my buttocks with his palms. "Great ass."

"It's the swimming, I guess."

He lets his hands wander up the small of my back and around to my stomach - then strokes the curves of my bare breasts. "Great tits, too."

For the first time ever, I push his hands away. I should feel complimented but a clutch of anxiety takes hold as I imagine his ex, Laura, to be so much more than me. She broke up with him – she must be something else. "You said you'd show me photos of Laura," I say, turning to face him.

"What, now?"

"Why not?"

"We should really be leaving."

"Just a quick glance. I'm curious about her."

"She's a special woman."

"Yes, so you keep saying." *What is this? Is he trying to keep me on my toes by making me jealous?*

We go downstairs to the living room where the giant fireplace and all the English books are. Madame Menager has left a tray on the table with a bottle of chilled champagne and some tasty-looking canapés. He pours me a glass. I sip the refreshing drink, savoring the bubbly taste, and I nestle onto the sofa, while Alexandre gets out a photo album.

"This is typical Laura," he tells me. "I don't have any printed photos myself – everything is on my computer and iPad but she used to make albums – very English that." He's holding a large, blue leather-bound book in his hands. My heart is beating with trepidation – why do I want to torture myself?

He puts the book on my lap and sits next to me. I start carefully turning the stiff pages. There, before me, is a young woman who can't be more than thirty, smiling into the camera, jumping in the air. She is tall, blonde, with a body like a swimwear model and a smile that takes up her whole face. She is gorgeous. On the page next to it is Alexandre looking really young, thinner and more boyish. I turn the page. Another set of pictures – them sailing at sea, soaked through – it looks like it's a wet day with clouds in the sky. They are both laughing their heads off.

"That was in Cornwall, the south of England. We called ourselves the Salty Sea Dogs. It was always raining, or so it seemed. We sailed a lot, Laura was practically Olympic level."

Now I understand. She was an all-rounder. Stunningly beautiful, smart (all those books), and sporty. She looks older than he does, perhaps she went off with someone more age appropriate. I turn more pages. A birthday party, she blowing out candles, her lips luscious, her eyes as big as saucers - she makes me look like Plain Jane.

"She's beautiful," is all I can muster.

More of Laura and him. Now they are in India riding elephants painted with flowers on their wrinkly skin. There are temples in the background. I feel envious – the love between them is so evident. I turn more pages and a jolt of shock arrests me.

"Who's that?" I ask, pointing at a blonde woman in a wheelchair. It looks like Laura. She must have broken her leg or something.

"It's Laura," he confirms, covering his face with his palms. He looks as if tears could well in his eyes.

I turn more pages. She's still in the wheelchair here. "What happened?"

"We lived in a basement flat in London. One night we came home late and the next door neighbor's child had left one of his toys on the steps. Laura tripped and fell. I couldn't catch her in time. She tumbled down the concrete steps and landed really badly. It was one of those freak accidents with a terrible consequence."

"Oh no. Was she really hurt?"

"Paralyzed from the waist down. Luckily, no damage to her head."

"Oh my God." I have tears in my eyes as he tells me this. "But she was a sportswoman and so active."

"I know. Life's unfair, isn't it?"

"And now?"

"She's a lot better now. She's walking with a cane. Limping, but the doctors had told her, originally, that she would probably be paralyzed for the rest of her life, so what she's achieved is a miracle. Her husband has been incredible, too. He's been by her side every step of the way."

"Husband?"

"The man she left me for. I was broken-hearted. He'd been her childhood boyfriend and had always been in love with her. I felt, at the time, as if she was dismissing me as useless, as if I wouldn't know how to care for her, or didn't care enough. But I would never have deserted her. Never. She knew what she wanted, though, and it was him. James. She was right, in hindsight. He's been fantastic. I couldn't have been there for her the way he has been."

"Had you started your business by that point?"

"Just. Of course, when she left me, I threw myself head-long into work to keep my mind off her. I moved back to Paris and did nothing else but get HookedUp off the ground. I didn't see daylight for weeks, holed up in my dark basement office, coding and working out formulas and ways to make it successful. Meanwhile, my sister was having meetings and getting backers."

"You said your stepfather helped you."

"He lent us fifteen thousand Euros and some of his friends pitched in, too. They've made their money back several thousand percent, I'm glad to say. They took a risk."

"And you and Laura are still friends?"

"Of course. She and James are coming here in a couple of weeks. I won't be here, though. I lend them the house every summer. We'd better get a move on, Pearl, or we'll be late."

I now see Alexandre in a whole new light. He is not the philandering, 'woman in every port' type, at all. He's loyal and a good friend. He was prepared to stick by Laura even when she was crippled, not out of a sense of duty but for love. He's a kind person who cares about people.

I want this man and his baby - more than ever.

14

We roll up to the party in the Murciélago, black as night. I would have felt self-conscious in such an outrageously flashy car, were it not matched by vehicles almost - but not quite - as impressive, lining the driveway. I can already spot some movie stars – I feel as if I'm in Hollywood at an Oscar party, not a place in the middle of the French countryside.

Alexandre walks over to the passenger side and opens the door for me. I ease myself out, careful not to expose my panties to the world. Who knows, there might be paparazzi here – they could be interested in Alexandre Chevalier's love interest. *Love interest? What am I painting myself as, an actress in a movie? I am his girlfriend, am I not?*

My insecurities are assuaged when he introduces me to the host and his friends, saying, "This is my girlfriend, Pearl."

The house is slicker than Alexandre's; more luxurious,

but that's to be expected of Hollywood royalty. Is that Charlize Theron I see over there? Beyond stunning. And is that Susan Sarandon, looking so elegant in a black sequined dress? The candlelit rooms are milling with the bold and the beautiful, spilling into the garden. Alexandre is holding my hand, leading me around.

Once in the swing of things, and after a few glasses of champagne, I feel completely at ease. After all, my main job as producer is communication. Chatting with people is easy for me and we've had a few stars doing voice-over work for us at Haslit Films. I'm not intimidated by fame.

After a while, we meander our separate ways. I get chatting to a woman from LA – shop talk, really, and Alexandre gets distracted by one of his neighbors – they're talking about their vines and lavender production. Before I know it, someone who looks oddly familiar has joined us and he soon overtakes the conversation. Who is he? That's the problem with actors - you think one is your neighbor or even your old friend, because you feel you've known that person all your life and then you realize you've seen them on TV or in a movie and you are a total stranger to them. Who *is* this man? Anyway, the woman has slipped out of sight now and I find myself discussing Haslit Films with him and my next, hopeful project. He's smiling away and I'm smiling away, too. Finally, he asks my name and I tell him.

"And your name is?" I ask. He looks surprised as if I should know and then says, "Ryan." He's thirty-something - blond, blue eyes. Handsome in a classic way although not my type. Funnily enough, he reminds me somewhat of my ex.

We are just beginning a conversation when I feel Alexandre grab my wrist from behind. "We have to leave," he says briskly.

"What, already? I feel as if we just got here."

The movie star is looking awkward so I introduce him to Alexandre. Alexandre nods and murmurs in a husky tone, "Pearl, we have to go."

"Bye," I say. "Nice meeting you."

"I was having a good time," I hiss at Alexandre. "Why are we leaving?" *Is he jealous?*

As we are walking out the front door, an elegantly dressed woman gives me a look of disgust like a dagger being thrown into my face. I recognize her but I can't place her. What is wrong with me tonight? As I pass her I hear, "fucking cougar," and wonder if the insult was directed at me.

Alexandre bundles me into the car and screeches out of the driveway. I feel like Batwoman in this thing. He's no longer in a happy mood and I fear that I've upset him by unwittingly flirting with that famous actor, although what he's famous for, I have no idea. Alexandre is silent, staring ahead at the road.

"You were right about your dress," he says in a cold voice. "It drew too much attention to you. It was too garish."

"I wasn't flirting. At least I wasn't conscious of doing so."

But he doesn't say a word. Twenty minutes go by and I'm aware that he doesn't take a turning I noticed earlier on our way here. Half an hour later and we are still not home. He's driving fast now, really fast. I can feel angry vibes emanating from every pore in his body. Jesus, if chatting with another man makes him jealous, this relationship of ours is not going to work.

"Are we going somewhere?" I ask.

"I'll get Madame Menager to send your things on. We aren't going back to my house."

Oh my God! I am being dumped! He's breaking up with me

for some harmless flirting. That's my job! I have to be charming, have meetings, lunches and sometimes, yes, they happen to be with attractive men. I'm looking over at him and see the rage on his face. Uh, oh. I'm feeling scared. Maybe it's best to break up with him, anyway, if he's going to be like this. I don't want some possessive psycho as my boyfriend.

"Alexandre, what's going on?"

"I don't like seeing you treated like that. Fuck, just because you were wearing a short red dress doesn't give people a license to be so judgmental."

"That guy, Ryan, was being perfectly friendly. He wasn't being lecherous or rude in any way at all."

"We are not talking about him, for fuck's sake," he shouts. He has never spoken to me with that tone before and it shocks me. "We're talking about you," he adds, ominously.

I can feel myself well up. "I was just being friendly. Discussing my work. I didn't even find him attractive."

But he doesn't reply, just mumbles, "fucking bitch," under his breath.

I want to sink through the floor of his car. If this really was the Batmobile I could press a button and be shot out into the sky or something. Tears are now spilling onto my dress. The dress, I realize that is causing all this turmoil. I knew I shouldn't have worn it. Too short. Too red. It's screaming out 'slut'. I feel humiliated and small. He's racing around corners now like some Formula One driver. He seems to have control but the speed and the way his temper is flaring has me crumbling into a wreck. I'm sobbing now, I have nothing to wipe away my tears but this vulgar dress. It's smeared with mascara which is also, no doubt, half way down my panda-eyed face. He looks over at me.

"Are you crying, baby?" he asks, his voice suddenly soft.

"Of course I am," I heave between sobs. *What the hell does he expect?*

He pulls the car over in a dark lay-by and turns off the engine.

"Oh, Pearl, I'm so sorry."

"This goddam dress."

"Well, I love that dress," he says, unclipping his seatbelt and mine. He takes me in his arms and draws me close. "You think I was angry at *you*?" he asks tenderly.

"You called me a 'fucking bitch.' "

He let out a small laugh. "Oh shit. No, Pearl. Not *you*, chérie. I was talking about my sister."

"Sophie?"

"She turned up at the party," he explains.

Duh, I click. That woman I saw was *Sophie*. Sophie, who shot me that look loaded with poison daggers.

"She called me a cougar," I tell him.

"In my book, that's a compliment. Cougars are beautiful, streamline, elegant and intelligent creatures."

"I don't think she meant it as a compliment."

"Why," he slams his hand on the dashboard, "can't she mind her own fucking business." He strokes my hair and kisses me on the forehead, then his mouth presses gently on my salty cheeks. "I'm sorry, baby. I'm sorry. That's why we're getting out of here – I'm really not in the mood for a scene. She'll be staying at my house. You don't want to be around."

"Why does she hate me? What have I ever done to her?"

"She's just jealous, that's all. She feels you're distracting me from my work."

"But you're still working your ass off, despite seeing me!"

"I know, but lately, she's right, my heart and soul are not in it. Since I met you I've been reminded that there is more to life than HookedUp. Besides, my work there is done. All the creative bit has finished, it's only about deals now and making more money. That's not what I'm about. Yeah, the money's great. I mean, look at this car, my properties and stuff, but…." he trails off, deep in thought as if an idea had just struck him.

"Where are you taking me now?" I ask.

"I'm taking *us* to Cap d'Antibes. I thought you should see a little of the French Riviera, the Côte d'Azur. I'll get our passports and anything important biked over to us tomorrow and then we'll fly to Paris from Nice the following day." He's now putting my seat back so I am reclining, the seat almost making a bed. "Let's just forget this episode, shall we? I'll sort things out with Sophie next week. I won't have her ruining things between you and me."

I take a deep breath and am placated, at least for now. No more tears.

He's running his eyes along my body and says, "You look amazing in that little red dress. Did you see how you were like a magnet? Everyone was looking at you. The best looking men in the room couldn't keep their eyes off you." His hand has moved its way between my legs and he pushes them apart gently. "And you know what turns me on? They want you - but you're mine. All mine." The next thing I know, he brings out the feather from his pocket. "It's had a bit of wear and tear," he says, "but it might make you feel more relaxed. Close your eyes, chérie. Think of lavender and rolling waves and just relax."

I lie back and he begins to trace the feather around my ankles and along my calves, and he tweaks my nipples with his fingers, rolling them between his thumb and forefinger. I can feel the pulse between my legs and I splay them open. He leans over and kisses me, flicking his tongue on mine and then kissing me hard on the mouth. I moan and start jiggling about in my seat. He traces his finger down my navel, around my belly-button and down to my panties. He presses the palm of his whole hand over my core, holding it there, still. I can almost hear the throb of it like a heartbeat.

"Are you feeling better now," he asks. "More relaxed?"

"Yes."

He presses my clit ever so lightly through my panties and holds it down for a second. I start pushing up against on his firm hand. But then he takes it away and starts the engine.

"What are you doing?" I gasp, longing for him to take me right here in the car.

"I'm hungry. It's a good hour away, yet, and I want to get us there in time for dinner."

"So French," I moan. "Your belly comes before anything else, even sex."

He laughs. "I know how to handle you, Pearl Robinson. I may be greedy for food but you are greedy in other ways. I'm just whetting your appetite - just making sure my chick is still clucking."

I'm clucking alright. "You bastard," I exclaim, pounding his thigh with my fist. "You can't leave me here like this, moist between the legs, tingling all over." I see the huge bulge in his jeans and it makes me catch my breath. *Why does he insist on this torture?*

He has a knowing smirk on his face as he drives off, the car noisy like a racing car. "You just sleep now, baby, we'll be there soon. Dream of me, and remember - be prepared, because I'm going to get you to ride me later. See how hard I am? That's all for you."

15

I've done it again. I've wasted a night sleeping! Last night, after a mouth-watering dinner, which was accompanied by both vintage red and white wines (so delicious, I drained every glass), I conked out on the sofa in our suite. Alexandre carried me, woozily drunk as I was, to bed, and here I am the following morning in the most beautiful place in the world with the most beautiful man in the world, nursing a hangover. What a fool. Except, right now, I appear to be alone in our sumptuous suite, which is decorated with pristine antique furniture.

I go to one of the two bathrooms, a marble affair, beyond luxurious, and look in the mirror. Uh, oh. My hair is wildly messed up and I have dark makeup around my eyes. Did he wake up to that unsightly mess? Poor guy. I splash water on my face and glug down some mineral water to clear my foggy head. I wander back into the bedroom and living room. Alexandre is definitely not around. I have a memory of last night's dream, quite Freudian, perhaps, that I was making love to a black horse. Well, not with his actual wiener, but riding his foreleg which was pressed in tightly between my legs, holding me up. I was worried I was too heavy for his leg as he was supporting all my weight, and I asked him if it hurt (of course, animals speak in dreams). The horse replied, 'no, it's fine - keep riding.' I was meant to ride Alexandre but ended up dreaming about a horse instead! I think I had an orgasm in my sleep. Well, in the dream I did, but does that make it really happen? I have always wondered that – when you come in your sleep are you actually climaxing, or just dreaming you are? For men it's obvious, they wake up with a sticky mess on the sheets, but for women it is more of a mystery. Sometimes, I still have my hands between my legs, still tingling and hot so I know it happened. But today, I'm not sure.

Alexandre has awoken my sensibility, my sexuality. To think that less than a month ago, I had resigned myself to a sexless, passionless life, centered around work, and little else. Yet, I am only forty – too young to give up so soon. Forty. Not long ago that seemed a lifetime away for me, and then the number crept up - and here it is. Four O. Four Oh! Like the pearls, I am made of forty shades, a different tone for every year I've been alive. Forty. For some that seems old, that I am a preying cougar, that I have no right to be with a man fifteen years younger than me. Yet, for centuries it has been accepted when the roles are reversed. How many people even blink when they see a man fifteen years older than his partner? Princess Diana was only nineteen when she met Prince Charles who was thirteen years her senior, and the whole world thought it marvelously romantic. Yet she was still just a teenager.

But I am seen as a Cougar with a capital C.

Cougar - Sophie's one word, spat at me like venom, is echoing in my ears. I should ignore her spite, but I can't. I feel I am being judged, and that eyes are upon me, not just Sophie's, but others, too. Will people be observing me here, thinking, 'how did she get that young guy?' *Shut up, Pearl!* He wants to be with you, just accept It. Be happy, stop doubting yourself all the time.

But I do doubt myself. I can't help it.

I gaze out the window from my balcony at the view, and tears well in my eyes. Tears of happiness, tears of despair. Have I ever witnessed anything so perfect? I look across the century-old grove of pine trees to the sea before me - a blue more profound than I thought possible. Even Hawaii cannot match this. I have heard all my life about the Mediterranean and here I am at the Hotel du Cap-Eden-Roc on the southern tip of the Cap d'Antibes, the pearl of the Côte d'Azur - no pun intended - where the glamorous and great have been coming for a hundred and forty years.

Here I am, me, Pearl, in this place that holds such mythical status, standing on my balcony listening to the sound of nature's summer music - the cicadas chirping in my ears - and breathing in the scent of jasmine, or something delicious, mixed with pine. Perhaps the great playwright, Bernard Shaw, stood right here, or the Hollywood legends, Tyrone Power and Rita Hayworth.

The turquoise water is shimmering with the morning sun and there is a sailing boat in the distance, its white sails like fairy wings edging on the deep horizon. The deep green of the pine trees compliment the glistening blue - his eyes and mine – green and blue. I think back to when I was a little girl putting my green and blue crayons side by side together – my two favorite colors, so pretty, peaceful, pleasing. Now those colors are part of my soul.

Only yesterday I was a little girl.

Today, I am a 'cougar'.

I take a shower to freshen up, wash my hair, but once dry, I realize I have nothing to wear but the fated red dress. There is no way I'm strutting about this hotel in that, garnering stares from the glamorous guests. I heard a rumor last night that Madonna is staying here. Eat your heart out, Anthony!

I call reception and order a blue and white bikini, a tennis skirt and T-shirt from the hotel boutique – something, for now, to make me blend in. Then I ask for breakfast to be brought to the room. It is ten o'clock – where is Alexandre? I don't want to go looking for him. I have my iPhone but my battery has run out and the charger is back at his house. I open the mini bar and drain a whole bottle of orange juice. Already I feel more alive and am grateful I have had this last hour to myself alone. No more drinking alcohol.

Famous last words, I know.

When Alexandre returns, he finds me in my little tennis outfit. He stands at the doorway and gives me a wolf whistle. I laugh.

"Hi Pearl, love the look. But isn't it a bit hot to play right now?"

"I have no intention of playing tennis," I reply. "All I want to do is get into that crystalline sea. I had to wear something so I got this tennis gear, and look," I say, flashing the bikini underneath. "Ready for a swim?"

He saunters up to me, kisses me on the mouth and lays his hand on my butt. "Absolutely."

"Where have you been, by the way?"

"Making some calls." By the look on his face I know who he has been speaking to.

"You talked to your sister?"

"I needed to get a few things straight with her."

"What's her problem, anyway?"

"She's possessive." He leads me to the sofa and sits me down. He obviously wants to explain things. Explain why his sister is such a tough cookie. Why she dislikes me. "Look, she was the same with Laura. Laura was never good enough for me. Until we split up, of course. Then, suddenly, the sun shone out of Laura's ass and she could do no wrong."

"Even when Laura was already married to the other guy - to James?"

"Exactly. Once safely ensconced with another man, Laura became the perfect woman for me. They're great friends now. For some reason, my sister feels that if I am in love with someone, she'll lose me."

I bask in his words. Does that mean he's *in love* with me?

"But Sophie has a step-daughter," I argue, "and a husband - she has a life outside HookedUp. You're not a seven year-old boy anymore. She doesn't need to play mommy to you any longer."

He's shaking his head solemnly. "She can't let go."

"And what about you?" I ask. I'm beginning to see his sister as a major obstacle to our relationship. Like a wicked, jealous mother-in-law with whom you'll never see eye to eye.

"She's had a tough life," he answers, as if by way of ex-planation.

"So have you, but it hasn't made you aggressive."

"Oh, I can be, Pearl. When crossed. Sophie's the same."

"But I haven't crossed her! I met her once for five

minutes." I put my hand on his knee and soften my voice. "Something you said yesterday has been haunting me. You told me she did a job that wasn't good for her soul - to help you with tuition fees. What was it?"

"I really don't want to go into that."

"Was it dealing drugs?"

"No, she's never had a drug problem. She's pretty straight. In fact, she was furious when I was loafing about smoking weed and playing video games when I was a teenager. She was the one who insisted I get my act togeth-er."

"So what was she doing that was so awful?"

"Pearl, I don't want to judge people, least of all my sister. What she did was just her way of trying to make ends meet. It was hard for her at age seventeen when she had to support me. She had to endure stuff she wasn't happy about. And years later she fell back on a profession that she knew could make money fast."

"She worked as a prostitute?" I guess, looking him in the eye.

He's tapping his fingers together in agitation. "I don't like that term. I prefer 'sex worker.' It's still work, whatever anyone says. And it's not the sex workers who are at fault but their bloody customers. All the perverts of this world who take advantage of someone in a weak, vulnerable position."

"I see."

"That sounds judgmental, Pearl."

"What? I haven't said anything! All I said was, 'I see.' "

"Just your tone of voice. Have you any *idea* how tough it was for Sophie?"

"No, I haven't," I say carefully. "I can try to imagine but

I cannot put myself in her shoes." I nearly say, *I have never fallen so low,* but instead come up with, "Life has never gotten that bad for me."

"Money is important to Sophie. She's terrified of losing everything we've built up. Scared shitless of going back to being poor, or in a compromised situation."

"Look, I don't know much about your finances, Alexandre, but it seems to me that you could both sell up and never work a day again for the rest of your lives - if you ever chose to."

"Tell me about it. Not a day goes by when I haven't considered doing that."

"Well, why don't you?"

"I can't just abandon her – we're business partners."

"You'd hardly be feeding her to the lions, Alexandre. She'd be set for life. You both would. You said yourself, it's all about deals now, and the creative process is over. You could start another company; create something new if you wanted. I mean, if you're not happy–"

"I am happy. Please, let's drop this, Pearl. Let's go swimming."

The water is heaven and it washes away that unpleasant conversation. The sea is smooth and refreshing but not cold. Rocks glimmer beneath us and we dip and dive about each other like children. Alexandre is a strong swimmer – thank God. I'm glad I'm not disappointed in that department. Snotty, I know, to care about something like swimming, but I do. A bad swimmer could be a deal breaker. How ridiculous is that?

Afterwards, we sun ourselves on the rocks like salamanders. He has a dark tan and doesn't seem to need sun-cream at all.

"How come you already had swim trunks with you?" I ask.

"I always keep an emergency overnight bag in my car. Dumb, really. It started in LA having to be ready in case of a fast getaway after an earthquake. I got caught out once and it shook me. Call me a geek, but I like to be prepared. Next time, I'll pack for you, too."

I smile. 'Next time' – I like that. "So what else have you got in your bag of tricks?"

"A shirt, shorts, jeans, cash and so on."

A man prepared for anything. I have a feeling this has less to do with any earthquake than a little boy of seven having to leave home at a moment's notice, never to return.

"We can have dinner here later, if you like," he suggests. "Watch the sunset."

"I'd love that." I start to giggle.

"What?"

"Already thinking about dinner, Monsieur Frenchie, and we haven't even had lunch yet."

"Just to prove I'm really French, I carry a corkscrew in my car, too."

We are back in our luxurious suite drinking chilled champagne (my no-drinking resolve didn't last a second) – I'm lying naked on the bed, admiring my tan.

"You can always tell an American girl," he observes, "by her tan mark."

I look up at him.

"Tits like vanilla," he explains.

"You think I should have taken off my top, don't you? Like the European women."

"I don't know about that," he says, running his eyes along my body and biting his lower lip. "It's sexy. Provocative. Those arrogant little breasts are asking to be sucked and played with, just asking for it."

I take a cube of ice from the ice-bucket and circle it around my nipples until they go hard. "Like this?" I tease. The melting water is trickling down my breasts and onto my stomach. "And what about my pale-skinned bottom and—"

"Your little, cream-colored pussy," he interrupts, coming over to the bed. But he doesn't touch me, just continues to drink in the view of my sun-kissed body. "All of it is asking for it," he notes, narrowing his eyes. "Asking to get fucked."

I take another cube and slip it in between my legs, up inside myself. I gasp at the chill but then it feels welcoming. I trace my finger up along my wet slit and watch his expression. He can't keep his eyes off me. I run my tongue around my lips, staring at him as I do so. He takes off his swim shorts and I watch his huge phallus spring free. It, too, is paler than the rest of him. Also, asking for it. Begging to be ridden. To get sucked. I want to get on top of it, feel it deep inside me. I want it to make me come again.

He takes a gulp of champagne, holds it in his mouth, and straddles me so his hard penis is resting in between my breasts. I am pinned to the bed. He leans forward, pressing his thumb on my lower lip, opening my mouth and then kisses it, letting the champagne run down past my tongue.

He slowly licks my mouth.

"It's so good to see you naked in the full light, Pearl. A few freckles have come up on your face, you look beautiful."

I look into his green eyes flecked with gold highlights, rimmed with black lashes. "You…you look like….sex," I whisper in his ear, the words falling out incomprehensively, and then I nibble his lobe which tastes of salt. I breathe in the smell of Mediterranean sun-on-skin mixed with Alexandre; a perfume designed just for me. I claw my hands about his butt and draw him higher, closer, and take his smooth erection in my mouth. It, too, tastes of the Mediterranean. I close my eyes and suck on it. It smells of sun and sea. I let my tongue flicker, rim and slap its round tip, sucking off the pre-come, tasting the love I have for this man, the surge of sexual desire and the hunger I feel, like an ache, to have all of him inside me, his soul, his body – all of him.

"Kiss me again," I demand. He pulls his hips back and grazes his lips along my throat, then lifts my wrists in the air and licks me under the arms. The sensation is so erotic and I sense my clitoris swell with excitement. I expect him to go to my breasts next, but he doesn't. His tongue journeys south all the way down, stopping to lick my thighs yet avoiding my pussy. Oh, no, not that again…the slow, tantalizing torture. It's throbbing now, my hips flexing and bending, wanting attention in that core centre, but he leaves it be. Instead, he lifts my legs high, one at a time, and licks me behind each knee. He carries on down my legs and takes my salty toes in his mouth, sucking each one, slowly. I am so relaxed, floppy as a soft doll.

I pop my finger inside myself and feel the heat, slick with desire. I tell him about last night's dream with the black horse.

"You want to ride me again, baby, is that what you want," he says, his face between my thighs. He is kneeling on the floor now, staring up at me from between my legs. His tongue flicks just once on my clit but not again. Teasing me. I can feel its pulse.

"Please fuck me," I beg. "I need it deep inside." I'm wriggling on the mattress.

He gets back on the bed and slips underneath me, lifting me up with his muscular arms, placing his head in between my feet, and he hauls me close to him so my legs are either side of his torso. He pulls my back up so I am sitting on top of him.

"Swivel round," he instructs, and he maneuvers me so I am straddling him, my knees either side of his hips. I'm sitting on his crotch but facing away from him. His view is my ass and I am looking at his feet.

"Now ease yourself on top of my cock."

I kneel up to position myself and take his erection in both hands. I aim it inside me, rimming it about me first. This feels great.

"Won't this hurt you, being at an angle?" I ask, slapping his hard rock against my clit and rimming it up and down and around the lips of my opening.

"No, this feels....delicious," he murmurs with a groan, pushing his hips forward so he is closer and slipping all the way inside me. "They call it the Reversed Cowgirl. You're in control, Pearl. You call the shots... with your pistol...with your pussy pistol."

I smile. I start riding him slowly, easing myself up and down. This is novel; I have never tried this before. His hands are on my waist, guiding me. I am looking at his strong calf muscles, his elegant feet. He has a bird's eye view of my curvy buttocks.

"Your ass is out of this world, oh yeah, keep that rhythm, this feels great, chérie. Love that peaches and cream ass, love that tight, wet pearlette moving so sweetly."

I lean forward now and slip my hand under his balls. I can hear his breath in gasps. I keep riding. Up and down. Up and down. Then I lift myself off his cock completely and squeeze his erection in a tight grip. "I need to get smacked about," I say, and I begin to slap his cock against my clit again, guiding it around my hot entrance and back on my clit. Oh yeah...this feels amazing. I observe my nipples darkening like crimson rosebuds. Then I ease myself on top of him again and press down so his erection slides deep, deep, deep inside.

"Rodeo me, baby. That's right, you Wild West American Cowgirl."

I want to laugh, but the sensation feels so intense, all I can do is concentrate. I'm pulling almost all the way out now, teasing my entrance and then making circular movements with my hips.

"You lak this?" I say in a faux Texan accent. I graze my thumbs across my nipples and they harden like bullets. I cannot see him but I can hear his murmurs. Oh yes, he does like this. Then I rest my hands back on his legs, impale myself upon him so he is deep inside me again, and I start to rock back and forth. He's stroking my butt cheeks with his hands, and just knowing how turned on he's getting, is making me hotter. I can feel that G-spot getting rubbed...oh yeah, this is nice. I arch my back. Alexandre lifts his hips a touch and....ah, he's hit that spot. I rock forward once more and start...

"I'm coming, Alexandre. You're making me come." I

clench my muscles tighter and feel another wave roll over me. He's pumping now, his hips rising from beneath in hard thrusts.

"Me too, I'm coming."

Feeling him thicken inside me brings on another surge of pleasure and I slam down on him. As I do so I press my clit with my middle finger and feel an intense roll of orgasm rush again to the surface. "It's happening again," I scream out, hardly believing this is real. Ripples and spasms rush through my body like patterns.

"I think I've accomplished my mission," he says in a low voice.

A wave of panic engulfs me. Does that mean it's over? *He's made me come with penetrative sex again, so that's it?* But I don't say a word. The aftershocks are making my body tremble. I'm like putty.

Alexandre is in my bloodstream like a drug.

While my nerves are still tingling, he pushes me off him so I'm kneeling on all fours. He grabs my hips from behind and shoves his huge erection into me from the back. I gasp. *More?* I hold onto the bead-stead as he fucks me so hard my head bumps up against the padded part. He's literally growling like an animal, ramming me from behind, punctuating his words with thrusts.

"Love. Fucking. You. All I can do is…. fuck you, Pearl. All I can think… about is… making you….come."

Then he pulls out slowly and starts sucking me so gently, so softly, his tongue darting between my thighs in tiny, almost imperceptible sweeps. The rough and now the smooth, the combination and surprise of it has me on the edge again. I find myself willing him silently to fuck me hard once more. And he does.

"This ass is….driving me…. crazy. This round, silky-smooth ass is…." he doesn't finish his sentence, just rams himself into me and starts pumping hard again. I feel another wave building up. He cries out in French and then more words that I don't understand. His hands are cupping my butt tightly, claiming it. Possessing it. "This ass belongs to me," he roars. He's thick and rock hard inside me. And then… he stills. Stationary. All I can feel is his throbbing, the rush of his release. It's filling me up. He's still, motionless, and the sweet soreness I feel inside me and the big pulse of his cock has me about to come. I can feel it. My head is down on the bed, my butt high in the air, his still erection pounding like a slow drum beat inside me. I touch my clitoris softly with my fingers, and feel the double-hot sensation build up, and I climax once more.

I'm quivering all over. "Oh, Alexandre," I whimper. "What are you doing to me?" I'm moaning and he starts moving gently back and forth again.

"I'm coming again, baby," he whispers, and I can feel a new surge of his release pulse through me. "Je t'aime."

He just said he loves me! But I don't reply. It's the moment of passion, I know - I can't be really sure if it's me he loves, or my body parts. Either way, my psyche is jumping up and down for joy. I remain still, lapping up my post-orgasm spasms.

Cool, calm and collected.

That's me.

16

We are having lunch overlooking the sea, and I am quietly meditating on what just happened. If I had read about my experience in a woman's magazine, I would have thought it was an invented fantasy to sell more copies, but it happened – it really did - multiple orgasms have rocked my world.

I, Pearl Robinson, had multiple orgasms. The notion seems extraordinary. Surreal. As if the new Pearl has been prized from her oyster shell and re-packaged as a shimmering piece of priceless jewelry. Pearl - the exquisite. Pearl - the treasure. That is how I now feel.

I think of all the wasted years in my thirties. My sexuality stagnant - sitting on a shelf like an unread classic book. Something of quality but ignored, or worse, in the hands of somebody who did not know how to read, or at least, did not know how to read me. My ex-husband - oblivious to the wealth inside my body.

It took a twenty-five year-old Frenchman to unleash my riches.

Now I feel cocooned in love. I sit here inhaling the salty sea breeze and watch a couple on their honeymoon swimming and splashing below us, next to the rocks. Once, that would have filled me with benign envy.

Not now.

Alexandre's lip is curved into a quiet, satisfied smile. Mind-blowing sex followed by grilled wild sea bass for lunch. At least, I think that's what he's pleased about, although it could be because he has arranged to pick up Rex from Paris on our way back to New York. He has, indeed, organized a private jet – Rex will be travelling in style. We're leaving tomorrow morning for Paris by helicopter, apparently. So much for Alexandre's 'ecological' carbon footprint – I have a feeling he gads about the globe this way a lot. Why did he make out he was so politically correct, never using private transport? What else isn't he telling me?

Alexandre is talking on his cell. I love listening to him chat away in French.

He slaps his phone on the table and says, "Today everything has come together," and we laugh at his double-entendre. Come together. So true.

"What else are you feeling cocky about?" I ask, smiling.

"A deal."

"I thought you were tired of making deals, that that side of things didn't thrill you anymore."

He laughs. He has a mocking look in his eye which disarms me, and I discern a slight sneer on his face. "Are you kidding? I'm making silly money. That turns me on, Pearl, as much as what happened today between you and me. A challenge complete."

My stomach drops like lead – a thousand stabs pierce my gut. Is this the same human being I thought I knew? The man with the black Labrador? The man who would have stuck by a crippled woman for love?

I feel like a gutted fish. Empty. Dead. But he's smiling away, unaware of the turmoil inside me. I am no more important than a money deal. A challenge.

"I've had too much sun for one day," I manage to say before my voice cracks. "I'm going back to the room."

"Okay, just got to make another call or two. I'll join you in a bit."

When I get back to our suite, I turn on my iPhone which has been re-charging. Five messages. The latest, from Anthony, who received my 'Madonna is here' message – although I can't be sure - still haven't seen her with my own eyes. I called him this morning, S.O.S as a joke. He's hysterical, wanting to know if I've done what he asked, namely, to chat her up and become her New Best Friend. Another two messages from him. Next, Natalie asking me to bring her a towel from the hotel, 'So chic,' she raves. 'So iconic. Must have.' My dad has also left a message, harping on about Natalie, wondering what happened. Men are so clueless. I really don't want to play piggy in the middle to their drama. Then, a voice I don't recognize, at first. Then it dawns on me who it is. The dagger voice - Sophie. She and her brother have something in common. They can slice your heart open with just one word.

"Pee-earl," she begins. "I don't know what the fuck you sink you are doing wiz my leetle brozzer almost twice is age, old enough to be is muzzer - but I sink I should warn you, you are barking up ze wrong tree. Ee does not give a fuck about you, you know? Eet woz a bet we made in ze coffee shop. Ee said zat he bet he could make you crazey about im, fuck you on zee first date. Zen ee told me ee ad a challenge wiz you. I know all about your sexual problems, Peearl. Your frigidity. Eet woz a game ee play wiz you. Game is over, stalker woman." There is a crackling on the line and then the Simon and Garfunkel song, *Mrs. Robinson* begins playing in the background.

Wow, what a bitch.

I stare blankly at the wall of this zillion star hotel. Dazed, out of focus. Alexandre has discussed my private secrets with his *sister*. It makes me feel nauseous. As if there has been some incestuous tryst between them. How dare she know about my sexuality? How dare he tell her? A bubbling heat is consuming me, too furious, now, for tears. I rummage about the room and find what I am looking for: my bag with passport and the clothes wrapped inside a plastic bag. The suitcase would have been too big to bring by bike courier. Never mind, they brought all the essentials. I grab it all, put on the same 1950's dress I arrived in, and some flip-flops. I run out of the room. I dare not even ask for a taxi at the front desk. They could alert Alexandre. I race from the grounds, leaving the scent of pines, the chirping crickets and the Mediterranean paradise, behind me.

I am now at Nice airport. Luckily, there is a flight to Paris and I can change there with just a few hours wait for a flight to New York. I'm listening to Beyoncé on my iPhone – *If I Were a Boy* – you tell'em, Beyoncé. I wish I could understand how certain men's minds work – how some will stop at nothing to puff up their egos even if they know they're breaking someone's heart.

Just before take-off, I do the decent thing. I call Alexandre to let him know I have left. Just in case he reports me missing to the *gendarmes* or something. Thank God his voicemail picks up and I can just leave a message.

"Alexandre – what can I say?" I start in a small voice. "I have left. Obviously. I received a message on my cell from Sophie who seemed to know every intimate detail of my sex life. I'm glad your 'challenge' worked out for you, and for me, too. It was a real eye-opener, an experience of a lifetime. It was beautiful. Beautiful because I believed in it. But... now I have found out that it was all a game for you, I know that it could never be the same between us again. As you said yourself, the biggest sex organ is your brain. And my brain is shot to pieces right now. Goodbye, Alexandre. Good luck with Rex, shame that cute dog and I will never meet. Bon voyage."

I end the call, sit back in my economy seat and let the tears fall. The catchy tune to *Mrs. Robinson* is playing over and over inside my head like background music to my misery – a tune I used to love.

A reminder of who I am.

And what will never be.

17

When I walk into my apartment, its walls feel like a fortress - a welcome haven, safe from the evils of the outside world. Whatever happens (God forbid, a tsunami should strike New York City), this is my security. My nest.

I haven't even turned my cell back on. I don't want to know what Alexandre's reaction may be. I just need to feel at peace. It's four in the morning European time, ten pm here – time for bed; I have to go to work tomorrow.

I keep going over everything in my mind; could there have been some sort of mistake? No, Sophie knew intimate details about my sexuality. I feel humiliated as if I were some sort of experiment. Not to say I didn't enjoy being Alexandre's guinea pig - I cannot deny that, but I feel dishonored by him.

I call Daisy, give her the lowdown on my latest drama

and ask if there's any way she can do an early breakfast tomorrow. I need to talk to someone – get a second opinion about this whole crazy mess. We are meeting at 8am at the café next to my workplace.

I run a bath and rummage around the kitchen for something to eat. I land on some potato chips which I dunk into cream cheese. I scoff the whole packet. Comfort food. I'll need to watch myself in the next few weeks. No bingeing – I'll get rid of those calories tomorrow with a long swim.

The bath feels soothing, only, it reminds me of our time together. Will I ever get this French bastard out of my system? I hear the house telephone ring. I'll ignore it. The doorman? Anthony? Who cares – I can't be dealing with any of that now.

I mull over the sheer arrogance and inflated ego that Alexandre seems proud to own. A cliché of his own making. Yes, French men have a reputation for being great lovers but also, arrogant shitheads. Why was he playing games with me? To feed his vanity? I dry myself and moisturize my body all over, and then look through the playlist on my iPod. I find the perfect song for him. "This is for you, Alexandre," I shout into the air. *You're So Vain* blares out and I start to dance about the bathroom. I feel energized. I can get through this.

By the time I flop into bed, I'm exhausted. Did I dislocate my shoulder blade by punching my fist into the air too hard?

I fall into a deep sleep which feels like five minutes. The alarm on my iPhone goes off and I get ready for work. I have failed both Anthony and Natalie. I did not become Madonna's NBF and sorry, Natalie, I did not feel inclined to pinch a towel from the hotel. You can buy one online, my dear, from their E boutique.

Daisy has lost weight in the space of one week. Incredible. Less Annie and more Nicole Kidman. I order a bagel, lox and cream cheese for my breakfast (uh oh) - and she, a fruit salad and tea.

"Well, you look great for someone who has just had her heart broken," she observes, glancing me up and down.

"Don't be fooled by the tan."

"Look, you had a good innings. Inning? Innings? I never know if that word should be singular or plural."

"I don't know either," I say. "But you're right, it lasted longer than I expected."

"Did you get to keep the pearl necklace?" she inquires with raised eyebrows.

"No, I left it at his house and he never gave it back."

"Oh well. You win some, you lose some."

"What would you have done?" I ask.

"If I still had the necklace?"

"Yes."

"Tough call. Pride would make me want to return it, but then…well…there is such a thing as severance pay."

I laugh. "Anyway, I don't have it - so luckily, I'm not in that predicament."

"How are you feeling?"

"Humiliated. But strangely grateful."

"Don't sell yourself short, Pearl."

"Look….sex," I whisper, lowering my voice, "was out of this world with him. I am now hoping that he has awakened something in me. That I can find another great relationship with someone else. In the future. I'm also more open to younger guys, something I never would have dared to consider before."

"Watch out, mothers, lock up your sons, here she comes! Just teasing, Pearl, don't look so horrified."

"I'm just a little sensitive to the cougar insult that Sophie spat out at me, that's all."

"Not every woman can pull a younger guy."

I squint my eyes at her.

"Pearl! Where's your sense of humor?" Daisy takes a large mouthful of strawberries and banana. "So, what's Plan B?" she asks with her mouth full.

"Do you think there's any way all this was a mistake?"

She shakes her head. "I doubt it. Those two are as thick as thieves. He obviously confides in her. Sorry, Pearl, I'm just giving my honest opinion. Bitchy as Sophie has shown herself to be, there must be some truth in what she said, or how would she have that information about you? I'm sure she made it sound worse than it was, but still. She knew stuff about you that she shouldn't have been party to. Can you imagine telling Anthony intimate stuff about your boy-friend?"

"Eew, gross, no!" I glug down the rest of my orange juice. "You know what gets me more than anything?"

"What?"

"Not hanging out with his dog, Rex. I had visions of us all together - walks in Central Park, you know, the whole family dream thing."

"Were you imagining a real family with him, too? Babies and everything?"

I haven't told Daisy about the condom-less sex. I know

she would disapprove. A faint shiver runs through me and then I take a deep breath. *No, Pearl, that ship has sailed.*

"Well, you know, a girl can have her flights of fancy," I say.

"It all seemed so on the cards, Pearl. Until this sister crap messed it all up. I'm surprised. No, shocked, actually. I really believed he was into you. He had me fooled."

"You never met him, Daisy."

"I didn't have to. The pearl necklace spoke volumes, the trip to France et cetera. It seemed he went to extremes to make you happy – he didn't have to do all that, he still could have accomplished his 'challenge' without all those extra trimmings. The truth is, the more I think about it, it doesn't add up. But then….he is French, I suppose. Maybe he wanted to do it all with flourish and style."

"I guess we'll never know."

"Hasn't he called you a million times?"

"I don't know. My cell is switched off. Between him, and Anthony obsessing about Madonna, I don't dare listen to my messages."

"You'll need to give Alexandre a chance to at least explain."

"Explain what? That his only sister is a psycho bitch from hell who once stabbed her father in the groin, and who has it in for me? To be honest, maybe it's better like this - I'm well out of it. Do I really want her on my tail? Sharing my life with her? I mean, she's his sister and they're business partners. I wouldn't want to test her temper."

"Alexandre did say, though, that the father was a monster, didn't he? Maybe he deserved to be stabbed," Daisy reasons.

"Whatever - I don't want to be on the wrong side of her.

Perhaps it's best I keep well away from Alexandre."

"Probably. If you see him, you'll only get tempted again. And this Sophie character sounds like bad news, whichever way you look at it." Daisy checks her watch. "Crap! I'm really late! We'll speak this evening, okay, Pearl?"

"I'm late, too. Thanks for listening, Daisy. Thanks for being there for me. And you look great, by the way. Ten pounds slimmer."

"Don't exaggerate, Pearl, but thanks."

We both get up from our seats, pay the check and dash off our separate ways.

When I get home from work, Luke, the skinny doorman who I thought had been fired, presents me with a box. I recognize it – wrapped with the same type of white velvet ribbon in the gray box. I think I know what it is. My heart is thumping through my chest, adrenaline pumping through my veins as if I'm preparing to run from a wild beast. Funny how nature has adrenaline kick in whether we like it or not.

I have a quick shower to ease the day away and when I pick up the box again I am a little calmer.

Déjà-vu. I set it on my bed and open it. The pearl necklace wrapped in one of his T-shirts which I pick up and smell. Bastard. He knows just how to get to me. He hasn't washed the shirt and I can smell him all over it. Sunshine, salt, the odor of his skin. I inhale it and feel a surge of desire sweep through my body. There is a long note in his handwriting and attached a typed, printed note on different paper. It reads:

Darling, precious Pearl,

You are my pearl, you are my treasure. Don't deny me this. Don't deny me the love I have for you.

When you left my heart broke in two. The Spanish describe their soul-mate as 'media naranja' the other half of the same orange. And that is what you are to me, the other half of me, the perfect half that matches me. I have never felt this way before about anybody. Ever.

You think I betrayed your trust. No, I would never do that. Sophie snooped at my iPad and saw my personal notes. They were written in English so I never imagined she would bother to translate them. Call me a jerk, call me a nerd for making notes concerning you. But here they are. (I have copied and pasted this). This is what she saw:

Problems to be solved concerning Pearl:
Needs to reach orgasm during penetrative sex. (My big challenge).
Needs confidence boosted - age complex due to American youth worship culture.
Need to get her pregnant ASAP due to clock factor. (Want to start a family with her.)

I feel embarrassed showing this to you but it is the only way I know how to explain myself. I write lists and notes – I write them for everything – you know that.

When I first set eyes on you in that coffee shop, I was smitten, instantly. I remarked to Sophie how beautiful you were. Sophie commented on how easy American girls are, how they jump into bed with anybody at the drop of a hat. I told her, that in your case, I thought I stood very little chance – that you looked sophisticated and classy. (Given that I had never been with an American woman I had no idea if what she said was true). It was disrespectful of me to discuss this in French with her while you were standing right there before us when we were all waiting in line. I apologize. But that was then.

This is now.

Now I have found my Pearl I do not want to let her go.

I will fight for you. I want you in my life.

I have made a decision. I am giving over HookedUp to Sophie. I will still keep shares but will no longer be involved in the daily decisions of running it. I'd like to start up a new enterprise – a film production company and I will be looking for someone to run it (production skills mandatory). I wondered if you would consider yourself for the job?

Here is the necklace. It belongs to you, and only you.

A squadron of kisses,

Your Alexandre

P.S Rex has arrived and wants to meet you.

P.P.S For the present time my family members will no longer be staying at my apartment when they visit New York.

I smell the T-shirt again and go all weak. His natural scent is like an elixir of love. Before I have a chance to consider the contents of his note, the telephone rings. It's Luke, the doorman.

"Ms. Robinson, did you call the Fire Department?" he asks nervously.

"No, I didn't. Is there a fire in the building?" My voice flies up two octaves.

"Not as far as I know, Ms. Robinson, but a firefighter is on his way up to take a look. Somebody must have called 911."

"Well, it wasn't me. Mrs. Meyer from the eleventh has been known to call emergency services. They came once to retrieve her cat from the fire escape - did you ask her?"

"I'll call her now."

"Or that guy on the second floor, what's his name? Oh yes, Mr. Johnson. He is always burning his food."

"Okay, ma'am, thank you."

I go to the kitchen and look out the back door to see if I can hear a commotion. Nothing. All is silent up and down the back stairs. Why only one firefighter? Usually they come in pairs. I hear some clanging outside my kitchen window and I look over with a start. The firefighter is right there on the fire escape, peering into my apartment. Is he about to smash my window? I race over to open it – I don't want shards of glass everywhere. I lift up the window, raise my eyes and cannot believe the vision before me. I break into a smile.

Hot. Hot. Hot!

But not from any fire.

"Excuse me ma'am," the voice exclaims, "I heard there was fire in this apartment."

I observe the sexy outfit, the dark pants with yellow stripes. But the firefighter isn't wearing a top. His muscles are ripped, shining with perspiration, his cheeks dark with yesterday's stubble. Any girl's fantasy.

I open the window wide and his big black boots jump down into my apartment followed by his drop-dead gorgeous body.

"You nearly had me fooled," I laugh. "But your accent gave you away."

Alexandre is standing there, legs astride, holding a Fire Department helmet. It's not such a crazy idea - the electricity between us really does have me on fire.

"I heard there was a lot of heat coming directly from this apartment," he says with a big grin on his face. He takes a step closer and stares into my eyes. I can feel his breath on mine. Mint, apples, sun, Alexandre. He takes my chin in his hand and lets his lips graze my mouth. I respond with a gasp. I can hear him take in a gulp of air, inhaling the scent of me, of my hair. It feels like a century has passed since we were last together, yet it was only one night away. I open my mouth a little and his tongue finds mine, letting the tips meet. The connection, like lightening, goes straight between my legs.

"A lot of heat is coming from right down here," he tells me. He palms his large hand on my crotch and I feel a rush of blood pump through me. "I'm sorry, ma'am, but I'm going to have to put out this fire any way I can."

He gets down on his knees and places himself underneath me. He unzips my skirt and lets it fall to the floor. He pushes my legs apart and hooks his fingers inside my panties, peeling them down. Very, very slowly. He blows softly in between my legs, then flicks his tongue for just a second on my clitoris. Then he blows again.

"If you knew anything about fire, Mr. Firefighter," I gasp, "you'd know blowing on a flame just gets it more excited."

"True," he murmurs, letting his tongue lap along my slit. "Perhaps it needs some help cooling down."

He presses his tongue flat against my buzzing V-8 and I hold onto his head, my fingers running through his soft dark hair. I push my hips forward, pushing myself so the lips rub up and down against his mouth. I am so stimulated - so hot and horny. I'm moaning. I am still wearing a bra, nothing more, and I look down to see my breasts held like cupcakes in a demi push-up. I pull out one breast and play with my nipple, watching it turn hard. Alexandre begins to stand up and circles his right arm around my thighs, lifting me up over his shoulder in a fireman's lift! He's so strong - the way he does it so effortlessly makes me feel as light as a feather. I'm hanging upside down over his shoulders, gripping on to the waistband of his sexy fireman's pants with one hand, and with the other, cupping his cute, tight butt. He's taking me to the bedroom.

"Are you abducting me, Mr. Fireman?"

"I need to teach you a lesson, Ms. Robinson."

"What kind of lesson?"

"To teach you not to play with fire. To trust me, and not play silly, girlish games. Or you could get burned."

He lays me on the bed. As he does so, the telephone

rings.

"It could be the doorman," I say. God knows what chaos Alexandre has caused.

"Answer it. Tell him I'm showing you some fire safety tips."

I laugh, and do as he suggests. Poor Luke is confused. Half of the building is in a panic. I assure him there is no fire here, that everything is under control but he did the right thing letting the firefighter into the building.

Alexandre stands on the edge of the bed and undoes the zip of his pants. Like a cobra, his erection comes free, proud and magnificent. The black pants, the big heavy boots, the clinking of the bits of metal on the waistband have me mesmerized in a Playgirl Firefighter Fantasy. I walk on my knees and take his erection in my hands, letting my loose hair brush back and forth, swishing across his shaft. I kiss him there, up and down, mini nips and kisses all over, and on the tip.

"It's beautiful," I breathe, and I mean every word.

I take it in my mouth, rimming my lips about his hard shaft and look up at him from under my lashes.

"Turn around," he says and swirls my body using his hands to control my hips, so my butt is facing him. I am on all fours.

"I'm going to have to spank you, Pearl You did wrong abandoning me in France the way you did. You had me desperate, distraught. I have to punish you so you won't do it again."

He pulls my thighs further apart.

He's into hurting women, after all, I think. I brace myself. How bad can a spank be? He pulls me closer to his pelvis. I'm waiting for his hand to come down on my ass.

Instead, I feel a thud right up between my legs right at my entrance. I don't know what he is doing, exactly, but it feels so erotic, the thud, whack, thud. I bend my head all the way down and push my head under my thighs. I look up from under myself and see his cock slapping me. His dark pants against the color of his smooth flesh, has me throbbing with excitement.

"Pearl, I'm going to have to bite you now. Bite that creamy ass of yours." I feel his teeth nipping into my flesh, all over my butt, and then at my wet entrance where he gently tugs my lips with his mouth.

"Keep punishing me," I murmur in a faint whisper. "This feels incredible."

"Greedy... (bite)... Girl.... Greedy.... (slap).... Girl."

I'm groaning.

Suddenly, he lifts me off the bed, holding me in his arms like a baby. *What? Don't stop now!*

"You've been punished enough," he says seriously. "I want to make love to you now. I think we've fucked enough, don't you? I think we need a bit more commitment from one another. No more games."

"But I am committed," I protest.

He sets me back down so I am sitting on the bed, and he gazes deep into my eyes. "Undress me, Pearl. Get me out of this gear. I feel claustrophobic trussed up in this outfit."

I smile wickedly. "Not so fast, Mr. Fireman. I think Mr. Firefighter needs a little dance first. A little lap dance to ease his tension." I find my iPhone and go to my play list and select the most sensual song I can think of - a French song - *Je T'aime....Moi Non Plus.* I start slowly gyrating my hips to the rhythm of the music, the deep voice of Serge Gainsbourg, the breathy, ecstatic sighs of Jane Birkin – a love song if ever there was one.

Alexandre's erection is jutting out from the uniform pants and I dip down on it, parting the lips of my cleft as I do so, sitting on it then rising up, pressing my pelvis against his stomach, rising all the way up and impaling myself on him again to the beat of the music. But he grabs me tight, his hands immobilizing me.

"Pearl, that's enough now. Get me out of these. Game's over. I don't want my future wife doing a lap dance for some dirty firefighter."

I burst out laughing. "But *you're* the firefighter."

He's trying to suppress a grin. "Some dirty firefighter who broke into your apartment uninvited."

I smile, realizing what he just said: *future wife*! I unbutton his waistband and pull the pants down over his hips, stopping to gaze at his navel, kissing it, tugging gently at the hair there with my teeth. I peel the pants down past his muscular thighs and stroke his arms until my hands are resting on his. He holds my hands, squeezing my palms and caressing my fingers. There is a stillness about him, a calm. I see such tenderness in his eyes – an expression I have not noticed before. I bend down and unlace one boot, and then the other. Then I stand up, and push him backwards onto the bed with a hard shove. He topples back and laughs with surprise. I tug each boot off and throw them, one by one, on the floor.

"Now you're free," I say.

"Take off that bra. I want you naked. Naked the way you were at Cap d'Antibes. Let me see those pearly breasts that are trapped inside."

I unhook my bra and throw it across the floor but carry on with my dance. I can't stop, the music is making me feel very sensual. *Future wife....oh yes!*

"Be still," he beckons with an intense look on his face. He steadies my moving hips and pulls me to him. "Lie beside me."

I lie down at his side so we are facing each other. He is motionless - just gazing at me. He strokes my hair and lays his long fingers on my shoulders, fondling me softly, studying my face.

"You're unique, Pearl. I've fallen in love with you."

I say nothing, just watch his expression.

"I want to marry you. To start a family. Is that what you want, too?"

I nod. My heart is beating so loudly he must be able to hear it.

He draws me close to him, pulling me into his arms, hugging me tightly, and plants small, whispery kisses on my neck and shoulders which send shivers all over me. He smoothes my wild hair away from my forehead and traces his finger along my eyebrow, my nose. I curl my arm around him and stroke the small of his back, tracing my nails lightly on his coccyx and on the cheek of his butt. I edge up closer to him. His breath is coming in long, slow sighs. Sighs of contentment, of feeling at peace.

His fingers are stroking my inner thigh with such a light touch I can hardly feel them and then they tap on my clit as lightly as the heartbeat of a bird. Tap, tap, tap.

"A little spanking," he says with an ironic smile. "For being so wayward - for escaping from me."

I edge up the bed higher so his erection is resting at my entrance and I sense the head there, soft yet hard. I clench my inner muscles into mini contractions, needing him, wanting him – I know he can hear my desire through the pattern of my breath.

He eases himself into me, stretching me open and I cry out in surprise. He feels huge.

"So wet," he whispers, pulling himself back out so he is only an inch inside me. He stills, doesn't move again.

I use his biceps as leverage to move myself in little circles so he is rimming me. I have this carnal need within me but the look on his face is about love, tranquility. I keep moving, his tip is soft on my clit, then my entrance, all the nerve endings - the nexus of pleasure connecting my entire body - are alive with hot desire. He kisses me softly, parting my mouth with his tongue. He flexes his hips towards me which makes him enter another inch. I hold the pulse between my legs. He is still gazing at me.

He narrows his eyes slightly, and says, "Will. You. Marry. Me. Pearl?" When he says each word he gives tiny punctuation thrusts which are like mountains moving inside me. I grab his butt and pull him deep into me so he is close. He stills and I can feel his throbbing. Something about his heartfelt words bring on a rush of pleasure, fireworks inside me, the waves of bliss roll through me, the unexpected orgasm upon me now in flashes of white stars. Intense. Sublime.

I cry out, "Yes, oh yes."

He juts his hips forward and I feel his release, filling me. He holds me tighter, closer. "Yes, what, Pearl? What are you saying yes to?"

"Yes, Alexandre. I will marry you."

"That's what I wanted to hear," and he kisses me again.

Shadows
of
Pearl

(Book 2)

1

I'm lying between the glorious Egyptian cotton sheets in Alexandre's bed, relaxing against the plumped-up, down feather pillows. I feel satiated. Complete, both physically and spiritually. Beyond satisfied. More glorious love-making has left me feeling like the luckiest, most appreciated woman in the world.

Of all people, I know what it's like to be stuck in a sexual desert – without another human being to fulfill my needs. For almost twenty years I had convinced myself that work could be a substitute. I'd given up. I'd learned to be self-sufficient in every way – yes, in *every* way - and I never, in a million years, believed that at forty years old I would meet anyone special, let alone a man fifteen years my junior. And not only a younger man, but ridiculously successful, kind, devastatingly handsome, and last but not least, a veritable god in bed.

And to top it all off; completely in love with me…

Alexandre Chevalier.

I still feel as if I have walked into a modern day fairy tale.

It's tough when you're riddled with insecurities the way I am. Hard to believe that a man so gorgeous can covet you and feel the same intensity of passion that you feel for him. Yet, there he was, Alexandre Chevalier, co-founder of the Internet sensation HookedUp – a company which has taken the world by storm and, at the tender age of twenty-five, has made him into one of the wealthiest men in the world. There Alexandre was - wanting to date me.

And if that wasn't enough, he has chosen me, Pearl Robinson, a forty year-old with my just-above-average, girl-next-door looks, to be his *wife*.

Yes, I do believe I'm dreaming.

I look now at my left hand which I'm turning this way and that and admire my diamond engagement ring - proof that all this is real. It's glinting, catching rays of morning sunlight which are pouring in through the long bedroom window. The ice-blue silk drapes are half open. Alexandre hates to sleep with them closed - as if darkness could swallow him up at dawn.

I've learned a lot about Alexandre in the two months since we've been engaged. There's a shadow that lives within - a mood which can encompass him at times, and it frightens me. I can never be sure when it will possess him but it is there, deep inside his soul. He's a damaged man - that much I know. Yet he seems to be an expert at hiding the phantoms which lurk within.

So far, I have only seen glimpses.

I too, try to hide any gremlins from my past. Some things are better left unsaid. We are still getting to know each other.

I can hear him now, next door in the en-suite bathroom. The faucet has just been turned off. I picture him in my mind's eye; water trickling from his lightly tanned chest, his biceps flexed deliciously as he dries himself, his strong, muscular thighs, the ripples of his stomach and his wet, almost-black hair - wayward and mussed-up - which frames the even features of his handsome face.

I think of our lovemaking just ten minutes ago and a shiver of lust shimmies through my body. I cannot get enough of him. He possesses my psyche. I have never needed anybody as I need him. But I try to keep myself cool, calm and collected, even though I'm on fire inside. He mustn't know the apprehension that envelops me - fear that I could be flung back again into the desert, abandoned with no water - on my own once more. And when I say 'on my own' I don't mean literally so. No, you can be with a man and feel like an island – as I was with my ex-husband, Saul. I blamed myself for my frigidity, my inability to reach orgasm through sex which, if I remember correctly, happened in my early twenties after I'd split up with my first boyfriend, Brad.

I thought I was a lost cause until I met Alexandre. He intrinsically understands me and my body. Maybe that's why I'm hooked on him. Sexually. Mentally. But I try to keep that to myself. There's nothing like a needy woman to scare a man away. Especially one as hot as he is. I have to hold onto my independence, my self-possession.

Or I could lose him for good.

My fiancé saunters into the bedroom and fixes his eyes on me, running them along my naked body with approval. I cannot believe he is actually mine. *My fiancé.* How I relish those words.

I'm now willing him with my gaze to come back to bed,

just for ten minutes, but I know that his drive and ambition rarely lets him lose restraint. He has a plane to catch – a business trip is waiting; clients hanging in limbo with baited breath for a decision to be made, a deal to be signed. I've learned that Alexandre is a ruthless negotiator, a tough cookie when it comes to business – nobody gets to be as successful as he is by accident.

I drink him in. A white towel is hanging about his washboard abs. Beads of water are gathered about his buffed-up chest. His green eyes are gazing at me.

"Come with me, Pearl," he says, his French accent full and rich.

"I told you, I really can't."

"I'd love to show you my favorite haunts in London, take you to the theatre, a walk along the South Bank by the River Thames."

He moves over to the bed and sits beside me, fondling my chin with his long fingers. He tilts my head back a touch and presses his lips to mine. His tongue explores my mouth, the tip of it gently probing, running along my lips. He holds my head in his hands and teases my tongue with his. I feel the electricity of it - tingles shoot between my thighs. I groan. My sound makes his kiss more intense, hungrier. The towel moves - his huge cock is flexing against it. I rest my hand there and feel how stiff it is. Always ready for me, even with just a kiss or at the sight of my naked body. Nobody has ever desired me the way he does.

"Why are you tormenting me like this?" he whispers. "You know I don't like us being apart."

"I can't just leave Anthony alone – he's come all the way from San Francisco to visit. Besides, I told you, I have that important meeting this morning."

"It's just work, it can be postponed."

"No, it can't. Samuel Myers has flown in from LA. You can't start up a company for me, Alexandre, and then expect it to run itself. HookedUp Enterprises needs me more than ever right now – it's my baby."

"So têtue," he teases, his French accent rumblingly deep.

"What does that mean?"

"Stubborn."

I laugh. "I know you, Alexandre Chevalier. You told me once yourself, that the last thing you wanted was a woman to be hanging onto your 'every word, your every movement' – that's what you said. You'd get bored of me if I didn't have my own projects, my own life."

"Perhaps, but sometimes I think you push it, Pearl. Like the wedding, for instance. Why are you making us wait until December? It's absurd – we could get married as soon as I get back from London." He grazes his tongue along my lips and kisses me again.

"I told you - I've always dreamed of a winter wedding," I whisper.

"The ice princess."

I trace my fingers along his cheekbone and smile. Let him think I'm the ice princess. Let him think I'm cool. He can't know that my insides are made of marshmallow – that my need for him is more than life itself.

"You'll be late," I warn, running my fingers through his thick, soft hair.

"What I like though, is when I fuck you I make you melt," he murmurs, his hands trailing down my back along my spine. "I love your dimples, these adorable dimples in your back, just here...and here." He makes circular motions around my little dips and then runs the tips of his fingers further south, cupping my buttocks in his large hands.

I feel the tips of his fingers as they lightly, so very lightly touch my cleft, lifting me off the mattress, pulling me towards him. "So wet," he says. "Even when all I do is kiss you. Funny how you and I get each other so worked up - you've made me rock hard."

"Yes...isn't it?" We both laugh.

"Shit, damn it! You're so tempting, Pearl. Damn my meeting." He nips my lower lip softly between his minty teeth.

The tease - I'm used to this. He keeps me in check – always leaving me begging for more, my heart racing. I throb with desire, aching for his return – even before he has departed. Or even when he's right beside me, I'm on red alert, ready for sex at a moment's notice. Alexandre says he likes it this way. My resolve must stay intact, though. I need to stay strong. I cannot lose myself in him one hundred percent.

Or he'd swallow me whole.

I study him. It's not just sex that has me in his hold. It's the way he is inside; his kindness, generosity, his sense of humor, the love he has for me - even his damn French pride which makes him a touch possessive and jealous. Not too much - no, but just enough to make me feel desired and treasured. All this makes up a complex personality - a character I'm still trying to work out.

He walks over to his closet and opens the door. That same closet where, just three months ago, I hid myself behind rows of hand-tailored suits and racks of silk ties – where I childishly played Hide and Seek. A tremor fills my body now, remembering that sexually-charged moment. Alexandre caught me and then tied my legs to the bedposts with two ice-blue silk ties, splaying my thighs apart. I thought he was going to play bondage and he did. His style. Sweet - but terrifying as I couldn't imagine what would happen next. I had nothing to fear; he 'beat' me with a Kingfisher feather and tied my wrists together behind my head with the price-less Art Deco pearl choker he bought me in Paris. The excitement tipped me over the edge – the trepidation, the lust, the sensitivity all mixed together in a delicious cocktail of sex. A cocktail which has turned me into an alcoholic of love. A drink which I need every day just to function at my best.

I am addicted to him.

I watch him now. Six feet, three inches of pure, virile male. What is it that makes me want him to take charge in the bedroom? To overpower me? I love being beneath him, strong and dominant as he is – on top of me, pushing me to my limits, making me scream his name when I come. He has control over me sexually and he knows it – I can't let him also dominate my life. He's testing me. I can sense it. Testing me to see how strong I can be. He made it clear that he wants an equal. I have to match him; I cannot let myself sink into oblivion. He once told me he was attracted to me for my maturity and that he was into 'women not girls' – I need to act my age – keep my composure. It's a battle I fight every day. I still feel like a vulnerable child inside and sometimes find myself acting like a teenager with her first love. Passion is a powerful thing – hard to control.

"What's it to be today - T-shirt and jeans, or a suit?" I ask him.

He pulls on a pair of boxer briefs over his tight, perfectly formed butt. My eyes then focus on that fine smooth hairline that goes from his abs down to his groin. He still has a semi-erection bulking out his underwear. He looks at me. "I don't know, what do you think?"

"Both are sexy. The second you put a suit on I want you to fuck me, though - you fully-clothed with just your cock free. You could take me up against the wall. I love it when I'm naked and you're dressed in one of your chic, tailored suits. I love it when you slam me from behind." I bite my lip. "Hard as a rock. Just thinking about it makes me so—"

"Stop tormenting me, baby, or I'll have to put you over my knee and spank you." He winks at me.

"That'll be the day."

"You know I could never do that, Pearl, not even in jest."

I observe him as he pulls out a pair of jeans and a black T-shirt from the rack in the closet. "Jeans it is, then," he says assertively, "or I'll never get to London on time."

"Bastard," I say with a grin.

"It's not as if I haven't asked you to come with me. It's not too late to change your mind."

"No, I'm staying."

"Sure? Last call—"

"I'm sure," I say, already regretful.

I slip out of the bed and glide towards him. "I'll miss you." I place my arms about his warm, strong torso and hold myself close to him. I breathe in his faint smell of lavender, hand-picked from his fields in Provence - crushed into heavenly oil - and the famous wish-I-could-bottle Alexandre smell - his natural odor that has me completely intoxicated.

As if on cue, Rex bounds his way into the bedroom, excited from his morning walk. He often barges in on our intimate moments. His black Labrador-mix tail spins about like a windmill; his tight muscles rival his master's.

"Oh Rex, how I'll miss you my boy," Alexandre says, bending down to hug his dog. "Look after him for me, Pearl. Don't let Anthony spoil him with too many treats. I'm late, I have to rush. See you in a couple of days." He embraces us in a family trio and then looks into my eyes and says, "I love you, Pearl. You're my everything - my light, my future. Take care now." He plants another kiss on my lips and makes his way down the corridor to the elevator where his ready-packed case is waiting. I don't follow as I'm still naked. Anthony is staying in one of the guest rooms – God forbid my brother should see me with no clothes on.

Anthony is in his element. He arrived late last night and couldn't believe that Alexandre's chauffeur was there to meet him at the airport. He tells me that he's moving in (joke). Or is it? Anthony could get used to this lifestyle. Not to mention his boy-crush on Alexandre.

I get dressed and find breakfast waiting in the kitchen. Coffee, cereals, home-made yoghurt and jellies, fresh fruit and a spread of croissants and pastries sit temptingly on the table. I begin to set things on a tray to send up to the roof terrace. Sun is streaming through the windows and the sky is crystal blue. The perfect Fall weather. Cool, sunny and crisp but warm enough to still eat outside. Patricia, one of the staff, finds me rummaging about the kitchen and a look of dismay shadows her face. She's wearing a neat, black and white uniform – her choice – she says she feels more professional that way.

"Ms. Pearl, please, what are you doing? You'll make me lose my job if you insist on serving yourself."

"I doubt that, Patricia. I thought Anthony and I could sit on the roof terrace, have breakfast up there, today, but I don't want to be a nuisance."

"That's what the Dumbwaiter's for," she says with a wink.

"Best invention ever," I agree.

She loads everything into the mini-elevator which sends food or forgotten cell phones up and down between floors. Anthony has not yet set eyes on this marvel. I can hear him now in the living room screaming and yelping.

"Thanks, Patricia. I'm going to take my excitable brother upstairs."

I find Anthony sitting on the piano stool, breathless, his mouth open so far that his jaw is practically horizontal to the floor. He catches my eye as I'm standing in the doorway.

"Oh my GOD!"

"I know," I reply simply.

"Pearleee—"

"Do you want me to call 911?"

"Oh my freakin' God!"

"Yes, I think God has gotten the point."

"What is this place? A *museum*? I mean, this room is the size of mine and Bruce's entire apartment in San Francisco!"

"It is pretty awesome."

"Awesome does not even begin to describe this *palace*."

I watch his eyes scan the room; the walnut wood paneled walls, the delicate cabinetry and integrated bookshelves, the parquet floor, the picture windows with views of Central Park on one side and of The Plaza on the other - and the massive marble fireplaces. Rex is wagging his tail as if in agreement. He came from humble beginnings - from a dog pound in Paris – where the poor thing was waiting on Death Row. I get the feeling that he, too, appreciates his luxurious surroundings. Anthony is now caressing the piano keys; whimpering sounds are emanating from somewhere deep within his body as if he were sick with fever.

"Can you imagine having a grand piano like this?" he gushes.

"I don't have to imagine it, Anthony – it's a reality."

"Have you pinched yourself? Are you sure you're not just dreaming?"

"Sometimes I do wonder."

"A Steinway? Seriously? I really do have heart palpitations - you need to call an ambulance."

"Play something, Ant."

"Are you talkin' to me? Are you talking to *me*?" he jokes, imitating Robert de Niro in *Taxi Driver*. "Are you talking to *me*? Well, I'm the only one here!"

I burst out laughing. Anthony couldn't look more unlike Travis Bickle if he tried. My brother is heavy, blonde – okay, not heavy - he is actively overweight. And when I say actively, I mean he cannot stop eating, even though every day he swears he has started a new diet. I've missed him – he does make me laugh. Except when I'm the object of his humor, which is often.

He begins to play and within seconds my eyes well with tears from the beauty of the sound. The way he strokes the keys with such a whispery touch makes me remember what a novice I am compared to him in the musical department. He has so much talent I find myself holding my breath.

"Mom used to sing this to us to get us to fall asleep. Do you remember?" He's playing *Lullaby* by Brahms.

"I miss her so much," I tell him quietly.

But he doesn't reply. His answer is all in his playing. His fingers caress the keys and his eyes, half closed, speak of nostalgia for a life cut short; a woman we both loved beyond measure who was taken from us too soon – her bones ravaged by that evil disease which begins with C and ends in heartbreak. Before I know it, I'm weeping, as if all my pain has finally unleashed itself. Pearl, the Independent One can finally let loose her pent-up sorrow.

"Why her?" I mumble. "Why her..."

Anthony stops his playing short. "I know. I know."

I take his hand and try to change the mood, "Breakfast, come on! You think this room is cool? You ain't seen nuthin' yet," I joke, "wait till you see the roof terrace."

I lead him upstairs, Rex excitedly at our heels, and listen to Anthony's oohs and ahs as he flips out about the décor, the priceless antique furniture and works of art. His eyes settle on a giant, red, heart painting with a multi-colored background. "That's a Jim Dine," he observes, "isn't it? A. Goddam. Jim. Freakin. Goddam. Dine!"

"Alexandre gave that to me a few weeks ago. An engagement present."

"Oh, so like, the rock of a diamond solitaire you're wearing on your finger wasn't enough already?"

I laugh. "Obscene, isn't it?"

"Well, it is *big*, to say the least."

"It belonged to a Russian princess."

He raises an eyebrow. "Of course it did."

"The diamond was part of a pendant and Alexandre had it made into a ring."

Anthony's reaction to the roof terrace with its real lawn, trees and sumptuous views across Central Park and the Manhattan skyline is even more extreme than mine was the first time I laid eyes on it all, back in June. "So the view wasn't enough... there has to be a freakin' *park* on top of this roof *as well?*"

"All for Rex," I say.

"I'm going to dress up as a dog."

I pull my cardigan tighter about my waist. "It's a little cool, let's go into the orangery and have breakfast."

"Don't we need to take Rex for a walk in the park first? Do his poops and stuff?"

"Don't worry, he's been out already."

"You took him out this morning so early?"

"No, Rex has a kind of nanny. She comes every morning at 7am sharp. Then again at eleven and every four hours if somebody's home. If I'm at work then his nanny – her name's Sally - she hangs out with him. Rex is never alone."

"You're kidding me."

I giggle. "No, really. Rex lives up to his name. He's a king."

"I'll say."

"Come here, Rex, let me see that new collar you're wearing." He wiggles up to me sporting a smart, electric blue collar. He's wagging proudly. "Sally must have bought him that; she's always getting him gifts."

"So who else is running the show, besides Rex's nanny?"

"The housekeeper, Patricia, two or three cleaning ladies, a chef who comes and goes if Alexandre isn't in the mood to cook and—"

Anthony interrupts me with a waving hand. "Stop! I've heard enough, I can feel myself turning green."

I pour some coffee for us both and he's staring at me as if dissecting my very being. Uh, oh, what now...

"Pearl, what is wrong with you?"

"Excuse me?"

"What the hell are you playing at with this winter wedding bullshit. Winter - hello - is two months away. What are you waiting for?"

"Look, Alexandre and I have only known each other for just over four months. I want to be absolutely sure."

"Sure of what? That you're even luckier than Kate Middleton?"

"I don't want to make a mistake. I want for us to really know each other, warts and all."

"You want him to know about your *warts?* Are you crazy? Snap him up now before he realizes what's happened. You don't want him to see your goddam warts or he could change his mind!"

"Thanks for the vote of confidence, Ant. Actually, that expression is kind of gross. Let's just say I want us to be great friends as well as lovers before we tie the knot. I want to be open about everything and anything concerning my past and for him to do the same with me."

"Are you *insane?* Keep your goddam mouth *shut* about anything at all that makes you seem less than perfect. Keep any skeletons you may have locked firmly in the closet. You cannot jeopardize this golden opportunity."

"I want us to be honest with each other."

Anthony doesn't hear me – he rattles on, "Okay, I get the whole fairytale wedding thing in Lapland. I do. The whole reindeer pulling the sled, the white, silk-velvet ribbons on their antlers, the powdery snow – I get it, but please, don't be a fool – you need to get on with this marriage already and stop dithering about."

"You want me to settle for a quick wedding just in case my fiancé changes his mind? If he changes his mind, then I would have done the right thing. If he's that mercurial I shouldn't have been thinking about being with him in the first place."

Anthony rolls his eyes. "What's the worst that can happen? The marriage fails and you end up with a nice settlement, thank you very much."

"No, Anthony, that is *not* the plan. I would never marry for money, you know that. I refused to take a dime from Saul. In fact, I ended up lending him a ton of money which he never paid back and I never even asked him for it. I've suggested to Alexandre that we do a pre-nup. That way, it's clear from the outset that I don't want a cent if it turns out we aren't made for each other."

Anthony buries his head in his hands. His exasperation is palpable. "Please, Pearl, stop. I just can't *bear* hearing you throw your life away."

"I'm being practical. Realistic. Strong."

"You're being a dumbass – burning all your bridges. What does Alexandre say about this pre-nup nonsense?"

"He says no, and that he doesn't even want to discuss it."

"Phew, that's lucky."

"Try one of these Danish pastries – they melt in your mouth," I say, offering him a platter of tempting goodies, knowing that's the only thing that will shut Anthony up - at least for a while.

But all he does is stuff the pastry in his gob and talk with his mouth full. "And what's with all this business you've started together, this HookedUp thingamyjig?"

"HookedUp Enterprises."

"Yeah. Why can't you be content with just being a trophy wife, so to speak? You'd never have to work again in your life."

"That is *so* not my style and you know it. Besides, Alexandre secretly likes me being into my career. He bought up Haslit Films. It's all under the umbrella of his new company, HookedUp Enterprises, run by me. And he and I are the directors of it, except he's a silent partner. He doesn't want any say in how the company's run day to day – it's all up to me. So he *says*, but I'll need his help. I want him there – I'm not that proficient with the business side of things. We've started doing feature films, keeping on Haslit for the documentary side."

"So where does that leave your boss, Natalie?"

"She's on board, too. She came with the package."

"So wait, that means you are now technically Natalie's boss and the tables have turned and you're like, some big shot who's going to hang out with Tom Cruise and Matt Bomer and all those sexy TV and movie sirens?"

I laugh and breathe in the heady scent of winter jasmine entwined about the trellises of the orangery. "Who knows where it could lead – it's exciting though."

Anthony taps his finger on his nose. "Just exactly how rich is your husband to-be? That is, if you move your skinny ass and hurry up and marry him and don't blow it all, somehow."

"Alexandre is a very powerful man. Much more powerful than I had first imagined."

"Not to mention drop-dead gorgeous. If he wasn't going to be my future brother-in-law, I swear I'd–"

"Anthony, please – you'll shock Rex."

"Sorry - go on, you were saying…"

"I actually had no idea how wealthy he was – his T-shirt and jeans look kinda had me fooled."

"Doesn't he wear a suit to meet clients?"

"Very rarely. Only if the clients are way older."

Anthony narrows his blue eyes. "Isn't everyone way older? I mean, he's only twenty-five, right?"

"He's very laid back about the way he presents himself.

On the outside, that is. But I've overheard him speak business on the phone. I wouldn't want to cross him, that's for sure. Although he never raises his voice and he's always polite and friendly, but there's a kind of chilling power he holds over people. I can't explain it."

Anthony is still devouring his Danish. "A computer coder, huh?"

I take a sip of coffee. "That was what he led me to believe when I first met him. He's very modest - it's his French upbringing. He never discusses money or boasts about his wealth. He likes to make out he's just a regular guy."

"And what about Psycho-sister – does she get a stake in this new company of yours?"

"Sophie? No, this has nothing to do with her." I look at my watch. "Oh my God, Anthony, speaking of my new company – I need to run or I'll be late for my meeting. Will you be okay on your own?"

"Hell yeah, are you kidding? I get to play king of the castle."

"Sorry, that's Rex's role, isn't it sweetheart?" I say cupping Rex's wide black head in my hands and giving him a kiss on the snout.

"Ha, ha, Rex means king in Latin – very cute."

"Be good, big brother and don't get into mischief. If you need anything Patricia can help. See you later."

"Later, baby sis."

2

This is my first official meeting with a new client at HookedUp Enterprises. We have spoken several times on the phone already and even signed a preliminary deal but this is the first time we are to meet face to face.

I'm obviously nervous but I feel poised in my sharp, navy blue suit and high heels. I'm meeting a big Hollywood mogul named Samuel Myers – the old-school type who smokes a cigar and calls women 'sweetheart'. But he's friendly and easy going. A little too much for my liking.

As I approach him he looks me up and down but then his eyes wander to my engagement ring and he clears his throat as if to say, 'okay, never mind'. I smile at him. I'm used to these types - one of my first jobs was a stint in LA as a casting director's assistant. This man doesn't faze me at all.

He has been waiting for me in our lobby, a cool, modern

269

space with vast opaque glass doors that smoothly open as you approach them. We shake hands and introduce ourselves and I lead him into my office. The windows here look down onto Fifty Seventh Street. There's a large glass desk and sleek sofas and chairs all in off-white or cool-gray leather. It is the antithesis of Alexandre's apartment. Here we are talking state-of-the-art, Italian - very contemporary.

Just as Samuel Myers has eased himself into one of the brand new designer couches and I have sat myself down and crossed my legs neatly on my swivel chair, my cell buzzes. I look down and see a message has come in from Alexandre. I know I shouldn't but I can't resist. I quickly read it.

Just remembering you naked on the bed this morning has made me hard. Can't stop thinking about your tits and ass and making you come. Can't wait to get home and fuck you senseless. X

Bastard – he knew exactly what time this meeting was. He has ways of keeping me in check. Or is it another test? To see if I'll break? See if I'll be able to remain composed. A second ago I was cool and poised. Now I feel a rush of adrenaline and heat surge through my body. I squeeze my legs together. Uh oh, no, I mustn't do that or you-know-*what* could happen. My heart's racing from Alexandre's schoolboy message, my breath short. Who would think that a forty year-old could be knocked out like this every time the one she loves comes on to her? But 40 is just a number. When you're in your twenties it seems like light years away. You imagine a forty year-old to have all the answers, never to lose her self-possession – basically, to be a grown-up. But it's not like that when you're in love. Especially when it catches you off guard the way it did for me. When you feel the way I do about someone all your barriers come crashing down. I was a woman when I met Alexandre and he changed me into a teenager.

Get a grip, Pearl.

I switch off my cell so I can't be distracted again and continue with my conversation with this important producer. I take a deep breath and say, "I read the script changes." Samuel Myers is now lounging comfortably – his weighty body spread out like a sea lion. "I think they're great," I add.

"I'm so pleased," he replies with a grin.

I sit erect and try to turn my imagination into a blank canvas – erase the image of Alexandre and his erection. "I know we signed on this project already but have you considered the leads going to women?" I ask calmly.

The producer's eyebrows shoot up. "W*omen?*"

"Yes, women."

"But, sweetheart, this is a *buddy* movie."

"Flipping gender roles works in a buddy movie. Think about *Thelma and Louise*. It beyond worked - it's a classic. You get my point."

He temples his fat, sausage-like fingers. "I hadn't even considered that."

"Would you like to think about it? Sleep on it?"

He gets up and pads his heavy frame over to the high window and looks down onto the street below. The usual background of New York City can be heard – muted by the thick triple-glazed windows, but still evident - the sirens never sleep, not in Manhattan. People below are rushing this way and that like ants on a mission. Samuel Myers snorts. "What are you saying? That if I don't consider the leads going to actresses you'll be unhappy?"

271

"Let's just say that HookedUp Enterprises will be less enthusiastic about doing future projects with you unless we feel we can make our mark. We want to put our stamp on the movie industry – shake things up a bit, not just churn out the usual run-of-the-mill, same-old-same-old blockbuster. We'd like to see more females in lead roles and less ageism when it comes to actresses. There is no reason why beautiful leading women always have to be in their twenties. That message is getting worn and tired, and frankly, you're losing a big chunk of the audience that way."

"Oh."

I edge towards this powerful man and say, "There are some amazing, very sexy actresses in their early forties: Charlize Theron, Jennifer Aniston, Cameron Diaz, Cate Blanchett, Gwyneth Paltrow, Nicole Kidman, Catherine Zeta-Jones, Lucy Liu—"

"Lucy Liu is Asian."

"So? She'd be right for the part of Sunny. She's beautiful as well as feisty."

"I don't know, I can't afford two names, Pearl."

I keep talking. "Those are just the big stars. There's a lot of other talent out there, too."

I can hear his heavy, considered breathing.

"There's nothing in that script that dictates to us that a man should play those roles," I go on, "a woman can kick ass just as easily, excuse the expression. I see *women* playing those parts."

"Okay, Pearl, let me think this through. I need to make some calls. This has taken me by surprise. Quite a ball-buster, aren't you?"

"No, Mr. Myers, I'm a pussycat."

He looks at my ring and then says, "Does your fiancé

know what he's letting himself in for?"

"No, he doesn't. I thought I'd surprise him."

He chuckles. "Call me Sam, by the way."

I shake hands with him to denote the end of the meeting. I mean, there really isn't much more to discuss –either he goes for my pitch or he doesn't. "Okay, Sam, let's take a rain check. Call me as soon as you've thought this over."

"So you're not flexible on this woman thing?" he asks.

"I'm always flexible but the 'woman thing,' as you describe it, is an important factor, like it or not. We females do make up almost half of the world's population and we're pretty bored of playing second fiddle all the time."

"A feminist."

"Not a feminist, just a woman. But you can't be a woman in today's world without busting the odd ball here or there." I give him a wry smile and he laughs. "We'll speak later," I say assertively. "Call me."

I walk him to the elevator and when he's out of sight I punch my fists in the air. "Yes!" I never imagined he'd even *consider* letting the roles go to women. I call Alexandre to tell him the good news. No answer. He must be in the air. As I pass back by the lobby, Jeanine, our receptionist, an ice-cool brunette who matches the décor perfectly she's so glamorous, tells me in a husky voice. "Pearl, there's a video clip waiting for you."

Alexandre and I have instructed everyone who works here to call us by our first names. No pretentions here. We want to make everyone at HookedUp Enterprises feel like extended family.

"Samuel Myers brought in a video? He forgot to mention that."

"No, your fiancé," she says emphasizing the F of fiancé.

273

"Alexandre? When?"

He called me ten minutes ago. You weren't picking up, he said. Check your email. There should be a video in one of your messages."

"Thank you, Jeanine."

"You're welcome."

I go back into my office and look through my emails. There is an attachment. I click on it. I simultaneously laugh and cover my mouth with my hand in shock. I should be used to this by now but Alexandre's shenanigans still take me by surprise. He's lying on a bed in the private jet. Then the focus zooms in on his huge penis taking up the whole screen. He must have shot this with his iPhone. There it is - smooth as silk in its full glory, hard and thick as granite, the head proud. His hand grips it as he lies on the bed propped up against cushions – the self-held camera pans up - he's languidly seductive, his eyes half closed, his tongue running lustfully along his dark red lips. I hear his deep voice. "Chérie, I'm on the plane before take-off in this private cabin thinking of you, kicking myself that I didn't force you to come with me today. I miss you already."

I'm hot and feel a throb between my legs. The sight of Alexandre's huge penis has my heart beating fast, my whole body tingling. I press my fingers on my clit and give it a hard push. Oh yeah. I look at the screen and am transfixed as he fondles himself and starts moving his gripped hand tightly around his erection. He goes on, "I'm thinking of your wet pearlette, Pearl, and your beautiful face when you come for me and your erect nipples and that pretty waist and soft skin and I'm thinking how when I get home I'm going to tease you with my cock. I'm going to bend you over the arm of the sofa and flutter my tongue around your clit. Just the tip of my tongue. Really gently. I know you baby, you're gonna get all wet and hot and be begging me for it. And I'll make you wait. I'll make you moan with anticipation."

I swallow. I can feel my pulse speed up hearing his words, imagining myself in the position he describes. I press 'pause' and go over to my office door and lock it. Jeanine always knocks, but just to be sure. I go back to my laptop and press 'play' again.

"See how hard I am?" he purrs. "I'm thinking of you sucking me – your pretty lips wrapped around my cock, running your tongue up and down and making it even stiffer."

I unzip my skirt and let it pool around my ankles on the floor. I take off my suit jacket and fling it on the back of my swivel chair.

Alexandre continues. "Have you got your fingers in your pussy, baby? Is it all wet for me? I want you to sit back in your chair with your legs wide open…"

Wait a minute, I think, how does he know I'm next to my chair? I sit down, my heart pounding, and yes, I am wet. Very wet.

"Let's get back to the other position I had in mind for you, eh?" he says, the focus now on his face which is grimacing from pleasuring himself. "You bent over the sofa arm, your peachy ass in the air. I'm gonna have to spank that ass, baby and then I'm going to take you from behind."

He has never spanked me, ever, but he talks about it in his fantasies – does he do that to please me, or does he secretly want to punish me? I still don't know.

"I'll slip my cock in just an inch, no more. Thrust it in all the way, and then out, and then tease you again with just a centimeter of my cock. You won't know when I'm going to slam you. Maybe I'll pump you good and hard, maybe I won't. Maybe you'll be screaming for me to fuck you."

My fingers are deep inside myself now. I'm hooking them up against my front wall against my G-spot - a place I didn't even know existed until Alexandre found it with his magic thumb. My left hand is on top, both adding pressure now to my clit and my special zone. I make circular movements and press harder now. I can feel the build-up. My eyes are glued to the screen. The camera is back on his rock-hard cock and he's moaning now, almost growling – he's about to come – I can sense it.

"All I can think about is fucking you. I. Love. Fucking. You. Pearl. I love fucking you hard, fucking, you, really slow."

I suddenly hear a knock as I'm about to reach orgasm. The panic of it makes me climax in a thunderous spasm. But then I realize the knock's coming from Alexandre's home-made porn movie as I hear him shout out, "hang on, just coming."

"We're about to take off, sir, I need you to buckle-up," a muffled voice says through the cabin door.

He groans. I watch his face, now shown up by the camera in twisted ecstasy, and I laugh at the madness and irony of it all – 'just coming' he said - and I'm still coming, too, with delicious, powerful contractions – never were words more aptly spoken.

Then the video goes dead.

Why does Alexandre continually make me feel like a naughty schoolgirl?

I try to compose myself, which is difficult as now all I have on the brain is my sexy fiancé. I'm not the jealous type but I wonder at my foolishness of letting him roam free in

London without me there by his side. I trust him, I do, but at the end of the day he's still a guy. Women throw themselves at him. Women, girls, mothers, dogs; this is a man who enjoys popularity. He's easygoing and nearly always has a gentle smile on his lips which makes him very attractive to everyone. But there's also something commandeering about him that make people sit up and pay attention.

Funny, he says the same about me – that people listen. I do a good job of pretending – shoulders back, head up (and all that) but inside I feel the same as when I was twelve years old. You think getting older would make you qualify in the extra confidence stakes, but it doesn't. Perhaps all that happens is that you get better at acting. If I have him fooled, that's fine by me. If I have Samuel Myers fooled – all the better.

I go to the bathroom to freshen up. One thing Alexandre has had installed in every bathroom in his apartment and here is the old-fashioned bidet. At first, I thought it was archaic but now I'm a convert and wince every time I go to a bathroom and there isn't one. How civilized they are – perfect for a quick clean-up at any moment, especially if you've indulged in a little afternoon sex and don't have time for a shower. I have found they are perfect to use as a foot-bath, too.

I look in the mirror and see a happy woman staring back at me. Her skin is glowing, her blue-gray eyes bright. Lots of passionate sex – the perfect cure for anyone.

I turn my cell back on and see I have three messages. Alexandre? No, Anthony. My mind flashes through a series of disasters that could have befallen him. Has he set the kitchen on fire? Did he try and squeeze his huge body into the Dumbwaiter? Has he smashed something, broken a chair? Fed Rex the box of hand-made chocolate truffles that were on top of the piano? Has he spilled a hot drink onto the piano keys? Anthony has two left feet and is always crashing into something, and putting his foot in it either verbally or literally. I call him without even listening to the messages – God knows what's happened, I dread to think.

He picks up. "Pearl, thank God."

I can hear outside sounds – sirens, cars, horns, cries. "Anthony, are you on the street?"

"I'm getting into a cab."

"Oh, where are you going? Shopping? Wait for me, I'm on my way home."

"Pearl, I'm catching a flight back to San Francisco. Bruce is ill, it's an emergency."

I roll my eyes. Bruce did this last time. He is incapable of being without his boyfriend for five minutes. Co-dependency does not even begin to describe their ten year relationship. "Anthony, you know what a drama queen Bruce is."

"No, this is an emergency. Seriously. An. Emergency! He's had an aortic aneurism. Something to do with the heart. He's in intensive care. Oh my God, I'm like, freaking out, I think he's going to die," he wails.

A wave of guilt washes over me for my dismissive atti-tude. "He's not going to die. Calm down – if he's at the hospital they'll get him through this. Have faith, Ant. Stay strong. Why are you taking a cab to the airport? Suresh could have driven you there."

"He was running errands, I couldn't wait."

I hear the cab door slam and the vehicle screech off. "What can I do to help? Do you want me to come with you? I have money – let me sort out the medical bill."

Anthony seems as if he is going to burst into tears. "No

and no. There isn't any point you coming and hanging around at the hospital – there's nothing you can do. And Bruce's job has great benefits – he has full insurance. Thanks, anyway, Pearly – I appreciate the offer."

"Well let me know if there's anything you need."

"I will. Shame, I was having such a ball at Alexandre's palace. I mean yours and Alexandre's palace – if only Bruce wasn't afraid of flying and he'd have come too -maybe this would never have happened."

"Life happens when you're busy making plans," I say.

"John Lennon said that."

"Yes, he did. And that was before he got shot. There's nothing you could have done, Anthony. Life throws stuff at you sometimes – things that are beyond your control."

"Shit happens, huh?"

"Exactly," I whisper, thinking of our mom.

"Listen, I've got to go – I need some time to think."

"Good luck, Ant. I'm praying for Bruce. Call me later."

"Bye Pearl." The line goes dead.

I mull over the fragility of our existence. One second everything can be perfect and the next, bam, anything can change and there's not a lot you can do about it.

Except - live each day as if it were your last.

3

I need someone to talk to. Bruce's aneurism has really knocked the wind out of me. Not that I am a huge Bruce fan but he is everything to my brother and I can't bear to see Anthony's life fall apart. It brings it all gushing back again; my mother's unexpected death. You'd think the pain would go away after all these years but that feeling of abandonment never leaves your side – the eternal lurking shadow which accompanies even your happy moods.

Alexandre is still en route to London so I can't talk to him.

I dial my best friend - poor long-suffering Daisy. I say long-suffering because she always talks my problems through with me. That's just the way she is. Even if I try to discuss *her* she somehow swings the conversation back round to me. It's in her nature, and besides, it's her job. At least it *was* before she got married and had a child. She was a full-time counselor cum therapist when she lived in London. Now that little Amy's at school all day, Daisy is back working again. Or will be soon. She has set up an office in the maid's room in her pre-war apartment block. A lot of these old apartments come with small 'box' rooms – that once were maids' quarters in the days when people rang bells for service, had their baths drawn and drinks brought to them. These days, only people like Alexandre live this way. And now me. I still can't get used to the luxury of my new life and feel guilty every time I see his staff running around for us. It doesn't seem right. Indecent, almost. But Patricia gets cross with me if I don't act the complete 'lady'. She winces when I put plates in the dishwasher or begin to scrub a pan. I need to act more like the princess people expect me to be in my privileged situation.

Daisy picks up on the first ring.

"Hi Daisy, it's Pearl, are you busy, am I interrupting anything?"

"Hi gorgeous. Right now, I need to take care of a few calls but my eleven o'clock has just cancelled on me, so come over then."

"You have appointments already? That's fantastic!" I cry out.

"Joel - he's my charity case, I don't charge him a penny," Daisy tells me in her British drawl. "Getting back into the swing of things, you know. But I do have my first paid patient, I mean *client*, coming in next Thursday. Come on over – see my nest-like office. Just got a new couch – it's a bit squeezed but I look pretty professional in my new surroundings."

"Can't wait to check it all out. See you at eleven."

I grab my gym bag where I keep my swimsuit and decide

to go for a workout at the pool. I usually do fifty lengths. Gets the lungs working, and the blood pumping – it keeps me in shape. Although Alexandre has installed a gym at his apartment, working out with him is a disaster – I can't concentrate. Apparently, Barack and Michelle Obama exercise together every morning. *Do* they work out or just leap on each other? Because when I see Alexandre pumping those biceps, sweat beading on that toned chest of his, his cute, tight buns clenched in action, all I want to do is jump his bones. No, I need a nice peaceful swimming session *alone* to keep my concentration in check.

Daisy has done wonders with her tiny space. It's intimate but it works. The walls are painted burgundy. I wonder if people will imagine that they are back in their mothers' wombs – safe, protected. It certainly makes you feel you could tell her any inner thought - although Daisy has that effect on people, at least on me. The burgundy clashes with her natural red hair and, as if on purpose, she's donning an orange dress. Very Autumnal. She has two framed certificates of her diplomas on the wall and a photograph on her desk of her daughter Amy and her husband together in an embrace. There's a small library of books on a shelf behind; Freud, Carl Jung and titles like *Stage Theory of Psychosocial Development* and *Eponymous Influences in Therapy.*

"What d'you think?" she asks proudly.

"I think you'll have a line of people clamoring down your door."

"Really? I feel so insecure, you know, I've been out of

the picture for ages but Amy's just turned five, is at school all day now and I need to get my independence back."

I lean back on her couch. "My father once gave me a great piece of advice. He said, 'Pearl, whatever happens, whatever you do, even if you end up with someone wealthy you always need to have your own 'fuck-you' money. Money that's just yours that you can do what you like with. Women need to have their own fuck-you money at all times. You never know when you'll need to catch a plane or treat yourself to something special.' "

Daisy laughs and throws her curly head back and swivels in her therapist's chair. "That's brilliant and so true. That's why I'm doing this! I need 'fuck-you' money, too. I mean, Johnny's very generous and earns enough for us all but if I want to go on a wild underwear splurge at Victoria's Secret or pig out at the gourmet bakery at Dean & DeLuca, that's my prerogative, right? I don't want to feel guilty about it. 'Fuck-you' money, I love it! What about your 'fuck-you' money, Pearl? Do you feel as if Alexandre is being too controlling, still? A couple of weeks ago it seemed to be really bugging you. Is he still pushing you about getting pregnant ASAP?"

"Yes, but it hasn't happened so we'll cross that unlikely bridge if we come to it. The truth is though, I'm relieved I'm not pregnant right now. It would all be too much going on at once."

"What about the wedding date?"

"Alexandre's cooled off a bit about that but just can't understand why I need a bit more time. And he gave in about the company. As far as money goes, I get a generous director's salary from HookedUp Enterprises plus a percentage of any future projects that I orchestrate. It's all been drawn up legally with lawyers. I refused to be given a stake in the company, much to his irritation. If at a later date my projects go well then I can buy in. I want to know I deserve the money I earn."

"Wise. What about your apartment? You're not selling that, are you?"

"No, I'm subletting. It's a nice, regular income that I can rely on."

"Fuck-you money."

I laugh. "Exactly. Just in case I have to take off running," I joke.

"Good girl. Smart move. You need to keep your autonomy."

"Exactly," I agree. "I don't want hand-outs. I've always earned my own living. Anthony thinks I'm nuts, though."

"Yes, well - he would. I know Anthony's your brother but he's such a wanker. Why are you always so forgiving with him? You've got to face it, he really is pretty cruel to you Pearl."

"I know. He doesn't really mean it though."

Daisy arranges some papers on her desk. "There you go again – always defending him. Do you ever tell him to F off? I wouldn't stand for such continual negativity."

"We had a huge fight once and I did, I told him to get out of my life. Well, guess what? I've never told anyone this, Daisy, but…well, he attempted suicide…took a load of pills, so you can imagine how I felt. It wasn't because of me that he did it, but still."

"Oh, shit. How long ago was this?"

"About two years after John died. So you know, John died of an overdose, my mom died of cancer, I hardly see my dad so…"

"I see. Guilt and fear. Guilt is powerful."

"Anthony is incorrigible. He thinks I should 'snap up Alexandre before he realizes what's happened' – those were his very words. Oh, and become a 'trophy wife'. Do younger men have trophy wives who are older than they are? Don't you have to be arm candy to be a trophy wife?"

"You *are* arm candy, Pearl, believe me. Arm candy with intelligence. Age doesn't stop anyone being beautiful. In fact, I think you look better now than you ever did. And you seem so much more self-possessed lately, not so needy."

"What d'you mean?"

"Well when you first met Alexandre you were practically wetting your knickers over him – sorry I didn't mean that," she bursts out into a cascade of giggles. "No - but I mean you were behaving as if you were the lucky one, completely dismissing the fact that he, too, was getting a great deal."

I put my hand on hers. "Oh, sweetie, you think I'm a great deal?"

"I think you're a *bargain* and he should be bloody grateful. Just because he's loaded and gorgeous and younger than you doesn't make him more special than you are. And you need to be aware of that. The truth is, Pearl, you were behaving like a teenager. I can tell you now because you seem to be pretty much back to normal but I was a little worried for a while. I mean, I know you basically hadn't had any decent sex for twenty years and never thought you'd meet anyone ever again, so I do understand why you went so gaga over him, but still, he really had you under his thumb."

Little does she know, I think, and find myself humming *Under My Thumb* again, remembering what Alexandre did with his magic touch. Is still *doing* with his magic touch.

"Yes, but he wasn't aware of my Jell-O insides," I say.

"One of the reasons he was attracted to me was that I was 'mature'. Luckily, because of your wise advice of acting 'cool, calm and collected' he wasn't party to my insecure, self-doubting internal dialogue or I think he would have dumped me."

Daisy arches her delicate eyebrows. "You worry about that a lot, don't you? Desertion. Being dumped…left in the lurch?"

I tell Daisy about the whole Bruce saga, how I fear for Anthony, and how it has triggered the dread of abandonment and loneliness – memories of my mother's sudden death. Then I add, "I don't want to go into this marriage for the wrong reasons. I want Alexandre to really know me and love me for *me* – the good the bad and the ugly."

To my amazement, Daisy takes Anthony's side on this topic and warns, "Be careful, Pearl, he's a Latin man at heart. I'm speaking as your friend, you understand – professionally I'd probably urge you to be completely honest, but you're not my client, you're my best mate. Latin men can be jealous and possessive – believe me I know, I dated one. They have that virgin/whore complex going on. I really, *really* would think twice about coming clean about divulging sexual history – there are some things better left unsaid."

I bite my lip. Maybe she's right. Although, the truth is I had blanked it all out. I can't even remember, anyway.

She goes on, "You don't want him to know about what happened that time. He really doesn't need to be privy to it all–"

"But I was a different person then."

"You were cocky and sassy and brimming with self-confidence – you were only twenty-two."

"Exactly," I agree, remembering how I then didn't suffer

from insecurities - that at that age I felt I owned the world.

"Still, best to keep it all under wraps, don't you think? Let sleeping dogs lie," she advises.

I cross my legs almost in self defense. "It's a blur, anyway, Daisy. I genuinely can't remember what happened but it *is* a part of me still, whether I like it or not. I suppose I just feel like really opening up to Alexandre, that's all. I don't want us to hold secrets from each other."

Daisy strokes my cheek and brushes a tendril of hair away from my eye. "You want to talk about it, how it messed everything up with Brad...empty your heart and soul, re-open painful wounds? That's fine - I totally get that, me more than anyone. But talk to *me* about it, or any other close friend, or even another therapist - I could recommend a colleague to you - but your future husband who happens to be a proud Frenchman? I'm thinking, no, bad idea, or you could really screw things up. Look, maybe I'm wrong and totally overreacting; maybe he'd be understanding, adorable and wouldn't give a toss. But I'm just speaking from my own personal experience. It's up to you, Pearl, but my gut feeling is this: he's crazy about you – he thinks you're perfect. Why risk jeopardizing that?"

"I guess you could be right," I mumble.

There's an awkward silence and then Daisy says enthusiastically, "On a brighter note – tell me about your wedding dress; have you chosen the designer yet? Let me know if you want me to come along and help you pick something out."

"I forgot to tell you, Daisy – it's all arranged. Zang Toi is doing my gown."

"You're joking? But won't that cost a fortune? You told me you didn't want Alexandre paying for your dress and I know your father doesn't have a bean. I read somewhere that

Zang Toi dresses like…Saudi princesses…and Bill Gates's wife – *that's* when he's not too busy with the likes of Eva Longoria and Sharon Stone."

"He does, but Sophie's paying. It's her wedding gift to me. She has insisted and won't take no for an answer. Zang Toi was *her* idea."

Daisy goes white. You. Are. Kidding. Me."

"No, really, she's being as sweet as pie at the moment."

"And you trust that?"

I grimace. "No, but what am I meant to do? Tell her she's a scheming bitch and that I suspect her of foul play? If she insists on spending sixty-three thousand dollars on me and it makes Alexandre happy and I'm going to get the most stunning wedding gown in the whole wide world, then who am I to disagree?"

"Sixty-three thousand dollars?? But that's insane money! I know Sophie and Alexandre are loaded but−"

"Alexandre," I interrupt, "is rich and powerful but Sophie? Oh my God, that woman has her money invested everywhere - Vegas and half way round the United States and Latin America, and Lord knows where else. She *oozes* wealth. Alexandre spends his money on cars and property, but her? She *invests*. She plays the stock market. Who knows what pies her bony fingers are stuck into but I wouldn't be surprised if she's involved with Russian mafia or something. I know sixty-three thousand is a fortune for you and me, but for Sophie it's not even a morning's work."

Daisy presses her thumb up to her lips in thought. "Hmm, I wonder what her plan is. Maybe, knowing she's going to be your sister-in-law has made her turn over a new leaf and the wedding dress is her peace offering."

"You think?"

Daisy sniggers. "No, not for a second, I was being sarcastic. I think she could be plotting and scheming something. Watch out."

"Me too. I mean, I'd love to believe that she genuinely wants to be friends - of course - but my little voice inside tells me not to trust her."

"If I were you, I'd listen to that little voice." Daisy narrows her eyes. "I smell a rat."

I saunter through Central Park on my way back to the office, taking my time, mulling over what Daisy has said. I think of Sophie and her dark past, how she worked as a prostitute when she was only seventeen. Alexandre never judged her for that and even got angry with me when I made a benign comment. So how then, would he judge me for one thing that happened in my past? Would he think less of me? Would it spoil everything? Both Daisy and Anthony seem to think it's not worth the risk. But Alexandre is a forgiving person. He'd love me anyway.

Or would he? Perhaps things are better left unsaid.

The day's still beautiful. I take out my iPod and find *Autumn in New York* and put on my headset– what song could be more perfect? I have on my lightweight sneakers, which - as any New Yorker knows - is part and parcel of living in this city - walking is one of the great pleasures of living here. I kick up the crispy, golden leaves as squirrels scatter in front of me. I observe them leap up boughs of American Elm trees; a variety which has been decimated all through its range by the ravages of Dutch elm disease, but miraculously still alive and thriving in Central Park.

I feel the warmth of sun on my back; the sky is crystal blue. There are people sprawled on park benches reading newspapers, Smartphone texting and snoozing in the morning rays. Dogs are charging about trying their luck with a squirrel catch. I regret that Rex isn't with me. Dogs complete a real walk. I decide to pass by the apartment to collect Rex and take him to the office. He loves hanging out there and is a star amongst the staff; his treat every now and then to come to work and lap up the attention they lavish on him – his white cravat of a chest stroked, his ears caressed. I'll order something in for lunch – some Chinese perhaps – I have a lot of work to catch up on, and Natalie needed a second opinion about a project she's working on.

I'm singing along to *Autumn in New York* and making a mental list when I feel the buzz of my cell. I fumble about for it and pick up.

The voice is familiar but I don't recognize it straight away. I switch off my iPod so I can hear better.

"Pearl?"

"Speaking."

"Sam."

"Oh, hi Sam." Samuel Myers – that was fast. Such a quick answer can mean only one thing. A 'no' to my proposal.

"Lunch?"

"Oh, okay." I look at my watch. Lunch is now.

"You sound surprised," he snorts.

Uh, oh - the cool, sophisticated woman in the chic suit is now wearing sneakers, has damp mussed-up hair from swimming and is in a twisted mess of iPod wires tangled all over her head. I take a neat breath. "No, Sam, not surprised at all. I would love to do lunch. In fact, it'll be my treat. How about the Century Club?"

He chuckles. "The Century? You're a member? Too stuffy. Where are you right now?"

"In Central Park at about Sixty Third, or so."

"I'll book a table at Daniel. Is that good for you, sweetheart?"

"It's my local haunt but it's closed at lunch time."

I hear him breathing heavily. "Oh, darn. Let's just meet at The Plaza, then. Meet me there in… twenty minutes, say – in the restaurant at The Palm Court."

I start sprinting. I need to get there fast before he does – empty out my monstrous bag of tricks in the ladies' room and transform myself into the glamorous ball-breaking executive I was just a few hours before.

I emerge fresh from the powder room at The Plaza, looking composed and primed, and as sleek as a panther on the hunt. High heels back on, suit smoothed out, hair in a chignon bun, make-up perfect, just a touch of lip gloss.

Samuel Myers has something up his sleeve, I can be sure of that, or he would have just called, not suggested a lunch meeting. Or does he just want to get into my panties? Ha! Some chance. He's used to bimbos in LA - pretty young actresses who'll do anything for a break. He's fat and balding but he's powerful; the strongest aphrodisiac of them all for a lot of females. Not me, though. Money doesn't motivate me. Even if Alexandre had been a bus boy I would have fallen for him anyway.

The maitre'd shows me to our table, and to my amazement Samuel Myers is already seated, eagerly waiting for me. The room is massive, bordered with mirrored arched windows all around and fleur-de-pêche marbled columns. This airy room's crowning glory is a stained-glass yellow and green skylight way up high – the restored 1907 décor is breathtaking. Funny, how when you live in a city you neglect its best landmarks. I haven't set foot in The Plaza for years.

I find Samuel almost hidden behind a potted palm tree beaming at me.

"Pearl - we meet again," he says in a motion to get up, although he plunks himself right back down in his chair with the effort.

"Sam," I say, shaking his hand heartily.

"Not the most elegant cuisine in the city but there are some nice organic things on the Eloise menu. I can report back to my wife that I'm being a good boy and sticking to my diet."

"Diets are tough," I say. "Actually, I've never managed more than three hours of being on a diet."

He snorts with laughter. "I don't believe that for a minute, Pearl. You're so svelte, so slim and trim."

"I cheat."

"Oh yes? How?" he asks eagerly.

"I swim a lot. It's amazing what you can get away with when you go for the burn."

He sounds disappointed and says in a glum tone, "I wish I could admit to doing the same but I'm a lazy old man with a sweet tooth and a penchant for Cognac."

I suppress a grin. The waiter comes and we both order. The swim has given me an appetite so I ask for organic grilled chicken, mashed potato, carrots and sweet peas. Sam orders a hot dog.

"So should we get down to business?" he breathes.

My heart starts racing but I smile serenely, wondering what's in store.

"You got me thinking, Pearl. A lot. And I want to meet you half way.

"You do?" I ask, wondering where this is leading.

"You say Thelma and Louise. I say, just Thelma. No Louise. Because the other part needs to go to a guy. I need box office. I need testosterone. I'm obliged to hire a star which means I have to go easy on the budget – like I said before, I can't have two big names. That's where your Thelma comes in. The guy and the girl. A buddy movie with a twist."

I cross my legs, hold my hand up to my chin and listen intently. "Go on."

"What's the name of that woman who won a Tony Award for that play, *Seeking Sandrine* – the half-Italian actress? She was good."

"Alessandra Demarr."

He shakes his head. "Forget it. I've heard she's gay."

"So? She's a great actress. Even better if she's gay - we'd see the character from a different angle – it could really deepen the story. I mean, whatever happens, the script is going to need some more tweaking."

He ponders this and says, "I guess the advantage is that she won't be too expensive and the whole gay thing she's got going could work in our favor. The two leads can play off each other. Flirt but not get involved, you know. I like it, actually. I like it a lot."

"I had a feeling about you, Sam," I flatter him, "I knew you'd *get* it."

"My wife likes the idea of a female lead. My daughter *loves* the idea. We could be onto a winner here."

"And if Alessandra Demarr's not free?"

"Oh, she'll be free all right. Her agent will be chomping at the bit, guaranteed. Leave it to me, I'll sort it out."

"Really? That simple?"

"I have to leave for LA tonight but I'll set up a meeting. You two can get together next week or the week after."

"LA or New York?"

"Take your pick, sweetheart. You decide."

I look up at the glass ceiling and ponder my options. New York or Los Angeles? "I'll talk it over with my fiancé," I tell him, and imagine that a little trip with Alexandre might just be the tonic.

4

I've been parted from Alexandre for less than twelve
hours yet I still ache with his absence. I had gotten so
used to living alone before I met him that it seemed
normal to be doing everything solo, save a dinner here
or there with Daisy or with a group of friends. All I did was
work. Now I'm part of a busy household, loved by a fiancé
who calls me every few hours and I even have a dog. Everything has changed - I wonder how I survived before.

The day has been so full-on with those two meetings
with Samuel Myers, swimming and Daisy that I'm now
soaking in the tub with some magazines, a glass of wine and
some great chill-out music - *Play* by Funk. Heaven. Made all
the sweeter by Anthony's call to me earlier - Bruce has been
stabilized, the operation was a success and he's going to be
okay. Panic over. I'm searching online on my iPad for hotels
in Los Angeles when a Skype call comes through from

Alexandre.

"Hi baby," I say and wait for the video to come on. His handsome face appears on the screen and my stomach gives a little lurch. I can't believe that still, every time I see that face, or wake up with him next to me, it's as if I'm setting eyes on him for the very first time.

"Hey sexy," he says, his voice deep, his eyes heavy-lidded. You're in the bath?"

"Had a busy, very eventful day."

"Sorry, I couldn't call earlier – was in that fucking meeting forever."

"And?"

"All good. Sophie ate them alive. We're going to do extremely well with this. Got an edge on any future competition – got the British government eating out of our hands."

I think of how Alexandre promised me that he would sell his share of HookedUp to Sophie and concentrate on starting new projects of his own, but now I realize that may never happen. He and his sister are as entwined as ivy in this business together. It seems he needs her on some deep, psychological level. But I don't want to nag him on this issue so I have said very little lately. Especially as she's being so sugar-sweet to me - I really don't have a leg to stand on.

"What about you?" he continues, his eyes scanning my naked shoulders soothed with big white, foamy suds from the bubble bath.

"Well, after that little porn film that you whipped up this morning, right in the middle of my million-dollar meeting, thank-you-very-much, dear fiancé, I have to say it was a little tricky to concentrate, but Samuel Myers and I have made a deal."

Alexandre smirks irreverently; his wicked mouth a little crooked making a tiny dimple appear in his cheek. "I knew you'd handle it. Nothing can faze you, Pearl, not even my dick."

I laugh. "Of course Samuel Myers is delighted. He really enjoyed your video – thinks you could be a big star. He's branching out into doing porn movies and would like to sign you."

Alexandre's face flinches for a second but then breaks into a broad grin. "Very funny."

"No, but seriously, the meeting went better than expected. Two meetings, actually. We've got Alessandra Demarr on board," I tell him proudly. "An LA trip could be coming up shortly."

"Really, you're joking – Alessandra Demarr?"

A rush of surprise courses through my body. "You know who she is?"

"Of course I do. I saw her at the National in a play. She's an amazing actress - stunning too - she looks like a young Sophia Loren."

I smile sweetly but feel nauseous inside. *Why am I jealous? It's absurd.* Perhaps it's because I'm blonde and girl-next-door-ish and Alessandra Demarr is a ravishing beauty – the type that screams sex-siren and smoldering sophistication. "She's gay," I snap, not meaning the words to come out that way.

"So I've heard. Nothing like a sexy gay woman to turn a man on."

"You're *attracted* to her," I hear my voice creak out. I try to stay cool – after all, he can see every expression on my face, every nuance of emotion.

"I'm attracted to you, baby, and I know you have a penchant for pretty women. That first time, in your apartment, when you told me the story of your first real orgasm when your best friend stroked you with a feather? That was the sexiest thing I'd ever heard. Fuck, I'm hard now just thinking about it."

"I'd love to suck your cock right now," I purr, making sure he has *me* on his brain and not Alessandra Demarr. I know I'm going to have to keep him well away from her. Gay people can be swung and I'd rather not put temptation in his path.

"Tell me what you'd do," he says, running his tongue along his upper lip. His thickly lashed eyes sear into me – tiger's eyes – keen, intense as if he wants to eat me whole.

"First, I'd take your big, beautiful cock in both hands and bury my head between your legs," I murmur. "I'd run your silky smoothness around my nose, my cheeks and then on my lips, breathing in the smell of you, and just run my eyes all over you – this one thousand percent pure, unadulterated all-male, luscious helping of Alexandre Chevalier."

His lips tip up in that crooked smile of his.

And I keep talking, "I'd tease my lips along your balls and gently flick them with the tip of my tongue, letting it ride up your length - your thick, throbbing cock – thinking about how it's gonna make me come after I'm done with sucking it first – how it's so sexy and virile that even after that big bad boy has spurted in my mouth, it's ready again for round two."

He groans. "Always ready for another round with you, Pearl. Always ready to fuck your slick, wet, tight pearlette."

I smile at his poetic rhyme and continue, "I'll ring my tongue around your soft, satiny head, making it flicker over your one-eyed jack. I'll slowly lick off your pre-cum – you always taste so good, so sweet, Alexandre. The only man in the world I could ever do that to."

"Don't even put the idea of another man into my head," he growls. "I don't want to know who's touched you - I don't even want to *imagine* you having ever been with anyone else. Your *mine,* do you hear that, Pearl? You're *mine* - and you were born to be mine. "

I instantly regret what I've said – it's made him edgy. His gaze narrows – his green eyes on fire, covetous, greedy for me. I know I have to keep my secrets to myself or all hell could break loose – I can't risk letting him find out anything. But it turns me on – knowing his jealous flame is alight. I'm pounding with desire – I squeeze my thighs tightly together as both hands are holding onto my tablet and I don't want to drop it in the bath. That already happened a couple of weeks ago with this very same scenario – Sex-Skyping is getting to be a regular habit with us. I'm writhing now, squeezing, crossing my legs and clenching myself. I need this release.

"I want you to come in my mouth," I carry on in a whisper.

"Tomorrow night I'll be back and I'm gonna lick you all over, tease your clit – then I'll fuck you. Your. Tight. Wet. Pearlette is going to Make. Me. Explode."

"Alexandre, I'll be with you in a minute." I can't bear it anymore. I set the iPad down on the floor and turn on the faucet of the shower-head. I can hear him moaning now, groaning at the release of his orgasm. I think of his gorgeous face, his dark hair flopping about his defined cheekbones, his huge, smooth cock stretching me open and fucking me. I turn up the power of the water and let it pound my clit. I press the metal on my mound and it's enough to push me to the edge – the water's firing inside my slit, shooting at my clitoris like tiny bullets – I start climaxing in a shattering orgasm, rushing through me with continual spasms as the water continues to draw out the intensity of pleasure; my sensitive core coming in undulating waves.

I finally let go of the shower head.

I reach down for my tablet and observe the relaxed face of Alexandre, spent, orgasmed-out, but then my freaking battery goes dead. I set the iPad back down. I lie back in the bath and press my fingers on my clit to draw out the last little ripples of satisfaction.

I close my eyes and snooze off, the warm water lapping around me in a gentle swell.

I was looking hot. Really hot. Loved getting ready to go out. Madonna's latest hit, *Secret,* was playing on the radio and I was moving my hips to the rhythm, dancing around the room. I checked myself again in the mirror and tossed my teased-up curls about and then ran my fingers through my long, wild blonde hair. Eyes looking like smoldering fires – make-up just right. At least *some* guys appreciated me. Fuck him! Fuck Brad – I'll show him. He needs *space,* I'll show him goddam space.

We'd been dating for four years and now, suddenly, he was telling me he needed space! I knew it was because of his studies, I knew - med school looming, exams to get through. That, I could understand, but all that studying lately with Alicia – all those all-nighters. I'm not some Kleenex to be tossed aside, I'm your girlfriend, I told myself. He didn't want me to cramp his style? Two can play at that game, buddy.

Julia breezed into my dorm. "Are you ready?"

"What d'you think?"

"I think your skirt might be a little short," she said eyeing up my electric-blue mini, my legs going on forever in high, clunky heels.

I laughed. "If you've got it, flaunt it."

"You don't usually wear stuff so...so *revealing*," she stammered.

"I want to look sexy."

"You always look sexy, Pearl, you don't need to try so hard."

"*All I wanna do, is have some fun,*" I sang.

"Come on Sheryl Crow, or we'll be late. The boys said to meet them at the bar."

"*So* not my thing," I said, rolling my eyes, "football, frat boys from that dorky college but, hey, who knows? Maybe we'll have a good time."

I wake up with a jolt. The bath water's tepid. I must have dozed off. I bury my hands in my face as hot tears pool in my eyes. Memories are being unleashed but I'm not sure why. All this talk lately about keeping my past to myself is making me remember.

I let the plug out and stand up. I grab a warm towel and relish the cocoon feeling it gives me when I wrap it tightly about my cold body. I wish Alexandre were here. I need him. I need his strong arms to protect me, to envelop me with love.

I'd completely forgotten about that electric-blue skirt.

I get out of the tub, take another towel and dry my feet. My tablet's on the floor and I take it back to the bedroom and plug it in. The cell is sitting on the bed – I pick it up and call.

"I just want to hear your voice," I tell my husband-to-be but it's just his voicemail. *Where can he be?* I flop on the bed, slip under the down comforter and before I know it I've lapsed into a profound sleep.

I was leaning against the juke box – lapping up everybody's stares – all eyes were on me and my sexy dance moves. I'd lost count of how many shots of tequila I'd had. I was licking the salt seductively off my lips, then I tilted my head back to empty yet another glass. The blond guy – what was his name – he had his hand up my electric-blue mini; the other was fisting my hair. The music was loud – Snoop Doggy Dog singing intensely about something intense. The football player shouted in my ear, "Fuck, you're hotter than a bitch in heat," and then he said to his friend, "we all need to get out of here."

I'm suddenly in a lavender field and Alexandre is smiling at me. "Don't worry, baby, you're with me now. I won't let anything happen to you."

"But it already *has* happened," I say. "It's too late."

I wake up with a start and feel the small of my back drenched with sweat. The bottom sheet is soaked. I peel off my silk nighty, toss it, and shift my naked body over to a fresh part of the bed. Blurry-eyed, I look at my watch. Two twenty-five a.m. I swivel it around; it's a Reverso, (another extravagant gift from Alexandre) and the other face, the London-time side, says seven twenty-five – five hours ahead. Perhaps Alexandre is having breakfast; like a true Parisian, drinking a strong dark espresso. Should I call? And say what? My dreams are keeping me awake but I can't tell you what they are.

As if he could smell my angst, Rex comes wagging into the room. His basket is next to the kitchen but he comes to say good morning every day. Today he's five hours early. He nuzzles his nose next to my hand which is dangling over the mattress. Dogs know when things aren't right – they *know*.

"Alright, Rex, but don't tell Daddy - come on up."

He gazes up at me with his almond-shaped eyes as if to say, "Really? Truly?"

I'll get in trouble for this. Rex isn't allowed on the bed but I'm sad and lonely, so who cares. I pat the mattress and he jumps up excitedly, his windmill tail in motion, digging his paws into the comforter, not believing his luck. Tomorrow, I'll change the sheets so there's no evidence. He crawls almost on top of me and I put my arms about his solid black body and squeeze him tight. "Just this once Rex, as a special treat – I could really use a hug right now," and I kiss his soft, silky ears. I need him close to get through the night. He's my bodyguard to chase away the bad dreams.

I fall fast asleep with my doggie-love in my arms.

"Ah, ha! Caught you, you naughty boy!"

I rouse from my sleep and there's a big commotion going

on around me, Rex padding about the bed, wild with happiness. Alexandre has tried to sneak into the bedroom without waking me but got more than he bargained for.

I look at my watch - 7a.m. "You're back early," I mumble into my pillow, my eyes half closed.

"I wanted to surprise you," he replies, planting a soft kiss on my lips, "but it looks as if you got there first - while the cat's away—"

"I couldn't sleep – I needed a French lover by my side. You were gone so Rex offered himself up."

Just then, I hear the elevator door open and Rex leaps off the bed and into the hallway. Sally must have arrived to take him on his morning walk. I rouse from my sleepiness and stretch my arms languidly in the air. "I've missed you, Alexandre."

He throws his raincoat on a chair. "Next time I go, you're coming with me. I don't like us being separated." He moves towards me, his eyes flashing with passion. He strokes my head and then folds me in his strong arms, pressing his face to my throat and breathing me in as if his life depended on it.

"I felt empty without you," I whisper. I relax into him, his natural scent is intoxicating, and my heart beats with anxiety at the thought of being away from him again. Ridiculous; it's been less than two days. I bury my head in his wide, warm chest. He lifts my chin with his hand for a kiss but I slip away from his clutch. "I'll be back, hang on a sec," I tell him, sidling underneath his embrace.

"Meanwhile, I'm getting straight into bed," he says.

I go to the bathroom to pee, freshen up and brush my teeth. When Alexandre tried to kiss me just now I closed my mouth tightly, lips sealed – morning breath, the horror of it.

Why is it I always want to be perfect for him? I want to be his princess – faultless, blameless and flawless. I want to reach unattainable heights. Yet at the very same time, I yearn for him to love me just the way I am and for all my faults, even my wrong doings. A paradox. I'm asking for the impossible.

When my teeth are squeaky clean and I've washed my private parts in the wonderful bidet that Alexandre had specially installed, I feel ready to come back to bed. I stand at the bathroom door and just survey the scene around me, realizing that my luck is a chance in a million. How many people get to love someone in their lives? I mean, really fall in love, not because of habit, or convenience or security but for passion – get to experience a real romance? I observe him now lying in bed and imagine there must have been angels fluttering about me that day when I bumped into him at the coffee shop four months ago. Was Cupid there, himself, with his bow and arrow? What were the odds of that?

Was Puck from *A Midsummer Night's Dream* sprinkling love dust in Alexandre's eyes?

Because what were the chances that a ravishing, twenty-five year-old Frenchman with the world at his feet would fall in love with a run-of-the-mill, forty year-old American woman?

"What are you staring at?" he asks with a grin.

"You."

"You're so beautiful, Pearl. Even when you're all ruffled up and half asleep – especially when you're ruffled up. You're like a fluffy chick, all sweet and innocent. Come here, I need to hold you."

I scurry over and slip under the comforter. Nestling myself next to him, I wonder where he gets these notions that I'm so unblemished. If he knew otherwise, would he do a one hundred and eighty degree turn?

He takes me in his arms again and strokes my hair. "You're my jewel, my angel – your hair's like spun gold in this morning light."

I run my fingers underneath his T-shirt; I need to feel him, to own his flesh and blood, press my fingers against his heartbeat to make sure this is all real. He lifts up his arms and I ease the T-shirt over his strong shoulders and fix my eyes on the rise and fall of his pecs moving with the rhythm of his breath. I touch his smooth skin and marvel at the fact that this gorgeous man before me is going to be my husband.

He gazes at me for a moment, his green eyes tender and warm, and then rests his defined lips on mine, softly at first. Then his tongue begins to tease me, running quietly along my upper lip. I let my mouth open and close my eyes in response. My tongue meets his and the tips tantalize each other in little flutters, like wings of a humming bird above a flower full of nectar; quivering, flickering. I moan and grip my arms tightly about his shoulders – I can't be near enough to him – close enough – this is beyond desire; it is an aching need for Alexandre to own me, to possess me. I abandon myself to him completely. I tilt my head back and melt into him; relaxed like a rag doll as his lips devour me, wet and all-consuming into a deep, insatiable kiss - our mouths as one, our tongues tangled in love and want for each other. I pull back for a beat to catch my breath, then nip his bottom lip playfully and open my eyes to observe his all-male beauty.

"I love you, Pearl. I need you." He pulls me into him and cups his hand under my butt forcing me even nearer. I feel his solid erection up against my belly and a bolt of desire shoots between my legs making me moan again. He licks my tongue with fiery lashes, the passion growing as if this kiss were alive - a being with a heart and soul all of its own. "You're mine, Pearl," he growls like an untamed panther. "Only mine – you have never belonged to anyone else – you were made for me, God created you just for *me*."

I pull myself up a little higher so that his erection is poised at my entrance. "I've been waiting for you my whole life, even when I didn't know it," I breathe through the kiss. "All my unhappiness, my loneliness before I met you was so I'd know what it was to really feel loved. You can't appreciate true love until you've been in a desert, looked Despair in the eyes. I don't want to be like that ever again."

"I'll never let you go, I promise."

A hot tear trickles down my cheek and Alexandre licks it before it falls. We're now lying side by side and I feel him enter me slowly. I gasp. I'm throbbing, my nipples hard and rosy. He thrusts himself into me and I cry out at the surprise.

His eyes flutter half closed in ecstatic reverie and he murmurs, "Jesus, you're so tight but so warm and juicy - coupled with that kiss - I think I'm gonna come." He holds his hips still. I can feel the pulse of his cock flexing inside me, stretching me, blood pumping through his taut veins, filling my walls – but he doesn't come, he has too much self-control. "I don't want to fuck you," he whispers, "I want us to make love." I sense myself shudder at the deliciousness of his lips grazing against my ear, sending shivers all through my body.

He may have self-control but I don't. The shaft of his penis is rubbing delicately against my clit and I start to make little circles tilting upward with my pelvis, my arms hooked about his neck. I can feel it building – the double pleasure of his huge girth inside me pushing all the right places – still motionless – and my clit rubbing against the thick base of his penis - pushing me to my limits.

Then Alexandre starts licking my tongue again in slow swipes and under my tongue, too, at its sensitive root....faster now - little flicks as if he's fucking me with it. The sensation is exquisite. My clit is tingling like a thousand little bells – as if there's a golden thread linking it to my nipples and tongue. Never has a kiss been so sensual. He then presses his thumb on that little space just behind the base of my entrance and I climax in a shudder, riding myself up and down his huge cock, the only movement made by my own friction – he's still motionless. I'm moaning. He clasps both of his large hands around my buttocks and pulls me on top of him in one smooth movement - "That's right baby, ride that orgasm all the way - ride my big, hard, throbbing cock." I'm still climaxing around him when he lunges at me from his position underneath. "Pearl–"

"Alexandre," I moan. I can feel the zealous spurt of him shoot inside me, squirting into my depths in a hot fountain of desire. Both of us are as one – an extension of that kiss now melded into an orgasmic zenith of emotion.

Fucking is great but making love is even better. And that is what I feel emanating from Alexandre's psyche, his soul – the force and power of pure Love with a capital L.

We stay like this for a long time. He's still hard inside me but relaxed as miniscule ripples fade little by little contracting deep inside me. His breath is on mine; he's still looking into my eyes – the orgasm spent but the love surrounding us like a halo of light. No words are needed for how we both feel. I can behold it in his gaze and my core is flashing with a radiant energy from within. I am alive. If I were to die right now I would have tasted Heaven on Earth. My gentle smile creeps into a grin paired with my teary eyes. My emotions are raw and so are his. Like me, he is vulnerable. He, too, has misty eyes but a smile is also dancing on his lips.

We are united in every way.

The essence of true love.

5

A week has gone by, both of us busy with work but having lunch every day together and then meeting up later at home where we usually order something in for dinner. In New York City you are spoiled for choice; whether it be Thai, Indian, Chinese, Mexican or Japanese - even Ethiopian; you name it, you can get the best of it all in Manhattan. Sometimes, Alexandre whips up something mouth-watering himself. He has a knack with any type of cuisine, but especially French and Italian. Alexandre's chef, Vincent, is on vacation.

I need to start getting used to saying things like, 'our chef' and 'our apartment' but it's still taking a while for it all to sink in. Also, this is not my money paying for all this luxury so I find it difficult to use the word 'we' when it concerns 'necessities' that most human beings live quite happily without.

Alexandre set up a mini movie theatre in the apartment so we get to watch movies on the big screen and eat popcorn. Occasionally, Sophie's step-daughter Elodie comes over, still painfully shy and only just eighteen. Alexandre refuses to speak French with her so she's learning fast. He's also paying for her to have private English lessons, so movie night is extra tuition as far as he's concerned – nothing like a good film to make you absorb a language. With a head on her shoulders for anything technical and frighteningly nerdy, Elodie is being groomed as a future heiress to HookedUp – at least that is how it appears to me, although it's unspoken. Alexandre even wants her to spend some time working with me. He's set her up in a pretty apartment in Greenwich Village. He suspects that she rarely goes out and neither of us has seen any evidence of her making friends, hence the choice of Greenwich Village; he thought it would be the right ambience for her to mingle and meet people. So far, she seems to keep to herself, though.

Anthony was right. I feel like Kate Middleton must have felt preparing for her big day. The thought of Sophie spending $63,000 on my wedding gown brings goose-bumps to my flesh. She's an old client of the Malaysian-born designer, Zang Toi – a star who dresses stars and who's been based in New York for the last thirty years or so. I was nervous at first but then I met him and knew straight away that he was special. He's adorable with an infectious laugh and a sense of humor that brings out the child in you. Like many Chinese people, he looks way younger than his fifty-one years. The first time I saw a photo of him he was wearing a mini kilt. Now he usually goes about in a black suit.

Today, I'm off for my first fitting at his showroom, an atelier on Fifty Seventh Street, just a few blocks over from

HookedUp Enterprises. He has already promised me that I'll look like a princess on my wedding day. When I saw some of his designs, both vintage and new, I knew that he was right. He's a genius.

I take the elevator up to his floor and am greeted by one of his assistants, a sweet, unassuming girl who could be a teenager but no doubt isn't – those Asian, wrinkle-free genes again. She ushers me into his showroom where there are floor to ceiling windows overlooking Fifty Seventh Street below, and rows of to-die-for gowns and outfits draped from hangers. There is a large desk in the center of the room where he is sitting, his blue-black glossy head bent, busy and in deep concentration. I've heard that he's a shrewd businessman as well as an artist – he learned from a young age, helping out in his parents' grocery store when he was just a boy. He is the seventh child and his lucky number, Sophie told me, is thirteen.

He looks up from his task, rakes his eyes over me quickly and smiles, saying, "You are making my life very easy, Pearl, you're perfect sample size, so no snacking before your wedding!"

I laugh but know he's probably serious. This is not going to be the type of dress to favor a last-minute nip and tuck. "Tell me, Zang, what do you envision for me?" I ask, kissing him on both cheeks. Somehow a handshake seems too formal for such a friendly person.

"I have planned for you a floor length ivory, silk velvet cape with dramatic train and ice crystal beaded blossoms cascading down from the shoulder, and matching strapless gown with ice crystal beaded blossoms cascading up the dramatic flared hem."

"Wow, it sounds beautiful."

"You will be the perfect ice-princess for your handsome French prince," he says with a giggle.

We spend the afternoon discussing the design and all the different options for shoes. He has me there like a manikin, being draped with muslin cloth, pins going here and there - the fabric itself, the silk velvet, will not be touched until later. He loves the idea of a winter wedding in Lapland and asks me a hundred questions about what food and drink will be served – but even *I'm* not sure about that yet - this is all stuff I have to decide with the wedding planner.

Elodie, of course, will be my maid of honor – she has yet to come in for her fitting, but slim as a pencil, I'm sure Zang will love her – no chance of her pigging out before December; she's like a little waif. With her long brown hair styled with crystal beads, Zang is confident he can transform her into a character from a fairytale.

I leave late, bubbling with excitement and hope – Zang's giggly demeanor is catching and I'm in the highest of spirits.

That's until the elevator door to his showroom opens and Sophie is standing there with a fixed grin on her face.

My heart sinks.

She looks ravishing, impeccable - but then Sophie is always impeccable. She's wearing her thick dark hair loose, the cut chic with Parisian perfection. Her pinstripe pantsuit is tailored. I instantly feel straggly and unkempt next to her mature sophisticated demeanor, even though she's five years younger than I am.

"Pearl, *darling*," she says in her heavy French accent and air-kisses me on both cheeks.

"Sophie, what a lovely surprise, how long are you in town for?"

"Didn't Alexandre tell you I was coming?"

"He must have, but I guess I lost track of time," I lie. I don't want to give her the satisfaction of knowing I fear her and that Alexandre is keeping anything from me. No, he did not let me know she was coming to New York.

I smile sweetly. I feel like the two of us are in that scene from Oscar Wilde's *The Importance of Being Earnest* – two women's saccharine smiles and sweet-talk hiding dagger-like intentions. Although *my* only intention is to avoid her as much as possible. What her plans are for me, I still cannot begin to guess. Except I'm sure they include ousting me from her brother's life in whatever way possible.

She says excitedly, "I thought I'd pop by and see what Zang has designed for Elodie."

"Sophie, I can't thank you enough for this generous gift. I mean, you're really pulling out all the stops."

"Pearl, you're going to be my sister-in-law. Part of my life. If you make Alexandre happy, zat's all I care about." She wrinkles her nose cutely and I wonder, for a second, if she can twitch it like Samantha on *Bewitched* - something I practiced as a child watching endless re-runs on TV - but never mastered. I wouldn't put it past Sophie to be able to come up with a few sorceress tricks, or to cast some sort of wicked spell on me.

Or am I being unjust? Maybe her intentions are good and I'm just a jaded, unforgiving bitch.

Time will tell.

I go back to the office to work and when I get home I find Alexandre on the roof terrace with Rex.

"Hi Pearl, darling," he says, "come and sit on my knee. I'm just finishing up a couple of things." He's tapping away distractedly on his tablet, making lists.

I run my fingers through his thick dark hair and tell him, "I bumped into Sophie at Zang's showroom. You never told me she was coming to New York."

"Sophie's here, in Manhattan?"

"Yes, didn't you know? She said you knew."

"I can't remember her telling me, no."

"Oh," I say, wondering which one of them is fibbing. Sophie, no doubt.

As if the Devil herself were listening in on our conversation, Alexandre's cell rings. I can tell it's Sophie by the way he talks – not just because he's speaking French but the easy expression on his face; the relaxed way you speak to an old friend. My French is getting better every day, namely by hearing him chat on the phone. They're discussing dinner. Great. Just when I was feeling more at ease than ever, our lives perfect, Sophie has to nuzzle in on us. I tense. Is Alexandre now telling her, that yes, I will make dinner tonight? Please, God, no. He knows cooking is not my forte. He ends the conversation and looks at me, his slightly crooked smile showing a hint of irony.

"Did I hear right?" I ask him. "Did you just tell Sophie that I'd cook supper?"

"She asked especially. She wants to taste typical, home-made, American food."

"Well, there are a lot of restaurants that do it way better than I do."

"Nonsense, your cooking is great."

Little does Alexandre know that it's Dean & DeLuca's and Zabar's cooking which is great, or our local delicatessen.

Not me.

He brushes a lock of hair from my face. "Make your hamburgers, they're delicious."

"Really? You like them?"

"I love them. Or you could do your BLTs – the best this side of New York."

"But Sophie will be expecting something fancy."

"No, she won't. She gets gourmet food in Paris. Give her BLTs." He presses his mouth on mine and whispers through his kiss, "You're my Star-Spangled girl, remember? I don't care if you don't cook flashy, haute cuisine. I love you just the way you are. Don't ever change."

Sophie and Elodie arrive at eight o'clock sharp. Needless to say, every second has been spent by me preparing for their dreaded arrival. Patricia helped me lay the table with the best silver and crystal champagne glasses – BLTs in style with match-stick French fries and Bollinger Champagne. Because I'm the only native English speaker, the language du jour is soon French. Sophie has ways of looking as if she's the most charming person in the world while quietly stabbing me simultaneously. Alexandre doesn't seem to notice and Elodie is so busy stuffing her face with the BLTs, that she is blissfully unaware.

"So Pearl," Sophie begins. "How is everything going in zee Enterprise's department?"

"Great," I reply sweetly.

"She's just made a deal with Samuel Myers," Alexandre interjects proudly. "He's a tough nut to crack and Pearl got what she wanted, namely a woman for one of the leads in *Stone Trooper.*"

Sophie smoothes her manicured hand over her sleek, chignon. "No! You're kidding me? Very talented actress, Alessandra Demarr."

The way she says that makes me wonder if she knew about this already. Although I do remember telling her I wanted women for the lead roles I don't remember anyone mentioning Alessandra Demarr. I wish Alexandre hadn't let her in on my business but answer simply, "Yes, I'm very pleased with the way things are going."

"I'm sure you'll be even more delighted as sings unravel zemselves to you," she says ominously - although the ominous vibe could just be my imagination. She's French – the translation may have come out wrong – 'things *unravel* themselves' – *what things?*

Alexandre puts his hand on mine. "Pearl's going to do some re-writing of the script, aren't you, darling? She always wanted to be a script writer and now's her chance."

Sophie's hand envelops both of ours, her eagle talons cupping us, her nails long and sharp. "Let's have a look at your engagement ring. Beeeootiful," she coos, gawking at it, her eyes wide.

"Thank you."

Alexandre looks pleased. "It belonged to a Russian princess, a lady in waiting, so to speak, to Catherine the Great."

Sophie cackles. "Cazerine zee Great - isn't she zee Empress who used to fuck horses?"

Elodie almost chokes on her champagne. "Maman!"

"No, seriously, rumor has it zat zay had to lower zee horse on top of her as no man's penis was big enough nor insatiable enough for her. Zay said she was a 'beastite' – I think zat's zee correct term. She died, in fact, trying to have sexual intercourse wiz a horse – she got crushed to death in zee act."

Alexandre bursts out laughing. "Nonsense. That was a myth, gossip spread by French aristocracy and her Polish enemies at the time to belittle her."

"Well, she certainly had a voracious sexual appetite which contributed to her downfall." Sophie turns to me and stares, her last sentence directed at me, for sure. I think of the Freudian dream I had about a black horse at the hotel in Cap d'Antibes, after Alexandre had been talking about getting me to 'ride' him. *Can Sophie read my frigging dreams?* She knows that I can't keep my hands off her brother. She knows my sexual appetite has been awakened. I look down at my empty glass awkwardly. Alexandre doesn't seem to notice what she has said and Elodie looks hazily at the *Tromp l'Oeil* of the dining room, settling her gaze onto the painted lake with swans and the fake view beyond that looks so disconcertingly real, obviously choosing not to follow the conversation.

"Well, I *love* your ring, Pearl," Sophie continues with a syrupy smile. "But why didn't you want a new piece of jewelry?"

"Pearl and I didn't want a blood diamond," Alexandre breaks in.

"A blood diamond?"

"A conflict diamond," I clarify. "A war diamond. A lot of top-grade diamonds are mined in war zones, particularly Africa. We didn't want to contribute to that in any way so Alexandre chose a vintage piece instead, and I'm glad he did."

Elodie pipes up, her pretty eyes wide, her interest piqued.

"It's true, Natalie Portman does not wear real diamonds to Oscars or red carpet – she wears fake knock offs for five bucks for same reason."

I'm marveling at Elodie's colloquial English, using words like 'knock-offs' and 'bucks', and add, "It used to be a pendant and Alexandre had it made into a ring."

Sophie lets me know in a soft voice, "Well, I don't sink wearing someone's old jewelry is so lucky – bad Feng Shui, you know, could be bad vibe."

For the first time Alexandre looks angry. His mouth tenses as he says quietly between his teeth, "Actually, Sophie, I had the ring cleansed by a priest. By two different priests, in fact. Blessed with holy water. The ring is as pure as snow."

I look down at my achingly beautiful ring and wish Sophie hadn't laid her hands on it. As if her touch could pollute it in some way.

Swallowing a mouthful and then smiling sweetly she says, "These BLTs are so delicious, Pearl, you must tell me zee recipe."

Recipe. The recipe is in the *title of the sandwich.* BLT - bacon, lettuce and tomato. Of course, Sophie's irony is not lost on me but does seem to go over Alexandre's head. Men are so clueless when it comes to women's sharp claws disguised in white kid gloves. I tell Sophie, "The secret is in the bacon itself, Sophie. It's from a small farm Upstate where the pigs roam free in fields and lead a happy life."

Alexandre gets up from the table to get another bottle of champagne and Sophie whispers to me out of his earshot:

"Pearl, make sure you don't wear zat pearl choker my bruzzer gave you on your wedding day, itself. Pearls are unlucky for a bride, you know." Then she adds in a hoarse whisper, "I hope zat doesn't make *you* unlucky, having Pearl as your name."

I couldn't even remember how we got there. I guess it was by his car – what *was* his name? Later, I blanked that name out. Later, when it was all too…

Late.

My friend, Julia, had somehow slipped out of the equation. I was left with both boys, lascivious, like hungry dogs drooling for their dinner. But I was lapping up the attention, thinking of Brad studying with his new *girlfriend* – well I, too, could have some fun – two guys at once. An erotically-charged night – a threesome. A one-time pleasure adventure - just the once. Isn't that every girl's secret fantasy?

"Baby, what's wrong?"

My breath is short, my back is drenched with sweat. My eyes fly open and Alexandre is there beside me in bed. I heave a sigh of relief.

"You were having a bad dream, Pearl." He holds me close to him and kisses the lids of my wet eyes. "It's okay, everything's okay, baby. You can go back to sleep."

Alexandre brings me breakfast in bed the next morning. He sets down the tray and pours me coffee, adding steaming hot milk – a change from just the usual black caffeine fix that I always drink at work – he thinks the calcium is good for me. He knows just how I like it and it's always more delicious when he makes it than when I do it for myself. In every way he is the most sensitive man to my needs and desires, except in one aspect:

Sophie.

She is like the cliché Italian mother-in-law who wants to protect her son from the wicked influence of his wife or girlfriend. He is the eternal baby. Forever suspicious, she will always be jealous, no matter what you do or how you prove yourself. Sophie may be just his *sister* but because these siblings are so embroiled in HookedUp together this is a tough battle. She's a sister who is unfortunately embedded in my life, whether I like it or not. I am doing all I can not to nag. I have to be smart about this. My long game plan is to get her out of our lives.

"Alexandre," I begin, wondering how to broach the subject. "No, never mind."

"You want to tell me about these bad dreams you've been having, my darling?" he asks, sitting beside me on the bed. He's already dressed, ready for work.

I look at my watch and see I overslept. That dream has turned me upside down. "Actually," I venture, "I wanted to ask you if you noticed how...how spiky Sophie was being yesterday evening. I mean, she covered it up well with smiles but her intention was to make me look small."

He holds my hand. "Yes, I did notice. But the best thing to do with Sophie is ignore her when she's being like that. She wants to get a rise out of you – if you react it'll just feed her desire to overrun you even more. It's her way of getting your attention. Be flattered she's investing so much of her energy in you."

"Flattered? I'd like you to stop her behaving that way."

Alexandre shakes his head. "I can't stop her."

"Alexandre, why do you weaken when it comes to So-phie? If she's going to be like that, I don't want to see her. Period."

"Look, Sophie loves you."

"What?" I say incredulous. "Are you serious? She hates everything about me!"

"She was saying only yesterday how good you are for me. Singing your praises. That you're beautiful and have the face of an angel. She thinks your eyes are...what was the word she used? Yes, that's right...'soulful'. She loves you, Pearl. Believe me, if Sophie didn't like you, you'd soon realize. It's just her manner. Plus, her English comes out a bit strange sometimes...the translation goes a bit awry and things sound critical or odd but she doesn't mean it that way."

"She's playing us both, Alexandre." I sigh, exasperated. We are going nowhere with this conversation. "I wish I'd never agreed to the wedding gown gift."

But he just kisses me on the forehead as if I'm his little daughter who hasn't had her rest and is cranky from lack of sleep. "She adores you, Pearl. Now, I've got meetings all day so I'll see you later this evening. I'm taking you to the opera tonight."

"Wonderful," I mumble grumpily but then realize how spoiled that sounds so I ask with more energy, "What are we going to see?"

"Surprise."

I walk to work with Rex and decide to spend the day with Natalie. For some reason, I thought that working on feature films would be more exciting but I'm finding that I miss the detail of documentaries. There is something satisfy-ing about delving into a world you would never normally encounter and unveiling truths and horrors that the normal public would never find out about. Sharing real life stories rather than selling fantasies – that is fulfilling.

Natalie's latest venture is into the dark cavern of modern slavery and human trafficking. This is something she feels passionate about as her ancestors were African slaves shipped to America. She's horrified that with all our education, this travesty is still happening all over the globe; the difference being that it is undercover and illegal, but nevertheless rife. I agree with her and think this project is crucial.

I find her in the editing room. The light is low and I study her concentrated hazel eyes set amidst her smooth café au lait-toned face. She is staring at the screen in the semi-darkness.

She clicks her fingers. "Cut right there," she instructs her assistant, John. "And then pick it up again at the voodoo dance bit." She looks at me out of the corner of her eye, "Hi, Pearl. We have so much footage I don't know how to squeeze it all in, in under just one hour."

"Make it ninety minutes, then."

"Can we get away with that?"

"Why not? I think people will be riveted by this story. We can do a special on it. I mean, this is world news. Most people think slavery finished with Abraham Lincoln – they need to know what's going on right here in New York City. Also, in London and Rome and in so many of the 'civilized' cities of the Western world."

Natalie wipes a tear from her cheek. "It breaks my heart."

Just as she says those words, Rex comes wagging up to her.

I laugh at his adorable dolphin face. Dogs can smile. "Mention the word 'heart'," I tell her, "and Rex will be at your side. He has an uncanny instinct when it comes to emotions. He can feel it when people are sad."

Natalie holds Rex's wide head in both hands and kisses him. "You sweet boy, just what the doctor ordered."

"By the way, sorry to change the subject but while it's on my mind, Dad called."

Natalie raises an eyebrow. "Did he now."

"He misses you and wonders why you won't return his calls."

"Men," she sighs.

"I think he loves you, Natalie."

"*Think* being the operative word."

"No, really, I'm sure of it. Every time Dad and I speak he wants to talk about *you*."

"Look, your dad is gorgeous. Very sexy, very attractive but as a human being he has a lot of failings. A lot. One of them being that he clams shut when it comes to his emotions. I'm sorry, Pearl, but I need a man who is more demonstrative."

"Well, I'm just passing this information on. Feel free to consider giving him another chance. You know, he is just a *guy*."

We laugh simultaneously.

"What about co-living with Alexandre? Any better with psycho sis?"

I tell her about my Zang Toi visit, my wedding gown and Sophie's snarky comments about my ring.

Natalie responds, "Clever woman. She has you over a

barrel. Buying you with an amazing gown – now she feels she has control over you."

"You make it sound as if I had a choice in the matter."

"We always have a choice, Pearl."

"I wish I could be more assertive like you, Natalie. You think I should cancel the gown, then?"

"It's a little late for that now. But don't have her over to your home anymore. Meet her at a restaurant, if need be – keep her at arm's length."

"I can assure you, there's no 'need be' – I'd be delighted if I never set eyes on her again."

We both fix our gaze on John for a moment as he prepares to show us more footage, and then Natalie says, "So pleased about Alessandra Demarr and that you came out on top getting a female lead."

"Girl power," I joke.

"You may laugh but it's true – we women need to look out for each other. When are you going to meet her?"

"It looks like Alexandre and I are going to Los Angeles in a few days. He's just waiting to hear back on something."

"Well, watch out for her."

"What do you mean?"

"She has a reputation, Pearl. She's a seductress."

"I have confidence in Alexandre – I trust him."

Natalie chuckles. "Not him, dummy. You. Be careful you don't fall for her charms."

The opera was awe-inspiring. A new soprano (whose name I can't pronounce) has everyone enthralled with her angelic voice. Afterwards, Alexandre and I went for a late supper and came home well after midnight.

I'm lying in bed unable to sleep. Not even sex has been able to calm my nerves; in fact, it made things worse. Natalie's film has been playing over and over in my mind. All I can think about is how men control so many parts of the world and women are their victims. Poor innocent girls, some as young as thirteen are being sold by their husbands or families in Nigeria – lured away for a 'better life' in Europe or The States, being promised lucrative jobs or an education but ending up working for the sex industry. An 'industry' it is with no thought for their feelings or their well being - like cattle they are being herded in droves.

How can there be so many monsters in this world? The image of Sula, one of the children in the film who was later lucky enough to have been saved, is turning over in my thoughts. Her large, doe-like eyes, her long, elegant neck; a sweet child who was abused by hundreds of men out for a cheap thrill. Cheap. As if she were worthless; just two holes - orifices for them to abuse. It makes me sick.

Finally, I drift off to a worrying sleep....

I lay down on the futon in just my bra and panties. The room was dimly lit with just a flickering candle. I felt nervous but excited. This was a first. I could hear them mumbling between themselves, discussing me. It was exhilarating to be the center of attention. I lay back, the tequila whooshing through my veins. I told them my name was Jane. Jane Doe. They were from another college, I'd probably never see them again but still, I didn't want to get a bad reputation – didn't want to be gossiped about. This was going to be a one-off, a secret. I wouldn't even tell Julia.

Jane Doe. I smiled to myself – I wondered if these boys

believed my silly fib.

A firm hand touched my ankle, stroking me gently. Then a different hand, a little rougher, on my other calf. "Fuck, she's got a body on her," one said.

I looked at them hazily and saw the blonde one had his shirt off. He, too, had a body on him. He was a football player. They both were. I was in for a treat, I thought. My boyfriend Brad's body was different from these two – he was lithe and slim. He hated sports – he was too intellectual for that. These guys were hot. Dumb, from the basic way they spoke and the things they'd been saying all evening like, 'stoked' and 'dude' - their vocabulary was limited, but they were hot, nevertheless.

One hand trailed up my leg and lingered on my thigh. I felt myself clench inside and I gasped.

"Turn over," the blonde one said.

I turned on my stomach. He unclasped my bra and I felt some warm oil being rubbed on my back. Four hands were massaging me and it felt incredible, the knots in my shoulders being kneaded away. One set of hands was working on my upper body and the other traced down to my ass, cupping it, squeezing it; the fingers brushing past my crack. I moaned. This felt amazing. The same hand parted the cleft in my butt and trailed an index finger along it, resting at my entrance. I could sense my moistness gather, my clit tingling with pleasure. The hands moved down my thighs, and then up again, I could feel a hand press against my panties and his finger exploring my opening.

"She's as wet as a wetback, dude," one said and they both laughed.

Blood rushed to my head for a second, riled by the racist comment - normally something I would have jumped at - but

I felt so good, so relaxed, the liquor coursing through my body, throbbing in my groin.

The other pair of hands moved underneath me, caressing my belly, then cupping my whole mound, the base of his palm pushing in just the perfect spot. I groaned and took his hand, thrusting it against my clit and I lifted my stomach upwards off the futon and pressed hard back down on it again. I felt so aroused.

"Jesus, her pussy's wet," this one said. He opened my legs apart and slipped his fingers inside me with one hand and peeling my panties off with the other.

"Turn back over," the other one said. "I want to suck those hot tits." He pushed my body so it rolled like a heavy stone. He pulled off my bra. I felt woozy. I was now on my back, my eyes closed. I could smell some patchouli incense coiling in the air, rich and thick. My head was propped up by cushions.

The blonde one edged further down the bed and prized my thighs apart with his hands. "Gotta chow down on this pussy," he told me with a sexy groan. His tongue darted out at my clit and I could feel my body, almost as if it didn't belong to me, writhing with desire. He engulfed me with his entire mouth and began to lash his tongue up and down my cleft then circle my clit with his flipping tongue. I arched my back up high and moaned, pressing myself against his mouth.

The other guy was sucking my nipples. Nibbling on them, gently tugging with his teeth. "Christ, this feels incredible," I whimpered, the alcohol drumming through my veins.

I flexed my hips even closer to the blonde one's mouth. I could feel the need building, the need to be penetrated as the guy working on my torso flicking his tongue again on my hard nipple making it pucker. He then kneeled up and I saw his erection press towards my face.

"Suck my dick," he commanded.

I could feel the other guy's finger slide inside me. "Gotta fuck this pussy," he said.

The other one shoved his penis in my face. I held my breath – the reality of what I had got myself into suddenly hit me.

I heard him say to his friend, "Wait up, dude, she's gotta suck my dick first. I wanna come inside her mouth. I want her to lick her sweet tongue all over my cock and suck it till my hot, creamy cum jets out to the back of her throat. Then I'm gonna fuck her, fuck that tight, horny little cunt – fuck it till she's begging me to stop."

"Dude, *I've* gotta bone her first – she's got my dick so pumping and hard – gotta fuck that wet cunt – gonna make that cunt come all over my cement-hard dick."

I need air. I need space.

"Wake up!"

I don't want to open my eyes. I don't want to see.

"Darling, wake up!"

I dare to peel open my eyes and see Alexandre's concerned face staring at me. I let out the breath I've been holding in – my lungs expire with relief.

Alexandre shakes his head. "There's something wrong. I don't understand. Why all of a sudden these nightmares? Baby, what's wrong?" He grips me tight and covers my face with kisses.

"Just a bad dream."

"You were moaning – muttering in your sleep. Everything seemed fine at first, your lips were even curved in a smile but then you started thrashing about the bed and crying out. Tell me about your dream, Pearl, baby. Maybe if you speak about it, these nightmares will go away.

"I can't remember," I lie. "I don't remember. Please just hold me, Alexandre."

*

6

Los Angeles has not let us down. The sky is so blue that just looking at it makes you feel warm and happy, as if you've never had a problem in your life. The palm trees line Sunset Boulevard, the leaves shimmering in a gentle breeze as we cruise along in our rented 1960's Cadillac convertible. It's powder blue. Only in LA.

I remember that when I lived here, brief as it was, I felt that I was on vacation every single day, even though I had a nine to five job. People are easy in Los Angeles and constantly in a good mood. They don't call it La La Land for nothing. Beneath the veneer of perfection lie secrets and a dark interior but why delve deep when you can savor the trappings of glitz? At least for a little while.

Sunset Boulevard is a winding road, over twenty miles long linking the urban streets of downtown to the grand and glamorous residential avenues of Beverly Hills, Bel-Air and Brentwood. It continues to the Pacific Coast Highway in Malibu, passing some of the most beautiful properties that money can buy. Why take the freeway when you can soak up the ambience of the old-style Hollywood allure along this stretch? Gloria Swanson immortalized this place with her 1950's film, *Sunset Boulevard* – I imagine the debauched parties that were held in the exquisite homes here, the deals, the passion and the back-stabbing divorces that followed.

Alexandre's left elbow rests languidly on the sill of the open window, a content smile on his handsome face as the wind laps his dark hair – neither of us speaking, just enjoying the music; a golden oldie, *Hotel California*.

We're headed to Alessandra Demarr's house in Topanga Canyon, an interesting choice for an abode, once famous for being an artists' colony. She has invited us for lunch. I don't know why but I'm feeling nervous.

We arrive at our destination although it's not quite as elegant as I had imagined. Our low automobile has trouble on the bumpy, pot-holed driveway which crosses a creek where frogs are croaking – not your typical Hollywood mansion. Who is this woman? Everybody has been raving about her acting abilities and her brooding beauty. I'm already intimidated by her.

Alexandre parks the car in an opening where the driveway seems to come to an abrupt end. There are no houses about, or at least, none that I can see.

"Did we make a wrong turn?" I ask him.

"This is where the GPS directed us," he answers looking about. There are some lemon trees and rolling, scrubby hills in the distance and exposed bedrock. I even see a vegetable plot and beyond it a sort of shack. There's a black vintage

Porsche, dusty from passing along this makeshift driveway, no doubt, parked in a corner.

Just then, a figure appears from behind a hedge. A sunbeam of light catches her and she's wearing a long, black dress. She's slim and when she walks she glides as if she were not part of this world. For a second, I think I must have seen a ghost. But it must be Alessandra Demarr.

She grins at us and calls over, "You made it! Shows you must be in the top four percent of the intelligent population – you'd be amazed how this place has most people flummoxed." Her accent is vaguely Italian but obviously she has mastered the English language with a word like flummoxed. I look at Alexandre to see if he's as bowled over as I am by her beauty but he seems nonchalant as if seeing stunning women is part of his daily routine. He walks over to greet her and she immediately offers both cheeks.

I do the same. When I kiss her, her skin is soft as down and she smells delicious, of flowers and sweetness; femininity seeping from every pore. I step back and my breath hitches. Her thick, wavy hair is almost wild, like a teenager who hasn't brushed it in days. The dark locks hang down her bronzed back, her shoulders are strong but slight, her breasts pert but not large - you can see straight away that she isn't wearing a bra. Again, my eyes flit over to Alexandre to gauge his expression but he seems unimpressed by her. Her teeth are flaming white and her smile stretches across her face – a Julia Roberts sort of smile, warm and friendly.

"You know what? I'm starving," she cries, "as I skipped breakfast. D'you mind if we eat something straight away? I've prepared some antipasti to nibble on. Then I have a home-baked pizza cooking away in my wood-fired pizza oven."

I lick my lips. "Wow, you have a special pizza oven?"

"Made by hand by an Italian guy who lives nearby."

"Count me in!" I say.

"Where are you guys staying?" she asks.

"In Santa Monica," Alexandre tells her, edging towards the old Porsche. Is this car yours? It's a 356B, isn't it? Let me guess, 1962?"

"Yes, you're right. Poor thing, she needs a wash," Alessandra says with a laugh, and then links her arm in mine and pulls me towards the gap in the hedge from where she emerged five minutes ago like a dark angel. "Boys - always obsessed by bits of metal. Sniff about her, Alexandre, why don't you. Take her for a spin if you like – the keys are under the matt. Meanwhile, I'm going to feed your fiancée some snacks and give her a Bloody Mary. Come join us when you've finished with your testosterone boost. Anyway, I want to have your beautiful Pearl all for myself for a while and talk shop. Go for a drive, Alexandre - take my car along the coast."

Alexandre laughs out loud. "I can see you're desperate to get rid of me."

"Just for a little," she says, tossing her dark mane. "Come back in half an hour." She pulls me close and walks me away from him. I look behind and he winks at me in amusement, settling himself in the driver's seat of her classic car.

"See you in a bit," he calls out but Alessandra ignores him and rakes her gaze over me from my head to my toes. I'm wearing just a dress and some flat Greek sandals. A frisson of nervousness shoots through my body. No woman has ever looked at me this way before.

Once through the secret entrance in the hedge, I set my eyes on her house; a glorified barn made of wooden clapperboard and with a garden surrounding it of roses and more lemon trees. There's a little tree house looking like something out of *Robinson Crusoe* and a hammock resting between two small oaks. Beyond, I see a swimming pool, the water shimmering and breaking up into fragments of wavy light from dark blue mosaic tiles. The place is magical and from another world. The antithesis of 'Hollywood' or how you imagine it should be.

"He's cute your husband-to-be," she notes. "Very sexy French yet with a body like an American movie star – before and during filming, you know, when they're in perfect shape." She throws her head back and laughs. "He's very Alpha male. I bet he's a great fuck."

My mouth hangs open at what she just said. I'm speechless. I've known her for less than ten minutes. I reply simply, "Yes, he is."

"Of course, that's something I don't do anymore, but sometimes I miss that, you know, I miss that hard rod between my legs. But the whole man thing is such a bore. The pride, the bullshit and they just don't *smell* like we do. There's nothing like a woman's touch to make you feel like you've come home."

At the words 'woman's touch' she places her hand on the small of my back, letting her fingertips linger on my butt. I think of Natalie's warning and know that this woman is just beginning. I feel scared but thrilled and mostly, curious. Not even Alexandre came on so strong when he met me. Then it suddenly hits me. The names:

Alexandre.

Alessandra.

The yin and the yang.

Why is this woman making me feel as if I have no control? As if she's running the show? What happened to Pearl the ball-buster? Is it because Alessandra has no balls *at all* that I am at a loss for words?

I wriggle away from her contact but she grabs my hand instead and leads me to the pool.

"I'm hot," she says, and pulls her slinky dress over her head. She isn't wearing anything underneath. I glance awkwardly at her body. It's perfect. Her legs are smooth and long, her golden arms hang cool beside her hips. Her breasts are perfect and not surgically enhanced like so many actresses here, but curve upwards like full but perky teardrops, the nipples pert and small. She catches me watching her and smiles seductively, the dimple on one cheek reminds me eerily of Alexandre when he looks at me that way. It's uncanny. She's like a female version of him. He may be Alpha male but she's an Alpha female, all woman. Tough but whimsical, strong but softly feminine. Her eyes are also green like his but more feline. The similarities between them are frightening.

"Come in, the water's perfect," she entreats after she has accomplished a perfect swallow dive. Her hair is now sleek on her head and her eyes dark from run mascara – it makes her the epitome of a Hollywood 'femme fatale'.

I take off my sandals and dip my toes in the water. It really is warm and I'm tempted.

"Come on, don't be shy. Nobody's allowed in this pool with a swimsuit – only skinny-dipping here at all times. Come in, Pearl."

I slip my dress over my shoulders and stand there in my bra and panties. A matching, pale pink lace set from La Perla that Alexandre surprised me with the other day. I suddenly feel awkward and embarrassed – *I don't know this woman!* "You know what? I think I'll just dangle my feet in and wait until Alexandre gets back."

Her eyes narrow. "I won't bite, you know," and then she dives down and does a handstand, her elegant toes as pointed as a ballerina. She emerges from the water and looks like a Bond girl, all sex, heat, and temptress. As if she were designed by God to do nothing but seduce. I turn my eyes away and reach for my dress and struggle back into it – I should never have taken it off in the first place.

"Come, I'm going to make you the best Bloody Mary you've ever tasted," she tells me, water dripping off her tanned body as she grabs a towel.

I follow her to the kitchen which is country-style with a large pine table in the middle and baskets of dried flowers hanging from rafters and wooden beams. She takes a jug out of the refrigerator and pours the mixture into two tall glasses, garnishing them with sticks of celery and lemon slices. She hands me a glass. "Here, try this, it has a kick to it, a touch of horseradish. And help yourself to my spread of cold meats and *bruschetta*. The basil's fresh from the garden and the tomatoes from my greenhouse. Oh, and the olive oil I brought from Sicily where my grandparents are from. It has a nutty taste – quite delicious. Actually, let's take it all outside on the porch."

We put everything on a tray and take it outside where there's a wrought iron table and chairs. I delve into the *bruschetta* and can taste the sun in the tomatoes. It's true, the olive oil is sublime.

"So Pearl, Sam says we need to get to work on the script straight away."

"We?"

"You didn't think you'd be doing it all alone, did you?

No, no, my darling, this needs to be team work. I want the script to feel natural to me. You know, be part of who I am."

But you're an actress, ACT! "Oh, Sam made out that I'd be working with just the script writer, he never mentioned that you wanted to be involved," I say as politely as I can.

"Nuh, uh, I want to put in my twopence worth - I want to have my say."

"With all due respect, Alessandra, that wasn't part of the deal - it wasn't written into your contract."

She pouts her lips like a child. "But Sam wants me to be happy. Don't you?"

I take a sip of my Bloody Mary and then reply, "Well of course I do. I think an actor's input is very important but you know, too many cooks can spoil the broth."

"I just need a week with you. Just so you get to know me. I thought we could do a little improvisation, you know, have some fun."

"But we're only here for three days and then we have to get back to New York."

"Who has to get back to New York?" It's Alexandre. He comes up behind me and massages my shoulders. His touch is warm. I feel a wave of relief wash over me.

"Hi Frenchie," she says. "Hope you had fun with my car. Just trying to persuade your other half to stay on a few days. You know, we need to work on the script together before the others get hold of it. I want it to be our baby."

Alexandre laughs. I can see her flirtatiousness toward me is amusing him for some reason. Even calling him *Frenchie*. I feel as if I'm being fed to the wolves when he says to me, "Stay, darling. Enjoy this beautiful LA weather - relax a little. I can't as I've got a meeting in Montreal but there's no reason why you shouldn't."

"No way," I state assertively. "I have to get back to Manhattan. Natalie and I are working on something very important. She needs me in the editing room."

"Nonsense. That was your old job, remember? You're on features now, not documentaries. Natalie can take care of it all herself."

Whose side are you on? But all I say is, "I'll call Sam later and discuss it with him."

Just then a black cat shimmies its way around my bare legs. Its soft fur seductive, its purr intense.

"That's Lucifer," Alessandra tells me. "He's an Oriental. Isn't he the most handsome thing you've ever set your eyes on?"

The cat continues to purr and rub itself against me. Why do I have this ominous feeling that between Lucifer and Alessandra I don't stand a chance?

On the way back to the hotel Sam calls and confirms my worries. He wants Alessandra to 'assist' me with script changes. He tells me that the buzz is out and he wants this film to not only be a blockbuster but 'a classy blockbuster' - to have a chance to be nominated for an Academy Award. He feels that Alessandra is going to put it into a higher category because she's a 'real actress' and that we need to respect her wishes. He persuades me that I need to stay on a few more days, work with her before handing our changes over to the main script doctor. It all feels odd but as I am a virgin to the world of movie producing, I have to take his word for it.

Alexandre and I are sitting on the balcony of our luxurious room which overlooks the ocean. We're listening to the rhythmical sound of the surf and enjoying the feeling of being on vacation. I'm using this opportunity to discuss Sam and Alessandra with him and the rather bizarre situation.

Alexandre kisses my hand and says, "You make it sound as if it's some sort of punishment, Pearl – don't be so worried. How bad can it be to hang out in the sunshine with a beautiful actress while you fiddle about with the script?"

I sigh and fix my eyes on some surfers in the distance waiting to catch the next big wave. "She's just so persuasive, so...so..."

A mischievous smile spreads across his gorgeous face. "You're worried she's going to try and seduce you."

I look into his sparkling, amused eyes. "Yes."

"Ooh, how *dangerous*," he teases. *Don gaire oose,* his accent says.

"You're laughing about it now but what happens if she succeeds?"

"Sexy." He grins. "You can sex Skype me - the pair of you. I can't think of anything that would turn me on more. Two beautiful women getting it on together – two sexy female bodies entwined. Feel my cock," he says, taking my hand and putting it on his crotch, "I'm hard just thinking about you two together."

I rub his huge stiff erection through his jeans but I take my hand away and say, "Seriously, Alexandre, she means business, I can tell."

"Have some fun and come straight back home. I'm not worried, Pearl - not in the least."

"What, even if something were to actually happen? If she kissed me or...or...something more?"

He laughs, then presses his lips lightly on my temple.

"You're acting like this whole thing is a joke," I blurt out, a touch annoyed. "You might get jealous if something really did *take place*."

"Baby, she's a *woman*. How could I feel threatened by a woman?"

"What if a guy was coming on to me like this?"

Alexandre's smile fades and a flash of irritation dances in his green eyes. "That would be a whole different story. I wouldn't be allowing you to stay on in LA if some good-looking movie actor was demanding to co-write with you, I can tell you."

"But this is my *job*, you can't dictate to me who I work with!"

"I'm your fiancé. Didn't anyone ever warn you that Frenchmen have a possessive streak?"

I think of Daisy's wise advice: *He's a Latin man at heart.* "So you speak for the whole of France?" I ask with a laugh. "Or is it just a small minority of you who suffer from jealousy?"

"Not jealous, just claiming what belongs to me, that's all."

"Yet a woman couldn't possibly pose a threat? A woman isn't as powerful as a man, is that what you're saying?"

"Now you're twisting things. A woman doesn't have a penis."

I roll my eyes. "Ah, so it boils down to that, does it? The testosterone factor!"

"Maybe."

"So how would you feel about any of my past instances with men? How would you feel if you knew I'd been... promiscuous once upon a time?"

"Well, I happen to know that you weren't. You had a steady boyfriend, what was his name? Brad, that's right, the brother of your best friend…you dated him for four years and then you got married several years later. I don't see someone graduating summa cum laude and doing as well as you did academically, running around fucking lots of guys. Besides, it doesn't go with your personality."

"But let's just say, for argument's sake, that I *had* been running around, but it was—"

His cell rings and our conversation is over. It's his sister. Of course. As if she can hear what we're saying. Sometimes I wonder if she isn't sneaking recording bugs into the room to spy on us. Alexandre ends the call and now I feel compelled to speak out. This time, about Sophie.

"Alexandre - before we became engaged, you told me that you'd be opting out of HookedUp, that you and Sophie would go your separate ways."

"That's my plan. But all in good time, darling, all in good time. That's what HookedUp Enterprises is about – you and me. The two of us veering off in a new direction without Sophie."

I knit my brows. "When will 'good time' be?"

"As soon as the moment is right."

Getting nowhere with this, I return to Conversation One. "So to be completely clear, if something happened between me and Alessandra, hypothetically speaking, because I have no intention of letting her get her way, but if it did, you wouldn't consider that I was being unfaithful to you, or cheating on you in some way?"

"No, not all at."

"Just double-checking," I say.

Later, Alexandre goes surfing. He's dressed in a black, rubber, short-sleeved suit; his pecs defined and the bulge of his biceps accentuated by the outfit. I sit on the beach, a cardigan wrapped about me with my headphones on, listening to the perfect soundtrack by the Beach Boys, *Surfin' USA* as I watch my fiancé take each wave, moving his body in elegant swivels and jumps, flowing with the surf, bending and straightening his body at each perfect moment. He makes it look effortless, gliding with precision under each barreling wave, never flinching, never falling. He surfs as well as my father and that's really saying something. My stomach flips at his prowess – there's nothing like watching a man excel at sport.

I feel warm inside. I love this man more than ever.

7

It was pressed up against my face - I was gasping for air.

The boys' repeated use of the word 'cunt' was drumming in my ears. I hated that word – it was vulgar, demeaning to women - it made me feel cheap. I opened my eyes and saw the guy's long, skinny penis and his hand fumble again on my face. I could almost smell his hyped-up hormones - the whole scenario was suddenly grossly wrong – disconnected from the person I was inside. How did I get to this point? What happened? I felt sick at myself. I had only slept with Brad up until now. What had I been *thinking?*

Needle-dick pressed his thin, lanky erection on my mouth once more and shouted, "Suck my goddam dick, goddam it!"

I tried to maneuver myself up against the pillows but my head was spinning fast. The other guy was on top of me now and I could hardly breathe with his weight. "Guys," I said, "I don't want to do this. It was a bad idea. I'm drunk – I had too much tequila." I pushed my arms out at the blonde one's chest to get him off me but I couldn't even see past the other guy who was prizing open my lips with his clammy, smelly fingers trying to stuff his needle-like erection into my mouth. I gagged with repulsion.

"I'm going to be sick," I moaned, flailing my arms about and then tried to lever myself off the futon. "Please you two, I want to go home now...please somebody drive me home...I don't want to do this." My words were slurring but they understood. "Guys, I apologize for leading you on but I don't want to do this anymore. I made a big mistake, I just wanna go back to my dorm."

"Fuck you, bitch, suck my fucking dick!" He was pumping his hips into my face now, his hand grabbing my long hair like rope as his hot, sweaty balls were squashing against my closed lips.

"Get off!" I screamed, shaking my head and protecting my face with my hands. "Get the fuck off me, don't you *get* it, the party's OVER!"

"Get the fuck off her dude," the blonde one said pushing Needle-dick away from me.

Thank God, I thought, and I took a desperate lungful of air, so relieved his crotch was out of my face. But the blonde one then said, "I'll fuck her first and then you can have her after me."

"Fuck you, asshole, she was gonna suck me off!"

"She's wasted, dude, can't you see that? The slut's off her fuckin' face. It's really taking effect now. Let me have her first."

I started to scream and thrash about but the blonde one held my wrists together in a tight vice and the other one

345

muffled my mouth with his stinky palm. The blond was powerful, his football-trained muscles rippling beneath his chest. As I tried to sit up in one great burst of effort my head started to spin and I saw stars trail about the room in waves. He crashed back on top of me and forced my legs open with his knees. I tried to free my hands to scratch him but I was still immovable. He started pumping into me, his elbow still holding down my arms. My legs were kicking in the air but my attempt to get him off me was pathetically weak. This guy was super-strong. The more I shouted and thrashed the more turned on he got.

"That's right, fuck that horny little slut, dude – you know she wants it," Needle-dick chanted, getting a vicarious thrill out of watching his friend pound me while he simultaneously played with himself.

The blond's breath was hoarse with whiskey as he panted his way to a fast orgasm. Jesus, I realized - he wasn't even wearing a condom. He pulled out immediately and rolled off me. I lurched up to stand but the other one grabbed my ankles in a rugby tackle and I went flying face-down on the futon, my head slapping hard against the pillows.

"Don't think you can run off, you cock-teasing slut! I haven't even started yet." He rolled me over and smashed on top of me, lustily pinning me down. He too was brawny, my inebriated body, now feeling almost numb, was no match for his big, clumping frame. I clasped my legs tightly together so he couldn't enter me but he wrenched my thighs open and poked his weapon inside. I bashed his back with my fists but it was like pummeling a brick wall. Grunting, he thumped himself further inside my vulnerable spot forcing my legs further open. I screamed but nobody seemed to hear. Where was everyone? By this point, I blanked out. I held my head to the side and closed my lips tight. Of all the horrors, being kissed seemed the most disgusting of all. If I could at least keep my mouth untainted, I'd be winning on some level. I felt repulsed at myself, horrified that I got my sorry ass into this mess but all I could concentrate on was survival and somehow getting out of there. I eyed my clothing strewn about the floor and planned my getaway. The second he was done, I'd grab my stuff and charge out of the door. My shoes I'd leave, I'd need to be barefoot to move fast.

But then I heard another voice; a new guy barging into the room. My heart leaped into my stomach with both hope and dread. Would he save me? Or were things about to get much worse?

My lungs are heaving, my chest tight - I feel suffocated. I open my eyes and hear the reassuring sound of the surf and feel a cool morning breeze wafting through the window. The sheets are crumpled in a mess. I've been kicking, tossing and turning. I hear the shower next door – thank God, Alexandre is in the bathroom - he hasn't been witness to yet another of my nightmares.

I get out of bed, holding my stomach. I feel nauseous and think I may throw up. I sit on one of the comfy chairs on our balcony and breathe in the fresh, salty air. I already feel better. All of my past is surging back – the buried memories which I thought had been blanked out of my life. No wonder men grossed me out for so many years. Holy shit!

Alexandre finds me on the balcony. He's dripping wet with a towel tied around his middle of his toned abs. I look at him, taking in his physical beauty and wonder if he would have once been capable of doing what those boys did. Are all men pigs at heart? Is it just a question of circumstance?

Perhaps those guys are all happily married now with sweet, adoring children who look up to them and think that they're the best dads in the world. Wives who would never believe you if you enlightened them to what their husbands had once done in their college years.

Nobody would blame them. Guys are guys. Girls should know better, shouldn't they? Women should be smarter, not put themselves in precarious situations, not 'ask for it'. Not behave like 'sluts'.

Alexandre comes over to me and gives me a hug. "You look very pensive, Pearl. What's on your mind?"

"Just looking at the beautiful view thinking how wonderful it would be to live by the ocean."

"Funny, I was thinking exactly the same thing. I feel a real estate goblin knocking at my door. Shall we buy something here?"

"I still can't get used to this," I murmur.

"What?"

"Buying whatever your heart desires. It makes me feel guilty somehow."

"Hey, I work hard for these privileges. You do, too."

"I know. Just…well, we're still so lucky."

He holds my hands and pulls me off the chair. "Come to bed for a little while. You look so sexy, Pearl – I love you in the morning all ruffled up. It makes me want to get as close to you as is physically possible."

His body is so beautiful, my heart yearns for him, but the truth is that sex is the last thing on my mind, even with the man I love more than anything in the world. I melt into his strong arms and nuzzle my face against his warm chest and lick off a few droplets of shower water. He smells of soap and his own natural Alexandre magic – he is my elixir, the potion I need to keep me healthy and sane. I kiss him all over with sweet, girlish kisses. I want to be loving, not sexy, but it makes him groan and I can feel his erection press up against me.

I peel away the towel around his waist and see his beautiful anatomy, a penis that is substantial but wonderful because it has never tried to hurt me or force me. Even that time that he was angry with me, after I hadn't been honest with him about who I was and he came barging into my apartment...even then when he took me in the kitchen and ravaged me right there and then...he knew I was desperate for him and if I had told him to stop he would have.

I bend down and kiss him below his waist and breathe him in - his kindness, his patience, his genuine love. And then I let out a sigh of relief; gratitude that he is the way he is. I look up at him like a puppy.

He strokes my hair. "Pearl, darling, what's with the tears?"

"Tears of love," I reply.

He takes me over to the bed. I feel a tingle in my groin and realize that I'm moist between the legs. He does that to me because I trust him with every fiber of my being. His finger glides between my slickness and he slips it gently inside me, letting just a hint of pressure tantalize my clit. "You're so sexy, so wet. I need you baby, I need to be inside you. How I'm going to get through this week without making love to you, I don't know." His mouth is on mine, pressed hard over my lips and I respond with desire, meeting his tongue with little licks. He groans again and pushes me on the bed, his strong body covering me whole. I feel all-feminine underneath his strapping frame.

I open my legs and cling to his firm torso, my arms gripping around his muscular back and I claw my nails into him without meaning to. "Please fuck me," I beg, confused as to the double emotions I feel inside. I want to prove to myself that everything's okay. That no past ghosts can come between me and the man I love. "I need you and only you," I murmur.

He slips inside me, his mouth again on mine and he slowly pushes his way further between my cleft, his erection taut and full, stretching me open, his pubic bone pressing deliciously on my clit. He's staring into my eyes. He takes my clawed hands one by one away from his back and holds my wrists together above my head with just one hand. He is claiming me, dominating me - I can't escape from this position but it's okay because it's him. I feel the power of his extensive thick cock cramming me full, pumping into me. I push my hips higher to meet him and we thrust together in a natural rhythm, each time we meet all my nerves are tingling with need.

"Don't stop, I think I'm going to come – keep doing what you're doing," I moan.

"I'll never stop. Never."

I can feel it building, feel that glorious sensation of blood rushing up inside the core of me when he says, "I love being inside you, baby…fucking you…and you know what else?"

"Tell me," I plead. "Tell me what you love." I'm gyrating my hips now - I need to be as close as is humanly possible.

"I love kissing you, running my tongue along your sexy lips when I'm deep inside you." His mouth is on mine as he says this.

I'm thrusting hard, pressing my clit against him…this feels incredible. "Tell me what I can do to please you," I say with urgency. "Tell me what you love."

"When you suck my cock tightly with your pretty lips, when my cock is deep inside your hot mouth."

Suddenly, a vision of the needle-dick guy flashes through my mind. I catch my breath but not in a good way. I was on the brink of orgasm but not any more...I close my eyes to make the image go away and then open them again to drink in Alexandre, to reassure myself that he is different, that he has nothing to do with these repulsive snap-shots. I get back to my rhythm – I need this release - but more images come crashing through me...being forced, pushed, pulled, not being able to escape. Needle-dick again, suffocating my mouth. I feel panicked and smothered. Alexandre is pressing his body against me passionately and all I can think of are dirty, smelly cocks and rape and tequila and my body as weak and helpless as a rag doll....

"Alexandre, I can't...sorry, I feel sick...I think I'm going to barf....please..."

He freezes his position and releases my wrists but it's too late...I can feel his cock swelling and hot rush spurt deep inside me. He is instantly contrite and says, "I'm sorry, baby, I couldn't help myself; you're so fucking sexy the way you move. What's wrong, chérie?" Slowly, he pulls out. He rolls off me to give me the space I crave.

I lie there hyperventilating.

"Are you okay, baby?" He looks shocked with concern, puts his hand in mine and kisses my fingertips softly. He pulls me off the bed and ushers me to the bathroom. I stand there with my face in my hands, my head bent down. I turn on the shower faucet. I need to get clean. I need to wash this morning's dream away. I feel the sticky mess of Alexandre's cum trickling down my inner thighs and even though it emanates from pure love and goodness, from a man who would lay his life down for me, I feel sickened.

Penises. Cocks. Dicks. Blowjobs. Semen.

I am disgusted.

I'm hoping this feeling will fade but as the day draws on it gets worse – the straw that breaks the camel's back is a video clip Natalie sends me of her documentary about child trafficking for the insatiable sex industry. Men are pigs whichever way you look at it. Aided, sadly, by women sometimes, even by mothers selling their own daughters - but still, who is fucking these young girls (and sometimes boys) - women? No, men are the devils with their penises ruling their brains. Not women but *men*.

Poor Alexandre is the innocent victim of my sudden re-pulsion towards all things male, although when I look into his beautiful eyes I don't feel anything but love and compas-sion for him. My heart aches – he is my everything. None of this is his fault.

But the idea of being penetrated, right now, revolts me. Please God, let this feeling go away. I love sex with him so much...

Luckily, he's flying out late tonight so I won't have to explain myself. On two occasions this afternoon, my whole story nearly escaped my lips but something held me back. Why subject him to my baggage? Give it a few days – let the memory ride itself out and I'll be back to normal. At least the dreams are unleashing it all, revealing the truth of what really happened that night – things my conscious mind had blocked out.

It wasn't my fault as I had always led myself to believe. Or was it? If I tell Alexandre I'd have to explain to him how I got myself into that predicament in the first place. A threesome with two footballers? His vision of me as the perfect summa cum laude student with the unblemished past would be shattered. No - let his perception of me remain untainted, at least until I feel confident enough to reveal everything. Remembering all this is bad enough, but if he finds it hard to accept? If he has it lurking in the back of his mind every time we have sex, then what?

I need time. I need a few days to think this all through.

We spend the day walking along the beach and then pass by Venice to see the wild and wonderful attractions. There's a hippie guitar player zipping along on roller-skates and a bottle-blond Tarzan character working out in an outdoor gym with massive weights, right by the Boardwalk for everyone to see. There are volleyball and paddle tennis courts and funky shops, cafés and vendor booths lined along this long stretch on Ocean Front Walk. We meander, people-watching, taking in the sights of colorful street performers and beautiful young things strutting their stuff in skimpy outfits – Venice Beach is an exhibitionist haven.

The distractions are perfect; enough for Alexandre to not realize that anything is particularly wrong. When he asked me earlier what happened in bed this morning and I told him that it must have been the smoothie I drank the day before - a mild case of food poisoning - he believed me.

And like food poisoning I *will* kick this out of my system. I will. It is in the *past*, something that happened so long ago it has no business screwing up my life now. I won't let it dominate my thoughts; I won't let it make me bitter and angry. I was a different person then, anyway – I made a foolish decision, and I paid a price for it. Does that mean it has to affect my life now? That I have to keep paying that price? Affect the person I am today?

As Alexandre and I continue our walk - arm in arm, I notice people looking at my fiancé, eyeballing him up and down with come-on stares and I feel proud. Yes, he's handsome, girls and boys, and you know what? He's *mine*.

Perhaps the break of a few days will be good for us. I can sort my scrabbled head out. I'll call Daisy and talk it through with her – maybe even see a therapist here.

I crook my arm tighter with his. "I'll miss you."

He winks at me. "It's only five more days. You'll be so busy you won't even notice."

"And you? What will you be doing?"

"Making money for us to get a pad here."

"A pad?"

"Something wonderful. Further up the coast in Malibu. A house overlooking the water where I can surf and you can walk along the beach with Rex and swim if you're brave enough to brace the cold – would you like that?"

"No, it would make me miserable. Too much of a punishment."

He laughs and pulls me closer. "You don't have to go to work, you know."

"What d'you mean?" I ask, confused.

"You don't have to prove yourself to me. I know you're clever at your job but if you feel like packing it all in and do nothing but read novels and lie about in the sun, I wouldn't think any less of you."

I grin. "I don't know how long I'd last doing that. Sounds tempting, though. But I've always worked. Even at school I had a Saturday job – I don't know if lazing about is my style."

"Well, just letting you know that you have a get-out clause. Just because we started HookedUp Enterprises doesn't mean you have to be chained to it for forever."

"What about you? You wouldn't ever have to work another day in your life if you didn't want to, either, but you keep going with all these endless meetings all over the place."

"Just say the word, baby, and we can go and live in a tree-house in Thailand. Or join your father in Kauai."

"You mean that?"

"I think so. Although, the truth is, I've always worked, too. I had jobs from the age of nine."

"But that's illegal in France, isn't it? Children working?"

"Nothing about my life was legal when Sophie was playing mother to me after we left home – after we left that monster," he spits out between his teeth, his mouth bitterly tight.

"Your mother must feel so guilty about not having come with you when she had the chance."

"She does. Her guilt is almost tangible. Every time I see her, her eyes spell out regret."

"You know that Edith Piaff song?"

"Why is it, Pearl, that you and I can read each other's minds? I was just thinking the same thing! *Non, je ne regrette rien…*"

He starts singing. He has a good voice, perfectly in tune.

"*Do* you regret anything, Alexandre?"

He squeezes my hand. "I regret not having kissed you sooner."

"No, seriously, if you could re-live your life what would you choose to do differently?"

"I am who I am because of all my choices, the good and

the bad. Perhaps if I'd done everything in the perfect order I'd be married to Laura, and you and I would have never met."

"D'you still think about her?"

"She's a dear friend, we shared a past, of course I still care for her and worry about her wellbeing."

A clown comes bounding in front of us, interrupting our heart-to-heart conversation. *Not Now!* I glare at him and his painted face and turn my head back to Alexandre, "So you don't agonize over choices you made in the past or about things you wish you hadn't done?"

"Sometimes you don't have a choice, Pearl. Sometimes external forces choose for you."

"Natalie says we always have a choice."

"Well maybe Natalie's had a relatively lucky life. Perhaps she's never been a victim of circumstance or ever had to battle with personal demons."

"Your main demon being your father?"

"And the tidal wave he left behind."

"What happened to your father, anyway?" I ask, relieved that for the first time Alexandre's opening up about his past. I need to strike while the iron's hot – I may not get this opportunity again.

"He disappeared."

"Really?"

The look on Alexandre's face is a chilling mask when he says, "Yes, really, Pearl. The nasty piece of shit just disappeared into thin air."

"Aren't you worried he could re-surface one day? I mean, not that he could hurt you now that you're a grown man, but psychologically speaking. He could come back to haunt you in some way."

"No. He won't come back. He's gone for good."

"How can you be so sure? Sometimes when you think something's buried it can come back with a vengeance just when you least expect it."

"Because as far as I'm concerned, that bastard's buried for good." Alexandre's eyes are cold fire, the green in them flicker to a pale, icy gold and for just a second I feel as if I'm looking into the gaze of a man capable of murder.

8

Two days have passed. I've been working with Alessandra at her house in Topanga Canyon. Her attitude has changed. She's less cocky than when we first met, as if she had something to prove then – as if she felt competitive with Alexandre in some way. Since that first day, she hasn't been coming on to me or flirting. Thank God. We've made huge headway with the script. She has a sharp sense of humor and has managed to slip in a lot of great one-liners. They still haven't chosen her leading man – everything is up in the air while Sam awaits decisions from tough-cookie agents and managers. Whatever, whoever, the actor will be a star. If this film is successful, I'll get a nice percentage of the box-office. This is a win-win situation for all of us.

I've been so busy that I haven't had a chance to speak to anyone about my nightmares.

When I get back to the hotel after a full day's work, I call Daisy. I need her sound advice. It's strange – when you get older you become more and more picky about who you spend time with and in whom you confide. I used to wear my heart on my sleeve and had never since associated bottling up my feelings with that dreaded night. But when I think about it, it was after that that everything changed – when I lost my trust in people. I had never put two and two together. Because I had not been aware, until now, of how it affected me psychologically.

I lie back on my deliciously comfortable hotel bed leaning against the padded headrest and I stretch out my legs. Daisy takes a long time to pick up.

"Amy stop that," she finally shouts into the receiver.

"Daisy?"

"Oh, hi Pearl. Sorry, Amy's being all needy right now. One sec. Amy - if you want my attention then you need to sit quietly with your coloring book for ten minutes and then we'll choose your Halloween outfit together. Is that a deal? Ten minutes only, I promise, then I'm all yours."

I can hear Amy's willful voice soften and she says, "Okay Mommy, but just ten minutes. I'm watching the clock, you know."

"Sorry about that, Pearl. Johnny's away on a business trip so she's being really demanding. He's been away a lot lately."

"I'll try to squeeze everything I have to say in ten minutes," I say jokingly.

"I know. Foolishly I taught her how to tell the time and now she's got me on a tight leash. She doesn't miss a trick."

I lay bare to Daisy the details about my nightmares and how I've been keeping their content a secret from Alexandre - bearing in mind, I let her know, about what she said about him being a 'Latin man at heart.'

"Okay, Pearl, first off, since we had that conversation in my office? Things are not the same as I had previously imagined."

I plump another cushion behind my head. "What d'you mean?" I ask - sure that whatever advice she gives me will be sound.

"Well, how you are describing the situation now colors things very differently. You'd always led me to believe that you had been totally up for that threesome with the two footballers but you were so out of it, that later, you couldn't remember what happened."

"Yeah, well that's still true. I mean, it's only since these flashbacks - these dreams, that I realize there was more to the whole story."

"This is what you have to figure out — were these actual *flashbacks* or are they just dreams, figments of your imagination?"

"They're so detailed, so in depth that I think it's what went down that night."

"When you confided in me years ago about this, I remember you saying that Brad found you alone in the boys' room drunk as a skunk, naked in a stranger's bed with used condoms strewn about and vomit all over the bedclothes. And he freaked out but took you home and then, basically, never spoke to you again and that was the end of your relationship."

"That's what I thought. I mean, yes, that's what happened afterwards when he found me, but before that I can't be sure what took place. At the time it was just a blank. I'd blacked-out."

"So now it's all coming back to you? What triggered the

memory?"

"I don't know – my upcoming marriage, all that talk we had about being honest with Alexandre and...this color...electric-blue...Rex was given an electric-blue collar and it must have just made something click – I remembered this skirt I had that was also electric-blue. I wore it that night. Something about remembering that color must have activated a part of my brain that had been shut off all that time."

"So then what happened after the third guy came through the door?"

"That's what I can't remember."

"You said your body was practically numb? Like a rag doll with no strength in your muscles?"

"Yes. I remember that clearly. I had no strength to move – I must have been really inebriated."

"Sounds like a lot more than just tequila to me."

"But I didn't smoke any weed or anything, I wasn't stoned."

"Sounds to me as if you'd been slipped some Ecstasy or something, maybe even Rohypnol or Valium."

"Ecstasy?"

"I took it once, twenty years ago. Big mistake. Well, a lot of people were doing it then, it was all the rage – I thought it would be a laugh. I remember being exactly like that, like a flopsy marionette. I couldn't move a muscle. Everybody else was dancing all night but with me it had the opposite effect. I spent the night with this guy who I thought was God's gift to the human race but when I woke up the next morning I was horrified. HORR. IF. IED."

The way Daisy tells me this with her exaggerated British accent makes me chuckle. Comic relief from a serious subject.

361

"That's why it's called Ecstasy," she goes on. "People are convinced they're madly in love. You see everything with rose-tinted glasses while you're high. But actually, those bastards probably gave you Valium or something. These types of drugs affect everyone differently but mixed with all those shots of tequila? You wouldn't have stood a chance, Pearl."

I twiddle my hair in thought, retracing my nightmare. "Maybe you're right…in the dream one of them said something like…what was it? Like…'It's really taking effect now.' You think they spiked my drink?"

"Hey, it happens all the time at colleges and parties, that's one of the reasons they call it 'date rape.' I *bet* they slipped something in your drink. It can cause retrograde amnesia which is obviously what happened to you. I mean, it's common for people to wake up the next morning without any memory of huge chunks of the night before. It's really rife in Britain with all this binge drinking going on with young girls. There are so many cases of fake taxi drivers raping them – you know, they get into a car thinking they're going home and end up being violated. Some even murdered. But I'm digressing – what happened to you was a classic case of date rape. Even if you had gone to the doctor for a test the next day, a lot of these date rape drugs don't even show up in urine samples."

"How d'you know all this?"

"It was part of my training. Date rape is way more common than people think and it usually goes unreported – but often it's revealed years later in therapy sessions. Like with incestual rape, people often don't want to admit to themselves that they were abused, let alone confide in someone else – it can take years to resurface sometimes. Or like with you, the victim genuinely forgets about it – blocks it out and something triggers the memory years later. It could be a smell, a word, a movie or book – in your case it was a color that was the trigger reminding you of that skirt and everything that followed."

"The truth is, though, I asked for it, Daisy. I was dancing around in that little skirt coming on to them, flirting like crazy. And I agreed to go back to their place – they didn't force me. I was even looking forward to having a threesome. At first it seemed like a great idea."

"Oh so you think you asked to be basically, *gang raped?* This was not your fault, Pearl. This was *not* your fault. *Do you hear me?*"

"I felt so ashamed at the time and I still feel ashamed even speaking about it now."

"You and every other person who ever gets raped. It's classic – the victim feels like somehow it was their fault and they were asking for it. Their lipstick was too bright, the skirt too short, they shouldn't have worn high heels that evening - they should never have got into that car. The list goes on."

"The worst thing is that I suddenly feel repelled by sex – the repulsive details are all flooding back and I feel grossed out."

"That's why you need to tell Alexandre about what happened."

"But you said—"

"Pearl, that's when I thought this was about a fun, wild night out during your university years - something he really didn't need to know about. But this? This is affecting your *relationship*. This is a whole different kettle of fish. It was *rape*. Just because it happened ages ago doesn't make it any less serious."

"He might think it was my fault."

"I doubt it very much. We all have a past – we've all done crazy things. This was eighteen years ago, for fuck's sake."

"Just yesterday he said how he couldn't imagine me ever having been promiscuous or wild – he thinks I was perfect."

"Well, wakey, wakey, Alexandre Chevalier, you are engaged to be married to a mere mortal! Pearl, if he can't stomach what happened to you and if he can't deal with it in an adult way then you really shouldn't be marrying him anyway. Listen, Amy says my time is up and I don't like breaking promises. Call me tomorrow and we'll finish this conversation. It's good you're letting it all out, anyway."

"Bye. Thanks, Daisy, thanks for listening. Say thank you to Amy for being so generous with her mom's time."

"Please, stop making yourself sound like a bore. Of course I'm listening, This shit is serious and you need to sort through it. We'll talk tomorrow. Love you, and thank you for trusting me with all this, I know it's painful."

I get out my iPad and look up the words online that Daisy mentioned, 'retrograde amnesia.' I always thought that was a nifty trick they used in soap operas but never could have imagined it would happen to anyone in real life – to totally blank something out. At least, not unless you've had some sort of physical head trauma from a car accident or something. Although, I understand now that it *was* trauma - only mental.

If I'd remembered the course of events at the time I could have defended myself – Brad would have seen me in a different light, not as some complete slut with no morals at all. Not that having a threesome is wrong, no. But I was going steady with him. The fact that he admitted he had slept with Alicia didn't let me off the hook. I broke his heart. Broke his trust in me. We would have gotten married if he'd been able to forgive me. Maybe we would be together now.

I take a deep breath and try to stop the self-blame flooding over me. It's true what Alexandre said, that you have to accept your mistakes, the good and bad because they define who you are as a person. Perhaps if that had never happened with the footballers I wouldn't be with Alexandre today. Then again, maybe I would have had children. Who knows which path would have been the 'right' one. Are our lives destined by fate or does every single choice we make offer a gamut of possibilities like a CD with several different tracks? I chose that song, *All I Wanna Do Is Have Some Fun*…and that's where it led me that night.

I am mulling all this over and thinking about a light dinner in tonight at the hotel restaurant, when my cell rings. It's Alessandra.

Her smoky voice sounds languid and rich. She doesn't even say 'Hi, Pearl' but begins, "All we ever do is work, you and I. I think we should just hang out this evening together."

I'm taken aback. "Well, I—"

Her voice is almost a whisper. "Actually, I'm cheating. I'm already here - down in the lobby – thought I'd take a chance."

"Wow, Alessandra, what if I'd been busy?"

"I figured you'd be free. I'm on my way up to your room."

When I open the door a few minutes later, I'm stunned. It's like action replay, except the seductive person standing before me uninvited is not Alexandre but Alessandra. She stands there dressed in a clingy, silky dress – almost see-through - her nipples erect, her cascading, dark hair wild and untamed about her shoulders. She's holding a chilled bottle of Dom Pérignon and some pink roses. Déjà-vu. Except, she also holds a glass vase for the flowers.

It plops out of my mouth, "You look pretty," I say. My eyes fall on the roses. "These are for me?"

"No, they're for your alter ego, the Pearl who takes work way too seriously, the Pearl who needs a little sweetening up."

I try to stifle a grin. It's true, we've been working non-stop on the script and not spoken about anything else. "Come in, Alessandra – sorry, it's a little messy, I was just choosing something to wear. I always end up rooting through every piece of clothing I have, never knowing what to put on. I thought I'd go downstairs and eat in the hotel restaurant – the food's great here –join me if you like."

"I love this place," she says in her husky voice – "so romantic. Let's open the champagne while it's still cold. Oh look, you have a balcony, how lovely." She steps onto the balcony and surveys the ocean view. The breeze blows her dress revealing the outline of her thighs and ass. No underwear. Another thing she and Alexandre have in common. Oops, maybe we won't be dining downstairs after all; her dress is no better than a negligee. Unless I lend her a pair of my panties. No, far too intimate, perhaps room service is a better idea.

I fill up the vase Alessandra brought with water and place the flowers inside and then grab a couple of flute glasses by the mini-bar. "Thanks so much for the roses, they're beautiful."

"The rule is - this evening we won't mention the film, is that a deal?"

"It's a deal," I agree. I look at her, my eye like a camera

and know that this woman is on her way to movie stardom. It's obvious. Her beauty is breathtaking. Her skin is olive-colored but flawless, an advantage these days with high definition cameras showing up every blemish. Her eyes flick up at the corners and her dark lashes are like frames making the green greener, the flecks of gold more pronounced.

She pops open the cork and some of the champagne bubbles over. She licks her fingers, her tongue slowly rimming her top lip. It's as if she and Alexandre are twins; their mannerisms are the same. Am I in the middle of a soap opera? First this retrograde amnesia business and now this. Am I about to discover that Alexandre's mother gave up one of her babies for adoption and Alexandre and Alessandra are long-lost brother and sister? She and I have been working so hard on the script, I haven't had a moment to really observe this woman but everything about her fascinates me, mostly because she reminds me of him.

We clink glasses and make a toast to the success of the film but burst out laughing simultaneously when it occurs to us that we've both broken our rule to not mention it this evening She tells me about her hybrid upbringing, that she was born in Chicago but then moved to Italy when she was six, raised in Florence by her single mom who had at that point divorced her father, an American. She spent her summer vacations with her grandparents in Sicily. She returned to the States when she was sixteen and modeled in New York before landing a commercial and an agent. Little by little, she found her way into the theatre although it was a slow progression. Finally, she got the part that won her the Tony Award and things have been going skyward from there.

She takes another sip of champagne. "The problem is I still have my Italian accent - it's hard to shake off one hundred percent."

"But it hasn't harmed your career up until now, has it? I mean, people love an accent, it makes you exotic."

"So far I've been lucky, but I want to be in the same league as Charlize."

Tough, I think. Trying to compete with the best of the best. "Well you can have elocution lessons. There must be so many voice coaches in LA. I like your accent, though. I think it would be a shame to lose it completely."

She puts her hand on my thigh. "You do?"

"Yes, I think European accents are sexy."

"Well, I suppose you would, Pearl. Tell me about your husband-to-be. Is he really as hot as he looks?"

"I thought you were gay," I reply with suspicion. *Keep away from him, femme-fatale!*

"I am. But you know what turns me on? Lying in bed with my girlfriend and watching a man fuck a woman in a porno movie. Seeing a big, hard, thick cock stretch open up a sweet tender pussy and fuck her. Or even two guys together making out."

I'm feeling the effects of the champagne and I laugh.

"Why is that funny? Didn't you know that that's a lesbian fantasy? A lot of us still love to imagine big cocks but we want to be once-removed from them, if you see what I mean." Alessandra picks up the hotel phone and nonchalantly dials room service. "Hi, can you bring us an ice-cold bottle of Dom Pérignon and some sandwiches? A mixture of snacks, I don't care, a mixture of vegetarian and whatever. Thanks."

My eyes widen. *So cocky! She didn't even ask me.*

"It's on me," she lets me know. "Now, where were we? Yes, big, huge, throbbing cocks—"

Cock...the word brings unwelcome images to my brain and I feel my eyes well with tears. The needle-dick memories flash back and a recollection of that third guy who came into the room envelops me like a blanket smothering me to suffocation. He was fat, sweaty, his penis repulsive; I remember him struggling with a condom...I cover my face with my hands in disgust – the twisting agony of what happened wrenching memories out of my body...I start hyperventilating again, my breath short. I try to suck in a lungful of air.

Alessandra steadies my shaking shoulders. "Pearl, what the hell is wrong?"

And it all comes gushing out; the whole story from beginning to end. I reveal everything to her. I'm in tears now, the memories of what happened to me thick with sordid details. The faces of the guys, how they held me down, how their repulsive penises poked and prodded as if I were nothing more than an orifice.

"The one with the fat, flaccid walnut of a penis couldn't even get it up – it made him angry," I wail in between sobs.

Alessandra is holding me in her arms. "That's right, Pearl – let it all out."

"He felt humiliated in front of his friends. There were more. I can't remember how many...but there were more. I puked up – that's when they finally left me alone. They left me there covered in vomit and semen and–"

She holds my trembling body close against her. "Now, now, my beautiful Pearl, they can't hurt you anymore."

Room service arrives and I pick at the food, hardly being able to swallow. Telling Alessandra all this was the last thing I wanted to do. So unprofessional, mixing my private life with a work situation. I should never have agreed to allow her into my hotel room, letting her look into my heart and soul. I've been an idiot.

I sit up straight and try to compose myself but I feel exhausted, spent, all my energy sucked out of me.

I don't protest when she takes control and says, "I'm going to run you a bath, Pearl, and you can just lie back and relax. Think of lovely things. Any time you have a nasty image in your mind replace it with this bunch of pink roses."

The bath is just what I need. I recline my head back, unwinding in the hot bubbly water and do as Alessandra tells me. I picture the pink roses climbing up the stone walls at Alexandre's house in Provence and the scent of lavender, the intense purple-blue of the fields, the white butterflies fluttering about like confetti. I remember the buttery croissant I ate for breakfast, the taste of homemade cherry preserve – from the cherry trees in his garden.

Alessandra puts on some music – *Woman* by Neneh Cherry – a powerful song. I close my eyes. It's healthy that all the bad memories have resurfaced but now they can go back where they came from, six feet under where they belong. It's done. It's over – I don't want the past taking over my perfect world, screwing up my life.

My lids are shut tight when I feel the bath water ripple. I open them and see two smooth, golden legs in the tub. Alessandra is joining me. *This is not what I planned!*

"Scoot over," she says, slipping herself behind me before I have a chance to object. She eases her slim body to the back of the tub and maneuvers around me so I have no choice but to lean on her, my back pressed against her breasts, her legs splayed open on either side of me. *Double déjà-vu!* But this time with her, not Alexandre.

"Use me as a cushion. Just relax," she says soothingly,

pulling my shoulders back.

I'm too tired to disagree. I lean against her. She begins to lather my back with a delicious-smelling body wash as she sings along to the song…about being a woman's world. Her hands are firm but soft as she massages my shoulders with her fingertips, kneading out the knots – the stress.

"This feels good," I tell her, realizing it's past the point of protesting. Anyway, who cares? What's the worst that can happen? Alexandre said himself he wouldn't mind. She's a woman – she can't hurt me. A little rubdown can't be a bad thing.

She continues with this wonderful massage for a good ten minutes. I'm like putty in her agile hands. Then her fingers run themselves from my shoulders to my front and tantalizingly across my breasts. She isn't touching the nipples, just circling around and around – all part of her skillful massage. But my body does things my conscience can't control: my nipples pucker and to my surprise I'm silently begging for her to tweak them – the massage has got me really turned-on. I don't want her to know but she senses something as her hands graze across each nipple. I feel a shooting desire connect the pulse with my core and my clit starts to throb. She begins to flutter her fingers on my nipples and I can't help it – a little moan escapes my lips and I lean back closer against her. Uh oh, that's done it.

"I thought you'd like that," she whispers, her lips grazing my ear. I shudder with secret, quiet desire. "Your tits are beautiful, Pearl. People pay thousands to get their breasts to look just like yours."

"They're real," I tell her trying to feign a normal conversation.

She flickers her pinkie seductively on one erect, rosy nip-

371

ple. "Yes, I know, I can always tell."

Her hands have moved back to my shoulders and neck as she continues her soft touch. She's running the very tips of her fingers along the base of my hairline – my hair is pinned up in a messy bun. Shivers tingle through my entire body.

"I'm not gay you know, Alessandra," I blurt out, trying to convince myself that this has nothing to do with me. *I am an innocent bystander in all this!*

"No," she murmurs, "of course not, but who's going to arrest you, huh? Just relax, I'm just giving you a little massage, that's all. You're holding in a lot of tension."

She begins to brush my neck with her lips with whispery kisses and then her fingers are back on my nipples again. I feel the need build up inside me. Being with Alexandre has awoken my sexual appetite, a yearning for orgasms and now is no exception. She's getting me worked up. Her hand moves under the water now, searching between my thighs. My breath gasps in anticipation. *I don't want her to stop… yet this is…wrong!*

My conscious mind wants to tell her to leave me be but I can't, I'm simply too turned-on. Her finger taps my clit gently making me flex my hips. I want more and she can sense that. Oh yes, she can sense it alright. She presses her palm flat on my pussy and the pressure of it has me moving up against her hand. She makes circular motions almost imperceptibly but it's just enough to feel myself throb as if my heartbeat were right down there. With the other hand she tugs at my nipple, kneading it softly between her fingers. She slips her index finger from her right hand inside my slick opening, continuing with the pressure on my clit.

"I'm not gay," I repeat, sensations unspooling, my hips

grinding on her hand in a ripple of carnal desire, "but this does...aah...oh yeah...feel...so...good."

"Doesn't it? Your pussy's so sweet, Pearl, I'd like to flicker my tongue against your clit." She presses her hand harder on my purring V-8 now and I feel myself come in a thunderous pound. My back arches as I rock my hips forward pushing on her hand - the orgasm pulsates deep inside me, her finger still there exploring my G-spot, making the double-sensation linger and flutter in waves of orgasmic bliss.

"The best way to relieve tension is through climax," she says quietly. "If you ever have a migraine you know what to do."

Sensations of shameful bliss are still pulsing through me, my clit tingling with aftershocks, the base of me beautifully released. *I am not a lesbian! How has this happened?* "Alessandra, this was a one-off. I can't let this happen again."

But she just laughs. "Don't be so serious, Pearl. It's just a release, that's all. Your body needed it."

"I'm not going to reciprocate," I warn her. I can't see her expression as she's behind me but I can imagine it. I have a picture in my mind's eye of a cool smirk etched across her beautiful face.

And it scares me.

No woman has touched me like this. Ever.

And I'm shocked at how I responded with so much desire.

I awake to the sound of the Skype ring on my iPad and

hazily turn on my side. I didn't have any nightmares last night, I had night mares, or should I say, a night of *mares*. No stallions. I dreamed about females - beautiful breasts, slender long legs. *This is crazy!* Still, I guess it's better that visions of women erase the grotesque, panting images of what was there before.

Ugh, I can't even think about it.

I unlock my tablet. It's Alexandre.

I quietly recount my adventure yesterday evening – I'm wondering if he'll be as delighted as he said he'd be. Perhaps he might get jealous.

But no - jealousy doesn't seem to hold a place with him when a woman is involved. He responds huskily, "If my plane wasn't about to take off right now, I'd want a full recount of every single, tiny, sexy detail and I'd pleasure myself while you recounted each horny moment. I swear to God you've got me all worked up thinking about it."

I can hear the jet's engines roaring in the background. "I'm not proud of what I did," I say tentatively. "It just sort of….unfolded. It won't happen again, I promise."

"Pearl, have some fun, don't take it all so seriously."

I freeze. Isn't that exactly what *she* said? "I have some-thing really important to tell you. Something that's been responsible for my bad dreams….hello?…Alexandre?"

The line's gone dead. I call him back on both Skype and his cell number. Nothing.

I roll out of bed and amble to the bathroom. I miss Al-exandre – it strikes me that all I really want to do is be with him and Rex, cozy together watching a movie or a walk in the park. Work used to be so important to me but now less so. I mull over the 'lady of leisure' fantasy he sold me yesterday, lying by the beach reading novels. Or the pair of us escaping to Thailand and living in a tree-house – leaving the 'real' world behind. Usually when you cook up a fantasy it's unattainable but for us it could be a reality. A sweet thought. But the Devil makes work for idle hands, doesn't he?

With this in mind I shower quickly, get myself ready and set off for work in my outrageous low and vast, powder blue Cadillac that feels like a ship. I swing by my favorite smooth-ie stall feeling cruel that I blamed it for my 'food poisoning.' In a few hours I'll be able to speak to Alexandre and we can have a long talk. I want to get these dreams off my chest, I want to lay it all open – I'm sick of harboring this secret.

As I cruise along Pacific Coast Highway, sipping my strawberry smoothie, I wonder if I could adapt to this city – smoothies, the ocean, palm trees swaying in a warm breeze, beautiful people everywhere – what isn't there to love?

This is my last day with Alessandra – our last day work-ing on the script. I have to admit that it's been fun but right now the last thing I need is the possibility of more complica-tions. It was a highly pleasurable one-off experience in the bathtub but I mustn't let her have her seductive way again. *Watch out Pearl, be on your guard.*

It's cooler today so we write inside. We settle in the liv-ing room, which is an extension of her open-plan kitchen. The place is decorated with Navajo hand-woven rugs and an eclectic mix of oil paintings that are copies of Klimt and Frida Kahlo. There's a wood-burning stove in the corner with a brick surround and bookcases stuffed with self-help books and...dare I say it, Russian novels. Spooky...a woman after my own heart.

"You have the same reading taste as me," I remark, set-ting down my bag and sitting on a big arm chair.

"I knew we'd think alike, Pearl. We're mirrors of each other."

I want to tell her that she's the female image of Alexandre, not me, but I say nothing. The less we talk about my fiancé, the better.

She pulls back her long, dark hair into a ponytail, settles cross-legged on the sofa and says, "I told you so much about my life, my family in Italy and stuff but you've revealed nothing about yourself."

Only the most personal thing ever. "Oh, my life has been very normal," I hedge. "You know, school in New York, college, jobs, marriage, divorce, and now I'm engaged."

"Engaged to one of the richest men in the world."

"Well, I don't focus on that aspect. Money doesn't motivate me."

"What does motivate you, Pearl?"

"Passion. In work. In love. In ideas. I think you have to really believe in what you do on every level. You know, morally and spiritually speaking."

"Do you believe in *Stone Trooper?*"

Her question grabs me by the throat. Do I believe in this Hollywood blockbuster? Is it important on the grand scale of things? Or is what Natalie is doing so much more significant? "Of course I do," I reply with a half lie. "I mean, I think the fact that your character Sunny is gay is important. A movie with a message. So many people are homophobic."

"Are you homophobic, Pearl?"

"No! Of course not. I believe in gay rights, I believe in same-sex marriage, I believe in—"

"You kept trying to convince me last night that you weren't gay. Why is it okay with you that others are gay but not yourself?"

"But I—"

"Why label things? Why is it so important for you to limit yourself, to pigeon-hole yourself?"

"I….I…" I stammer, "I guess I've never thought of myself as being locked in some pigeon-hole." For some strange reason I feel hurt by her accusation. *I am liberal-minded!*

Her voice softens at my injured expression. "You're so tender, Pearl. So vulnerable. I hope your husband-to-be realizes how lucky he is."

"He tells me every day."

She locks her eyes with mine and says quietly, "When you came by my hand yesterday in the bath, I could feel you tremble, feel your beautiful little pussy-pearl quiver – you know, just the thrill of it, the excitement gave me an orgasm too."

But how? You didn't even touch yourself.

She goes on in her husky voice, "All I had to do was give myself a tight clench and I felt little ripples of pleasure. Not a bumper-big, mind-blowing orgasm but, you know…a little thrill. Touching your hard nipples and those beautiful boobs of yours – seeing how turned on I got you…well…you got me horny, Pearl." She bites her lower lip. "My pussy flutters a little when you look at me with your big blue eyes. But you know that, don't you? You know you penetrate me with your intense, come-on stare, don't you?"

"Alessandra! I'm not trying to seduce you!"

She chortles with laughter. "Just kidding. Where's your sense of humor? Lighten up."

I sigh with relief but am alarmed when I can sense my panties have got a little moist after what she just said. I shuffle my position on the couch and sit up straight. "We need to finish this script," I say assertively. "I'm leaving tomorrow morning."

She pouts her full red lips. "Such a shame. We've had so much fun together."

I spend the next twenty minutes with my legs firmly crossed listening to what Alessandra has to say about *Stone Trooper* and the ideas she has for the love scenes. Somehow, she has convinced Sam that a full-on sex scene between her and her onscreen girlfriend in the film is a must. "To titillate the audience," she explains.

I have Lucifer purring away on my knees while I'm also trying to type on my laptop. I look up. "Alessandra, there's no way our kind of audience will be up for that."

"Oh, stop being so backward-thinking. People are more open-minded these days. Mid-American housewives are reading about bondage and sex toys for God's sake – hell, they're even experimenting with it all."

"Yes, but *gay* sex in a mainstream movie? A blockbuster, buddy movie?"

"Why not?"

"Because, because…"

"It hasn't been done before?"

"No, I don't think it has. This is not some French or Italian art-house film. This will be screened in shopping malls across the USA."

"Then give them something to talk about with their popcorn and soda."

I put my laptop aside and gently unhook Lucifer's claws from my skirt. I get off the couch and stretch my arms. "I'm going to have to talk to Sam about this, Alessandra. Personally, I don't think it will work. I mean, I know that gay characters in movies are either marginalized or made the punch-line for degrading jokes a lot of the time and so having your character being gay, and you, yourself, being gay, is already a big leap forward. We can hint at sex, show a kiss or something but a full-on lesbian love scene?"

"I thought a little light BDSM."

I laugh. "Okay, now I know you're kidding me. It's that crazy Italian sense of humor. You Europeans - really. Alexandre does the same thing to me…you know, that poker face thing? Which is what you're doing now. Very funny. You guys are expert at getting us Americans all worked up for nothing."

I think back to that time when Alexandre tied my ankles to the bedpost when he said I'd been disrespectful and needed to be punished – his wacky sense of humor had me fooled at first.

As if reading my mind, Alessandra says, "I think we should play it out. Do a little improv acting – we thespians love that."

I burst out laughing at her unintentional (or perhaps intentional) onomatopoeia with the word, thespian. "Lesbian bondage?"

She still dons her poker face. "Yes, why not?"

"Not even my fiancé would approve of that."

She widens her eyes innocently. "He's not into a little dominance play? A little S&M? He looks the type. So manly…so controlling Alpha male."

"No way. He won't come near me with a whip. Personally, it's something I wouldn't mind experimenting with - but him? Not a chance."

She rolls her eyes. "My ex girlfriend is like that. Can't play Dom and Sub with her ever – she has an aversion to any kind of physical power play. Except, I think in the past she's got pretty tough with men. You know when she was kinda straight. But she would never lay a hand on me."

"Yeah, well, in my fiancé's case, he has good reason. A violent childho—" *Shut up, Pearl!* I stop my sentence midway and change the subject. "Who did these paintings on the wall? They're lovely copies. Got the colors just right."

"I did."

I raise my eyebrows. "You're an artist as well as an actress? Why does that not surprise me?"

I wander about the room feeling extremely uneasy. I promised Sam we'd get this script done and dusted but now I'm feeling like I want out of this part of the project altogether. This whole movie process is giving me the willies. Something about it just doesn't seem right. The procedure doesn't feel normal…both of us tinkering about with the script and we're not the official script writers. Then again, having only ever worked on documentaries, who am I to judge? This is Hollywood, not a world I know well.

"Do'you mind if I make us some coffee?" I ask, stalling my decision as to whether I should throw in the towel and let her get on with it with the script doctor. I don't have time to play her silly games right now, nor second guess what's going on in her nutty mind. Besides, I find her disconcertingly attractive, mixed with my anti-male mind-set after my needle-dick nightmares – I'm an easy target right now. I don't want to succumb to her sexual charms again.

Alessandra gets up, the folds of her dress falling like ripples of water about her willowy body "Let me help you."

"No, really, I can do it. You relax. You take sugar, don't you?"

"Just half a teaspoon."

"Sure."

I slip off to the kitchen, relieved to get away from her for a moment and her quirky, oddball demeanor. I take two funky pottery mugs down from a shelf. They look like they were hand-painted by a child. I turn on the coffee percolator. The kitchen is chaotic. There are piles of scripts and baskets of fruit also stuffed with stray papers, magazines and bills. Lucifer comes in and jumps on the kitchen table, his tail up vertically swishing from side to side. He leaps across to the kitchen counter landing on a pile of papers in one of the baskets which he then begins to use to sharpen his claws. "Lucifer, you naughty boy." I prize his paws away from the basket and take him in my arms. But something catches my attention. A name.

Sophie Dumas.

My heart is beating fast. It's a business letter about *Stone Trooper* from Samuel Myers to Alessandra.

Producers: Sophie Dumas / HookedUp Enterprises.

Executive producer: Samuel Myers.

Sophie is not meant to be involved with this project! In any shape or form. I stand there for a moment staring at the letter, a rush of blood pumping in my ears – I can feel myself redden with fury. This must be some sort of mistake.

I march into the living room, still with Lucifer in my arms and say to Alessandra. "Who is the producer on this movie?"

She sits up and looks at me surprised. "Sam Myers with HookedUp Enterprises."

"He's the Producer or executive producer?"

"Oh, you must have seen some paperwork in the kitchen."

"Yes. I wasn't snooping. Lucifer landed on a very interesting piece of information which I - as co-producer and director of HookedUp Enterprises…" I stop myself short.

This is so unprofessional. Alessandra has been hired as an actress – she doesn't need to know about this cock-up. It makes me look incompetent to be so in the dark. To have been hoodwinked like this. To have been such a frigging, freaking *idiot*.

"Do you know Sophie Dumas?" I ask, trying to sound casual.

"I know who she is and we once spoke on the phone. She's one of the producers of *Stone Trooper*. I mean co-producer with Sam and HookedUp Enterprises – you're partners, aren't you? I mean, HookedUp Enterprises is Sophie Dumas and Alexandre Chevalier fifty/fifty, isn't it?"

I want to scream. I want to shout out, *No, actually, that meddling bitch is not part of HookedUp Enterprises at all*. I can feel my knees trembling but I try to stay calm. "The coffee sounds like it's ready. One sugar, you said?"

"Half a teaspoon."

"Oh yes, that's right." I set the cat down and go back to the kitchen. I cradle my head in my hands and wonder what I should do next.

I need to see Samuel Myers - find out what the hell is going on.

9

I t takes a while to park my shark of a car in the garage of Samuel Myers office building Downtown. I haven't warned him of my arrival in case he detects the anger in my voice. I have been duped – I need to get to the bottom of this without losing my cool. If that's possible. Once I've got an answer from him I'll call my sweet sister-in-law to find out what the fuck she's playing at. On second thoughts, no. I won't give her the satisfaction. I don't want her knowing that she's getting to me.

And then I'll call Alexandre.

I take the elevator up to the seventh floor. I was not prepared for this. I look very casual in just a pair of jeans, T-shirt and Converse sneakers. I'm not even wearing make-up; I wanted to dress down for Alessandra, to try and keep her advances at bay.

I needn't be worried, though. The receptionist and everyone at his office is very laid-back, LA style, although a little put out that I don't have an appointment. I'm in luck. Sam is here, just finishing up a long distance call, they tell me. The setting is not as grand as I had imagined and a little dated with big old couches and a wooden and glass coffee table piled with out of date magazines. They offer me a drink and I glug down a glass of water – the heat I feel inside needs to be quenched. I sit there flicking through an old Vanity Fair. I hear a door open and I look up.

Sam waddles towards me – his smile beaming as if he's delighted to see me. He ushers me ahead of him into his office, pulling the door closed behind him. The book shelves are lined with movies and there is an Academy Award in prime position. There are family photos in gold frames on his large desk and at one end of the room a basketball net. I can just imagine him making million dollar deals while simultaneously scoring a goal.

"Siddown, Pearl. Did they offer you a beverage?" He eases himself into his large leather swivel chair, panting with the effort.

"Yes, thank you, Mr. Myers."

"Hey, sweetheart, what's with the Mr. Myers? You look pissed."

"Well, yes, I've had quite a shock and I'd like you to explain yourself and the situation. Perhaps there's been a typo on a letter I saw. I'm hoping that I'm completely wrong, hoping this has all been a mistake. However, if I am not wrong I think your prerogative to call me 'sweetheart' will be null and void."

His eyes look shifty – he twiddles his fat, caught-in-the-cookie-jar hands.

I pin my eyes on him like darts. "Please can you explain

why Sophie Dumas is one of the producers?"

"Okay Pearl, firstly, she is only *technically* a producer. She is not involved in any decision making at all. Not a bit. That's just you and me. It's just money, that's all. She's fronting the money – she's a silent partner, so to speak."

"So to speak? So to lie, more like."

"Hey, Pearl, nothing has changed between you and me! Sophie Dumas is not calling the shots here."

"Oh no? So if this is *her* money, not yours, she is kind of like your boss, wouldn't you say?"

"It's not like that."

"What is it like then, Mr. Myers?"

"You are the director of your company, HookedUp Enterprises but you are not the owner, am I right?"

My blood is boiling. *What has HookedUp Enterprises got to do with Sophie Dumas?* I try to remain calm. "Sophie Dumas has nothing whatsoever to do with HookedUp Enterprises, Mr. Myers. It is owned by my fiancé."

"And I signed the deal with him."

"Co-signed by me."

"Nowhere in our contract did it stipulate that I could not bring in money from my side from whatever source I chose."

"That's not true. You signed a deal saying that no backers would be involved in politically incorrect dealings—"

"Sophie Dumas is not laundering dirty money, Pearl. Hey, she's your sister-in-law, what's the big deal? She told me you two were close."

"Don't bullshit me, Sam. If we were so close you wouldn't be red in the face from embarrassment right now. You would have been straight with me."

"What was the point of telling you? Money is money. The point is, the movie is going to get made – we have the money. You will make a lot from this - you still get your cut just the same - your percentage. Nothing has changed, Pearl, sweetheart.

"My trust in you – that's what's changed."

"Okay, okay, I admit it. I screwed up - I should have let you know sooner. But she only just came on board a while ago. I've been having a rough patch and she came along at the perfect moment. She's bailing out my ass. I had an unexpected loss on a project recently – as far as I'm concerned, Sophie's doing us all a big favor. Your fiancé isn't upset about this so why should you be?"

I feel as if I've just been hit over the head with a baseball bat. *Alexandre already knows about this??* I need to get information so I can't let him know that this is such a shock. "What were Alexandre's words to you exactly? And at what point did you discuss this?"

"Just after he landed back in New York. The other day, I guess."

"I see."

"He told me it was best if he discussed it with you first. That's why I didn't mention it to you, Pearl. You know, I didn't want to get out my big wooden spoon and stir about someone else's family affairs."

I notice my fists are scrunched into balls as my nails are digging into my hands. I say between my teeth, "You and I are business partners – we are meant to tell each other about anything that could affect this movie. This is not some freaking *family affair*! I resent that you just said that!"

"Calm down, Pearl."

"No, I won't calm down! I could sue you for breach of contract. I won't because I don't want to waste my time and energy but this is the last time you will be doing business with HookedUp Enterprises. I will finish this movie because I'm a professional. The show *will* go on. But I do not want to have one single meeting with Sophie Dumas. Is that clear? I do not want to hear her name, nor see her at the premiere. If I so much get an inkling of her rootling about my business I will get my lawyers on to you. You are a powerful man, Mr. Myers, but my fiancé is even more powerful and richer than you are."

His eyes look down ashamedly.

"By the way," I spit out, "I don't want Sophie knowing that we've had this conversation. I don't want you running off tittle-tattling to her about what a bitch I've been."

"You can count on it, I won't say a word."

"What you did was wrong. It wasn't unethical. It was sneaky and dishonest."

He smiles at me weakly. "Welcome to Hollywood, Pearl."

I take the flamboyant powder blue Cadillac back to the car hire and swap it for a BMW. I don't want to advertise my whereabouts to the whole of LA. I go to the hotel and check out and call the airline to cancel my flight to New York.

I will not be returning home tomorrow. I'm not sure what I should do now – I need to come up with a plan. Sitting in my new rental car in a parking lot near Santa Monica Pier, I call Alexandre. Over the phone is hardly the best way to manage problems in a relationship but I have had enough. I cannot live my life with mistrust. I cannot have this as-good-as incestuous relationship between him and his freaky sister barging in on me with every breath I take. He knew about Sophie producing *Stone Trooper* and he didn't call to let me know! I'll give him a chance to explain himself but if he doesn't come up with an airtight answer, then that's it.

It's her or me.

He cannot have us both. He will have to choose. Now. Not tomorrow, not 'when the time is right but – N.O.W.

I need to have this resolved or nothing will ever change. This is the most painful thing I have ever done in my life but I have no choice. If I don't stand firm now, this Sophie nonsense will never end.

Shaking, I press in his number. His plane will have landed by now.

"Hello?" he says. Just hearing his deep, melodic voice has me trembling all the more. I am so in love with this man. But I am so furious with him, too.

Without saying 'hi' I screech out, "Why didn't you tell me, Alexandre?"

"Nice to hear your voice, chérie. What's up?"

"What's up is that I have just come out of a meeting with Samuel Myers. Nice to be working on a movie where I am the last person to find something out. And I say, *find something out,* as in, not be enlightened by people around me whom I am meant to trust, one of those people being my *fiancé,*" I cry out, my voice rising as I splutter out that last word.

"Calm down, Pearl. I was going to tell you when the time was right."

"If you use this 'time-is-right' crap on me anymore I'll–"

"I was going to call you right now, in fact. It totally slipped my mind, chérie. I just didn't think it was *that* important because the source of where the money was coming from was not going to affect you in anyway personally."

"What is *wrong* with you? This is meant to be a HookedUp Enterprises project. That is the *whole point!* HookedUp *Enterprises* is not part of HookedUp. This is not supposed to have anything to do with your sister *at all!*"

"It's just money, Pearl. Nothing more. I've already spoken to her about it. She swears she won't get involved in the creative side. Sam Myers is in financial straits."

"You know what? I wouldn't be surprised if that's all a big fabrication – an excuse for Sophie to wheedle her way into my business. Because one minute Samuel Myers is one of the most powerful producers in Hollywood and suddenly he's in a quagmire and Sophie just happens to bail him out at the perfect moment – sounds very fishy to me."

"Pearl, you're reading way too much into this. He was in a bad way and, yes, maybe Sophie saw a good business opportunity and she snapped it up. She's getting a chunk of his company in exchange. In the long term it could be a great deal for her."

"Well bully for her! But it is not a great deal for *me!* Or, I might add, for our future marriage. Or should I say, to be more precise, our *ex*-future marriage!" I am stumbling now, spurting nonsense but I mean every word of my jumbled phrases, however higgledy-piggledy they come out.

There is silence. *Has he hung up on me?*

"Alexandre?"

I can hear his breathing. "You don't mean that, baby. We're going ahead with this wedding and nothing's going to stop me. Sophie's separate from all this. You have got to stop obsessing about her and just ignore her."

"Me obsessing about *her?* I think you'll find it's the other way round, Alexandre. You know what? That's *it*. I thought maybe we had a chance to sort this problem out but I see that you are not budging – stubborn as ever. You are so fucking wrapped up and wrapped around your older sister's devious little finger that you might as well be fucking her for all I care. You two can carry on and live happily ever after because I'm *out*. OUT! Do you hear me? Our relationship is over! I love you but I do not love her and I do not want her burrowing her way into our marriage. You said you were working on ways of extricating yourself from her with HookedUp and in your personal life. Like a fool I believed you. I trusted you. But it was all *bullshit!*"

"Pearl, please, darling stop. I know she had good reason to do what she did. She—"

"Alexandre, you can make excuses till the cows come home. I am not going to listen anymore. If the day ever, ever comes when you and she are one hundred percent separated businesswise, then give me a call. Meanwhile, we are over. I am not returning to New York. I'll finish *Stone Trooper* from a distance by email and long distance calls. Once I have started a project I don't think it's professional to abandon ship. However, after that…well I don't know yet…I'll need to work that through but—"

"I'm coming to Los Angeles tonight to get you. This is crazy. We're getting married. We'll get married in Vegas tomorrow and we can do the white wedding, too, if you want. I'm not standing for this, Pearl. I give you my word I'll dissolve my part of HookedUp. I'll make it go public or Sophie can buy me out but it will take time, I can't do something like that overnight. We can draw up a contract with lawyers if you don't believe me."

"Oh, like the HookedUp Enterprises contract we drew

up? Fat lot of good that did! Sophie found a little loophole to slip her way in like the sly snake she is!"

"You're not listening to reason, Pearl, so I'm coming to get you. I'm calling on my other cell right now and cancelling my meeting here in Montreal. I'm turning around as we speak. I'll hire a jet and come right now to LA. We'll go to Vegas and—"

"You're not listening to me, are you? You deal with your sister and HookedUp *first* and when you can prove to me that it is *finished,* signed, sealed and delivered, then give me a call. Until then, adieu, Alexandre." And I add with a tone of spite in my voice, "Besides, the last thing I want is to have a relationship with a *penis* right now."

His voice is incredulous, tight with anger. "*Excuse* me? Is that what I am to you? A *penis?*"

"Men are pigs. All of you. Deep down inside all you do is rule your lives by your dicks! You rape women. You even rape babies to 'cure' yourselves of AIDS which, hello, you got from fucking prostitutes in the first place – underage, abused prostitutes who should be in school or playing with dolls—"

"What has that got to do with me? What are you *talking* about?"

"The rape ratio in South Africa? One in four men there have committed rape!"

"Pearl—"

"Oh, and that sick, pedophile British DJ who's dead now? Have you heard about him on the news? Men are sticking their dicks everywhere – they have been since time immemorial - they don't care who they hurt both physically and mentally – children, disabled people - as long as they get themselves and their stinking dicks off!"

He replies softly to my accusations, "My darling, where's all this coming from? *What* is going on?"

I'm weeping now, yowling. I sound like a braying donkey as I suck in air between sobs, my head resting on the steering wheel, my body shaking. I manage to get out, "I can't talk about this anymore. Call Daisy, she'll... tell you... what...h...happened... to...m.... me."

I hang up. I can't even think straight. Here I am sitting in my parked rental car with nowhere to go. I can't return to New York right now – I've sublet my apartment. I need a break from Alexandre. Okay, I know, I'm being dramatic – even childish. But it is the only way of getting it through his head. *I do not want Sophie in my life!* Why can't he get that? The one thing I hung onto was my autonomy, my work. And even *that* she is trying to snatch away from me.

My cell goes. It's him. It keeps ringing. I let my blood simmer a little, dry my eyes, take a deep breath and pick up.

His voice is steady. "I've cancelled my meeting. I'm on my way."

"Don't do that because I won't be here when you arrive."

I can hear the clipping sound of his purposeful footsteps. He's talking in motion, his long legs striding towards his goal which happens to be me right now. "Stay where you are, Pearl. You're being absurd."

"I need some time to think all this through. I don't want to see you for a while, Alexandre."

He sighs. The anguish in his voice is palpable. "What happened to you? It's about those nightmares, isn't it? What happened, baby? Please tell me. Please trust me."

I close my eyes and draw my knees up to my chest, and sink into the seat of the car. "A long time ago when I was at university…" I break my sentence.

"Go on, baby. I'm here for you. I love you," he cajoles. "Please, share your pain with me. Your pain is my pain. I can help. I can help you through this."

"No, you can't. You're a guy. I'm disgusted by men right now."

"I understand. I swear I do. I know that men can be vile. You don't think I know that after my father? But we aren't all bad, Pearl. We can be kind and caring. What happened, my angel? Please," he begs gently.

"I was… gang raped," and I add quickly, "but I asked for it. I wore a micro-mini skirt. I went back to their room willingly – I thought it would be fun, me with two guys. I invited it to happen, Alexandre. But it turned into something else. Something sick and gross."

I can hear the echoey announcements at Montreal airport and Alexandre's quiet breathing. I knew it. The idea of me behaving like a slut is too much for him, even if it happened eighteen years ago.

"Who did this to you?"

"You think I remember? I blanked out. I blocked it out. All this shit has been resurfacing in dreams. I can't even prove it happened. I was zonked out - drunk. Daisy thinks they may have spiked my tequila. Who knows? I behaved like a slut and I got raped."

His voice is edgy: "You did *not*," and he says between gritted teeth, "behave like a slut."

"Thank you," I reply quietly.

"We'll get through this together. We don't have to make love, baby. I won't touch you, I promise. Not until you're ready."

"Please don't come, Alexandre. I'm serious about what I

said. Deal with Sophie and HookedUp first. I need some time alone. I'll call you in…like…a week or something. Bye."

I switch off my cell and take a deep breath. If any of this is to work between us I want Sophie out of our lives. Poor Alexandre – he's being understanding…but still. He is part of the male species and for now I don't want a penis near me bringing back visions of needle and walnut-dicks. I need some time to myself.

I get out of the car and start strolling towards Santa Monica Pier. The sun is setting - the sky swirling in moody blues, streaked with orange, making shimmering reflections on the ocean. To the north, the view of the Malibu mountains is spectacular. I walk briskly until I arrive at the pier. A trapeze school, The Trapeze School New York, is offering classes to anyone daring enough. Their logo reads, *Forget fear. Worry about the addiction.* Hmm….addiction. That is how I felt about Alexandre - completely addicted to him. But now that the sexual craving has waned on my part – at least for now – how will that affect our relationship? Before, when there was a problem we worked it out through sex. The infatuation and carnal desire we held for one another was so all-consuming, so powerful, it overrode everything. Will that need and desire return? The compulsion to have him inside me? Fucking me at every opportunity? Right now I need space, freedom. I can't bear the idea of being smothered, my body invaded - even by him.

My cell is off. He'll be frantically phoning now. I feel cruel. But then I remember Sophie again slithering into our lives in her oh-so-subtle way.

I watch one of the trapeze students, a little girl who can't be more than eight-years-old - swinging back and forth high above me and I'm tempted to give it a go myself. Anything to clear my mind of its present turmoil.

I ask the young woman standing there, "I guess all the classes must be booked up way in advance?"

"Well actually, someone just cancelled. Lost his nerve."

"Could I take his place?"

"Sure. Have you ever done this before?"

"Only in my dreams."

She laughs. "Well, now you can know what it's like to fly for real. You wanna try?"

"I sure do."

I whip out my credit card, pay and sign a waiver agreeing to take full responsibility for my own risk.

She instructs me, "Okay, you'll need to tie up your hair in a ponytail and have you got anything other than jeans to wear? Something more comfortable that gives you room to move better?"

"I have some yoga pants in my handbag."

"Perfect. You can put them on behind here." She leads me around to the side where there is a makeshift changing room.

This is crazy. Here I am in the middle of some existential crisis and I'm about to risk my life on a trapeze. Actually, that's a wild exaggeration – there's a safety net to catch my fall but I guess anything could happen or they wouldn't have asked me to sign that waiver. I'll be upside down, hooked onto the bar with my knees, swinging back and forth until the 'catcher' can get me, our hands linking. It'll take a few goes but let's see if I can be as good as that child up there.

When it comes to my turn I climb the ladder in my harness and stand on the platform about twenty-three feet up. I feel vertigo but am determined to go ahead with it. I look out over the dark blue ocean and the streaky sky. It's cooler up here, a light breeze catches me and the nervy heat I'm feeling inside is momentarily at bay. My heart is thumping – I feel so high up.

A topless man wearing what look like white pajama bottoms hooks the trapeze with a pole and brings it towards me. He connects another rope to my front. Uh, oh, here we go. I launch out into the air pushing my legs forward horizontally with great momentum and then hook them above my head, under and around the bar. This is scary. I have the choice to stay doubled up or let go. Will my legs be strong enough to hold me? After a few seconds, I do let go and feel my arms and torso drop like a big lead weight. I am completely upside down. I haven't done this sort of thing since fourth grade! The woman below me is screaming instructions, "forward, backwards, forward, backwards," and I swing my legs like a pendulum. Then I drop myself into the net. End of go one.

I wait my next turn, adrenaline pumping and wish Alexandre were here to share this experience with me. It reminds me of our first date together when we went rock-climbing. He'd be proud of me now. My cell is in my purse in the trapeze school's office. I can't call him now. Should I later? Or just leave it? I need him to know I'm serious about Sophie. I must remain strong or the next forty years of marriage or as long as we all live, will be one frustrating-as-hell compromise.

After a few more turns on the trapeze, taking my turn between the eight year-old girl, a couple of surfer dudes and another woman around my age, I manage to do the swinging circus 'catch.' Hooray!

This whole experience has given me a sense of strength.

I walk back to my car. The sun has set for the evening leaving the sky a deep cobalt blue - a lone star is flickering on the horizon and I make a wish. Star light star bright, first star I see tonight... *I wish that Sophie would get the hell out of our lives for good.*

An overriding feeling of emotion hits me and I start crying again.

Alexandre said he's on his way to get me. But the only man I can bear spending time with right now is my father.

I need my dad. I make a snap decision.

Kauai here I come.

10

I decide it's only fair to swing by Alessandra's to say goodbye and explain the situation. She's going to get wind of it one way or another so I might as well inform her that I won't be returning to LA for meetings – that I'll be emailing and Skyping, if need be, but distancing myself emotionally from the movie project. What I thought was 'my baby' now has a surrogate mother:

Sophie Dumas.

I've been betrayed on so many levels and it has made me bitter towards Hollywood. It has brought something to light: I want my old job back - I feel the urge to do documentaries again. I don't care about movie stars and big budgets. I care about those little Nigerian girls who are being sold for sexual slavery. I care about the fourteen year-old girl Malala, shot in the head by a Taliban man for championing education for girls. By some miracle she's still alive.

These are the things that drive my passion. Not some blockbuster, even if it does have a gay rights message.

I call Alessandra just to make sure she's going to be in. And on my way I swing by a Thai restaurant and pick up some Tom Yam soup and other treats. I'm hungry after my trapeze exertion and I'm sure Alessandra will be up for a bit of Thai food.

She is. When I walk into her house I realize that I haven't been here before when it's dark. She has lit her wood-burning stove and it smells of firewood and rose incense. She's delighted that I brought take-out and we begin to heat up the soup as we stand in the kitchen chatting.

She's wearing tight jeans and I can't help my roving eye. Women are always checking out each other's buns – but I'm not comparing myself to her; I'm admiring her sexy curves. I can't help it. I myself, though, still look a bit disheveled and truthfully need a shower. I know I look anything but hot.

"You wanna watch a movie or you want to talk about *Stone Trooper?* she asks, stirring the Tom Yam.

"You know what? I'm a bit Troopered-out."

I reveal to her the whole Sophie saga, keeping the tale simple and not too dramatic but explaining why I'll be bowing out gracefully from any more script tweaking and future get-togethers. I tell her about my plan to see my father and that I'm flying to Hawaii tomorrow morning.

"I'll miss you," she says, her eyes mournful. "So it's your last night at that cool hotel, huh?"

"Actually I checked out. I was in a flustered state, I thought I might be getting on a plane that very second but then I got distracted by the trapeze school on Santa Monica Pier."

"Oh so that's what the sweaty appearance is? I wondered

why you were looking so mussed up."

"Would you mind if I took a shower?"

"Sure, of course. You wanna eat now or wait?"

"I'll take a quick shower first, why not – I don't want to stink up the kitchen."

She gets out some plates from a cupboard. "I like the smell of your sweat. It's sexy."

I snigger sarcastically. "Now that *has* to be a lie."

"No it's not. My ex…well she goes crazy for underarms, you know?"

"Well I have to admit, I like the smell of Alexandre's day-old T-shirts so I do understand."

"She likes it when I have hairy armpits, it drives her wild. I mean *crazy* wild."

I grimace. "Each to their own, I guess. You're still seeing her? You refer to her as your ex yet you speak about her in the present."

She looks uneasy but doesn't answer directly. "Whenever we have….whenever we *had* a fight I'd shave to get her pissed."

I laugh. "Shaving your armpits was a big punishment?"

"I know, isn't it crazy?"

"What was she like…what is she like, your ex?"

"Beautiful. A tigress between the sheets."

"Does she live in LA?"

Alessandra looks uncomfortable. "Actually, I don't really want to talk about her, d'you mind? Let's talk about *you*, Pearl. Any more nightmares?"

I'd forgotten that I'd laid bare my soul before our bath-tub 'event'. "No, no more nightmares, thank God."

"Pearl, can I ask you a very personal question?"

"You can ask but I'm not sure I'll give you an answer."

Alessandra chuckles and tosses her mane. "Do you have multiple orgasms?"

Where did that come from? I remember the shock of when it happened in Cap d'Antibes with Alexandre. "Do *you?*" I ask boomeranging her question.

"No. Never. And I never had an orgasm with a man. I wanted to…but…I tried…you know, but it just didn't happen."

"Well, that's nothing to be ashamed of. Lots of women go through that," I say carefully, not wanting to reveal anything too personal. "You know what? I'm going to grab that shower and then we can eat. I hope you like cold sesame noodles. There are puffed rice cakes, vegetable spring rolls and there's some spicy prawn curry as well."

"I'll heat up the oven."

"I won't be long."

I feel her eyes on my back as I saunter to the bathroom and she shouts after me, "Do you want to borrow a robe? Hey, Pearl, if you already checked out of your hotel, why don't you stay here tonight?"

I turn around. "No. Thank you for the offer but I can check into an airport hotel. I'm flying out at the squawk of dawn."

"As you please. Grab a terry-cloth robe from the bathroom. You know, you can chill out comfortably while we watch the movie. Have you seen *All About Eve?*"

"One of my favorite Bette Davis films - '*Fasten your seatbelts, it's going to be a bumpy night,*' " I say, quoting my favorite line.

"Oh dear, well, we can put on something else."

"No, that's perfect - I haven't seen it for years."

I shower and then we eat watching the movie. Eve Harrington – what an insidious character - and Bette Davis's Margo Channing who's just turned forty. Oh, how I identify! Eve Harrington - a seemingly sweet-as-candy actress usurping her idol's position in such a scheming, clever way. The whole scenario reminds me of Sophie. The story is different but the intention is there: to slowly silently take over, to push out your rival with a smile on your face. Buying me my wedding gown, telling Alexandre she loves me, yet plotting behind my back. Yet she hasn't actually done anything *actively* bad so it looks as if I'm paranoid. Sure, she called me a 'cougar' and a 'stalker' a few months back but I shouldn't hold that against her forever. She did apologize, too. But I know she's up to no good.

So far, Sophie is winning. Getting her way with Alexandre - pushing me away from him.

We'll see if she succeeds.

Alessandra has been plying us both with champagne and because of the spiciness of the Thai food I've been glugging it down without really noticing. Uh oh, I have an early plane to catch and now I'm feeling woozy. But I'm so relaxed by the cozy log fire and she has a way of making me laugh with her ironic and direct sense of humor that I'm loathe to leave - just yet.

All About Eve ends and I'm sprawled out on the couch in Alessandra's terry-cloth robe, my hair still damp. She's gazing at me, her lips slightly parted.

"Pearl, this is our last ever moment together. Probably."

"Yes, it is. I don't think I'll be returning to LA."

She pouts. "Why?"

"It's too tough here. I mean, New Yorkers can be rough around the edges but at least what you see is what you get. Here things are subtly sinister – I can't explain it but I feel this place is a little Machiavellian - sugar-coated with a seductive sheen, which makes it all the more dangerous. Los Angeles is a magnetic place and you can get sucked in all too easily."

Alessandra temples her hands to her chin as if digesting my opinion and then says softly, "I sense you have a dark side to you, Pearl. And I think you need to be punished for being a little slutty in the past."

I stare at her in amazement. At first I want to slap her – what she has just said is way too close to the bone and I feel hurt - betrayed even. She's a woman, she should understand - know how tortured I am by my own guilt and self-blame about what happened to me. But then I'm overcome by...I can't even explain it...a sort of morbid intrigue. There is something fiendish and sinful about Alessandra and it draws me in.

She continues, "Before you leave this wicked town for good would you like to experience one last thrill?" She runs her fingers through her wavy hair. "You like living on the edge, don't you, Pearl? Experimenting? Today on the trapeze, for instance, and all those years ago putting yourself in danger with those horny, out-of-control footballers. What were you expecting? You knew it would end in tears, didn't you? You knew, yet you did it anyway."

My heart is pumping with both irritation and curiosity. I narrow my eyes. "Where's this leading?"

"Do you trust me?"

"Not really," I reply coolly.

"And that makes it all the more titillating, doesn't it? I know you want your fiancé to spank you, to flick a whip on your wet little pussy."

This woman is something else. What a nerve! I want to laugh out loud but what she's saying is secretly turning me on. The champagne has made me so relaxed that I feel fearless and a shiver of excitement shimmies through me. I tell her, "Like I said - Alexandre would never play S and M games with me even if I begged him. Anyway, I don't like being hurt."

She raises an eyebrow. "We would use a safe word."

I try to suppress a smirk. For some reason this conversation is amusing me although Alessandra has a dead-serious expression on her face. "*We?*" I ask.

"I'm going to blindfold you, Pearl. We can play a little fantasy game. You pretend in the darkness beneath your blindfold that I am Alexandre. See if you like it. If you don't then just shout out the word, *Sicily*."

"Sicily?"

"You wanna choose something else?"

"You're serious about this, aren't you?"

"You need to purge your guilt about your past – extricate that feeling of culpability. I'm going to help you do that by punishing you. Then you'll be free. Call it witchcraft, think of it as a little spell, if you like."

As she says the word, 'spell' Lucifer jumps onto the couch and rubs his soft black fur against me. His tail brushes onto my slightly open robe and it touches my flesh seductively. He purrs loudly as if agreeing with his mistress.

"Pussy," she spits out.

Does she mean pussycat? Is she talking to Lucifer?

"You're a coward, Pearl," she clarifies.

"Alessandra, I'm not into being hurt. It's one thing reading about this kind of stuff in an erotic novel or seeing it in a film, but another doing it in real life. Okay, I admit, I'm curious but…"

She rolls her eyes. "Forget it. I thought it was a good idea

– something to ease away your mental anguish – a way of striking out those bad dreams by administering a little light punishment - but if you're not into the idea…"

My mind is ticking over. Maybe she has a point. Perhaps this could be the answer - the champagne part of my brain thinks so, anyway. What harm is there in at least trying? This woman is slight, not as strong as I am - she can't hurt me. "Okay, Alessandra, but on one condition: no handcuffs. If I don't like it I want to be able to stop instantly."

"That's what the safe word is for."

"No restraints, I mean it. And only five minutes, just to see. No kissing. I'm not gay - kissing would be way too intimate."

She takes another swig of her champagne and grins wickedly – her full lips breaking into a smile that spreads across her whole face. "You're on."

She glides over to the other side of the room, her bare feet noiseless on the parquet floor. I watch her out of the corner of my eye. She stands on a chair and carefully brings down a long box from the top of a free-standing closet. She blows some dust off the top of it. A treasure trove, obviously unused for a long while. Or, more likely, Pandora's Box. Will evil things fly out when she opens it? My curiosity makes me sit up. *What am I doing?*

The lights are already dimmed and Alessandra lights several candles and some more rose incense. She puts on some music – Frank Sinatra's *Witchcraft* (how fitting) and sways her hips slowly to the rhythm. She's still in her jeans and I in her robe. Obviously, she wants to play Dom and have me as her Sub.

She's right, I'm a sucker for adventure. Most forty year-old women don't go rock climbing and swing from trapezes, let alone get engaged to a man fifteen years younger than they are. And most women, period, forty or not, do not decide to experiment with a dose of lesbian bondage. *Am I nuts?* My sensible side yells at me, 'yes' but my curiosity drives me on.

"Okay, Pearl," she whispers, her lilting Italian accent catching the R of Pearl, "lie flat on your back."

The L-shaped sofa is large and there's plenty of space for me to sprawl out. I do as she bids. The room is blissfully warm and I feel comfortable. The champagne has eased away the fury I felt for Alexandre earlier. I suddenly wonder - is this my way of getting back at him? Yes, he told me that he'd find it sexy for me to be messing about with another woman, but S and M? *I don't think so.*

I observe Alessandra open up her toy box and take out a whip. It has tassels at one end.

She stands over me and presses it up to my nose. "Smell this."

I sniff it in; it smells of perfume. She runs it gently about my face and the tassels tickle.

"Now let's get your dressing gown off. You won't be cold, will you?"

"No, it's lovely and warm here."

She helps me off with my robe and stands back as if admiring all of me. "You have a very sexy body, Pearl. I was looking at your ass earlier. So round and shapely, but not big. I bet that ass drives Alexandre wild."

"It does."

"Tell me what he likes to do to it."

I have my eyes closed now and I conjure up one of our last love-making sessions before my mind went pear-shaped with nasty memories. "He likes licking me there along the crack, pinching my pussy lips at the same time and teasing my clit until I'm begging him to fuck me."

She bites her bottom lip. "Tell me more, it's making me horny."

"Sometimes he beats me with his cock. It's so big and always rock-hard – he slaps me with it on my ass and right up at my opening. Until I'm so wet I can't stand it anymore. Then he fucks me from behind until I come."

"D'you have anal sex?"

"No," I whisper. "He's never tried. He's very old-fashioned that way. He thinks men who do that must be secretly gay or something. Doesn't understand why anyone would do that to a woman."

"Very vanilla."

"Yes, very. But sex with him is incredible. Well, when I'm not having needle-dick visions of that horrible night, that is."

"That's what we're going to deal with now, Pearl. Beat away your guilt about that night with needle-dick and company."

Her accent makes me laugh. Not that the needle-dick thing is funny but it suddenly strikes me how ridiculous this whole scenario is. Both of us about to do this nutty experiment. I observe her graceful movements. She has now got a blindfold out of the box of tricks.

"Sit up a second, Pearl, let me put this on you."

I ease up from the couch realizing how floppy and re-laxed I feel. I'm about to be whipped and I don't care. *This is madness!* She adjusts the black silk blindfold so I can't see a thing.

"Now lie back," she commands in her husky voice.

I lie back down. I can feel the tassels of the whip run up

and down my flesh but surprisingly it's soft and soothing. She circles my breasts, not touching the nipple and guides it around my navel fluttering it about my clit. I moan with pleasure.

"I can see you're getting wet, Pearl," she sing-songs, slapping me between the legs very slightly. But it doesn't hurt. "You're naughty, aren't you? Playing around with me behind your fiancé's back?"

"He wouldn't mind," I whisper, flexing my hips to meet the sweet brush of the tassels. But it's trailing back to my breasts now leaving my lower region bereft and needy for more. Then she stops and bends my knees up. I lie there in the darkness of my blindfold. I hear her getting something else out of the box.

"What are you doing?" I ask a little scared. Maybe this woman is crazy. People in Los Angeles have guns. She's a woman living alone in semi-countryside – she probably packs a pistol in that box of tricks. Uh, oh, am I about to have a snub-nose revolver held up to my head?

"Ssh," she says pressing her thumb against my lips, parting them and then grazing it along my front teeth. I lax my mouth. Being blindfolded is scary, but sexy.

Then I feel her hand on my wet slit and she's gently walking her fingers along my cleft and parting my lips down there. She doesn't touch my clit which is begging for attention, tingling with longing. She has something in her hands, what is it? Then I feel her slip something large inside me. I'm throbbing with pleasure. What is this she's putting inside my opening?

She tells me, "These are jiggle balls. Don't worry, they're new, never been used before. You can wear these all day – prescribed by gynecologists to strengthen the pelvic floor muscles but what I use them for is to make my pussy extra sensitive. Wear these about and by the time evening comes your orgasm is super intense."

I can feel the chilly metal slipping inside - alien but welcoming. I'm so wet they slide in with relative ease. I'm already feeling stimulated. Nice.

Her fingers are lightly stroking my clit now and I'm feeling double pleasure. She goes on, "They're called jiggle balls because they jiggle once inside – they contain weights so they vibrate gently when you move around. You know, you can go about your business, do your shopping, whatever, and nobody knows the little smirk you have on your face is because you've got a sexy little secret going on south of the border."

I moan quietly as Alessandra presses my clit deliciously.

She continues, "These balls stimulate your G spot for discreet arousal." She bursts out laughing. "Except, you know, Pearl, once I climaxed in the grocery store so it wasn't so discreet. I was feeling really horny and you know those big chest freezers they sometimes have? I'd had the balls inside me all day long so I was already pretty worked up and all I needed was a little nudge, you know? So I pressed my pussy up against the corner of it and had like, this mind-blowing orgasm right there in the store. Nobody saw me - supposedly - but I bet it got caught on camera. Some guy in a control room somewhere getting his rocks off, watching a video of me coming like crazy. These little silver balls work wonders. You can keep these when we're done. As a memento."

I'm lying back in a zone of sexual bliss. Jesus, this is sexy, I'm so aroused. She slides her finger inside me and circles it very, very slowly. The balls are warming up now – hot in fact from my burning core which is pulsating around them and clenching with anticipation. It's true, they're making me needy. She's got me, Alessandra has. I'm at her mercy – I need an orgasm. I'll do anything now to feel that release.

"Right, now I want you to sit up, turn over and get on your hands and knees doggy style. Stay on the couch."

"But this is so great, I'm so happy where I am just like this."

"Do as your told, you naughty girl. Up!" She taps the whip between my legs and it brings me to attention.

Still blindfolded, I crawl into the position she has described. I feel really vulnerable now – naked, my ass in the air. I sense the tassels tickling my opening as she guides the whip up and down.

"Get ready, slut!" and she brings the whip down on me. The tassels lash at my pussy lips. Ouch, it stings. Then I feel a soft stroking finger sooth my cleft. I'm clenching myself, I feel the balls inside me move – I'm still smarting from the sting. She's stroking my butt cheeks softly with her palm in circles and then, whack! She brings her hand down on me hard. I think it's her hand – it feels different. "That's for wanting too much cock at one time!" she warns.

I cry out, "That hurts!"

"So it should. But I'll be nice and kiss it better."

I feel her soft mane of hair tickling between my thighs and her lips are blowing at my opening now, her warm breath making me shimmer and pound in all the right places. She kisses me there. Oh God, oh yeah...I feel her tongue flickering at the back of me right at the base and move north towards my butt slit. Glad I had that shower and lathered sweet-smelling oils over my skin. She's running her tongue up and down and I'm bucking my hips at her – I can't help it. I'm teetering on the edge. Then there's a lull. Oh no, the punishment again? The trepidation is only making me all the hornier. *This is nuts! Why am I enjoying this?* Then I feel the whip thrash on my ass and then immediately tapping so softly against my clit as contact is made and then lost...trailing the whip softly from there up to the cleft of my butt...she does this over and over. The anticipation is killing me. My hips are gyrating - my V has morphed into a veritable humming V-8, buzzing with desire. My breathing is profound - I'm moaning, "Please Alessandra, please."

"Please what? You want me to whack you again?"

"Touch me, press it, make me come."

"Not so fast you bad girl who thinks cocks are the answer to her prayers." She slips what feels like her thumb into my wet slit and starts moving it around. The balls are doing their thing. I can feel the build-up...all she needs to do is stroke my clit...

But whack! Down comes the whip with the tassels. It really stings this time.

"That freaking hurt!" I have tears in my eyes.

"That's for getting gang raped, that's for putting yourself in so much danger. Tell me you won't do it again."

"Of course I won't, are you crazy?"

"I'm crazy about your sexy ass that makes me want to rub myself all over it and make my pussy come hard but I have a job to do and that's to make you never forget why I'm punishing you. To whip those filthy needle-dicks out of your memory." SLASH! The whip comes down on my ass again and I shriek this time. I must be sore as hell. "That's enough!" I yell at her. Should I scream *Sicily?*

"Tell me you'll kiss me first."

"That wasn't the deal, Alessandra!"

She pinches my pussy lips hard just at my entrance. The

smarting pain is mixed with desperate carnal lust as I feel myself about to come. But my clit is begging for just a nudge of pressure. I need that release so badly. Suddenly the idea of kissing her soft lips and licking her full, beautiful tits fills me with horny desire.

"Do what you did when we were in the bath and I'll come, please...I *will* kiss you Alessandra, I promise."

She trails the whip up along my stomach and on my nipples brushing the tassels over them. I groan with desire. She softly strokes my cleft with her hand and pressures my clit firmly with her whole palm with a few hard rubs. I rock back and forth to meet her hand. I feel a thunderous rush of blood well up and my orgasm bursts from deep inside. The silver balls, her palm, the image of her breasts, Alexandre's gorgeous, sexy face when he's fucking me - all unite into a wave of ecstasy. I push hard on her hand, the waves undulating through my core and I'm moaning, still blindfolded, all the sensations doubled by not being able to see.

My legs are trembling and I collapse face-down on the couch. I press my own hands between my legs to eek out the post-orgasm quavers. Like musical notes they are dancing through me, chiming and jingling, the balls heavy inside me, the tingling and shivers now light and feathery after feeling so deeply intense from within.

"Girl power," whispers Alessandra. "Tell me you liked that."

"I loved it," I murmur. "Well, not the beating bit but−"

"Stay there, I'm going to get some balm for that poor sexy ass of yours."

She goes off to the bathroom and comes back with some calamine lotion. I know because I recognize the smell. It reminds me of when my mother would rub it on me when I was a child after too much sun, which just makes the reality of what I've done hit home. *I am playing sex games with a lesbian!* Is it wrong? Now I've had my orgasm I regret saying what I did – I really don't want to kiss her - it's too intimate. I think of Julia Roberts in *Pretty Woman* and remember that's what her character said. I should go soon, anyway. Get out of here. I feel a wave of shame mixed with exhilaration. What a paradox!

I'm still lying on my front. Alessandra takes my wrists and ties them together with what feels like a bandana. *Why am I letting her do this?*

I say weakly, "I said, *no restraints*, Alessandra."

"Oh this is nothing. I just want to ensure you don't go trying to pleasure yourself. That's *my* job."

I chuckle. *I've just had an incredible orgasm, I don't need another!* "I'm good. My whole core has just exploded, believe me, Alessandra, I'm done. The last thing I need to do is pleasure myself."

"We'll see about that."

"What are you going to do now?"

She says nothing but begins to gently rub the lotion on my butt, careful not to hurt me. It's sore but not too bad. I'll live. But…oh God…here she goes again. Her massage is turning me on once more. *This is insane!* Her fingers gently open my cheeks and with a little pressure she rests her thumb at that sweet spot where my thighs join my ass – she's slipping her thumb inside me. Holy Moses – she's circling it now and those sexy jiggle balls are still there. Oh wow. Multiple orgasms are not something that happen often, not even with Alexandre…but…this…Holy Heaven…….this feels amazing.

Her thumb is inside, the balls are doing their thing –

she's got her four fingers resting on my mound, on my clit…the pressure…oh wow….any second now I'm going to come again. I'm rubbing myself hard on her hand. This feels so horny. It's coming…it's coming…

But she stops.

What is she playing at?

My nails are clawing into the material of the couch, wrists in front of me tied with the silky bandana. She has me so worked up. Teetering on the edge. *Please!*

"Please Alessandra," I plead in a desperate voice.

"Quite a selfish lover, aren't you?"

But I told you I'm not gay. I don't do girls.

"Turn over," she commands.

I do as she says. I feel my wetness hot between my legs. I bring my arms down to touch myself. I just need that little push and…

"Not so fast." She grabs my wrists and puts my hands above my head. I'm on my back again. Ouch, my butt is sore. "Bend your knees up and press the small of your back into the couch, it'll take the pressure off your ass," she instructs.

I do as she says, all my nerve endings tingling with trepidation, my clit pounding…wanting round two. Not round two of a beating…no, I think I'm done with that little experiment for good, but round two of….oh wow, I can feel her warm breath on my inner thighs. She splays my legs apart some more and I detect her mane of hair nestling between me. Softly. I flex my hips up higher to meet what I can feel is her tongue. Oh wow. She's licking me now with long swipes using just the tip of her tongue. I'm writhing and pressing my groin into her – her tongue is resting so, so gently on my clit – I'm going to come, I'm going to come…

But she stops.

Pussy-teaser. "Please," I beg.

She's moved away from her position now. What's she doing? My blindfold is still keeping me in my dark little world, each movement is multiplied a hundred times – each sensation more pronounced. I smell the rose incense and calamine lotion and her sweet minty breath – she must have brushed her teeth in the bathroom. She's licking my tits now, flicking her tongue around my nipples, nibbling them gently with her teeth. I sense her hand on my head and she slips the blindfold off me in one quick movement. The room is dimmed but suddenly everything seems bright. Her cherry-red lips parted seductively, her dark hair falling like a cascade about her bare shoulders – she has taken off her shirt and her breasts are full, the nipples erect - but she's still got her jeans on, straddling me, not sitting on me, just kneeling on the couch. Tendrils of her long hair rest on my cheeks. She is breathtakingly beautiful and I gasp at this unusual situation of not just having an upcoming movie star desiring me and pleasing my desires but a *woman!*

"You really are stunning," I hear myself say.

Her lips graze me lightly on the chin and then linger on my mouth without moving. *I shouldn't do this!* But she smells so sweet, her skin soft as silk. I find myself parting my lips and offering her the tip of my tongue. Slowly – so slowly we lick each other, playing with just the tips, flickering together like a flame of a candle. Desire shoots like a current of electricity down to my groin. I moan into her mouth.

Her lips are lightly teasing - her finger tapping my clit as she kisses me. Oh, yeah. Her kiss gets deeper, more sensual and I think, *I am loving this.* She's making little circles now with her fingers flat against my mound, pressuring me in all the perfect places. I'm gyrating against her and yes, oh yes, the build, the stairway…I start climaxing in a rush of rapture – Seventh Heaven - ignoring any preconceived notions of what a woman should or shouldn't do with another female. My tied hands are grasping, fisting in her wild hair as she pleasures the fuck out of me. I see stars of color flashing through my brain. The orgasm is long, it keeps going - rolling over me, under me, through me, the jingling balls wriggling about inside as I cry out with intense gratification.

Finally, the waves roll into ripples and the ripples begin to fade. Alessandra gets off the couch and adjusts her position. With one leg firmly on the floor and one still on the sofa she holds my knee and thrusts it between her crotch – the material of her jeans pressing hard into my knee. I feel her heat. All it takes is a few dry rubs and I see the expression on her face change to a clenching of the teeth, her nipples hard as nuts and with one last push she screams out. "I'm coming Pearl, coming hard."

This is a first! If Alessandra weren't so beautiful I would laugh out loud at the madness of it all but her vulnerable face as she looks at me with such an expression of bliss and her tight, peachy ass thrusting her crotch on my knee in such a sexy way as she tips herself into ecstasy, makes it all okay.

I Kissed a Girl and I Liked It. The song captures my imagination as the tune hums about in my head.

But Alessandra is looking serious. Like a guy who has just got what he wanted, she gets off me and slumps herself down into the armchair opposite. I'm relieved. The idea of post-coital cuddles with another woman would be going too far. It was curiosity. Sex. Carnal desire. A physical release. An adventure. But it's Alexandre I want, not a woman. That's clear to me. Crystal clear - however much fun I've just had.

I still stand by my resolution, though. I won't accept

marriage if I have to live in a proverbial threesome with Sophie.

I observe Alessandra. She's lying back in the chair, her legs stretched out before her, her pretty toes pointed, her bare golden torso smooth as caramel.

"I have extremely intense orgasms, Pearl," she whispers. "Afterwards, I feel drained – wiped-out. This one's been building for a long time, thanks to you. Excuse me, I just feel like resting a while,"

I take the terry robe which has been strewn over the back of the couch and put it back on. "That's fine," I whisper back. I notice her eyes are closed now. Good. I can leave - slip away and she won't get upset. Phew.

I tiptoe to the bathroom, untie my wrists and gather my clothes together. I check out my butt in the mirror. It's red, alright, with a couple of obvious welts. Lucky Alexandre won't be around to see. I pull the jiggle balls out, wash them with hot soapy water and leave them by the sink – somehow I don't think I'll be using these again, fun as they were. I get dressed back into my panties and jeans, gently easing each article of clothing over my sore behind, trying not to graze the sensitive skin. I quickly put my bra and T-shirt back on. My sweater must be in the kitchen.

I tiptoe past her. "Bye," I say quietly but she doesn't hear me. Or she's pretending not to. What a fascinating character. It seemed like it was her mission to kiss me and now she got what she wanted she feels as if she's won me in some way. But I won't be returning.

I grab my sweater and handbag from the kitchen. I check inside for my car keys, but now I remember...I didn't put them there because they always get lost in an ocean of darkness. Where did I leave them? By the stove? In a bowl? Where? Lucifer trots into the kitchen, light on his paws, and starts doing a pole dance against the furniture and my legs.

"Where did I put my keys, Lucifer?" I whisper. I don't want to wake Alessandra, I need to hightail it out of the scene of the crime – yes, I do feel as if I've broken the law. CSI could be arriving any minute to scan for evidence. I am a naughty girl, no two ways about it.

As if by magic, Lucifer jumps up onto one of the countertops and starts clawing at another basket piled high with bills. "You clever puss," I marvel, finding the BMW rental keys right there. "Are you a warlock pussycat? Do you understand human talk?"

He meows as if answering and stares at me with his shimmering green eyes. *Jesus, this cat really is magic!* I grab the keys from the basket and then something catches my eye. Again! But this time it isn't a letter. It's a photo peeking out from under a bill. I freeze. Is it really...? No, surely not. My hearts starts pounding. I ease it out from the pile.

Alessandra...and yes, unmistakably...Sophie. Nude bodies entwined in an intimate embrace, Sophie's hand on Alessandra's breast - both grinning away at the camera. The picture tells a story...best friends? Nuh, uh - I don't think so. They look like a couple in love.

I grab the photo and shove it in my purse.

And run.

11

I drive the car over the creek very carefully as frogs have gathered for their night time chit-chat and I don't want to run any over. The noise is impressive as they croak in the pebbled rush of water amongst the bulrushes. Once I am safely out of sight from Alessandra's lair, I pull the car over at the end of the potholed driveway, kill the engine and turn on my cell which has been switched off for hours.

There are six voicemail messages. I listen to the first.

"Pearl darling, we got cut off. As I said, I'm on my way to LA. I've organized a plane. Can you meet me at the Van Nuys Airport in…I don't know, five hours or so?"

No mention of Sophie. As if he hadn't heard a word I said.

Next voicemail: "Pearl, chérie, why aren't you picking up? I'm about to take off. I'm gutted about what you told me. Hang on in there. We'll talk about all this when I see you. It was not your fault, baby. We all have a past. It's nothing to be ashamed of. And don't think I won't hunt those fuck-heads down for what they did to you. But first we have our marriage to attend to. I've organized it all and we're going to Vegas tonight. Meet me at the Van Nuys Airport and I'll pick you up there. The pilot will wait and we'll fly to Las Vegas."

Again, nothing about Sophie or separating the business. *This guy has not heard me.* He thinks we can just marry and that will be that - everything sorted, solution over! *No, Alexandre, I will not just marry you in Vegas before you've dealt with HookedUp first! Especially now that I know Sophie has been screwing with me and my movie deal right from the beginning – she is Alessandra's LOV-ER! A coincidence – I don't think so!*

Next voicemail – sent five hours later. "Landed, baby. Your cell is still switched off, what the fuck is going on? I'm really worried now."

Finally, the penny is dropping.

Next voicemail: "Okay, baby, I get it; you're really pissed off about Sophie. I swear I'll deal with it but please, please trust me on this. I just want us to get married. We'll be a team and we can sort it out together. Where are you? I've hired a car, I'm on my way to the hotel in Santa Monica."

Next voicemail. His voice sounds as if he's almost in tears. "Baby, they say you checked out. I'm so worried, you alone in LA and stuff. The only thing I can think of, right now, is that you're at Alessandra's. But she's not picking up her phone, either. I'm on my way there now. Please don't leave. Please, Pearl. I beg you. I need you. I'm coming to find you."

Next voicemail...hang on, this isn't him. A woman's voice. An English accent. Educated, softly-spoken. "Pearl, you don't know me. I'm sorry to bother you like this. I finally tracked down your number. My name is Laura. Alexandre's ex…maybe you know who I am?"

My heart is pounding through my sweater, my hands burst with a sheen of sweat - a prickly nausea envelops my entire body. Why I feel so nervous I'm not sure…a premonition?

The urgent but friendly voice goes on: "I'm calling to warn you. Sophie is really crazy. She could be out to hurt you. I'm sorry but…." There's a long pause…. "I had a terrible accident several years ago and could have died. It wasn't an accident at all. Sophie tried to kill me."

I press my ear closer to my phone. There's a slight pause and the voice continues:

"Why do you think I broke up with Alexandre? I had to keep well away. Stay away from her, too, Pearl. I know you love Alexandre but your life is at stake. She's powerful. She's even more dangerous now than then. She knows people…she could have you topped off at the click of her fingers. *Do not go to Vegas.* It's too dangerous for you there. She owns great chunks of it… hotels et cetera, corrupt police officers, officials all in her pocket like little pawns doing whatever she asks. Sophie could do anything and will, believe me. I won't bother you again but as one woman to another, I thought I owed you this. Goodbye, Pearl. Good luck."

I feel sick - all this information flooding into my exhausted brain like sewerage. *Sophie tried to kill Laura?* Then why does Laura still go to Alexandre's house in Provence with her husband for vacations knowing she might bump into Sophie? Alexandre told me they were friends and that Sophie thought 'the sun shone out of Laura's ass.' Unless…he was lying, sticking up for his sister, as usual. Painting her with a rose-tinted brush when in fact, Sophie still hates Laura. *Jesus – she tried to murder her?* That nutcase will stop at nothing!

And that's just the tip of the iceberg. Sophie and Alessandra are a *couple?????* Or if not a couple, best friends/lesbian fuck buddies. Alessandra lied to me, pretended she'd only ever spoken to Sophie, that she didn't know her personally. *I was totally set up by Sophie. It was all planned out!* Alessandra Demarr was suggested for the movie role by Sam Myers. Meanwhile, Sam Myers was in cahoots with Sophie from word go. Clever. Really clever. Knowing I wanted a female lead for the role, Samuel Myers put the idea of Alessandra Demarr into my head – made it look like it was my choice all along. Or *was* it my choice? Now I can't even remember our conversation.

Alessandra and Sophie lovers? But Sophie's married! She has a step-daughter. Alexandre never mentioned anything about his sister being *gay*.

Never before have I felt such a fool. So dumb. Summa cum laude? They got that wrong, alright. What a dense dumbass I've been, congratulating myself on getting a gay female lead who is not only Sophie's lover but who also seduced me! No, *worse!* She didn't even have to seduce me – I was up for it. Like putty in her hands. Acting like a little slut again.

I got snagged right into Sophie's spider web. Tangled right in the middle of her Black Widow trap.

Laura's right, Vegas would be suicide.

I put the car into drive and move off. Great, I told Alessandra where I was going. Sophie could have me tracked down in Kauai. But I guess Sophie would find me anywhere in the world – she has the means and with GPS as sophisticated as it is nowadays hunting me down would be a piece of cake if she set her mind to it. She wants me to back off from Alexandre. And I want *her* to back off. Who is going to win this duel?

It depends on him. Who does he love more? His own flesh and blood? Or me? He once told me that the expression, *blood is thicker than water* doesn't exist in the French language. If so, he'd better prove it.

As I'm moving off, a car is pulling into Alessandra's driveway but I can't see the face of the person behind the wheel. Alexandre? Jesus, maybe it's Sophie. Either way, I rev my engine and double my speed. I look in my rear-view mirror and think the driver hasn't seen me, but I'm wrong. The car is screeching in a U-turn and coming right after me. I hang a sharp left on PCH in the direction of LAX, just getting the green light in time and flatten my foot on the accelerator. If it's Sophie, I need to outrun her. Alexandre, ditto. I know him – he's so persuasive he'll have me on that plane, abducting me and whisking me off to Vegas to tie the knot. He's used to getting what he wants.

Well not this time, buddy.

My foot is all the way down. I'm cruising fast. This BMW is smooth and speedy – thank God I traded in the Cadillac. I'm outrunning the driver, way ahead but can see its head-lights flashing at me. I feel as if I'm in some car chase in a movie and it gives me a wicked thrill as a surge of adrenaline spikes my veins. The driver is careering about corners with a keen, formula one style. Uh, oh, I recognize that technique – that easy panache, those gear changes. I see what kind of car it is – a sleek, black Mercedes – yes, that's him, that's Alexandre. I don't stand a chance. We are both hell bent for leather, flying two times past the speed limit as if we were on a German autobahn. We'll both be arrested, for sure. He's catching up with me now, zooming between two other cars. He has overtaken me and I can't do a U-turn.

I'm busted. If I don't want us both killed I'd better pull over. I see a safe spot up ahead and pull into a restaurant parking lot. He does the same a little way ahead. My heart's pounding but I'm secretly enjoying the attention. A twenty-five year-old sex-god, babe-magnet, the best looking man in the Universe is tracking me down and wants to take me to Vegas to marry him! Hello? *Am I dreaming?* He's running towards my car now and I can't help it; a huge grin is spread right across my face. I zap down my window, trying so hard to stifle my beaming smile, biting the insides of my cheeks. But he's got my number.

He leans into the open window of my car. "Quite a madwoman, aren't you? Trying to get us both killed?"

"I meant what I said, Alexandre," I say, pursing my lips to stop myself laughing, my only ammunition against his drop-dead gorgeous smile – a smile that's giving me butter-flies and turning my stomach inside-out. "I'm not going to Vegas with you; I'm going to visit my father in Kauai."

He opens my door and leans in, his apple-mint breath on my face. He says in a soft, low voice, his face touching mine, "Correction. *We* are going to Vegas. Now. I'm going to marry you tonight or," he looks at his watch, "early tomor-row morning as it's already ten-thirty. "Then *we* are going to Kauai for our honeymoon."

"NO!" I shout. But it's too late. He grabs the keys out of the ignition and scoops me out of the driver's seat and hauls me over his shoulders as if I'm a weightless doll. He walks round to the trunk.

I'm kicking and flailing about. "Put me down Alexan-dre!"

"No. You're acting like a child, Pearl, and need to be treated like a child." He opens the trunk and takes out my suitcase - awkward but he manages. His determination and strength have him holding the suitcase in one hand and the other clamped about my rear in a tight vice. He locks the car with the remote. He's marching forward now towards his rental car, his arm still clenched around me. Ouch, my sore, whipped butt hurts! I can't escape, he has me in a firm hold. The fireman's lift. Oh yes, he knows I love this fireman thing, however much I'm screaming and kicking.

"Let me down!" I cry, pummeling his back with my fists.

"No, Pearl. Stop behaving like a wayward teenager. You're coming with me. I'm fed up with this nonsense."

"I'm not marrying you, Alexandre Chevalier! Not until you sort—"

"Stop telling me what to do," he barks, his gait strong as he strides towards his car. "You're marrying me and that's the end of it."

I suddenly think of something. "You can't marry me, you don't have my divorce papers. So there!"

"Oh no? I've had Suresh get them couriered over to the hotel we're saying at in Vegas. All will be quite legal, I can assure you."

We arrive at his car. With one hand he opens the trunk, chucks my case in and, keeping a tight grip on me with the other arm so I can't escape, lowers me into the back seat and lays me inside as if I were a child not allowed in the front seat with her daddy. Then he locks the door. I try to open it from inside but it won't let me out. Child safety locks, no doubt. I pound on the windows.

He comes around to his side, opens his door and jumps in. "Not so fast, Pearl Robinson, soon to be Pearl Chevalier.

You are *not* running out on me. You did that once in France and I won't let it happen again." He starts the engine, puts it into first and revs forward, Formula One Style.

"So I'm your prisoner?"

"Yes. And then you'll be my wife."

"Also in jail. Do not pass GO - DO NOT COLLECT $200."

"There'll be more than $200 to collect, of that you can be quite sure."

"But still in jail."

"Yes." He smiles and adds, "A very pretty, gilded jail where you can have anything you want."

"Except my freedom."

"Believe me, you'll be there of your own free will."

"Like now? Trapped in the back of this Mercedes being abducted into marriage?"

A gentle smirk edges his curvy, dark red lips. "I know what's best for you, Pearl. Trust me. You need to marry me."

The arrogance! I would laugh but it's not funny. I'm crying now, tears trailing down my cheeks. "You're taking me to my death."

He laughs out loud and changes smoothly into fourth.

"I'm not kidding, Alexandre. Laura called. She says Sophie tried to kill her."

"Nonsense."

"She did! She says it was no accident and that Sophie owns chunks of Vegas and will have me murdered."

He doesn't say anything. Just keeps his eyes on the road.

"What is *wrong* with you? You sister is insane and you're too blind to see it!"

"I agree, my sister is a little eccentric, shall we say, but she's not going to try and have you killed."

"How do you *know*?"

"Because I know her. I know how her mind works."

"Like she stabbed your father in the groin? She is *dangerous*."

He turns his head abruptly to me. His lips close tightly, bitterly – his eyes flash with rage. "He deserved what he had coming to him. Don't you *dare* defend that vicious monster."

"It doesn't let Sophie off the hook. She's out to get me."

"She's jealous, Pearl, that's all. She'll get used to you."

"She will *not* get 'used to me' because I'm bailing, Alexandre. I value my life too highly, however much I love you. I'm not going to marry you with your whack-job sister in the picture."

"I made some calls tonight. I'm selling her my share of HookedUp. Once and for all. Satisfied? Most men wouldn't let their girlfriends pussy-whip them the way you have with me about this, but because American women have a history of dominating their men, I'll forgive you. But just this once. It won't happen again, Pearl. This is the last time you tell me what to do. Do you understand." *No question mark but a statement.*

I am speechless. Pussy-whipped? I don't know whether to laugh or cry. Instead I blurt out, "I got pussy-whipped tonight. Literally."

He looks around at me with a wry smile and then back at the road. "Oh yes?"

"Yes, A bit of lesbian S and M." *There, said it.* "Surely you don't want to marry a quasi lesbian who got beaten by your sister's lover? Oh, and by the way, thanks for letting me in on the fact that Sophie is gay. Another secret you've been hiding from me."

"I didn't think it was my place to reveal Sophie's sexual

preferences. It's something we never discuss – she's very private. It was up to her to tell you. What do you mean, 'my sister's lover?' "

"What?? So it's true then, she's gay?"

"Yes, she's gay. She kept it quiet from me for years but I always had my suspicions. What do you mean, 'my sister's lover?' Are you talking about Alessandra Demarr?"

"Yes, I found a photo which I stole for evidence as I'm fed up with you telling me I'm imagining things. They are lovers. At least that's what the photo is spelling out loud and clear."

He changes the music. *Leaving on a Jet Plane*. How apt. "Interesting," he mumbles.

"What?? Why do you not seem shocked by this?"

"Sophie must have got together with her when we went backstage that time at the theatre - when we saw her in that play."

"What? Alexandre, why didn't you tell me this?"

"I did. I told you we saw a play of hers in London. Sophie wanted to congratulate her so we went to the green room backstage afterwards, but I got bored waiting so I left. Sophie stayed, though. She never told me the two of them had anything going on, or that they'd even met. I had no idea. And you had a little fun with Alessandra, too? Oh well…keep it in the family." He laughs.

"Stop it!" I yell leaning forward, still riding in the back seat. "I am *disgusted!* I feel used and dumb and a total freaking idiot. Why did I not see this? She seduced me, Alexandre, *and I let her.* My ass is so sore I can hardly sit. She whipped me, she made me come, she…she…" I find myself wailing through angry, shameful tears.

He turns the music down. "Ssh, now chérie, it's so not

important in the great scheme of things." But he still has a slight smile on his face as if the whole thing tickles him somehow.

"Why the hell do you want me anyway?" I sniffle. "I had a threesome with two guys that went all wrong. I'm a quasi lesbian. I can't do a work deal without being totally screwed over. I can't look a penis in the eye, excuse the pun...I'm a basket-case. I am a disaster. This is all wrong, Alexandre, this is all screwed-up. *I* am screwed up. Really, I'm not the person you thought I was. I'm not Miss Sweetie-Pie, Star-Spangled American Cutie, Golden Girl. Look at me, I'm all over the place."

He changes gear again. "I know."

"No, you don't *know!* You thought I was perfect."

He threads his arm to the back seat and holds onto my hand. "Perfect for me, chérie. You think I want Miss Good-ie-Two-Shoes? That I could relate to someone like that with my fucked-up past? I know who you are, Pearl, maybe even better than you know yourself. You're a contradiction, a paradox, a mix of all things messy and delightful. We've only known each other four and a half months but you are my *media naranja* – my soul mate - I knew that the second I laid eyes on you."

"The other half of the orange?" I snivel, grabbing some Kleenex from my purse and blowing my runny nose. "That Spanish expression you wrote me in your love letter?"

"That's right. We fit perfectly together. We're two separate orange halves that make up one whole."

I exhale with frustration but climb forward and maneuver myself into the passenger seat so we can have a more normal conversation. All Alexandre's love and forgiveness still doesn't solve the Sophie problem. This is exasperating. I feel as if I have been left to bubble and boil in Sophie and Alessandra's witches' cauldron. With Lucifer purring away, observing the whole crazy scene.

"Well, this is all a big shock for me, I can tell you," I say buckling up, remembering Bette Davis's line in *All About Eve*, 'Fasten your seatbelt, we're in for a bumpy night.' "I mean finding out about Sophie being gay, being Alessandra's girlfriend and, oh yes, P.S. Sophie is married."

"So? You think she's the first gay person to be married? It helps her social status, not to mention fiscal benefits. In France, being single's expensive. It's way more cost-effective to have a spouse."

I glare at him. "Is that why you want to marry me, to save on tax?"

"I file in America, chérie. My primary residence is New York, in case you haven't noticed. And no, I would never marry for financial reasons, you know that. Sophie's different – she's obsessed with money, as you are well aware."

"I feel grossed out. I might as well have had sex with Sophie herself. I kissed Alessandra. I let her whip me!"

He looks at me for a second, still vaguely amused. "And are you over it now? Cured of your bondage curiosity? Because don't ask *me* to get the handcuffs out and spank you."

I shuffle in my seat trying to find a comfortable position that doesn't chafe my tender butt. "Yes, I'm over it. It hurts. No more, thank you very much, my derrière is really sore."

His lips curve very slightly. "Good. Now can we get on with our relationship or do you have some more sniffing about to do?"

"Are you pissed at me?"

"What I had envisioned in my obviously very boring

male imagination was a little kissing between two beautiful women, some light sexual entertainment, not my fiancée being beaten with a whip by my sister's lover.'"

"Yeah, well, I regret it now, that's for sure."

I suddenly remember all the dirty details that Alessandra shared with me about her 'ex' liking hairy underarms. The 'ex' obviously being Sophie, the 'tigress in bed.'

"It was an experiment," I say, excusing myself. "I wanted to beat out those nasty memories of that fateful night – wipe out my past."

Alexandre takes in a deep breath as if to say, *Good luck.*

"What, you think that's crazy?"

"Revenge is a dish best served cold," he replies ominously.

"What are you trying to say, Alexandre - what are you telling me?"

"Nothing, just quoting a rather fitting line from Shakespeare – or maybe not Shakespeare at all; perhaps it's some old Sicilian proverb."

Sicily. Alessandra. Yes, come to think of it I've heard that expression in *The Godfather* – Michael Corleone talking about how his father gave him that very same advice – *Revenge is a dish that tastes best when served cold.* I remember what Alexandre said to me on the phone earlier about the footballers - that he'd 'track those fuck-heads down' - and then I wonder, is that what he did with his father - serve him up a cold dish of revenge years later? His father's 'disappearance' – a cold payback dish that Alexandre took out of the freezer, thawed and served up when his dad was least expecting it? I'm dying to ask but every time I mention his father he gets riled. Now is not the moment to press him.

The car breaks smoothly to a halt. I can see the private

jets clustered together a way off – Van Nuys Airport isn't a maze like LAX. "We've arrived," Alexandre lets me know in a serious voice.

"I'm not going to Vegas."

"Yes you are."

"I'm not getting out of this car."

He laughs. "Do you want me to carry you in a fireman's lift again?"

"I'll scream and attract attention so you'll let me go."

"Not a chance. I'm keeping a firm grip on you until you've got that ring on your finger. I'll gag you if I have to. You want a bit of rough play, a bit of bondage? – you've got it, baby."

"What good will a dead wife be to you?" I shout. "Sophie will have me 'topped off' as Laura put it. Yes, that was the expression she used."

"Laura and Sophie get on fine – this is all ridiculous, I can't believe Laura called you and said that."

I fumble in my handbag for my cell. "Right, if you don't believe me, I'll play you the message!" I squeal.

He pretends he hasn't heard. "Where shall we go for our honeymoon? Anywhere in the world – you name it, baby, we can go. Kauai or Bora Bora. We can leave straight after the ink is dry on our marriage certificate if you don't fancy hanging about Vegas."

I want to scream. *Why is he ignoring me?* I grapple about for my phone in my oversize bag. *Where is it?* "Alexandre, why are you not listening? Your nutcase sister is going to kill me and all you're doing is laughing and in total and utter denial! She tried to kill Laura! Where is my goddam phone?"

"Calm down, Pearl."

I try to unlock my car door again but he grabs my wrists.

I stamp my legs on the floor. "I will NOT calm down!" Then I fish about in my bag again and finally locate my cell. Suddenly, a brilliant idea flashes into my brain like a torch-light. I take a deep breath and say. "Okay, fine, Alexandre. I'm coming along. I'll be quiet and behave but please keep an eye on me until we have gotten the hell out of Vegas. I'm scared."

"Good girl. And don't worry, I won't let you out of my sight. Ready now?"

"I think my cell fell out of the side pocket of my hand-bag," I lie.

"What a bummer, there's nothing worse than losing your phone. I'll buy you another. That one was outdated anyway."

"Never mind," I grumble.

He gets out of his side and quickly dashes around to open my door. I generally love that about Alexandre; he has such gentlemanly manners; always treats me with such respect, opening doors for me – except for *now*, throwing me over his shoulder like I'm a little girl – ignoring my plea. He's so dominating it worries me. Do I want to marry this man? As things stand at the moment, no, I don't. I can just see myself lying dead in a ditch somewhere in the suburbs of Vegas or in a dumpster with a bullet through my brain, or covered in liquid cement like some Jane Doe in a CSI Las Vegas episode. Alexandre admitted Sophie was 'eccentric' but he still won't stop her mad games And now he's putting my life in danger! I glare at him furiously.

He helps me out of the car and puts both his hands about my waist. "Christ, you're beautiful," he murmurs with hooded sex-eyes, raking me up and down as if he wants to eat me alive.

"Thank you," I mumble, bowing my head to stop his

burning gaze - loathing him and loving him simultaneously.

"C'est normal," he says in French and then takes my face in his large hands tilting my chin up and planting a firm kiss on my mouth. My heart is racing. His devastating good looks, his flashing green eyes, his soft, dark red lips…but more than all that, the adrenaline rush of what I'm about to do…

I break the kiss. "I really need to go to the bathroom."

"You can go when you're on the plane."

"Don't we need to go through some sort of security though?"

"Lately they've got a little picky – sometimes they frisk you with the metal detector thing before you board."

"That's what I was afraid of," I say, thinking I have metal balls inside me jiggling away. But then I remember that I took them out.

He smiles wryly. "Why, have you got a pistol on you?"

"No, just…well, I've got my period. I would really like to use the bathroom now before we board."

"You're just saying that. You'll try to do a runner."

"That's one of those British expressions you picked up from Laura, isn't it?"

"I have a feeling you'll try and slip away, Pearl."

"Don't be silly," I assure him, holding his hand and leading him to the building where some double doors are. "I just want to freshen up a bit and those airplane toilets are so squished – even on private jets - you can hardly turn around. Anyway, we have to drop the rental car keys off, don't we?"

"All I have to do is make a call and someone will come and pick up the keys."

"But I need to use the bathroom to clean up."

"Alright, but don't dawdle. This is already taking far too long."

We find the ladies room.

"Why don't you drop off the car keys while I go to the toilet?" I ask, knowing he'll say no.

"Some chance. I'll wait here."

Alexandre hovers outside the door watching me suspiciously as I go in. I rush inside to have a scout about. No windows.

I come out again grimacing. "It stinks in there - half the toilets are blocked up. I need to find another."

"Come on, this is ridiculous, just go on the plane."

"I have blood all *over* me," I hiss at him.

I march ahead, desperate to bring my plan to fruition but it looks as if I'll be getting on that jet, like it or not. I find a new bathroom and do a quick check over. Bingo, there's a tiny window high up. I go over and see if I can open it. Just. It'll be a real squeeze but I'll try. I search in my bag and get out what I need. All my cash and my passport. I stuff it in my jeans' pockets. I casually come out of the ladies room. Alexandre is standing there, legs astride in his Alpha male stance, watching my every movement. I smile nonchalantly.

I edge up close to him, fingering the expensive material of his sharp, charcoal-grey suit jacket. "You look so handsome. How come you're wearing a suit today?"

He strokes the knuckles of my hand. "I didn't get a chance to change. I double-backed on that meeting in Montreal, remember? Chasing about after you, Ms. Pearl Robinson. But not for much longer though," he glances at his watch, "before I make you mine. You won't be Robinson any more. *Pearl...*" he says, rolling his tongue around the R of Pearl... "*Chevalier.* Sounds good, doesn't it?"

"Can't wait," I answer sweetly. "Hold my handbag, will you? There aren't any hooks on the back of the doors in there. Disgusting, I hate putting my handbag on the floor with all those germs everywhere." I give him my bag and hug him closely, slipping my hand surreptitiously into his jacket pocket until I find what I need. I distract him meanwhile with a kiss, gliding my teasing tongue along his lower lip and then I nip him there with my teeth. I lock my eyes with his. "I love you, Alexandre Chevalier, whatever happens, remember that. You'd better call the pilot and tell them we're on our way. I'll be a while in there, though. I need to change my panties." I hold a 'fresh pair' up at him (which is, in reality, a bunch of Kleenex scrunched in my hand with his car keys inside) …but it does the trick.

"I'll wait over there," he says, awkwardly handling my bag, as if it were a bomb. Why is it men find a woman's handbag so embarrassing? But he seems relaxed now, getting out his cell phone as he makes a call.

I race into the ladies room making a dash to the window. I climb on the toilet seat trying not to make any noise and raise my leg up, twisting and contorting myself into yogi-like positions until I am able to squeeze myself through the window. Better this than dead in Vegas, I think. It's dark out there and it's hard to tell where I'm going to land. All I have is the wad of dollar bills in my front jeans' pocket with the car key, my passport in the back pocket. My cell and everything else is in my handbag with him. There's no point bringing any of it - he could trace the movement on my credit cards and cell phone - and would. My heart's pounding in my chest. I'm falling head-first, now, and manage to twist my torso back around so I land on my feet the other side. My eyes dart about to fix my location. Luckily, this airport is fairly small and I spot the position where we parked the Mercedes. I sprint like crazy until I reach it.

I leap inside, turn on the ignition and drive like a bat out of hell.

12

Anthony's apartment is up on a hill in a beautiful tree-lined street in Pacific Heights. He and Bruce live in part of a stately Edwardian house which has been divided into three condos. His is the first floor sporting huge bay windows that look out over the city of San Francisco. It is light and roomy, decorated impeccably with graceful feminine furniture and walls painted in robin's-egg blue and whites that are not white but tinged with subtle tints of ivory - worthy of a spread in a designer magazine. There are two large fireplaces and detailed crowned moldings that run around the ceiling. Dead centre, an elegant crystal chandelier hangs like dripping jewels – a 'souvenir' that he and Bruce brought back from Venice, Italy. Which is where my eyes are fixed now, as I lie on the sofa in the living room contemplating what I should do next. It's nine a.m. - the morning after the night before, and I still haven't gone to bed yet.

Bruce, thank God, is visiting his parents in Napa Valley so I don't have to make small talk with him. I am not in the mood to make an effort with my brother's other half and am exhausted from last night's long drive. I look like hell, too.

I drove without stopping. At every moment I half expected to hear a helicopter above me searching with headlights for a Ms. Pearl Robinson, 'belonging to' a certain, Mr. Alexandre Chevalier. But I made it through the night. I guessed he would have suspected that I got on a plane to Kauai. Sorry, Dad, next time. Besides, Sophie will be expecting me to be there and I'm too freaked out to risk it – I want to stay out of her radar. Alexandre has called here, of course, but Anthony did a great job of sounding shocked and worried. I feel terrible, thick with guilt but what else can I do? Anthony seems to be enjoying all the drama but thinks I'm nuts not to have snapped up the wedding opportunity in Vegas. That's what he says but his ironic sense of humor can have you easily fooled sometimes.

Anthony minces into the living room in his pink silk pajamas. I am still in a trance, staring at that flickering crystal chandelier which is catching beams of morning light flooding through the bay windows. He brings in two large mugs of steaming drinks –coffee for himself and cocoa for me.

He sets the mugs on the coffee table on top of a thick book about Renaissance Art. "Just hire a bodyguard, Pearly. Get the marriage over and done with," he says carrying on with this morning's no-sleep conversation. I still haven't got any shut-eye at all.

I cover my yawning mouth. "Dead in a dumpster somewhere with a ring on my finger? What good would that do?"

"As long as I'm your next of kin and can inherit half of

Alexandre's empire," he jokes.

I glare at him.

"Seriously, Pearl, he's behaving like a total, control-freak asshole. Of course you can't go through with this union as things are right now. He can't just *abduct* you into marriage, that's insane. Even I get that."

"Yes, well, he's a man who's used to getting what he wants."

"To me it screams insecurity. A man who is so hooked-up on you, HookedUp, pardon the pun – so obsessed with you that it's scary. Like you're his possession. It won't be long before he arrives here, or sends someone – I could tell by his voice on the phone that he didn't quite believe me when I said you weren't here. There's probably someone watching the front door as we speak, waiting to pounce on you. Lucky the rental car is parked in the underground parking, anyway. I'll warn the neighbors not to say a word."

"He'll think I've gone to Hawaii."

"Nuh, uh, he's already checked all the flights out of LA and has people on the case. He said so on the phone."

I sigh. "I feel mean and guilty. I should call and tell him where I am."

"I bet he already knows where you are."

"How?"

"He has a whole team of private detectives working around the clock – that's what he told me, or warned me, more like. If you stay here he'll be on the front doorstep any minute now throwing you over his shoulder again and riding off into the sunset with you on his galloping black stallion."

"You make it sound so romantic."

"Well, it is romantic, in a way. Who wouldn't dream of a guy so in love with you that he's willing to take you hostage?

Especially one as drop-dead gorgeous as Alexandre. However, this psycho sister shit is no joke and I totally see, Pearly, where you're coming from."

"You do?"

"Yes, she sounds like a total fruitcake. And a dangerous one at that."

"But he just doesn't *get* it. He refuses to take it seriously, just tells me that she'll 'get used to me'. The fact that she wheedled her way into Samuel Myers and my movie deal doesn't faze him at all. Alexandre acted like I was over-reacting and P.S. he forgot to let me in on the fact that he knew about it."

"It sounds as if he and Sophie are so close after what happened when he was a child that no matter *what* she does he will always forgive her and make excuses for her until the day he dies. Blood is thicker than water, and I'm sorry, Pearl, but you are the water and she is the blood. He's obviously crazy about you but he wants to have his cake and eat it too. He wants you both in his life and is juggling everything to keep it so."

"Yeah, well, I won't be in his life much longer if she has her evil way – I'll be dead."

"You really believe she could try and *kill* you?"

"I told you, Laura called to warn me. She sounded really kind. Really concerned. She supposedly tripped down some stairs because the next door neighbor's child had left some toys there. But she ended up in a wheelchair because of it – she could have *died*. The whole scenario sounds suspicious to me."

"She's still in a wheelchair?"

"No, apparently she's all better now. Just has a vague limp. But it was a miracle that she was able to walk again.

Poor thing."

"What's she like?"

"Very nice, I think – does a bunch of stuff for disabled charities. Despite what happened, she hasn't felt sorry for herself in any way. From photos she looks like a supermodel. Legs that reach up to her armpits, about five foot ten tall, a body to die for, a face like an angel, long blonde hair and sporty. At least she *was* sporty once before the 'accident' – I think she's doing round the clock physical therapy and is doing really well. Alexandre mentioned that she wants to sail again. To compete - so she's dedicated to getting a hundred percent better. So brave. She sounds like a really admirable person."

"They're still in contact?"

"Yes, they're still friends. He still cares for her."

"Does that make you jealous?"

"It would but she's happily married with a husband who dotes on her. Her childhood sweetheart who she knew before she met Alexandre. Of course, that pang of envy is there, knowing how in love Alexandre was with her once and, as I said, she really is beautiful but you know, it was a long time ago."

Anthony takes my hand in his and says softly, "*You're* beautiful, Pearl."

I look at him in shock. "That's the nicest thing you've said to me for years."

"I know. I'm sorry. I owe you a big apology. I've been a total ass for so long. I'm *really* sorry, sis, I guess I must have been envious of you and holding in a lot of anger about John."

"Envious? Of *me?*"

"I always felt that Mom loved you more. She always confided in you, not me, especially towards the end. It made me resentful inside and I blamed you for all sorts of things. I now realize I was wrong. Will you ever forgive me?"

My eyes are prickling with tears and I feel a lump in my throat. "Thank you, Anthony for that. It means the world." I hug him, his bear-like body is now trembling as his tears come gushing out. "Pearly, I feel like such a big, fat failure. When Bruce nearly died it knocked the wind out of me. I thought I was going to be alone forever and it was then I stopped and thought about you. Really took responsibility for the way I've been acting towards you. I've been unfair and snarky and bitchy and you've...you've been so patient with me." He's blubbering now, his large body shaking with emotion. My heart goes out to him and I, too, am crying.

I stroke his pale hair and say, "Because I knew that it wasn't really you saying all those negative things. That you were hurting after John died and then Mom, and all that guilt you felt inside. You were taking it out on me because I was the closest person for you to lash out at."

"How come..." he asks between sobs, "you're so wise?"

"Because I felt angry, too. I felt guilty, crazy guilt about the tough love thing we were doling out to John. Those goddam meetings we were going to that encouraged us to look out for ourselves more and not pander to him and stop the co-dependency...you know, I felt mad at myself because I didn't call him back that time - like if I'd been there more for him he wouldn't have taken that overdose. I was mad at you because you and he had had that fight... and worst of all? I felt mad at Mom for abandoning us - even though it wasn't her fault. Can you imagine? I felt furious at her for *dying* – how screwed-up is that?"

Anthony wheezes out a little laugh. "I guess we're both

as fucked-up as each other, huh? We probably need several sessions with a therapist. Can we be friends now? Can you forgive me for being such a jackass?"

I squeeze him tightly and say, "Of course I forgive you and we have always been friends, no matter what. I have never given up on you, Ant. Ever."

We nestle in each other's warm embrace. I feel the softness of his pink silk pajamas and smile. What a pair we are. He - the consummate drama queen and I, a basket-case disaster in every possible way. I can't hold a deal together, have hand-picked a stalking Frenchman as my future husband who probably murdered his father, and I don't even know if I'm bisexual or if I can even ever have sex with a man and his penis again.

Anthony's breath hitches from his weeping, he draws back from me asking suddenly, "Well, did you call her back last night and ask for details - about her accusations about Sophie? Proof?"

"Call who back?"

"Laura, of course."

Oh okay, so we are back to that conversation. Heartfelt sibling reunion over. Fine.

"I didn't have time," I answer. "The second after I'd listened to Laura's message, Alexandre and I had that crazy car chase and then he threw me over his shoulder and took me to Van Nuys Airport to catch the private jet to Vegas. I didn't have a second."

"And then you escaped through the toilet window."

"Exactly."

"Leaving your cell behind with her number on it so you can't call her back."

"Yes."

"Laura could be making it up or accusing Sophie of something she never did."

"Whose side are you on, Anthony? You sound like Alexandre! I'm going to end up in an asylum like in one of those psychological horror movies where nobody believes the heroine and sends her stark-raving mad!"

"Sorry, just I haven't met this Sophie but I have to admit she does have a pretty face from photos and looks kind of nice."

I pound a feather cushion with my fists to stop myself from smashing my brother in the face. "Shut up!" I yell.

"Sorry but all this is kind of... I mean, Alexandre loves you, right? He must *know* his own sister. If she were really going to harm you physically, he'd stop her in her tracks."

"She stabbed her own father in the groin, Anthony."

"After he'd repeatedly raped her and beaten her – the father had it coming to him."

"That's exactly what Alexandre always says."

"What happened to their dad anyway? Where is he now?"

"Oh, right, get this...he just 'disappeared'."

Anthony laughs. "Wow, you really are entangled in a family affair, aren't you? You think Sophie killed their father?"

"Maybe," I reply, secretly thinking that Alexandre was in on it too, but not daring to say that to Anthony. I think of how Alexandre mixed rat poison with his father's food when he was only a small child. Killing him could have been the next step. Alexandre could be capable of anything, especially recently with all his money and power. He could have even paid someone to do it for them. And that's why Sophie has such a hold on him. They share a guilty secret. I'm wondering at what point the father disappeared. Hmm…it would be interesting to know that.

Anthony breaks my train of thought, "It sounds to me as if, deep down inside, you *like* the fact that your fiancé could be a killer."

I stare at him incredulously. "What?" *Can Anthony read my mind? How does he know I think Alexandre could be guilty of murder?*

My brother raises his pale blond eyebrows. "Who are your favorite movie characters?"

I roll my eyes. "What's that got to do with any of this?"

"You love fucked-up tough guys, Pearl, let's face it. You like bad boys, menacing, unscrupulous men."

"Alexandre is not bad, he's sweet and kind."

"Who are your favorite movie characters?" he sing-songs. "Travis Bickle and Michael Corleone, aren't they? I think that says it all, don't you?"

"Okay, I love Robert de Niro and Al Pacino just because they are great actors, nothing more."

"No, what you love most is the mysteriously sinister characters they portray, their ice-cold, ruthless interiors mixed with their dark, brooding, panty-melting eyes. The irresistible villain. Well, in *The Godfather* and *Taxi Driver* Bobby and Al were in their prime, of course – they're grandfathers now but–"

"Alexandre's eyes are green, anyway," I interrupt.

Anthony takes a swig of coffee. "Your fiancé doesn't have me fooled for a second. Oh, he's Mr. Perfect on the *exterior,* alright, with his textbook French manners, opening doors for ladies and pulling out your chair at dinner and giving to charity et cetera et cetera, but *within* him lurks a dangerous man, believe me. Let's face it, you've always gone for the typical bad boy."

"That is so not true! Brad wasn't a bad boy."

"He started fooling around on you and you gave him the perfect out by having that little adventure with those foot-ballers. Which means, maybe he wasn't bad *enough* for you. You sabotaged the relationship because you secretly found him boring."

"How d'you know about the footballers, *anyway*, I never told you."

"I overheard Mom talking on the phone to you."

"You *eavesdropped?*"

"You know how she used to whisper so loudly that it attracted attention? That, *'no you don't say'* voice she had that made you instantly stop what you were doing and prick up your ears? Well, she had that voice on when she was on the phone to you, and I….well, I just overheard, that's all. You were not cut out to be the perfect doctor's wife anyway, Pearl."

A wave of sadness engulfs me remembering my mother and I feel heaviness weigh down my heart like a dull ache. "Well Saul was good. He wasn't a bad boy."

"Oh no? Mr. Tax Evasion himself! They nearly sent him to jail and would have if you hadn't bailed him out. But again, he wasn't bad *enough* for you so you divorced him, and that's why you're so crazy about Alexandre and so addicted to him. He's your Michael Corleone."

I think back to my conversation with my mom and how she was always there for my problems; I could tell her anything, she was like a sister to me. I'm tempted to share my saga of the recurring nightmares with Anthony and reveal the real story of what happened with the rapist footballers, but I keep my mouth closed. The thought of my brother knowing anything about my sexual life repels me. "Listen," I yawn, "I need to get some sleep; I can hardly keep my eyes open."

"Your bed is all made up with fresh sheets. The bathroom has everything you need. I'll guard the front door as I'm sure Mr. Possessive will be knocking at it any moment now. But don't worry, he'll need a warrant first, I won't let him in."

"I don't know what to do next, Anthony. I'm being cruel to him – he'll be worried about me."

"Let him suffer for a while. He needs to understand you mean business about getting that nut-job sister out of your life first. If you don't stand your ground now, the next thing you know she'll be moving in to your apartment."

I flinch. Needless to say I haven't shared the worst of it with Anthony about my adventure with Alessandra. The too-close-for-comfort mess I got myself into, never mind the kinky business. Curiosity killed the cat, that's for sure.

"Just get some sleep and then we'll think of the next step," my brother continues, his voice sounding sensible. "Meanwhile, I need to call the office. This is the second time in two weeks I've played hooky."

I take a long, hot shower, then collapse into bed and fall into a profound sleep, not dreaming about needle-dick or any nightmares at all but hot, hot sex with Alexandre. I hear myself coming in my sleep, feel the damp heat between my legs - wanting him, yearning for him. He's fucking me from behind, me on top, me underneath, Cowboy style, 69 – every which way and I can't get enough. His soft dark hair is flopping about his face which is beaded lightly with sweat. I can smell him, even his cock I have in my mind's eye, hard as a rock, fucking me, making me come in thunderous spasms.

I'm hungry for him, ravenous for his touch, for him to be inside me. I'm moaning in my sleep. I need him. Want. Desire. A burning passion has me on fire.

Can I be strong? Keep my resolve? Or am I so addicted to him that I'm a lost cause?

13

Several hours later, while Anthony is working from home, I slip out the back door and use the neighbor's entrance in their garden to make my exit. I still don't know what to do about Alexandre. I need more time to think before I call him. I'm in love with him, no doubt about it and I want to marry him but every time I'm tempted to give in I think of my naked body sprawled in a ditch, or in a shallow grave. Dead. Maybe even chopped up and distributed all over the United States. Or perhaps Sophie would meddle with the brakes of my car or slip cyanide in my drink. She has people working on her payroll all over the country – she could do anything.

I spend a couple of hours at Anthony's gym, swimming – letting out all my steam and stretching my aching limbs from that long car journey last night. The water feels great and I feel so much better afterwards.

As I'm approaching Anthony's neighbor's back yard, carefully looking out for Alexandre, I hear steady footsteps behind me. My heart is racing, I feel a spike of adrenaline rush through my veins and turn around. It's HIM. He's standing there in jeans and a white T-shirt looking beyond stunning. His jaw is set firm and he has a five o'clock shadow and hooded eyes of a man who hasn't slept all night. He's not smiling. His face is stern, unflinching but he doesn't look angry, just immovable. Uh oh, this is scarier than anything.

I walk over to him, stretch out my arms to hug him, donning a limp smile. But he steps back as if he doesn't want me to touch him. His body language shocks me.

"Alexandre, I'm so sorry, I didn't know what to do last night."

"Oh, I think you did, Pearl. You had it all nicely planned out. You knew exactly what you were doing."

I edge closer but he steps aside, narrowing his eyes at me. All I can think of is how handsome he is and that I don't want to lose him. "I'm sorry, I—"

"Did you stop for even one second to think how I'd feel? Can you imagine what an idiot I looked; standing there with a lady's handbag while my fiancée had climbed through the window of a fucking *toilet*? To escape from me? How debasing that was?"

"I had no choice, I—"

"I wanted to *marry* you, Pearl. I wanted for us to be together forever - didn't that mean anything to you?"

Oh my God! He's speaking in the past tense!

"Alexandre, I still want to marry you, I still want to make this work, I still—"

"Pearl, don't you get it? It's too late for that now. I can't be with a woman who's going to bolt on me every time my

450

sister does something that she isn't a thousand percent okay with. What kind of a man do you think I am? That I'd abandon my own family for some crazy notion of yours that my sister's got it in for you, that she's going to kill you? It's just insane."

"She is!" I yell. "Laura called me. She told me not to go to Vegas, that Sophie caused her accident—"

"The night the accident happened, when Laura tripped down the stairs, Laura was tipsy and yes, it was Sophie who had taken us both out to dinner and ordered that extra bottle of wine... so was Sophie responsible? No she wasn't, but at the time Laura felt angry – she has two left feet and was always tripping up and usually never drank alcohol, but Sophie didn't ply her with wine on *purpose* so she'd have an accident – you must have misinterpreted what Laura said."

"I didn't! Laura said on the phone last night that—"

"Well we'll never know exactly what Laura said," he interrupts, "because your phone's missing. I was in such a state last night, calling the police - who didn't fucking want to know, by the way - so I had to hire private detectives to try and find you. I was out of my mind with worry. I thought something could have happened. Anyway, I'm sorry, but with all the commotion I left your handbag by a take-out place in LA near the police station, and when I went back for it, it was gone. Stolen. Don't worry, I've already reported it all missing—"

"Alexandre—"

"And I know your phone was inside because straight after the toilet escape fiasco I tried to call you and you can imagine the surprise when it rang in your fucking handbag. I had a look to see what else was there. Your wallet, everything left behind. I figured, a woman who leaves her fiancé

451

without her credit cards and cell phone is a woman who's on the run. As if I were some wife-beating bastard who wanted to hurt you - someone you had to run and hide from."

"No! It wasn't like that. But I was scared. Scared to go near Vegas. I'm still scared of Sophie. Laura was serious. Your sister wants me out of your life, she—"

"Sophie would never hurt you, chérie, believe me."

"I wanted you to stop her to—"

"Imagine yourself in my shoes, Pearl. You and your only brother. You'd abandon Anthony just like that? He's behaved like an asshole with you ever since I met him, yet you have still stood by him because he is your *flesh and blood*. You can't just trash your own family! My sister and I have been through Hell and back together and we're close. But that doesn't seem to register with you. Yet I still listened to you. I have made so many concessions. I have even started to dissolve my own fucking company for you. Even agreed to sell HookedUp to Sophie so I will be out of it one hundred percent. But you know what, Pearl? I'm done. What you did to me last night pushed me to my limit. You demonstrated to me, loud and clear, that you *do not want me* and you know what else? I think you're using Sophie as an excuse. An excuse to run from me."

My heart is pounding. I can't believe what I'm hearing. He is dumping me! Dumping me in favor of his crazy sister.

"I love you Alexandre. Please. Please let's work this out."

"Work what out? As long as Sophie is breathing you're going to nag on and on at me about her. What do you want me to do? Have her killed? So you can be free of her?"

"No, of course not. I just wanted her out of your business."

"And then what? The next step will be you demanding

that I don't see her at all. What has she actually *done* to you? Called you a cougar. Ooh, how terrible! It's her manner, Pearl, she has a sharp tongue. If you only knew some of the stuff she's said to me over the years you'd laugh out loud—"

"She called me a stalker and said you didn't give a shit about me, that I was frigid and…and…"

"But that was over four months ago - she apologized several times and has been trying to make up for it ever since – she's been trying, Pearl. Somebody who buys their future sister-in-law a one-of-a-kind Zang Toi wedding dress is not going to try and hurt you."

"She's been messing with my mind, sneaking in on my movie deal—"

"She came in on a bad movie deal that was sinking to save our asses! Why did she bail out Samuel Myers? Not just because she saw a good business opportunity but because *you and I fucked up*. We hadn't done our homework. Samuel Myers was going broke! Yes, that's right, the whole movie would have gone under because Samuel Myers wasn't good for the money so Sophie came in to make things right. He told you, himself, that he was having financial difficulties but you wouldn't have it, wouldn't believe him. You were so obsessed with Sophie doing a number on you that you wouldn't listen to reason."

"At what point did Sophie get involved?" I'm still trying to work out the Alessandra connection.

"I don't know exactly but the timing was perfect for us all. Why did Sophie not tell us both, earlier? To save us from embarrassment. She thought she could subtly stay in the background and not get involved, except financially. She knew how much this project meant to you. And why did Samuel Myers, himself, not mention it earlier? Because of his pride. He's a big shot producer, or at least was 'till some deal went sour – he was hardly going to admit to you his state of affairs."

My brain is racing a thousand miles an hour. "But that doesn't make sense. It was my idea to have a woman for the role, my idea to take a chance on a gay actress."

"Exactly, Sophie knew all that, knew how you wanted a woman, a more mature actress to play the lead – you'd mentioned that to her yourself at some point – why do you think Samuel Myers was so open to the idea? Because he didn't have a choice. But as far as a gay actress was concerned it was Samuel Myers who put the idea of Alessandra Demarr into your head, wasn't it? When Sophie found out about the mess he was in she took the opportunity to use Alessandra as leverage to make it all work out for everybody. And yes, now I realize that my sister did have an ulterior motive – to give Alessandra a chance to break into the movies – Sophie was giving her a leg up with her career. Sophie was doing all of us a fucking favor by coming on board. Me, you, Sam Myers, Alessandra – all of us would benefit."

"Why did Alessandra pretend she didn't know Sophie?" I ask with suspicion.

"Because Sophie hasn't come out of the closet. She doesn't want her marriage breaking up. She doesn't want her step-daughter knowing she's gay - Elodie has no idea. Alessandra was being discreet."

"Did *you* know about Alessandra, that she and Sophie were lovers?"

"No, of course not or I would have said something when I saw how flirtatious she was being with you. Sophie never discusses her sex life with me anyway, why would I have known about Alessandra?"

I stammer, "She….Sophie…she had it all worked out…to demean me. To get her girlfriend to seduce me so I looked like a fool."

"You're really scraping the barrel now, aren't you, Pearl. She got Alessandra on board the movie because a.) she was cheap and b.) she wanted her girlfriend to get a leading role in a film. Alessandra was basically going to do the part for free as long as she could rework the script. That was the deal. The fact that you then got into Alessandra's panties had nothing to do with Sophie."

"I didn't get into her panties, she got into mine!"

"Six of one, half a dozen of the other, what difference does it make – you two made out, which, by the way, Sophie has no idea about."

"Bullshit! Sophie set me up! They were in on it together."

"Oh please. You think my sister is into BDSM after what she went through with our father? Or she'd want her own girlfriend fooling about with another woman? With whips and shit?"

"To punish me to—"

"Oh come on, Pearl, you've been gagging for a spanking ever since I've known you. You were up for it, Alessandra didn't force you."

I'm lost for words but know that I must be right some-how. I'm all tongue-tied but blurt out, "Sophie was mean to me when she and Elodie came for dinner, she was hinting that things were going to go wrong to 'unravel' themselves and…"

"You know Sophie's English is bad and the translation comes out all wrong sometimes."

I'm standing there stupefied. Everything Alexandre is

saying makes sense yet…

"Come here, chérie. Let me give you one last kiss before we say goodbye."

What?? Goodbye? I can feel my breath short, my stomach churning with terror. He's leaving me. This is real. Anthony was right, I should have snapped Alexandre up when I had the chance. *Oh my God!*

He walks towards me and holds me tightly in his arms and then runs his fingers through my swimming pool-wet hair and says, "I'll miss you baby, but there's no way you and I are going to work out. I don't want to play this cat and mouse game any longer. I want a stable relationship, I'm not into roller-coaster rides, sorry."

"You're splitting up with me?"

"*You* split us up last night, Pearl. Not me. You. You broke my heart. You made it clear that our two orange halves will have to go their own separate ways."

"No! That's not what I want at all!"

"You can say what you like, baby, but actions speak louder than words. You made your choice when you escaped out of that toilet window last night, leaving a waiting jet and a waiting fiancé like two pieces of discarded trash. Not to mention the reverend in Vegas, and a special surprise I had planned after our wedding."

"What surprise?"

"It doesn't matter now, it's water under the bridge, it's the past."

The past? No, this can't be happening!

He tilts my head back and kisses me. He presses his lips firmly on my mouth and I open it, craving his tongue, desperate for him, his taste, his everything. I wrap my arms around his back and hold him as close as is feasibly possible.

Tears are burning in my eyes; my heart feels as if it's ablaze. Our kiss gets deeper, more ravenous. Tingles dance in my groin, my panties are slick – I need him. I need him inside me, our bodies to be one – I need for us to make love. "Please, Alexandre, give me another chance," I breathe into his mouth.

He pulls me off him slowly but with a firm grip. "No."

"Is that all you can say? No?"

He steps backwards but stops and says, "Bye, Pearl. Keep that Mercedes, by the way. I bought it for you - bought it from the rental company, I figured you needed a car. They'll be in touch. Later today you'll receive a package from me. A new handbag, cell phone and other stuff. The diamond ring is yours to keep. And I've bought you a covered parking space around the corner from your apartment in Manhattan so you won't have to move the Mercedes all the time when they do street cleaning – you know, otherwise you'll end up with millions of parking tickets. Oh yes, I got you a pretty condo near Cap d'Antibes overlooking the Mediterranean – not far from where we stayed at the Hotel du Cap-Eden-Roc; the deeds are in your name. In case you fancy a vacation now and then. You'll love it. It comes with a parking spot, too, because the royal blue Porsche that you drove that lives in my house in Provence? She's yours now – drive her with care. I'll have her delivered there."

I can't believe what I'm hearing. Is this all a joke?

But he continues on in a monotone, hardly stopping for breath. "Oh, and of course your Jim Dine and everything you've left at my apartment, your clothes and books and stuff I'm having delivered to your new place on the Upper East Side. I'm renting somewhere for you because of your apartment being sublet. If you prefer it, let me know and I'll buy it for you. Oh yes, and HookedUp Enterprises? I've done a sweet deal with Natalie. Sweet for her, that is, not me. You and she will be partners, fifty/fifty – I thought you'd be more comfortable that way. I know how you feel about Hollywood and the movie business so you can get back to doing what you're truly good at – documentaries. My lawyers will send all the paperwork to you. You decide if the business idea appeals or not."

I'm speechless, my jaw drops, my eyes are stinging with tears about to flood out at any moment. He has had this all *planned out*. Spent the day organizing everything to buy me off! He's breaking up with me and giving me a 'divorce' settlement all in one go. There's no going back now, he's serious. I start sobbing. I think about Rex – no more walks in the park with him. My life as I know it is over - *I've lost Alexandre forever.*

A voice from above shouts into the garden, "What the fuck is going on down there? What have you done to my sister?" It's Anthony leaning out of his living room window glowering at Alexandre. But Alexandre ignores him.

"Bye Pearl, take care." Alexandre squeezes my hand and walks off with purpose as if he can't get away from me fast enough. The fact that he has been so generous when he didn't have to be has made it all so much worse. I collapse on the lawn and roll into a fetal position howling with painful tears as if someone has stabbed me in the heart.

Because someone just has.

14

The only good thing that has come of this black hole in my life is my rekindled relationship with Anthony. We are closer than we ever have been - even before our mother died. He has made a three hundred and sixty degree turnaround – we have talked things through; the anger, the guilt, the blame on both sides about John. I'm clinging to him like never before.

Right now he's my lifeline.

I stayed on several more days with him in San Francisco, moping about his apartment mainly, nursing my wounds. Alexandre only called once, to check a delivery had arrived: a beautiful red, Hermès Birkin handbag, replete with gift vouchers for Neiman Marcus and Barneys ('to replace make-up or anything lost – about time you had a bag that suited you', his note said) a new Smartphone and the keys to my new apartment. After making sure the number was going through okay, he hung up. He was polite but matter-of-fact as if I meant nothing to him at all.

I wailed for hours, cradling my designer bag like a dog with a bone – a sad reminder of what a fool I'd been to crawl through that ladies' room window. Surely I could have done things differently? No wonder he'd had enough. Normal people don't escape through toilet windows. Normal people don't behave the way I have done.

A Birkin – all those times I'd been going about with my over-sized handbag and now, finally, this one was perfect. Still big enough to fit everything I needed inside but so stylish and chic. The perfect pocketbook named after the Francophile British actress, Jane Birkin, who fell in love with the sexy French singer, Serge Gainsbourg. It brought back with nostalgia the moment when *Je T'aime....Moi Non Plus* was playing, after Alexandre had dressed up as a fireman and just before he asked me to marry him.

He sent me the perfect purse at a price, not because of how expensive those bags are but the price of unhappiness - a continual *aide memoire* of the fool that is me, Pearl Robinson. Ms. Pearl Robinson. I held the Birkin close to me and started crying again. How I wished I could turn back time. He wanted to make me Pearl Chevalier and all I could do was run.

I knew then that I could not possibly accept any of these 'pay-off' gifts – I called to say I wanted to give everything back but he never picked up.

Just when I was thinking that the world couldn't get worse,

Hurricane Sandy struck. Entire coastal stretches along the east side of the country were destroyed, five million without power, and the death toll rising daily. Scores of people died in New York City alone, more than in any other previous natural disaster to have occurred there.

It quickly shook me out of my self-pity, realizing that I was/am one of the lucky ones in the world. Natalie, not so. Her aunt was a victim of the superstorm's wrath. She lived in Queens in a neighborhood which was first ravaged by flood waters before a raging fire burned everything to the ground leaving nothing but a pile of ashes, debris of wrecked cars and dead trees reflected in the oily, knee-deep water.

Natalie is broken-hearted. I thought of what Alexandre had said a couple of weeks earlier when we were talking about choices we make in life and he said something like: *"Maybe Natalie's had a relatively lucky life. Perhaps she's never been a victim of circumstance or ever had to battle with personal demons."*

Poor Natalie, she's certainly been a victim of circumstance now and will be haunted by demons for the rest of her life.

When Bruce arrived back from visiting his parents, I knew it was time to leave. I had options. Go back to New York and settle into my new apartment, the one Alexandre has organized for me. Luckily, the Upper East Side is still in working order, not the case for some other parts of Manhattan where the storm wreaked havoc. I had only seen photos of the apartment, a stunning two bedroom pre-war co-op just around the corner from where my place is (which is sublet for another ten months and I can't break the contract). He said he'd buy it for me if I liked it. I can't even imagine what it would cost, but a lot, and I don't feel comfortable with all these 'gifts' he has showered me with – I want to return them: a condo in the South of France, two incredible cars, a parking space in the city. Things which remind me of him, remind me that I played it all wrong – that I screwed up yet again. Things which I don't deserve.

Another option for me was to drive across America. I had to take the Mercedes to New York so I thought I might as well make a trip out of it.

At one point Daisy said that she and Amy would come too, because Johnny was on business in Phoenix, but then it was cancelled so she changed her mind. A ten day drive just with me on my own didn't appeal at all, especially with the way I'm feeling right now.

I spoke to Natalie several times and she advised me to stay away from New York, just for now. Meanwhile, all she wants to do is spend time with her family.

The third option was to visit my father in Kauai, which is what I decided to do.

That's right, Alexandre *did* call a second time but only briefly to ask what arrangements I had for the Mercedes and how I was planning to take it back to New York. I told him I didn't want the car but he was adamant I keep it. He came up with a plan. Elodie and a friend of hers were going to fly to San Francisco, pick it up, and deliver it to New York for me. They'd drive across the country, very carefully, he'd instructed them, with utmost respect for the car, he'd warned. I consider it his car, anyway; his money paid for it. Elodie and her friend stayed with Anthony and Bruce for a couple of nights before setting off on a sightseeing trip of a lifetime. By that point I had left for Kauai.

So here I am now at my father's in his romantic house made of bamboo, away from the aftermath of Hurricane Sandy, away from the aftermath of my messed-up life. 'At least you're still *alive*,' Anthony reminded me. 'And not, as you feared,' he said, 'some victim of Sophie's.' Perhaps he had a point.

I have thought about Sophie a lot. Mulled over every-thing. Maybe Alexandre is right...I'm paranoid, being unfair, I've watched too much *Dexter* and *CSI* on TV. Whatever, I made my bed and have to lie in it now. He doesn't want me back. I could hear it in his voice when we spoke those two times. Businesslike - polite but cold. Unemotional. How it kills me to hear him talk to me that way.

Now I spend the days looking at the ocean, watching the waves rise and fall, listening to the surf and sound of birds. I have penned several letters to Alexandre. Not emails but real letters on paper. But they end up in the trash, crumpled up – like my thoughts, confused, shocked, as if the last five months have been one long dream, as if this phantom Frenchman never existed at all, that he was just a figment of my imagination.

Speaking of dreams, I am possessed. Not by needle-dick and company. No. That seems to be over. I am possessed, obsessed by Alexandre. Not only does he occupy my thoughts in the waking hours, but when I close my eyes, too. Constantly there. He is in my subconscious, my conscious, flowing through my veins, beating in my heart. He is every-where. I see his peridot-green eyes sparkling with happiness looking down on me while I sleep. But when I open my lids, there is emptiness; my soul is like a void of black, a deep, dark cavern of misery. Misery I brought upon myself.

I have been trying to reach Laura all this time. I even asked Elodie if she could get her number for me, I was that desperate. Finally, I got it and left Laura a message but she hasn't called back. I need answers. Is Alexandre just in denial? Denial about how crazy Sophie is, or was he speaking the truth? Whatever, I realize that I was no match for his beloved sister. As Anthony pointed out, I am the water and she is the blood. Ironic that. *Blood is thicker than water* doesn't exist in French yet Alexandre is taking every word of that to heart, polishing each letter of that phrase like a soldier polishing his boots. Until it gleams and shines like a mirror. *Blood is thicker than water.*

"What's up, Pearl?" I nearly jump out of my skin but it's only my dad coming up behind me. He lays his warm hands on my shoulders and gives me a little squeeze. "You've been very silent lately, sweetie, very introvert – that's not like you at all."

I turn around, holding one of his hands on my now bony shoulder – I can hardly eat at the moment. "I'm sorry Dad, sorry I'm being so dull and boring."

I look up at his handsome, rugged face. His sand-blond hair falls limp about his high cheekbones, his crow's feet are etched in hard lines about his dark blue eyes which reveal a man who has lived life. Suffered and pushed himself to the limits. His face is a map. He has a reckless air about him mixed with a soft vulnerability which makes him hard to resist. I think about Natalie and see how she must have fallen head over heels in love with him but ran because she needed to protect herself. He could break a heart because you want more from him and he isn't able to give more. He is a self-absorbed person, yet kind and caring. Self-absorbed because it's hard to penetrate his shell. *What is he thinking?* she must have wondered, *why can't he open up?*

"It's time you learned how to surf," he says in his deep voice.

God he's handsome. I suppose I'm not meant to notice

things like that because he's my father - but I'm not blind. Natalie must be crazy about him however much she's in denial.

"What happened between you and Natalie?" I ask, ignoring the surf request. He has been pushing that one on me for as long as I can remember.

"I tried, sweetie, I tried."

"Why did she come running back to New York so soon, then? What did you do?"

He lets out a sigh. "The way I see it? She was scared. Scared by her strong feelings for me. Natalie is a woman who has always been in control of situations. She's a tough business woman, a negotiator. She wanted to negotiate me, didn't want to lose herself in me."

"So you were hard on her?"

"Not at all. I felt that she was trying to manipulate me into being somebody I wasn't."

"She's so beautiful," I say.

"She's that, alright."

I frown. "Poor thing. Hurricane Sandy has really knocked the wind out of her. I was going to go back to New York to help her in any way I could but she wants just to be with her family."

My dad answers sadly, "I've called her several times to try and comfort her but I guess she's just not willing to talk about it. She still won't return my calls."

I sit there pensively, his hands still cupping my shoulders. The view is spectacular – a carpet of emerald green stretching to the deep blue of the ocean ahead. Coconut palms sway like ballet dancers in the gentle breeze and a cockerel crows for the fourth time in a row. An early morning mist is rising almost like smoke it's so thick, dissipating into the air as it ascends into the cobalt blue of ice-clear sky. It's just after dawn. As usual, I couldn't sleep and my father has gotten up early so he can get in some surf time.

"Come with me, honey. Come and surf. Surfing will clear your mind – it's the zen of life. Surf and all your troubles will melt away."

"It's your addiction, isn't it?"

"It's my sanity, Pearl."

"Maybe tomorrow."

And then he does something that he has never done before with me. His voice deepens into a commanding, strict tone. He suddenly sounds like an old-fashioned father from the Victorian age who might spank his children or put them to bed with no supper. "No, Pearl. I've had enough of you moping around like some lovesick, surly teenager. You are *coming surfing* and that's the bottom line." He clutches my hand and pulls me up out of my chair with a strong jerk.

I stand there stupefied.

He barks, "You are my *daughter* and I'm going to make you a surfer, once and for all. When you next see that French boyfriend of yours you can show him just how good you are. Give him something to be impressed about. You think he'd like to see you as you've been all week, hunched over in that chair staring at waves all day long? Or making work calls? No, honey, he was attracted to an active girl full of *joie de vivre* when he met you - a woman who went rock-climbing on that first date. Show him what you're made of."

"It's no good, Dad. It's over between us. He doesn't want me now. He's not going to give me another chance."

"Nonsense. You're coming surfing, young lady. Soon you won't even be brooding about him anymore anyway - you'll have better things to occupy your mind."

I pull back but he keeps yanking me toward him. "Besides, have you seen the talent out there?" he continues. "Have you set eyes on the bodies along that beach?"

"What do you mean?" I ask, still surprised by his sudden air of authority.

"There are, like, at least ten dudes on that beach who are good enough to compete around the world. You think your French guy is handsome and can surf? Wait until you set your eyes on this bunch of kids."

"Kids?"

"There are some good-looking young men out there, some in their late twenties, early thirties – perfect for you if you're attracted to younger guys - a few of them interesting, too. Everybody thinks surfers are dumb but we're not, we have the key to the secret treasure box, the potion to the essence of life."

I've heard all this before but I listen anyway. I watch him as he continues with his spiel.

"Meanwhile, most other people out there are too busy running about in a rat-race in some concrete jungle somewhere, so preoccupied with 'ambition' and getting ahead that they can't appreciate what real living is all about. We surfers know - we have the wisdom." He tells me this with an ironic smile, although what he says he truly believes from the bottom of his heart.

"Surfers with brains?" I tease, although my dad is extremely smart. He can tell you anything about philosophy or astronomy and is an ace at mathematics. You wouldn't know it, though. At first sight he's so startlingly 'cool' and so buffed-up you'd take him for…for what? An old hippie? No, he's too in shape for that, his eyes too focused. An ex-bodyguard? No, he's too graceful, too ethereal. Who is he? I wonder to myself. I observe the flexing of his biceps as he turns his surfboard upside down. His fifty-nine year-old body could pass for thirty-five. A thirty-five year-old in great shape, no less.

I reflect on what Alexandre said about living in a tree-house and wonder, is that what my dad is doing, basically? Not that his bamboo house is a shack, no – it's pretty state-of-the-art and modern; he designed and built it himself. But living the simple life, no frills, no 'needs'. He doesn't care about the car he drives or impressing anyone. He is who he is and he makes no excuses for himself.

He squints his eyes as he gazes at my left hand. My engagement ring is making reflections on the walls and ceilings like a mirror, twinkling in the morning light. "But take that rock off your finger, first," he tells me, "or it could get washed away with the pull of the surf. I have a safety deposit box in the house - you can put it in there." I am still wearing the ring even though it's officially over between Alexandre and me, as if the ring is a symbol of hope that somehow everything will work itself out. He refused to take it back. So I carry it about on my finger like a wish.

My dad and I leave the porch to its spectacular view and go inside. My father taking me in hand the way he has is almost a relief. I don't have to think anymore; he can do my thinking for me. Isn't that what parents are for sometimes? To ease the pain? To shake you out of a stupor?

"Change into a whole piece swimsuit or you could scratch your belly on the board," he advises me, waxing up his surfboard.

"All I have is that bright red Baywatch-type thing from years ago."

"So? What's wrong with that?"

I raise my eyebrows. "I'll look like a Pamela Anderson wannabe. I'll attract attention."

"You'll attract attention no matter what, honey. They all want to meet you."

"*What?*"

"You think it's normal that you live by the ocean and you've been tucked up in hiding in this house for nearly ten days? Every morning when I go down the boys are asking where you are. They're curious. Curious to meet my only daughter. Besides, I need your help at the shop today. We'll surf all morning, have lunch and then you can help me organize my book keeping. Your lady of leisure days are over, Pearl. From now on, it's hang out in my shop, surf, or swim. No more moping about. Is that a deal?"

"Okay, it's a deal," I agree and then my mouth breaks into a huge grin.

"That's better. That's what I want to see. I want to see that big, beautiful smile of yours."

15

The surfer guys are really friendly and greet me with a warm welcome as if the top of the hill where my father lives were on a different planet. Their dedication to the surf is as forceful as the Pacific waves, unrelenting - they don't venture far from the beach during the day.

My surf lesson begins on the sand, itself, and then once in the ocean I find out that 'paddle' is the magic word. With my torso pressed on the board, I paddle with my arms feverishly out to sea and am then spun around by my father at the right moment to catch the wave and ride it to the shore. The idea is to stand up on the board as soon as possible. Easy on land, but nigh impossible with a fast-moving crashing wave. I do several tries, toppling over immediately into the water, each try more exhausting than the last, especially after the paddling; my arms and shoulders feel as if they are about to snap off, but in the end, after a long morning, I get there and I manage to ride the wave upright on my shaky legs all the way to the beach.

"Not bad for your first try," my father says approvingly. "Not bad at all."

"I don't know if I'm cut out for this, Dad," I say looking off to the rolling green hills in the distance and then back at him. "It's really hard, all that paddling – I'm wiped out. No wonder you surfers have such big pecs and biceps."

"It's just a question of building up your stamina, honey, that's all. What d'you make of the kids here? Anyone that takes your fancy?" he asks, gesticulating at the guys expertly riding the waves.

"Where are all the girls? The women surfers?" I reply.

"They're about, just not today. Shame Zac's not here, he's a great teacher. Sometimes it's best when someone who isn't next of kin shows you the ropes," he tells me with a playful grin.

"Who's Zac?"

"You'll see. You won't be able to miss him. He's one of our local champions. He could show you a few tricks of the trade."

Later that evening after dinner, Daisy calls. I can tell immediately by her quivering voice that something is wrong. She usually speaks with such bravado and confidence that I'm instantly troubled.

After both of us have discussed the horror of Hurricane Sandy she blurts out, "Johnny is having an affair."

I take my cell onto the veranda where the reception is clearer. "Wait, hold up, Daisy...an affair or a one-night stand."

"A one-night bloody stand that developed into a full fucking-blown affair!"

Fucking being the operative word, I think. "But that doesn't make sense, Johnny's crazy about you."

Daisy blows her nose into the receiver. "That's what I thought, too, but I was obviously dead wrong. Wrong and blind, to boot. I trusted him."

"Well of course you did. He's your *husband.* You had no reason not to trust him."

"I should have seen the writing on the wall."

"What writing?"

"The increase in the amount of 'business' trips he was making. The stupid cow lives in Phoenix, doesn't she?"

"Phoenix? Who *is* she?" I ask taking in a deep breath.

"Another married woman."

"Oh, my God."

"Which makes it worse. The pair of them are as bad as each other. She has two kids. She has a husband who's just as much in shock as I am."

"You've spoken to the husband?"

"It was him that called me. He was the one who discovered what they were up to."

"How did they meet? What's her name, how old is she? *Why is she doing this?*" I shout out all in one breath.

"The worst? She's not even pretty. I don't understand, Pearl. She's plain, homey-looking, the type that might bake bread. Not that bread bakers can't be attractive, but you know—"

"What's Johnny playing at?" I screech with disbelief.

"You ask me. This has been going on for six months. She's a secretary - oh sorry, not meant to use that word these days...she's a *personal assistant* to one of the guys in Johnny's company. She must give really good blow jobs, or something, because I don't get what he sees in her!"

"You've seen her?"

"Her husband made friends with me on Facebook so I could check out their family photos. Two kids - not to mention Amy. All these little hearts being broken. Can you believe it? The husband is devastated, of course."

"Does Amy know?"

"No, of course not, but even at five years old she's guessed something's up. Mummy can't stop crying, Mummy has got red, swollen eyes, so she knows Mummy is in a terrible way."

"Oh, Daisy, I'm so, so sorry."

"So am I."

"What excuse has Johnny given? I mean, is he in *love* with this woman?"

"He says he needs time."

"So typical - as if you're just meant to sit about twiddling your thumbs while he works out his inner man-whore."

Daisy laughs faintly. "He's still at the apartment. Can't make up his mind what he wants to do."

The *wanting the cake and eating it, too,* syndrome. Sounds familiar. An idea suddenly occurs to me and I say, "Daisy, why don't you and Amy come out here for a break? Get away. The airports are all open again, aren't they?"

"I can't, Daisy's in school and stuff."

"She's only five - it's not the end of the world. What she misses in school she'll make up for by seeing Hawaii. What could be a better education than that? Seeing the Fiftieth

State?"

"Tempting, Pearl, but I really can't afford it right now. If I'd known this was coming I'd have saved some 'fuck-you' money."

"It'll be my treat. I'll get your tickets and once you're here it's cheap. We'll eat in – there's not a lot to spend your money on, the surf and sun are free – life's simple here."

"I don't know, I really–"

"Come on," I cajole. "You need a change of scenery. Get away from Johnny. He needs time? You need a vacation!"

"Good point."

"I'm going online as we speak and getting you two tickets."

"Pearl–"

"I won't take no for an answer. Then maybe Johnny will realize what he's missing not having you both at home. It'll give him the kick up the butt he deserves."

"You don't want to listen to me miserably droning on about my problems."

"Oh, please, Daisy, like it isn't always the other way round. As if you haven't had years of me sharing some drama or other of mine while you've sat there patiently giving me wise advice. It's time I did something for you in return."

Finally, after hours of lying awake, staring at the ceiling and wondering how I could have done things differently with Alexandre, I fall asleep. I dream about white surf and 'killer' waves. I'm riding fast on the surfboard moving my body in balance with the swell and Alexandre is watching me from the beach, a proud grin on his handsome face.

So I'm irritated as hell when my happy dream is woken by a noise. Is it one of those feral pigs? Sometimes they come snuffling and grunting about my father's garden. The legend goes that Captain Cook introduced them to the islands; a source of nourishment for shipwrecked crews. Now they are proving to be a nuisance. The hogs (in their ongoing quest to find something to eat) dig and rootle about in the undergrowth trying to find worms and roots. Whole chunks of land and mountain slopes are being stripped of native vegetation making it easier for invasive weeds like ginger to get established, and the puddles in the mud wallows they create breed mosquitoes with avian malaria that kills the native birds. Hence, their appearance on local restaurant menus.

I lie in bed, stock-still, my ears pricked up like a dog. Scary thoughts of wild, long tusked, razor-backed, boars pillaging my father's garden, breaking and entering the house and attacking me, fill my racing imagination. I decide I should do something and scare them away. I get up and move over to the window and look out. The sky is dark as black ink. I listen. No hog-like sounds at all. No grunting, just a gentle rustling in the bushes.

I nearly have a heart attack when I hear a man's low voice.

It is Alexandre.

"Hi, chérie," he says casually as if no time has passed, as if I had never escaped from the airport ladies' room window.

I lean out of the window into the shadows and catch a glimpse of his face lit up by a waxing moon. My heart is racing so intensely I think my knees are going to give way beneath me.

"What are you doing here?" I ask amazed. "How did you find this place in the dark?"

"I have my ways; modern technology offers all sorts of solutions these days."

"You came," I say simply. "You're not still furious with me then?"

He bends forward into the open window. His breath is on me, I can taste the smell of him; his Alexandre elixir. "I thought I'd never see you again," I murmur into his face.

"As if," he breathes into my hair. "I could never abandon you, Pearl." His soft mouth presses on mine and he begins to lick along my lips, parting them. But then his gentleness turns like a cat who suddenly becomes over-excited, and he nips my lower lip. I can feel the salty taste of blood.

"I need you, Pearl. I have to make love to you. Don't you know that? I can't live my life without you, without being inside you, without—" He doesn't finish his sentence but continues with his rough kiss, playful and needy all at once. He rams his tongue deep inside my mouth and I groan. I can taste the blood, the sweet saliva of his minty apple breath and I return the kiss with passionate fervor.

"Alexandre," I moan.

"Aren't you going to invite me in?"

"Of course. My father's sleeping so don't make a noise."

"Are you ashamed? Worried he'll disapprove of me?"

"He's not so keen on you right now," I say with a sly grin. "He wants to hook me up with one of the surfers. He doesn't think you deserve me."

"That's why I'm here, baby. I got thinking about what you might do here in Kauai. You think I want my future wife fucking some sexy surfer?"

Tears fill my eyes. *Future wife? So he has forgiven me!* I rush to the front door and open it quietly. He's standing there, legs astride and I fall into his arms. "Alexandre, I've been so miserable without you." *And I think, even if I die from Sophie's hand, I'd rather die than be without him.*

He scoops me in his arms like a baby and carries me inside the house. "Nice place," he whispers approvingly. "I love the huge open-plan space. Great taste your father has."

"He built this house with his own bare hands," I reply proudly. "My room is just around the corner here on the ground floor. Actually, I've just remembered, my dad is out for the night seeing a friend."

"A fuck-buddy type friend? I thought he was dating Natalie."

"She's not interested. Won't return his calls. He's an attractive man, my dad, he can't be expected to live a monk's life."

"No, of course not."

We go into my room and Alexandre lays me gently on the bed, all the while kissing me ravenously. By the time he slips his fingers inside me I am a pool of liquid jelly.

"Always so ready to be fucked by me, aren't you?"

"Yes," I whimper. "I need you even more than you need me."

"The only problem is, Pearl, you've been a really naughty girl."

"I know."

"I'm going to have to punish you."

More feather beating, I think. I know there's no Nutella in the house so...

"This time I mean business, though."

"What kind of business?" I breathe into his hot mouth.

He says seriously, "Look, you know about my fucked-up past. You know how I feel about men hitting women after what that fucker did to my mother and sister—"

"I know, Alexandre, I'm not asking you to—"

"Let me finish," he interrupts. "Secretly I want to raise my hand to you and give you a good hiding." He pauses and then adds, "Let's put it this way, I'm a clandestine Dom, but you must have guessed that about me already with your female intuition."

"I had my suspicions," I admit.

"I want to beat you and then fuck you. Fuck you really hard. I need to punish you for hurting me, Pearl, for humiliating me so badly."

"Why have you kept this Dom side of yourself so secret?" I ask. "It's not as if it's illegal, lots of people—"

"Because I felt ashamed. Ashamed inside. I felt as if I would be betraying my mother in some way, betraying Sophie, too - as if I was psychologically sick ever wanting to hurt a woman in any way."

I can feel a gush of new wetness gather hot and horny between my legs. I want him to do it. I want him to dominate me, to punish me. I want to be all his even if it means getting hurt.

"When you disobey me Pearl, it makes me angry. But it also excites me, gets me hard and makes me want to sort you out, fuck you, punish you and fuck you again." He trails his hand along the nape of my neck and a delicious, shimmering shiver courses along my spine. "Do you understand why I want to punish you?"

"Yes," I whisper.

"You're a spoiled Star-Spangled brat. Independent, testy and always doing what you think best. Not your fault, of course, you American women are born that way. It's in your pioneer blood. But it makes me want to fuck it out of you. Beat that disobedience out of your peachy ass, fuck it out of your tight little pearlette. And I don't want anyone else coming near you," he says with a threatening gaze, eyeing up my Baywatch swimsuit which is slung over a chair. "You've been prancing about in *that*?"

"Yes. All the guys on the beach have been staring at me; it makes my tits look great, you can see my nipples really clearly," I tease knowing that I'm riling his jealous side.

He laughs. "An insecure man would get flustered by that remark, but me? I know it's me you want. All those men can stare at you all they want but it's me you want to fuck. But just to be clear, Pearl. You're mine." He strokes the inside of my thigh with his long fingertips and slips one inside my wet hole. "Do. You. Understand."

He's hovering over me. My high bed is on the same level as his crotch. I take his fly and open it letting his erection spring free and pull his jeans down. No underwear. "Yes, I understand, Alexandre."

"Good girl. Now be an obedient fiancée and suck my cock. Are you over that penis phobia, baby? Do you think you can suck me so I come hot and heavy in your pretty mouth?"

"Oh yes," I murmur. "Oh yes," and I take his erection in my hands and then run my lips over his soft, warm crown. My tongue flickers on his one eyed-jack and I lick off the pre-cum and taste his welcome salty-sweetness. I take his cock and tease my nipples with the top of it and then pop it back into my mouth. My groin is on fire and even more so when he groans and thrusts his hips forward into my face so it goes deeper. "That's right, baby, keep sucking, oh yeah, oh yeah, just like that. I'm going to really fuck you like you've never been fucked before. That little lesbian fiasco? I knew it wouldn't last because you crave cock at the end of the day, don't you, Pearl? You like a huge, hard cock inside you, fucking your hot, tight pearlette, isn't that what you want?"

"Yes, I want 'ock," I say, gagged by his massive size, hardly able to get out the words coherently.

"Whose cock, baby? Whose cock inhabits your brain every waking hour and in every wet dream?" he says rocking his hips forward.

"Yours, Alexandre. Only yours," and I wrap my lips tightly about his huge penis sucking as tight as I can as I claw onto his firm butt with my hands drawing him as close as possible to me.

"Good girl," he groans and I feel him expand inside my mouth. A rush of cum shoots at the back of my throat. He continues to moan and gently thrusts back and forth, fucking my mouth very leisurely as his orgasm slowly fades. I swallow desperately, lapping up every drop, savoring his taste.

"This is just the beginning," he warns. "I haven't finished with you yet."

He pulls out from my mouth and he's still erect. Round two 'coming' up. I run my eyes along his rock-hard abs, that sexy fine line of hair from his belly button seeping into his crotch does things to my brain. He still has a faint tan left over from the summer, his golden skin soft and smooth. I stroke my hands around his ass, his thighs – feel the strength of him, his powerful body, his flexing muscles. I practically come myself just drinking him in (ha, ha, yes I giggle to myself at my pun). Alexandre is Beauty incarnate. I have genuinely never seen a man as handsome as he is. No male model or movie star can compete. He is incredible in every way. It's true; all those pumped-up surfers can stare all they want at me but it's Alexandre I desire.

And only Alexandre.

As I'm gazing at him he suddenly spins me around so I am in a letter L on the bed, my torso spread out flat and my butt on the edge of the mattress, my feet almost touching the floor. He's standing over me, lording it over my wetness, my trepidation, my excitement. He starts circling my ass softly with his palm and trailing his index finger over my opening, at one point dipping it inside as if it were nectar. I can feel myself clench. Oh wow, I'm so ready for this, whatever 'this' may be. Then he ties my hands together with a silk scarf he seems to have in his jeans' pocket and puts my wrists above my head. Did he plan this? He seems so prepared. He takes my hair and gathers it in his hands, tugging at me so I can't move.

He starts a rhythm, chanting a tune that I learned as a child, a song from the American War of Independence. How does he know this song?

> Left, right, left, right left
> I left my wife with forty-eight kids
> On the verge of starvation without any Johnny
> cakes
> Oops, by golly, by left
> Right, left right left....

At the 'left' he smacks me on my left butt cheek and then on my right... wallop! Both with his right hand. His left hand is still fisted in my hair making sure I don't escape. And then, on the last 'left' of the song he crams his erection into me hard and then withdraws immediately. Each time the smarting spanks are a warm-up to what I'm craving more than anything – the hard thrust into my opening on the last 'left'. The pain is bearable…in fact…delectable and I await each plunge.

I'm groaning. Waiting with baited breath, screaming Alexandre's name. On the next thrust I know I'm going to climax. This is so sensual so…erotic despite the hard stinging slaps. And then it comes, that last hard shove inside me and it tips me into an ecstatic roll of emotional, orgasmic fervor, my brain and body ringing and trembling from deep within. This time he doesn't pull out but lets himself rest within me as I spasm around him, my muscles clenching onto his length like a limpet clinging to a rock. He comes too, his enormousness filling my walls, pulsating inside me with his groaning climax as he empties himself with a cry.

"Pearl—"

I hear bells sounding in my ears - no not bells, music so sweet. I blink my eyes. What's the music? It's coming from above. It's *She's a Rainbow* by the Rolling Stones…'she comes in colors everywhere'….

Yes, I think, I come in colors. I see flashes of red and gold - the orgasm is still sparkling within my body lighting me up like a firework display.

I lie there panting and open my eyes from my sexual stupor. It's no longer dark outside but dawn is creeping slowly through the bedroom window. I move my wrists…but wait…why aren't they tied? My eyes fly open and I feel my hands, not above my head but between my hot, wet thighs, my post-orgasm still tingling through my core. My wrists are free. I am not splayed across the bed - no, I am tucked up under the sheets. I turn over to feel for Alexandre. The song is louder now. It's my father's 'alarm' – he likes to wake to music instead of a clock.

I sit up with a jerk. Alexandre is nowhere to be seen.

Of all the nightmares I have had, this is the worst of all.

Because this was nothing but a dream.

16

Daisy and Amy have been here for two days. She is like the sister I never had and I'm so grateful to have her in my life. Coming here was just what the doctor ordered. She needed to get away and gain a little perspective. Being under the same roof as Johnny, while he procrastinated about what he wanted or didn't want was not doing her any favors.

Johnny. Johnny Cakes. Funny how dreams mix up everyday occurrences and names and places with fantasies. There I was the other night dreaming about bondage accompanied by an American Civil War marching song about Johnny Cakes (sung by a Frenchman, no less). Needless to say, I haven't shared that with Daisy – a little too bizarre, especially as Johnny played a symbolic role – *'without any Johnny Cakes.'*

When we walked into my father's house, after I had collected Daisy and Amy from the airport, I noticed something I hadn't anticipated:

My father's expression the moment he set eyes on my friend. He has known Daisy for years but hadn't seen her for ages. He wasn't expecting a new, slim version of her. He still had the Annie girl in his mind, the chubby-cheeked redhead. At least, that is what I deduced judging by the way his jaw dropped when she walked through the front door. All he said was, 'My, how fabulous you and Amy both look.' But I could see a sparkle in his eyes. I am not sure how I feel about my friends and co-workers (Daisy and Natalie) being offered up as love fodder for my father. Luckily, Daisy hasn't noticed and I have kept silent. The last thing she needs right now is more complications, but still, nice to have someone be so attentive even if he is twenty years older than she is.

Amy is in Seventh Heaven. Coming from a city it's a big change; she is free to roam about in the garden and when we go down to the beach she has no end of admirers. She has a sassy sense of humor and it isn't long before she has a throng of people gather about her, keen to hear a five year-old's outtake on life. She has an old soul for such a feisty child, and even though she doesn't seem to know what is going on with her parents, she comes out with things like, 'Don't worry, Mom, everything will work out just fine,' and 'Look at the waves, Mom – sometimes nature can be really powerful, more powerful than we are so don't sweat the small stuff.' She has made friends with one of the surfer's children; a little boy named Pete.

As Daisy and I are having a light picnic on the beach and Amy and Pete are busy making sandcastles, Daisy tells me about a new plan she has hatched. Payback for Johnny.

"I'm not actually going to *do* anything, God forbid, but

I'm going to let him know how it feels."

"What do you mean?" I ask, trying to catch on to her runaway train of thought. Every day she comes up with something different. A new-fangled plot to punish him.

"I want him to feel what it's like being in my shoes. I'm going to pretend I'm having a fling with a surfer."

I try to suppress a grin. Daisy is being dead serious.

She raises her eyebrows. "Maybe that will shock him into action."

"Yes, but what kind of action? It could make him run into the arms of Mrs. Phoenix all the faster."

"You have a point there."

"The truth is, Daisy, honesty really is the best policy. Playing games is not the best line of action. At least if you are honest with your feelings you can hold your head up high with dignity. Because if you lie to him, or to yourself, it could catch up with you in the end."

"Maybe you're right."

"But at the same time you can't be Johnny's doormat. You need to be strong and have barriers. There are things you have to let him know that are not acceptable. It is not acceptable for him to expect you two to remain under the same roof while he makes up his procrastinating mind."

"I wish I had some of that 'fuck-you' money you told me about. Then I could get my own place."

"Yeah. That's what every woman needs. You never know when things can change. It's always good to be prepared. A woman needs to be like a one-band army. Ready with her ammunition, ready with her armor, yet actively seeking and living a peaceful existence. But if she is attacked emotionally or physically she has the tools – the strength to protect herself."

Daisy pulls her curly red hair into a high ponytail which sets off the cheekbones on her pretty freckled face. "In a perfect world," she says with a sigh.

"I know, easier said than done."

"I'm just not making enough money yet. I have a few clients but I depend on Johnny's income. I can't just get up and leave."

"Such an archetypal scenario," I say. "Women the world over are in this predicament. Worse. Many of them are being physically abused or have five kids to feed. Think about it, Daisy. Maybe you and Amy should move in with me to my new apartment."

"How do you feel about that? Alexandre paying for your apartment when you aren't even with him anymore."

"I told him I couldn't accept it, that I wouldn't move in."

"And what was his response?"

"He said it was too late, that all my stuff had been moved there and if I didn't take it, it would sit there empty. That's why I came here. I needed time to sort my head out. I still don't really know what the next step is."

"Maybe we should all move here to Kauai," Daisy suggests with a giggle. "Life would be so much less complicated."

"That's what my dad keeps telling me."

"So what are you going to do about Alexandre?"

"There's nothing really I *can* do, he's decided for me."

"For your own peace of mind, I think you need to talk with Laura."

"I've tried calling. I've left messages."

"Well maybe you need to go and see her. She might be ignoring your messages because she's scared of Sophie finding out and doesn't want to attract attention to herself.

You need to talk to her face to face. Sort out all this Sophie stuff once and for all."

"What difference does it make now? Alexandre and I aren't together anymore."

"You say that, Pearl, but do you remember last time you split up? He came back to you. He was still in love with you. If that happens again, the Sophie problem will still be there. You need to know for sure what happened."

"She tried to kill Laura and pretended it was an accident."

"You really believe Sophie would have *risked* that? That's attempted murder, Pearl. Surely Alexandre would have guessed?"

"Not when it comes to Sophie. He can't see the wood from the trees. He protects her no matter what. His loyalty is unwavering."

"Well, I still think you need to see Laura - one on one."

"Fly to London?"

"You can stay with my mother, she'd be thrilled. I can set you up with some mates of mine – they've all heard about you – all dying to meet my beautiful, American, best friend, Pearl."

"You've told them about me?"

"Yes, of course. Only terrible things, though."

I laugh, then grab a handful of sand and let it run through my fingers like an egg timer. "I need to get back to New York, though. This 'break' has morphed into too long a vacation. But still, at least I've been able to spend time with my family. Anthony and I have patched up our relationship and I've gotten to know my dad better. We've bonded with the surfing. It's been a very healing time for me. Adversity sometimes brings hidden gifts."

"So what's happening with HookedUp Enterprises?" Daisy asks, her eyes fixed on Amy as she rushes towards a wave with her little bucket.

"Natalie and I are carrying on the company. I'll finish *Stone Trooper* which has now started filming."

"Who was the movie star they picked in the end to play the male lead?"

"Nobody famous – the budget simply wasn't available even with Sophie's input. But he's an excellent actor and very handsome. I received the final script. It's good, actually. I think it will turn out well."

"And then what?"

I pour some iced-tea from a thermos flask into a paper cup and hand it to Daisy. "Back to documentaries. There are so many topics that deserve attention."

She takes a sip. "Good for you, Pearl. Do you feel deflated? Disappointed by all this?"

"It's been a learning curve. I always wanted to write scripts but the truth is, there is no better script than real life. Documentaries suit me way more."

"And what about Alexandre? If he came back to you, even if it meant the whole Sophie saga going on forever, would you want him anyway?"

"Some days I feel the answer to that question is a definite 'yes' I'd want him, despite the risks, but I don't know, I think you're right, Daisy. I need to go and see Laura and talk to her face to face. She and Alexandre were together for at least a couple of years. If anyone knows Sophie, she does."

"Well if it isn't Pearl, the jewel of Kauai."

Daisy and I look up abruptly from our girl-talk. A deep voice has interrupted us and for a moment I'm irritated. *Go away, I think. Leave us to our privacy.* But Daisy's mouth hangs open and she quickly pulls her hair loose from its ponytail so I know the interruption must be worth it.

"My name's Zac," the man says. His huge frame towers above us. Floppy blonde hair half covers his sparkling blue eyes. His toned and muscular legs are covered in sand and he grins down at us with a dazzling white smile.

"You must be our local champion," I say, my neck craned up at him, noticing his defined abs, not an inch to pinch anywhere.

He crouches down on his haunches and shakes both of our hands. "Finally I meet Billy's beautiful daughter," he says, gazing at me. "And who have we here? Her gorgeous friend, Daisy. There should be a law against having such stunning women grace our beaches. We're trying to surf here, and you two women are way too distracting."

We both titter like teenagers. The fact he knows our names is very flattering. He must have been talking to my dad. And who doesn't like a bit of male attention, especially when we are both nursing broken hearts and especially when it's coming from a god-like apparition with a deep tan.

"Perhaps we can hook up for a drink later?" Daisy suggests bravely.

"Nothing would please me more," he replies. "You two ladies have a good day now." He stands up. "I'll see you around. Excuse me, I need to catch a few waves while the going's good."

He strolls off and we both trail our eyes after him. His neat butt in long, black surfer shorts saunters along the shoreline and he picks up his surfboard, his rippling muscles moving as he lifts it up from the sand and carries it with him to the ocean.

"There you go, Daisy, the answer to your payback plot.

Maybe you can give Johnny something to *genuinely* worry about."

"It's you he fancies," she tells me, an eyebrow raised.

"I don't think so. Didn't you see the way he eyed you up? Anyway, I'm too hung up on Alexandre." I sigh. "Still - can't complain about the attention."

Daisy lets out an exasperated groan. "And I'm too hung up on my bastard of a husband. Mind you, I wouldn't kick Zac out of bed on a cold rainy day."

We both burst into a cascade of giggles.

17

It's raining in London. Gray, dull and depressing. No wonder Alexandre prefers New York; even if it's cold in winter, the skies are so often blue back home.

Daisy's mother is a sweetheart. She lives in a little house in Hampstead near Hampstead Heath, a wild and sprawling park where people take their dogs for rambling walks or play soccer on Sundays. Although part of London, Hampstead is like a village full of adorable pubs and quaint shops. Daisy's mum, Doris, has set me up in a cozy room at the top of the house decorated with flowery wallpaper – quintessentially English – and she's treating me like a daughter – she misses Daisy so much.

I've done some wonderful sight-seeing here: the Crown Jewels, Big Ben and the Houses of Parliament, Portobello Rd, a street market on Friday and Saturday mornings where you can pick up silver for nothing and vintage clothes.

Actually, despite the weather, this city really does have its charm. It feels like dozens of villages melded together, each with their unique character. I've been going out with some of Daisy's friends who are more than welcoming. They have been taking me to local pubs, the theatre and walks along the Thames. The food in England is not the way it was when I came here as a teenager. Now, the cuisine is eclectic and plentiful with fabulous restaurants on every corner, the best of all being Indian food, inexpensive and delicious.

I have had some business meetings here, too. I couldn't justify to myself coming all this way to basically stalk Alexandre's ex-fiancée. I needed a better reason so I have visited some television stations – making a few connections and fanning about some ideas. The British have always done great documentaries – so far, I have been taken seriously and given a list of people to contact for future projects. Natalie needs my input more than ever.

I flew here straight from Hawaii with just a stop-over in LA. I couldn't face New York so I still haven't ventured into my new apartment and I haven't worked out what I'm going to do. I have called Alexandre several times but he is always too busy to discuss things in detail, or doesn't want to. He simply won't let me return the gifts. The Mercedes must be sitting in the garage in New York by now. I called Elodie. She had a wonderful trip with her friend driving across the States. It was she who provided me with Laura's address.

It is my final day here in London.

I have left the most daunting task until last.

I stand by Laura's front door nervously. It doesn't look dissimilar to number 10 Downing Street where the British Prime Minister lives, with a big brass knocker and letterbox. The wood is painted in a high gloss black, flanked by matching wrought-iron railings. It is all extremely 'grown-up' and intimidating. And it screams serious wealth. I wonder if Laura bought this place with all her modeling money or if her husband is rich. I seem to remember Alexandre once mentioning that he works in the City; a hedge-fund manager or something – the type that makes a million or two just for his Christmas bonus.

Finally, I pluck up the courage to rap the door knocker: the threatening head of a hefty brass lion.

Nobody answers.

My heart is pounding. Is it because I'm uninvited? Or that Alexandre was once so in love with Laura all those years ago? I don't know the answer but blood is drumming in my ears and my hands are clammy with trepidation. Finally, I hear footsteps.

The door opens slowly, guardedly. A head peeks out. By the way the person is dressed I guess that she's a member of staff. "May I help you?" the voice inquires with suspicion.

"Hi," I say beaming to try and hide my nerves. "I've come to see Laura."

"Mrs. Heimann?"

"Yes, is she in?"

"Do you have an invitation?"

Er, no. "I tried calling," I manage with a dry throat. *Why am I so nervous?*

"Who should I say is paying her a visit?"

Jeez, this is so formal. "Pearl."

"You're a pearl salesperson?"

"No, my name is Pearl. Pearl Robinson."

"Wait one moment please."

I am already feeling as small as a sparrow but when the door is closed on me, I feel as if I might as well be invisible. I wait. Five minutes later, the door opens. Wide. My jaw drops. A tall woman in her early thirties stands before me who is achingly beautiful. She must be at least five ten or eleven because I am like a shrinking violet in comparison. She's dressed in tight jeans, her legs go on forever. Her hair is wavy, long and blonde, her smile broad, with perfect, movie star teeth. She holds a black cane in her hand with a mother-of-pearl handle.

She greets me like a long-lost friend. "Pearl, come in."

I step into the immense hallway. The floors are white marble and a huge bunch of calla lilies adorns a big round table in the middle of the entrance, the table draped with pale blue shot-silk.

"Sorry, I wasn't expecting company, the place is a mess," she says with a faint giggle.

The 'place' is immaculate. Laura is immaculate.

I offer her my hand. "So nice to finally meet you. Alexandre always speaks...always *spoke*," I correct myself, "so fondly of you."

"Well, I'm sorry he's not here right now but he's been in a meeting all day – you know how it is with him? Always jetting off on a plane somewhere to make another deal, always wheeling and dealing. Come through, would you like some tea?"

Did I hear that right? 'Sorry, Alexandre isn't here right now?' No, she must have said his name by mistake. It must be her husband she's referring to.

I follow her through to a grand room. She has a slight

limp but nothing you'd hardly notice. I look about me in awe. The walls are hung with what look like grand masters, the vast sash windows are letting in an afternoon glow. I notice she's wearing a huge ring on her engagement finger, not unlike mine.

She sits on a sofa and jingles a little bell. Her back is erect, her posture perfect. "I'll call for some tea and cake. I always get a bit peckish at this time of day," she says in a plummy British accent (like some aristocratic character out of the TV show, *Downton Abbey*).

"Did you mention Alexandre not being around?" I venture edgily.

The same woman who answered the door to me earlier comes in to the room. "You called, Madam?"

"Yes, Mrs. Blake. Tea for two please. Lapsang Souchong. Oh no, actually that might be a little too fancy for our American guest — make it basic PG Tips or whatever builders' tea we have." She smiles sweetly at me and I wonder if I have just heard correctly - *Too fancy for our American guest?? Builders' tea?*

"Where was I?" she continues in her posh accent. "Oh yes, Alexandre is out. He'll be so upset he missed you."

Alexandre? This is crazy, what does she mean? "Where's your husband?" I creak out, my mouth dry and parched. I need that tea even if it is only fit for builders.

"My soon to be ex-husband, you mean? Or are you referring to Alexandre, my fiancé?"

"You...and...Alexandre...are *seeing* each other again?" My brain is thumping with blood, I feel as if I'm about to collapse.

"Didn't he tell you?"

"I haven't spoken to him...I—"

"We're going to be married, Pearl."

"But...but...that's impossible! He was engaged to me, he was going to marry *me*. You're not divorced yet, Alexandre would never—"

"Well, we're an item again. He had a little...what should we call it...a detour. With you. You were the rebound, Pearl, his solace after a broken heart. I'm sorry, it must be very painful to hear this but...well...he's always been in love with me, surely you guessed that?"

My hands are shaking, my breathing pinched. I think of all those books of hers still at his house in Provence. "But you were happily married to—"

"We never stopped loving each other, Alexandre and I."

"You're *sleeping* with him?" I cry out, trying to keep control of my frayed nerves.

She cackles with laughter. "*Sleeping* is not exactly the word I'd use."

"But he was...he was in love with *me*."

"No, Pearl. He was in 'lust' with you, for a brief spell. But he never had me out of his thoughts, not for a second. You were – oh, I'm sorry, would you like a tissue, there, there, don't cry now."

But I can't help it. Tears are flowing down my cheeks. She hands me a box of Kleenex and I snivel and blow my running nose into a wad of them, but there aren't enough to soak up my gushing tears. I'm making a complete spectacle of myself and am about to get up and leave but her cell phone rings. My curiosity is piqued. She answers and starts speaking perfect, fluent French; laughing and joking. I feel sick. Her French is perfect, *she's* perfect. Stunning. Intelligent. And the worst thing of all? Alexandre has been in love with her the whole time. She ends her call and beams at me.

"That was Sophie, she's coming over in an hour. Do stay, I'm sure she'd love to see you."

"But you said Sophie was dangerous. That she tried to kill you!"

"No, surely not?"

My voice hitches and heaves, "You called me, Laura, and told me not to go to Vegas, that Sophie could 'top me off,' that she had politicians and police in her pocket and…and…"

"Oh, poor Pearl, so gullible. I just didn't want Alexandre to marry you. I had to stop him somehow."

"So it was all a lie about Sophie?"

She lays her cane down and smoothes her slim hand over her luscious blonde locks. "Sophie's a pussycat at heart. Okay, she can be a bit frosty sometimes but it's just her manner. In fact, if she says mean things it's her way of communicating. It's when she's silent you have to watch out. I can't believe you thought she was out to kill you." She laughs raucously. "Alexandre told me as much - that you were suffering from delusions about Sophie. Tut-tut, Pearl, not the best way to warm him up, you know how close they are. You couldn't have picked a better way to alienate yourself from him. Oh, and bossing him around the way you did. Not the best of moves."

I can't believe what I'm hearing. Sweet, charity-giving Laura is a total bitch!

She widens her huge, blue eyes and talks on. "Ironically, Sophie actually rather likes you, likes your quirkiness. It took me *years* for her to warm up to me, yet you…well, you two could have been friends if you'd given her more of a chance. She's had a shit life so she's a bit tough on the outside but actually, she's really sweet when you get to know her."

I am silent now. The sound of my tears has been taken over by my heartbeat which feels as if it's about to explode in my chest.

"So how did your accident happen? Nothing to do with Sophie, then?" I ask.

"Of course not! It was bad luck, that's all. A load of children's toys had been left on the steps. I was tipsy. I tripped. I fell. End of story."

"But it's not the end of the story! You split Alexandre and me up! You told me a lie!" I screech at her.

"Far better that you broke up before that silly marriage of yours took place. Alexandre would have come back to me no matter what, even if it meant divorce. He's been desperately in love with me Pearl, from the day we met. And I with him."

"Then why did you marry your husband…James?"

"Because I was a cripple, for fuck's sake. You think I wanted Alexandre to look after me, to shackle him like a slave to a disabled person? I loved him too much for that. Besides, he had no money then. He was just starting up his company, he didn't have a bean – I needed stability, someone who could look after me properly."

"You *used* your husband?"

"James wanted to be with me. It wasn't 'using' him. But the moment I was really better, able to lead a normal life…well, it seemed right that Alexandre and I should get back together. I mean literally, all I had to do was click my fingers and he was waiting for me. He'd been hoping all along, that's why he's always been in touch and remained friends just in case, in case I changed my mind. All this physical slog I've put my body through - the physiotherapy I've been slaving away at - has been so we can be a normal,

499

functional couple again."

She used her husband as a means to an end. I want to shout at her but all I can do is start blubbering again like a child who has fallen off a bicycle she realizes is too big for her to manage.

"Now, now Pearl, don't cry. You've come away with all sorts of goodies – he's been more than generous when he didn't need to be. Two fuck-off apartments, two fuck-off cars, a ready-made business, all sorts of gorgeous jewelry, oh, and let's not forget that Birkin bag I see you carrying. Obviously you could never afford to buy that for yourself. Alexandre offered me a Birkin but I thought it was too passé – preferred a Kelly, myself. But still, do you have any idea how much that's worth? That color is unusual – looks like a one-off. That handbag must have cost a bloody fortune, not to mention the fact that there's a queue as long as my arm to even get one in the first place. Alexandre must have pulled some serious strings. That pretty bag probably cost him...ooh, I don't know, upwards of forty grand. Fitting, really, that it should cost forty grand when you're forty. Beyond generous, I'd say. So why, Pearl, are you feeling so sorry for yourself?"

The way she uses 'fuck-off' as an adjective to describe something fabulous is typically British – I've heard it before - yet it rings in my ears as if I have been punched in the head. 'Fuck off' – that is basically what Alexandre has done – told me to fuck off, yet sweetened it with all his amazing gifts. But nothing has been sweet, just sour and bitter. And this is the sourest news of all.

I manage to get out in a rasp, "I don't *care* about material stuff, it's Alexandre I want."

Laura tosses her head. "Well, you're too late. And anyway, he was fond of you, it's true, but he thinks you're a total loony. All that lesbian bondage nonsense - oh and your slutty past. So not his style."

No! he would never share that – it's my personal life! "He told you?" I ask incredulously.

"Of course he did, we don't hold any secrets from each other."

"But that's not like him, he would never do that."

"I'm his best friend, Pearl, as well as his true love – he tells me everything, he confides in me. He can't believe he took you so seriously. Look, I have to be cruel to be kind here..." she lowers her voice almost to a whisper... "he *doesn't* love you. He never really has. You had a laugh, that's all. You had some steamy sex, maybe, but it's *me* he loves. And besides, you couldn't even give him a child. He wants a family. You and he were all wrong right from the word go. Do yourself a favor, Pearl, get over him, find yourself a nice American boy with whom you have something in common."

"Alexandre and I had so much in common!"

"Bollocks. You Americans don't get our acerbic sense of humor. You're all so earnest and, 'have a nice day'. We're different from you lot. You need someone more your own age, too. Ah, look the tea's arrived. Do you take milk?"

Mrs. Blake waddles in with a tray. I get up, unsteady on my feet. I feel as if I'm going to faint. "No thank you, I need to go."

"Please yourself. I'll tell Alexandre you dropped by."

I turn around. I need to know one last thing. "What about Rex?"

She throws up her hands. "Rex? Well, we'll have him shipped over here, of course. I hate New York, wouldn't dream of living in that shithole so we'll be in London full time. That's when we're not wintering in the Caribbean, that is. I'm not big on dogs but you know, he's Alex's pride and joy so I suppose I'll have to deal with the creature."

The *creature*? *Alex*? I want to slap her face and would but she'd probably beat me with her witch's cane.

I slowly begin to slink out of the house feeling like the most worthless human being alive.

Laura remains cheery and nauseatingly jolly, waving as I leave. But just as I reach the door she calls after me, "Shame about your divine Zang Toi wedding dress - what a waste."

I pretend I don't hear. It's as if she has sucked out all my energy with her painful words. I have no gumption, no force or ammunition left inside me to defend myself. There I was talking with Daisy about women needing armor and I had none. I feel shamed. My head is slung low like a beaten dog, I pad out of the house, my misery trailing me like a murky shadow.

I am so crushed and weak that I decide to sit on a park bench by the square that faces her grand house to regroup my fragmented dignity. I get out my iPod and put on the first song I see – the Blues - Billie Holiday, *Foolin' Myself.* How apt. I stay there for a good few minutes mulling over all the cruel but probably truthful things Laura has told me, or rather, fired at me like a relentless machine gun. I agree with Billie Holiday, I *am* through with love and I'll have nothing more to do with love. What's the point ever opening myself up again? Even if I had gone through with the marriage in Vegas with Alexandre, it would have, at some point, come to an abrupt end. Alexandre is still in love with Laura. As she said, I was just a 'detour'. The 'rebound'.

I think of my beautiful wedding gown probably being worked on right now. Crystals being hand-sewn on the train, the exquisite silk smoothed and pressed, a myriad of tiny, feminine fingers working on all the details. I noticed Zang Toi had mostly women in his atelier, busy as dedicated bees, their keen eyes supervising every fine stitch, every delicate fold. What am I going to do about that dress, that work of art? The truth is it would be better off in a museum.

And just when I'm praying that there may have been some mistake, some misunderstanding, or that it could all be a fantasy on Laura's part, Reality slaps me in the face. I see the thing I'm dreading most in the world - Alexandre approach Laura's front door.

I observe the scene, wishing I could look away but I am transfixed. He's holding what looks like a gift-wrapped box. She opens the door, tosses her golden mane and throws her loving arms around his broad shoulders.

Then the glossy black door with its brass lion's head shuts with a bang and I feel as if it has slammed right in my face.

It wasn't Sophie who was my enemy. No.

It's been Laura all along.

Shimmers
of
Pearl
(Book 3)

1

I'm still staring in disbelief at Laura's sinister, black, front door. I have not moved from this park bench. The only thing that has changed in the last ten minutes is the music I'm listening to on my iPod. The Blues have been replaced with Patsy Cline's *Sweet Dreams*. That is all I have left – dreams of Alexandre and memories of how it used to be between us. Could I really have just imagined the intensity of our bond, our passion? 'He was in lust with you,' Laura told me, just twenty minutes ago, and I now see that what she said was true. Alexandre walked through her door. What more proof do I need that it is over between us?

He is still in love with her, his ex fiancée. This horrific fact is seeping through my veins like green poison, sapping me of energy, rendering me drained, making me feel as if my life has been nothing but a lie for the last five months.

Laura's words, 'rebound' and 'detour' to describe who

and what I am to Alexandre are ringing in my ears. Twice, I have tried to get up from where I'm sitting. I want to rap at that foreboding, black door and confront him, but my muscles are weak – I can hardly move. Laura has been plotting and scheming to get him back all along and he was waiting, as she said, for her to click her fingers.

Click.

And he rushed back to her like an eager dog.

I fumble about in my beautiful, red Birkin bag for my cell phone. I need to speak to Alessandra Demarr. Maybe she can clear a few things up for me.

My memory slides back to that moment when I fled Alessandra's house, when I found that photo of her and Sophie together in an intimate embrace. I had the notion that they had set me up and that Sophie was trying to destroy my life by wheedling herself in on my film projects; infiltrating her way into HookedUp Enterprises. Alexandre testified to her innocence, swore that her motivation came from nothing more than her desire to help out her girlfriend and get us out of a sticky situation when Samuel Myers wasn't good for the money. I didn't believe him. But now I see that Alexandre could have been telling the truth. I have been so 'hooked up' on Sophie that I was blind to what was really going on… Laura, my real enemy from word, Go.

Laura told me that Sophie actually liked me, confirming what Alexandre had also said. Either I am living some sort of Hitchcockian nightmare, where everyone is conspiring to drive me to a loony bin, or they're right – I have misjudged Sophie – wrongly accused her. There I was, obsessing about my future sister-in-law, when it was Laura I should have been looking out for, all along.

Alessandra picks up her phone after several rings. She

sounds groggy and I realize that it's only eight a.m. Los Angeles time; she isn't an early riser. Too bad, I can't wait. Rise. And. Shine.

"It's Pearl," I say with urgency. "Sorry to wake you."

I hear a growling yawn. "Can you call back, I was sleeping - I thought it was a family emergency." Her sleepiness is evident - her Italian accent is more pronounced than usual.

"Well, considering that you and I could have been family, it is."

"What are you talking about, Pearl?"

"Alessandra, I'm so sorry to wake you and everything, but I'm not in a good way and I really need to talk."

"If this is about *Stone Trooper—*"

"It's about Sophie, your girlfriend, my ex-to-be sister-in-law." I am aware of how crazy that sounds. I do up the top button of my coat – the London humidity is getting into my bones. My eyes are still fixed on Laura's front door as I hold my cell next to my ear in my other shaky hand. I need answers and I need them now.

Alessandra's voice suddenly perks up with interest. "Did Sophie tell you that she and I were a couple?"

"I found a photo of you two in your kitchen, and Alexandre confirmed to me that Sophie was gay."

"Don't you *dare* say anything to Sophie about us, Pearl - about that night. *Please!*" She is pleading; the desperation and fear in her voice takes me by surprise.

"So you and Sophie weren't playing some game on me? Some, 'let's screw with Pearl's head' kind of game?"

She chuckles – her laugh is laced with irony. "What? Are you *insane?*"

"It just seemed all too much of a coincidence; that I was working on *Stone Trooper*…suddenly Sophie gets involved…

you coming on board at the perfect moment and then seducing me..."

"Look, can we talk about this later? I need a coffee. I can't even think straight right now."

"Alessandra. I'm sitting outside Laura's house in London and she just so happens to be - not only Alexandre's ex-freaking-fiancée - but his *present* fiancée as well. He's inside her house, as we speak. He's involved with her again. No, let me spell that out − *he is going to marry her*, she is divorcing her husband. She's all buddy-buddy with Sophie and−"

"What? Sophie hates that money-grabbing bitch!"

Did I just hear that right? "But Alexandre said they were friends."

"Sophie puts up with her," Alessandra informs me in her husky voice, all the more husky for being the morning. "She's never liked Laura. Anyway, I don't think she's seen or spoken to her for ages."

I squeal out, "But I was at Laura's house, just now, and she said Sophie was coming over! They spoke on the phone. In French, no less."

"I doubt that, Pearl. Look, I'm sleepy, can we speak later?"

"Wait! No. Alessandra...why, when we were in LA were you referring to Sophie as your 'ex' if you're still together?"

"Questions, questions."

"Please Alessandra!"

"We had a big fight − she said I was using her to get ahead in my career. All because, I was too busy to speak to her one time. That was just before you arrived in LA She told me it was over. So I had some fun with you to spite her."

"You were planning on telling Sophie about us to make

her jealous?"

"No, of course not. I'm not that dumb. She'd come after us both with a carving knife. But it made me smile inside – you know, knowing I had the last laugh. Sorry, Pearl, I have to admit...I was using you to make myself feel better. Can I hang up now?"

"No! I need to know more about Laura."

"I've never met her," Alessandra replies boredly, punctuated by a yawn.

My heart sinks. I remember Laura's words: *'He was fond of you, it's true, but he thinks you're a total loony. All that lesbian bondage nonsense - oh and your slutty past...'*

I had assumed Sophie had enlightened Laura, but from what Alessandra says, obviously not. The only other person that knew about my adventure with Alessandra Demarr was Alexandre, himself. *How did Laura know those intimate details of my sex life?* Simple – he must have told her. She was speaking the truth. He confides in her, even when it comes to me. I feel so belittled.

Belittled. And cheap.

Alessandra pipes up, "Anyway, Pearl, as I was saying, Sophie is not a big fan of Laura's. Apparently, Laura has been sniffing about Alexandre again showing real interest. Her husband has lost a lot of capital in the stock market, or is being done for some dodgy dealings tax-wise and no longer has the kind of money he had before. So Sophie thinks she's after Alexandre because of what he can offer her."

"What does Sophie say about *me?*" I ask, wondering if Sophie is suspicious of everyone who comes near her brother.

"You really want to know?"

My heart starts pounding – might as well hear the worst. "Yes."

"She thinks you're the best thing to happen to Alexandre for years. At first, she suspected that you were like all the other women after him – interested primarily in money. But when you told him you wanted to do a pre-nup and refused to take a stake in HookedUp Enterprises, she knew you loved him for *him*."

Wouldn't everyone love him for him? "Why is she still so bitchy, then?"

"It's part of her DNA, Pearl. But if you made more of an effort, you'd find she'd be a good friend to you. She said that, too. That you didn't like her, that you still hadn't forgiven her, and that you were a hard nut to crack."

"She said all this in English? Hard nut to crack?"

"Of course not. You know how bad her English is – we speak in French."

"You speak French? I didn't know that."

"Well, Pearl – there's a lot you don't know about me. Just keep quiet about our little evening, will you?"

"Are you kidding me? Of course. Anyway, I don't have anyone to tell even if I wanted to. It's over between Alexandre and me."

"Nonsense. Latin passion can escalate or descend at any moment – he'll be back."

"That's just it, Alessandra. He broke up with me in a cold, passionless voice. And now he's seeing Laura again. Not just seeing her but sleeping with her. She's like some top model...I don't stand a chance."

"You say you're outside Laura's house and Alexandre is inside? Go and knock at the door, silly. I'm going back to sleep, Pearl. Remember, don't you *dare* tell Sophie about what happened or you'll regret it."

"Is that a Sicilian threat?"

"You bet."

Revenge is a dish best served cold. "Don't worry, Alessandra, my lips are sealed. You think I want Sophie running after me with a carving knife? Thanks for talking to me - things are a lot clearer now. Good night, morning - whatever. Sleep well."

The line clicks dead.

I take a deep breath and stand up. I have a head-rush – black stars flicker behind my eyes. Laura's front door is giving me heart palpitations. Black as the Devil himself, it beckons me and taunts me mockingly. *Come, come and humiliate yourself.*

But Alessandra's right. I need to see Alexandre face to face.

I stand at the door, once again. It is so glossy I see my warped reflection before me. A disheveled woman who is forty whole years old. No wonder Alexandre has gone back to glamorous Laura. I rap the lion's brass knocker head. The lion is saying to me, *I challenge you, go on – make a fool out of yourself, see if I care.*

I knock three times. Rap, rap, rap. My heart…pound, pound, pound.

Nothing.

I'm planning in my head everything I'm going to say: *Alexandre, please be honest with me, please…*

The smooth black door swings open. Not Mrs. Blake but Laura, herself.

I will not cry, I will not cry. Be strong, no tears, no scene…be strong.

She's standing there, looking like some figurehead on a

ship; tall, willowy, in a royal blue, silk-satin dressing gown shimmering about her slim body like ripples of water. My heart sinks. She has that just-fucked look – the afternoon love-making flush glowing in her cheeks. Her hair is all mussed up. She says coyly, "Pearl, what a surprise!" Her smile is set like a plastic bride on a wedding cake. "What can I do for you?"

"I need to speak to Alexandre," I reply bravely.

"Sorry, but he's not here. He just left."

My composure melts into the damp sidewalk. "Don't lie to me, Laura. I saw him come in through this door twenty minutes ago. He's here!"

"My word, have you been spying on us?" Her smirk is victorious.

I try to stick my foot in the door. "Let me in. I need to see him, just for a few minutes and then I'll be on my way."

"Pearl, I'm not making this up. He left five minutes ago."

"BULLSHIT! I've been watching your front door. Nobody has left, least of all Alexandre."

"You don't know much about London houses, do you? This house's garden backs onto our mews house and garages. He went out the back."

"Laura, you've gotten what you wanted. Why are you tormenting me? Please, I just want to see him for–"

"God, you're a bore. Do I have to spell it out? HE. IS. NOT. HERE! Go round the back and see for yourself if you don't believe me."

"What was he doing here?" I demand, my body shaking with rage.

"Now you're being naïve. He just fucked me senseless, if you must know. You're not the only one who likes a little afternoon sex, Pearl. Now run along, I have stuff to do." She begins to push the door in my face.

And then I shout out something cruel. Something I know I'll regret. Words spill uncontrollably from my mouth:

"I wish you'd stayed in your freaking wheel chair forever!"

The lid is firmly in the coffin now. Not only am I jilted, I am despicable. When Alexandre hears what I have just said, he'll be shocked and never want anything to do with me again.

It's official.

I'm a jealous, spiteful, malicious bitch.

Laura slams the door in my face.

I scamper around the block to see if what Laura said about a mews house and garage is true. It is. Only the extremely wealthy could afford to have their garden sandwiched between two stunning houses in one of the most expensive areas in London. The mews is cobbled – in the olden days this is where the stables for horses and carriages were but now, of course, just a mews house alone in this Chelsea neighborhood would set you back millions, let alone adjoining garages. I imagine Laura's husband, James, beavering away in the City to buy all this for the woman he's in love with, for whom he sacrificed his life – and now she is about to dump him because he's no longer rich enough for her. Does Alexandre know who he is dealing with? That Laura is as ruthless as a razor blade? Like most men who are smitten, he probably doesn't see through her sweetness and light act.

A thought suddenly rushes to my brain. Uh, oh. I just insulted her, said the worst possible thing somebody can say and she'll be out for revenge. Laura knows about me and Alessandra. All it takes is one phone call to Sophie.

The carving knife...

I call Alessandra again.

She sighs into the phone, exasperated. "What d'you want now, Pearl?"

"Laura knows about us. About...our evening," I stutter. "Just warning you."

"Deny, deny, deny. And I suggest you do the same. How the fuck would Laura *know* that?"

"Alexandre must have told her."

"Thanks, Pearl, for sharing that with him - now I'll have *him* after me with a carving knife, too."

"No, you won't – he really didn't...doesn't care. I'm history."

"I didn't know he was the tattle-tale-tit type."

"He's not. He's usually very discreet; it's not like him at all."

"Well thanks for the warning," she says grumpily. "Bye."

I amble back to Sloane Street and walk towards Knightsbridge. I have a couple of hours to kill before I need to go back to Hampstead for my suitcase and make my way to Heathrow for my flight. I get my iPod out of my bag and go through the playlist. Got it. The perfect 'fuck you' song ever written, Gloria Gaynor's *I Will Survive*. The music feels great. Powerful. Encouraging. Hell, I even feel like disco dancing along the street. I punch my arm in the air. Yes, I *am* strong and I *will* survive. I refuse to mooch about and feel sorry for myself. Life goes on and we women can be tough. I *am* tough. I'm a New Yorker for crying out loud! I can do it. I will survive, I sing out loud and I don't care who hears me, even if I'm out of tune.

Where to head now? Harrods, why not? Probably the most famous department store in the world. I'll go there and buy a gift for Daisy's mother to say thank you for my stay.

Perhaps some home-made chocolates or some fancy bath salts.

I step through revolving doors, greeted by uniformed doormen and make my way through the vast labyrinth of the store to the Food Hall. There is no place like it; I could be stepping into a museum. My mother brought me to this emporium and I vowed I'd return one day. It's a work of art. This was the original part of the shop, opened in the first half of the nineteenth century. Now Harrods is comprised of seven floors and spans an incredible four and a half acres. I have never seen such opulence and grandeur where food is sold. It is like a food court at a palace – something worthy of Louis IV or some bygone monarch's banquet feast.

The black and white marble floors stretch before me like a long yawn and the imposing molding decorating the ceiling reminds you that this building is a majestic legend – a true London landmark. Hall after hall is grandly overflowing with beautifully presented gourmet food delights. My eyes and nose are already feasting. The sheer volume and selection of British and International goods is awe inspiring - artisan chocolates, lavish cuts of meat and seafood - even exotic things like sea urchin. Unusual cheeses, Dim Sum, Beluga caviar, truffle butter, pistachio and rose Turkish delights, gourmet terrines and drool-worthy patisserie - all presented in breathtakingly beautiful displays arranged behind gleaming glass counters. It is like being in the hall of mirrors in Versailles, only with food, reflected twenty-fold by mirrors set in arches, made glorious by mahogany and brass light fixtures – everything twinkling and glittering in gold.

Foolishly, I thought I could whip in and out of here, but I am mesmerized by the beauty of the place, the surreal Willy Wonka and the Chocolate Factory I-want-it-all attack. Where to begin? What to buy? You could spend a week in the Food Halls alone, not to mention the rest of Harrods. I get some exquisite French truffles for Daisy's mum, Doris, and meander towards another tempting counter.

I'm staring at cupcakes now. I need some kind of American comfort food after the Laura 'encounter.' What to choose? – Banana, Mocha, Strawberry, Rocky Road, Sticky Toffee…or the chocolate torte sprinkled with gold dust? Edible art if ever I saw it.

"Pearl, is zat you?" a voice exclaims behind my shoulders.

I nearly jump out of my skin. I see a familiar reflection in the mirror before me.

It is Sophie.

I spin around in amazement, my sneakers squeaking on the polished marble floor. A nervous guilty churn makes my stomach dip. Sophie with her carving knife…does she know about me and Alessandra?

Obviously not, because she is smiling, and for the first time her happiness seems to be genuine. Or is that just me? Now that I know she doesn't hate my guts, I can observe her with fresh eyes, devoid of judgment and suspicion.

"What are you doing in London?" she asks, kissing me on both cheeks. I inhale her usual, heady scent of *Fracas* and notice how pretty she's looking, her eyes are like pools of dark chocolate and she's dressed immaculately in a chic, navy blue pantsuit. Hand-tailored, no doubt. I know she and Alexandre get all their suits cut on Savile Row, here in London.

"I came…I…I had some work appointments," I splutter.

"What a wonderfool surprise. Alexandre never told me you were both here."

Wonder Fool. Fool being the operative word. *So you don't know we broke up? That he dumped me? That he's gone back to Laura?* "I'm leaving today," I say simply. "Back to New York."

"What a shame, we could have hooked up. Isn't zis place marvelloose? I come here to get my Jelly Belly jelly beans. Cannot get zem anywhere, you know. My little American addiction." She holds up the bag of candy. Jelly Belly – my favorites, too.

I want to spill it all out and tell Sophie my woes. I want to discuss everything and ask her about Laura; tell her that Laura warned me that she would 'top me off' in order to stop me marrying Alexandre in Vegas - but I am dumbstruck, not least by the bizarre coincidence of bumping into Sophie here at Harrods – what are the odds of that?

"Where do you go now? You want a coffee? Or razzer, in England a cup of tea, no?

"I have a plane to catch, I need to get back to Hampstead, then get my case and catch the tube to Heathrow," I reply uneasily.

"Hampstead? Alexandre usually stays at zee Connaught."

Sophie doesn't know?? "I'm visiting a friend," I say uneasily. "Alexandre isn't with me."

"My driver, he can take you to Hampstead and zen airport, okay? Save so much time. I have a friend in Hampstead I've been wanting to see forever. We go togezzer." She links her arm with mine and ushers me through the crowds, and out of Harrods. Her embrace is warm and I wonder…was it me? Was I the one, all along, who has been spiky and defensive? Maybe Alexandre was right. Sophie has been trying to be my friend for months.

I caused all that trouble for nothing. I wish, now, I could

jump into a time capsule and travel back to the waiting private jet at Van Nuys Airport.

But it's all too late.

2

The limousine is waiting for Sophie around the back of Harrods like a panther on the prowl. Or rather, a Jaguar, because that's what kind of car it is. The uniformed chauffeur opens the door for us as we slide onto the sumptuous, leather seats, and then he drives us off into the London traffic. I try to peel my gaze away from Sophie as she calls her friend, so I fix my eyes on the beautiful shop front window displays along Sloane Street (especially Harvey Nichols) as we glide through the shimmering wet streets - the traffic lights reflecting globes of color in the windows of passing cars and on the road. There is a thin haze of drizzle - bad for depression, good for skin, I think, having noticed the peaches and cream complexions of so many young British girls.

Sophie is now arranging an assortment of shopping bags and feasting on her Jelly Belly beans. She offers me a handful and I chew the mixture of flavors thoughtfully together, too afraid to speak because I really don't know where to begin. It seems she thinks that Alexandre and I are still together. *How can that be?*

Finally, she breaks the silence. "I haven't spoken to Alexandre for days - so you came to London all alone, Pearl?"

I swallow. A mélange of root beer and cinnamon swirl about my mouth. It tastes of America and I feel momentarily soothed. "Yes, I'm alone." *Is she testing me?*

"How is your wedding gown coming along? Is it finished yet?"

Oh God, what do I say? "I'm not sure," I hedge. And then I blurt out, "Do you know Laura?"

"Laura?"

"Alexandre's—"

"I don't see her anymore," Sophie interrupts.

But when I was at Laura's house Sophie called her and said that she was coming over! "Do you phone her from time to time?" I ask, the conversation fresh in my mind; Laura chit-chatting in perfect French and telling me it was Sophie who'd called.

"No, not for ages."

Oh. Strange. Someone's hiding something. Laura? Sophie? Laura, probably.

I ask, "Do you like her?"

"No, but she was in a wheelchair so I had to be nice."

"I see."

"She's been calling my bruzzer again?"

"They are seeing each other…a lot," I mutter. I want to tell her about Laura, what she said – I want to spill all the beans but stop myself. I suddenly think of Alessandra's warning once again…that carving knife… If I tittle-tattle on Laura she'll tell Sophie about me and Alessandra. Actually, she might tell Sophie anyway…I'll be in trouble, no matter what.

Then Sophie says with her mouth full, "You and me got off on wrong foot, Pearl. I'm sorry. We need to talk."

My heart begins to race but I reply, "Yes we really do need to talk. I'm sorry, too, if I've been…" I trail off – I don't know how to express myself – how much should I tell her?

"Zee last time I spoke to my bruzzer he tell me you know about me and *Stone Trooper*."

Uh, oh, here we go.

"I guess you know why I got involved?" she asks narrowing her eyes (the way her brother sometimes does).

"Not completely," I say, giving her an opening. I need to see which direction she's going to take with this conversation.

"Alessandra."

"Yes."

This is beginning to sound like some enigmatic scene in a Harold Pinter play. How much longer can I beat around the bush?

"Alessandra is my girlfriend."

I look down at my sneakers."Yes, I know."

"She tried to seduce you?"

I can feel my face burn like glowing coals, although I have been told by people I don't go red. But I feel like I'm on fire. "Why do you ask?"

"Because it's her nature…Italian. Flirt. I have a husband, you know – I can't blame her for a little extracurricular activity."

The carving knife comes to mind, yet again. "You don't get jealous?"

"Yes, but I cannot have my cake and eat it too, you know?" Sophie looks at me and throws some more candy into her mouth. "Sorry, very rude, I eat zee whole packet. I get very greedy with this Jelly Belly. So if she flirts I'm not cross – I know you both spent a lot of time togezzer on zee script."

"Alessandra thinks you're very jealous," I venture, my heart still hammering inside my chest.

"She loves drama. She likes zee idea zat I scream and shout, you know?"

"So if she did something with another woman you wouldn't come after the other woman with a carving knife?" *Oops, I didn't mean to be so blunt. Blunt about something so sharp.*

Sophie bursts out laughing. "She tell you zat? No, Pearl. Only one time in my life did I come after someone wiz a carving knife and zat was my fazzer."

I seize this rare opportunity to find out more – my Sherlock instinct piqued. "What happened to your father?"

"He's around. He lives in Rio, I sink."

"He's *alive?* I thought he disappeared."

"Yes, he disappeared - to Rio." She's staring out the car window now – I can't judge the expression on her face.

"How d'you know he went to Rio?"

"A friend of Alexandre say she see him zaire one time."

Interesting. I change the subject. "So how long are you in London for, Sophie? How come you haven't spoken to Alexandre? I thought you two spoke every day."

"Not since I bought him out."

"He sold you his shares in HookedUp?"

"You didn't know zat? I buy but I cannot pay for it all in one go. HookedUp is worz so much money, you know? Even I cannot afford to buy in one go."

We sit there in silence both licking our lips after our Jelly Belly binge. Then I exclaim, "Sophie, I may as well tell you...Alexandre has left me. He's gone back to Laura. We haven't seen each other for over two weeks."

She stops chewing and her jaw drops open. I see a mélange of blues and yellows of the candy stuck on her perfect white teeth. Her usually flawless composure slumps into disbelief. Her eyes widen. She is genuinely shocked – this is not an act.

"I knew zat fucking beach was up to no good."

It takes a beat for me to realize that 'beach' means bitch.

"I went to Laura's house today. The reason I went was because...because she told me that you caused her accident, Sophie...that you wanted me dead...that you would have me killed... 'topped off'—"

"*Merdre! Poutain!* You believe I would do zat?"

I drop my head in shame and a smart of pain shoots through me – I realize, too late, I have nipped my lower lip. Tears start spilling from my eyes, "I'm sorry, Sophie. I thought you hated me. Yes, I believed her – she was very convincing. I was going through a rough patch and well...I was vulnerable."

Sophie, to my surprise, folds me in her arms and draws me close to her slim frame, hugging me like a long lost friend. Her gesture makes me shake with unbidden emotion.

I made Alexandre sell his share of HookedUp to her, and I caused him, through my nagging and suspicion, to run back to Laura. I dug my own grave. I have nobody to blame but myself.

I spill out my woes and tell Sophie the whole story, omitting only the kinky stuff with Alessandra – I come clean about everything else. She apologizes, too, tells me that she is sorry for having slipped into the *Stone Trooper* deal without warning me.

Finally she cries out in anger, "Anyway, I don't believe Laura for a second. Alexandre is crazy about you. Zaire is no way he start fucking zat skinny gold-digger beach again. No, Pearl, he loves you too much – why would he go for hamburger when he has steak at home?"

Alexandre once said that to me. I try to smile but I feel so raw inside. Raw like the steak I'm supposedly meant to be. I tell Sophie, "Laura says they're getting married."

"You know sumsing about that skinny, asparagus beach? She's a good liar."

I wipe my face with my coat sleeve. Asparagus must be the French equivalent to bean-pole. Normally I would be laughing but none of this is funny. I reply, "Laura had me fooled, that's for sure. But she could be telling the truth. Alexandre was there at her house, I saw him – it looks as if he's moved in with her."

"You spoke to him?"

"No, I just missed him. And whenever I've called his cell, his voicemail always picks up."

"You leave zis to me, Pearl. Sumzing is not right. He loves you – he is crazy about you. I know my bruzzer, believe me."

I burst out crying again. Something about having Sophie on my side when I thought she was my arch enemy stirs my deepest sentiments.

She takes her arms away from my shoulders and says, "We have arrived."

I look up from my blurry-eyed vision and see that we are in the heart of Hampstead Village, crawling along a beautiful tree-lined street where houses are like country mansions.

Sophie fishes her cell phone from her purse and calls her friend.

"I get out here, Pearl. My driver, he takes you wherever you want to go and he picks me up later. We speak tomorrow, no?"

"Thank you, Sophie."

"It's normal," she says with a smile as she eases her graceful way out of the limousine. And then she turns and fixes her eyes on my face as if she is studying me. "I'm sorry, Pearl for zee names I called you once."

"It's water under the bridge."

Water under the bridge. It brings a memory to mind - when I was a little girl playing Pooh-Sticks with my brother, John; throwing the stick off the bridge upstream and rushing to the other side to catch the stick bobbing along the foamy water. The memory makes my eyes prickle again. *Get a grip, Pearl, stop the waterworks already.*

"Bye, Sophie. Thanks so much for lending me your driver."

"What time is your flight?"

"About ten twenty, I think."

"Who are you flying wiz?"

"American Airlines."

"Bon voyage, Pearl – see you in New York. Soon."

Sophie must have called the airport because when I board the plane I find I have been upgraded to First Class. The irony is not lost on me. Finally, she and I have a chance to be friends – she is making so much effort - but our friendship has come too late.

I mull over everything that Laura said about her and envision Laura clicking her slim fingers and the hot, passionate embrace that she and Alexandre must have shared, knowing that their relationship was back on course. A rush of jealousy floods through me and for a moment I feel the urge to plot some kind of Sicilian revenge on her, but then I sink back into my plush airplane seat and appreciate the fact that she knew Alexandre first. She must feel she has priority, and however strongly I feel about him is neither here nor there. It is Laura he has chosen, not me.

Traveling First Class reminds me of how my life would have continued had I been the wife of a billionaire. That word, 'billionaire' sounds ridiculous – out of my league – even out of Alexandre's league because he's just a young guy in T-shirt and jeans who likes to surf and rock climb. But he *is* a billionaire – that's who he is - and Laura is claiming him for her own because of it. His wealth is letting our love down. I think of the tree house option in Thailand and wish I had snapped it up there and then; away from Laura and her treacherous, gold-digging claws.

Alexandre doesn't love me, it's clear. He doesn't even pick up the phone anymore.

It is over. I will just have to go back to how things were before – back to The Desert. Because the only person I want is him. I cannot even imagine kissing anyone else, let alone sex.

I stretch back on my comfortable seat and close my eyes. I can feel his touch; the way he strokes my inner thigh, brushing his finger lightly against my panties which are always soaked by the time we make love because he waits until I'm begging him – screaming for him. He is always rock-hard, even when he just kisses me, even when all he does is look at me. *Stop, Pearl! Stop torturing yourself!*

"Would you like a beverage, ma'am?" I look up from my reverie and a pretty flight attendant is looking at me sweetly.

"Yes, please. Bring me a Bloody Mary with extra horse-radish and one of your best Russian Vodkas – you choose."

"Certainly."

Perhaps I can drown my sorrows, one last time, before I land in New York and start my life afresh. I have already arranged things with Daisy. She and Amy will be moving in with me. I'll be back working on documentaries and back to being the self-sufficient woman I was before.

Life happens when you're busy making plans. So true.

3

I fumble with my new apartment key, already impressed with the grand lobby and its plush décor below. I'm feeling really nervous now. It seems a lifetime away when I last spoke to Alexandre in the back yard of my brother's apartment in San Francisco. Here I am now, standing by the door of one of the 'fuck-off' farewell gifts – part of his guilt package that had him running back to Laura and brushing me off with money to ease his guilt.

Then my mind gets working…no…would that be possible? Would it have been possible that he wanted Laura back, all along, and they were in it together – that he knew about her telling me that Sophie was out to kill me? He knew that would have made me run for the hills…a sure way of getting me out of the picture….

To my amazement, the door swings open before me, and I nearly jump out of my skin. I tumble into the open gap and a pair of muscular arms catches my fall. My apartment being broken into, already, and I haven't even started living here yet? My heart is racing and I yelp at the surprise of a stranger in my new building. I trip forward in a double stumble and dare to look up at my adversary. I expect a masked robber in a balaclava but instead, I see a pair of peridot-green eyes that are inches away from my face.

"Alexandre."

"Pearl, baby."

My stomach is flipping and folding in on itself. I fall headlong into him, gasping with desire, lust, happiness and relief. But then my inner voice warns: L.A.U.R.A.

He loves another woman. *Be careful, Pearl.*

He's holding me now, tightly in his arms as he tilts my head up to kiss me. Tears are in his eyes. "Jesus, I've missed you. I can't live without you, Pearl. I need you. I've been climbing the walls."

I try to push him away. "Get off me! What are you play-ing at? You're with Laura now. Leave me alone, Alexandre. Why are you torturing me?"

He grabs me in his embrace, again, and presses his lips to mine. His eyes are hungry, roaming and boring into me, the green flickering like the color of lit brandy aflame. "What are you talking about? I'm not with Laura." He breathes sex into my mouth.

I turn my head to the side and hiss, "Don't screw with my head, Alexandre! I saw you enter Laura's front door today. You fucked her in the middle of the afternoon. You took her a gift in a big box. You're living with her. You're going to marry her – she said so!" The words come out in screeches and squeals. I must be waking up the whole building – not the best start to my new life here in this apartment.

To my horror, Alexander says nothing, just shakes his head as if in disbelief. I step back away from him and observe a huge bulge in his jeans and a look of libidinous need in his eyes. Laura was right, he's 'in lust' with me. He loves her and wants to be with her but he wants to 'fuck' me. His hand cups his crotch as if to adjust his massive, uncontrollable weapon – a weapon that wants to claim me and posses me. He's wearing one of his hand-tailored, made-to-measure suits. I wonder if the Savile Row tailor instinctively knows he needs to give extra space in that area – room for Alexandre's 'weapon' to flex and maneover itself.

I feel dizzy, nauseous, because my desire is as potent as his. I want to stay strong – I need to protect myself but all I can think of, right now, is ripping off my panties and spreading my legs for him. He's so good looking and sexy that I'm melting before him like the pathetic ice cream cone that I am. *Where is my will power?*

He edges closer to me, brushes his lips along my neck so I quiver with longing. I'm trying to hide my craving. He whispers in my ear "You have to trust me, baby. I don't want Laura. I haven't fucked Laura and I'm not living with her – that's crazy, please believe me."

"It's not crazy! She said so. And I saw you with my own eyes at her house!"

"Well she was talking nonsense. I just zipped by her house to drop something off."

"Bullshit! You haven't even called me, you haven't picked up your cell – you've been avoiding me!"

His voice is gentle. "I haven't called you because I knew you needed time to sort your head out. Let's face it, Pearl, you were all over the place. You needed time alone to reflect;

not only those nightmares and all that shit, but on the whole Sophie issue, which I hear is resolving itself nicely. She told me you bumped into each other." He cups his large hand on my butt and I'm too mesmerized by him to move. "I didn't get in touch, chérie, because things were too haywire." He breathes into my ear and adds huskily, "But it's been hell for me; I've missed you like crazy. You're all I can think of night and day. I'm obsessed with you. I've been going around with a hard-on for two weeks. Please Pearl, calm me down. I feel like an animal – I need you – I need you, baby."

My heart is racing and my stomach's churning in nauseous waves. I'm so crazy about this man, it is literally making me feel sick. "You just want to fuck me and then go right back to Laura," I spit out. "What were you doing bringing her that massive box? A gift, no doubt – perhaps a Kelly Bag?"

Squint lines radiate from his face as if he's amused but he notices the set fury on my face and states quietly, "I was bringing Laura her books from my house in Provence, that's all. You didn't like them being there – I wanted to make you feel more at home."

"That's crap and you know it! Why didn't you get Madame Menager to just Fedex them?"

"Because the last time I used Fedex, the package, which happened to be worth a lot of money, went AWOL for three weeks. Madame Menager had put Royaume Uni on the address and it went back and forth to Romania three times – they used the first two letters, the RO. Customer service in France is a disaster -I didn't want to risk it. I needed to pop by my house – the pool's being worked on - so I picked up the books while I was at it."

"Why was it gift-wrapped, then?"

"The hotel did that. I'd bought some cashmere scarves and things that I was going to have sent to my mother, so they took the liberty of wrapping the box of books, obviously assuming it was also a gift."

I flinch and eye him suspiciously. I so want to believe him. "That doesn't explain all the information Laura has about me. How did she know about me and Alessandra Demarr? Laura said nasty things to me, Alexandre. That you think I'm a 'loony' with a 'slutty past' – she knows stuff about me that only you could have told her." I push my hands fiercely at his chest to shove him away but another rush of desire floods through me when I touch him - that chest, those abs and his smooth skin.

"She said *what?* I sure as hell didn't say any of those things. How could I say them when I don't even *think* them?"

"Well, you told her about Alessandra!"

"No, I didn't."

"Well someone did and it wasn't Sophie and it wasn't Alessandra and it wasn't me. *You* are the only other person that knows."

"This is insane!"

"That's why it's time for you to leave now, please. I don't ever, ever want to see you again. Please exit from my loony, lesbian, slutty-past life."

He holds my shoulders. There is no point trying to push him away – he's too solid, too strong, too determined.

His eyes flit about as if recalling something. "Alessandra must have said something to Sophie, maybe to rile her up, it doesn't make sense—"

"No, Sophie doesn't know - if she did she would have hardly upgraded my plane ticket to first class. Please go now,

Alexandre."

"She didn't upgrade you. I did."

"Did Sophie tell you my flight time?"

"She did, but I knew it already."

"What? How? You're spying on me?"

His mouth tips up crookedly as if he wants to smile but he stops himself. "Was it comfortable enough for you in First?"

"Yes, thank you for the upgrade, but I would have been quite happy in Economy had I known it was you and there were strings attached and that you were stalking me."

His mouth is tilted into a very subtle smirk when he tells me, "I know, it was wrong of me, baby. It's something I would never normally do – I respect people's privacy. But I was worried about you; I just wanted to know your whereabouts, just in case." He steps closer and murmurs, "Anyway, deep down inside, you secretly like me keeping an eye on you Pearl, admit it."

It's true, I do like the fact that he's been thinking about me and wanting to know where I am. But the question is, why? What does he want from me? I glare at him and say, "Stalking me - but with only one thing in mind - to get into my panties when it's actually *Laura* you want to be with." The idea that he desires me so much physically is a real turn-on. I try to hide it with my furious scowl but what's going on down south of the border is giving me away – even if only to myself.

He flings his arms in the air with exasperation. Boy he's a good actor. "I do not fucking well want to be with Laura! I want to be with *you*. I want to marry *you*. Please, baby – I'll get to the bottom of this; something strange is going on. I'll talk to Laura–"

"Oh yes, I *bet* you will."

He lays a hand gently on my shoulder and tells me quietly. "Pearl, chérie. I love you. I've missed you so much. I *love* you; *you* are the only woman I want."

I shrug my shoulder to shake off his hand and roll my eyes in disbelief like a sulky teenager.

He roars at me, "You *have* to believe me!" The neighbors would have heard that outburst, for sure.

Something about his hot-blooded anger, not only tickles me, but jolts me into action. I do want to trust him and in that split second, I decide that I have to let him hold me, at least one more time, even if he is lying. I can't stand being in The Desert. I need him, his touch, his breath on mine. I *need* to believe his lies.

I stand there weakly, succumbing to him as he unzips my jeans and puts his hand down into my panties, pushing his finger into my soaking wet opening. He scoops me up in his arms and says, "That's it, you want this as much as I do. No more games, Pearl."

He takes me into the bedroom and throws me onto the soft mattress, his massive bulge flexing through his elegant pants.

"What if I said 'no', what if I said I couldn't do this?" I mumble, only too aware that I can't resist him, knowing this whole Laura issue will have to sit on the back burner because I can't hold out anymore.

"Then I'd know you'd be lying," he rumbles, casting off his tailored jacket and unbuttoning his beautiful, bespoke pants.

I gasp at his size – his raging angry cock wants all of me – I start to frantically pull off my jeans and panties. I too, feel like an animal. I lie there thrashing about the bed - wanton like some Babylon whore, my legs spread wide. "Fuck me, Alexandre, please," I whisper – "I need you, all of you. Fuck me."

"You bet I'll fuck you." He licks his lips lasciviously, crawls between my legs, laying his naked body on top of me. He's beautiful – how I've missed this. His dark floppy hair, his lean, sexy body, his flashing green eyes wanting me, needing me. But I suddenly feel as if I've been too easy, so I close my legs – a bit late, I know, but I need to show some semblance of pretense – so I squeeze them together to try and make myself seem less like a cat in heat. A ridiculous attempt to gain back a sprinkling of dignity.

His strength overpowers me – he knows I want this as much as he does. His mouth is on mine, his tongue probing me as growls are rumbling from his throat "Don't suddenly play the chaste damsel in distress with me, Pearl. I know what you want, chérie. You want me to fuck your brains out."

He eases his hard erection between my unyielding thighs and I close myself tightly around him, still feigning the 'hard to get' female. But within seconds I'm whimpering with pleasure. He doesn't slam himself inside me, which is what I'm expecting, but starts fucking my clit. *Oh my God…*it feels out of this world. He's not even an inch in but just ramming me back and forth, pummeling me there on my sweet spot – why haven't we tried this position before? This is amazing. I'm groaning, thrusting myself at him as I sense my wetness pool with arousal.

"Alexandre, this is…wow…oh my *God!*"

His hands are clutching my hair as he fucks my clit over and over and over, groaning with each thrust, his mouth on mine, his tongue searching my tongue, tangling and lashing at each other as his cock thrashes my clit relentlessly. I always thought it ridiculous when I read about women being 'pounded' to orgasm but I think it's about to happen. The rhythmic sliding, up and down has me on the edge. I don't want to climax because this feels so fucking amazing that I want it to last forever – it's *so* hot, s*o* sexy, *so* incredible - but I open my legs a touch because my body is doing its own thing. He goes in further. He hits the perfect spot and that's it. Yes, Pearl Robinson is being 'pounded' to orgasm.

"Alexandre…aaahhhh" I can hardly say his name as his mouth is hungrily all over mine. "I'm coming…oh wow, I'm coming really hard."

I can feel my slickness oozing through the core of me as spasms overtake the center of my body. He fastens his mouth on my throat and sucks, also changing the angle of his hips as the root of his erection presses into some other magical spot and I feel another wave crash through me. He pushes my thighs apart with his knees and I'm wide open – my nails scraping his back as my orgasm flutters down from its peak. He rams himself into me, filling me with his immense size and I cry out, desperate for the whole of him.

He's growling like a lion, really 'fucking my brains out' – it's true, I am no longer coherent. He's now nipping my neck, covering me with ravenous wet kisses, pumping me deep, ruthlessly – both his hands are cupping my ass tightly as he thrusts me rhythmically, bringing me as close to his groin as possible with his grip. My hands rake down his back and claw down onto his butt as I bring my legs up and wrap them around his neck. He's in so deep now, it hurts, but I'm relishing the sweet, sharp pain as he pumps his thick length into my womb.

"I. Love. Fucking. You." His mantra is almost cruel,

punctuated with each thrust. "So. Fucking. Wet. So Fucking. Horny. My cock thinks about you. All...Day. Long. All. Fucking. Day. Long. Your. Wet. Pearlette. Your. Tight. Horny. Pussy. Always ready to be...Fucked. By. Me."

Our mouths are frantic, tongues lashing out at each other, licking all over, biting, sucking. This is not love-making, this is dirty, carnal sin. It's verging on painful but I want it this way. I want to feel him. To own him. Laura doesn't elicit this kind of desire from him. I do. I'm his addiction. I'm his drug.

"Why did you leave me?" I murmur as he rams all of himself mercilessly into me. "Why didn't you phone?" I push my butt up higher as my ankles close fast about his neck.

He pulls almost all the way out, tantalizingly slowly. "Because you needed to know how much you wanted me. And I needed to have you desperate for me." He's licking my tongue, speaking only between kisses which are carnal pools of frantic desire.

"I am desperate," I breathe.

He slams back into me. "I know - your body's telling me. Do you think about sex with me all day long, Pearl?"

"Yes." He pulls out teasingly slowly. Sooo slowly.

"Are you cured of your penis phobia?" He thrusts himself in really deep and hard. I groan. I feel so dominated. Then he eases a tiny way out and speeds up, circling his hips. *Oh yes. Oh yes.*

I can hardly speak but burble, "Yes, I'm over it. At least *you* override any hang-ups I have. You..." His movements are doing things to my brain, I can hardly get the words out...."You are different. You...*oh, God,* I need you Alexandre."

He slams himself all the way in, brutally. "I know you do.

And I need you to need me. Are you done with your lesbian fantasy, too?"

"No, I'll never be done with lesbian fantasies," I tease.

His growl is deep with appreciation with what I've just said. "Tell me...tell me, baby, what you did with Alessandra," he asks gyrating his hips again. I can feel how thick he's getting, feel him spreading inside me even more, filling my walls.

"I kissed a girl and I liked it."

"Oh yeah – tell me more."

I raise my butt up a touch so he's in even deeper. "She licked her tongue in between my legs – she made me come."

"Like I'm coming now, baby. Oh fuck this is intense!" He rams himself hard up inside me and I feel a scalding rush of cum shoot into my womb – profound and powerful. Then he thrusts again and I sense another charge of semen burst deep within me. "Aah," he's moaning and crying out. "Jesus, Pearl, only you can do this to me. Fuck!" He's groaning as if in pain.

We remain like that for a good five minutes and then he pulls out, very slowly. I lie there, still doubled up, my butt in the air. There's a marsh between my legs – it's seeping everywhere. Slowly I stretch myself out but Alexandre's arms are wrapped about me so I can't escape.

He's stroking me gently, running his fingertips along the curve of my ass. I'm no longer being devoured but savored. "Your skin is so soft and flawless, Pearl, so beautiful. You're intoxicating...really...I just can't get enough of you."

He presses his muscular thigh into my crotch and I move myself gently up and down. At first, it feels like a small comfort after being ravaged by him but as I rub myself languorously back and forth on his muscular leg I feel desire building up again until it reaches a new crescendo – another climax shudders through me. I feel his semen hot between my satiated thighs as we both fall into a deep sleep, entwined in each other's arms.

Several hours later, my eyes spring open. Alexandre is still fast asleep but my own worry and angst have woken me. Trickles of dawn light have made the darkness fade, but it must still be very early. *Am I insane?* Nothing was resolved last night! Nothing. The fact that Laura lied to me about Sophie, telling her she wanted to 'top me off' - the fact that Alexandre must have told her about my naughty tryst with Alessandra (because nobody else knew except for Alessandra herself) – is all registering in my slow, sex-numbed brain – he really did 'fuck my brains out.' Duh! As usual, Pearl Robinson jumped into the flames without wearing a fire-proof vest.

How did Laura have that information about me? Because that bastard, who's lying beside me now, *must* have shared it with her, despite his denial. He deserves an Oscar.

I observe him as his breath rises and falls, his pecs strong and firm, the V of his sexy torso ending with his sex tool which he uses to make me weak. Anger starts to flood through me, more at myself than with him. *Why did I let him have his way with me last night without talking things properly through?*

I get up and tiptoe to the bathroom. That's right! My suitcase is still outside the door (I hope) – everything was dropped (including my mind) when I saw his green gaze and his drop-dead gorgeous body which, I hasten to add, had broken into my apartment, no less! *Pearl Robinson, you are a disaster!*

I pee and wash my hands before going to find my abandoned case which I wheel inside. I go back to the bathroom and run the shower faucet. So preoccupied was I last night with the vision of Alexandre and my lusty appetite, that I didn't even have time to appreciate the lovely and sleek modern furnishings of my new apartment. It's all cream and white with soft carpets and smooth silk curtains. It looks like a five star hotel – a place where you wouldn't call home but where you'd lounge about in pure luxury wishing it were yours. It is too perfect to call home – too sleek. The bathroom is all pale Italian marble with his and hers wash basins and a massive mirror. Uh oh, inspection time. I have definitely lost weight through nerves, despite my Jelly Belly binge.

I jump into the hot, steamy shower and lather away at my hair and body with some delicious vanilla-scented shampoo and body wash. Did Alexandre organize all this? As I'm exiting the shower all wet, there he is. He's been watching me like a Peeping Tom. I know because his boner tells me so.

"Beautiful. Just beautiful," he says running his tongue along his lower lip. "You've lost a little weight, though."

"I guess you were so busy fucking me you didn't notice that last night," I remark, bitterly angry with myself, knowing that I'm going to give into him all over again.

"Oh, I notice everything Pearl. Everything. Like how tight and wet you were last night. How much you needed me inside you. Bend over."

"No! I won't."

"Don't be disobedient. Bend over. I just want to see how much weight you've lost."

"Alexandre!"

"Bend over and touch your toes."

Here we go again. A pool of desire gathers in my stomach. *In for a penny, in for a pound.* I bend over. Actually, the stretch to my backbone after the hot shower feels good.

He comes up behind me and I feel his erection press up against my ass. His thumbs part my butt crack and he gets down on his knees. I sense his tongue lashing in great sweeps up and down and then flickering at my entrance and the soft hair on his head tickling my inner thighs. I can hear myself moan involuntarily - he's got me again.

He stands up. Then the slapping begins, his cock walloping my opening. He's guiding it with his hand – I can sense it teasing me. He pulls away. Then suddenly, I feel a hard slap right in my hot spot with his palm. It stings. I cry out in shock.

"What are you doing?"

"A little spank, that's all. You hurt my feelings, Pearl, when you ran off at Van Nuys Airport."

I'm dreaming again. Please no. Please don't say this is all a goddamn dream and that, in fact, I'm still fast asleep on the plane in First Class. "Pinch me," I tell him.

"What?"

"Pinch me hard. I want to know I'm not dreaming."

He pinches me on my pussy lips and it hurts. Almost. But seconds later, I feel the urge. The urge to be claimed again. "I need you, Alexandre," I pant, sticking my butt out further.

"I know you do. Hold on to something. I have to fuck you again, Pearl."

I'm still doubled over and I hold onto the edge of the bathtub. I'm sore inside, yet I still want more. What is *wrong* with me? Why am I such a push-over?

He cups my breasts with both hands, kneading and playing with my nipples. I can feel desire shoot through the back of my molar teeth – all connected – my groin, my mouth, my nipples. I jut my ass out towards his erection. With one hand tight around my waist he pushes his cock inside me but just an inch. I can hear my wetness ooze about him and I cry out like the little slut that I am. Even if I have to share Alexandre with Laura I'd rather do that than not have him at all. I'm so hooked on him and his body parts – I can't deny him. He's my drug.

And he knows it, too.

He starts with shallow thrusts just sliding in an inch or two but it's so huge that even just a little of him is a stretch. Then he takes it all the way out and slaps it on my clit, fucking my clit so it's rubbing it up and down. Then he jabs it at my entrance again without entering. I'm screaming now.

"Ssh, baby, we don't want the neighbors to hear."

He pushes inside me again and tweaks my nipples between his thumb and index finger, rhythmically pumping me but still hardly entering. Then he rams it all the way in. Hard. Then pulls back out. Again, just the tiny thrusts. I'm whimpering. He's unpredictable – I don't know if I'll get the whole plunge or not. And then, as if by perfect osmosis, just as I bring my own hand up to pressure my clit he thrusts once more all-in, deep from behind and I feel myself coming in a burst of unbelievable pleasure, his thick cock pushing out against my walls, filling me with tingling spasms as I contract all around him like one of those fly-eating plants, sucking him in, eating him whole. He stills his movements and I really sense his swelling inside me, which makes me come even harder. Then I feel his own release, hot and quiet as he groans gently with hushed arousal, his fingers exploring my butt, snaking them up around my waist which he grips harder as he bursts inside me.

"I love you, Pearl. You're my treasure. I love you and I always will." Then he cries out with another hard thrust, "Fuck you make me come hard – can't keep away from you. Gotta keep fucking you for the rest of my life. Is your wedding gown ready yet?"

My legs are tucked beneath me on the couch and Alexandre's head is in my lap. He thoughtfully stocked the refrigerator for me before my return and we're sipping freshly squeezed orange juice. He knew exactly when my plane had landed. He has had my every move monitored since I last saw him. How? Through my cell phone, he now admits. Duh. It was Alexandre who bought me that Smartphone – it's as good as a GPS; I should have thought that might happen, although assuming he had lost all interest in me, it hadn't occurred to me that he'd be tracking my movements with modern technology.

I've been trying to make sense, all morning, of what is going on between us and I'm still confused. For hours we've been talking things through, about Sophie, about Laura, about the fact that he left me broken-hearted for two weeks believing it was all over. Now he says he wants me to return to his apartment and leave this place to Daisy and Amy. He iced me out, now he wants all of me back. I'm still recovering – still assimilating what has happened. I'm not ready for this. Well, I am; all I've been daydreaming about is getting back with him – but I still don't trust him a hundred percent. Maybe not even seventy-five percent.

I plump up the cushion behind my back. "Is that *really* true, what you say, that you followed me to Laura's through my cell phone?"

"Yes. But I got there too late – I did a quick detour to my hotel to pick up Laura's box of books but I wasn't fast enough - you'd already left."

"There I was, watching you, sitting on that park bench listening to heartbreaking lyrics by Patsy Cline and thinking we were over and that you were back with Laura for good."

He threads his fingers through mine. "And I thought the same. She told me you'd had a talk and that, as far as you were concerned, we were finished."

I want to scream. *She had me fooled and tried to do the same to him!* "And you believed her?"

"No. That's why I'm here now. I knew in my heart you still loved me."

I throw my hands in the air. "You're so cocky! I wish I was that sure of myself. There *you* were, all cool, calm and collected and I was a friggin' basket-case!"

"Not cocky, just confident. I thought, if I can fuck Pearl just one more time, she'll remember how much she needs me." His lips flicker into a subtle but wicked smile.

I shake my head and raise my eyes to the ceiling. "So un-believably cocky! By the way, Monsieur God's Gift to Womankind, I'm not done with this conversation yet. I still have quite a few more questions. I mean…I'm sorry, Alex-andre, but *someone* must have told Laura about me and Alessandra Demarr. You swear it wasn't you – then who *was* it?"

"I have no idea."

I take a long sip of juice and say coolly, "Wouldn't it just be easier to tell me the truth?" I make a mental note to myself that next time I want information I should hold back the sex. I have zero bargaining power now.

"Look, baby, I swear I don't know, but everything that Laura told you is bullshit. I can't believe—"

"Believe it! Don't you fucking dare," I snap, "doubt me again when it's my word against Laura's. She lied to you, *too*. I should have recorded the conversation at her house with my Smartphone. I should have—"

He presses his lips to my temple. "Okay, calm down, I believe you. But why would she say all that when it just isn't true?"

"She wants you back, Alexandre."

"Well, I don't want her back."

I finish my juice and ask, "Why were you in London, anyway?"

"I was curious as to why *you* were there. I wondered what you were up to."

"I don't believe that for a second. You could have simply phoned me and asked me straight."

"I was forcing myself not to call. Trying to let some time pass – you needed a break. Feel it. Suffer a little so you realized how much you missed me." A faint smile touches his lips. *He knew what he was doing. He was being calculating.* This man knows me too well!

I pout. "You could have just come and gotten me."

He shakes his head. "Sometimes pursuing something you want is the fastest way of losing it. I learnt that a long time ago. If I had chased you relentlessly, Pearl, I could have lost you for good. You needed time to reflect and sort yourself out."

I observe him cautiously. I so want to believe this. *Is he telling the truth? Or is all this a crock of horseshit?*

"Why else were you in London?" I grill.

"Business."

"Not true. HookedUp didn't have any meetings or Sophie would have said."

"I told you, I have other projects in the pipeline."

"Like what?"

He hesitates. Glugs down all of his orange juice in one go, and says in a flat voice. "Don't ask me about my business, Pearl."

"Don't ask me about my business, Kay. My God, can you hear yourself? You sound like Michael Corleone!"

"You regret meddling between HookedUp and Sophie. It won't happen again. From now on, what I do is my concern and you, chérie, need to keep your pretty nose out of my business affairs."

I bite my tongue. It's true. I got myself into a real pickle with Sophie; my imagination running wild. I still can't work out, though, how Laura would have private information about my sex life. Is Alexandre lying to me? Does he want us both?

"Why was Laura wearing a silk robe and told me you'd just had afternoon sex?"

He bursts out laughing. "She said that? I suppose I should be flattered that two women are fighting for me but—"

"I'm not fighting for you. If you want her, go! Go on…fuck off out of here and fuck that skinny bitch for all I care. But you have to choose—"

He laughs even harder and I scowl with fury. I stand on the couch, now, kicking him with my bare foot. "Fuck off!" I scream, realizing that I've said the word fuck way too many times. "Go on, go back to her if that's what you want, but my *'pearlette'* is off limits forever. Do. You. Understand?"

He grapples me and pulls me back down on the couch and pins me beneath him again.

"No! Alexandre, I'm sore."

"That's just how I like it so you can spend the day hobbling about, feeling like you've still got my cock inside you."

"You're disgusting! Obsessed with fucking. Obsessed!"

"Look who's talking – you can't get enough of me."

The arrogance! I pummel his head with a cushion and the next thing I know we are at it again, this time he's rolled underneath me and pulled me on top of him, slipping himself inside me - I find myself riding him – my anger boiling (even though I'm smiling) but because I have control and can dismount any moment, I take a long, deep breath and decide I can use this to my advantage. Yes, I have control! Now is the time to ask some more questions. I ride him for a while until he's really aroused and then slow down.

He scowls when I stop and flexes up his hips. "Keep going baby, it feels incredible."

I mustn't let him win this round. It's my turn to take the reins. "When you left Laura's house, how did you leave?" I test him.

"What do you mean?"

I freeze my movements. "Which door?"

"Out the back."

"What back?"

"Through the garden, through to the garage."

"Why did you go to the garage?"

"What is this, *Homeland?* Why are you cross-questioning me?"

"Why did you go to the garage?" I repeat, punctuating my question with a thrust.

"Because I keep my Aston Martin there."

"What! You have stuff at her house?"

"My Aston Martin is not 'stuff' – it happens to be a 1964 DB5, the same Bond car, I'll have you know, that featured in *Goldfinger* and *Skyfall*. Anyway, the last I heard, it wasn't Laura's house but *James's* and Laura's house. Yes, I keep my car there, for now. They have the space – they borrow my house in Provence for summer vacations, I use their garage from time to time, what's the big deal?"

I relax into him for a moment and go back to my stallion ride. I feel sore but then I drag my sleepy eyes over his body and get a renewed rush of desire. Christ he's handsome. His wide chest is smooth, warm, his biceps chiseled and strong, and the cords of his forearms flex as he holds me around my waist, making me feel petite and feminine. His dark hair is mussed up about his face and when I lift up my butt and plunge back down on him he groans, biting his beautiful lower lip, red and lush. He grabs my ass and starts pumping from underneath.

"Not so fast, cowboy," I scold. "I'm sore, remember."

I lift myself almost off him and rest my body forward so just the tip of his crown is inside me. I tease myself with just the big satiny head of his cock and no more, all my nerve endings are gathering in a sensuous dance at my aroused entrance. My eyes flutter and I keep my rhythm as he groans beneath me. I pile cushions behind his head so he's in the perfect position to suck at both of my nipples, pleasuring each one in turn, flicking his tongue over the puckered areolas. My clit's rubbing up and down on his taut stomach with my rhythmical, almost horizontal movement, while his erection pushes in and out just a couple of inches inside my wet hole. Mixed with the tit sucking it's driving me crazy with desire... I plunge hard back down and that's it... I start coming in both places - a deep vaginal spasm mingles with a massive clitoral orgasm slapping against his hard abs, pulsating through me. This is a Mighty Big O and I start screaming. How I love the fact that every time I come, Alexandre's button is also pushed. It's impossible for a woman to come on command – our bodies just don't work that way - but men are different; at least Alexandre is. My excitement always gets him hot and he, too, is crying out my name, his release intense – there seems to be no end to the semen inside him.

He starts kissing me, his tongue probing, pulling and sucking on it - he breathes into my mouth, "Pearl... Pearl, forever. You're mine forever, please never leave me baby, I'm so in love with you."

"Me too," I cry out. "I love you, Alexandre," as another wave rolls right through the core of me making me clench and contract with unbelievable tremors.

9.8 on the Richter Scale, this one.

4

It strikes me that I have a real problem. We both do. Alexandre and I are hooked on each other sexually. I think back to my marriage with Saul. He was completely faithful to me. Yet I was in The Desert. If Alexandre is not being faithful and he's cheating on me with Laura, what do I do? Which would I rather be... in The Desert with a faithful man or in the flames with a cheater?

Cheating Flames...Alexandre?

Safe but Lonely Desert...Saul-type of man?

My head is opting for The Desert but my heart...

Not to mention my nether regions...

Because maybe the twain cannot meet. Maybe the sex-god, Mr. Good-Looks-Charmer only comes with the cheating strings attached.

It has been a week now. Alexandre wants me to move right back 'home' he said, (his place) but I have managed to resist. I'm still in my new apartment. Daisy and Amy have moved in, sharing the second bedroom. I have managed to keep a modicum of autonomy. Because a little voice inside my head is warning me to be cautious. All it has done is make Alexandre even keener.

Because of my insistence, the wedding and the gown are on hold. I want to hear it from Laura's lips that there is nothing going on between them and find out how she knew private stuff about me. Alexandre is on probation. The southern part of my body (the Deep South) may be foolish but I, the cerebral tough nut up north (the Rocky Mountains) am not.

My brain, at least, must stay intact. For the moment I have told him it's just Sex, nothing more. No marriage, no living together officially, until this Laura nonsense gets sorted out. The only problem is that she isn't answering my calls nor replying to emails and snail mail letters. I want to ask her why she's pretending that they're together if they aren't.

I have also tried contacting her estranged husband, James, although rumor has it that he has slinked off to the Cayman Islands. Alexandre, too, tried to contact him but he won't respond. Did Laura feed her husband the same story and now James hates Alexandre's guts? For good measure, Alexandre's precious, classic Aston Martin (how men love their cars) has been moved – collected and driven by his driver, Suresh, over to his house in Provence. That was one of my demands and he obliged without flinching.

Alexandre swears that he won't see Laura again, not even as friends, and that all connection has been severed for good. Still, I am biding my time. In my head, I have moved our marriage to St. Valentine's Day. It will still give me my white winter wedding but let me sort things out. I'm not telling

Alexandre about my secret plans. Let him teeter on the edge – let him be the one to feel insecure for a change. I have thought long and hard about this. I imagined that if I ever got Alexandre back, I'd snap him up, rush to the altar just to seal the deal, but I want this marriage to be secure. I really do need to clear up the Laura issue – be one hundred percent sure.

A marriage is for life, not just for Christmas.

To my surprise, I'm enjoying being the Sex Only woman. I feel liberated – free. I hold the cards. I have control...

Except, of course, in the bedroom. Alexandre still seems to have jurisdiction over my body. It has a mind of its own as if it were a marionette - he being its puppet master.

To think that I spent eighteen years without anyone being able to give me an orgasm and he can just ease them out of me, every single time, like falling drops of rain. It's a miracle.

Work is better than ever. I am still in contact with Sam Myers via Skype and have decided to keep the HookedUp Enterprises fifty/fifty deal going with Natalie – even with feature films. If a good movie script comes in, I'll take it. But I will not get so emotionally involved again, and I certainly won't tamper with any script, nor have private meetings with movie stars.

Natalie and I could have changed the name. After all, Alexandre severed any connection to HookedUp Enterprises by bowing out gracefully and handing the business over to us. We can buy him out over time – although, luckily, no money had yet come in before he and Natalie did their 'sweet' deal so, in effect, we are just buying options, rather than anything that exists. The features can help us budget our documentaries which, bit by bit, are gaining more recognition. Not to mention the favor Alexandre is granting us: HookedUp Enterprises gets free advertising on his social media site. Another reason to keep that name.

While I'm busy doing a spurt of cleaning, organizing, chucking out the old and in with the new, Laura calls. Finally. About time. Now I can get on with my life – my plans; get a few facts straightened out. I can tell, right away, by the tone in her voice that she's feeling triumphant.

"Hello, Pearl," she purrs in her upper class British drawl. She sounds like Cruella De Vil. Perhaps if she got her hands on Rex, she'd turn him into a fur wrap. "Sorry I haven't got back to you but we've been busy."

We've.

"Laura, stop trying to pretend that you and Alexandre are an item. I'm not buying it."

She groans. "God, I hate that American expression, 'buying it'. You lot should really learn how to speak properly. You've got *us* now infected with your way of speech - all your inane TV shows…going up at the end of perfectly normal sentences as if they're questions when they're not. Saying cute instead of sweet, warranty instead of guarantee, kidding instead of joking. Next thing you know we'll be calling our knickers panties."

"Speaking of panties, Laura, stop throwing yours at Alexandre. It's over between you two and it has been for three years. You're acting like some deluded fan who won't take no for an answer."

"Ooh, Pearl, I can see your claws are really out for the kill."

"You bet they are, Laura. Just keep away from Alexandre, okay?"

"How can I keep away from him when he won't keep away from me?"

"Stop bullshitting me, Laura."

"I think you'll find out in time, Pearl, that you're the deluded one, not me."

"I want to ask you a few direct questions and I'd like direct answers, please."

Silence.

"Laura? Are you still there?" I ask between gritted teeth.

"I really don't think I owe you a thing after you insulted me. Do you know what it's like being in a wheelchair? To imagine never being able to dance again? Or sail. Or even walk. Can you imagine that?"

"I apologize - I do, for insulting you at your front door. It was a gross, unkind thing to say and I'm glad that you are no longer in a wheelchair, but it doesn't give you license to lie to me. Pretending that Sophie was out to kill me. Lying about you and Alexandre, telling me that you were sleeping with him again and getting married and—"

"What makes you so sure that's not true, Pearl?"

"Because Alexandre swears it's not true, that's why."

"He'll swear his father just 'disappeared,' too. He's a good liar, Pearl. Anything to get into your 'panties' - as you so vulgarly call them."

I can see this conversation is going nowhere, fast. "Why

did you lie to me about Sophie?"

"For your own good."

I sit on the edge of my bed, kick off my shoes furiously and hold the phone closer. "Something tells me, Laura, that you are so *not* concerned about my welfare."

"Listen, it's only a matter of time until Alexandre and I are back on track. It was kinder to nip things in the bud between you two - sooner rather than later."

This woman is something else!

"You don't give up, do you?" I spit out.

"Alexandre and I are meant to be together. One day, you will accept that. Really, Pearl, give up. I'm stronger, mentally, than you are. I'm like a Rottweiler with a bone. You'll see. Soon, you'll be so exhausted by this whole ordeal that you'll be handing me Alexandre on a platter, relieved to be out of it. Do you really want to go into battle with me? Do you *really* want to find out what I'm capable of?"

"I don't take threats lightly."

"Oh, please, don't get me wrong – this isn't a threat. Oh no. This is a friendly warning."

I lean against the headboard. Maybe this conversation will be longer than planned. "Where's your husband?"

"James is indisposed right now. He's having a holiday."

"Why isn't he returning Alexandre's calls?"

"You know how it is, Pearl...sometimes people just go AWOL. Bit like Alexandre's father...just slipped off one day never to be seen again."

"What are you telling me, Laura?"

"I'm not telling you a thing. You're a bright girl...summa cum laude and all that – I think you can work it all out for yourself. Especially with your penchant for super-sleuthing." She bursts out into a demonic cackle.

"Speaking of sleuths, Laura, how did you know about me and Alessandra Demarr?"

"Alexandre told me."

"No, Laura. You know that's a lie. Tell me the truth."

"You are a bit thick...I'm amazed you passed any exams at all."

"Just tell me, Laura, I need to know."

"Well, because I don't *need to know* what you're up to anymore, plus I really couldn't give a toss now that I've got Alexandre's attention back...well, I'll give you a clue."

"I'm listening."

"I really shouldn't be divulging my secrets."

I sigh into the receiver.

"Alright, but this is just between you, me and the gatepost."

I claw my nails into a cushion.

She whispers, "I'll give you a itsy, bitsy, little hint...does your phone have trouble shutting itself off or stay lit up after you've switched it off, or does it light up even when you aren't using it at all?"

Yes, I think. All of the above, which surprises me because it's new. "My Smartphone. But how? You've never had my cell in your possession."

"As I said, you're a bit slow on the uptake. You're so 1972, Pearl. So Watergate. But I suppose it makes sense for you, at your age, to be locked in a time warp. Anyway, must dash. Lovely chatting."

"Wait! That means you've hacked Alexandre's phone too? Maybe even Sophie's...hello? Laura are you there? Laura!!"

In a frenzy, I go online and look up cell phone hacking. The British newspapers did it, so why couldn't Laura?

Especially with all her money and contacts.

I read hungrily:

Cell Phone Spying: Is Your Life Being Monitored?

It connects you to the world - but your cell phone - anyone from your boss to your wife could be monitoring your every move.

The same modern technology that keeps you on the move and in touch with everyone could also be your road to ruin – without you suspecting a thing.

Long gone are the days of simple wiretapping when all you could fear was someone listening into your conversations. The new generation of cell phone spyware provides a lot more power. Eavesdropping is easy. Your calls and text messages can be monitored – systems can even be set up so the spy is automatically alerted when you dial a certain number. Anyone who can perform a basic internet search can find the tools and figure out how to do it in no time.

Even more worrying is what your phone can do when you aren't even using it.

Location – simple surveillance.

A service called *World Tracker* lets you use data from cell phone towers and GPS systems to pinpoint anyone's exact location any time – even with the phone switched off – as long as the person has it on them.

I think of Alexandre – knowing I was at Laura's and when I would land in New York – upgrading my plane ticket. But he had my phone in his possession so that makes sense. It hadn't occurred to me that I could be a technology target of Laura's. Scary. I read on:

All the spy has to do is log onto the website and enter the target phone number. The site sends a text message to the phone that requires one response for confirmation. Once that response is sent automatically by your phone the spy is locked into your location and you can be tracked. The response is only required one time – after that, you, the cell phone owner, can be monitored – pinpointed on a Google map, without even knowing it.

Eavesdropping.

So once that person has been located they can also be spied upon. Even if you are not talking on the phone, the eavesdropper can still listen in to conversations.

Dozens of programs are available that can turn any cell phone into a high-tech, long-range listening device, undetectable to the average person. A phone's microphone can let the listener hear any conversation within earshot. The program can be installed from afar – the spy does not even have to come into contact with your cell phone. Once your number is dialed it taps into your phone's mic and can hear everything going on. Your phone won't even ring and you will have no idea that

the listener is virtually at your side.

It is now also possible for the spy to recover your deleted text messages and last dialed numbers – even deleted contacts.

I sit there stunned. My cell, that nice new Smartphone, and my old one – especially my old one (lost with my handbag) with even more unprotected technology - have been unwilling traitors to my every move, my every word. My phone, a recording device even when switched off? Laura could have practically been in the bath with me and Alessandra; been privy to our bondage madness, heard everything about my night with the footballers, not to mention all my intimate text messages and phone calls to Alexandre and Daisy! Maybe she's been in on my emails, too. And if she has me tracked, who's to say she hasn't done the same to Alexandre, or anyone she chooses?

I'm horrified, yet relieved. Alexandre has not lied to me. He did not betray me. Laura is psychotic. And dangerous. *Dange-air oose,* as Alexandre would say.

Anything I say, I do, can be used against me. Not in a court of law, no – the woman is breaking every ounce of the law, what she is doing is highly illegal. But her knowledge is her weapon. There's only one thing to do. Take my phone to some techie-genius to be swept clean of her spyware and get a new chip not registered in my name. And phone Alexandre – let him know that his ex is a total nut-job. Speaking of techie-geniuses, how come Alexandre, himself, didn't catch on to the fact she was hacking my phone? He must know all about that sort of stuff. How come he didn't guess?

All that Laura was saying about her husband, too? Being

AWOL. Has she topped James off??'

I need to be careful. She's not only jealous, bitchy and determined...

She is terrifyingly dangerous.

I take my phone to a specialized shop and the man confirms that yes, it looks as if it has been hacked. He restores the factory settings, changes the chip so I have a new number and warns me to watch all text messages coming in which could be new attempts at breaking into my conversations and messages.

As I'm opening my front door, my landline is ringing. It's Alexandre. His voice sounds shaky and very apologetic. "Your cell isn't going through," he lets me know in an agitated voice.

"That's because I changed my phone number. It had been hacked. By Laura."

"I gathered."

I chuck my coat on the hall table in fury. "What? You're not surprised?" I shout out. "Why didn't you warn me?"

"Because I didn't put two and two together until it was staring me in the face. I was being very blind, Pearl, and I'm sorry. I'm so sorry about Laura."

"She's been listening to my conversations! Maybe yours, too. I don't trust my cell...even now after I've just had it swept clean. And you – you've been tracking me too – I don't like it, Alexandre, I don't like it one bit."

"I feel safer when I know where you are, chérie. I just want to look after you, know you're okay. Listen, baby, I have to take a trip – at least a week."

"What about Christmas?"

"I have an emergency; I have to see my mother."

"Oh my God, is she okay?" I think of my own mother – *please don't say it's the Big C.*

"Physically, yes, she's fine but…well…we have a family emergency."

"Is Sophie alright? Elodie?"

"This has nothing to do with Sophie. It's just between me and my mother. Something's come up."

"What? What's wrong?"

"When we're married, Pearl, I'll tell you all about it."

This mysterious and enigmatic comment leaves me speechless. Suspicion nips at my heels.

"Pearl, are you still there?"

"I don't understand, 'when we're married.' Is this some kind of moral blackmail to speed up the wedding?"

"No."

"Then what are you saying something like that for?"

"When we're married we'll be a team."

"We're a team now, Alexandre," I say, hurt. I slump onto the chair and take off my sneakers.

"Not quite. I need to know…look, I don't want to discuss this over the phone."

I'm rendered silent, still trying to digest this weird conversation. Laura calling, telling me she finally has 'Alexandre's attention' and Alexandre's mother who isn't ill, yet has a mysterious emergency. *What* emergency?

"Look, I'm flying to Paris in a couple of hours."

I wait for him to say more. Wait for his invitation. He says nothing.

"Christmas?" I ask.

"I'm in a real mess right now, a real bind. I'm sworn to secrecy."

"Christmas?" I repeat, my heart pounding with disappointment and anger.

"Baby, of course you're welcome to come for Christmas in Paris but..."

"If there's a 'but' involved, I don't think I want to," I reply tentatively, my throat swelling up.

"Yes, there is a very big but."

I take a deep breath. My eyes are prickling with tears. I had imagined Christmas here, in New York, both of us alone with Rex. If his mother were ill of course I'd understand, but this...this is beginning to sound like some strange excuse. "What's going on?" I croak through my wooden throat.

Alexandre's voice sounds as pained as mine. "Something I have to sort out. I don't want to lie to you, Pearl, so please don't ask me any more questions. Just know I love you and want to marry you the second you say yes."

"Why would I want to marry someone who has secrets from me? Someone who's hiding something?"

"It's a Catch 22, isn't it?"

I try to stop my voice from breaking. "It certainly is."

"I love you."

"Are you going to London, by any chance?" I ask, not wanting to hear the answer that I'm dreading.

"Please don't ask me any more questions - I don't want to lie to you."

"I take that as a 'yes.' So you're going to London," I state flatly.

"Look, I have no choice."

"We always have a choice, Alexandre."

"External forces are trying to pull us apart."

"Laura."

"Yes.

"You're going to see Laura?"

"Please, Pearl, don't make this harder for me than it already is."

I hang up. There is no more to discuss. I don't want to humiliate myself, scream and cry down the phone. All I know is that he will be seeing Laura again after he promised not to. Her phone call…she knew she had him back. She was right; *I'm* the deluded one, not her. For whatever reason, whatever hold she has over him, he just can't keep away from her. And he's not even offering to explain why – everything shrouded in some big, enigmatic secret. Well, fuck him!

This time I know it's over between us, once and for all.

5

Christmas zipped by, Alexandre spent it in Paris. Anthony came to stay (Bruce went to his parents in Napa Valley because his father was ill). Here, at my new abode, it was like one big slumber party. Daisy and Amy, Ant and I all snuggled together in our two bed-room apartment, Ant on the couch and Amy in her special Wigwam in the bedroom which was a gift from Anthony. It was fun.

We watched endless children's movies which we loved, particularly the *Toy Story* trilogy. Embarrassingly, I found myself weeping in *Toy Story 2*, identifying with the toys being abandoned by their owners. I still have all my old teddies; I never did have the heart to get rid of any. It feels to me that only yesterday I was a child, playing tea parties and doctors and nurses the way Amy does now.

She, Ant, Daisy and I all played cowboys, too – a toy gun

and western outfits came along with the wigwam kit, although Amy refused to kill any Indians – a politically correct tomboy. Christmas is all about children and Amy had a ball.

I kept waiting for Anthony to slip into his old sarcastic, jaded demeanor but he didn't. He was adorable and very loving towards me. I am so glad the troubled part of our relationship is history.

The troubled part of a relationship….namely, Alexandre. He called on several occasions and each time my brother picked up and chatted merrily away, but never handed over the phone and told Alexandre that as long as he had anything to do with Laura I was not interested in seeing him. Alexandre didn't push it; he just seemed pleased to have news of me. He has been flitting from Paris to New York to London. I keep half expecting him to be waiting outside my door but it hasn't happened.

I guess he has made his choice, after all.

And that choice is Laura.

Made all the more complicated by something I have been feeling for two whole weeks. Swollen breasts, sleepiness, occasional vomiting and a strange longing for pickles.

Perhaps my old teddies will get unpacked, after all.

Yes, I'm pregnant – at least that's what a home pregnancy test has confirmed. I called my gynecologist and booked an appointment for next week. Meanwhile, I thought it was time to pamper myself, so I also booked a massage.

The Ayurvedic salon is not what I had imagined. Daisy recommended this place to me – a friend of hers comes here on a regular basis for soothing massages. Daisy's friend had described in detail *a warm herbal oil massage designed to bring nourishment to the tissues, deep relaxation to the muscles and calmness to the mind.* Hmm...sounds perfect. However, this place seems like less of a beauty parlor and more of a doctor's office. I am given a form to fill out with my medical history – *Jeez, all I wanted was a relaxing massage with oils!* But because the book I'm reading on my e-reader has me hooked, I remain in the waiting room patiently; in fact, happy that I have this peaceful excuse to devour my novel.

Finally, a large woman in a white coat brushes out of her office and says a warm goodbye to the lady before me. She smiles and ushers me in. She's Indian and dons a happy, friendly face with cheeks like ripe apples.

"Come in, Ms. Robinson, sorry to keep you waiting."

"No problem, I caught up with some reading."

"Please sit down. Let me see your medical history," she says, and I hand her the piece of paper.

She adjusts her spectacles and peruses it with great interest, although I'm not sure why – I'm your pretty average type. No allergies, no epilepsy, no addictions – except, of course, for sex with a particular Frenchman, if you count that. Right now, you could say I was going 'cold turkey.'

"Now, what can I do for you?"

"Well, I...um...I came here for a basic massage."

"Nothing is basic about our massage therapy, Ms. Robinson."

"Oh, I see. Please call me Pearl, by the way; I hate formalities."

"Pearl – what a lovely name. Tell me, what's troubling you? Are you feeling tired, sluggish, depressed?"

"Yes to the first two things you mentioned. Depressed?

Well, I would say I feel more anxious that depressed."

She says nothing, just nods her head as if to say 'go on'.

"I'm pregnant, for starters."

"Congratulations, that's wonderful news." She beams at me, her sparkling white teeth are set off against her coffee-colored skin.

"Thank you. Well, yes." I want to explain to her that I'm not with the baby's father; I want to burst out crying, fling my arms about her ample shoulders and unleash my inner turmoil, but I chew my lip instead, and fight back any impending tears.

"Well, of course, you know that *any* kind of massage therapy is out of the question for you right now, don't you?"

I'm stunned. Who is this woman? *I just want a goddam massage, lady!*

"But why? That's why I'm here."

"Well, perhaps it's divine intervention – you don't want to lose your baby. How many weeks are you?"

I think back to the rampant, sex-fueled night with Alexandre when he practically pierced my womb he went in so deep. I can't be sure if that was the qualifying moment, there have been so many since.

"I think about five weeks. I'm not sure – I just did a home pregnancy test this morning."

We discuss my periods, dates, medication and so forth for a good ten minutes. I'm wondering why I'm offering all this information about myself to a massage therapist when she informs me, "I run this Ayurvedic practice but, you know, I'm just as much a doctor as I am a masseuse."

"No, I had no idea. So you don't practice regular medicine here in the States?"

"Ayurvedic medicine is not recognized officially in this

country but where I come from – Kerala in southern India – well, it is an important part of our culture and taken very seriously. But I am also a qualified GP. My mother was a doctor and also my grandmother; all of us GPs with a particular interest in preventative medicine."

"But I have nothing to prevent," I venture, still confused as to how I got myself into the doctor-ish situation when all I wanted was a freaking massage.

"I see here that you are forty years old."

"Yes."

"With a history of two miscarriages – one D&C," she says, reading my notes.

I remember that awful time; when I went in for an ultra-sound and they discovered the baby had no heartbeat. I had been carrying about a dead fetus for two weeks and they had to operate immediately. "Yes, I had a D&C," I say, suddenly profoundly grateful that I'm now pregnant, that God has given me another chance even if I am to be a single mother forevermore.

"How many times have you had sexual intercourse with your partner in the last few weeks?"

"Er…none."

She nods with approval. "Good. You must abstain from sex for the first three months of pregnancy or you risk suffering another miscarriage."

Well, that will be easy now that Alexandre is with Laura and I can't even look at another man, let alone bed down with one.

The doctor continues, "Any penetration is dangerous for a woman of your age with your medical history. You will not find this written in any textbook and most modern-day doctors would poo-poo this idea but, believe me, old wives' tales are very often true."

569

I stare at her bemused. *Abstain from sex?? What has this got to do with my herbal massage?*

She goes on matter-of-factly, "No penetration but you can do other, non-invasive sexual practices. No massages, least of all with powerful oils that can upset the body's hormone-balance. You must not even indulge in reflexology; too much stimulation. Some doctors believe abdominal massage is good as it gets the blood flowing. I do not, unless it is very gentle and with your own hands – do not go to a massage therapist for the first three months or you could lose your child. You're forty; this could be your last chance at pregnancy, you need to take all the precautions you can."

I eye her suspiciously. Is she some kind of quack? "I've never heard of this before. It seems so extreme."

"Once, my dear, people thought it was extreme when they were advised not to smoke and drink whilst pregnant. Believe me, I have been in this business all my life, since I could walk and talk – I have breathed it – every single member of my family, the men included, are doctors. We have picked up a few tips over the years." She waggles her head in a figure of eight.

I observe her warily but I'm also fascinated by this information. My mother would have loved this woman – she hated conventional medicine.

"Now, what I'm going to prescribe for you, Pearl, is simple. One baby aspirin a day. This will safeguard you against any premature clotting. Stay off caffeine, alcohol and away from second-hand smoke - eat plenty of fresh vegetables and protein, but you probably already know all that. No heavy exercise at the gym, no jogging."

"Is swimming okay?"

"Swimming is perfect but don't train for the Olympics."

570

She smiles. "Folic acid in a multi-vitamin, B6, B12 and omega 3's," she states briskly.

"I already bought all that at the pharmacy, and fish-oil tablets."

"Good. I'm going to give you a painless saliva test to see your progesterone levels and if they are low I'll prescribe a completely natural progesterone cream. Progesterone is responsible for creating a healthy environment in the womb by creating and maintaining a healthy uterine lining. If more people used this treatment a lot of miscarriages could be avoided. All you need is a pea-sized amount of cream on your finger which you can rub into a different area each time, just once a day - somewhere the skin is thin; your breasts, face, upper thighs. It's completely natural, no synthetics, no harmful ingredients."

She sticks something into my mouth to do the saliva test. My mind wanders off to my baby-to-be - that is, if it can survive the next couple of months up until the first trimester, the most precarious. Will he be blond or dark? Will she have Alexandre's curvy red lips and his crooked smile? Will she be proud like him? Will he break hearts like his father...

"Oh, and one more thing," the doctor says assertively. "Try to keep your cell phone calling to a minimum. Radiation levels are harmful and can impair fetal brain development. Nobody will tell you this and few people want to listen but—"

"No, you know what, doctor? I think it would be a great idea to dump my phone, once and for all. It'll be safer for both me and the baby."

Alexandre may have been stalking me through my cell but I am stalking Rex. I miss that dog. I can't break our bond. On my way back home, I get off the bus at Central Park South and walk into the park, listening to Michael Jackson sing *Ben*, the best love song ever written about an animal. But instead of 'Ben,' I sing along with the word, Rex.

I know Sally's schedule – she and Rex will be somewhere near the big bronze Alice in Wonderland statue, chit-chatting with her dog owner friends discussing their 'children's' behavior and comparing notes. Will I be doing the same soon? Only, with a human child, not a four-legged one? I guess I should join prenatal classes and discuss breastfeeding options and which is the best brand of diapers.

Maybe I'll be coming to this spot, myself, watching my child climb on Alice. Unlike most sculptures, children are invited to climb, touch and crawl all over Alice and her friends. In fact, through the decades, thousands of hands and feet have literally polished parts of the statue's bronze surface completely smooth. I observe Alice now, sitting on a giant mushroom reaching toward a pocket watch held by the White Rabbit. Peering over her shoulder is the Cheshire Cat, surrounded by the Dormouse, Alice's cat Dinah, and the Mad Hatter and yes, I see Rex and Sally not far off, just behind this landmark, Rex sniffing a fellow mate.

Sally loves to pass by here every day. With her shocking pink pigtails and punk rocker outfits, Sally is an eternal child. Alexandre found her walking dogs with one of the dog walking companies that roam the Upper East Side. The handlers typically walk ten dogs at a time all leashed, making sure their right hand is free for picking up dog poop with wads of newspaper stuffed in their back pocket. Sally makes three times the money, now, being Rex's personal nanny.

"Hi Sally," I shout, rushing over to Rex to hug him.

"I wish you'd come home, Pearl," Sally grumbles with a sad pout. "Alexandre is a bit mopey without you there."

"Really?" I ask, thrilled to know he may be suffering a little (obviously not enough, though, to stop seeing Laura).

"Yes, really. He's always on the phone doing business – doesn't smile much these days, his temper's short; he seems to have lost his sense of humor."

"Have you seen Laura?"

"No, who's she?"

I try to sound casual but fail miserably. "Do you ever hear him speaking to a woman on the phone – you know, sweet-talk."

"The only person he's been talking to more than usual is his mother. I know it's her because he has one voice for his mom and one for Sophie. You know his 'mom voice' is super-protective – it's very cute. Not that I understand French but I can hear the tone."

"No lovey-dovey talk with other women, then?"

Sally shuffles her big biker boots along the muddy grass. "No way! He obviously misses his precious Pearl. Sometimes I hear him say so to Rex, discussing how lost they are without you. Not that Rex can talk, but you know, I think he understands. And the other day, Alexandre gave me a whole bunch of photos of you – I was asked to drop them off at the framers. Like I said, he's either working or moping about you all day long. Rex is sleeping in his bed now."

"You're kidding?"

"I know! Alexandre snuggles up with Rex everywhere. He's now allowed on all the couches, even the bed. Since you've gone all Alexandre wants to do is be with his dog."

"Has Alexandre been traveling lately? To London?"

"Yes, he went to London last week."

"I see." I am now reminded of my mission. To forget about Alexandre for good and let him go - move on with my life. He has Laura now – he can't have us both. *Be strong, Pearl.* "Oh, Sally, I have something for you." I bring out my Smartphone and hand it to her. "A gift for you. It's already unblocked."

She jumps up and down and her pigtails swing as if in celebration. "Wow! Really! But this is like, brand new – this Smartphone is the best!"

"It's a great phone. It has advantages. You can keep your gloves on when you dial a number – not all Smartphones let you do that. Handy here in New York with the cold winters."

Sally's Cheshire Cat smile is spread across her whole face. "This is the greatest gift ever."

"Don't let Alexandre know I was asking about him."

"Okay, sure."

"And if you hear any information about Laura, pass the word along." *Oops! I have just broken my own resolution to put him out of my mind.* I add hastily, as if to excuse myself, "I just worry about him, that's all."

"Of course. You have my word this is just between us."

Sally, Rex and I meander about the park for a good half hour before I wend my way back home.

I am cell phone-less and it feels great. After all, once upon a time we humans made dates with people, arranged a time in advance and turned up. We couldn't cancel at the last second and flake-out when a better deal came up. We were responsible people, once. We could spell: see you tonight, not C U 2 nite. We had attention spans of more than five minutes at a go. We painted, sketched and wrote in note-books, not just flicked like mindless idiots through our Facebook and HookedUp pages, worrying about what everyone else was doing and living vicariously through them. Yay! I am no longer shackled-down with invisible chains to my social-media addiction!

It's a wonderful feeling with no cell to know I am not being spied upon nor stalked. I feel liberated and brain tumor-free. Most of all, I feel protective of that tiny bundle inside me; not that there is much evidence; no more swelling than a large bowl of pasta or rice wouldn't do. There is life within me and it feels incredible, especially as I am so in love with its maker, despite Alexandre being a heartbreaking bastard, I will still love everything about his future off-spring...

Because deep down inside me (call me a clueless fool), I feel there must be some mistake – he cannot be lying to me, he does love me.

Yet – I need to get a grip - all the evidence is there, clear and sharp as crystal – he still can't give up Laura.

A week has passed by. Sneaking off for my secret Rex *rendez-vous* has become a regular habit. If I can't have Alexandre, himself, I can feel close to him through his beloved dog. Today I've arranged to take Rex alone.

I meet Sally at the entrance at Sixty Forth Street by Central Park Zoo. Rex is there waiting, all excited. Funny how Labradors and Labrador mixes wiggle the middle of their torso when they wag their tails. He's ready for his tour around the park.

I kiss Sally hello and give her a one hundred dollar bill. "Have a nice breakfast."

She shakes her head; her Cerise-colored pigtails swing in surprise and her wildly plucked eyebrows, which seem no more than painted curves, shoot up. "Pearl, this is way, way too much."

"I don't have change," I lie, wondering if she has caught onto my not-so-subtle bribe. It's good to have Sally on my side, to get snippets of information about Alexandre, know where he's going and when he'll return. "Treat yourself to something delicious. I'll meet you back here in an hour and a half."

"Are you going to the Central Park Paws event this morning?"

Only dog-mad Sally could know about such a thing as Central Park Paws. "No," I answer, "but tell me more, I'm intrigued."

"Well, Central Park Paws hosts regular events for dog owners in the park. Today is Monthly Bagel Barks – it gives dog owners the chance to meet, talk and have breakfast while the dogs enjoy some off-leash playtime. It starts in fifteen minutes until nine o'clock."

"I'm so sorry, Sally, am I robbing you of your meeting? We can go together if you like."

She looks at the hundred dollar bill and says, "No, it's okay, I've always wanted to go to The Carlyle for breakfast …well, thanks so much, Pearl. Have a nice walk."

The Carlyle – where Alexandre and I had that dreaded

breakfast when I hadn't been honest with him about wanting to do a documentary about HookedUp and he lost his temper with me. This is the third time we have split up and this time I fear it's for good. It still doesn't make sense – he doesn't strike me as a person who would lie but the evidence is there – he can't keep away from Laura. She has some kind of emotional hold over him, no matter how in love with me he claims to be. I want him so badly but this time I must keep my resolve.

I wave Sally good bye and Rex and I go into the park. It is covered in a blanket of fresh, untrammeled snow and looks like a fairy-tale; the sky a clear, icy blue. Some pale crystal flakes flutter through the air – it's snowing, but only just.

We start wending our way across the twisting paths and buried grass towards Bethesda Fountain to the other side of the lake, now frozen, near to the woods and where I can confidently unleash Rex to run free and sniff about. I love New York. Here in Central Park, you are allowed let your dog off the leash before nine a.m. and again after nine at night. Not that I would brave Central Park at night alone – just in case. I let Rex loose; he's so well behaved that I don't have to worry about him escaping, unlike Zelda, the beautiful Husky of my childhood years.

We walk at a fast-paced clip, my thermal boots squeaking on the powdery snow, my huge, floor-length overcoat brushing against itself, whooshing and shuffling in muffled silence. Hardly anyone is around, just a few other dogs and people walking with purpose as if they are going home after an all-nighter or cutting through the park to work. It's still only seven thirty.

"Stop it, Rex," I scold, as he pees against a lumpy, half-melted snowman with a drooping carrot for its nose. I take the carrot between my gloved fingers and push it further inside its head. "There we go, Mr. Snowman, you'll last a little longer."

I zip along swiftly in the direction of the woody grove – New Yorkers walk fast – no meandering ever; you can get mugged that way. I wear eyes in the back of my head. This part of the park is remote. When I hear footsteps behind me I am aware of what a risk-taker I am. Rock-climbing, trapezes, going with two footballers to their dorm alone and dating a man too young for me with such a rampant sexual appetite he desires more than one woman to satiate him; he'd date us both simultaneously if he could get away with it. When will I ever learn? The footsteps are male, booted, tough...Holy crap! I spin around, my fists in balls and call Rex over to my side. I need to clip him back into his leash to show the world I'm a woman with a black Pit-bull mix...DON'T MESS WITH ME!

It's HIM. No less dangerous than a mugger. He's dressed in a long military coat that looks as if it's from World War One and big, black boots. His hair is damp and ruffled from the snowflakes, his dark eyelashes sparkling with moisture, his curvy lips red from the cold, tilted up into his signature crooked smile. He looks delicious, sexy, mysterious. Uh oh.

"Pearl, stop!" Alexandre rushes up to me and grabs my arm forcing me to stumble into him. His breath is on my face, hot mist clouding the tiny space between our mouths. He has the 'I'm going to fuck you' look written all over his face and I know I'm in trouble.

"What do you want Alexandre?" Stupid question. I know what he wants.

"I can't bear this any longer, Pearl – please." He starts

kissing my eyes, my nose and the animalistic groan deep within him makes my stomach flutter. I know what will be beneath that military coat. A big, huge, rock-hard Weapon of Mass Destruction.

"Christ, I've missed you."

"How's Laura?" I hiss from my tightened mouth. My white, steamy breath is like a dragon's; no less furious.

"Please let's not argue. Please, chérie, I'm going crazy without you. I need you."

"You just want me for my body, Alexandre."

"That's not true. I need you, baby. I need—"

"You can't have your cake and eat it, too."

"You're the only cake I want, I swear." He takes my gloved hand and pulls me towards him. "Come over here, we have to talk."

"We can talk right here."

"Too public, please baby."

He draws me behind him towards a large elm tree and pins me up against the solid trunk. "I have to kiss you."

"No."

But he starts with his trademark wispy kisses on my eyes again, on my icy cheeks and then my temple. I quiver all over and can feel my panties moisten. "Leave me alone, you bastard. How did you find me anyway, now that I don't have my phone?"

He breathes in the scent of me. "I have ways."

"Did Sally sell me out?"

"No, annoyingly Sally is on your side." He slips his black leather-gloved hand through a small opening in my coat and around my waist. Then the other hand. I can feel him un-glove himself and his warm fingers are tracing their way about my bare flesh. My skin tingles. He starts a familiar journey down the back of my butt cheeks but I slam my behind against the tree, trapping his hand. He was inches away from knowing how wet I am, and how I long for him inside me.

"Ouch, tigress, that hurts."

"Take your hand away, Alexandre."

"I know that you secretly want me, chérie, but as you wouldn't let me see you, I thought I'd better come and claim what's mine wherever I could - and it happens to be here in Central Park."

"Get it through that arrogant, ego-inflated head of yours that I do not belong to you! I am not your soul mate, nor your *media naranja*. You have all that already with *Laura*."

"You *are* my soul mate, my *media naranja*, my wife-to-be, my everything, Pearl. You're Rex's mother, too. We're a family."

Little does he know there's more family on the way. "You ruined and destroyed all that by seeing Laura again!"

"How many more times do I have to tell you that I don't love Laura? I don't want her - haven't for years and certainly not since I met you. The truth is, I don't even *like* her anymore."

I bellow at him, "Love and like have nothing to do with it for you. You covet her because you can't bear to give up any of your women. You're like a cock with his hens. You *are* a cock! One big walking, talking, cock! You have a Weapon of Mass Destruction which you go around using at every opportunity!"

He strokes a loose tendril of hair from my cheek. "I swear, believe me, it's been tucked away, unused except by my own hand since I last made love with you."

"You haven't 'made love' with me for ages, you *fuck* me!

'Fuck my ass off' 'fuck my brains out' as your expressions go."

"Come back and live with me again and we'll be making love again...just...I go crazy when I see you...this *diet* of sex - of us not living together is making me go insane so the last few times we got together I felt like a beast."

He takes my hand. "Feel it. Feel how hard it is. All I can think of is your voice, your smile, Pearl, your face, your lips, your ass, your tits and most importantly, your soul - your essence, your very being. I can't live without you, chérie. Every waking moment, every sleeping second I'm dreaming of you, Pearl, I'm so crazy about you, it hurts."

"Then fucking stay away from that asparagus stick bitch, Laura!" I yell, remembering how Sophie had described her as an asparagus.

Rex comes bounding over and jumps up. My screaming has alerted him and he starts to bark at his master. "You see?" I screech - "even Rex is on Team Pearl. He knows what a prize jerk you are. A lying, two-timing jackass!"

"Look, I'm dealing with Laura—"

"*Dealing* with her? You are unbelievable. Unbe-fucking-lievable!" I try to break away from his devouring gaze which is swallowing me whole.

But he has my wrists in a clasp so I can't escape. Christ he's sexy.

"I swear I haven't lied to you. I swear I've been faithful – I haven't touched Laura – please trust me, Pearl. Please have faith."

"Then why have you been seeing her?"

"I can't tell you. But trust me." He breathes into my face seductively – he smells of apples and sweetness. "I was just protecting someone I love."

"Someone *else* you love? How many of us *are* there, Alexandre? How many more women have you got hooked on you with your panty-melting antics?"

"I'm sorry, chérie. But I had to see Laura – I had no choice." He looks down at his boots. "And I'm afraid I'll have to see her again."

His words stab my heart. *I'll have to see her again.* I shout out in a jealous rage, "What is it that Laura has that I don't?"

"Something I need from her. Once I get it, I'll never go near her again, I promise."

I try to struggle free. "You are quite something, Alexandre Chevalier. Wow! You really win the prize for being a French, macho SHIT-head!"

He keeps hold of my wrists. "Please, baby, trust me. I can't say more, just trust me." He pushes his soft lips onto mine and kisses my closed, bitter mouth. He begins to lick me very gently and an unbidden low moaning sound escapes my throat which I know is my downfall. He pushes his wavering tongue inside my longing mouth and parts it. My jaw drops open. Even through his thick military coat I can feel his erection pressed up against my thighs.

"Hey, you two! No indecent behavior in public!"

I open my eyes from my reverie and say a little prayer to St. Lucy. Thank you, Santa Lucia, for saving me; for shining a light on this situation and showing it up for what it is…madness. It's a police officer and now he's making his way over towards us, half smiling as if he was kidding about 'indecency' but I take this opportunity. I slip from underneath Alexandre's clutches and dash towards the uniformed stranger.

"Bye, Alexandre. Rex! Come boy, come!" I start galloping at full pelt in the direction of the East side.

Rex runs behind me, following at racing speed. Rex has chosen me over his master and I feel triumphant.

I don't look back.

Daisy and I are sitting on her bed with our legs tucked under us while Amy's playing with her teddies in her wigwam.

"It's just my body he wants, Daisy, nothing more. Laura was right; he's in 'lust' with me."

"Nonsense, he wants all of you."

"All of me *and* all of Laura. He wants her for...I don't know what...and me...just to fuck."

"Rubbish. Look, Pearl, if all he was after was a sexy body...well... I don't mean to sound harsh and you do have an incredible body and you really are beautiful but...well...if all he wanted was a body, he could flick his thumb through any Victoria's Secret catalogue and pick off any top model he wanted – well, anyone who Leonardo di Caprio hasn't already claimed, that is. With his money and looks Alexandre could, literally, have any *body*. But he's chosen you."

"I suppose you're right. It's true, he could be going out with a supermodel. A supermodel who wants world peace and plays chess, to boot. He could get anyone. Some-times...no - not sometimes, often - I wonder what he sees in me."

Daisy rolls her eyes with irritation. "Stop sounding so poor-me and buck up, woman! He sees your good heart, your soul. And you may not be a supermodel but you look bloody amazing for your age. You have a better body than most twenty-five year-olds, and a beautiful face – sometimes you remind me of Grace Kelly. It really pisses me off when you start all that, 'I'm just an average-looking girl next door' nonsense. It's bollocks. Plus, Alexandre feels at ease with you, likes to hang out. You both love dogs."

I suddenly think of Laura (Cruella De Vil) calling Rex a 'creature' and it makes me seethe. "Alexandre swears nothing is going on with Laura and that I should trust him."

Daisy sucks in a lungful of air. "Well, I'm obviously not the best person to discuss this with after what Johnny did to me. And to Amy. I trusted him implicitly – I don't think I'll ever be able to do that again with any man."

"At least he wants you back and he's groveling."

"But I don't want him back now. How could I live with that uncertainty again?"

"What about Amy?"

Daisy looks over at the wigwam. Amy is muttering to herself in different voices and playing 'tea party' inside. "That's my only concern. Amy loves her dad, obviously, but at the same time it's no good if we're unhappy together – that's no good for her at all."

"You need more time to think it through. Let Johnny wallow in his misery a bit, it'll do him good. Make him appreciate what he's lost." I realize I sound like Alexandre – that's exactly what he said to me.

"Coming from you, the eternal forgiver, that sounds tough."

"Well, some men deserve the cold shoulder, now and then. If you're too nice they walk all over you."

"Actually Pearl, I have a confession to make."

"Really?" A gamut of possibilities runs through my mind. Perhaps she's been having private conversations with Alexandre and has been holding out on juicy information.

She looks at the wigwam and whispers, "About Zac."

"Zac, the surfer? The good looking one we met on the beach?"

Daisy looks down; her face flushes pink. "We kissed."

My jaw drops open. "You are *kidding* me? Daisy – that's so exciting…"

"It gave me confidence – made me realize I was still attractive."

"Are you kidding? You're gorgeous. Especially since you've lost all that weight. He should be so lucky."

Then she squeals quietly, "But wait. There's more!"

I laugh. "You sound like one of those infomercials…'but wait, there's more.' "

"I shagged him."

Shag - British for 'fuck'. I scream, "No!"

Amy pokes her head out of the wigwam. "Why are you shouting, Auntie Pearl?"

"Nothing, honey. I thought I saw a spider but I was wrong."

"I like spiders. I would never kill a spider."

"That's because you're an angel, sweetheart. Don't worry, I don't kill them, either."

Amy slips back inside her wigwam and continues her tea party.

Daisy whispers, "I haven't been able to get him out of my mind since."

"I'm not freakin' surprised. He was gorgeous. When did this happen? You're such a dark horse, Daisy."

"That day when you three all went on a walk in the woods. Remember? When I said I'd stay behind? Zac popped over."

"Sounds like he did a lot more than just pop over."

"Well, yes. It started with a kiss and then…well, I thought, 'I'm on holiday, what the hell.' I didn't mean it to go so far but my hormones took over, I couldn't resist him."

"And? Was it worth it?"

"Let's just say that he woke up a certain part of my body that had lain dormant for a long while."

"You were very brave to just *go* for it like that."

"Like I said, I was on holiday - I felt reckless. As far as I was concerned it was a one night stand…I mean a 'one *day* stand'…but he had other ideas."

I'm still grinning at this gossipy news. "Like what?"

"He told me he wanted more. Well, I left him hanging - you know, it wasn't exactly the right time in my life to be jumping into another relationship. When a woman doesn't give a damn, it makes a man all the more interested. I told him I wasn't ready for a relationship."

"*Relationship?* You'd even consider Zac as *boyfriend* material?"

"He's gorgeous, Pearl. And he's a really sweet guy. And not dumb either – he's interesting. Yes, I see potential there."

"But… but… he's a *surfer* - the non-committal type - he'd drive you nuts."

"That's what your dad's like. Zac is more demonstrative."

"Really? What did he demonstrate?" I laugh at my silliness and wait for a detailed description of the nitty-gritty.

Daisy replies in a serious tone, "Nothing like 'absence making the heart grow fonder.' He wants me to think about moving to Kauai and living with him."

Stunned doesn't even begin to describe how I feel. "You'd consider leaving New York? Living in *Hawaii?*"

"You bet. I mean, it's so beautiful there, so peaceful. A great place for a child to grow up. You get a tropical life but it's still part of America – the best of both worlds."

"Are you sure it wasn't something he just *said* – the way guys do sometimes. Empty promises and all that?"

"We've been in touch by email. No calls. I told him not to call – I don't want to upset A. M. Y."

A little voice pipes up from within the wigwam, "Mommy, I know you're talking about me."

"Just saying how pretty you are, Amy," I shout out. "My God, she's bright for her age."

Daisy whispers, "He's invited us to stay with him at his house. A three month trial period, he suggested."

My mouth hangs open. "I can't believe I'm hearing this. A surfer with *plans*?"

"Well, he said it. It was his idea. Maybe not every surfer is as flaky as your dad when it comes to relationships."

"And you're *considering* it? Seriously? What about your practice? What about your job?"

"I'm self-employed, I can go anywhere. I could start up something there. I may earn less out there but the cost of living will be so much less than New York City. I mean, Amy and I wouldn't move in with him straight away. I think that would be foolish. We could get something small nearby. See how it goes first. It would be an adventure – a life change. I'd keep my autonomy. Then, if it didn't work out with Zac it wouldn't be the end of the world and if it did, well…hello? Book Two of my life."

"What about Johnny?"

She lowers her voice to an almost inaudible whisper, "Johnny can fuck right off."

"Really?"

587

"The only reason he wanted us back is because Lady-love Phoenix has gone back to her husband. He had the perfect life with me and Amy and he blew it. We can't be left-overs. Anyway, don't worry, I won't do anything rash. But I am weighing things up." She clears her throat. "And what about you, Pearl? D'you think you'll have the willpower to stay away from Alexandre when he's still expressing undying love for you?"

"This time I have to, Daisy. I have no choice. I can't be left-overs, either."

"I just don't get it. *Why* is he still seeing Laura?"

"He says he needs one more thing from her and then he'll never see her again."

"Is that code for one last goodbye, d'you think? One last shag?"

"That's what I fear but he's been taking his time about it – this Laura thing has been dragging on for weeks."

"It must have been painful for you not spending Christmas with him."

"I had an amazing Christmas here with you and Amy and Ant."

"Yes, but still. Have you spoken to Sophie, by the way?"

"Yes, she called the other day. So strange. She asked me what was going on with Alexandre. She asked *me*."

"But surely she must *know* if it's to do with their mother - this big 'emergency' Alexandre was talking about."

"Exactly, that's what I'd presumed. But no. She's as much in the dark as I am. That's why I'm beginning to think this mother emergency thing is a fig leaf of an excuse to keep seeing Laura."

"But what you told me – the stuff Sally the dog walker said. It sounds as if he's miserable without you. None of this makes sense."

"Maybe he's miserable because he can't make a final choice and it's ripping him apart. I'm so glad you're here to protect me, Daisy, or I know what he'd do. He'd be at my door wooing me with kisses and flexing his huge great Weapon of Mass Destruction until I succumbed. He knows how weak I am, how I can't resist him.

"You're really hooked on him, aren't you?"

"I'm head over heels in love with him. I have never, ever felt like this about anybody."

"Are you going to let him know you're pregnant?"

"No. I want to know it's *me* he's choosing if he finally makes his mind up. If he knows there's a child involved he might come back to me just for that reason. It has to be me, and only me he wants."

"Did you tell Sophie about the baby?"

"No. I can't trust her not to tell him. You know how close they are."

"I wish I had a crystal ball, Pearl. I wish I could offer great advice but I've screwed up with you on more than one occasion. I was just as suspicious as you were about Sophie and if I'd kept my bloody mouth shut maybe you and Alexandre would be married by now."

"And what? Be divorced ten minutes later because of Laura? Having a ring on my finger probably wouldn't have changed a thing. Maybe he's like all those ex French presidents and aristocratic types who have a wife and also a mistress at the same time – maybe that's what rich French men do."

Daisy frowns. "He didn't strike me as that sort. I still can't believe he's with her. I mean, he swears to you that he hasn't touched her – why would he say that if it weren't true?"

"Because, as you know more than anyone, men can be very convincing. Listen, some women fall in love with serial killers and have no idea. I have obviously fallen for a pathological liar who can't keep it in his pants."

6

Alexandre felt as if he had been sliced in two. This whole situation was a fucking nightmare. He had never imagined that Laura could do this to him - have this hold on him just as everything seemed so perfect with Pearl. Crap timing - that was for sure.

He sat in his parked car, watching as snowflakes drifted across the windscreen... waiting, his heart pounding fast...with rage. He hadn't done anything like this for a long while; hadn't got into any fights for years because he knew what he was capable of. Anger and excess energy had been building up steadily over the past few weeks and this fuck was going to get it – he deserved it. He'd show that fuck, once and for all, that you just can't go through life treating people like garbage, especially women. Jim was his name. Probably thought that, because he made a killing on Wall St, he was above it all. He needed to be taught a lesson.

Alexandre's eyes were fixed on the man's front door. It was still decorated with a crown of holly, the imposing white brick house boasting expensive Christmas lights; tasteful, not overly done. Must have cost a mint, this place; Mystic, Connecticut was not cheap. He imagined the man's wife and 2.2 children, perfect and with no clue to the monster that lived within their loved one. Alexandre wouldn't damage him, no. He wouldn't do that to a man with kids but he'd scare the living shit out of him. Make him pay. In more ways than one.

He smiled to himself as it struck him that he'd never let onto Pearl that he was a black-belt master in Taekwondo. He hated people who boasted about their prowess at martial arts or sports. But after his father, he swore nobody would ever have the power to hurt him again physically. He remembered his teacher, Sophie's first serious boyfriend. He started to train her, and then Alexandre took an interest. The man was a real grand master, a genius; had been trained in Korea as a child. Alexandre remembered the mantra he had been taught, 'I shall be a champion of freedom and justice' and 'I shall build a more peaceful world.' Justice – that's what he would set right tonight. And as for a more peaceful world, Alexandre would ensure that this fuck, Jim, made his contribution to help abused girls in need.

Alexandre noticed the front door open. Fuck, there he was, that little shit. Just seeing his enemy made the thigh muscles in Alexandre's leg twitch. Those legs that had been trained to kick like a weapon; break a concrete block in two – even if he hardly trained anymore, it was second nature, his leg could fly up and smash any opponent in the head, knocking even the strongest man to the ground without even trying too hard. He'd have to control himself, though – he could kill, just with his thumb on someone's pressure point. Peace before combat at all times – except now, this bastard had it coming to him for nearly twenty years.

Alexandre briskly eyed his opponent's cocky way of walking and could see straight away that he was brawny – yes, he had a footballer's shape, but an ex-footballer who'd had too many lunches on his big fat banker's budget. Good, just as he'd been told – the man was going out alone. His family would still be inside watching TV. His contact had told him as much, that Jim liked to go out to a particular bar down by the Seafront on Saturday nights, usually coming home about ten thirty.

Alexandre watched as Jim got into his SUV and snailed out of the driveway. He waited a beat and when the vehicle was far enough ahead of him, he started his car and drove cautiously behind. He thought about people feeling repentant - how it was only possible to forgive someone when they were truly sorry for what they'd done. That's why his father had ended up dead – because he could never admit culpability, could never say he was sorry. That's all it would have taken, that one word beginning with S to save his life – but the shit couldn't even say it.

So he'd ended up electrocuted in his bath, the electric appliance zapping him until his body's spasms jittered like a live wire. Finally, like a huge wet fish he lay silent, his reign of terror over for good.

Jim parked his car near the bar. Alexandre did the same and swiftly got out, calmly walking over. Luckily, nobody was around; a couple had just gone inside the bar. Alexandre stepped up beside his target, grabbed the man by the shoulders and stuck the pistol into his back.

The man tried to spin on his heel but he was locked in a

vice. "What the fuck?"

Alexandre murmured quietly, "I've got a gun pointed right into your spine. If you don't do as I say, I'll pull the trigger and if you don't die you'll be paralyzed for life."

"Who the fuck are you?"

"Your shadow. Now get back into your car – we're going for a little drive. Don't fuck with me, this gun has a silencer. I'll pull the trigger, walk you over to the water and throw you in. Nobody knows I'm here, nobody has seen me. Nobody will hear a thing. You'll be fish food."

The man flinched and swallowed hard. Alexandre could smell his fear, the man was a coward. Bullies are always cowards.

"Get in the car, Jim."

"How d'you know my name? You're accent...are you like... one of those Romanians, the guys from the mafia? Look, I already said I didn't want to do that deal−"

"Shut the fuck up, Jim, just get back into your vehicle. If you do as I say, I won't kill you. If you fuck with me, I will. You're driving by the way."

"You must have me mistaken for someone else."

Alexandre pushed the gun in his back a little harder. "I don't think so. It's payback time, buddy."

The man let himself be bundled into the driver's seat and panted with fear. He had tears in his eyes and sweat dripping from his brow. Alexandre carefully got into the back seat, keeping the gun pointed at his spine – maintaining the pressure close so there was no doubt he meant business.

"You know, this country's gun control laws really need to be revised. Where I come from, you have to be part of a sporting club or a hunting club to get a gun license. They don't let any Tom, Dick or Harry go around with arsenals of lethal weapons."

The man stuttered, "Where are you from?"

Alexandre replied quietly, "That would be telling. Now start the car and drive."

"Where are we going?"

Alexandre's gloved hand pushed the weapon harder into the man's back making a dent in his cashmere overcoat. "Somewhere nice and quiet. Don't try anything smart, remember. This baby is still nuzzled right on your spinal cord.

Jim squeaked, "I swear I won't try a thing."

"So you live here just on weekends?"

"Weekends, holidays. I work in Manhattan."

"Yes, I know. You do well?"

"I'm proud of my capabilities, yes."

"Capabilities…hmm, that could be disputed. How much money do you earn a month, Jim?" Alexandre already knew the answer to his question.

The man's breath hitched. "It depends. You know, on bonuses and stuff, but I make a good fifty grand a month."

"That's a lot of money."

"Yes, it is."

"It's how much I make every thirty minutes, more or less."

The man sniggered uneasily as if he thought Alexandre was joking. He wasn't.

Alexandre went on in a low voice, "I don't like people telling others how much money they earn; I think it's tacky. But I thought you might be interested so you understand who you're dealing with. So you understand that, not only could I have you killed at any moment, but right now, I have an alibi. I have three people who can testify I am *not* here now… with you. That is, should you get any smart ideas. Should you want to call the cops at a later date or tattle-tell on me. You see, I am way, way richer than you are. And you know what money buys, don't you, Jim?"

Jim nodded.

"It buys power," Alexandre whispered.

"What do you want from me?" the guy asked edgily.

"I want you to make a donation. Not much at all. I'm going to be really fair. All I ask is that you donate two month's salary."

Jim squealed, "I can't give you a hundred thousand dollars just like that! I don't even know who you are!"

Alexandre replied calmly "Oh, I think you can, Jim. Here's the thing. I'll make you a deal. You give me the names and phone numbers of all your rapist friends who were there that night – when was it, yes, about eighteen years ago. All those assholes who violated a beautiful young woman called Jane Doe, and I will give you a ten percent discount."

"You're nuts. Completely nuts."

Alexandre poked the gun into the man's back even harder. "You're absolutely right. I'm so nuts, I'm capable of killing you."

"I can't even remember who was there."

"So you admit what you did?"

Jim wailed, "She wanted it, man. We were all drunk. She was asking for it. I can't even remember that far back."

"So all these years have gone by and you've never felt a drop of shame or remorse?"

"What would you have done? A naked chick with her legs splayed open…ouch, that hurts!"

Alexandre released the pressure of his middle knuckle just under the man's ear lobe and spat "Okay, your choice. A hundred and fifty thousand, then. Or you die here tonight."

"Okay, okay, I'll give you names and take the ninety grand discount option. How do I know you won't kill me anyway?"

"Because I'm a man of my word. And right now that's all you've got. I want the payment wired tomorrow."

"Tomorrow's Sunday," Jim squeaked, his voice like a terrified boy.

"I'll give you until Wednesday. If it doesn't arrive I will hunt you down, Jim, do you understand? You can hire bodyguards but I am a very patient man. I will wait quietly. Silently. You will never know when I might strike. It could be years from now, it could be days. Do you want to live that way? Constantly in fear?"

The man's breathy response was weak. "No."

"Do you want your wife and kids to know who you are, what you did?"

He shook his head pitifully. "Where am I to send the money?"

"To young girls who have been abused by men like you – I'll give you the details. Men who thought their actions held no consequences. Now, pull the car over, right here."

They were on a remote beach miles from anywhere. With one hand still holding the pistol, Alexandre handed Jim a bit of paper with the bank account number of the charity he had set up. "Now, you have a choice. We are going to get out of the car. You can either strip naked and walk home in your bare feet in the snow or we can fight this out, man to man. Whichever you choose, the donation will go ahead as planned." Alexandre chuckled facetiously. "Hey, don't look so glum, it'll be tax deductable – the fact I need you to make that donation means I'm not going to kill you now."

"You have a weapon!"

"I'll put the gun in the trunk of my car. We can fight it out weapon-free just using the tools that God gave us. Or, Jim, you can strip naked and walk home."

"I'd catch hypothermia, are you crazy?" The man began to wheeze.

"That's just what I thought you'd say."

"Give me a break, man!"

"Oh I *am* giving you a break. You'd already be dead if I weren't such a reasonable man."

"This is crazy. It was nearly twenty years ago. What kind of fucked-up vendetta is this?"

"The Sicilian kind. You know, if you'd just said one simple word beginning with S and showed some kind of remorse, some kind of feeling for the woman you hurt, I would have felt so much more compassion for you."

"Jesus! I'm *sorry*, okay."

"Too late, Jim. I know what kind of person you are. The kind who thinks he's the master of the universe, the kind whose ego gets the best of him. Now find those numbers of your friends in your Smartphone and tell me their names and any extra details you have. Here, you can write them on this piece of paper." Alexandre got out a scrap of paper and handed the man a pen from his coat pocket.

Jim was shaking uncontrollably but managed to scrawl down some names.

"If none of this makes sense, if these names are false or you happen to be playing any kind of game with me, remember, I know where you and your family live. I also have your New York address. I know where you work. I know everything about you, Jim. Give me your cell phone."

"Why?"

"I said we'd leave all weapons behind. I leave my gun, you leave your phone. Get out of the car...slowly."

Jim opened the car door and exited carefully. A gust of icy wind blew into the vehicle. It was crisp outside and pitch-black. Alexandre quickly got out, too; he noticed the man's large shoulders were shaking. "Hand me your phone," Alexandre said quietly. His breath was making steam in the frosty air.

Jim handed over his cell. Alexandre's black gloved hands took it and he proceeded to frisk him all over; just in case the guy had two phones, or even a gun or knife on him. But he was clean.

Alexandre said, "Now hand me over your car keys."

Jim obliged. Alexandre took the Smartphone, then threw it with the gun into the trunk, took off his long coat which he chucked over the back seat, closed the car doors, zapped them locked and pocketed the car keys. "We're both weap-on-free now." He smiled.

"You still have my car keys, man!" Jim replied with a sneer.

"Come and get them. Come on, you're a big man - throw me one of your best punches and you can have it all. Me, the car keys, your car, your phone – even the gun."

Jim eyed him suspiciously and rocked from one heavy foot to the other as if weighing up his options.

"Come on, you pussy," taunted Alexandre. "If you're the big, bad money-maker, Wall St. master of the universe footballer, come on! Show me what you're made of! Come and get me."

Jim launched himself at him, flailing his fist as it caught the air because Alexandre ducked and side-stepped so fast. Jim swung again and Alexandre dodged to the left. A third swing had Jim's punch meet the edge of his SUV and he shouted out curses then shoved his bashed hand in his mouth to ease the pain of his bleeding wound. He then pushed his feet on the side of the car to give himself momentum and threw himself at Alexandre smashing hard into his torso, but Alexandre didn't fall. Alexandre simultaneously elbowed his adversary in the face and drew up his knee sharply into Jim's crotch – Jim stepped backwards, buckling up in pain as he cupped his testicles protectively.

"You need to lose weight, you rapist scum," shouted Alexandre.

Then it happened so quickly: Alexandre moved his body with fierce momentum as his leg swung in a semi-circle landing like a bolt of lightning on Jim's head. Jim toppled over instantly, groaning in agony. Blood was pouring from his ear.

Alexandre bent over to check the damage. "You'll live. That was for Jane Doe. Remember, the money. No fucking about. You might want to warn your rapist buddies to have their money ready, too. Two month's wages, each one. They would be advised to give a little extra as a bonus just so I know they're showing good will; call it a heartfelt apology. In fact, I'll leave it to you, Jim, to collect the money. Within a few hours, I'll know who they all are, what they all do for a living, how much they earn, so no bullshit." He gave the man one last kick in the kidneys. "Have a nice walk home, scumbag."

Jim was moaning in pain hunched into a fetal position, the icy ground was blotched red with his blood. He moaned, "You can't leave me to walk back, it's freezing!"

"Leaving people lying like garbage when you're done with them? You'd know all about that, wouldn't you, Jim?"

Alexandre zapped Jim's SUV unlocked, got in and drove off. In his rear-view mirror he saw Jim get up and collapse on the ground again still cradling his groin. Alexandre sped off back to his own rental car. He'd rented it in a false name, just in case. Jim couldn't prove a thing and he'd be an idiot if he tried.

He parked the SUV, took the gun out of the trunk, leaving Jim's cell phone inside and the keys on the windscreen wipers, changed vehicles and screeched off back in the direction of New York. He smirked to himself about the gun. The 'gun'. It was one of those cigarette lighters – pretty convincing, but if you pulled the trigger all that happened was that an orange flame ignited. Alexandre laughed out loud and then turned on the radio. It was that song again. The one Elodie kept listening to: *Little Things* by that boy band, *One Direction*. It was uncanny, as if the song had been written especially for Pearl, *the dimples on her back, the crinkles by her eyes* – the lyrics spoke of a woman's insecurities but how the guy loved her despite her faults, even *for* her faults. A beautiful song....

Pearl...fuck he missed hanging out with her; it was driving him crazy. He could feel his cock expand, now, just thinking about her face, her peachy ass. He had in his mind's eye her soaking wet pussy and he could almost taste her, just thinking about it. So sweet. Always trimmed and neat, always tight and hot, and always, always ready to be fucked by him. Nothing in the world gave him more pleasure than making Pearl come – nothing. No woman had ever desired him as much, and that was the biggest aphrodisiac of all.

Jesus! His cock was rock hard now and it ached. He thought of that last time when he had her moaning as if she had a fever, squirming on the bed beneath him. He loved the way she was always so vulnerable; tried to act like a tough cookie but always gave in, in the end.

Except for now. Lately, she was being really stubborn. He wanted to fuck that stubbornness out of her, make her scream his name. He'd have to get her alone without Daisy there. Damn Daisy, always hovering about, and Amy, too – even worse. He could hardly just barge into the apartment with a five year-old there, even though he still had keys. His mind ticked over, thinking of ways he could get Pearl alone, whisper into her ear, push her up against a wall and kiss her so she couldn't...wouldn't want to get away. His heart was beating like a drum out of rhythm, imagining how he would fuck her again, how he'd tease that little pearlette, prize open that glistening oyster with his big hard cock. He needed to control the beast in him, though. Needed to sweeten her up a bit more before he pounced. He *had* to have her, had to fuck her...Jesus, this was torture.

His cock was flexing and throbbing. He stopped the car and pulled over. He unbuttoned his jeans. He freed his cock from its prison and it sprang through his boxer briefs, rock hard and wet with pre-cum. It was huge, even he realized that. He knew the size of men's dicks in general – seen them in the gym - he knew he was big (the only decent thing he had inherited from his father). Girls had told him all his life, too. More than once, he'd been too much for them to handle – he'd even scared some women away on occasions.

He let the car seat go all the way back and relaxed into it. He thought of Pearl now, kissing Alessandra Demarr and he gripped his hand about his pulsating phallus and squeezed hard. Ah, that was better. He moved his hand up and down his smooth length, with images of Pearl's wet pussy and her mouth sucking his cock flitting like photos through his brain.

He imagined the two women kissing and wished for a second he had been there, too, not enjoying a threesome but just to be a fly on the wall – because a threesome would have hurt Pearl. Not in the moment, no, she would have been turned on - but afterwards – she was too sweet, too easily wounded. Other men had screwed her over enough for several lifetimes – he wouldn't go there. She was too vulnerable to experiment with. Besides, he'd been there, done that - had his fun with threesomes in his late teens; they weren't all they were cracked up to be – two's company, three's a crowd. He didn't like it when women felt hurt or jealous from feeling left out, which is invariably what happened, at some point, when there were three.

And right now he, ironically, found himself in this situation of *three* with Laura right there in the middle. He knew how poor Pearl's heart was bleeding, but what could he do?

He thought of all the women that had come and gone over the years. *Come* and gone. There had been too many to count. How he was taught – no *trained*, by a professional - how to make love. How to really get a woman turned on. It was Sophie's co-worker, Hélene, the one who pulled his sister into the game when she was seventeen. Sophie worked with her for years. By the time Alexandre got to be broken in, the woman was thirty - Alexandre was fourteen. His hand was moving fast, now, remembering his first fuck-orgasm, how mind-blowing it was for him as a skinny teenager and how he feared his penis might explode with pleasure.

He and Hélene needed each other. It had been the perfect symbiotic relationship. She taught him everything about the art of sex. *Because never forget, great sex is an art...*How to take his time, how to wait until she was really wet and never enter her too early. She taught him that if he had to use lube then he must be doing something wrong. She explained how women want to be told sweet nothings and dirty talk but nothing too crude. To be dominant, but never aggressive…to hold out until the woman was begging for sex, take his time; it wasn't a race – that if the man could be patient he'd get paid back double-fold by her passion.

She explained to him that many men were fools…so obsessed with the chase that they lost focus. Forget the chase, she said. That's 'old-school.' Don't end up with a woman just because she says 'no' to you or plays hard to get. Just because she says no doesn't make her any more special. Look into her soul, her eyes. Don't judge a woman by her past. A woman in love with you, she let him know, was a woman who would be sexy as hell. And loyal, too. Loyalty, she said, was like a sovereign coin - never abandon family…never abandon those who truly love you.

Hélene told him how all women were different; there was no blueprint and how he must pay attention to the girl's whole body not just her orifices and breasts. Stroking and caressing – foreplay was imperative. Any man could 'stick it in', she said - and don't be fooled into thinking you were good in bed - women were good at faking orgasms. She'd warned him about this on countless occasions.

She drummed it into him that the woman must always come first – well, he'd got that wrong once or twice with Pearl. Fuck, with her sometimes, he couldn't control himself - even just one of her kisses could drive him wild. No woman ever had gotten him as horny, no woman could hold a candle to Pearl in the sack. Why? Even he couldn't explain. Was she the most beautiful woman he had ever dated? No. But she had something, something irresistible. The smell of her skin. Her flavor. Her humor…her sweetness…her smile.

An image of Pearl's tits flashed through his head – couldn't put a pencil under those. No – too pert. Her ass, her tits, her face, her wet pussy – which was his very own little private pearl, his pearlette - her lips, those big blue eyes....

He groaned out loud and felt the spurt of his climax pulsing through him. Fuck, his cum was all over the seat. But it wasn't enough – he needed the real thing. He couldn't stand it anymore – the minute he got back to New York he'd have to fuck her.

Fuck her till she screamed.

7

H ere I am in the kitchen again, eating ice-cream. They say just as much ice-cream is sold in the winter as in the summer months, and I believe it.

Daisy and Amy are fast asleep. That will be me, soon….a single mother with my child…although, I suddenly remember…Daisy and Zac – wow, that came out of left field. She may not be a single mother for long. I have mixed feelings; delighted for them but…well. Time will tell if he's good enough for her.

My ice-cream reverie is interrupted by the sound of the front door opening - I forgot to lock it with the safety latch. A rush of adrenaline surges through my body but then I remember… Alexandre still has keys. I pray it's him and not some armed robber, although Alexandre is just as dangerous, in another way. I go to grab the first thing I can think of for protection; a kitchen knife – just in case it really is an intruder. No, that's dangerous; it could be seized from me. I see Amy's cowboy gun lying on the kitchen table, snatch it up - it looks quite realistic - and tiptoe quietly down the hallway towards the front door. It isn't a thief. Well, it is. A thief of my emotions...Alexandre.

There he is....gorgeous as ever.

He turns on his heel and observes me with wry amusement stealing across his face, ready with my toy gun.

"Sorry, baby," he whispers, "I didn't want to wake anybody so I thought I'd slip through the door quietly."

I should be furious but all I can think is, *what took you so long, I've missed you.* My heart is racing with left-over fear of thinking I was being broken into, and renewed fear of being broken into...my body being broken into. No sex, the doctor forbade it. I keep saying this mantra to myself in my head. Despite all this, desire is circling me like Cupid with his arrow and I'm only too aware of an aching need for Alexandre to hold me.

Until I remember the L word.

I'm wearing pajama bottoms and a thin cotton tank top and his glittering green eyes stray to my swollen breasts. A low rumble comes from deep within him like a lion about to devour his prey. He doesn't say anything, though, but I can see the rise and fall of his chest – his heart is also pounding. His desire for me is palpable and I sense the familiar tingle between my legs.

"You need to leave, Alexandre." My voice is weak, laced with yearning. My sexed-up pregnancy hormones are not helping one bit.

"I need to hold you, baby. To breathe you in." He comes towards me. I'm still grasping the gun and his half-cocked smile breaks into a grin. "But I think you'd better put that gun down, don't you?"

In a moment of foolishness I grip the handle even tighter and wave it in front of me.

He grins, "Love the toy gun. You and I have more in common than you can possibly imagine."

But I'm not smiling back. "I mean it, Alexandre, you need to leave me alone and stop torturing me this way."

His smile fades and he says sadly, "yes, it *is* torture – you're right. I just can't go on like this – I can't stand it anymore." He slumps against the wall and slides down so he's sitting on the floor. His big boots drip with melted snow on the polished parquet wood. Tears are welling in his eyes. I've never seen him look so vulnerable and it's breaking my heart.

I set Amy's gun on the hall table and sit down opposite him. He holds his dark ruffled head in his hands. He's wearing the long World War One overcoat. He looks so handsome, like a movie star – the Hollywood legend kind, the kind they don't make anymore.

"Why are you doing this, Alexandre?" I speak in a whisper because I don't want to wake Daisy and Amy. "Why can't you stop seeing Laura?"

He looks up at me and a tear falls down his cheek. I want to hug him but perhaps this is all part of his little-boy-lost act, the act that makes dumb women like me swoon and lose all reason. Talk about Hollywood. This guy's a good actor.

"My plan was to come here and fuck you, Pearl. But I can't play that game anymore. It isn't fair on you."

My heart starts thumping like an oil well. What's worse than him wanting to use me for sex? Not wanting me at all. A lump gathers in my throat. "What's going on, Alexandre? Why are you…practically crying?"

"Because all I want in the world is to be happy with you and it doesn't seem possible."

"But that's your choice, Alexandre. It's *you* that's putting up all these barriers. All I want, too, is for us to be together but I can't be in a relationship with three people. You have to choose – me or Laura. You simply can't have us both."

"That's why I keep asking you to marry me, baby....despite Laura. So you'd be my wife and you couldn't testify against me."

I flinch. "What the hell are you talking about?"

He temples his hands over his nose and lets out an exasperated puff of air. "I literally don't know what to do! With all my money and influence...yet still, she has me beat...I swear I don't know what to do."

"You're being so obtuse and enigmatic, right now, I'm completely lost."

"Please come here, chérie – I need to hold you. I swear I won't do anything. I won't even try and kiss you. I promise."

I tentatively shuffle my behind over to his side and sit close to him. He puts his arm about me, his fingers squeezing me tight. He smells of the night air and his Alexandre elixir that weakens me every time. I stroke his head and he sighs, closing his wet eyes and biting his lips...perhaps to stop himself from actually weeping. I'm dumbfounded by his demonstration of emotion and understand now that it is for real. I lay my head against his shoulder and we just continue sitting there on the floor in silence with only the sound of our breathing between us.

Finally I say, "Why?" I don't even know what I am referring to but 'why' seems like a good thing to ask.

"Remember I told you I was protecting someone I love?"

"Yes," I say bitterly, conjuring up a host of ex girlfriends. Or is he talking about Laura, herself? The idea of him loving someone else sends a wave of jealousy to course through my veins and circle my stomach.

"I was talking about my mother," he says in a grave tone.

I exhale with relief but then ask, confused, "What on earth does Laura have to do with your mother?"

"Laura's threatening her."

"What? *How?*"

"Laura has something that belongs to her, something incriminating, something...Look, Pearl, I've already said enough. I made a promise to my mom that I wouldn't ever say a word and..." His eyes tighten as he starts chewing his lip with worry.

"Your mother did something and Laura has evidence?"

"I knew if I said anything you'd pick up on it straight away. I've revealed way too much, I need to go, I—"

"You can trust me. I don't care what your mother did, or what you did — I love you," I plead. "I would never say a word. Never."

"Please come back with me tonight. I need you in my arms, baby. I need to sleep with you. I've been going crazy without you."

I take his head in my hands and say, "Look me in the eyes and tell me the truth."

He nods.

"Have you had sex with Laura since you've been with me?"

He fixes his gaze on me and I feel sick for a moment. The dark flecks in his green eyes flicker with hesitation. Can I bear what I'm about to hear?

"I swear by my mother, by Sophie and Rex and all those

who I love. I swear by you and the moon and stars, I have not touched, nor even kissed any woman since I met you, least of all Laura."

The relief I feel right now is indescribable. I search his eyes for clues – he's telling the truth, I'm sure of it. Now it's my turn to well up. A hot tear rolls down my cheek.

He continues, his mouth pinched, "I despise Laura. She's trying to ruin my life. If it were just *my* life she wanted to butcher, I might be more forgiving, but she's threatening my mother. And you."

"Me?"

"I know you, Pearl. I know that if you don't spend the rest of your days with me you won't be truly happy. I don't mean to sound conceited saying that but deep inside me, I feel exactly the same. If we can't be together we'll both go through life half dead. Without you, I feel my flame has been snuffed out. I function on auto-pilot. Without you I am half the person I should be."

I take his chin in both hands and tilt his mouth towards mine. I run my tongue along his upper lip to ease the tension in his angry mouth and we kiss gently. To my surprise, he's not ravenous for me but just returns the kiss sweetly. Innocently, even.

He breathes into my mouth, "If I can't marry you, Pearl my life will be running on empty."

"I want to marry you more than anything," I whisper back. "I love you. I can't be without you, either."

"Will you come home with me tonight and we can talk?"

"If you promise to tell me the whole story. If you promise to trust me. I don't care *what* you've been hiding from me," I say honestly. "What hurts me is that you've been hiding it."

"If I tell you everything, will you promise to marry me, Pearl? No more running away?"

For some reason, his request causes a rush of adrenaline to stream through my body. Fear? Excitement? Panic? This is it. I've been running from him, using every excuse. But I can't run anymore. I need to trust him, to show my loyalty. I take a deep breath and reply, "I promise."

Alexandre gets up onto his haunches and lifts me up, cradling me in his arms as if I were a baby. His eyes stray to my pregnant breasts again. But I don't care if he has sex on the brain - I want him even more than he wants me. I can feel my nipples pucker with desire, my breathing's shallow. He sets me down and kisses me lightly on my temple. I grab my long overcoat from the hall closet, my Birkin bag and slip into my thermal boots. I can't get back to his apartment fast enough.

"You're coming just like that? In your PJ's?" he asks, surprised, yet eyeing up my ass with a look of lust.

"I think we've both waited long enough, don't you? I just want to be back in your bed even if Rex *has* taken it over."

He laughs. "You've heard, huh?"

"Yes, Sally told me."

"I've been lonely. Missing you like crazy."

As I'm scrawling out a note to Daisy so she doesn't think I've been abducted, I say, "Are you going to tell me everything, Alexandre?"

He nods.

"*Everything* about Laura?" I ask again, double-checking that this isn't a trap of seduction to get into my panties (or PJs).

"I promise. Let's go."

The whole time I have been in my new apartment it has felt like Limbo and, now back at Alexandre's, I know I've come home. We're sitting on one of the huge white couches in the living room, snuggled up with Rex. I'm keeping the bedroom at bay, for fear of letting desire get in the way of my mission; to find out everything I can. If Alexandre doesn't come one hundred percent clean about this insidious situation with Laura, which has been eating into our relationship, then I will give up for good. This is Make or Break time and I think he senses that.

My eyes stray to the bald patch on the wall where my engagement gift was; the Jim Dine painting of the big red heart that is now hung in my new apartment, and I feel a wave of sadness. So much time has been wasted because of our own fears. It has all boiled down to trust. I have not trusted him; not trusted his judgment about Sophie – of course he would never have put me in danger; of course he knows his own sister. And now, he has been keeping secrets from me for fear I might abandon him, or worse, report him for whatever wrong he or his mother has done – that I would betray his family.

I lie back with my head in his lap as he strokes my hair, the soft touch of his long fingers caressing me, making me remember that I belong to him and nobody else.

"I'm breaking my promise to my mother but if I don't tell you, I know that our lives will be ruined. I'm trusting you to keep this to yourself, take it with you to your grave, Pearl."

"I swear." I make a cross sign on my heart.

"You know what I told you about my father? That he disappeared?"

I hold his hand to let him know that I'm on his side, no matter what he tells me. "Was it a lie?"

"Yes. Not all of him has disappeared – that's the whole problem."

"What do you mean?" *This is sounding really crazy.* "Sophie told me that he had gone to Rio - that he'd been spotted there."

"That's what she still believes. I told her that a friend of mine had seen him there. This friend doesn't exist, of course. My father's dead, Pearl."

"Did you kill him?"

He says nothing for a beat and then answers in a cold voice. "No. My mother did. No, let me be completely honest here. She didn't just kill him, she murdered him."

I try to sound unemotional. I don't want to spook him away. "Was Laura witness to the murder, then?"

"No. It happened when I was only nine."

"Well what does Laura have to do with it? Even if you told her, she has no proof!"

"Oh, but she does. She's got proof that he's dead. And he has never been declared dead. No death certificate, nothing. Officially, he's still alive. And there are some people still wondering where he is. His brother, my uncle, for one."

"I don't understand – how does Laura *know* he's dead?"

"He was lying peacefully in his bath. Ironic that. Some of the only times when he was being truly peaceful was when he was wallowing about in warm water. My mother had bought him his favorite Scotch. She was plying him with it so he was completely relaxed. She'd had enough, and knew that the only way to be free of him, once and for all, was to kill him. He'd threatened her that if she ever left him he'd hunt her down and kill her – then search for us, too." He looks at me and hesitates.

I absorb all that Alexandre has said. It sounds crazy but you read about these people and see them on the news often…the nutters that shoot their families down, killing each and every member, or massacring them in a stabbing frenzy before doing themselves in, too. I squeeze Alexandre's hand. "I empathize, Alexandre. I really do. Please go on."

He stares into space as he reels off the story in a monotone, hardly stopping for breath. "She had the electric heater plugged into the wall with the extension cord. She'd planned everything. When he was lying back with his eyes closed she came into the bathroom with the pretense to top up his drink and threw the heater into the water to electrocute him. She was even wearing rubber shoes and gloves just to take extra precaution."

I gasp. What a scene that must have been. "Did he die instantly?"

"I don't know. My mother had assumed she could pretend it was an accident but there were huge burn welts where the water level was. It was obvious it was cold-blooded murder. She had to think on her feet. Had to get rid of the evidence – there was no way she could pass it off as an accident."

"So then what happened?"

"Luckily, she had some French doors in her apartment that led onto a balcony. She unplugged the electricity, drained the bath, hauled him out, little by little, and rolled him into bed sheets, wrapping him like a mummy. Then she pushed him off the balcony in the dead of night. Once she was sure nobody had woken from the thud of the body landing on the ground – she was two flights up – she dragged him to the car. Amazingly, nobody saw her, or if they did, they never said a word. The neighbors hated him anyway – even if they'd seen something they would have probably been relieved. She managed to haul him into the trunk of her car."

"That must have been hard. Was he tall and strong like you?"

"No, my height comes from my mother's side of the family. But still, it was no mean feat. She drove to the countryside. When she found an isolated place, miles from anywhere, she made a bonfire and set him alight."

"Oh my God. Nobody saw? No farmer or anyone?"

"She doused him with gasoline – he went up fast."

"I still don't understand what Laura has to do with all this."

"Not everything burns, does it?"

"There were remnants?"

"My mother waited for the fire to burn all the way down but there were two things left over – his teeth and bits of his hip replacement, both identifiable through medical records. There was the titanium part of the fake hip and a ceramic ball bit that didn't burn either. They have identification numbers, not on the parts themselves, but from the factory where they make the prosthesis. These are kept by the hospital on a register with the name of the patient and the date of operation, in case of problems like breaking or premature loosening. They can be traced back to their source. It's the same with teeth and dentist's records - a common way of identifying corpses."

"How the hell did Laura get her hands on those?"

"Years ago, I found them in my mother's house in a drawer when I was looking for something – I put two and two together; that's how I knew he was dead. I'd always suspected, anyway, because I knew if he'd been alive he would have hunted her down. Anyway, I had a long talk with my mom and she told me the whole story. I've kept it a secret all these years; I never even told Sophie."

My nose is prickling with tears as Alexandre's voice sounds as if it's about to break at any moment.

"But what on earth was your mother *doing* with all that evidence? Why didn't she chuck it all in a river or take it out to sea?"

"That's the multi-million dollar question, but she had a reason, crazy as it was. Having the remnants, she said, reminded her that he was truly dead – that he could never harm her again.

Anyway, I took away the bits of evidence and took them to Provence with me – I didn't want my mother having them in her house, in case her husband found them. But at the same time, I didn't throw them away because I didn't feel it was my right to if they were so important to her. I was an idiot. A fool. I should have taken it into my own hands. Instead, I hid the teeth in a multi-volume Encyclopedia. Call me a heathen but I'd cut out the centre of one of them and placed the evidence inside. Nobody looks at Encyclopedias anymore with the internet and Wikipedia – I thought they'd be safe there. And the titanium bit of hip was wedged behind the book. Laura knew exactly what it was because she, too, had a hip replacement a couple of years after her accident. And I'd mentioned to her once, years ago, about my father having had one – tried to assure her that they worked."

"She discovered them?"

Alexandre looks down at the floor ashamedly.

"But even if I found that stuff, I wouldn't know that they were *body parts of a dead man.* How did she *know?*"

"When I started dating you, Laura became obsessed. I didn't realize this, of course, until just a few weeks ago. I thought we were friends, I had no clue that she wanted me back, that she was still in love with me. Although, when 'love' is that warped it's hardly a word I'd use to describe her feelings for me. Basically, she became obsessed, possessed - and will stop at nothing to get me back."

"I still don't understand. How did she *know* for sure that those things were parts of your father?"

"You've been her victim, as I have. She had my cell phone hacked, too. Really dumb of me to not have caught onto that, especially in my line of business. A joke, really. I think she must have been in on a text message or conversation or even an email to my mother – we've never mentioned the murder in a call or message but Laura's not dumb. Who knows? She's a smart woman – she put two and two together. I've never admitted a thing but she has all the evidence in her possession. With forensic labs the way they are these days – medical records; all it takes is one call from her."

"When did she get her hands on all this?"

"When she and James were there last summer."

"You didn't notice it missing?"

"No. I wouldn't have thought to look. I'd pretty much forgotten all about it, actually."

"If she's had everything since the summer why has she waited until now to tell you?"

"Good question. She must have thought things with you and me would die down - fizzle out. It didn't, she tried that stunt pretending Sophie was responsible for her accident, which nearly did the trick to split us up, but when she saw that you and I were back together, she pulled out all the stops."

"What does she want, exactly?"

"She wants you out of the picture and for me to marry her."

"But that's *insane*, especially as you don't even love her."

Alexandre closes his lids as if locked into a deep thought and continues in a grave tone, "The truth is, after her fall she was never the same person. I did understand why, though, at the time. Shit, your whole life changes after an accident like that. They said her head wasn't damaged in the fall, but when I think of it now, I think they were wrong. I'm convinced something changed in her brain. She was so sweet before, so loving and fun. After the accident…well, I didn't spend much time with her afterwards, we didn't see each other for a couple of years, anyway, so it was hard to gauge−"

"But I thought you two were bosom buddies."

"She left me immediately for James. Said I couldn't look after her properly, that I was too young and she needed stability. What she really wanted - even I wasn't stupid – was someone who was rich enough to take care of her. That's why I worked my ass off − determined that HookedUp would be a financial success. I became driven with the idea of proving that I, too, could look after her, could be wealthy enough to take care of her. Not just her but any future relationship – any future girlfriend or wife. I felt very proud – I still do. I'm old-fashioned in that respect. I'm the type of man who wants to be able to support my partner financially."

"Well, why didn't you both get back together as soon as

you'd made all that money?"

"By that time, I'd become good friends with James and I just wasn't in love with Laura anymore. They came to stay in Provence and stuff. I genuinely had *no idea* she was still into me, until recently. I think the second you came along she became competitive and wanted me back. At first, she was convinced you and I would split up, but the moment she heard about our marriage she went wild with jealousy."

"What about James? How does he feel?"

"He still hasn't returned my calls. He got busted for dodgy tax dealings and is in financial straits. That made Laura nervous. I don't think she loves me at all, really, I think she loves my bank balance. Plus..." he hesitates.

"What?"

"James can't have children and she's fixated on the idea of getting pregnant. She wants me to father her child."

A stab of fury seizes my heart making it skip a beat. "Jesus. Why can't she pick on a single man? Why *you*?"

"I know."

"So she's blackmailing you, then?"

"Exactly. But in her warped brain she believes it's for my own good and we'll live happily ever after."

"Where has she got the evidence hidden?"

"She says it's in a safety deposit box and if anything happens to her, any accident or mishap, she has instructed her lawyer to open the box and its contents with a note revealing everything."

"What a monster!"

"Tell me about it."

"But that's insane! If you don't love her, how could she have a happy life, even if she did get you back?"

"As I said, I think some chip in her brain went doolally

when she had that fall. The girl I dated would never have done this. Her behavior is totally irrational. I just didn't see it before because James was always about. He's a good guy. We've done some Aston Martin and Austin Healy rallies together, he's a nice man. It's crazy what she's playing at." Alexandre buries his head in his hands and lets out an exasperated sigh.

"So her idea is to have the evidence sitting in that safe deposit box forever, blackmail you throughout your 'marriage' so you'll never leave her or else your mother goes to jail?"

"Yeah, that's more or less the plan she's got up her dirty little sleeve, although she's not coming out and saying it directly. She pretends it's for my own good, just in case the evidence got into 'the wrong hands', she says."

"That's terrifying. I mean, if she were to get run over by a bus tomorrow, out comes that goddamn safe deposit box."

"Exactly."

"What are we going to do?"

Alexandre smiles at me. "Thank you, chérie, for using the word 'we' - although that's why I've been so secretive - I didn't want to get you involved in this mess."

"Till death do us part. For better or for worse. We may not have said our vows yet, Alexandre, but I'm with you one hundred percent, whatever your decision."

He puts his arms about me and holds me close to his chest. I feel his slow, strong heartbeat. His voice is low and quiet when he tells me, "I love you, Pearl."

I breathe him in. "I was so scared you wanted her back, that you were still in love with her – all those parting, 'goodbye' gifts you gave me; the Porsche, the Mercedes, the apartments—"

"It was never goodbye, baby, not for a second. You needed some space to sort out your head. We needed to be apart for a little, but goodbye? Never." He smiles and I notice the roguish dimple on his cheek makes its signature mark. "I knew I'd see my pretty Porsche again and that we'd be vacationing in that apartment in Cap d'Antibes. You and I are forever, Pearl."

I bite my lip just thinking about how it could have been. The agony I would have suffered. "I was scared that everything we had was a fantasy, a figment of my imagination."

He kisses my temple. "I'm sorry I've put you through all this. I kept thinking I could reason with Laura, make her see sense – that's why I saw her face to face, but she's being impossible. Inflexible. I just don't know what to do."

"What does your mother say?"

"She wants to have it out with Laura – she's furious."

"So your mom's husband has no idea about any of this?"

"No. Not a clue. He's a very straightforward guy."

"But if he loves her why would he care what she'd done? It was self-defense."

"That's *you*, Pearl. You think that way. But other people are more wedded to the law. A lot of men don't get it. They don't understand what it's like to be bullied, day in day out, to be humiliated, threatened and abused. My step-father's a great guy but he just wouldn't understand. Besides, it's one of those things she should have come clean with straight away when they first met – maybe he would have forgiven her, but she didn't dare test him. And if she let him know now what she did it would look as if their entire marriage had been a lie all these years."

"Do you believe Laura when she says she has it all in a safe deposit box? Maybe she's lying."

"Maybe she is, but I'm not in a position to risk it, to call her bluff. My mother's life is on the line, or at least, life imprisonment which would amount to the same thing for her."

"I thought France was lenient with crimes of passion."

"I'd rather my mother didn't even spend one minute in a jail. So many years of her life were hell and finally she's found happiness. Plus, this is all my fault. If I'd just bloody well left the evidence with her and hadn't meddled with it all, we wouldn't be in this mess."

I look at my watch and then stretch my arms in the air. "We should go to bed. It's three a.m. Let's see if either of us comes up with a brain-wave in our dreams to sort out this fiasco."

"You dream a lot, don't you?"

"You have no idea."

"What have you dreamt about me?"

"There was one dream in particular that had me squirming with pleasure," I tease, remembering the Johnny Cakes March with the sexy spanking session.

His eyes light up. "Oh, yeah, what was that?"

"It's my secret."

He gives my wrist a small squeeze. "Come on, tell me."

"No, but I will tell you another secret, if you like."

"I'm listening."

"I'm pregnant – you and I are going to have a baby."

He kneels before me and gathers my hands in his, softly kissing each finger. His eyes are brimming with emotion. "You've made me the happiest man alive, Pearl. If I could jump over the moon, I would. And as far as secrets go? That's the best damn secret I've ever heard in my entire life."

8

Waking up next to Alexandre is pure heaven. We dozed off, intertwined together like ivy, last night, listening to each other's heart beats, soothed by one another's breath. I fell asleep, dreaming of ocean waves. His smell...it's intoxicating, and I was reminded of how much I had missed him. The idea that I have spent so many nights alone is heartbreaking. All those wasted hours. When we needed each other - when we could have helped each other. Perhaps that's what an engagement is all about. A test to make you stronger. Although I doubt any other couple has endured what we have – unwittingly putting each other through such turmoil.

I observe him now, his lids closed in deep slumber, yet beneath the sheets another story is being told; a huge penis, smooth as alabaster, proud as the Washington monument, is puckering up the bedclothes with its rock-hard stance. I

624

don't want to wake him but I can't resist. How I've missed that core of him. I've dreamed of it, come in my sleep thinking of it.

I nestle my head on his stomach and let my tongue flicker on the end of his crown. It's bigger than my dreams had allowed me to remember. I nip the rounded end of it and he groans quietly. Then I guide my tongue down his length in semi darkness under the sheet. I take one ball in my mouth and suck on it languidly. I can feel his arms now stroking my hair. He flexes his hips up a notch and I hear him say, "Oh fuck, oh wow, I've missed this." My tits are alive with desire, my nipples aflame with sensation and I need him to play with them. I wriggle up the bed until I'm straddling him.

I lean my breasts over his erection, take it in my hands and tease my nipples with its smooth head. Holy hotness, I'm wired like an electric cable – everything is connected and desire shoots through me in pulsating tingles and spasms. My breasts have always been sensitive but lately, since pregnancy, even a breeze of cool air can get them excited.

Alexandre's eyes spring open, "Jesus, Pearl, your tits… I need to fuck those beautiful big, pregnant tits."

When I told him last night about the Indian Ayurvedic doctor I thought he'd think she was a quack but he said, 'old wives' tale or not, I'm not going to be the one to put it to the test'. He swears, even if I beg him, that he won't penetrate me. I wonder how long I can hold out, though.

I suck on him, then move my body up a bit and swirl his cock about my nipples again, mewing softly with pleasure. The wetness of my saliva makes them pucker into tight, dusky-red buds; I re-position myself and rub my clit against Alexandre's muscular thigh as I continue teasing my nipples. I start moaning – from my head to my tail bone, this feels amazing.

"Fuck, your pussy's soaked," he murmurs, thrusting his leg at me, keeping up the pressure.

I rub against his solid thigh, back and forth, and he pushes it hard against me so my clit is getting a real massage. I continue teasing my nipples, slapping them now, using his penis like a whip. He starts rubbing his leg rhythmically against me; I graze his erection round and round in circles on my nipples, taking it in turn with each one, as I feel the build-up and I start coming hard – a series of long, slow convulsions and spasms explode inside me, my nipples harder than bullets, stimulated beyond imagination. I'm letting out moaning wails with every sweet spasm.

"That's right, baby, let your little treasure come on me – I'm going to keep you coming for the rest of your life."

I collapse on top of him, my afterglow alight like burning embers, and after a few minutes of relaxation, he rolls me over gently, straddling me without any of his weight. I see his taut stomach ripple with lean muscles and his huge cock nestle itself between my tits. He pushes them carefully together, almost enclosing his hard shaft. I take over, pressing my breasts tightly around him and he begins to fuck my chest, his balls rubbing lightly against my skin, his cock pressing hard against my breastbone, the tip almost reaching the hollow in my neck every time he pushes northwards. I keep my breasts squeezed together, putting the pressure on his thick, long length.

His movements are languid as if he's really making love to my breasts, his eyes transfixed on my swollen boobs, his sex mantra punctuated by thrusts. "These. Hot. Horny. Tits. Making. My. Cock. So. Fucking. Hard. My. Seed. Exploded. In. Your. Hot. Pearlette…Fucking. You. To. Pregnancy. So.

Fucking. Sexy." He groans. Scorching, creamy cum starts spurting on my face, my tits, my neck - shooting out like a fountain. He's crying out, "Pearl, baby, I love you." His orgasm is super-intense – I can tell he's charged with passion; his face twists as if he's in pain.

He stills as his climax slowly fades, his cock flexing in spasms, and then laughs out loud and shakes his dark head of hair, "Fuck, that was fast."

I smile. "For both of us."

"Did you notice something? We didn't even kiss. We were both so hungry to release weeks of sexual build-up and tension, that we haven't even said hello properly."

I laugh, and run my finger over my sticky breasts, scooping up a taste of him and popping it into my mouth. "Powerful stuff this," I remark. "It can make a woman pregnant."

His mouth flicks into a broad grin. "Hang on, chérie I'll get a towel." He kisses me lightly on the nose, goes to the bathroom and comes back with a damp washcloth. He gently wipes his sea of pleasure off my chest. "I just want you to know something, Pearl…"

A panic of fear sweeps through me; a twisting, chilling knot in my solar plexus. Another secret? Something else he's been holding back?

But he laces his fingers through mine and whispers in my ear; the soft wind of his breath sending shivers down my spine, "Of all the women I've ever been with, you are the most spectacular, the most beautiful, the *most* in every, single way."

The knot unfurls and my heart feels as if it will explode with happiness.

"And I'm not just talking about sex. I'm talking about

love, chérie. I love you, Pearl. Even in the days when I was happy with Laura, I *never* felt so serene, so at home with her as I do with you. I have never experienced this deep, bottomless ocean of love with anyone but you. It's almost as if it hurts, there's so much love bursting inside of me."

"Semen bursting inside of you," I joke, but then immediately wish I hadn't made less of what he has just shared with me, opening his heart up the way he has. I tighten my grip on his hand, "I feel that bursting love, too."

He takes a loose, sticky tendril of my hair and parts it away from my face. He lifts his head from my ear and his crooked smile seems thoughtful as he squints, honing his gaze on mine. "We both need a shower, I think."

I enter the steamy shower with Alexandre. It is almost like a little room. It is all tiled in white mosaic, including the built-in bench The heat suddenly gets to me and I sit down. He's standing before me; my eyes are level with his beautiful, muscular ass. He is like one of those Greek statues but so much better endowed – oh yes, this art is more exquisite than you would see in any museum, his sculpted thighs, his taut, flexing gluteus maximus, the glorious V that runs from his waist to the core of him – the core that has me lightheaded, that has created the living seed inside of me, the tiny being that belongs to us both.

"He holds my hand as the hot water rains from above. "Are you okay, baby, you looked a bit dazed."

True. I am in a daze. This is real. We are together and in love. We are going to have a baby. "I'm fine, I just get a little dizzy in the mornings."

Alexandre lathers up his hands with some lavender body wash and begins to cleanse my shoulders very gently, moving his hands softly about my breasts and under my arms as he lifts each up to massage me. This is crazy…his soapy hands softly kneading my breasts is turning me on again. I am like a hormone machine. I don't know if it's because that crazy Indian doctor forbade intercourse that I have it constantly on the brain, or if it's my pregnancy playing havoc with my body parts, but flashes of Alexandre claiming me, pumping me with heavy thrusts into my wet hole has me squirming. His penis has hardened with every one of his gentle strokes and his fingers gently tug on my nipple, shooting tingles directly to my pulsating clit. I grab his butt and pull him close to me, nipping softly on his balls as the water falls on my face and breasts like a cascade. Just the pressure of water is doing things to me, let alone the vision I have before me – the veritable piece of art that is my fiancé.

"Alexandre," I moan into his thick, hard cock, licking the under-shaft with long sweeping strokes of my tongue.

"Pearl, oh yeah, baby." He's holding my hands, his legs astride to lower the height of his body so he is at the right level for me. My lips nibble his length and my tongue flickers all over the enormity of his smooth, dreamy cock. Not even Michelangelo could have created a penis so beautiful as Alexandre's. I think of riding him, how he fills up my walls, pressing all the right places which effortlessly brings me to mind-blowing orgasms every time, and just the memory of it makes my core pulsate, swelling with needy desire.

"I need you to fuck me, Alexandre," I breathe into his groin.

"Not a chance, until these three months are up, baby."

I take some body wash on my hand and begin to lather his balls, tracing my fingers up the crack of his butt, exploring the dips and valleys of his solid boulder of an ass. I turn him around so it's in my face. Water is cascading over us and

I let all the soapiness rinse away before I part his butt with my fingers. I begin my tongue's journey from his swollen, hard sacks up his crack, lashing my tongue up and down. I can hear his low moans beneath the rush of water. There it is, that scar. Once, I asked him how he got it and he wouldn't tell. I kiss him there, now – licking the old wound with all the love I have inside me. Then I trace my tongue up and probe his hole – only a woman beside herself in love would do anything so intimate. I hear a low growl emanate from deep within him. His right hand is on his erection now, fisting it into a tight vice.

"Come on my face, Alexandre. Come on my lips, come all over me, baby." I guide his body back around so I can see his glorious cock as he slides his hand up and down from the huge crown to the root, his long fingers gripping tightly about himself. All I can think of is it inside me, fucking me, slapping itself on my clit when it withdraws, then ravaging me with hard, ruthless, pumping thrusts. I'm aching, tingling, delirious with the space that is between us. I need my fiancé inside me.

Alexandre's tongue runs along his parted lips, his green eyes hooded with pleasure as if he is thinking exactly the same thing...fucking me...owning me...ripping through the core of me with his relentless virile masculinity. The fingers of his left hand are in my mouth and I suck them, imagining my mouth is my man-eating pussy; that his fingers are his cock - I pull them in, my lips a vacuum. I also cup his balls with my hand. My gesture makes his hips jerk – his hand jacks his cock back and forth at a feverish pace.

"Pearl," he cries out as cum starts spurting everywhere like the Trevi Fountain.

Rivers of white-hot cum snake over my still seated body

as the water washes it away. Alexandre catches back his breath, gets down on his haunches and takes my face in his hands. He starts with a flick of the tongue and I moan into his mouth, opening my lips letting the kiss go deeper, tongues tangling and probing together, sending direct hits to my clit. I see his penis harden and I whimper at how horny I feel. I want that between my legs. His kisses brush my jaw, my neck and then my breasts. My legs splay open in readiness and I cry out—

"Please, I beg you, fuck me!"

He sucks each nipple in turn, and I throw my head back in ecstasy. He turns on the hand-held shower and directs the water at my ready, horny vulva and the power of the spray has my juices oozing with excitement. I jut my hips forward to meet the tingling pressure on my clit and jerk with spasms of pleasure, feeling I could come at any moment. Every bit of my body is alive with sensation. Then he holds the shower head away and nestles his face between my thighs – his hair tickling my flesh as he begins his slow, languid tease. He doesn't touch my clit with his tongue, no, the water has already made it super-sensitive. He avoids it, flicking and wavering his hot lips everywhere else so I am moaning and begging.

"Please, Alexandre."

"See how wet you are for me, baby? When I fuck you your tight pearlette is like a welcoming haven for my cock, clinging onto it like a tight glove, contracting around my cock - never wanting to let me go." Then he slips his magic thumb inside my glistening hole, slowly lingering there until it finds its way to my lush Garden of Eden - my G-spot.

"I *never* want to let you go," I scream out, tortured by pleasure.

Every part of me is clamoring for attention. Just as I thought it couldn't get more intense, Alexandre starts sucking at my nipples again, his thumb still inside me. The familiar electricity sparks my connected inner-wires – tits, clit, mouth, all quivering in unison, building up to the Mighty O. With his other hand he presses my clit with his flattened fingers, gently rubbing in small circles – his thumb on the nub of my G-spot, the pressure on my clit, his tongue on my tits – it's as if there are three Alexandre Chevaliers all at once... as if I'm in the sexiest threesome in the universe. I arch my back and push out my hips, moving my ass up and down, pressing hard against his fingers.

"Alexandre!" The force of his touch – his lips on my tits, his thumb, his fingers, has me coming in a rush of frenzied contractions. I hold his head to balance myself - I feel as if my whole body could detonate with bliss and pleasure-pounding gratification. "Aah...Alexandre," I scream out like a banshee.

Half a minute later, I feel weak; my orgasm has sucked all the life out of me as it pounds its way to a plateau, and finally calms itself like a gentle heart beat.

Alexandre turns off the faucet, cocoons me in a warm, larger-than-life towel, and carries me to the bedroom. He lays me on the mattress like a sleeping baby and says, "You rest, my angel, I'm going to make us some breakfast. You need your strength as I'm not done yet, certain parts of my body are aching for more of this. Call me a beast...I am...I can't get enough of my pregnant fiancée. After we've eaten, I'm going to tease you into another orgasm, but this time we're going to come simultaneously."

He pats me dry with the towel – I see his erection is full-on again. Hearing me scream, watching me climax so intensely has gotten him hot once more. We are both insatiable. I lie there, feeling very pregnant and yes – still horny as a rabbit in spring. *How does he know I want more?* As if he can read my body. I cannot believe I am so wanton. And I know Alexandre. His Latin blood has been bubbling away. Aware that his seed is inside me, growing every day, makes him want to claim me whole – possess me even more. Never have I been so turned on. Never have I felt so ravenous for sex.

And *never* have I wanted a man to own me. Until now. I ache for that wedding ring to be planted on my finger. I want Alexandre's hard cock inside me whenever he wishes it. I need to be dominated by him. Enjoyed by him. I want to be a vessel for his pleasure. Forever and ever. *Does that make me crazy?*

A revelation strikes me. This is the first time I have really truly been in love and wanted to put another person's happiness before my own. Everything else has been a dress rehearsal.

This is it. Now. This is the final act. And I'd better not blow it.

9

We sit on the bed eating breakfast – the usual mouth-watering selection of *patisserie,* freshly squeezed juices and fruit. No coffee for me, at least for now. I know that a woman in her twenties could probably guzzle down whatever she chose, but I have to be vigilant; this could be my last opportunity to be pregnant – I shouldn't take any risks, even with something innocuous as coffee.

Alexandre brushes the back of his hand along my cheek. "Thank you, Pearl, for letting me forget about my quandary for a while."

I kiss his hand. "I know. Sex and sleep are the only two temporary cures."

"Every time I wake up, I'm okay for a few split seconds, and then I remember the mess I'm in."

"*We're* in," I correct. "We're in this *together.*"

"I wish you weren't involved in this fiasco. My mind spins in circles all day long; I just can't come up with a solution. Laura's threat could cause havoc. My uncle, my father's brother – if he got wind of this...he's never believed my father just disappeared; he's always been suspicious. If he knew about this, he'd be down on my mother like a ton of bricks."

I feel so bad for Alexandre – the searing regret he must feel at not having destroyed the evidence when he had the chance. "It's in a safe deposit box in the bank, right?" I ask.

"That's what Laura says."

"We have two options: to steal it back or to *make* her give it up." I take a long swig of apple juice.

"She won't, there's no way. Even if, hypothetically, I gave her everything she wanted, she'd still protect herself; still wrap up her blackmail like a neat burrito."

"Then we must steal the evidence. Well, not *steal*. It doesn't belong to her in the first place."

"It's in a vault in the bank. I may have a bit of money and can pull some strings but I'm not Tom Cruise in *Mission Impossible*. Nor can I pay anyone to do it for me. The job's too...too bloody difficult."

"Not do a robbery in that way, silly."

He stares at me and shakes his head. "No way, Pearl. Don't even think about it. I already said I didn't want you to get involved."

"I'm already involved. Look, Laura and I don't look that unalike. Well, she's taller and skinnier than I am but we're both blonde, both have blue eyes."

"What about I.D?"

"Steal her passport, or we can make a duplicate."

"You've been watching too many thrillers."

"Alexandre, you're ridiculously wealthy; now's the time to really *use* some of your money, your clout; pull some of your weight. I'm sure you can work something out – you have all kinds of people on your payroll."

His crooked smile makes the dimple in his cheek stand out more than usual. "*Now* look who sounds like Michael Corleone."

I reply seriously, "We have to *do* something. She's going to want an answer sooner or later, you can't stall her forever."

He sighs and stretches his long legs out. He's half dressed but his feet are bare. I never tire of looking at those elegant feet. He leans his head against the headboard of the bed and mumbles in a tired voice, "But I don't want to see her again."

"You'll have to. At least to get your hands on her passport. Or do you have a connection at the British Embassy?"

"I don't work for the MI5, Pearl."

I take another long swig of juice. Thinking about all this is making me thirsty. "Then you need to swipe her passport and find out which bank holds the evidence. Then find the safe deposit box key."

He raises his eyebrows. "And then you'll go personally to the bank masquerading as her?"

"It's the only thing I can think of. If I get arrested, though, you'll need to find me the best attorney in the world. O.J. Simpson's lawyer would be perfect," I joke.

He shakes his head. "It's too risky."

Another idea flashes into my brain. "Laura hacked our phones, you need to hack hers; get all the info you can – keep us abreast of what's going on."

"That part will be a piece of cake." He squeezes my wrist

as if he's afraid I'll run off and do something crazy without him by his side. "Pearl, I don't want you to put yourself in the middle of this. You're pregnant, this is insane – there has to be a better way. In fact, *no* – there's no chance I'll let you do something so crazy."

"Then hire someone. Hire an actress to be Laura for an hour or so." I bite into another mouthful of croissant.

"If the impersonator got caught she'd let the cat out of the bag, though."

"That's why we'd need to keep who we are a secret – not show our faces. Pay the actress in cash. Half up front, half later."

He chuckles. "This is beginning to sound like some crazy suspense movie. Worse, a Woody Allen film that could go laughably wrong."

I don't say anything but in my mind I think, *what Alexandre's mom did was pretty nutty.* Not the killing part, so much. I can see how that could happen in a state of black desperation, fearing for your life - but not getting rid of every scrap of evidence? Not such a bright move.

As if Alexandre can read my mind he says, "I know it seems as if my mother did something really dumb but for her it was a reminder that my father was dead and gone, that he couldn't hurt her anymore."

I bite my lip. "I understand," but I think to myself secretly, *what a nut-job family I'm marrying into. And, worse, what a mad person I must be, myself, to identify with a murderess as much as I do.*

"Tell me about your father," I probe – a question I have been trying to ask for ages without any definitive answers.

"I think you can read between the lines."

"Alexandre, I am going to be your *wife*. I need you to open up to me, to share your pain and your past. I shared mine with you."

"True," he admits. He takes a deep breath as if he needs an extra dose of oxygen to remember the worst. "The scariest thing about my father was that he wasn't always a monster."

"I figured, or your mother wouldn't have stayed with him so long."

"They had a connection – very physical. He was extremely handsome. She was sort of... hooked on him."

I don't respond but I can imagine. After all, Alexandre is his son.

"He was witty, charming, very charismatic. Clever, too. He could walk into a room and everyone would pay attention. People wanted to please him, be loved by him."

"But he was violent."

"Not at first. They had several happy years. He was Bipolar, you know, what they used to refer to as 'manic-depressive.' Everyone is affected differently. Some Bipolar people lead almost normal lives and are pussycats; never show an aggressive side at all. Others...well. When my father was nice he was great, very loving. But when he was in a manic state, he became a complete monster."

"A real Jekyll and Hyde?"

"He was violent and very sexual if he drank. Drinking sent him over the edge."

"And that's when he sexually abused Sophie?"

"Yes."

"And you, too?"

Alexandre lowers his head and nods. Pain is wavering between us, filling the room. "That's when Sophie knew she had to take me away. She could deal with him – but when he started on me, she lost it. That's why she stabbed him in the groin. She was outraged that he could sink so low."

I lay my hand on his. "It must have been hell for you, I'm so sorry."

"I blanked it out mostly. The same thing happened to me as to you…just blacked my mind from the whole ordeal."

But I know what he is telling me is not completely true. Muscles have memories. When we first started spending nights together, when Alexandre was fast asleep, I would cuddle into him in the spoon position, me behind. A couple of times he woke in a panic, elbows and knees crashing everywhere, flailing his legs and arms about. Someone edged up behind him still means only one thing: sexual abuse. My heart aches for him so badly. What happened to me was horrific but at least it wasn't *betrayal* of the first degree.

"Didn't your mother realize what was going on?" I ask, tears pooling my eyes.

"She was in total denial."

"Does that make you angry?"

His face is impassive, although his calm demeanor doesn't fool me for a second. "I was too young at the time to be angry. But Sophie still feels bitter towards her. She has tried; gone through God knows how much amount of therapy, but Sophie will never be able to *truly* forgive her. That's why I've never let on to her about the murder. I couldn't trust her a hundred percent."

"Just awful to have that treachery come from your own father. I can't even imagine." I bring Alexandre's hand up to my face and rest my lips on his long fingers.

He frowns and says, "Have you noticed that whenever they deal with incestual abuse in films or novels they always have a *step*-father or *step*-brother? Never blood parents or blood siblings. Why? Because it's such a taboo topic that nobody wants to talk about it, let alone believe it. It's such a shameful subject. I've felt shame all my life. Illogical but that's how it is for victims, I don't need to tell you that."

"I know," I say quietly.

"But you know what, Pearl? I'm not the only one. Believe it or not, there are lots of us out there. More than anyone would dare to imagine. Fathers fucking their daughters and sons, brothers, uncles, even mothers doing it to their sons. And within wealthy, privileged families, too – this disease isn't a class, race or monetary issue. It's happening all over the world even in nice, tidy, middle class households."

I know that he's right, although it seems impossible to accept, but it's a vicious, insidious truth eating into society, ruining many people's lives - sometimes forever.

"Why wasn't your father on medication? Lithium or something?" My question seems redundant, ridiculous, but Alexandre is discussing this, finally. He is trusting me with his dark, buried secrets and opening up. I know how painful that is.

"Oh, he *was* on medication at the beginning, but pride got the better of him. He felt he didn't need it, that he could fix himself. Of course, he couldn't. When he came out of the manic episodes he could never explain why he'd done what he did, and he'd always feel guilty, sad and remorseful. My mother always used to end up forgiving him."

A spike of fury stabs me in the heart. How could she do that? Forgive such a monster? But I remain calm. Alexandre loves his mom, however sick she makes me feel. I ask simply, "So what tipped her scales finally?"

"The violence. He was raping her, repeatedly. His condition got worse and worse. He was beating her up, continually. Broken ribs. Nose. You name it. That's when she decided to leave. She tried, once, but she ended up in hospital. He said if she tried again, he'd kill her next time. And us, if he found us – we were in hiding by that point. That's when my mother hatched the plan to get rid of him, once and for all. But deep down inside? She's still in love with him, even now. The good side of him. She kept the teeth and stuff to remind her that he was dead but she also has photos of their happy times in a secret box in the attic. She sneaks up there, sometimes, when my step-father's out of the house, or she pretends she's spring cleaning."

"Pretty screwed up, huh?"

"You bet."

As much as I hate her for what she did to Alexandre by not protecting him, I do identify with Alexandre's mother. Falling in love with someone you think is the perfect man and then he turns? That must be hard. What would I do if Alexandre suddenly changed his colors? Women all over the world face this predicament, especially if they have kids. It's easy to spot an abusive man as an onlooker, but when he is living with you every day and you love him? Not so much.

I look at my fiancé and wonder. What would I do? Because the truth is, Alexandre's dominance turns me on. It's only in small ways that he demonstrates it and he has never, ever made me feel scared of him physically, but I do enjoy being beneath him (no pun intended). I know it's crazy but being submissive makes me feel sexier and relieved that I don't have to make all the decisions – he can take command. But it also causes me to feel frustrated with myself, as if I'm putting the clock back on women's rights by a hundred years.

We sit there in silence. I know this must be the first time he has really opened up to someone about his past. He's been carrying this all on his own shoulders. No wonder he has been so protective of Sophie. She's the only one who has been through hell and back with him. She truly *knows* him. I think of how understanding he was about what happened to me, horrified that I'd even considered that it had been my fault.

I get the feeling that he is all talked out. He's revealed so much about himself, laying his wounds open to the elements. It's time to change the subject. I slip my hand under his T-shirt, maneuver myself so my head is on his stomach, look up at him and say in a soft, seductive voice, "I had an erotic dream about you when I was in Hawaii."

He narrows his green eyes that seem to be twinkling with amusement. "Oh yeah, you mentioned you had a little secret. Tell me about it."

"I dreamed that you were spanking me."

He gives me a wry, wolfish smile. "And?"

"I woke up the next morning, soaked between my legs, nursing a post-orgasm after-glow. After-shock, more like. Pretty high on the Richter scale, it was. The truth is, what you did in the dream really turned me on."

He licks his lips. He's the wolf and I'm Red Riding Hood. "Is this an invitation?"

"I'm curious," I whisper stroking his navel.

"You girls have been reading too many erotic novels. You think you want it but, in reality, it would freak you out."

"I might. I might love it. I did in my dream."

"Because it was a fantasy, baby. Some women fantasize about being raped but would be horrified if it happened in real life. I don't need to tell *you* that, of all people."

"I enjoyed my little adventure with Alessandra, though."

"Because she's a woman. You knew you were equals in strength. Neither was the *dominante*."

"Oh, I don't know, she wielded that little whip with *panache* and relish," I joke, remembering that mad evening of lesbian bondage as if it only happened yesterday, although I realize now that she really did take advantage of me. She sensed that I was weak and vulnerable and honed in on me.

Alexandre's eyes scan me from head to toe and settle on my breasts. I know this conversation is turning him on, even if he won't admit it. I add, "I'm just curious, that's all, about a little BDSM."

"So am I."

My eyes widen. "Really?"

"Of course. But I would never *act* on it."

"It wouldn't mean that you were like your father, Alexandre. Not if it's consensual and both parties are up for it."

He runs his fingers along my collarbone. "I wouldn't dare, Pearl."

"Why not?"

"What if I liked it? What then? What if I got a taste for it and it took me over?"

"It wouldn't."

"Don't be so sure," he tells me with a dry smile. "I might develop an addiction for putting you over my knee. Whipping that wet little pussy of yours. Whipping it, then sucking it, then fucking it."

I can feel moisture flush through my hot kernel.

"Enough of this conversation, chérie, it's dangerous. Although, I have to admit, it's a good distraction from our dilemma." He rests his hands on his huge hard-on. "And you've got me in the mood again."

"To fuck me?" I purr, stroking him through his pajama bottoms, feeling that comforting ridge that never lets me down.

"No, baby, you know the rules."

I squeeze him a little. "But my gynecologist said it was fine to have intercourse! Only if I was spotting was it risky. She said—"

"I don't care what she said. I'm going by the Indian woman's advice. Delicious sex comes in many forms; it doesn't have to involve penetration. It's like martial arts - training with your hands tied behind your back – your footwork gets better, so do your kicks."

"Do you know anything about martial arts?" I ask, running my hands along up his solid thighs – he must have gotten those sinewy muscles from some kind of hard training.

"A little." He winks at me.

"By the time we have sex I'll be desperate."

"You'll be like a virgin on our wedding night. I'll fuck you then. When *is* our wedding, by the way?"

"It's a surprise. Just make sure you don't double-book. Keep your calendar open until the end of February, at least."

"From now on, chérie, you *are* my calendar. You take top priority."

"What about your business?"

"We're going to be even richer."

I raise my eyebrows. "What have you got brewing?"

"You disapprove of video games so I won't tell you."

"*Video* games?"

"You see, I knew you wouldn't understand."

"Okay, tell me. You know I'm not a video game kinda girl but I do respect the creative process that goes into them."

"As well as that side of things, I'm not selling HookedUp to Sophie, after all. She simply can't afford to buy me out –

she pulled out of our deal at the last minute. We might both sell at a later date – strike while the iron's hot. You can be a lady of leisure if you like, Pearl."

I feel relieved that the family business hasn't broken up because of me. I think back to our other conversation, fondle his cock and say, "If you spanked me, Alexandre, tell me how you'd do it."

He strokes his thumb languidly over my lower lip and I suck on it, letting my teeth graze across the ball of his thumb, flickering my tongue on his shiny square nail. He takes my other hand and presses it against his erection.

"See how hard you get me, Pearl, lying against me with your pregnant tits, those nipples like silk bullets? But you're wrong if you think I'd spank a woman with my child inside her."

"Please, just humor me. Just pretend. Tell me how you'd do it." I walk my fingers under his PJ's and squeeze his penis, feeling the throb of it in my fisted hand.

"I'd bend you over my knee with my arm over your shoulder so you were locked into position and couldn't wriggle away. With my right hand I'd stroke your hot little pussy-pearlette, tickle it, tease it until it was glistening wet. Until it was begging me for more."

I run my tongue along my lips and stroke the length of his smooth erection, softly. He bucks his hips up a little so I can roll his pajamas down, and I hear his quiet moan.

He talks on in his deep voice, "Once you were really aroused, I'd bring my flat palm down hard on your ass with a stinging slap. It would shock you, might even hurt you a little, but it would also make you want more. Then I'd tap your hot, juicy little pearlette so gently, letting my fingers dip inside."

I grip him harder and begin to jack his cock up and down, concentrating on the crown of it, teasing the bulbous tip.

"Then I'd slap you again, this time the tips of my fingers would land on your pussy. You'd be moaning for more. I'd plunge my fingers inside. Then slap you again with my other hand. Then stroke you softly. You'd be going crazy because my rhythm would change. You wouldn't know if you'd get the tease or the slap. Then I'd throw you on the bed and fuck you so hard from behind while your own fingers played with your clit. I'd ravage you like an animal. Bad boy style. Play the ruthless, selfish bastard. Girls like that. Pump your pussy until it was numb. I'd fuck your ass off, thrusting in and out till I came really hard deep inside you, emptying all my seed. Then I'd pull out before you had a chance to come."

He's really rock solid now and I'm soaked hearing him describe this particular brand of torture, my clit pounding with arousal.

He's grinning now, enjoying this game. "You'd be confused, chérie. Almost in pain, but wanting more. I'd leave you there for a few minutes. You'd spread your legs begging for me to come back."

I lick my lips. "Yes, I would."

"I'd spank you once more, just so you'd know who was boss. Then I'd turn you over. I'd fuck your clit with the tip of my cock till you screamed. Then I'd enter you again. You in the missionary position. But really slowly and gently, this time. I'd cup your ass with my hands tightly so it was all mine, bringing it as close to me as possible. I start a slow fuck, hauling your peachy ass up towards me with each thrust. My pubic bone would be rubbing on your clit, or I'd change my position so the root of my dick would massage your clit - and my cock would be pressing against your secret places, those places that drive you wild. I'd keep my motions as rhythmical as a metronome, the thing musicians use to keep the beat..."

I feel I'm about to come just listening to his description.

"Come here, Pearl." Alexandre grabs me about my waist and maneuvers me so I am above him, my pussy on his face, my butt in the air, doggy style. He flickers his tongue up beneath me, lapping at my opening - he's groaning. "Fuck you're wet," he murmurs.

We commence our 69. I wrap my lips about his steel rod and start sucking the tip and then put as much as I can into my mouth, sucking in like a vacuum, riding my head up and down, letting my mouth fuck him as if I were mounting him. It's hard to concentrate because his tongue is doing magical things to me, also sucking in a vacuum, drawing out my juices.

My eyelids flutter – I'm entering another realm. "Alexandre..."

His hands are clamped on my thighs so I can't escape – not that I want to. He's pulling my groin closer to his face and taking me whole, fucking me now with his tongue. Then with his right palm, he brings it up between my legs and cups my mound, keeping the flatness of his hand hard against my clit and rubbing in small circles. His tongue lashes at me from behind as I relish the pressure of his hand on my clit...aah...Incredible.

I compress my lips around his broad length and fist my hands about the root....there's too much of him to fit in my already stretched mouth. I can feel him thicken...

"Jesus, your wet, sweet-tasting pussy is driving me wild,"

He groans. The throbbing expansion of him inside my mouth is giving me all the clues I need...he's going to come any second.

I grab his hand and push it even harder against my clit and start coming in a powerful rush. His hand is moist from my oozing and I slap my groin into his palm, my mouth trying not to leave his cock – I need to keep the pressure up. He needs me but my orgasm is making me selfish. "Aah, baby, I'm coming so hard," I cry, releasing my own hand from his.

Whorls of bright colors spiral in my brain as intense spasms crash through my core. I tighten my lips about him and he's coming too, spurting inside my mouth. I swallow eagerly, sucking it all in.

"Je t'aime, Pearl," he groans. *I love you.*

"Moi, non plus," I scream out, aware I'm quoting Jane Birkin in the song and what I've said is mad nonsense...'me, neither' is the translation.

He pushes my legs further apart, holding his tongue flat against me as my aftershocks fade slowly, my orgasm riding on its vibrating plateau. Alexandre can read my body like a memorized book – he always knows what to do, always senses when I need extra pressure or when I need stillness. It's as if he has studied the art of lovemaking somewhere along the line. He knows when to fuck hard and when to be gentle. When to be a pirate, and when to be a gentleman. Right now, his tongue is motionless – just what I desire. As my climax shimmers like the glistening pearl he tells me that I am, I collapse my face into his crotch, licking all the droplets of cum from there and his solid thighs. Whoever imagined that carnal lust could be so beautiful...

I am totally spent.

10

Two days have passed and I still haven't been back to my apartment. It feels good to be at work knowing that 'home' is at Alexandre's place with him - that at the end of the day, I have my partner waiting for me. Finally, I can concentrate when I'm at work – doing something else other than obsess over lost love. Although he and I still have a lot of making up to do for lost *time,* or should I say, 'making out' to do. Like teenagers freshly fallen in love, we can't get enough of each other.

I think back again to the way I behaved, crawling out of that toilet window at Van Nuys Airport and it feels as if it was someone else, not me. I don't think I had fully appreciated the toll that the rape had on me; the memory flooding back in such detail – gang rape – being abused, used and made to feel like trash, as if I had no importance in the world whatsoever. People imagine it's the physical violation that is so devastating, and although it's true, it is nothing to what goes on inside your brain. I had hidden it deep in my sub-conscious, but it was still there – the feeling of worthlessness that ate into my psyche every single day for eighteen years. And whatever anybody says, however hard they try to assure you, deep down inside is that feeling of culpability - even if you know, logically, that it's nonsense.

No, I don't think I took it all on board and the effect it had on me. Remembering everything brought me back to that moment, that night. It made me vulnerable, a pawn for Laura. Had I not been in such a sorry state, I don't believe that I would have been so naïve, so blind – making rash, foolish choices based on nothing but fear. I have always prided myself on being astute and on the ball, but I was like a helpless beetle that had been flipped over, flailing my weak legs in the air. My armor was on my back, not on my under-belly where I needed it most.

Or perhaps the way I handled things with Alexandre was a subconscious desire to continue punishing myself because I didn't believe I deserved better. Alexandre said so at the time; that I was using Sophie as an excuse to run from him. It was only when I felt I'd lost him completely that I could see the situation for what it was. Me – all alone for the rest of my life. Back in The Desert. Thirsty for love. For sex. For self-worth. I'd lost the one thing that was true: Alexandre.

Alexandre *gives* me that sense of self worth. Having a man be so intimate with you, telling you that your private parts are 'sweet' and 'delicious' is a real gift. Few men do that. Few men make you feel really special and treasured. Yes, I am hooked on the orgasms he feeds me every day, but it is the intimacy, the connection that gives me those or-gasms in the first place. He is accepting every part of me, even the 'dirty' bits that he finds beautiful. He finds my vagina so beautiful he calls it my 'pearlette' – because for him it is a little part of me – a little part that is like a jewel. Yet for me those 'bits' caused such inner turmoil for so many years making me feel I was bad and unworthy. Alexandre has restored the faith I once had in myself before that dreaded event.

As he once told me, 'the biggest sexual organ is your brain' and he is, little by little, convincing me that I am precious – that I count in this world. Being sexy is all about self-confidence. It's all a question of how you feel inside. Alexandre took my dull nub of a diamond and he polished it until it began to shine.

I have even given nicknames to my vagina: V, V-8, and the sweet sounding "pussy" – that's how confused I've been about sex and my own sexuality. Like a little girl not being able to call it by its real name. Both ashamed and amused, all in one. Tittering about its naughtiness like a child in the classroom with a secret joke. Too fearful to come out and say the real word. Vagina. There, I said it. Was that so difficult? God gave females vaginas yet I was subconsciously shameful of having one because of what it brought me. That rape left me ashamed of having a vagina, of being a woman.

Sex is not everything but it is, literally, the core of us. We are born from sex. The world lives on through sex. We can feel ecstasy through sex.

Or misery.

And I never want to return to that place again.

It's all abuzz at HookedUp Enterprises today. Natalie is putting the final touches to our documentary, *Child Traffick – Red Light Alert* - (a double entendre on traffic lights and the red light districts in the sex industry). It's looking great. Well, 'great' is not exactly the best word to use with such a heart-breaking topic – let's just say, the film is brilliantly put together. We have already sold the rights in ten countries and it has been entered into several competitions. I have high hopes for this film.

I'm in my office sorting through paperwork when Jeanine, our receptionist, buzzes me.

"Hi Pearl, Natalie wants to come and see you, are you free right now?"

"Absolutely," I reply, curious as to why she's paying me a visit – usually we meet in the editing room.

Ten minutes later, she bursts through the door, looking stunning, as usual, yet with a girlish restlessness about her which I haven't noticed before – Natalie is usually so composed, such a 'grown-up'.

"Hi Natalie. You look amazing – like ten years younger or something." I rake my eyes over her outfit: tight jeans; not Natalie's usual attire.

"Or something," she says with a laugh. "Do you want to hear the good news first, or the good news second?"

"The good news second."

She sets her tablet on my desk and plunks herself in my swivel chair giving it, and herself, a little spin. Boy, is she in a good mood. "Actually, I can't make up my mind which is better," she gushes.

"Tell me either way, the suspense is killing me."

"Okay. Firstly, your fiancé has started this foundation for us – a charity.

"Oh yes?" I ask with curiosity. *How come he never mentioned this?*

Natalie goes on, "It's called the Jane Doe Foundation. It has been set up for sexually abused girls and young women. Because of all our research and experience with the girls we've met through our project, he thinks HookedUp Enterprises is the perfect vehicle, although I have been sworn that HookedUp Enterprises will never be mentioned at any time. The Foundation is financially independent.

"I guess I shouldn't be surprised. He's rich; he can afford to give money away to worthy causes – good for him."

She nibbles on a pen lying on my desk. "No, that's what's so cool. This isn't his money but has come in from four, other, private sources."

"Jane Doe, you say?"

"That's right. Because abused girls are handled like Jane Does, identities unknown, or treated like they haven't got a name; they are victims, not just because they've been abused but because so many people don't even know who they are. Or worse, they don't care."

"Jane Doe," I repeat. "Was that his idea?" Natalie has no clue about what happened to me all those years ago. Primarily, ours is a working relationship.

"Yeah, not even I could have come up with such an original name."

I raise my eyebrows. Is she being sarcastic? I study her expression.

"No, really, I think the name is cool," she says, tapping her legs eagerly as if she's ready to talk about her other good news.

"Who are these benefactors?"

She beams at me. "Anonymous."

"And they all came in together with the money? At one time? Or was this charity set up a while ago and this is the first we're hearing of it?"

She's still grinning. "It was set up, oh, I think less than a week ago."

"And we are to distribute the funds as we see fit?"

"That's right."

Revenge is a dish best served cold. What has Alexandre been up to?

"Do you want to hear my other good news?" Natalie asks, impatience dancing in her eyes.

I blink to concentrate on what she's about to say. "Yes. Yes, of course."

"I'm dating someone new."

I give her a cheeky smile. "Hence the sexy jeans?"

"You like my new look?"

"Any look suits you, Natalie," I say, trying to get Alexandre and his Robin Hood shenanigans out of my head. I wonder how he did it. The coincidence is too much. Four benefactors, Jane Doe…

Natalie jiggles her boot. She's wearing heels. "Aren't you going to ask who it is?"

"Let me guess. That lawyer guy you saw last year that you kind of liked?"

"No-o," she sing-songs.

"That doctor who your friend, Gail, wanted to send you on a blind date with?"

"Not even close."

I throw my hands in the air. "Okay, I give up." Natalie swore she would only ever date a man who earned a six figure salary. With all the commotion with her aunt after Hurricane Sandy, I'm amazed she has even found time to date anyone at all. In fact, this is the first time I have seen her so giddy with happiness – she deserves it after the Sandy aftermath and all that she has been doing for her family.

"A firefighter," she says and then laughs. "I know...not what you expected." She gives the chair a three hundred and sixty degree swivel.

"Probably not what *you* expected, either," I joke.

"He was cleaning up the devastation where my aunt used to live. Broken gas pipes, et cetera – the place was dangerous, you know. He told me to clear off. Then we got talking."

"What's his name?"

"Miles. After Miles Davis."

"I'm so happy for you," I tell her, trying to hide my surprise.

"You don't think I'm crazy?"

"Are you kidding? They're the bravest, coolest bunch of people in the world. Not to mention..." I trail off.

"What?"

I try to suppress a grin. I think of Alexandre in his firefighter get-up and a sexy-memory frisson runs up my spine.

"You have such a dirty mind, Pearl."

"Well, let's face it - a guy in uniform? A *firefighter* in uniform is every woman's fantasy."

"Well, I have to say..." she arches a neat eyebrow.

"You *haven't, you didn't?*" Natalie and I rarely talk about anything other than work. But she's in the mood to reveal all, obviously.

She widens her hazel eyes. She looks like a little girl who's had way too much candy. "He was very apologetic. I went to his house for dinner and he hadn't had time to change. I flung myself at him."

"I bet you did. So what does he look like? No, that's

wrong – I should be asking you if he's kind and caring–"

"Imagine a young Denzel Washington with a bit of Wesley Snipes thrown in."

"Very nice, indeed."

"Miles is a sexy cocktail, alright."

"Yeah, you look a little tipsy," I joke, "that's for sure. How old is he?"

She sighs. "A little younger than me."

"Join the club. So is this serious, like *relationship* serious or just….exercise?" I ask.

"That's what's so crazy. At the beginning I thought it was just for fun but he's like…so sincere, so genuine. I think I'm falling for him."

"Does he know that?"

"No way! I'm not like you, Pearl. I don't wear my heart on my sleeve. I'm playing it cool. You know, not always available. Making sure he knows he has to book an evening with me way in advance. No last minute dates."

I think of my rock climbing date with Alexandre…so last minute. Boy, was I easy. "Poor guy," I say making a face, "You've probably got him pining for you."

"That's the idea."

"You're such a catch, Natalie. I bet he feels he's in over his head."

"I don't think so. He's very confident and pretty cocky."

"Well, he's met his match in you."

She giggles. Natalie never giggles. "Am I that bad?"

"You can be pretty formidable."

"Is that what your father said about me?"

"No, Not at all."

"The truth is, there was no way I was going to move to an island in the middle of nowhere and leave New York – it would never have worked out with your dad."

"I know. My dad got that. Speaking of moving to Hawaii ...no, never mind." I walk over to the window and look down at the street. People are rushing this way and that, buzzing about in the post-holiday sales.

"What? I hate it when you do that – give me half a secret and then take it away again."

I turn around. She's still swiveling in my chair. "How do you know it's a secret?"

She glares at me playfully. "I can tell by the look in your eye."

"I'll tell you when it's a sure thing."

"See? There you go again, Pearl."

I hesitate. Would Daisy mind me telling Natalie? No, she wouldn't. I say, "Well, okay. It looks as if Daisy might have something going on with someone she met there."

Natalie claps her hands. "That's fantastic! Who is he?"

"A surfer dude. But very cute."

"You see, there was no way I could be part of that world. I guess I'm a city girl at heart. About your dad – I've been feeling a little guilty, you know, like I was a bit unfair to him. I didn't call him because I didn't want him to think we were...you know...still on. But I realized that I was being a bit cold."

"He'll live. He knew you'd never settle in Hawaii. You don't want some zen hippie like him, anyway – that's not your style."

"A New Yorker born and bred - that's me."

"Exactly. My dad wouldn't last more than three days here."

"Can you envision Daisy there, though?"

"When she came to visit, she was like a duck to water. It

might be just the thing for her and Amy."

Natalie's smile fades. "What happened to Johnny – she doesn't want to get back together with him?"

"He's repentant." I feel my hackles rise on Daisy's behalf. "But he's too late."

"Hell hath no fury like a woman scorned," Natalie chirps.

I've heard her quote that before. Shakespeare? No, the Restoration playwright. "Congreve, I believe?"

"You're a poet and you don't know it," she replies, laughing at my rhyme and making another.

"Actually, Daisy's being very nice to Johnny. Considering. But she can't trust him anymore. Plus, I think she's up for a real lifestyle change."

Natalie inspects her manicured nails and then raps them on the desk almost as if she's playing a tune. "What about you and Alexandre? You told me there were issues with the ex."

"Resolved," I say quickly. "You know what, Natalie? I really think we need to go through the credit titles again. We've been chit-chatting way too long – we should get back to work before the day's gone. I'm so thrilled for you about Miles. Keep him guessing – keep him on his toes."

She springs from my chair and picks up her tablet. "Oh, I will."

"I still can't get over those donations that came out of the blue." I'll need to find out what Alexandre has been up to.

We start our slow amble as we exit my office. "You don't mind that Miles isn't a six figure earner?" I ask, wondering if Natalie remembered the vow she made a year ago.

"He's a nice guy and that's what counts most. My daughters like him."

"They've met him? Okay, I see this really *is* serious."

Then she whispers, "The truth is, Pearl, he's a magician in bed. He takes his time, he's so *into* me, you know – he makes me feel like I'm the most incredible woman who's ever walked the earth."

I nod knowingly. "Yup, you're hooked, alright."

Then we both burst out at once, "HookedUp!"

I add, "It amuses me no end, the name HookedUp Enterprises. It's like Star Trek, you know, as if we're on a space ship."

"We're on a journey alright. The journey of our life. They say 'life begins at forty' and you know what? I think they're right!"

A few hours later, just as I am grabbing my coat to leave the office, my landline rings.

Jeanine informs me, "The person wouldn't tell me who she was."

"A woman?"

"A *British* woman."

"Thanks Jeanine, put her through."

I hold the receiver with trepidation. "Hello?"

"Sorry to bother you at work, Pearl, but I had no choice."

It's HER.

"What do you want, Laura." No question mark.

"I realize I was rash when I told you my secret about your mobile." Mobile...ah yes, British for cell phone.

"So you couldn't spy on me anymore, you mean?"

"Just keeping tabs."

"Well, I'm no longer using my 'mobile' anyway."

"So I gathered. That's why I'm calling you at work."

"I know what you're up to, Laura. Alexandre's told me everything."

"Ah, yes. The hip replacement. And the rather sorry-looking teeth. Why is it that Americans have such perfect knashers and we sad Europeans get lumped with bad dental care all our lives? Well, not blowing my own trumpet, or anything, but mine were sorted out and are in mint condition. But, you know, in general. Especially the French. Not Sophie and Alexandre, though, their sparkling white teeth are pretty perfect, except for that oh so slightly crooked one he has, but that, of course, is part of his charm—"

I cut her short. "Why are you calling, Laura?"

"I feel lonely. Left out. Alexandre's not answering my calls and I want to know what he's decided."

I take a deep breath and tell her, "He doesn't love you, Laura."

"He loved me once and he can love me again. Once I've had his child then we can be happy again. I mean, let's face it Pearl, that's something you can't give him. He wants to be a father."

"He's going to be a father," I blurt out.

"Come again?"

"I'm pregnant, Laura. Alexandre and I are going to be parents." *Oh God, why did I say that?* Why did I let her know that? I feel instantly foolish – this woman is nuts. This information could drive her over the edge of reason.

There's silence and then she replies with a hiss, "Bollocks. You're just saying that to rile me up!"

I don't answer.

"Pearl? Are you there?"

I want to hang up on her, but also don't dare to.

"Pearl?" Her voice sounds tearful. *Laura crying?* That I cannot imagine.

"I'm still here," I answer.

"Did you do IVF?"

"No, Laura. He fucked my ARSE with an R off, and his sperm shot inside my womb and I got pregnant naturally." *Oh no, now what have I said?*

She slams the phone down on me.

My moment of triumphant glory is overtaken by an overwhelming feeling of stupidity. Uh, oh. I've really gone and done it now. My heart's racing. That little payback instant felt sooo good....but....

The telephone rings again. I grab it, morbidly curious as to what will happen next. I hope my outburst isn't going to land Alexandre's mother in jail.

"It's the British woman again," Jeanine lets me know.

"Thanks, Jeanine, we got cut off, please put her through." I sit down in my swivel chair.

"Okay," Laura begins, "I'm willing to negotiate."

Negotiate? "I'm listening."

"This relationship seems to be far, far more serious than I had imagined."

"What relationship?" I ask tentatively.

"Yours and Alex's, of course."

"We're in love, Laura." *Ooh, that felt good, too.*

"His dick has obviously got the better of him. But that's by the by. I'm not a home wrecker, whatever you may think of me. How far gone are you?"

"Three months," I lie. "It's all happening, Laura. The

doctors are delighted with the scans. I'm carrying a very healthy fetus – no chance of miscarriage now." I hope I haven't jinxed my pregnancy by saying that. I wince at my words.

She puffs, "I see. Well, that will change the course of events somewhat."

Somewhat?

"Look Pearl. I'm willing to do a deal. You can keep Alexandre and your baby. But I *also* want a baby. You know, James couldn't have children and before that…well, I was in a bloody wheelchair, thank you very much. Having a child has been a dream of mine and I want that dream to come true at any cost. Do you understand, Pearl? I am *not* giving up on my dream. We can do IVF. Alex won't even have to have sex with me. Just his sperm, that's all I want."

This woman is a real nut-job. If this were a movie, I'd be laughing by this point. "Why don't you go to a sperm bank, Laura?"

"Ugh, that's disgusting. Some smelly old sperm from someone I don't know?"

"Don't you have a handsome gay friend who could help you out?"

"I'm not a fag-hag. I don't go round with poofs, and besides, d'you think I want my baby to have homo genes in his DNA?"

"Well, what about a one-night stand with some gorgeous guy?" I suggest.

"I want brains as well as beauty. I want it *all* for my baby."

I propose an idea which I'm sure she'll shut down. I go ahead and suggest it anyway, "There are lots of clever, handsome men. You can afford it – advertise – you could even do it on eBay. I'm sure Alexandre would pay for any costs involved. Or I can help out."

"You think I'd degrade myself like that, Pearl? Purr...lease."

"There must be a better way, Laura - a way that doesn't involve Alexandre doing something against his will."

"Pearl, I think you've forgotten something key here. I hold the cards. I have the power. I want Alexandre's sperm in that little test tube - and nobody else's - and if I don't get it I might just be inclined to make a very big scene!"

"Don't do that, Laura! You'll break his heart if you...you know....say anything."

"What about *me*? What about my bloody broken heart! I look at myself in the mirror and I see a fuck-off, babelicious blonde looking bloody good for her age – then I see you with your big forty year-old arse and wonder...what the fuck does he see in her?"

Big ass? I have to tread carefully here. I mustn't let this woman get to me. I force myself to remain calm and take another deep breath. *Breath in, breath out.* "We're both into dogs, Laura...things like that. We have a connection. A bond."

"Look, Pearl, I think I'm being bloody magnanimous as it is - I'm letting you keep Alexandre. All I'm asking for is his bloody semen!"

I'm speechless – I can't think of how to reply.

She carries on in her posh drawl, "You talk to him. Tell him that if he doesn't agree – in writing by the way – to come to the clinic with me, then I'll be perfectly happy to spill the beans about 'you know who', and what that 'you know who' did."

"Where is the 'you know what,' Laura?"

"The 'you know what' is in a safety deposit box in a fuck-off vault in one of London's most protected banks, so don't even think about fucking with me."

I try to sound composed. "I'm sure you wouldn't do anything rash, Laura."

"I always hated that silly cow anyway. To be honest, she's got it coming to her. What kind of a person would do what she did? Not the topping off part but abandoning her children."

I hate to say it, but Laura does have a point. I have never met Alexandre's mother but she doesn't sound like the most stable of people. Nor, the most loyal.

But I say, "We mustn't judge her. And whatever *we* might think, Alexandre loves her."

"Anyway, you need to have a chat with him and let him know where I stand. I'm thirty-three years old and I want that baby A.S.A.P. I've already started the hormone therapy and I want that French fuck's sperm in that test tube within the next few weeks."

"Laura, if you think he's a 'French fuck' why do you want his baby in the first place?"

"Because he happens to be the most intelligent person I know. He's a genius, Pearl. Do you appreciate how clever he is? His mind is like a quantum theory computer. He is also stunningly handsome with a perfect, well-proportioned body. With his brains and his beauty and my brains and my beauty we'll produce a wonder child."

She sounds like the baddie in one of those mad, science fiction movies. "And then what?" I ask.

"I get his sperm, wait until I have the actual baby - just in case. Might even have some extra frozen for the future just for good measure. I'll also want a nice trust set up for the child - several million's worth – *several* million – and then he can have everything in that vault and we'll never speak of the subject again."

"What about the child? You'll want it to have a father, surely? Is Alexandre expected to play daddy?"

"I haven't thought that part through, yet. I have to ponder what's 'best for baby'. Now *you're* pregnant. Pearl, it really puts a spanner in the works."

"What about James?" I ask, half imagining him lying dead somewhere, poisoned by her.

"I was getting geared up to divorce him but he could come in handy. Good point, Pearl. I need to mull all that side of things over. I really had imagined myself back with Alex until you and your fat arse got in the way. I'm sure he'll get bored with you, eventually. We'll cross that bridge when we come to it."

I want to scream and shout at her but I also don't want to rock us both out of the very wobbly boat we're in – we could capsize and end up drowning, the pair of us.

"What if the IVF doesn't work, Laura? There's only a fifteen percent success rate, you know."

Silence.

Then she replies chirpily, "I feel very confident. Oh yes, and Alex will need to do his bit, too. A multivitamin. He'll need to stop drinking, no soy products, eat organic, no food from plastic containers. The positive thing about you being pregnant, Pearl, is that it's proof that his semen is working just fine. I mean, it must be extra powerful to have got you, a forty year-old pregnant. I'll give him a list about the do's and don'ts when we speak later. Well, bye then. Nice chatting. Tell Alex to call me A.S.A.P."

"I will," I answer, my blood boiling. I hang up. *What a*

basket case. She really must have fallen hard on her head in that accident.

As soon as I get home, I search for Alexandre. He's in his study talking on the phone. Deadly serious. He shoots me a 'do-not-interrupt' glance. Normally, I'd slip away and come back later, but I hover. He's wearing a hand-tailored, charcoal gray suit and looks extremely dapper. I have to say, he really is one of the most handsome men I have ever seen in my life.

"No, I didn't say that. What I said was that we need to invest another twenty million. You know how these things are. If you want quality, you have to pay for it, and what we need is...what we need...look, what we mustn't skimp on is talent. If that's what his fee is, then that's simply what we have to pay. Green-light that, Jim, yes, we have to. She said what? That's bullshit. There's room out there for games that don't involve shooting people. You see, Jim, that's what I'm talking about. That's what I liked about it. It has an epic heart-tugging story, glorious environments, kind of a sweet light magic and dark magic and a simply stunning soundtrack."

I observe my fiancé as his face reveals a gamut of emotions between smiles, frowns and furious brow creasing – animated by this conversation which is obviously about the next big video game. I have gathered that their budgets are bigger than blockbuster movies.

Alexandre loosens his tie. "That's right. What consumers want are handhelds that run Android so they can have a nice portable emulator. Okay, Jim. Speak to them and get back to me in the next few hours. Thanks."

"Sorry to bother you, baby." I'm lingering at the doorway.

"You never bother me, chérie; I'm always glad to see you. Come here and sit on my lap - just give me a couple more minutes – I need to write something down before I forget."

But I can't hold it in. His wheeling and dealing may be important but nothing as life-changing as being, or not being, a father. I blurt out, "Laura called me. We need to do something. She's on the warpath, still." *The sperm warpath.*

He closes his lids as if that will wipe her from his mind. "I keep hoping she'll give up and go away."

"Not a chance. But things are looking up a little," I say, hopefully, as I settle on his knee.

He puts his arms about my waist and breathes in the scent of my hair. "What d'you mean?"

"She's given up on wanting you, yourself, although she still wants part of you."

He shakes his head. "She's such a nutter. What did she say?"

"She wants you to go to the IVF clinic with her."

"Oh Christ."

"Well at least she's stopped harping on about marriage with you and living happily ever after."

He raises his eyebrows.

"I told her I was pregnant."

He furrows his temple. "Was that wise? She's so off the rails she's capable of anything. I really want her to keep away from you, Pearl – she could get consumed by jealousy."

"Strangely enough, I think it's had the opposite effect – it seems to have cooled her down. She's delighted your semen is so potent. She says she's not a home wrecker."

"She's a wrecker, period."

I nuzzle into his embrace and squeeze my arms about his broad chest. "Maybe you should−"

"No, Pearl."

"I've got *you*, that's all that counts."

"I am not giving into her. She is *not* having my child."

"She says if she doesn't get what she wants - your semen in a test tube, plus several million, she'll make a scene."

"She can have the money − I'll pay her off, but she's not getting her way."

"She's determined. Nobody else's sperm will do. She wants yours and yours alone − she thinks you're a genius, wants a wonder child."

"I can't believe how insane she's being. This is not the Laura I once knew."

"I know, it sounds like some twisted black comedy or something − it's so far-fetched, so larger than life, I keep pinching myself to make sure I'm not floating about in one of my nightmares again."

He takes off his jacket and throws it on his desk. "She's totally out to lunch, she's morphed into a fucking lunatic."

"She wants you to call her tonight. Oh yes, and she reminded me about the evidence being in the bank vault."

He loosens his tie some more as if the Laura news is making him feel strangled. "You didn't discuss that over the phone, did you? She could have been recording it."

I run my fingers through his dark hair. It feels soft and comforting in the midst of the tangle of mess we're in. "We sort of spoke in code. Your mother was just referred to as 'she' and the evidence, 'you know what'. Something tells me

Laura's enjoying the drama of it all. The way she was speaking made me feel that if it came to the crunch she wouldn't actually go through with her threat. I think she might just be playing power games."

"Too much of a risk to take, though. I'm too nervous about this to call her bluff."

"Still no word from James?"

"No, he still hasn't returned my calls."

I grimace. "You don't think she'd be capable of murder, do you?"

"No. But then again, this new persona of Laura's is a total shock to me. I don't know who she is anymore."

"You really think she suffered brain damage in the fall?"

"Either that, or some mind-altering medication she's on. Maybe she's taking something for the pain, who knows. But she's not being rational, anyway."

"What if you humored her? Pretended you agreed? But give her someone else's sperm. Get the teeth and hip parts back and she'll be pregnant with an anonymous donor, thinking it's you. You'll still have to pay her the 'settlement' but at least it won't be your child she's carrying."

"I'd have to sign legal documents, though, wouldn't I? And we'd have to be in cahoots with the doctors. Doctors are hard to bribe or they could lose their license to practice."

"Not necessarily. If you can get the exact same container they give you, or bring in your fake sample in a sanitized container and swap it over, who's to know?"

"Laura's too savvy. She will have probably thought of that – would probably want me to masturbate into the container in front of her."

"Maybe, but you could try."

"How long does sperm live?"

"A few hours, I think. You could pay someone who looks like you to come to the clinic with you. Get it fresh."

He rubs his eyes. "Listen to us. This conversation is crazy! This whole situation is fucking surreal."

"We have to come up with some plan, though."

"What about our last idea? The fake passport idea – paying an actress to go to the bank?"

"That's riskier. It's breaking the law. Whereas with this idea we'd get a slap on the wrist, not slung in jail."

"True."

"Could we trust her to keep to her side of the bargain, though?"

"The way she's been behaving? I doubt it."

A question has been on my lips for a long time. "Just out of curiosity, what *was* it about Laura that you loved? Apart from her physical beauty? Before, the accident, I mean."

"Funny you should ask that. I've been mulling that one over myself, recently. You know, I think I was…I don't know."

"What?"

"Very young. She was my first serious girlfriend. I'd always been with older women, friends of my sister's."

"Prostitutes?" I ask.

"Sex workers, yes. They were high class hookers, if you like. Not the sort that lurked in an alley somewhere. Not at all. These girls were more like consorts – dined out with politicians and extremely wealthy, older men. They were vetted, tested regularly. Always impeccably dressed, often very educated, too. They knew all sorts, about good food, fine wines, current affairs and could really hold an intelligent conversation – it was part of their job. That was the kind of work Sophie did. Anyway, I had relationships primarily with them simply because they were friends of my sister's. I never paid for sex, obviously."

Obviously. They should have been paying *him*.

"Then I met Laura. She was a buddy really, like my best friend, at the time. Sophie has never really been a 'friend' because she was too busy playing my mother figure and I'd never stayed long in one school so I didn't have so many guy friends. Laura was my mate. But now I look back on it, I don't think I really loved her. I mean, I did, but nothing, nothing compared to how I feel for you. Physically, there wasn't that fusion, you know, and I never had that soul connection with her, not like I have with you, Pearl."

I thread my fingers through his. It's so good to feel close again. To know he's mine. What he's saying about loving me more than he loved Laura is like a cool breeze on a swelter-ing day.

"Thanks," I say.

"Sometimes my stomach wells up with jealousy when I think of Saul or Brad – Silly, I know, but I get furious knowing you've loved others before me."

My lips curl up. I love him being jealous – how childish is that? But I put his fears at bay and tell him, "Ditto, Alexandre. I never felt about them the way I do about you. But you don't know what love really is when you're with someone in the moment, especially when you're young. You're not aware how in love you are until you have some-one else to compare it to. If I hadn't been with them, maybe I wouldn't appreciate *you*, now." I think of men I have been with before Alexandre and a nasty memory comes to mind. Which leads me to my next thought: Jane Doe. We've been so consumed by the Laura drama that I had almost forgotten to ask Alexandre about the mystery money and the charity that he set up.

"By the way, Alexandre, I think there's something you have omitted to tell me."

He looks defensive. "I've bloody told you everything. I'm not holding back secrets about Laura, I swear."

I stroke his earlobe and say, "Tell me about the Jane Doe Foundation."

He nods his head with the faintest smile edging his lips. "Ah, yes. That."

I shoot him a sideways glance. "Yes. That. Where did the money come from?"

"From those fuckwits who nearly ruined your life."

"The footballers?"

"Yup, those fat fucks." His mouth puckers to show his disdain.

"How did you even find them? I mean, *I* don't even know who they are."

"And you never shall. I don't even want you to give them another thought, Pearl. They've had their comeuppance. Well, not exactly – they've been let off lightly, but I hit them where it probably hurts most – in their wallets, and reminded them that violent actions have their consequences."

I snuggle up against Alexandre's chest and snake my hand under his shirt. I feel his steady heart beat and feel at peace. "I don't understand. How did you get them to donate? Types like that rarely turn out to be saints."

"One of them seemed repentant. He donated quite a bit extra."

I pull my neck back and look him in the eye. "But nobody just goes round doling out that kind of money, even if it is to charity. How did you get them to *do* it?"

He cocks a dark eyebrow. "I made them an offer they

couldn't refuse."

I titter nervously. "No, seriously"

"I am being serious." *Serioose.*

"Can I ask how?"

"You can ask, but I won't tell."

"Don't ask me about my business. Is that it?"

He gives me a wry, mischievous smile. "Exactly."

The fact that Alexandre has protected me in this rounda-bout fashion – ensuring money is given to abused girls who deserve safeguarding - warms my soul. God knows what unorthodox method he used, but I feel strangely proud. Perhaps he's right; I don't want to give these men another thought. Knowing that justice has been served is enough. What he has done for me is, in effect, every woman's fantasy. He's stuck up for me. Fought for my rights - for women's rights in general. Showed his solidarity. He has demonstrated the extent of his love with actions, not just words.

"That's the sexiest thing any man has ever done for me."

Funny how words can have an effect. I feel his groin swell against my butt. He's getting hard. Hard as a diamond. I push my ass into him and feel the thick ridge of his erec-tion rub against me through the fabric of his pants in just my perfect spot. He clasps his large hands on my hips and draws me closer, rocking against me, his mouth resting tenderly on the nape of my hairline.

"You beautiful thing, Pearl," he whispers, kissing my neck. "Your skin is as soft as a dove's."

His warm breath makes me shudder; a tingle runs through me like the ring of a tiny, silver bell. Our clothes between us have me imagining - all the more - what will finally happen when he penetrates me again. Yes, I think - I'll feel like a virgin.

He guides my butt up and down his length, and the friction makes my nerve endings converge in a spool of longing, wanting and neediness. I edge my behind up higher, and his fingers walk their way under my silk shirt, up my belly to my breasts. He unhooks my lacey bra so my boobs are free, cups them, groaning a little as they fill his hands.

"So sexy, so full and sensitive, chérie." He flickers his fingertips on my tight nipples, pinching them gently as I continue my slow, steady rub along the seam of his fly opening, the bulge reassuringly, monumentally solid as it pleasures my clit. I can always rely on Alexandre; not once, even when he's been drinking, has he failed me. He's always ready, always turned on, even if all I do is give him a provocative look.

As my ass slaps up and down against him, I'm reminded of Laura's insult, 'fat arse' (with an R) and wonder if Alexandre sees me that way. I don't think so – he's forever telling me what a gorgeous behind I have. I lean forward so my clit is getting the full-on massage it craves, even though the finest, merino wool of his expensive suit fabric is between us. My lids start fluttering, my core tightens – I'm entering the seventh heaven zone, the zone where my mind blanks out, and colors and stars have me concentrating on nothing but my impending orgasm. Alexandre lifts my hair away from my neck and kisses me there again, tweaking the nubs of my sensitive nipples at the same time. I keep grinding against his solid form, turned on, even more, by his promises.

"You know how I'm going to fuck you on our wedding night, don't you, baby? I'm going to stretch that little pearlette open and fuck you so deep and slow, fill you up, chérie, fill up your Tight. Little. Pussy. I'll have to fuck you hard. I'll have to ravage you a bit, though; I won't be able to resist. I want you coming all around my stiff cock. I love it when you cry out my name."

My hips buck backward as he tilts his groin even more firmly up against me. I close my eyes. The image of him deep inside me has me revved up, and one last push against my clit makes my core spasm and has me coming in a rush of relief. I still myself as rippling waves shimmy through my center. I can hear my quiet moans tremble through my body.

"Alexandre…oh God, you've done it again."

"That's right baby, your body needs this - it's healthy for you. I love the way you whimper when you come for me."

His fingers are still tweaking my nipples so the aftershocks linger on; my moans fading slowly as I come down from my climax.

I let myself bask in the glory of my orgasm and after a while, I climb off his lap and kneel on the floor, dipping my head in his crotch.

He lifts my face up and looks into my hungry eyes. "You don't need to do that, chérie."

"Oh, but I want to." His erection is tight up against his pants. I unbutton them, letting my fingers linger on the fine, smooth fabric, and free him from his entrapment. "Raise your butt up," I order, and he lifts himself an inch so that I can pull the tailored pants free. I roll them carefully down his thighs. I bury my head in his crotch and smell the unique Alexandre elixir mixed with a sweet whiff of lavender, and Marseille soap powder from his freshly laundered boxer briefs.

His fingers tangle in my hair and he flexes his hips forward and groans. "Fuck, you make me hard."

I don't take off his underwear – not yet anyway. I nibble my teeth gently along the solidity of his length, nipping him through the soft, combed cotton.

His hands clasp my head and I know he's hot for me. His cock flexes as if it's a separate entity; a creature that's alive. Alexandre leans back languidly in his leather chair and I look up at him from under my lashes. His stomach is taut and faintly tanned and I lick that smooth fine line of hair that reaches from his belly button down to his core.

My God, he's gorgeous. I mean, *gorgeous*. Is there any movie star who can compete with his looks? Any rock star? Anyone at all? Not for me, anyway. Cary Grant is dead, so are Paul Newman and James Dean. Alexandre isn't like other modern men. He is *beyond*. He has the kind of charisma Hollywood actors used to have. Mysterious. Brooding. Just a look from him could weaken a nun. Never in my life had I imagined I would be attracted to a man so much younger than myself, yet here I am relishing the anticipation as I am about to go down on him.

"If you'd had an outie that would have been a deal breaker," I tell him with a naughty smile.

"An outie? What's that?"

"An innie or an outie – the way your belly-button is. I'm not a fan of outies – yours is perfect."

"Lucky, then."

"Very lucky."

I pull his boxer briefs carefully over his massive erection and wonder how other men must feel if they catch a glimpse of Alexandre – even 'resting' he's extremely well endowed. Love is like snow, you never know how many inches you're going to get. And I've lucked out.

He edges his butt up a fraction and I roll the boxer briefs down, taking my time. Eye candy. Deeelicious. I'm savoring every second of this sweet treat I'm about to devour.

I lean up and nuzzle my head against his strong chest. His torso's not 'pumped' like some men who work out. No, his is an integral strength, the muscles taut and lean but not bulky. I breathe in his scent, stroking my nose along his pecs. His nipples are firm and flat – I lick one, flickering my tongue around, sucking on it hard until he groans quietly. His erection flexes and he bucks his hips up a touch, as if that part of his anatomy is saying, 'me too'.

Don't worry, I think – you next, you perfect specimen. I'm still on my knees and I dip my head further south, tracing my tongue down his taut stomach, then taking his crown gently between my lips, nipping the satiny crest with just my pursed lips, no teeth, pulling and tightening them around the smooth head of his proud penis. A whimper of pleasure escapes my throat and I take it all in now, as much as I possibly can, holding the root of his shaft with my tightened fist, controlling it so I don't gag with his size.

Alexandre growls quietly. "Fuck, Pearl. You're incredible."

His words spur me on. I feel the pulse of my clit – knowing I'm driving him wild is my aphrodisiac. This is all about him now. This is my gift. I hollow my cheeks to create suction and move my head up and down along his thick length. My golden hair is falling over his stomach and he brushes it away from my face so he can see me work on him, as he bites his lower lip with pleasure.

"Nobody has ever given me such a good…oh fuck, Pearl baby, you're the best…oh fuck…I love this so fucking much."

'Baby you're the best.' I think of *The Spy Who Loved Me*…. *Nobody does it better…Just keep it comin'*…

One hand of his is gripping the nape of my neck and the

other clawing the chair. He's driving his hips upwards to meet my actions and he's moaning now, almost scowling. I flicker my tongue on the end of his crown and then suck hard back down. That's it - he bursts inside my mouth in a hot rush, emptying himself with a cry.

"Oh baby, can't get enough of you." His hands are on my breasts again, kneading them, cupping them. I suck harder, making sure I have all of his cum, every last drop.

His hard buttocks relax their tension and his climax is spent. A rumbling growl of contentment escapes his throat; low and satisfied. "Thank you, baby, for making me forget," he says. "And making me remember how insanely in love I am with you."

He then gives one last, unexpected thrust and another rush spurts into my mouth. I suck it all in, relishing him. I rim my tongue around the top to wash him clean, kiss him there, then lick my lips like a lioness savoring her prey, satisfied at a 'job' well done. Alexandre's sperm is mine, and mine alone. No other woman in the world is getting any.

His semen belongs to *me*, I think greedily – to swallow, to smear on my tits, to lavish between my thighs and all the way inside me.

That bitch, Laura, isn't getting one single drop.

11

Alexandre announced yesterday that we're going to Paris to visit his mother. I was worried about flying but I am past eight weeks, the most vulnerable period for clots or unforeseen problems and my gynecologist has given me the green light. I even rang the Indian doctor to double check and she confirmed it was okay, but to drink plenty of fluids and not sit in my seat without moving for too long a period. We'll be flying by private jet, anyway, so the stress factor will be almost nil. Call me a carbon footprint culprit, I am.

However, my guilt is alleviated as our plane will be full. We are taking a posse of people with us. Daisy and Amy, and some underprivileged twelve year-old girls from the Bronx, along with two of their teachers with whom Daisy has been working. They are planning a sightseeing trip; Alexandre is paying for everything; the accommodation and all expenses.

Five days.

That's one of the things I love about him so much. He shares his wealth. He believes in waving magic wands for people – one kind gesture, one experience of a lifetime for a child could change their outlook on the world, forever. That's what he believes, and I agree. Yes, we could both be sitting in our private jet (did I say 'our'???) sipping champagne and feeling gloriously glamorous, but giving something back is the biggest buzz of all. It may be chaos, though, eight kids (nine, including Amy) screaming and squealing with excitement. The Eiffel Tower, Montmartre, Notre Dame, The Louvre, La Place Vendôme (where my beautiful pearl necklace came from), and all the other delights and secrets of that magnificent city; whatever we can squeeze into five days.

I never have been to Paris. When I was a child, we went to the South of France, traveling from Italy by train and then back to Rome again where we were based. I imagine that everybody should visit Paris at some time in their lives; I hope it will be as splendid as people say.

While I'm in Paris, Alexandre will go to London to visit the dreaded Laura. They've spoken a couple of times on the phone, arguing, mostly. He has been trying to dissuade her, meanwhile, also trying to come up with some kind of plan in his head. She's adamant – she wants him to go to London and produce his seed for her, no matter what. He even told her that he feared he had a recessive genetic disease or sickle cell anemia - anything to try and put her off - but she's not buying it.

I feel powerless; all I can do is watch the show unravel. Perhaps a double bill. I'm on tender hooks.

Anyway, Alexandre has managed to not commit himself to any promise. One thing I've learned about him is that he doesn't like lying and he is, ostensibly, honorable. Okay, he may not disclose everything, may keep things to himself but, basically, he's an honest person. He's not going to promise Laura something and double cross her; it simply isn't his style. All those times I had accused him in my head of being untruthful when, in fact, he wasn't at all. He has never actually lied to me. He may have kept information at bay, but he has never *lied*.

He hasn't told Laura anything concrete, has made no promises except that he'll see her face to face and 'work something out'. He has told *me*, however, that she isn't getting one droplet of his sperm and that I must stop worrying – it's his dilemma and he'll sort it out. I wish I were the type of woman who could sit back and relax, just worry about what shoes I should wear, or what wallpaper to choose. Alas, I can hardly think of anything else except the Laura drama.

I just can't believe anybody would stoop so low, especially someone as proud as she is. I still have this vision of her standing at her front door like some glorious ship's figurehead in her blue satin robe, pretending that she'd had afternoon sex with Alexandre. Like a fool, I was gullible enough to believe her. The other day, I asked Sophie about the phone call (when Laura chatted away to her in perfect French when I was sitting right there in her living room). Sophie laughed and said that Laura must have been talking to the speaking clock. '*At the third stroke the time will be...*' Or perhaps, she said, she programmed a call to come through to herself from her cell phone. Whatever, Sophie said they hadn't spoken.

There is no doubt that Laura is a clever, scheming woman and, as she said herself, like a Rottweiler with a bone. I really don't want my fingers chewed off, but at the same time, how dare she get away with any of it? It just wouldn't be fair. Finally, at age forty, I have found love and have the chance to start a family and Laura comes along with her bacteria-laden, wooden spoon to stir it all up. If Alexandre doesn't manage to get rid of her, I will. I need to think of Plan B.

I wonder if her nature wasn't always like that, and Alexandre was too young, too sweet to see her true colors. I find it hard to believe that she has become this way from the accident or from medication. Her conniving demeanor suits her a little too well – she looks too comfortable in her own skin.

Meanwhile, James is still missing in action. Laura has told Alexandre 'he's taking a holiday'. I know I seem like some foolish amateur super-sleuth (not so super) but Laura was convinced that Alexandre would get back together with her – perhaps James was in the way? If she's capable of blackmail…what else could she do?

My suitcase is packed. What to wear? I have visions of sophisticated Parisian women tottering about in Christian Louboutins with chic haircuts, but Alexandre tells me that I may be disappointed, that Parisians are no more glamorous than anybody else.

There are so many paintings I want to see in 'the flesh'; the *Mona Lisa, Venus de Milo,* just for starters. So many pastries I need to sample, so many…of everything, I'm feeling giddy with nerves.

Alexandre and I are set up at the George V, one of Paris's most opulent hotels. It describes itself as 'located just steps from the Champs-Elysées, with private terraces that command all of Paris, lovingly restored 18th-century tapestries, and a defining spirit of elegance and charm, Four Seasons Hotel George V, Paris redefines luxury in the City of Light.'

Every word is true. He couldn't have picked a more stunning place.

So far, I am wandering around with flutters in my stomach, not so different from the first time I set eyes on Alexandre. The hotel, in itself, is a feast for the senses, let alone the rest of Paris. We are staying in the Presidential Suite – I dare not even imagine the cost, but Alexandre has insisted that I experience Paris in all its glory.

He didn't care to stay with his mother, as he wants us to be completely free and not feel obliged to hang out with them if we don't want to. I have mixed emotions about meeting her; I can't shake off the fact that she is a *murderess*. I am partly in awe that she had the guts to go through with it, but also horrified. Surely, there could have been another way? Why couldn't she have escaped in the dead of night and hidden in a small village in South America somewhere? But murder? I look forward to meeting her, with both trepidation and wonder.

Daisy insisted on staying with the group. Alexandre has rented an apartment for them, replete with kitchen and plenty of room for everyone to run about and make a mess. The girls have all been rendered speechless and are less wild than I had imagined; a lot of them never having left New York, let alone visit another country. One of them asked if French Fries came from France – a good question and it made me laugh. Although we'll be spending time with them,

I am primarily here to be with Alexandre and meet his family, except for when he goes to London.

This evening, Alexandre and I will be alone for a romantic dinner. As we walk into the foyer, a smell of flowers invades my nostrils – the floral arrangement of purple orchids is breathtaking. Bunches of blue hydrangeas, orchids and delphiniums are balanced on the edge of tall vases. Red dahlias are used sparingly for contrast. Indigo-blue, purple, mauve – all theses matching tones complement each other in a harmonious dance of color. I'm in a daze.

"You know why I always pick this place?" Alexandre asks me without waiting for an answer. "Because of the famous flower arrangements here, designed by the florist extraordinaire, Jeff Leatham. I can always be guaranteed to walk into another world when I arrive at the George V. After a tense meeting, it's what I always crave."

"So you never stay at your mother's or with Sophie?"

He hands over his credit card to the concierge. "Not often. I like to be free to do my own thing. Not be beholden to anyone. Besides, here it's all perfect. If I need to borrow an umbrella it's there. The towels are fluffy and plentiful, I can order room service when I want. The suite comes with my own private gym. The spa is relaxing, the massages exquisite – you get the picture."

"You've become a spoiled business man with a penchant for luxury."

"Yes, I'm guilty. Sue me." He gives me a sly wink.

"Bonsoir, monsieur." The concierge rattles away to Alexandre in French while I survey the beautiful surroundings. Our bags have already been whisked away from us, and we're free to meander.

We wander through the lobby to an inner courtyard open

to the elements, and I see that these same, stunning orchids in the floral displays have been suspended in the air by seemingly invisible threads, covering the expanse as if they are floating in the air. Instead of a carpet of color, it is like a cloud of color and reminds me of Alexandre's lavender fields at his house in Provence.

When we arrive at our suite, our bags have been delivered ahead of us. It is stunning. The walls are decorated in China blue and white brocade. The place is the size of a generous apartment with two bedrooms, a living room, a dining room, a private gym and three bathrooms. The rooms boast antique, Louis XIV furniture, crystal chandeliers, huge sofas, a dining room table and chairs, and even a marble fireplace overhung with a vast Italian gilt mirror. The master bedroom has sumptuous king-size bed which is majestically backed with swathes of the same blue fabric. The oversized, marble bathroom includes a steam room, sauna, bidet and a private walk-in dressing room, plus a guest powder room, no less. We could have fit Daisy's entire entourage in here but we have it all to ourselves. Really, it seems a shame that we have to leave this hotel for even five minutes. We are in *Paris* - that, in itself is enough of a treat - a broom closet would have been enough – but this? This is sinful.

Alexandre is eying me up with amusement. "Don't tell me you're feeling guilty?" He knows me so well – funny how he can read my thoughts just by my expression.

"Not guilty, just…well, this is overwhelming. Just coming for a cocktail to the George V would be enough, but this is—"

"You're not allowed cocktails, chérie."

"Don't I *know* it! Not allowed anything I yearn for."

"Only three more weeks, baby, till your trimester is up,

and then you can have what you want most."

The Weapon of Mass Destruction or, as I now see it, the *Tool of Creation.*

He steps closer and lays his arms about my shoulders, drawing me into him, inhaling me as if I were one of the sweet-smelling floral arrangements.

"You know how much I think about fucking you?" His eyes light up, then narrow into lascivious slits.

"Sometimes you frighten me," I say, the way Little Red Riding Hood might have said to the Big Bad Wolf, while licking his chops.

"I'll go slow, but boy, am I going to do things to you the moment I can."

"You could now," I suggest, gripping the collar of his shirt and pulling him towards me.

"I wouldn't trust myself. Anyway, waiting makes the prize all the sweeter, chérie. I'm a patient man."

His face meets mine and he kisses the corner of my mouth, letting his lips trail even softer kisses along my jawline. I tilt my head up and he runs his lips down my neck making little nips as he pulls me tightly to him, as if he never wants to let me go. I feel his erection pressed up against my belly and I part my mouth, my eyes closed.

"You smell so good," he breathes. One of his hands grips my waist and the other caresses my stomach, sketching his fingertips about the curves. "Nice, I can feel that there's life inside of you."

"It's too early to feel a heartbeat though, isn't it?"

"Not a heartbeat, but I feel a little belly growing. Very sexy. There's nothing more erotic than a pregnant woman. Well, a pregnant woman carrying *my* child, anyway."

My jaw suddenly clenches; his words make me remember

something extremely unpleasant. "When are you going to London?"

He winces. "I don't want to think about Laura, right now. I just want to enjoy this evening with you and savor every second with the woman I'm in love with."

He parts my lips with his tongue and begins a demanding but slow kiss, probing his tongue inside my mouth and then clasping his teeth gently about my lower lip. A deep growl stirs somewhere deep inside him. He lets go and murmurs, "Sorry, that was a bit rough - you bring out the beast in me, Pearl."

"I bring out the *best* in you," I whisper against his perfect mouth, and then return his kiss, clinching my hands about the back of his neck and pulling his head to mine so there is no space between us. Our tongues begin their erotic tango of tease and pull, tantalizing and coaxing, hot and sensual. I can feel my nipples harden, my stomach pool with desire. I stroke my tongue along his and he moans into my mouth. "I'd do anything for you, chérie. I'd kill for you - I'd do anything to protect you, my precious Pearl."

"Me too," I reply. "I'd do anything. And I swear, I'll never run from you again, no matter what."

"Dance with me."

"I didn't know you liked dancing."

"There are a few things about me you've yet to find out," he tells me in a soft, enigmatic voice. He takes out his iPod and puts on a song a slow, sexy salsa beat, sung in French.

"What's this?"

"*Mon Ami* by Kim. Listen to the lyrics – the words are perfect for us, chérie – they tell our story."

He places his hands around the small of my back and begins to languidly move his hips in time with the music. He presses his thigh in between my legs and keeps up a sweet pressure as he rocks his groin with the rhythm of the beat, leading me about the room in slow circles. He's a great dancer. I relax into him, letting him guide me. My French isn't perfect but I get the gist what Kim is singing about. Mon Ami – my friend. I listen to the words, catching snippets of bits I understand....*nobody can separate us....I'd do anything for us...I would do anything for you... ...I'll be there for you...you need me...you can count on me...only you can enter my secret garden...I want to share everything with you...the good and the bad.*

True, this song was written for us.

"What else are you hiding from me?" I whisper into his hair.

"I'm a black-belt in Taekwondo."

Ripples of excitement shimmer through me. There is nothing sexier that a trained killer who knows how to control himself. "That figures. I always wondered where those thigh muscles came from," I say, pressing myself even harder against his leg. Can you break blocks in two?"

"I can break a lot of things in two, chérie," he says, turning me with the rhythm. "I *can* but I usually don't."

"Just so long as you don't break my heart in two."

His lips curve upwards and he turns me again, leaning me back a little. I arch, relishing the sensation as he locks his mouth on my throat, kissing me there, then trailing his lips across my shoulders. I'm wearing a thin, cotton tank top and goose-pimples sprinkle themselves all over my sensitive body. He pulls me close again and nips my earlobe seductively.

"What other secrets have you been hiding from me?" I whisper.

"That I joined la *Légion Etrangère*."

The French Foreign Legion – some of the toughest men in the world. A fighting force designed to make use of prisoners and convicts, offering them a better life, people with no families and nowhere to go – men with criminal records. Nice.

"I thought only madmen joined the French Foreign Legion," I tease.

He sways his hips to the rhythm of the music, cupping my butt and murmurs, "We came from over a hundred and forty different countries. True, some of the men had very dubious pasts and criminal records, but they were some of the most loyal, trustworthy people in the world. They don't let axe murderers sign up any more, though. These days, they do screen recruits but yes, there are some pretty tough characters who join. It offers men a second chance. When you join up you get a new name, a new identity – you become a blank canvas."

"A killing machine," I say.

He laughs and then nibbles my ear. I get that brain-numbing feeling again, but I want to know more about this dark horse who is my husband to-be, so I don't let it distract me, which is obviously his intention. *Geez, how many more secrets does Alexandre Chevalier have?*

"So, how long were you in the French Foreign Legion?"

"You sign up for five years. I was fifteen but I forged my I.D. and managed to fool the recruiting officer. I was there for just under eighteen months when my mother found out where I was and reported them for recruiting someone underage. In the end, I got sent home."

"They didn't realize?"

"I looked older than my years. Maybe they did have an inkling but turned a blind eye, until my mother got on their case. I did well there. I was a force to be reckoned with at that age – I was pretty wild. They wanted me to come back when I was eighteen but I had other interests by that point."

"How come you never told me all this about your past?"

"I'm a businessman now – I left that part of me behind."

I have a feeling it must have been gruesome so that's why he didn't want to tell me - trying to forget. I want to ask him how many men's lives he's taken, but I stop myself. Do I really want to know? Killing obviously runs in his family's blood; makes up his DNA.

I tighten my hold on him, instead, "A businessman, huh? You're my own, private Michael Corleone."

He sniggers. "Is he your secret hero?"

"Al Pacino when he was young playing him. Yes."

"Very…um…what can I say? Quite a ruthless figure."

"He had to be. He had no choice."

"External forces."

"Yes," I agree. "External forces."

"Well, we both know about that, don't we?"

"We do," I reply, nestling my head against the crook of his neck. He smells so good and he is mine. All mine.

The song has ended. My heart's racing from the measured sensuality of our dance; we're united by the lyrics, understanding each other's dark passengers who travel beside each of us – our shadows, our alter egos. I like bad boys, obviously. Anthony was right. Nobody else had been dark enough for me…until I met Alexandre. Perhaps, in another era, in other circumstance, I could have been Bonnie to his Clyde. A fantasy, but one that I can almost taste.

"Dinner?" he asks.

"Yeah, I'm feeling a little hungry." I know he's taking me downstairs to *Le Cinq* – famous for its delicious cuisine.

"Me too – but I think I'll have a little snack first." His green eyes glimmer with irony.

He lifts up my top, unhooks my bra, pushing it away from my breasts very slowly and deliberately, then begins to suck my nipples, one by one. Our dance has me already turned on, as it is, but this...? My eyelids are doing their fluttering thing which means I'm entering the zone...oh my.... He holds my body steady as he feeds on me like a vampire - pressing that strong, Taekwondo thigh tight between my legs. I'm on fire. The dance was a prelude...making me desirous for more. Lately, I keep wanting more...oh wow...his sucking feels incredible. His soft hair is tickling my skin, my nipples might as well be my vagina, itself. I feel so turned on. This is numbing my brain...turning me into a sex zombie...oh my God...oh wow... he's feeding on me and it feels...out of this freakin' world. The next thing I'm aware of, in my semi state of unconsciousness, is a rippling orgasm pushing its way through my hot, moist kernel crashing in a giant wave. I cling to him and moan out his name.

"Alexandre....oh Jesus....aaah."

He stops suckling and just flickers his tongue against my nipple as I float down slowly from my pedestal amidst the clouds.

Déjà-vu all over again.

12

The next morning, Alexandre decides that the best way for me to get a feel of Paris is for us to just amble about and avoid the teeming tourist spots. He tells me that Paris is a *feeling*, not just a city. Interesting.

He's already dressed in jeans and a black T-shirt and I'm lounging in bed, propped up with a sinful amount of down pillows like a princess in a vast, sumptuous throne. We're enjoying a huge spread of breakfast, devouring mouthwatering *patisseries* – breakfast in bed. Half of me doesn't want to leave our suite, ever. I've had a long lie-in this morning and feel well rested.

This pregnancy is definitely making me tired. Luckily, I have only had a little morning sickness but the idea of rushing about the city, cramming in every sight is exhausting me just thinking about it.

"Don't worry, chérie, the best of Paris isn't very big. We don't have to go anywhere in particular. And if you get tired, we'll hail a cab."

I take a long sip of freshly squeezed orange juice. "I'll be fine; I'm not some fragile egg that will break."

"I don't want to take any chances. Daisy and her entourage have already set off – they'll be chomping at the bit."

"She called?" I still don't use a cell phone so Alexandre is taking all my calls. I feel as if I have some extremely handsome PA.

"I told her you were mine today and that I didn't want to share you."

"Oh."

"She insists, anyway, that we have our romantic break together, that you get plenty of shut-eye and she won't hear of coming along and disturbing the peace with nine unruly children."

"They were being so jaw-droppingly quiet yesterday, though. They were going about open–mouthed in total awe."

"Not anymore – they're rampaging through the streets of Paris. Last night, they took a boat trip on the Seine and today it's the Eiffel Tower followed by the Louvre."

I sink back again into the plumped-up pillows, secretly not wanting to go anywhere. "And what about us?"

"I'm tempted to keep you here as my hostage."

"I might be all too willing and not very hostage-like."

He pulls back the drapes and gazes out of the window. "It's sunny out. A rare treat in Paris in winter. We can meander through the Rive Gauche along the river, or just pass by La Place de La Concorde and through Le Jardin des Tuileries. Then I thought we could have lunch with my mother."

My stomach flips. I'd momentarily forgotten about his mother – *the murderess*. Maybe she'll hate me, the way Sophie did at the beginning. I say nothing and smile. "How lovely."

"Don't be nervous, chérie, she won't bite."

"You can tell I'm nervous?"

"Yes, Pearl. I usually know what you're feeling; you're not very good at hiding your emotions." His crooked smile edges across his face and his eyes crinkle with mirth.

"I amuse you, Monsieur Chevalier?"

"Yes, you do. You make me laugh. The first time I met you, you told me that you were into classic TV shows like *I Love Lucy* and *Bewitched*. I knew, right then, that you had a silly, self-depreciating sense of humor and that you were someone who didn't take herself too seriously. I thought that was very brave of you to lay your cards on the table, like that, when it was obvious you liked me."

"I was trying to play it cool. I felt like a total idiot afterwards, I can tell you. Thought I'd blown my chances."

He comes and sits at the edge of the bed. He's been up and dressed for hours. I'm still naked, wearing nothing but Chanel N° 5, bathing in the luxurious zillion-count sheets.

He strokes my face with the back of his fingers. "You're not afraid to show your girlish side – that's unusual. You'll make a great mother, Pearl."

"You think so?"

"I know so."

"What? Because I act like a little girl, myself? Connect so well to my inner child?" I joke.

"Don't laugh. People spend years of therapy trying to achieve that."

I sigh. "Therapy…that's something I've never even dared try. I really should have seen someone after my nightmares about the rape but…I guess I was too chicken. I use swimming to let it all out, instead."

He pouts and blows his mouth the way the French do when they're discussing politics or something important (food, sometimes), and says, "We're all fucked up, one way or another. At least you and I are in this together. We make a good dysfunctional team."

I giggle. "You're right, we've met our match, the pair of us." My eyes stray from his intense gaze to the classic paintings in the room and the elaborate décor and I say, almost in a trance, "You know, some people assume you have everything all neatly worked out as you get older. It's true that you become a bit wiser, yet I'm still the same person inside as when I was seven years old. Certain things never change. You can put on make-up and heels. You can have a kick-ass job, but if you're a sensitive soul you're still a child inside, no matter how hard you try to hide it."

I think back to our meeting in the coffee shop and add, "You saw my girlish side but you were meant to find me sophisticated and *glamorous*, Alexandre, and the height of….*je ne sais quoi*. I was wearing a suit!"

"The suit didn't fool me – which, by the way - I wanted to rip off the second I saw you and get my hands on that sexy ass underneath." He puts his warm hand under the bed clothes and gives me a little pinch on my butt.

"You don't think my ass is too big?"

"Why do women always ask that question?"

"Ah, caught you! Avoidance. You don't want to answer. So you *do* think I have a big butt."

He laughs. "There should be a Barbie doll with a wind up key that says," (imitating a robotic, high-pitched squeak), " 'Do you think my butt looks big in these jeans?' Your ass is perfect, Pearl. And you *know* it."

I want to say, *Laura doesn't think so*, but I stop myself. I don't want thoughts of that witch to spoil my reverie in Paris.

"What else did you think of me when we met?" I ask, waving my fishing hook about.

"In English, when you're describing something or someone really special you have that expression, 'gem'. Like, when I bought my apartment, the real estate agent described it as a 'real gem'. Well, in France we say a 'rare pearl.' So when I met you and you told me that your name was Pearl, it confirmed everything."

"What did it confirm?"

"That I wanted you. I decided, then and there, that I must have you." He winks at me and runs his finger along my neck.

"You were subtle about it, though. Pretty slow."

"Buying a woman a string of Art Deco pearls after you've only been on one date together is subtle?"

"No, you're right – that was pretty intense but…well…you didn't jump my bones straight away – you wouldn't even come in for a night cap – a knight cap," I say (pun on the word knight - his last name, Chevalier, ha ha ha).

"The 'wham bam, thank you ma'am' method isn't my style, Pearl. I knew you needed time. Needed to be wooed gently. I had a sense that you were damaged and vulnerable on the inside but fancied yourself as some tough-nut New Yorker. I wasn't mistaken."

"I *am* a tough-nut New Yorker! You should see me doing deals – I can be mean."

He presses his lips to my nose. "You can pretend to be mean but you don't have a mean bone in your body."

"I can be a bitch, trust me."

He laughs. "You and Sophie have a lot in common, funnily enough."

"Will Sophie be at lunch today?"

"If she is, she'll only be there to see us. As I said, she doesn't visit my mother so often."

"I guess I'd better get out of bed. What should I wear?"

"Sneakers, as we'll be walking. Jeans. You really don't need to make an effort."

"Are you sure? Your mother's Parisian."

"Actually, she's not. She's originally from the Alsace region in the east."

"German stock."

"Yes, well, many Germans like to think of that region as theirs, still. After all, that part of the world did once belong to them."

"So that's where you get your height from? And your penchant for be organized and making lists," I tease.

His lips curve slightly. "Amongst other things."

"What other things?"

"Ah, that would be telling. You'll have the rest of your life to find out."

"What? You have *more* secrets? I thought you'd told me everything!"

"It would be a bit dull if you knew *everything* about me, wouldn't it?"

"Something tells me, Alexandre Chevalier, that life with you will never be dull."

The sky is mostly blue and clear but the air crisp. I pull up the collar of my coat and link my arm tightly with Alexandre's. I don't say much as everywhere I turn there is some spectacular building saying 'look at me, how proud and stunning I am' and I amble along in a daze. Paris does not disappoint but it's hard to put it into words – Alexandre is right, it's a feeling. A feeling of majesty, grandeur and pride.

We come across the *Grand Palais*, a magnificent *Belle Epoque* landmark and museum with Greek-style columns and a glimmering, glass domed roof supported by heavy cast iron beneath. It looms ahead of us. The *Petit Palais* is nearby, arranged around a courtyard and garden – manicured and laid out symmetrically. I see that Paris is highly structured, nothing left to chance, nothing abandoned, at least, not here, where everything is neat and tended. The buildings face a beautiful arched bridge that crosses the Seine, the artery of Paris.

"That's my bridge," Alexandre tells me with a wink.

"Because it's so beautiful?"

"No, because it's named after me," he jokes. "It's called Alexandre III."

We cross the road and saunter towards it. At either end of the bridge are high stone columns topped with gilded, winged horses overlooking the river as if they are guarding the bridge. The whole way along the sides of the bridge, itself, are cherubs and ornate Art Deco lamps with globes of hand blown glass. Everything is in such tip-top condition, it feels like going back in time a hundred years ago. No filth or soot coats the surrounding buildings or bridge, despite the traffic. No, everything gleams and twinkles as if invisible hands were polishing the stone edifices and as if the horse statues had been gilded with gold-leaf, just last week. Alexandre tells me that it was all restored a few years ago, that the gold is real. I marvel, wondering if this would all still be in one piece if it were New York City. The Parisians must have real respect for their treasures, although he tells me the outskirts of the city are a different story with graffiti everywhere and tower blocks.

We make our way to the middle of the bridge. Behind, in the distance, is the Eiffel Tower and ahead the Seine meanders its way under more elegant bridges. There are some moored boats and barges below. The river swirls in little eddies and I instinctively clutch my belly knowing that there is life inside me; blood and fluids ebbing and flowing through my body just like the river, giving life to this newcomer – our baby. I lean over the bridge and stare into the water below, wondering what our child will be like, and grateful that I have Alexandre back in my life - that I won't be venturing into parenthood alone.

He notices my hand spread across my stomach and asks me, "Was everything okay with your last check-up?"

"It all looked great; the ultrasound shows a tiny beating heart. Just over two more weeks until the trimester is done and then I'll feel completely safe."

He lays his large hand on top of mine. "You'll be fine – it's meant to be."

Paris is one big superlative. Everywhere are tree-lined avenues and stunning historic buildings. I can see that it would take years to do this city justice. We meander slowly back, past the *Petit Palais* towards the *Place de la Concorde*. What I had imagined to be a quaint square is massive, boasting a towering obelisk in the middle, flanked by two grandiose fountains and more historic buildings at one end.

A frisson of excitement runs up my spine. The awesome

beauty and wonder of the architecture against the icy blue of the sky, and the way the square is ideally situated so that you see the most magnificent monuments of the city, including the Arc de Triomphe, the Champs Elysees, the Alexandre III Bridge, the Grand Palais, the Assemblée Nationale, the Tuilleries Gardens, and the Eiffel Tower, all at once, is a testament to how clever the design is. Looking at my little map, my eyes scan all around to find my bearings, even though I don't need a map, having Alexandre by my side. I'm your archetypal American tourist with my sneakers and sensible clothes, clutching a map. Just to add to the look, I whip out my camera and take a few snaps. Alexandre stands there, amused and happy that his city is obviously giving me goose bumps and spreading such a huge grin across my face.

A skinny man in glasses rushes up beside us - we look like sitting ducks; the quintessential sightseers, at least I do. He shuffles up next to me and gushes forth in a heavy accent at breakneck speed without stopping for breath:

"It is in this place that was signed on sixth of February 1778 the Treaty of Friendships and Exchanges between King Louis Sixteenth and the thirteen States Independents of America. Benjamin Franklin counted among the signatories representing the United States... Today at the place even where the King Louis Sixteenth was guillotined, is an obelisk offered by the Egyptians. Where many people came to see falling down the heads formerly, come much there today to admire the view of the Champs-Elysées..."

We both laugh when he says, 'Falling down of heads,' and then Alexandre blurts out something in French. The poor man is mortified and scurries off to see if he can nab some other, more bona fide tourists.

"Poor thing wanted to be our guide for the day, I guess,"

I say. "I forgot that it was you guys who invented the guillotine. Nice touch. So who got beheaded here in this square? I didn't quite catch what that man said."

Alexandre cocks a dark-winged eyebrow at me. "Everybody and his cousin, basically. Marie Antoinette, Louis XVI, Robespierre. They called it la 'Place de la Révolution' in those days. Just in one summer alone, I think it was in 1794, over a thousand people were beheaded here in this square, not to mention the bloodshed going on all over the rest of the country."

"All because of what Marie Antoinette said, 'Let them eat cake' when the people complained there was no bread?"

"Supposedly, she never said that, but that's right – the people were starving and fed up with the unfair tax system and lavish lives of the royalty and aristocracy. Everyone always imagines it was only the peasants that started the Revolution but it was several groups; the intellectuals, the bourgeoisie – even poorer members of the clergy."

I fix my gaze at one of the beautiful stone fountains with mythical bronze figures encircling the basin. In the water below, in the bigger basin, are more characters; their torsos dark bronze, almost black; their mermen and mermaid bottom-halves a beautiful green verdigris, and the fish they hold gilded with gold leaf. Water gushes from the fishes' mouths. Incredible.

Alexandre continues with his history lesson, which is almost drowned out by the sound of gurgling water. "But before all that, things were just as gruesome. Nobility were sometimes entertained by watching convicted criminals being dismembered alive. La Place de la Révolution was payback time when the people punished the nobility for their crimes - not the other way around, as it had always been before."

"My God, France has so much crazy history – enough to make you dizzy," I say as I stare up at yet another sight - the Egyptian obelisk decorated with hieroglyphics - a giant red granite column pointing erect like a rocket to the sky. I smile to myself and think of Alexandre's Weapon of Mass Destruction.

"What are you smirking about?" he asks.

"Nothing, just thinking about what you've been saying."

He's oblivious to my naughty musings and continues with his spiel. "Funnily enough, you lot contributed in some ways to the French Revolution. French troops who served as anti-British mercenaries in America during the American Revolution helped spread revolutionary ideals to the French people."

I laugh. "So you blame us?"

"Didn't you know? The French blame the Americans for everything. I blame you, Pearl."

"For what?"

"For causing a revolution in my heart."

"To have a sexy Frenchman telling me things like that in Paris, itself, is almost sinful."

"I can shut up if you like." He winks at me and a little tremor capsizes my insides. I think of my baby and wonder if he (or she) can feel what I feel; the thrill of absolute love.

I squeeze his hand, glove on glove. "Don't you dare. I want to hear sweet talk for the rest of my life."

Alexandre suddenly envelops his arms about my hips and lifts me into the air, the way my father sometimes did when I was a child. I wrap my legs about him and we kiss. When he sets me down he says, "It feels good, doesn't it, baby, knowing we're getting married? Knowing we share each other's secrets? I've carried such a burden all these years.

What my mother did, my abusive past. Now Laura. Thank God it's all out in the open, finally."

I reply, "I know. What a relief."

As unexpected as the lift was, Alexandre's cell rings. It makes us both jump. He fishes it out of his coat pocket, looks at it and connects the call. "Hi Daisy, where are you all? We're kind of slowly making our way to Notre Dame – very slowly, walking and talking about charming things like decapitated rolling heads and..." He pauses to listen. "You've done all that already? Jesus! Alright, we'll meet for ice cream. We probably won't have one as we're on our way to lunch – well Pearl should, ice-cream is good for her but...perfect. See you there in an hour and a half." He looks at me. "I know it's winter but this ice cream place is very famous." Just as he's putting his phone back in his pocket, it rings again. "Daisy?" But his smile quickly vanishes - a dusky cloud sweeps across his face.

"Who is it?" I mouth, fearing I already know the answer.

Alexandre's lips twitch with a mixture of sadness and anger. "Look, Laura, just calm down." He says nothing, just rolls his eyes. I can hear her screaming through the line, although what she's saying isn't clear. "I can't alright, I have commitments," he says through gritted teeth, his jaw clenched.

I look up at him expectantly, terrified Laura's going to steal him from me – steal our happiness away like the thief she is.

"I told you, I can't fucking well come right now. I have a meeting, I have–" he bites his lip, closes his lids and lets out a menaced groan. She has obviously slammed the receiver down on him. When he opens his eyes again, the green of his irises shine like wet moss. He shoots me an apologetic glance and says, "If I don't go now, she's going to do something crazy. She's going nuts."

"What about lunch with your mother?"

"You'll have to go on ahead without me."

"No way, Alexandre. No. I want to meet your mom with you there."

"Okay, I understand. Well, we'll just have to postpone it, then, and go when I return."

"When will you be back?"

He rakes his hands furiously through his hair. "As soon as I fucking can. Jesus, this bitch is ruining our lives - I could fucking kill her!"

"You mean, you're going to just leave, right now?"

"I have no choice. You could come with me if you like."

"Somehow, I think that might make things worse."

"You're right. If I can get back late tonight, I will. If not, I'll be back tomorrow by midday. I need to sort this shit out, once and for all."

"What are you going to say? Tell her you'll go ahead with the IVF?"

He shakes his head solemnly. "I just don't know."

"Are you going to the airport, right now?"

"That, or the train, which actually might be faster; it's so quick these days - just over two hours. I need to go back to the hotel to get my passport first, just in case I do end up flying. You can get some rest."

"If you're not going to be hanging out at the hotel with me, there's no point. I'll carry on with my walk and meet Daisy, as arranged."

"You're sure?"

"I'm a big girl. This is Paris not South Central LA."

"Well, if you're sure. You can't go wrong and you've got

your map." He points left. "Go through the park, Le Jardin des Tuileries – you'll hit the Louvre – then head across one of the bridges to Isle St-Louis. The ice cream place is famous, it's called Berthillon Glacier. The little island next to it, Ile de la Cité, is right where Notre Dame is. Here, take this." He stuffs a massive wad of Euro notes in my hand and a credit card. "My code is 1492 – Fourteen ninety-two, Columbus sailed the ocean blue. You can withdraw as much cash as you need or punch in that code when you buy things. Treat yourself to whatever you want; go on a spree."

"Don't be silly, Alexandre, I have money."

He widens his eyes as if to say, 'don't argue' and holds me tight against his chest. "I love you, Pearl. Have fun today. Don't exhaust yourself. Just jump in a cab if you get tired. I'll call you at the hotel later."

"I don't have a cell phone, remember."

"I know. But you can call me any time from the hotel and I think you should stay in tonight anyway, and take it easy."

"I will, I'll order room service. I mean, hello, how much punishment is it to slob out in one of the most beautiful hotels in the world?"

"Get Daisy and Amy over – they can spend the night; we might as well make use of that big suite."

"Good idea." I look square into his eyes which are flickering with fear. I have never seen him look that way. Ever. "I love you, Alexandre. Good luck with 'you know who.' I'll support whatever you decide."

"Thanks. I needed to hear that. Although, what that decision will be, I haven't the faintest fucking idea." He gives me a weak smile then hugs me again. We kiss but the kiss isn't romantic. How can it be with Laura as good as standing, right there, between us? He turns on his heel to go and we both look back several times, hardly bearing to let go of each other, even for one second, let alone the whole night.

13

Laura is infiltrating my mind, polluting the beauty I see about me like toxic waste in a meadow. Ten minutes ago, the world was awash with perfection but sank instantly with one jarring phone call.

The Tuileries Gardens are bleak in winter yet breathtakingly beautiful, but I walk along with misty eyes, wishing that Alexandre hadn't been snatched away from me and wondering how in the world he's going to extricate himself from Laura's tangled web. Is it possible that he can convince her to drop this madness? I doubt it. I can't see a way out of this. One thing I have learned about him is his fierce loyalty to his loved ones – he won't let his mother down, of that I'm sure. He feels responsible – had he not gotten involved, those stupid, hip bits and teeth remnants would still be hidden in her attic. It's true; in a sense it is his fault that Laura got her bony hands on it all. But poor man, how could he have envisioned what could have ensued? How could *anybody* have imagined? Not even the script writers for *CSI* could come up with such an insane scenario.

The only good thing about having my eyes on the ground, as I scurry along through the park (to avoid people's stares – I'm crying shamelessly now) – is that I miss stepping in some dog poop right in my path. Yes, I'd heard Paris was famous for that. Just like Laura, it is unexpected; a blight on perfection. The gardens have an air of formality with flower beds set out in a pattern; gravel paths lined with rows of trees, so the dog shit seems incongruous here where everything is in such order. A mess left to be picked up by some innocent bystander, or for someone to tread in and have smeared all over their shoe. I think of Laura again – it is as if the dog shit is a symbol of everything that has gone wrong.

I sit down on a stone bench to pull myself together and get my breath back. Not from the walk, but the torrent of emotions churning around my body, draining me of oxygen. I want my baby to feel serene and peaceful inside me, not all riled up and bubbling with rage. Surely they can feel everything?

I raise my head up to the sky as a cloud lifts with the breeze and the blue is once again revealed. A warm sun is welcome with the biting chill and I let it caress my cold cheeks. That feels so good. I think of our baby, again, and take my iPod out of my Birkin and go through my playlist until I find what I'm looking for – *Here Comes the Sun* by George Harrison. I mustn't dwell on Laura. Just a couple of months ago, I thought I had lost Alexandre for good but our bond is stronger than ever. I have *him* and his baby and that's what counts, no matter what happens with this IVF threat. Alexandre loves me, not Laura. *That* is what I am holding onto right now. And I need to trust him to make the right decision.

"This song's for you, little baby," I tell my belly, smoothing my gloved hand over myself. And it's true; the being inside me *is* the sun. Maybe even the 'son.' I don't care if it's a boy or a girl, I am just grateful, and pray that I'll make it to the first trimester, and there won't be any complications with the birth and that he, or she, will be healthy.

The song has lifted my spirits and I continue walking. I'm feeling positive and hopeful. If Alexandre can manage all the thousands of people who work for him in his multibillion dollar empire, surely he can handle Laura. I have faith. It *will* work out.

As I wander through the park, I have the sensation that I'm meandering through an open-air museum, and I'm glad for the distraction. There are classical marble sculptures dotted everywhere – characters from Greek myths and some modern ones, too. A few people are sitting on metal garden chairs placed along the paths or about the octagonal pond. It seems that it is forbidden to sit on the grass in this park, even in summer. I watch water spurt out of the pond's fountain but my gaze gets distracted by a huge Ferris wheel in the distance with the Louvre in the background.

As I approach, I soak up the pure majesty of the Louvre set like a horseshoe in an expansive courtyard – the space in front giving the facade the added grandeur it merits. The modern glass pyramid (that caused such a stir when it was first erected) seems like a rebellious teenager in contrast to the classical Renaissance of the Louvre - probably the most famous museum in the world, once a royal palace. The vast glass and metal pyramid is surrounded by three smaller ones. Being able to see through the pyramid is interesting because it doesn't block out the honey-colored stone of the old Louvre behind. But if I tilt my head, the reflection of clouds gives it a different feel. Do I like the Pyramid? I'm still not sure. There's no doubt in my mind that it's interesting and probably something that needs a lot of mulling over. I could stand here and pontificate all day long.

But I can't, and there's no chance of a visit or I'll be late meeting Daisy. So I continue on my merry way, still humming *Here Comes the Sun* and blanking out my thoughts from any word beginning with L.

I come across a little pedestrian bridge with wooden decking which I realize is the famous *Pont des Arts*. All over the sides are little padlocks clipped to the railings – 'love-locks' with names of lovers written or engraved on each one. One even says 'Bonnie and Clyde.' Another rusted one, has a pink lipstick mark with scratched-on hearts and the initials B and P at each end. Everlasting, locked love, left in Paris. I wonder how many of these couples are still together. As I am reading some of the messages, a man in a black wool hat tells me, "Zee Pont des Arts used to be one of my favorite bridges, now I can't stand to see it. I bet zaire is some jerk selling padlocks near ze bridge, with little hearts on them. He should be shot."

I turn around, surprised that he's talking to me in English. How does he know I'm not French? Do I look so obviously like a tourist? But then I realize I still have the map in my hand. "Oh, you don't like the padlocks?" I ask. "You don't think it's romantic?"

"Ze Pont des Arts used to be a beautiful, delicate bridge, now it looks like it's covered wiz some kind of metallic disease in zis mindless graffiti rusting on ze padlocks. Zis and ze dog crap everywhere." He gesticulates with his arms in the air and blows out air through his lips.

"Yes, I noticed the dog poop," I reply, and Laura shoots into my mind again. "Well bye, have a nice day. Au revoir," I say, and scurry off in the direction of Notre Dame.

I swing my Reverso watch around to Parisian time and see that I won't have a chance to go inside Notre Dame, itself, or I'll be late for Daisy and her gang. The cathedral looks majestic in its Gothic glory, commanding the ancient Île de la Cité with its flying buttresses and extraordinary gargoyles. It's both a chilling and comforting thought to know that heads once rolled in Paris, yet this great stone building still remains through all that turmoil – more real to us than what was once flesh and blood – people that are now no more than words in a history book.

I know I'll need time to explore Notre Dame to do it justice. I shouldn't be worried – I am marrying a *Frenchman*, for Pete's sake - Paris isn't going anywhere fast, so I shouldn't feel I need to do a whirlwind sightseeing trip all in one day. *Chill out, Pearl.* Take your time.

I pass a man playing Edith Piaff's *Non, Je Ne Regrette Rien* on an accordion, and I think back to the conversation I had with Alexandre in LA about regrets, life and external forces. The evidence he didn't destroy – that's sure to be one of his regrets.

The smell of something deliciously sweet wafts before me, and when I turn the corner, there is a wheeled cart with a knobbly-faced old man selling honeyed almonds. I buy a little bag – the last thing I want is ice-cream right now; it's simply too cold. Honeyed almonds are far more tempting.

When I arrive at the ice cream parlor, I see the posse of exhausted twelve year-olds licking their cones with great concentration. Daisy is in a heated discussion with Mary, one of the teachers, and Amy is looking up adoringly at the eldest child in the group; a girl named Vanessa.

"Daisy!" I shout. Amy rushes over and flings her little arms about my legs.

"Auntie Pearl!" I have been promoted to 'auntie' since Christmas.

"Hi guys, hi Mary, hi Susan – hey girls have you been having fun?" I ask the small crowd. They all start shouting at once, squealing about their adventures and discussing which of the outings has been their favorite, so far.

We chat about how beautiful Paris is, and they relay their activities which have been non-stop since dawn. A bus ride, the Eiffel Tower, Notre Dame – I'm exhausted just listening to it.

Then Daisy mouths to me silently, "Take me away from this, Pearl, I'm wiped out!"

I laugh and whisper, "Do you want to come and hang out in the lap of luxury?"

"Yes, I bloody well do! But just us, not the whole lot 'cause they're too wild and excitable." She turns to Susan and says, "Would you mind if Amy and I go off with Pearl for the rest of the day?"

Susan, a lanky woman with glasses and a Trilby hat (who reminds me of Diane Keaton in *Annie Hall*) replies, "Throwing in the towel already, you lightweight?"

"Yes I am, because I know what's next and I think Amy's a little young for it."

"What have you all got planned?" I ask.

"A bicycle tour around the city with a company called Fat Tire."

"*Tire* being the operative word," I joke.

"We saw them this morning by the Eiffel Tower, it

looked really fun," Susan tells me. "Perfect for the girls."

"Wow, you lot are going to know Paris like the back of your hands by the end of this trip. It puts me to shame."

"Shall we get going, then?" Daisy asks eagerly. "Come on Amy, we're going with Pearl back to her hotel."

"Mommy, I want to stay."

Daisy hesitates but then tells her, "No, sweetie, you're still too young. But you'll be back with the big girls tomorrow, all day."

"I hate my age," Amy grumbles to her mother with a pout. "It sucks being five."

"Rubbish. Five is the best age ever. Now come on, or we'll be late for lunch."

Mary, the other teacher on this trip, bustles up to me and says, "Thank you Pearl, you have no idea what this means to the girls - and to us, too. This is an experience of a lifetime." She is the antithesis to Susan and they look like a comic duo. Mary is so round and podgy, all you want to do is squeeze her; next to Susan's towering skinny frame, they could be a female version of Laurel and Hardy.

I smile and reply, "It's not me, but my fiancé. It was his idea. He's the one who organized everything."

"He's so incredibly generous! I mean, our apartment is divine. The spending money he gave us is way too much...I feel...I mean...I don't know how to *repay* that level of kindness, I don't—"

"Just knowing how much fun you're having in France will be payment enough, believe me. He's the kind of person who gets a real kick out of helping people and seeing he can make a small difference."

"I mean, these kids haven't even been out of the Bronx and now one of them is saying she wants to be a pilot, to fly a private jet, one day."

"You see, that's what seeing another slice of life can do," I tell her.

I can tell that Vanessa is Amy's crush. She's an elegant black girl with soulful, sparkling eyes. She bounds up to us and exclaims, "And I'm going to live here in Paris when I grow up, and learn to speak French."

Amy tugs on her mom's coat and asks, "Where are we going for lunch?"

"To the Marais. I'm treating you and Pearl."

"What's the Marais?"

"It's a neighborhood, darling. *Marais* means swamp in French – that's what it was hundreds of years ago. Now it has itty bitty winding streets and lots of galleries, beautiful medieval buildings and amazing boutiques. I'll buy you a present, if you're a good girl."

"I'm always good." Amy looks up at me with her large brown eyes as if to gain an ally and I laugh.

"I'll buy you a gift, too," I whisper, "and maybe you can choose something for each and every one of the girls."

"Cool!"

"See you guys later," Daisy says, linking arms with me and Amy, and pulling us off in the direction of Le Marais.

I wave the group goodbye and I feel relieved that I have a distraction from straying thoughts of Laura and the damage that she's sure to be planning. Let's hope Alexandre can stop her.

How, I don't know, but I'm sure he'll come up with something.

14

Alexandre forced himself to relax against the soft leather of the back seat of the Daimler; anything to ease the tension gathering like sailor's knots in his shoulders. He had Laura on his mind; He was now being driven to her house in Chelsea - she was expecting him.

He and Sophie always used this chauffeur when they came to London; it was so much easier than messing about with diesel-belching taxis with chatty Cockney drivers who wanted to talk about the weather. Not that he was knocking them, no – they were the most knowledgeable taxi drivers of probably any city in the world. They had to pass an exam called The Knowledge, could take you to any tiny corner of London by memory – but still, having a private chauffeur was one of the perks of having money to burn. And it was one of his secret pleasures.

It still felt at odds, that…being so bloody wealthy, yet it was something Alexandre never took for granted. It seemed only yesterday when he was rummaging through his jeans' pockets or picking coins off the floor to scrape up enough money to buy a sandwich or a cup of coffee. Being poor stank, but being rich and not appreciating what you had was worse. That's why he needed to justify that private jet – it made him feel too guilty to swan about the globe in jets without good reason. He felt it was only fair to spread the wealth a bit and share his good fortune. He hoped those Bronx girls were having fun and didn't see it as 'charity,' though. He hated that, being the magnanimous 'do-gooder'. No, it was simply a question of dividing things out, like buying a round of drinks at the pub – a British tradition that he liked. If you had the money, it was your 'round' and if you didn't have enough from your paycheck that week, never mind – you'd do it another day – your mate would pay instead.

Your mate. The pub. That's where he'd met Laura. She was there with a group of friends and they'd started up a conversation. Strange that – as beautiful as Laura was, Alexandre never did have that 'love at first sight' thing with her, the way he did with Pearl. It was more a case of feeling lonely in a new city, a need for companionship. They got talking and then soon started going out to movies together, or art exhibitions. It was a nice change from hanging out with Sophie all the time, and Sophie was in Paris, anyway. He didn't like male company so much, either – it reminded him of *La Légion* and all its madness. When he arrived in London all those years ago, he felt lonely, screwed-up; he needed a friend, wanted some female company, and Laura was right there.

La Légion…a part of his life he'd rather forget. He'd joined up at fifteen, an underage romantic idealist. Death seemed glamorous at the time – even welcome. The French Foreign Legion was infamous for having one of the highest fatality rates of any modern military. He wanted to be one of the 'chosen ones' - feel that he could stand amongst the world's hardest and not even blink.

There were three types of people who joined La Legion. The men who needed to be there, because they had nothing else, the fly-by-night dreamers, and the complete, fucking lunatics.

He never had been sure which category he fit into best – perhaps a mixture of all three.

Alexandre remembered the eerie words of one guy, an Australian, who said, 'I'll get a second chance at achieving something real, anything, even if it's just a shallow grave.'

Alexandre had seen enough shallow graves for a lifetime; bodies blown to smithereens. La Légion was tougher than any army, any professional fighting force. It was no fucking picnic. If he'd stayed, he would probably be dead by now.

He remembered the march of La Légion; *Le Boudin*. Eighty-eight steps a minute. 88, the magic number, the number of pearls on the Art Deco necklace he gave Pearl. He seemed to be wedded to that lucky number. Eighty-eight.

He now gazed out of the car window, humming the first verse of the marching song to himself:

Nous sommes des dégourdis,
Nous sommes des lascars
Des types pas ordinaires.
Nous avons souvent notre cafard,
Nous sommes des légionnaires.

Translated into English was:

We are crafty.
We are rogues.
We are no ordinary guys.
We've often got our black moods,
For we are Legionnaires.

Their motto was - *Legio Patria Nostra* - The Legion is our home. Thank God he had a real home, now, with Pearl. He had been searching all this time and knew he'd finally found what he was looking for.

An unwelcome image of Laura being pregnant flashed before him. He groaned and felt tension clamp at his jaw. He cursed the day she opened her bee-sting lips and asked him the time. He should have just kept her as a friend, not started fucking her. The truth was, that she was pretty unsexy in bed, anyway; all angles and bones - never letting go – too uptight, too neurotic. He felt bad judging someone like that but fuck, he felt no remorse now, in ripping Laura's personality to pieces – she was proving to be a bitch of the first order. But the worst thing was that she didn't even seem to be aware of what a monster she was being. As if all her demands were 'by the by' – the sort of, 'oh by the way, I need a baby and it has to be yours.' As if her actions wouldn't have consequences for all involved. Had she thought of the child, itself? He doubted it. Doubted Laura would have thought far outside the little box that was her own selfish head.

He'd told Pearl that Laura had become 'doolally' because of the accident, but he was now aware that that wasn't quite true. She had always been self-absorbed - it just didn't seem to matter when he was younger. Telling Pearl that – excusing

Laura's behavior - somehow justified having been with Laura in the first place. Modeling hadn't helped her, one bit. Take an egotistical person and shove them into the modeling world, and all it does is magnify the problem. And all that money she'd grown accustomed to with James. She'd become a spoiled brat, used to getting her way.

What a fuck-up! He still didn't know what he was going to say to her. He'd come up with a solution – he'd have to. As much as he had goals and wrote lists, he always played things by instinct. It drove Sophie nuts. Sometimes, he'd go in the opposite direction than planned just before an important business meeting. If he instinctively trusted someone... or the reverse; had a suspicion that someone would double-cross him, a gut feeling, then he might change his course altogether. It had made him a rich man and he wasn't going to change tactics now.

He'd play it by ear. Read Laura by looking into her eyes. Maybe it was all about money and she could be bought off.

He couldn't imagine her as a mother, anyway – surely it was some crazy fantasy of hers? The idea seemed preposterous - the woman could hardly boil an egg. Changing diapers? Forget it – she'd want a 24/7 nanny. Two nannies, in fact, a team of cleaners and God knows what else. He'd talk her out of it. Woo her with cash. Anybody could be bought at a price. Anybody.

Except Pearl, funnily enough. She was the one person he knew who really wasn't motivated by money. He believed that if he lost his whole portfolio, overnight, she wouldn't give a damn. Maybe, she'd even feel relieved.

Oh yes, you could add Elodie to the list. She was even embarrassed by being wealthy; a reaction, no doubt, against her mother – well, Sophie was her step-mother, but it amounted to the same thing. Poor Elodie – such a loner; he wondered if she had ever gone on a real date with a boy. Probably not. She was a nerd, like him, and preferred to stay in and play video games.

Alexandre looked out of the window at Trafalgar Square, home to the landmark, Nelson's Column, proud as ever, guarded by the four, famous lion statues and ridiculous amounts of pigeons. It was erected to celebrate the Battle of Trafalgar, a British naval victory during the Napoleonic wars over France.

It was a pain in the neck being French sometimes; especially in England; he wondered if the two countries would have a love/hate relationship forever. The French had a reputation for being cocky and arrogant and he suspected people saw him that way. Alexandre was fond of London; it was a beautiful city, so he'd asked his driver to take him the scenic route. If it weren't for his impending meeting with Laura he would be enjoying the ride.

His mind shifted to Pearl. His rare pearl. His gem. He missed her already, and it had only been a few hours. It felt great opening up to her the way he had the day before. But it had unlocked so many emotions, and not in a good way. He had never realized the anger he'd silently, and unwittingly, harbored for his mother. It was true – she had abandoned him, her own son at so young an age. But still, he couldn't let her down now, and wouldn't. It was strange the way children could sometimes feel responsibility for their parents. It was common with children of alcoholics, too. His mom had never been a drinker but she had an addictive personality. His father had been her drug and now she relied on Alexandre for emotional support. Not the healthiest of relationships, yet he felt responsible for her happiness, somehow.

Large raindrops, like tears, slid down the glass of the windows as the car crawled along in the traffic. The streets were slick with wet, as usual. When did it not rain in London? The double-decker buses were stopping and starting as people piled in and out of them. It wasn't long ago that Alexandre had been hopping on and off buses; a taxi was a rare treat in those days. He couldn't believe how lucky he'd been with HookedUp - an American Dream if ever there was one – even if he wasn't American.

The Daimler was now cruising through Admiral Arch and along The Mall towards Buckingham Palace where the road was paved in red. He'd like to take Pearl there one day – so many plans, so many things for them to do together. And now there was a baby on the way; it would be fun to watch the Changing of the Guard – children loved that.

Everything was perfect, except for this fucking Laura fiasco.

His buzzing cell jolted him from his rumination and he fished it out of his coat pocket.

"Oui, hallo?" For a moment there, he was in Parisian mode.

The voice was excitable and he recognized it immediately – Anthony.

"Oh Alexandre, I am going crazy with this no cell phone ban thing. I never get to speak to my sister, anymore!"

"She's worried about radiation vibes damaging the fetus."

"So like our hippie parents. Must be the genes. But, of course she's worried, I can totally understand - she's carrying what is going to be the most beautiful baby in the world inside that little stomach of hers. No wonder. I mean, pur-lease. Is she there, by the way?"

"No, she's in Paris and I'm in London."

"Oh my God! No! Alexandre what has she done now – please don't tell me she's leapt out of another bathroom window? What have *you* done? I can't stand the agony of it! Please tell me you two guys are not on some stupid separation thing again."

Alexandre chuckled. "No, not at all. I'm just here on business. Briefly. Pearl's at the hotel. At the George V if you want to call her there this evening. In the Presidential Suite."

"Well, excuse *me* your royal highness, Mr. President."

Alexandre's lips tipped upwards. Anthony always brought a smile to his face, especially recently, since he had changed his tune with Pearl and was being so sweet to her.

Anthony blabbered on, "I'm glad I got you, anyway, because I want to be reassured that your wedding is going ahead as planned and that my sister is not behaving like Lucille Ball or Rachel Green from *Friends*. Is she acting like a grown-up or is she-"

"She's being extremely grown-up," Alexandre interrupted. "Don't worry, everything's going very smoothly with us." *If it weren't for goddam Laura, that would be true.* Alexandre added, "In fact, we're crazy in love with each other, more than ever, so don't worry, Anthony."

Anthony sighed in a sort of sing-song. "Aah, so cute. Well, I'll call her later at the hotel, then. Good luck with your business, Michael."

Did he just say Michael? "Excuse me?"

"I said good luck, Mr. Corleone, with your business meeting."

Alexandre chuckled. "Thanks. I need it."

"Make, whoever it is, an offer they can't refuse."

Anthony's comment made Alexandre freeze for a second. *Make Laura an offer she couldn't refuse?* Tempting.

Very bloody tempting.

The car drew up at James's and Laura's house.

James...where the fuck was he? He hadn't returned one single call.

Alexandre rarely felt nervous but a foreboding feeling suddenly clenched his gut. Laura could be dealt with; why he felt so jumpy, he couldn't explain.

His long fingers gripped the brass doorknocker and he rapped at her black front door. He'd heard, once, that lions for doorknockers were a good idea; it kept the burglars at bay – a subliminal message – 'don't fuck with me'. Laura did have a way of alienating people. She never had been much of a girls' girl. Not like Pearl, who everyone warmed to, straight away.

He waited. No reply. Rain suddenly shot down like cold needles and he'd left his umbrella in the car and told his driver to come back later. He knocked again. Nothing. Where was Mrs. Blake? Fuck Laura. Making him wait like some lackey. Typical. He remembered that he still had his key to the garage; he'd forgotten to give it back.

He set off around to the back towards the mews. He unlocked the side door to the garage. It was empty and seemed sad without his DB5, as if crying out for companionship. If it was true what Laura said about James losing all his money, they'd be selling up soon. Who knew? Maybe the bank already owned the house.

The door to the garden was unlocked.

The grass was long and hadn't been mowed for a while; a sure sign that things with James and Laura had gone downhill. They'd always had a gardener. That meant she'd really want to take Alexandre to the cleaners, big time. That was, if he was able get this crazy baby idea out of her head, and pay her off instead.

He opened the kitchen door and thought how easy it would have been for somebody to break in. It was eerily quiet.

He shouted out. "Laura? Hello? Is anyone home?"

Nothing. Almost silent. Except the tick, tock of an old grandfather clock.

"Hell…o…ooo? Anyone in? Mrs. Blake?"

Just then, Alexandre heard a noise and nearly jumped out of his skin.

15

"To err is human, to loaf is Parisian," Daisy tells me with a rebellious look in her eye. We're lounging on my king-size bed in the Presidential Suite of the George V. Amy is sprawled out on the floor, busy with one of her coloring books. We ladies are drinking champagne (I am allowing myself two sips) and reclining like Marie Antoinette in the lap of luxury.

"To err is human, to loaf is Parisian," I repeat with amusement. "Who said that?"

Daisy sips her champagne. "Victor Hugo."

"The one who wrote *The Hunchback of Notre Dame?*"

"That's the one. What did you think of Notre Dame, Pearl?"

"I didn't have time to go in, just stood there mesmerized by its grandeur, gazing at those crazy gargoyles."

"Well, I have to say, I know it's wicked, and I'm only telling you this, because I know you'll keep it a secret, but I preferred just hanging out with you this afternoon. There's only so much sight-seeing you can do in one day. So glad I escaped." She takes another swig of champagne. "Let's have a butcher's then?" she asks, grabbing one of my shopping bags.

"What did you say?"

"Let's have a look inside that bag."

"No, what was that word you used?"

"Butchers. Butcher's hook. A look. Let's have a butchers. It's Cockney rhyming slang."

"What else can you say?"

"I can hail a sherbet."

"What's that?"

"A sherbet is a cab."

"How does that make sense?"

"Sherbert dab. Cab. Are you going to use the dog, then and call Alexandre?"

"The dog?"

"You're so slow, Pearl. Dog and bone. Phone."

"So you use the first word, but not the second?"

"Exactly, or it's too obvious. It was invented, or evolved, rather, to confuse people. Like a private language so nobody knew what they were talking about."

"So Cockneys are Londoners?"

"All Cockneys are Londoners but not all Londoners are Cockneys. I mean, I'm a Londoner but I'm hardly Cockney. I speak the Queen's English."

"So what makes someone a true Cockney, apart from their accent?"

"You have to be have been born within the sound of the Bow Bells; a church called St. Mary-le-Bow in the East End of London. So pick up the dog, then, Pearl. The dog and bone – pick up the phone. You've been itching to call him all day."

"You're right, I have."

This is so awkward. I'm dying to divulge all to Daisy but of course, I can't. If I tell her about Laura's blackmail she'll want to know the whole story, and I'm sworn to secrecy. She knows Alexandre is in London but I've told her he's on business and just had to drop by Laura's to pick something up. Even that got her suspicious. I realize that it wasn't the best plan, after all, to have her over this evening, although I love hanging out with her. I lean over take a deep breath and grab the receiver of the hotel phone. I dial Alexandre's cell. It rings and rings until his voicemail picks up.

"Why isn't he answering?" I grumble under my breath. I leave a message. "Hey honey, just calling from the hotel. We had a lovely long day having lunch in the Marais, hanging out and shopping. Call me, I'm worried about you." I slowly hang up and look at Daisy. "Just...you know, he had an important business meeting with some new clients."

I hate lying to Daisy. She arches her eyebrows and I feel instantly guilty, as if she can read my mind. I need to ply her with more champagne. All I can think about is what Laura is going to say and do, and what Alexandre's reaction will be. I pour us both another glass.

"Isn't this delicious?" I say, taking a long sip. "I love pink champagne. So girly."

"Yeah, men aren't into it, so much, are they? It *is* a very girly thing. Hey, Pearl, put the dress on you bought."

A little voice pipes up from the carpet. "Yes Auntie Pearl, put that pretty dress on."

"Oh, by the way," and Daisy lowers her voice to an almost inaudible whisper, "Zac has been pushing me to move to Kauai. He says he's falling for me."

"But he hardly knows you."

She's twiddling her red curls between her fingers. When Daisy does that it means she's excited. "I think he's very keen."

I widen my eyes. "Are you going to go for it?"

"I've been checking out schools on the internet, and apartments."

"No?"

"I think I really might go for it."

"Well, the good thing is, if it's all a disaster, my father is there as a safety net."

"I don't know how safe your dad is, Pearl." Daisy cackles. She's pretty tipsy now. Good, it'll keep her off Alexandre's tail.

"What d'you mean?"

"It never rains, it pours."

"He made a move on you, too? What is with my father cherry picking my friends?"

"Not a *move*, exactly, but he did his fair share of flirting. He's bloody handsome, your dad. Very sexy for an older man."

"He's not that old, he's only fifty-eight."

"Exactly. His body! Bloody Norah!"

"You are *attracted* to my father?" I suddenly realize I'm talking too loud. Some smart little somebody might prick up her little pixie ears.

"Talk about *sexy*," hisses Daisy in another hoarse whisper. "Wouldn't mind giving him one on a cold, rainy night."

"Daisy!"

"Just feeling a little horny, that's all. I'm ready for a shag.

Not that Johnny and I did it that much but when it's taken away from you, you miss it."

"Why are you two whispering?" Amy squeaks. "You told me it was rude to whisper, Mommy."

Daisy bursts out laughing. "So I did. So I did. You are absolutely right, Amy. I must not whisper!" She's slurring her words now and I know that they'll have to spend the night. Fine. This suite has an extra bedroom with en-suite bathroom.

She stretches her legs out on the bed and plumps up a couple of massive cushions behind her head. She lets out a sigh. "This is the life. You've really lucked out, Pearl. What a blast to be chilling out in hotels like this for the rest of your life. You'll never, ever, have to worry about paying a bill, ever again. Never have to do the washing up. Can drink pink champagne every bloody day of the week. What a laugh!"

The hotel phone rings. Thank God. It'll be Alexandre. I grab it eagerly.

"Alexandre?"

"Hello, Pearl?"

It's not Alexandre. It's Elodie.

"Hi Elodie. What's up?" Poor thing can probably detect disappointment in my voice.

"Why didn't you come to lunch today with my grandmother?"

"Alexandre couldn't make it and I didn't want to go alone."

"I was there."

"Oh, I'm sorry I missed you."

"I have so much news. I've applied to go to art school in London and I want to tell you about my maid of honor dress. I went to see Zang Toi for a fitting."

"Great! That's so exciting about art school, Elodie. And I can't wait to see you in the gown. What's it like?" *Ding, dong, it's my wedding, any second now.* Talk about fittings; I'll need my gown let out a little.

"It's so beautiful, oh mon Dieu. It's a Paris Pink, silk mousseline de soie fitted gown with a low draped back, caught with silk roses."

"Wow, it sounds amazing."

"Is the wedding still St. Valentine's Day?"

"Yes, Elodie. It is." I say this with confidence but I'm panicking inside. In fact, I have been so caught up in the Laura drama that I haven't been organizing my own freaking wedding. A good wake up call. I need to get moving. "Would you like to come over to the George V and hang out with us? Daisy and Amy are here."

"I can't, I have a rendezvous."

Elodie on a date! "That's great, Elodie, who's the lucky guy?"

"Nobody. Just a video game online with a bunch of people."

"Oh."

"Well, bye Pearl. Kisses to my uncle."

"Bye." I hang up.

Daisy squeals, "Oh my God! Your wedding! It's the fourteenth? Really? Still in Lapland?"

"Yes, I need to speak to the wedding planner again, but...yes. But hardly any guests. I woke up the other day and suddenly got a headache thinking about hundreds of people who, in reality, probably don't give a damn about us and would just be coming for the party. So we have a private jet booked and it's going to be just family and close friends."

"Am I a close friend? Am I invited?"

"And me!" Amy looks up from her coloring book.

"Of course you are, you silly fools. My dad, Anthony and Bruce – if he'll agree to fly. Natalie and her boyfriend-"

"She has a *boyfriend?*"

"A gorgeous hunk; a cross between young versions of Wesley Snipes and Denzel Washington, apparently. A firefighter."

"Very nice."

"I know."

"Who else is coming? Let's see…well, it's all a bit short notice so…oh yes, some old school friends, and then Alexandre's family, his new video game business partner, plus a couple of his old buddies."

"Not Laura, I hope."

"No. Certainly not." I wince. For a few minutes, thinking about my wedding, the dreaded Laura had slipped my mind.

"So I don't understand - *why*, again, is Alexandre going to her house?"

"He, um, he's dropping some books by."

"All those Folio novels she left in Provence?"

"Exactly," I lie. "Another glass?" Quick, I need to top her up before her brain starts working overtime again.

"What about food?"

"Are you hungry already? Shall we order room service?"

Daisy gulps down some more bubbly. "No, I mean wedding food."

"Well, it's Lapland – Finland, so they'll be a mixture of Scandinavian dishes and—"

"Will Santa Claus be at your wedding?" Amy stands up, rushes over, and leaps onto the bed.

"I think he'll be taking a well earned vacation, honey," I reply. "He worked so hard at Christmas; maybe he's by a beach somewhere drinking a cocktail."

Amy's mouth turns into the letter O. "Santa Claus drinks *cocktails?*" Whoops, I wish I hadn't said that.

"Non-alcoholic cocktails." A vision of Santa Claus on the beach flashes through my mind and it's wrong – very wrong. Poor Amy, what have I said? I quickly add. "Actually, no, Santa Claus never goes to the beach; he lives where it's snowy and cold and never leaves because he has to look after his reindeer."

Amy looks relieved. "Are you going to borrow Santa's reindeers for your wedding?"

"Actually, yes – he's lending them to me. Isn't that kind of him? And his sleigh."

"You spoke to *Santa*, himself?"

"Well, no. I don't think many people get to speak to Santa himself. Just his helpers." I suddenly feel terrible. I am outright lying. Is this what grown-ups do? Teach children how to lie – then we tell them how they must be honest with us. No wonder we confuse them – deceit starts early. I am about to bring a baby into the world and teach him or her, not only how to lie, but do it without flinching.

"What's your cake going to be like, Auntie Pearl?"

I gaze at her sweet, heart-shaped face full of innocence and wonder, and my stomach does a little flip. "Well, the traditional French wedding cake is made of chocolate profiteroles piled up into a big cone, like a tower."

Her eyes become pools of chocolaty desire. "Cool."

"And maybe we can have *two* wedding cakes, what do you think? One profiterole one, and a beautiful white one? White like my gown and with pink roses to match Elodie's gown...and you know what?"

"What?" slurs Daisy.

"I can't believe I didn't think of this earlier! Amy should be a bridesmaid. She can match Elodie. I'll speak to Zang Toi, I'm sure he can come up with something incredible for Amy."

"So glad you didn't rope me into being the maid of honor," Daisy murmurs, now half conked out, sprawled like a starfish across the bed.

"Well I did ask you but you didn't want to do it."

"I think a grown woman always looks awkward being a maid of honor. In England, we don't do the maid of honor thing, we have little girl bridesmaids."

"That's what made me suddenly think of Amy – she'd be adorable all in pink. I'll email Zang, right now, and tell him we have a beautiful little bridesmaid to dress."

Amy starts bouncing up and down on the bed, and for a moment, I'm envious. I remember doing that – the feeling of freedom and abandon, flying high underneath my light feet. Oh, to be five once more. "What will my dress be like?" she wants to know.

"I don't know, I'll ask him."

I grab my iPad and send Zang an e-mail which will go directly to his BlackBerry. "He's usually very fast at responding," I tell my eager audience. "So professional."

Then I pick up the hotel phone and call Alexandre again. No reply, just the goddam voicemail. He would have had plenty of time, by now, to sort stuff out with Laura – why isn't he picking up? I leave another message. Five minutes later, a message bleeps in from Zang:

How about a Paris Pink, silk taffeta baby doll, bordered with pleated tulle & organza & grosgrain ruffles and grosgrain ribbon sash?

Wreath (Hair) and tiny basket of baby ivy and pink roses.

I repeat the message to Amy and Daisy. Amy squeals with delight and gets back to her bed jumping. Daisy rocks about, oblivious in her drunken stupor. I call Alexandre again. Nothing. I mumble to myself...

What the hell is going on?

16

Alexandre and James stood there glaring at each other. Then they both, simultaneously, looked down at Laura. There she was at the bottom of the staircase, a pool of blood about her head. The stairs were wooden, all except for the bottom step, which was made of old granite.

"She must have careened down the stairs like a sled," Alexandre suggested. "Her feet forward and her body slanted backwards, bashing it on the bottom step."

James didn't reply. He bent down for the third time to feel her pulse, but there was no doubt that she was dead. Laura was wearing a crimson, silk satin robe with a sexy negligee underneath. One pretty heeled slipper - the Fredericks of Hollywood kind - was on one foot; the other had obviously skidded across the floor with the fall. She looked all dressed up with a sly touch of rouge on her cheeks and mascara enhancing her almond-shaped, blue eyes, which were wide open in shock, staring up at the ceiling like shiny marbles. She knew Alexandre was coming over; was this her one last effort to seduce him, he wondered?

He surveyed the gruesome scene. It was hard to see where the silk ended and where the blood began; except the blood resembled gloss paint. He'd seen death before, on many occasions, but not like this. Laura's exit had been a glamorous one. Stairs again, thought Alexandre – was that Laura's fate, all along? Maybe she had been destined to die, that time. Maybe that was just a dress rehearsal for this.

"You fucking cunt," spat James. "You sneaky fucking bastard." He laid his palm across her heart. "You killed my wife!"

Alexandre raised his hands in the air as if making a surrendering gesture. "James, no! What are you saying? That's crazy. I *just* got here, at the same time you were coming through the front door. I swear. This is just as much a surprise for me as it is for you."

James looked up at Alexandre; a sneer set on his angular face. His blond hair was a little longer than usual, and he looked less like a banker and more like a regular guy that mowed the lawn on Sundays. Except, he knew that James wasn't the lawn-mowing type. He was wearing corduroy pants and a dark green cashmere sweater. Usually, he wore expensive suits. Not today. But he still had that upper class air about him: his clipped accent, his Eton education – a man who had been used to money and privileges his entire life.

"What I don't understand, is why. *Why*, Alexandre? Did you try to kill her last time, too? When she had that supposed 'accident' and she ended up in a bloody wheelchair? I mean, it's obvious she fell down the stairs. One push, that's all it must have taken. You fucking bastard."

A surge of fury gathered in the pit of Alexandre's stomach. He thought of the evidence in the safety deposit box. Laura dead was all he fucking needed right now. "Okay, James...this is just great. You accusing me of murder? How about I accuse *you*? Where the fuck have you been for the last couple of months? Eh? Suddenly appearing like this. Maybe you *knew* that I was coming over. Laura knew. I called her. Maybe it was really bloody convenient for you to bump her off and then blame me."

"I'm going to call the police," James spluttered, his eyes wet with emotion.

Blood was pounding in Alexandre's ears. He didn't know what to do. The evidence. Laura's note stowed with her lawyer revealing everything if she ever had an accident. What a fucking mess.

James pushed a few strands of Laura's hair from her face. "Laura wouldn't just fall down her own stairs in her own house now, would she?"

"It is possible, she had those heeled slippers on."

"How the fuck did you get in, anyway?"

"Through the back, from the garden," Alexandre replied. "I still have your garage keys."

"That's right - your Aston Martin." James shook his head. "I forgot."

Oh Christ. Now Alexandre would have to admit that no, his Aston Martin wasn't there anymore. He had no excuse, whatsoever for coming through the back. He looked really guilty now. Oh fuck. He'd have to tell the truth; James would soon find out. "Actually, I moved my car a while ago. I knocked on the front door but there was no answer, and Laura didn't pick up the phone. She was expecting me. So I came through the back."

"Nice excuse, Alex. Tell that to Scotland bloody Yard." James took out his cell and dialed 999. Alexandre watched him steadily. His heart was pounding like an out of beat drum but trying to stop James would be suicide. Fuck. This was it now. He saw his life flash before him. He'd heard that happened to people when they drowned; and now both the beautiful and hideous, like snapshots, flew through his mind. His father jabbing him in the butt with a broken bottle. His sister's screams. Riding on the back of a bicycle with his dad, he was smiling and happy – they were going on a picnic in the sun. An IED exploding and blowing off his best friend's head, only missing Alexandre because he'd gone to take a leak around the corner. Pearl's face when he last kissed her when they were dancing. Pearl having an orgasm, her body juddering in ecstasy...

James's voice sounded distant, even though he was right next to him. James was giving them his address. "Yes, that's right, some type of accident but she's definitely dead. I'm here with her ex-boyfriend. Yes, I'm her husband."

Oh God, that sounded just peachy – the ex. The ex who just happened to be the object of Laura's crazy desires. James disconnected the call. Alexandre knelt down beside Laura. Why did he feel so little compassion? She was dead, after all. Flesh and blood. He'd loved her once. Tears prickled his eyes but they weren't for Laura, they were for Pearl. And him. What the fuck was going to happen now? He wanted to get out of there and run, but that would make him look as guilty as sin.

He got up from his haunches and leaned against the wall to steady himself. "Where have you been, James? I've been calling and leaving messages."

"I know."

"Then why the fuck didn't you get back to me?"

James sat down on the bottom step which was still smeared with Laura's blood. He didn't seem to notice. The image was surreal. James sitting by his dead wife, looking vaguely sad, yet with an almost imperceptible gleam of relief flickering in his eyes. Alexandre couldn't read him. Had James killed Laura?

"I was in The Priory," James answered solemnly.

The Priory – the British equivalent to the Betty Ford Clinic. Rehab for celebrities who take too many drugs, stuff their faces with too many cakes. Deals were made there – it was a pretty 'hip' place to end up. Some people exaggerated their problems just so they could say they'd been to The Priory. Sounded cool to some.

"I didn't know you had a problem."

James looked down at the corpse and buried his face in his hands. "Nor did I. Well, I did, but I was in total denial."

"What was your drug of choice?"

James swallowed nervously. "How d'you know it was drugs?"

"I figured. You've never been an excessive drinker."

"Smack."

"Heroin? Really? You could have fooled me. How did you get to work every day? How did you make all that money?"

James didn't flinch when he answered, "Well, most of my money went up my arm."

That made sense. He'd only ever seen James wear long sleeved shirts, hand-made in Jermyn Street. He wasn't a T-shirt kind of guy.

James went on, eager to share. Alexandre noticed that

people fresh out of treatment were always keen to tell their story. "I was a very controlled junkie. I had the budget for the high grade shit, you know. But things started spiraling out of control – I lost some money on the stock exchange; the tax men were after me. I needed to clean up my act so I went AWOL. My suitcase is still in the hall. I, literally, just got back five minutes ago. And I found *you* here. And Laura dead."

"So, had you spoken to Laura?" A loaded question. What Alexandre really wanted to know was, *how much do you know?*

"Of course. She told me she wanted to get back with you and that you were still in love with her."

Oh fuck! "And you believed her?"

"Well, yes. Why would she lie about that? It's one of the things that drove me into treatment. She was disgusted by me, and rightly so. I was a fuck-up, a disaster. A junkie. How could I have expected her to live with a man like me? There you were, all sorted out. Making a mint. Good looking. Together. And there was I like a fucking loser, jacking up every day."

Alexandre laid a hand gently on James's shoulder. After all, they'd been friends before. Sort of. "What she said wasn't true. I'm in love with Pearl, my fiancée. I have never wanted Laura back. Ever. You have to believe me, James."

James flinched his shoulder and Alexandre took his hand away. "I don't know what to fucking believe. Here we are, the pair of us, sitting next to a dead woman. My wife. The woman I was in love with. The woman I got clean for. I have a feeling you killed her but, obviously I can't prove it."

"James, you don't seem to be that distraught about Laura lying there dead. I could just as easily suppose *you* killed her."

He looked up at Alexandre, his brows furrowed. "And

why the hell would I do that?"

"Jealousy. Rage. Revenge. Or simply to stop her taking you to the cleaners. I don't know – you could have a million reasons." Alexandre thought of the evidence. Was it possible that it was right here, in the house? He was desperate to check it out before the police arrived. He knew how most women's minds worked; they always kept things of value hidden in their bedrooms. "I'm going upstairs to the bathroom."

"There's a bathroom down here, use that."

"I'd prefer to use the one upstairs."

"Why? So you can do a quick robbery while you're at it? Steal Laura's jewelry?"

"Don't be absurd, James."

"Do what you like, the police will be here any second and you can tell them your bullshit excuses about why you broke into our house." He sat like a stone, not budging from the bottom step.

Alexandre skirted around him and mounted the stairs. At the top, he made a right and followed the corridor all the way to the end. The master bedroom door was open. He entered, and scanned his eyes about the room. He'd been to this house on several occasions over the years, and knew his way around. He could hear sirens from two or three vehicles, outside. He looked out of the window, down onto the street. Two police cars and an ambulance had arrived. There was a frantic knock at the front door and he heard James opening it and talking in muffled tones to the police. The living room was filling up rapidly with more voices and commotion. Alexandre didn't have much time. He looked under the bed – nothing. Laura used to like keeping important things in her closet – letters and personal stuff. He opened the closet door, rummaged through hanging dresses, pants and shirts and he glimpsed something shiny at the back – was it the titanium hip? No, just was a silver sequin jacket.

"What the fuck are you *doing*?" It was James standing behind him. Alexandre spun around. James edged closer, a scowl set on his sharp face as if he was about to lash out.

"Nothing. Sorry," Alexandre replied. But James leapt at him, launching his slim body at Alexandre like a missile, his right fist flailing in the air aiming for his face. Alexandre ducked and clamped James's wrists tightly behind his back. Fighting was the last thing he wanted to do.

A policewoman quickly entered the bedroom, and a policeman rushed from behind, barging her out of the way and diving at the two men locked together; Alexandre was still immobilizing James who was thrashing about like a fish on a hook.

The policeman and another colleague, also pushing his way through the room, shouted out, "I want you two to come with us down to the police station."

James shouted out, "This bastard killed my wife! He broke into my house, uninvited. He must have shoved her down the stairs. They were lovers."

Alexandre shook his head and mumbled, "It's not true." What a fuck-up. He knew, though, that the best course of action was to remain calm and wait for his attorney. He'd call Sophie and get their legal team onto it. He had never needed a criminal lawyer before, but they had a good one on HookedUp's payroll, just in case.

Alexandre was silent. He released James's wrists and put his hands up peacefully. Oh shit. He needed his attorney, and fast.

"He basically broke into my house," offered James, nursing the burns on his wrists and glowering at Alexandre.

The policeman, a pale-faced man in his fifties, eyed both men up and down and said, "Look, there is a dead woman below and I don't have time to play Sherlock Holmes. I want you both down at the station, now, to make a statement and give interviews. I'll want to take DNA swabs – meanwhile, the forensic team will tell us if there's been any foul play."

"I know my rights!" James yelled. "Either arrest me now, or leave me be. You have no right to force me to come down to the station, let alone take any bloody DNA samples! I'll give my statement, right here, in my own house, thank you very much."

Alexandre noticed the policeman's thin lips quiver with rage. James answering back in his pompous Etonian accent, had really got his goat.

The officer, a small and 'important' man, told him, "Alright, so be it. I'm arresting you *both* on suspicion of manslaughter." He puffed up his chest and said in a monotone, "You have the right to remain silent, if you give up this right, anything you say can, and will be used as evidence against you in the court of law. You have the right to…"

The man's voice was a swirl of words spinning about in Alexandre's dazed head. He felt as if someone was smothering him with cotton wool. He tented his fingers in front of his face and mumbled, "This is crazy." But he noticed a sneer on the policeman's lily-white face. Damn. He shouldn't have spoken.

The other officer said, in a broad Cockney accent, "What *are* you? Bloody *foreign* or something?"

Alexandre was aware that he shouldn't have opened his mouth. His French accent would not go down well. At all. The English hated the French, it was common knowledge.

Frogs, they called them. The French, in return, nicknamed the Brits 'Roast Beef', not because of their national dish, but because of the color their bodies turned in summer as they slumped about Mediterranean beaches sporting agonizing sunburns.

James piped up, "It's him you should be questioning, not me! He broke into my house, I tell you."

Alexandre wanted to defend himself, explain he'd been invited, that the back door was open and he had a key to the garage but he bit his lip. He needed to stay calm, wait for his attorney to be present. He simply shook his head.

"So you don't know this man?" asked the policewoman looking at James.

"Yes, I *do* know him, I told you that, downstairs. He's my wife's ex-boyfriend."

"Is this true, sir?" the Napoleon complex officer asked Alexandre.

"I'd rather wait to give my statement down at the station with my lawyer present, if you don't mind," Alexandre answered quietly. He knew his rights. He couldn't be kept at a police station for more than twenty-four hours without being charged, although this could be extended to thirty-six hours with the authority of a police superintendent, and for up to ninety-six hours with the authority of a magistrate, which is exactly what could happen if they got wind of the whole IVF nonsense. He could hear them downstairs now, probably the forensics team – shit, now he thought about it, traipsing upstairs wasn't such a great idea. His footprints would be all over the staircase, proof that he could have pushed Laura. After all, it wasn't his house. James could have his footprints or fingerprints anywhere, and so what? But Alexandre was another story, altogether. That, plus coming in from the back when nobody was home, did not look good at all.

James cried out, pointing his skinny finger like a weapon at Alexandre, "It's him you should be worried about. He was having a bloody affair with my wife!"

The policeman smirked as if he's made a great discovery, and said to James, "So, sir, that would give you a good motive, wouldn't it?"

"Should I handcuff them, sir?" the female officer asked.

"Look, that really won't be necessary," James blurted out. "This is absurd. This is my bloody house! You think I'm going to kill my own wife? I'm the one who called *you*, for Christ's sake? You think I would have made that phone call if I'd been guilty of murder?"

"Actually, a neighbor called 999 before your call came in," the woman said. "She heard a woman scream."

The officer in charge shot her a poisonous look. She'd obviously said too much. She covered her mouth with her hand in embarrassment.

Laura screamed, did she? Alexandre mused. He didn't think that James was capable of murder, but who knew? His mother had killed - and he hadn't imagined Laura would be capable of blackmail. People did strange things under pressure. Maybe Laura was threatening James in some way, and he needed her out of the picture. It seemed strange that she would fall down the stairs in her own house, even with heeled slippers. It wasn't even dark.

"Look sir, we can either do this peacefully and you come with us nice and quietly down to the station for questioning, or we'll have to cuff you."

It was still very civilized in Britain, Alexandre thought. In the USA, he and James would be on the floor by now, wrists cuffed behind their backs and a gun held to their heads. Yet here, they were politely asking them to come along to the station for questioning. He knew a little about the law in Britain and the way the system worked. His new partner, the one he was starting the video game company with, had once been arrested for dealing marijuana. The police in the UK were able to arrest people much more easily than in the States. American police needed probable cause to make an arrest, but in the United Kingdom, officers could arrest just on suspicion.

Alexandre pushed out his wrists in front of him to show good will.

The police officer said, "That won't be necessary, sir. If you men can both come along with us quietly and do not resist, we won't be needing restraints."

"Sure," Alexandre told him, offering a limp smile. His mind raced back to the possibility of the evidence being in the closet. Damn, he'd like to have one more look but it would cause mayhem. James was already suspicious; Alexandre couldn't draw attention to the closet – not even look at it. He'd have no choice but to be led like a lamb to slaughter to the police station, and call Sophie to get his lawyer there ASAP. Meanwhile, he wouldn't incriminate himself, wouldn't give evidence – he had 'the right to remain silent' and he'd damn well use that right.

"Come along please," the small policeman ordered, ushering James and Alexandre out of the bedroom. Alexandre ambled along peacefully but James, disgusted by the Cockney policeman's hand clamped on his wrist shouted, "Get your hands off me!"

Alexandre knew that things would now get worse.

The Napoleon complex officer stood 'tall' and commanded, "On second thoughts, cuff them both. I really don't want any trouble." He pointed a fat finger at James and hissed, "You, sir, need to calm right down."

"He's upset, sir; his wife's just died," the policewoman suggested to her boss.

"Yes, well. I don't want any monkey business when I'm in charge, thank you very much."

It felt humiliating to be arrested and cuffed. Alexandre's mind traced back to the time when he 'cuffed' Pearl with the string of Art Deco pearls, and wondered if she had felt the same; humiliated. Christ, he hoped not, he hadn't meant it that way. Jesus, how embarrassing, his cock started throbbing just thinking about her naked, her hands above her head, her legs splayed open and bound to his brass bed with his blue silk ties – her pussy soaking wet as he licked and sucked her to her first, ever, oral orgasm. Pearl was all his. No other man had given her such pleasure sexually. He loved going down on her – she tasted so sweet. Shit! He felt himself expanding; it was as if his heartbeat was right between his legs. He knew that Pearl nicknamed it his Weapon of Mass Destruction and she was right – it could bring him to ruin if he wasn't more careful. Thank God he was still wearing his overcoat. Jesus, he had a full hard-on now. How he could possibly have an erection in the middle of being arrested was an enigma to him. Pretty fucked-up to be thinking about sex at a moment like this. He'd heard that when men got hung, they found it erotic. It was known as a 'death erection' and 'angel lust.' He'd read, somewhere, that Christ was depicted by several Renaissance artists with a post-mortem erection after the crucifixion. Maybe, that was what was happening now – he knew he was about to be hung, drawn and slaughtered, figuratively speaking.

As they exited, the housekeeper, Mrs. Blake, was bustling towards the front door with a bunch of grocery bags. She looked horrified.

"What on earth is going on?" She gazed at James. "Mr. Heimann, what's happening? I wasn't expecting you back until tomorrow."

"I'm afraid you can't go in there for the now," the policeman in charge said. "Not until the coroner has finished and forensics have done their bit."

James told her in a grave tone, "I'm sorry, Mrs. Blake, Mrs. Heimann took a fall. She's dead."

Mrs. Bake looked at the handcuffs and began to quiver uncontrollably. "But it was an accident, surely?"

"We don't know that yet, madam. Please move aside. I'm sure Mr. Heimann will get in touch with you when you're needed."

"But Mr. Heimann is innocent!" she screeched. "And this gentleman here, Mr. Chevalier. I know him. They would never have hurt Mrs. Heimann. Never! Handcuffs! You are *arresting* them? This is madness!"

"Please move aside, madam. This is being treated as a crime scene until further notice."

James stood erect and said, "Don't worry, Mrs. Blake, it's just a little misunderstanding, that's all. I'll ring you very shortly. Meanwhile, consider it paid leave."

As Alexandre was bundled into the police car and driven away, he thought of Pearl at the George V. He'd had his cell switched off all this time – he thought Pearl calling while he was dealing with Laura would add fuel to the already raging fire. Pearl had probably been trying to call. But now they'd only allow him one phone call and that would have to be to Sophie. In any case, he didn't want to worry Pearl in her delicate, pregnant state. Sophie could deal with everything. He hoped she'd pull out all the guns. Get him out of this mess.

Jesus. What a fucking nightmare.

17

Daisy is now sprawled out on the living room sofa, sozzled from all the pink champagne. I feel responsible, although she doesn't seem to care at all. I left her lying there with a grin spread across her face like the Cheshire Cat.

Amy was rushing about with excitement earlier. I ordered room service for us all, although Daisy was beyond repair and didn't seem interested in eating. I left her with a couple of large bottles of Perrier water on the coffee table and a ceramic bowl next to her to vomit in, just in case. The place is far too fancy to have a bucket and I didn't want to call down. I then gave Amy a sumptuous bubble bath in the grand marbled bathroom and put her to bed.

I return to the living room to check on Daisy and cover her with a blanket. She has miraculously perked up and is in the mood for a chat.

"You're not feeling sick?" I ask.

"No! I'm feeling simply marvelous. Bloody delicious champers – got anymore?"

"No, we've run out," I lie. "But there's lots of delicious mineral water."

"Bore Ring."

"I put Amy to bed."

"Good girl. You, not Amy. You're a good girl for doing that."

Yes, she's tipsy alright. "Okay, I think you're ready now for the delicious soup I ordered for you. Wait there and I'll heat it up. Organic chicken noodle soup with Shiitake mushrooms and ginger."

"Sounds delicious."

"Doesn't it? Give me five minutes and I'll be back."

I hear Daisy glugging down some water as I go to the kitchen. It really is like an apartment here. I could get used to this easy luxury; gourmet food on tap, flower arrangements changing daily.

Still no word from Alexandre. A frisson of fear runs up my spine as I think of all the possibilities. Why hasn't he called? It can only mean one thing: bad news. Laura has persuaded him to do the IVF and he's stalling. He doesn't want to hear me scream and cry about it. I swore to myself I wouldn't; that I'd remain cool, calm and collected, and accept whatever decision he made, but the more I think about Laura pregnant, the sicker I feel.

I return with Daisy's soup on a tray. It smells incredible and I'm tempted to order more, although I had a delicious Club Sandwich, earlier.

As I lay the tray on Daisy's lap, I feel as if I'm feeding an invalid. Chicken noodle soup can heal anything, even an impending hangover. "Are you sure you're not going to take a spoonful and vomit everywhere," I check.

"Ha! You think I'm a wimp, don't you? I used to drink quite a bit, in my day. You should have seen me down the pub; I could drink any man under the table." I spread a napkin like a bib about her neck and she slurps down some of the broth. "Oh my God, this soup is out of this world." She looks as if she's died and gone to Heaven. "Oh, by the way, I forgot to say. Remember when I slipped out of the restaurant this afternoon to go to the chemist to get some Advil?"

"The chemist?"

"Sorry, I mean 'pharmacy' – chemist is English. Anyway, I didn't have a headache at all. I went to buy us some naughty toys."

I widen my eyes with mock disapproval. "From that sex shop we passed earlier?"

Daisy giggles. "Yes. I slipped in and got something for each of us."

"You saucy wench, Daisy."

"I've never used anything like that before in my life, but now that I'm single I thought it was time to experiment."

"Well, I'll have to wait to use mine. I still have to be careful."

"Ah, but I thought of that, Pearl. Yours isn't," she lowers her voice to a tiny whisper, "a *dildo*...it doesn't penetrate, it *vibrates*. It's called the something deux, for the two of you. It splits in half – you'll see how it works." She giggles again. "The 'hers' part is convex and the 'his' part is concave, apparently. Or is it the other way round? Anyway, the saleswoman told me it was very popular with couples, and a best seller."

"So when Amy and I were innocently eating our choco-late mousse you were out buying *sex* toys?"

"I know, isn't it outrageous?"

"Where are they?"

"I left the bags in the closet by the entrance. I hope Amy doesn't find them." She slurps another mouthful of soup. "God this is good, you wanna try some?"

"No, it's okay, thanks."

Daisy studies me for a minute and suddenly comes out with, "Pearl, can I ask you a personal question?"

"Sure."

"Do you have multiple orgasms?"

I don't need long to recollect my memories. "Once or twice it has happened. Only with Alexandre, though. But the truth is, I feel so satisfied...so *satiated* after one, I really don't feel I need another. Why?"

"Oh, just because you're always reading about them and you feel like a kind of freak, you know, just having one, like all other women are having such fun and you, well, you're just...I don't know."

"What's your favorite dish?"

"What's that got to do with it?"

"Just hear me out. What's your favorite thing to eat?"

"Well, I do love a good Sunday roast with Yorkshire pudding and roast potatoes"

"Okay, imagine you've just eaten a full Sunday roast. And it was absolutely delicious. You are full. Best meal you've had for ages. Maybe years. And then you're offered another plate piled high with more of the same. Would you be able to wolf all that down, too?"

"I see your point."

"Believe me, you should be happy with one, good orgasm. Very happy. A lot of women - and it was how I was for so many years - are starved and don't even get the one, so count yourself blessed. Lots of women don't climax at all during intercourse. Don't believe all you read about multiple orgasms, anyway."

She considers what I've said. I can see the invisible cogs of her mind turning. I know what she's wondering – she's wondering if it's because Alexandre is a god in bed and that's why I've had multiple orgasms, or if I was born that way.

"So no word from Alexandre?" she asks.

"No." Uh, oh, the food is sobering her up; I need to change the subject. "So, tell me more about Zac; we hardly discussed it the other day because of Amy being around."

"Oh my God, Pearl. I mean, when Zac kissed me it made me realize what I'd been missing all these years, you know? He's so *sexy*...so...buffed up." She laughs too loudly and covers her mouth. Maybe she isn't sobering up, after all.

"Funny. You, Natalie and I have all ended up with younger men. Well, that's if you take Zac up on his offer."

"You're right! I hadn't thought of that!"

"We're getting our revenge on the world." I wink at her.

"What do you mean?"

"Well, it's always been guys who get the young girls. Now the tables are turning. There's so much more Girl Power about, have you noticed?"

She sips another large spoonful of soup and sighs at its deliciousness. "Like so many amazing women singers now, and stuff?"

"Exactly. Men need to watch out. Gone are the days when they can sit around getting beer bellies and think their women will be happily waiting for them if they behave like assholes. Women are beginning to call the shots now. I mean, look at *you*. You're not crying your heart out, feeling sorry for yourself. You've moved on. Moved on to a hot, sexy younger model!"

"Don't ya love it?"

I wrinkle my nose. "I hate that word, 'cougar' though, don't you? I find it offensive"

Daisy nods her head as if weighing up the options. "I don't know. I quite *like* the idea of being a cougar. It's a compliment. Cougars are beautiful creatures."

"That's exactly what Alexandre says."

Our girlie chit-chat is interrupted by the phone ringing. Thank God, it'll finally be him. "Oui, hallo?" I say, giving it my French touch.

"Pearl?"

"*Sophie*, is that you?"

"I'm in ze lobby, I'm coming up."

"Great-" The line clicks dead before I get a chance to say anything more.

Daisy arches an eyebrow. "*Sophie's* here? At this hour?"

"I know. A bit odd. Oh, well. We're friends now so…"

"Maybe she wants to come and hang out."

"You think?"

"I can't imagine why. She's so sophisticated. We're such…children compared to her."

"I'm glad you feel that way, too. She's five years younger than I am but I always feel so… so girly next to her."

Daisy laughs. "That's because you *are* girly, Pearl – you'll never be a real grown-up, not even when you're eighty. You're young at heart. You'll always be that way, no matter what happens." She starts singing *Young at Heart* in Frank Sinatra's croon. Actually, she does a pretty good imitation.

"I can hear a knock, that'll be her. I hope nothing's

wrong."

When I open the door I can see from the dour expression on Sophie's face that something *is* wrong. Very wrong. My first fear is that Alexandre has died in a car crash or something.

"Is he okay?" My eyes are already pooling with tears. "He's not dead?"

Sophie's lips twitch into a limp smile. "No, he's fine. I mean not fine, but he's not dead, not injured, don't worry."

My heart starts beating normally again. Well, almost. At least he's still alive. "Come in."

She walks in, casts off her sumptuous, cashmere overcoat and slumps herself onto the nearest armchair. "I need a drink."

"Sure, what would you like?"

"A whiskey. Make it a double."

"No problem. Is Alexandre okay?"

"Give me a drink and I'll tell you everything."

"Sure." *Crap, the news must be really bad.* "On the rocks?" I ask her.

"Excuse me?"

"Would you like ice with your Scotch?"

"Yes, lots."

I fix her the drink and gauge her movements from the corner of my eye. I don't know if she has a cold or if she's crying. I slip quietly next door to see Daisy. She has her iPod playing *Young at Heart* and she's spinning about in circles doing a strange sort of ballet. I whisper, "Daisy, I think you'd better stay in here; I have a feeling Sophie's not in the mood to socialize. Do you mind?"

"Actually, I think I'm off to bed now, anyway." She stretches her arms in the air and does a gazelle-like leap. "See you in the morning."

"Don't fall over."

I get extra ice from the kitchen, put some in a bowl and finish fixing Sophie's Scotch. I have no idea how strong a double should be.

I come back into the room and she's still sniffling, biting her lip as if to suppress full-blown sobs. I'm getting frightened now. "Here we go," I say, handing her the drink, my hands trembling. "It might be a little strong." She has been crying. Her dark eyes are like black coal, smudged by mascara. She still looks beautiful and put together, despite it all. "Tell me what happened," I ask, dreading the answer.

"Alexandre has been arrested."

Laura immediately comes to mind. "Oh my God. Why?"

"Don't worry, he's got a hotshot team of lawyers wiz him. Zey have nuzzing on him. I'm sure he'll be released soon."

"But what is he being accused of?"

"In England zey are very quick to arrest, you know? It means nuzzing. They'll let him go soon."

"But what—?

"Laura is dead."

My heart feels as if it's about to leap out of my chest. My first reaction is relief – how wicked is that? But then panic engulfs me as I wonder if Alexandre killed her. Sophie wipes her eyes and relays the story; tells me how Laura either fell down the stairs, or was pushed. How Alexandre slipped in from the back door. And that he and James practically collided into one another, seemingly spotting Laura at the same time, dead at the foot of the stairs; each accusing the other of murder or 'manslaughter.' That James called the police, and because of his finger pointing at Alexandre, they both ended up being suspects.

Sophie begins to weep out loud and I feel awkward. I hardly know her and her tears come as a shock because I have always had her in my mind's eye as a tough-nut. But she looks so tiny and vulnerable, like a fragile bird; and my heart is heavy with sympathy and surprisingly (given our history together), a sort of sisterly love.

"I love Alexandre so much, you know? He is everyzing to me. My bruzzer, my best friend. He is everyzing, Pearl."

I walk over and sit on the arm of the chair and rest my hand on her shoulder. I stroke her soft, dark hair, pulling a few salty strands from her tear-stained face. "It will be alright, I'm sure, Sophie. At least the attorneys are there." I say this calmly but I also have tears in my eyes. I picture the evidence in the safe deposit box, the note to Laura's lawyer if anything should befall her - a life sentence for their mother, even if Alexandre gets let off. *Should I tell Sophie?* No, I've been sworn to secrecy. "What can I do to help?" I ask in a quiet voice. "Should we go to London now? Get on a plane?"

She takes a gulp of Scotch. "Let's wait until tomorrow morning. If zey haven't let him free, zen we'll be in trouble. Ze lawyers will tell me more. We're waiting for ze forensic report."

I think of *CSI* and *Dexter* and am aware that we are now dealing with real life, not genius, fictional super-sleuths with state-of-the-art equipment that can solve cases within minutes and hours. This could drag on forever.

"What do you think happened?" I ask her.

"I don't care what happened. I don't care if he killed ze beach. I just want him home." She scrapes her slim fingers through her hair agitatedly.

I nod. She wouldn't care, either, if their mother went to jail, by the sound of it. She was her step-mother, anyway, not her own flesh and blood, and had betrayed them both when they were minors. From what Alexandre has said, Sophie has never quite forgiven her. I'm itching to tell Sophie about the IVF saga but worry that if I do, I could put my big wooden spoon in a broth with far too many cooks. I bite my tongue. I can do nothing more than comfort her. I wish I knew what Alexandre had told his attorney. Or rather, attorneys, plural. Let's hope his money and power will work miracles. How much, I wonder, do they know? How much of this crazy story has Alexandre revealed to them?

"So Laura's husband James suddenly reappeared, then?" I think of how, in my mind, I'd accused Laura of poisoning him. "Where's he been all this time?"

"Apparently, he went to rehab. He was a heroin addict."

"Heroin? But I thought he was an upper-crust banker!"

"You'd be surprised how people wiz lots of money and connections are ze biggest junkies of all."

What she says makes me remember what her old job was. She used to be a high class call girl, once upon a time, who mixed with the rich, famous and powerful. I guess she would know. "Do you think *James* pushed Laura down the stairs?"

"I wouldn't blame him if he did."

I don't know what else to say, so I offer, "Are you hungry, Sophie? The food's delicious here."

She gets up. "No. I'm leaving now, zank you. I just wanted to come by to see you in person. I'll call you when I have news. Meanwhile, here are ze numbers and emails of ze lawyers." She hands me a business card with extra, handwritten numbers scrawled on them in pen. "My driver's waiting outside. You know, Pearl, you could stay at my house next time. No need to get a hotel."

"I'd love that." *Next time.* Will there *be* a next time? Or is Alexandre going to spend the rest of his life locked up in British jail?

18

I can't sleep. The purple sex toy is lying next to me on my pillow. I thought it would be a good distraction but I wasn't able to bring myself to play with it. I need Alexandre, himself – nothing else can even come close. I need his flesh on mine, the scent of his skin, the taste of his sweet breath. The idea of spending my life without him is horrifying. It has taken me forty years to find true love and now it's being snatched away from me.

Did he kill Laura? Did he push her down the stairs in a rage? It's not his style but he does have a dark side to him; traits about his personality that I will never really know. He kept secrets from me. His Taekwondo, the fact he was in the Foreign Legion. He likes to keep the dark side in the shadows. Yes, he's capable of killing, but if he did kill Laura, I feel like Sophie. I don't care; I just want him safely home.

I mull over James. Not that I have ever met him, but he

sounded like a stalwart citizen. Maybe he's the killer; the nervous junkie who just couldn't take anymore of Laura's antics. He must have gotten wind of the IVF stuff. Maybe that's what drove him to use drugs in the first place. Yes, James could have been her killer. Or was it a simple accident? What are the odds, though, of falling down stairs twice in your life?

Finally, I drift off into a delirious sleep. I know I'm dreaming when I smell Alexandre on me, when I feel him part my thighs and run his hands along my breasts. I know I'm dreaming when I feel his lips on mine, pressing sweet kisses along my neck and my jaw-line, and when I hear his deep, sexy voice whisper in my ear, "I love you, Pearl. You are my life, my love, my rare, precious pearl."

I open my eyes but wonder if I am still in my dream. He's there, leaning over me, his dark hair flopping in front of his face, his five o'clock shadow framing the beauty of his even features, his peridot-green eyes twinkling with humor. "You look so serious, baby," he tells me and smiles; his dimple on one cheek furrowed with amusement. *Serioose.*

"I'm dreaming," I reply to the sexy phantom who has tricked me before. Who has given me orgasms in my sleep and even fooled me into believing he spanks me. This ghost is not the real Alexandre. He looks a little thinner in the face, a touch less hungry for sex.

"You're not dreaming, chérie. I swear."

"I know your tricks," I murmur. "Because I'm feeling it between my legs and my heart's racing. You're just a sexy spirit in my dream," I drift back to my other dream, the one about Rex. Rex is swimming in the sea, his doggie-paddle legs, wild with excitement. I have to spin him around and swim behind him so I don't get scratched.

The phantom crawls into bed beside me and trails kisses along my bare arms. His lips press my hand like a knight in shining armor. He is a knight; his name is Chevalier. Alexandre Chevalier. "Alexandre?"

"Yes, baby. I'm here. I'm back from London."

"But you were in jail," I mutter.

"Not jail, chérie, just at the police station giving a statement. They let me go."

I stir from my hazy slumber and sit up. "You're real? This is true?"

He laughs. "Yes, I'm real. This isn't one of your crazy dreams." He lays the back of his hand on my cheek. "Everything's been sorted out."

"But what about Laura?"

He exhales as if all that pent up fear of spending time behind bars is expelled in one long breath. "Someone made a confession."

"James? James killed her?"

"No, not James. He was telling the truth; he'd just got back from rehab, from The Priory."

"Who then? Who killed Laura?"

"The stairs killed Laura. Aided by lots of very slippery furniture polish."

I jolt up and lean back against a pile of soft pillows. I'm well awake now.

Alexandre goes on, "Mrs. Blake, the housekeeper, came to the station to make her statement. She'd polished the stairs that day. Laura was tottering about in kitten-heeled slippers. She fell down the stairs; slid down on her back, ending by crashing her head on the bottom, stone step. It was confirmed by forensics that there was polish all over the soles of her shoes."

"Who polishes stairs? Wasn't that a bit stupid?"

"Stupid or clever, depending which way you look at it."

"Mrs. Blake did it on *purpose?*"

"She told the police that Laura had asked her to polish the staircase but as you say, who polishes stairs?"

"But hadn't she been working for James and Laura for years?"

"Exactly. She hated Laura's guts. Secretly. But stayed because of her loyalty to James. She'd been working for his mother before. Years ago, when I was over there once, I heard Mrs. Blake complaining to the cook. After she made her statement, she asked the police if I could stop by the house. They'd given the case the all clear by that point and somebody had been sent over to clear up the blood. When I stopped by, she told me she had something that belonged to me. At first, I thought she must mean something to do with the Aston Martin. But no, it was the titanium hip parts and teeth."

"But Laura said it was in the safe deposit box."

"She was bluffing."

"But how did Mrs. Blake know that they were yours? How did she *know* that?"

"She said to me, 'Mr. Chevalier, I don't know why this stuff is important to you, or what it all means, but what I *do* know is that Mrs. Heimann was blackmailing you.' Household staff usually know what's going on where they work. She would have heard Laura make phone calls, probably eavesdropped here and there. The ironic thing is that it was stored in the garage, all along. I even had the key."

"The last place anyone would suspect? Especially you."

"Exactly."

"Mrs. Blake told me that she had been planning on calling me and letting me know. When she saw that James and I had been arrested, she was horrified and came down to the police station, straight away, to set the record straight."

"So in the end, you didn't need all those swanky attorneys?"

"The second they realized I was the owner of HookedUp they were putty in my hands. One moment, I was a 'frog', and the next their best mate. Two of them had met their girlfriends through HookedUp. Even if I *had* killed Laura, they were so impressed with me, I think they might have let me go," he jokes.

"What have you done with the evidence?"

"Oh, don't worry, I got rid of it."

My heart's palpitations have steadied now to a more even rhythm. My poor baby, with all the adrenaline swirling about my body, has sure been on a rollercoaster ride tonight. "Does James know about the IVF malarkey?"

"No, luckily Laura hadn't spoken to him about that, although she had told him that I was still in love with her and wanted to get back together."

"So he hates you?"

Alexandre's lips tilt up on one side into his signature crooked smile. "I showed him all the photos of you on my iPhone and shared with him the fact that you were pregnant. He calmed down."

"So you threw the teeth and hip parts away?"

"Too bloody right I did."

"Where?" I ask, fearing they could come back and haunt us like in one of those psychological thrillers. My stomach churns again…oops my baby's getting another ride on the Big Dipper.

"Hopefully, it's all sitting at the bottom of the deepest

part of the English Channel. I came back by helicopter."

"Ah, so that's how you got back so quickly. What about Sophie? Did you let her in on the details?"

"Not yet. I'm playing that one by ear."

My questions are like a machine gun. "Does she know you're free?"

"Yes."

"Why didn't she call me, then?"

"I told her not to. I wanted to surprise you, myself."

"So you chucked it all out of the helicopter into the sea?" He nods. "RIP Monsieur Chevalier."

"My father wasn't called Chevalier."

"Really."

"Sophie and I changed our names when we were in hiding."

Another little secret. "Chevalier - Knight. Whose idea was that?"

"Mine, of course. At eight years old, I fancied the idea of being a knight in shining armor galloping on my steed. I was into Sir Lancelot."

"Well your wish came true. Because you *are* my knight in shining armor."

He holds my head in his hands and kisses me gently. "I'm glad you see me that way." Then he leans back on the pillow, stretching out his long legs but his head lands on my new toy. I burst out laughing. "Oops, what's this hard purple thing?" he asks, inspecting the oval-shaped vibrator, the two halves meeting together like a cracked dinosaur egg.

I giggle. "That's a gift from Daisy. She bought it today at the sex shop. It's a 'his and her' design. The man gets his half and the woman hers. It splits in two."

He breaks it open, switches it on and it rumbles in his

large hands.

"It's called the Zini Deux. We both get to use it together, apparently, at the same time. You do me and I do you."

"Well, this will be a first."

"I know, me too. I always associated vibrators with lonely, sad women whose husbands can't get it up but, apparently they're big news these days, and very popular with couples."

Alexandre puts his arms around me and draws me close. "Oh, Pearl. You have no idea what's been going through my mind in the last twenty-four hours. It's been hell. First, wondering what the fuck I was going to do about Laura, then finding her dead, the police, James, all that time thinking the evidence was going to come to light, and even if I got off scot free, I thought that it was over for my mother. Jesus, what a rollercoaster of emotions it's been."

"I can imagine. I was going through the same. Thank God Mrs. Blake was so honest. She could have easily kept her mouth shut."

"They would have realized, sooner or later, that it was an accident."

"Yes, but you could have spent weeks, even months, worrying and waiting for that phone call from Laura's attorney – waiting for them to arrest your mother. And how do you feel about Laura being dead? That couldn't have been pleasant, seeing a corpse with her head split open."

"I've seen a lot worse, believe me. But still, I did feel a sort of sadness. Sad that Laura ended up being that way. But I also felt a great sense of liberation, obviously, that she was out of our lives for good. I know that's a cruel thing to say but it's how I felt; how I still feel. It also brought home to me how much I treasure you."

He rests his head on my shoulder, breathes me in as if I

were some deliciously scented flower, and we hold hands. This is a quiet moment for us both. Peace at last. We both slip our bodies further down the bed and, entwined in each other's arms, fall into a deep sleep.

Am I asleep? Awake? Alexandre's licking my nipples softly, making me moan. My eyelids flutter open and I remember that he really is here beside me. I lazily stretch out my hand and feel, not the Weapon of Mass Destruction but the Tool of Creation, hard as a rock. Ready. With my eyes half closed, I inch my way down the bed and take him in my mouth, licking, sucking, wrapping my lips about him – I feel a desperate hunger for something and someone who so nearly got taken away from me.

He's groaning, "Oh, yeah baby. Oh yeah, that feels so fucking good. I was thinking about you when I was arrested."

I drag my nails lightly over the delicate skin of his balls and he moans, his hands threading through my hair. I'm still half asleep and realize that we haven't even kissed hello properly, we were so busy talking in the early hours, and then fell asleep. I walk my way up the bed with my hands until our faces touch. I can feel his hardness against my mound and I'm lying on top of him now. He smells so good.

"It was like an eternity," I tell him in a whisper.

"I know."

The tip of my tongue flickers on his lips. He gives me that half-cocked smile, the dimple in his cheek making me remember why I was so smitten the second I laid eyes on him in the coffee shop. Light is pouring through the open parts of the drapes; it must be almost midday. A beam of sun is lighting up his head and I notice shimmers of auburn highlighting his dark hair, which usually looks almost black. He drapes his arms about me, squeezing me against his muscular chest. He gives me an 'Eskimo kiss' rubbing noses gently but what is going on down south is far less innocent.

"I'm trying to control myself, Pearl," he breathes into my mouth. He parts my lips with his tongue and moans. I feel his cock flex against me. His kiss is passionate but brimming over with need and love. I return it with equal fervor, my tongue sliding along his, stroking, flipping under and over and out until our tongues tangle almost into a sexual feast.

"Where's that egg thing?" I whisper.

He cups my ass and I feel his erection tight against me. "Really, you want to have a go?"

"Why not? We'll have to try it at least once, or Daisy will be disappointed. Speaking of Daisy, she and Amy must be up and about."

"I heard them leave a while ago," he tells me in a low voice. "We're quite alone and I put a Do Not Disturb sign on the door."

He leans over and takes the big purple oval from the bedside table and holds it up. He smirks.

"Pull it apart. Let's see how it works." I take one half from him and switch on the lowest setting. Even on 'low' it's still very buzzy. "This fits you right here," I say, cupping his balls with it. But it seems as if it's too ticklish for him because he jiggles about.

"Let's see what happens when we light you up," he says. He switches on the 'hers' half and pushes it underneath me so it cups around my form perfectly. The sensation is different from anything I've ever tried, not so unlike the shower head; intense, unrelenting. I slide further down his chest, back to my last position with my face resting on his erection and I begin to sweep the base of his cock with my tongue as vibrations massage my clit. I press another setting for me and it pulsates in waves. I look up at Alexandre and see him observing me, biting his lip as I run my tongue along his length. He simultaneously, from his half, must feel the vibrations on his balls.

"I need to see more of you, baby," he says sitting up, taking his half from me and switching it off. "We can do me another time. Right now, I want to concentrate on you. On your back."

"What?"

"Do as I say. Roll on your back."

He gets off the bed, pulls me by the legs so my butt is on the edge of the mattress. He grabs my ankles and hoists me up so they are resting on his shoulders. "Hook your pretty feet around my neck."

I do as he says. He's standing before me, a veritable vision of beauty; the Greek god again. That delightful V so prominent with the marble statues, but unlike their little fig leaf offerings I observe Alexandre's massive centerpiece, smooth and proud. His pecs flex as he maneuvers me into position. He wants to see all of me. I curl my toes about his neck and lift my arms above my head. The last time I did this he impregnated me, but now he brings the vibrator and presses it into its rightful position. It feels amazing – almost too intense. I buck back a touch and he gets the hint; he switches it down a notch and I'm writhing about – this feels great.

"Open your eyes, baby," he commands, and I do. I observe him, as with one hand he holds the gadget against me, and with the other he grips his cock. "In a minute, I'm going to come all over you." His index finger is massaging between my butt crack as he holds the Zini in place with his large hand. It's zapping my clit and vibrating at my entrance relentlessly. Meanwhile, I focus on his erection, tight in his fisted hand as he pleasures himself. I'm thrashing about, thrusting my hips at him, controlling the waves of pleasure by either pulling back a touch or grinding my hips forward.

"Lick your fingers and play with your nipples, Pearl." I do, and his hand works faster, jacking his cock with racing speed. I tug at my nipples and feel a rush of electricity shoot between my legs. Mixed with the intense vibrations, it feels amazing.

"I love watching you, so wet, so hot, so beautiful – when I fuck you, your pussy's so tight around my cock, your tits so sexy..." He presses another button and the rhythm changes to a pulse. I watch him grow even bigger, the crown swollen and full as his hand races up and down his thick length.

I push my hips forward and feel a spasm rip through the core of me. My legs are quivering like an out of control sewing machine. "I'm coming Alexandre."

"Me too," he shouts out. "Me too, chérie." Hot cum spurts out all over my stomach. Alexandre is still holding the Zini against me – it's too much, I want him to stop...but then..."Oh my God..." Another wave rolls over me and I realize that I'm climaxing again. My body jerks as if I've been electrocuted; my clit feels numb from the buzzing and he turns off the contraption. I slowly come down from my man-made orgasm and wonder if this little gadget could get addictive.

As if reading my thoughts, Alexandre says, "I can see I

might have competition. We'll have to keep this little minx of a machine under control." He kneels down below me and seals his mouth around my clit, pressing his tongue against me, hard and flat. I still feel the buzzing between my legs even though it's no longer there, like when you get off a boat and still feel yourself swaying. He flickers his tongue around my sensitive clit without touching it, and starts sucking hard. I can hardly believe it. Yet another spasm tingles through me and I climax again. This is insane.

"Alexandre, oh my….oh my God." He's growling into me like an animal eating its prey with his strong hands clinching my thighs apart, spreading my legs wide open. I'm shuddering as he lashes his tongue at my opening and I feel more contractions rolling through my core. All my energy has been stolen from my center as I slowly come down, moaning and whimpering like a dying person. There is nothing left of me. I am totally spent.

A wry smile spreads across my lips and I think about what I said to Daisy about multiple orgasms.

Sometimes God plays ironic tricks on you, and you have to laugh.

19

Even I have to admit, I looked beautiful today. It is St. Valentine's Day, the day of my wedding to Monsieur Alexandre Chevalier, also known as the knight in shining armor to a Pearl Robinson, now Pearl Chevalier.

Pearl Chevalier. Those two words roll off my tongue and take flight like tiny sparkles of snow-dust into the cool, Lapland atmosphere.

Pearl Chevalier.

All my wishes have come true and, as I look up at the sky above me and at the face of the man who is now my husband, I see that my wishes are *still* coming true every second.

Every millisecond is a moment to celebrate and cherish.

We are both transfixed by the swirls of color in the sky. I lean back in the open-air sled drawn by reindeer and nuzzle against Alexandre's shoulders. My feet are entwined with his as we gaze at the northern lights; nature's firework display. The sky looks like a pastel drawing that a giant has come along and smudged with his thumb. Blues and greens are dancing through the heavens in great twirls and whirls; ribbons of paler light ripple through the colors, creating surreal shapes and forms.

"Tell me why the colors are the way they are again, baby?" I ask my husband (how I love that word HUSBAND).

"Well as you know, the real name is Aurora Borealis. The northern lights are basically particles that are hurled into space after storms on the sun's surface. They're attracted by the magnetic North Pole, and the South Pole, and enter the atmosphere in a ring-like zone around the poles. We're incredibly lucky to see this spectacle; it's never guaranteed, you know."

"It's breathtakingly beautiful."

"*You* are breathtakingly beautiful," he tells me, his green eyes not so different in color from the northern lights. "You looked ravishing in your wedding gown earlier. Simply stunning. I have never seen a more beautiful bride."

A grin spreads across my happy face, proud that the day pattered along so flawlessly. We didn't need confetti because light snowflakes fluttered from the sky as everybody cheered. My white gown sparkled and shimmered. *I* sparkled and shimmered. Pearl, shimmering like my namesake.

Little Amy was clutching her basket of baby ivy and pink roses, and Elodie was holding my train, dressed in her Zang Toi gown, draped low at the back, also pink.

The ceremony was in a chapel made of ice and just our close friends and family were there to celebrate. They are still here enjoying the three-day party.

Alexandre's mother is not the dragon I imagined, at all.

She is charming. Tall and elegant and very quiet and unassuming. Alexandre's new video partner has come; he couldn't tear his gaze away from beautiful Elodie as she walked slowly behind me, making sure my gown was perfect. Amy's eyes were shining like an eager puppy, and Daisy looked on, mopping her tears. Even Sophie cried. Alexandre was right – she's not as tough as she pretends to be; she and I have a lot in common, after all.

My father looked so proud of me, and Zang Toi was also pleased with his creation, making sure that not a hair was out of place and that my gown was fit for a princess. I *was* a princess today. An ice princess. And Alexandre my prince. He was dressed in tails – he looked so chic, so elegant.

Alexandre's deep voice stirs me from my reverie. "How are those babies doing? Do you think they feel the colors of the northern lights?"

"I think they're swirling about in their own magical colors in there," I say patting my stomach.

"Well, I'm betting that our little boy and girl are feeling the vibe of happiness, no matter what."

"Monsieur Chevalier, the doctor said they couldn't be a *hundred* percent sure of their sex at this stage; that we needed to wait an extra week, or so."

"She said ninety percent, that's good enough for me. Anyway, my instinct tells me it's one of each. I'm never wrong. We have a girl and a boy cooking in that little oven of yours, I just know it."

"Is Louis still your number one boy's name?"

"I think Louis Chevalier sounds perfect, as long as Americans don't pronounce the S."

"Yes, I like Louis. It sounds quite regal, actually. Louis Chevalier...I love it. I can't decide between Angelique and

Madeleine. I think Madeleine because it works in both countries."

"In America and France, you mean?"

"Yes, of course; they *will* both grow up bilingual, I'll make sure of that. Madeleine. One of my favorite books as a child was *Madeline's Rescue* about the little girl and the dog Genevieve and their adventures in Paris. My mother used to read it to me over and over again."

"That was written by the artist Ludwig Bemelmans – there's a painted mural of his at The Carlyle Hotel."

"How funny. The Carlyle. I won't forget that in a hurry, when you stormed out on me during breakfast."

He throws his head back and laughs. "We've had our fair share of dramas, haven't we?"

"That's for sure. We've really put each other through the wringer."

He rests his hand on my thigh. "But here we are. To-gether. Married, till death do us part."

"And two little ones on the way." I breathe in the cool, crisp air. "Madeleine it is, then. I'll never forget how my heart broke in two that day. When you left me there, weep-ing into my linen napkin - everyone staring at me. That's when I realized how insanely in love with you I was. My whole world fell apart that day."

He grins. "Little did you know there was worse to come."

I raise an eyebrow. "And then I met Rex and I couldn't choose between you both. I have to say, you had real compe-tition there."

"Yes, Rex became quite the traitor."

"Because I had him on my side, in my heart of hearts, I knew that I'd win you back."

"You never lost me, chérie. I was yours from word Go. All yours. I always have been and I always will be." His words are sweet as music to my ears.

"It was like a fairytale today, wasn't it?" I say.

"It still *is* a fairytale. Look at that sky."

"Which reindeer is your favorite?"

"The pale one. The one with the soulful eyes," he says.

"I like the frisky one that tried to nip my bottom earlier. They look so cute with their white ribbons on their massive antlers. Wow, that was some ride sailing through the snow. We went so fast."

"And now we're doing it again." Alexandre tilts his head up to the sky. "What do you think they're all doing now?"

"The stars? The space people? The *Starman* waiting in the sky who'd like to come and meet us but he thinks he'd blow our minds?" I say quoting the David Bowie song.

He laughs. "No, our guests."

"Well, Daisy and Anthony were weeping. And drinking. I last saw them standing by the ice sculptures. Earlier, though, I did catch Daisy out of the corner of my eye flirting outrageously with my dad, so who knows what's going on. Or, they're probably telling embarrassing stories about us. Sophie and Alessandra had a midnight walk planned. Natalie and Miles will probably still be dancing." I laugh, conjuring up a picture of Anthony in his outlandish outfit. "How adorable did Ant look, squeezed into his pink suit? Oh my God, Alexandre! I forgot to tell you. Bruce proposed to him. While we were having the cake."

Alexandre licks his lips. *Those beautiful lips that I'm going to kiss later.* "Both of those cakes were out of this world."

"Weren't they?" I sigh with happiness. "This has been the most perfect wedding possible. The most beautiful day, ever."

"I have to admit, I'm glad we didn't get married in Vegas."

"What? Even though I escaped from you, clambered out of a toilet window and caused mayhem and heartbreak?"

"I caused you a fair share of heartbreak, as well, chérie. I think we're about even on that score."

"We made it, though."

"Yes, we did. We made it."

We are ensconced in our cozy, log cabin. There is a fire burning in the hearth. Outside, it is snowing lightly; a blanket of powdery white covers the ground and tops the pine trees.

I'm lying on the king size bed; nude, expectant and literally, feeling like a virgin on my wedding night. It *is* my wedding night. Alexandre hasn't been inside me for three months. My heart is in my stomach as it whips around in an eddy of emotions, twirling and swirling like the northern lights. I observe Alexandre, my husband, walking around the room naked, unwittingly parading his beautiful body. He is stoking the fire enjoying, perhaps, the latent fear that is mounting inside me. He must know how nervous I feel. The orange blaze of the fire glows on his golden torso; he bends down, his muscles rippling in his forearms and thighs.

I gaze at him, already moist between my legs, just imagining what he's going to do to me. He turns around, narrows his eyes and says, "You are so exquisite, Pearl." His legs are astride and I watch his erection flex into a hard rod. He's biting his lower lip without being aware that he's looking so predatory. A tingle of fearful adrenaline spikes me in my solar plexus.

"Do you have any idea how much I've been longing for this, Pearl?"

"I have a pretty good idea," I reply, blood pumping through me in a hot rush.

"Do you know what I want to do to you?"

The Big Bad Wolf, I think.

He saunters towards me slowly, standing above me as I lie there. His eyes trail up and down my body – just the thought of him has my nipples erect, but when he touches me, tingles shoot through me. He holds my chin in his hands, leans down and kisses me, parting my lips with his tongue; his glittering green eyes locking with mine, not leaving me for a second. "I want to kiss every inch of you. Your mine, Pearl, all mine." He straddles me, his strong thighs either side of my hips, his solid erection resting against my stomach. I grip onto his sinewy biceps, raise myself up a little to meet his lips once more, and I moan hungrily into his mouth.

"Please, Alexandre."

He inches his way down the mattress and I feel the tip of him resting on my clit, which is throbbing in anticipation. I begin to buck my hips at him in desperation. I need him inside me. He shifts his weight a touch and his soft crown rests at my entrance.

"You're so wet, baby. How I've missed this." He enters me just a millimeter and I cry out.

"Alexandre!"

"How does that feel?" he murmurs into my mouth.

"Incredible." I wriggle beneath him. "I want more."

"I know you do, and you bet I'm going to give it to you,

baby." He pushes himself an inch inside me, his mouth still on mine. "So juicy, so hot and ready for me."

"Ahh…" I groan, writhing under him.

He eases himself in further. "Are you okay? Is that too much?"

Are you kidding? "Please," I beg.

He groans and thrusts himself all the way in. "Oh, Pearl. Oh Pearl." He's stretching me, filling me slowly and I scream out. He circles his hips and pulls out a touch, waits a beat and then comes back down into me. I respond by grabbing his butt and thrusting myself at him.

"Alexandre."

He can't help it and nor can I. He's fucking me rhythmically now, and I rise up to meet each delicious plunge. I hook my feet around his ankles so he's in deep, and claw onto his butt tighter to control the pace. Each time he comes down on me I drive my hips forward, my clit rubbing hard against his pubic bone. I grasp his ass so tightly so our groins are united as one, and I freeze the movement so each time our centers meld, my clit slaps hard against him; tremors pulsating and ringing through me. He is thick and hard inside me, filling me on all sides, molded to my form.

"We were designed for each other, Pearl," he murmurs. "Made to fuck together. Forever and ever."

"Oh, baby, this feels so good."

His focus is just *me*. His forehead is on mine; his thrusts are making me delirious. His hands cup my ass possessively. We are locked together. He says, almost in a growl, "You. Are. All. Mine. This. All. Belongs. To. Me." Each thrust is punctuated by a word. "Love. Honor. And. Obey."

I want to laugh but maybe what he says isn't so silly, after all. Because on a hard plunge on 'obey' my inner fireworks explode – the northern lights of my core swirl and dance inside me like never before. I cry out in ecstasy and feel his hot release pounding through me, as his lips meld with mine.

"Yes, yes, *yes*," I scream into his mouth.

"What are you saying yes to, Pearl Chevalier?" he says on one last thrust.

"I swear to love, honor and obey you for the rest of my life."

"That's what I wanted to hear," and he kisses me again.

Epilogue

Eight months later.

The leaves have turned golden and the sun is lighting up a crisp, cobalt blue sky. Louis and Madeleine are dozing like two cherubic angels, their cheeks rosy and round, their eyelids fluttering into deep slumber, as I roll the twin stroller through the Ramble in Central Park. Rex is guarding the babies as if they were his very own, his ears pricked up expectantly, making sure no curious squirrels might leap upon them. I tilt my face up to the sky; the autumnal sun is shimmering in dappled shadows through the trees.

I love Central Park in fall - never more than now with my life being the way it is. Complete. Fulfilled. I am not here to stalk Rex, nor to run away from Alexandre. I am here as a mother to two beautiful, healthy babies, as a wife, and as a woman who has finally gained confidence in herself. I am enjoying my family, bathing in the caress of their unconditional love and a heartening sense of finality.

This is it. I have arrived. I am here.

Out of the corner of my eye I sense Alexandre watching me. I'm lapping up the sun's gentle, warm rays but I can feel the intensity of his peridot-green eyes upon me, his gaze focused - he probably wants to know what thoughts are flitting through my mind.

"What are you staring at?" I murmur softly without looking at him.

I can hear the smile in his voice when he answers, "How do you know what I'm doing?"

"Because that's what happens with husbands and wives; they get to read each other, even with their eyes half closed."

"What are you thinking about, Pearl, with that serene look on your face and that satisfied smile?"

I laugh.

"No really, what's going on in that pretty head of yours?"

A bird swoops above me and some leaves drop to the ground like golden confetti. "I was wondering when you'd ask me what I was thinking," I reply.

"Come on!"

"I'm not kidding."

I hear him sigh with contentment and he links his arm with mine. "You want to know what *I* was thinking?" he asks.

"Maybe about what we're going to have for dinner, even though we've just had lunch," I tease, knowing how he and his family are forever discussing *haute cuisine* recipes. He's been cooking up a storm lately, impressing me with his gourmet meals. I cock my head to see his reaction. His eyes glitter with amusement – a man who knows how to laugh at himself; one of the many reasons I fell in love with him.

He squeezes my arm. "Actually, no. Although I have to admit that did pass through my mind ten minutes ago. I was just going over the events in my head...you know, everything that led us here; all the trials we put each other through. I still wouldn't have had it any other way, though." He pauses, then adds. "Okay, perhaps a few less hours of labor pains for you would have been a bonus. But still, we've been rewarded nicely."

"We really are lucky." I stop walking for a minute and look at him. A little lurch causes my stomach to flip as if I've just set eyes on him for the first time. "Funny. I'd forgotten all about that, the labor pains. I think women are programmed to have a sort of amnesia after birth because I was just remembering how smoothly it all went, how effortless." I lean down to check the babies and tuck the soft blankets about their tiny, alabaster necks. "Madeleine's developing your dimple, Alexandre."

My husband's lips curve up and the dimple in his cheek confirms my observation. "I was just thinking how much like *you* she is, chérie."

"Like me? But her hair's dark. She even has your French pout. No, she's you in a nutshell."

"In character, I mean. She's a little indecisive."

"Give her a chance, she's only a month old." I frown. "Am I indecisive?"

He winks at me. "Hard to catch. You weren't easy to convince."

I love the fact that he sees me as having been hard to catch when I was so obviously *his* right from the second I set eyes on him in the coffee shop. I say nothing, although a tiny smirk sneaks its way onto my lips. I am unashamedly happy – the cat with all the cream. Double-cream, no less.

Alexandre turns to face me and folds me in his arms. I lean my head on his shoulder and feel the slow steady beat of his heart.

Madeleine makes a little murmur but then falls back into a deep sleep. I observe Rex who looks at her and then at Louis. Finally, his wide, black head checks up with us for approval. This is my family, dog and all. We are a team.

Team Pearl.

As if reading my mind, Alexandre says, "We're in this for the long haul. Are you ready for the ride, chérie?"

I hesitate for a minute and ask myself, am I really equipped for this, to be a good mother to my children, keep my autonomy as an independent career woman who can hold her own and also be a loving wife to a man as head-strong as Alexandre? Yes, I think. I *am* ready and more than capable. I have come a long way in the last nine months. Life is not about me anymore. It's about us.

I reply, "Am I ready for the ride, chéri? You bet I am."

Pearl and Alexandre's story continues...

A note from Arianne:

After I had finished *The Pearl Trilogy* (*Shades of Pearl*, *Shadows of Pearl*, and *Shimmers of Pearl*) I found Alexandre literally talking to me! He was keen to have his side of the story told. At first I ignored him, but as you know he's an insistent man so I started writing *Pearl*. It was so much longer than I imagined it would be and, so as not to make my readers wait, I had to split his story into two parts: *Pearl*, and then, *Belle Pearl*. As well as having a lot of questions explained in these novels, you find out a lot about Alexandre's past, learn about Elodie and Sophie, and are party to scenes that Pearl had *no* idea about in the trilogy.

Pearl starts off when they meet in the coffee shop, and *Belle Pearl* takes you beyond *Shimmers of Pearl* into the future, so has a different ending.

I had great fun writing *Pearl*, and *Belle Pearl*, creating many scenes and new characters that you do not get to see in *The Pearl Trilogy*. I worked hard to make sure that Alexandre's POV was not merely the same story told over. I wanted to give the feel of a new book with completely fresh scenes and a totally different voice (Alexandre's). The conversations between Alexandre and Pearl are worded differently on purpose.

Save by purchasing both books.

The Pearl Trilogy Playlists

Shades of Pearl Playlist

Pierre Bachelet and Herve Roy - Emmanuelle

Come To Me High - Rumor

Air - Bach

Under My Thumb - The Rolling Stones

Gymnopédie No.1 - Erik Satie

At Last - Etta James

Prelude in E-Minor - Frédéric Chopin

Black Cherry - Goldfrapp

Nothing Compares 2U - Sinead O'Connor (written by Prince)

Black Coffee - Julie London

Sex Machine - James Brown

Is This Love? - Bob Marley

What A Wonderful World - Louis Armstrong

Crazy For You - Madonna

Mrs. Robinson - Simon and Garfunkel

If I Were A Boy - Beyonce

You're So Vain - Carly Simon

Je T'Aime Moi Non Plus - Jane Birkin et Serge Gainsbourg

To listen to the Shades of Pearl soundtrack:

http://ariannerichmonde.com/music/forty-shades-of-pearl-sound-track/

Shadows of Pearl Playlist

Lullaby - Brahms

Autumn in New York - Sarah Vaughn

Hotel California - The Eagles

Surfin' USA - The Beach Boys

Woman - Neneh Cherry

Witchcraft - Frank Sinatra

I Kissed a Girl and I Liked It - Katy Perry

Leaving on a Jet Plane - John Denver (Sung by Chantal Kreviazuk)

She's a Rainbow - The Rolling Stones

Foolin' Myself - Billie Holiday

To listen to the Shadows of Pearl soundtrack:
http://ariannerichmonde.com/music/shadows-of-pearl-of-pearl-sound-track/

Shimmers of Pearl Playlist

Sweet Dreams - Patsy Cline

I Will Survive - Gloria Gaynor

Ben - Michael Jackson

Little Things - One Direction

Nobody Does It Better - Carly Simon

Mon Ami - Kim

Here Comes The Sun - The Beatles

Non, Je ne Regrette Rien - Edith Piaf

Young At Heart - Frank Sinatra

Starman - David Bowie

To listen to the Shimmers of Pearl soundtrack
http://ariannerichmonde.com/music/shimmers-of-pearl-sound-track/

Sign up (ariannerichmonde.com/email-signup/) to be informed the minute any future Arianne Richmonde releases, go live. Your details are private and will not be shared with anyone. You can unsubscribe at any time.

The Pearl series:

The Pearl Trilogy bundle (the first three books in one e-box set)

Shades of Pearl
Shadows of Pearl
Shimmers of Pearl
Pearl
Belle Pearl
Pearl & Belle Pearl (a 6 x 9 match for The Pearl Trilogy)

I have also written *Glass*, a short story.

Join me on Facebook
(facebook.com/AuthorArianneRichmonde)

Join me on Twitter
(@A_Richmonde)

For more information about me, visit my website
(www.ariannerichmonde.com).

If you would like to email me:
ariannerichmonde@gmail.com

Teaser for *Pearl*

It was raining in New York City. The sort of rain that felt vaguely tropical because it was summertime and the muggy heat was broken by a glorious downfall. Very welcome, because my sister and I had just given a talk at an I.T. conference and she was feeling hot and bothered—really getting on my case.

The rain eased the tension.

Sophie was driving me nuts that day. It wasn't easy going into business with a sibling, but if it hadn't been for her shrewd business savvy, I wouldn't have had the same luck. Sophie inhaled HookedUp. Exhaled HookedUp. Being as obsessed with money as she was, she wouldn't rest until we'd practically taken over the world. And, as everyone now knows, social media really *has* taken over the world so she was onto something big. Clever woman.

Sophie had moved our conference talk forward by an hour because she was in a foul mood—wanted to get it over and done with—get the hell out of there. I, on the other hand, felt bound by some odd sense of duty to share our success story; inspire people to jump into the deep end as we had done. To go for it.

At the conference, someone in the audience asked me how I would describe myself and I replied: "I'm just a nerd who found programming fascinating. With a keen eye for patterns and codes, I pushed it to the limit and got rich. I'm a lucky geek, that's all." People laughed as if what I said was a silly joke. But I meant it.

I'm still not used to being a billionaire. Even now, if I ever see an article written about the power of social media and HookedUp, it's as if I'm taking a glimpse into someone else's life; a driven, ambitious, 'ruthless businessman' (as I've often been described), when I'm still just a guy who likes surfing, rock climbing and hanging out with his family and dogs. Just an ordinary man. Others don't perceive me that way—at all. I suppose I should be flattered by their attention, although I'm a private man and hate the limelight.

I took a chance, worked hard, and got lucky. A Frenchman living the American Dream.

That's what I love about American culture. Everybody gets a shot if you get off your ass and have the will to succeed. Not so in France. It's hard to break away from the mold; people don't like to see others rise above their station. Maybe I'm being hard on my country, judgmental, but all I know is if I'd stayed there, HookedUp wouldn't be the megapower it is today. Not even close. The USA has given us all we have and I'm grateful, even though having this much money still feels sinful at my age. Or any age, for that matter.

Funny how Fate pans out; you never know what life has in store for you.

I nearly didn't go into the coffee shop that day. Sophie needed a shot of caffeine and I really wasn't in the mood to argue, so we dashed in from the rain and stood in line.

Our conversation had been heated, to say the least. We'd been discussing the HookedUp meeting we had scheduled in Mumbai in a couple of weeks time. It was a mega-deal that she'd been feverishly working on all year. I didn't think HookedUp could get any more global and powerful than it already was, but I was wrong. That deal was going to make us silly money. Really silly money. I knew I was going to be able to buy that Austin Healey I had my eye on. Hell, I could have bought a fleet of them. Aircrafts too. Whatever I wanted.

Sophie took out her Smartphone from her Chanel purse and said in French—her voice low so that nobody would overhear, "Look, Alexandre, this is the guy we're meeting in Mumbai." She scrolled down to a photo of a portly man with a handlebar mustache. "This is the son of a bitch who's squeezing us for every dime. He's our enemy. He's the one we need to watch."

"But I thought you said he's the one we're signing with—"

"He is," she interrupted. "Keep your enemies close." She brushed her dark hair away from her face and narrowed her eyes with suspicion—a habit I had myself. I remember thinking how elegant and beautiful she looked; yet in 'predator mood,' she was also formidable. I was glad to have her on my side.

Half listening to my sister gabble on about the Mumbai deal, I noticed a woman rush through the door—a whirlwind of an entrance. She was flustered, her blonde hair damp from the summer rain, her white T-shirt also damp, clinging to her body, revealing a glimpse of perfectly shaped breasts through a thin bra. I shouldn't have noticed these sorts of things, but being your average guy, I did. She was battling with an enormous handbag—what was it with women and those giant handbags? What did they carry in those things—bricks?

"Arrête!" Sophie snapped and proceeded for the next couple of minutes to berate me for not paying attention. She was rolling her eyes and puffing out air disapprovingly. Ignoring her, I wondered, again, why I had gone into business with her because she was really bugging me. She added, "If you want to fuck that girl you're staring at, you can you know—American women put out on the first date."

I hated it when my sister talked like that to me—it made me cringe—especially her sweeping generalizations about other countries and civilizations.

"She doesn't strike me as that type," I mumbled back in French. The pretty lady was now closer and I couldn't take my eyes off her. She had her head cocked sideways and was staring at the coffee menu, chewing her lower lip in concentration. She was beautiful, like a modern version of Grace Kelly—she looked about thirty or so.

My eyes raked down her perfectly formed body. She was dressed in a tight, gray skirt which accentuated her peachy butt. The slit on the pleat revealed a pair of elegant calves, but her chic outfit was marred by sneakers. Somehow, it made her all the more attractive as if she didn't give a damn. As my gaze trailed back up to her breasts, I saw that she was wearing an *InterWorld* button. *Good,* I thought, *we have something in common—I can chat her up.*

I cleared my throat and moved a step closer. "So how did you enjoy the conference?"

She jumped back in surprise; her eyes fixed on my chest. I felt as if I was towering above her, although she was a good five foot six. I looked a mess—T-shirt and old jeans with holes in the knee. So far, she was not responding. I knew that New Yorkers could be just as rude as Parisians so I wasn't fazed.

She flicked her gaze at me but said nothing. I was right—she hadn't answered my question, just continued to look at me; stunned, as if she really didn't want to have a conversation at all.

I smiled at her. I felt like a jerk, but dug myself in deeper. "Your name tag," I said. "Were you at that conference around the corner?" I decided that she obviously thought I was a total jackass as her response was clipped, terse.

"Yes I was," is all she said and then cast a glance at Sophie.

I realized that this woman—her nametag said **Pearl Robinson**—must have assumed that Sophie was my girlfriend—the perils of hanging out with my beautiful sister. Or maybe Pearl Robinson wasn't smiling simply because she wanted me to shut the hell up and leave her alone.

But I didn't back off. "I'll pay for whatever the lady's having, too," I told the girl serving our coffee. I wanted to say, 'Whatever Pearl's having' but thought that Pearl would peg me for some kind of stalker. Why I continued to pursue her I wasn't sure, since she was clearly not interested. But I couldn't help myself. "For Pearl," I added, wondering why I was not getting the response I was after. Not to be arrogant, but women did normally smile at me, if not give me the eye. They still do. Daily. But Pearl was not buying it. I wanted her to flirt, brighten up my dull day.

I went on, undeterred—for some reason I didn't feel like giving up; she had really piqued my interest. "Pearl. What a beautiful name." *Jesus what did I sound like? A typical French gigolo type, no doubt.* "I've never heard that before. As a name, I mean."

In my peripheral vision, I caught Sophie rolling her eyes, again, and she whispered in French, "Bet you anything you'll have that woman on her back in no time." *Shut up!*

Pearl Robinson finally reciprocated with a beautiful big smile. *Nice.* Pretty teeth. Sexy, curvy lips. She told me about her parents being hippies or something—explaining her name. I wasn't listening. I'd got her attention, that's all I cared about. I could tell she liked me. *Took long enough for her to warm up, though—all of forty seconds.* I felt triumphant. Why? I met pretty women all the time. But there was something about this one that really captured my attention. She was poised and elegant, yet unsure of herself. There was a childish, vulnerable quality about her which I found disarming, even beguiling. She was rifling through her enormous handbag, trying to find her wallet. Why are American women so keen on paying for themselves? Was she embarrassed because I was buying her a coffee?

"What's your name?" she asked, while simultaneously staring at my nametag.

Good…ironic sense of humor, I thought. I laughed and introduced myself. Introduced Sophie, too.

Pearl went to shake Sophie's hand and her wristwatch caught on my T-shirt. I looked down at her other hand. No wedding ring. *Good.* I felt my heart quicken with the physical contact of her delicate wrist brushing against my chest—the intimacy—and I knew….in that nanosecond, I knew; I was going to have to fuck this girl.

The way she was looking at me was giving me the green light. Yet her big blue eyes were unsure of me. She looked down at the floor, and then up again at me. She may not have even known it herself at that point—women rarely do—but she wanted me to claim her. I could almost hear her screaming my name. I pictured myself pinning her up against a wall, all of me inside her.

I wanted her. And I was going to have her. You bet. Every last inch of her.

"Remember to use protection," Sophie whispered in French, "she may look like an nice Upper East side WASP, but you never know."

I retorted, also in French. "Get your coffee, or whatever you're drinking, and *leave* because I've had enough of your snippy conversation for one day."

Sophie cocked her eyebrow at me and smirked. I turned my attention back to Pearl Robinson and prayed that her French was limited or non-existent. I gazed at her, right into her clear blue eyes. *Yes*, I decided, *I want this woman.*

And she wanted me. I was pretty damn sure. She was jittery, nervous, tongue-tied—couldn't get her sentences out straight. Why? Because I was running my eyes up and down her body, mentally undressing her, and she could sense the electricity. The heat. She was all flustered. She could read my mind. She was fumbling for something in her monster-bag again. Her apartment keys, she told me. Was she planning on inviting me over?

"Nice to meet you, Pearl," Sophie said, giving her the once-over. "Maybe see you around some time?" The innuendo was so thick you could have cut it with a machete.

Sophie sashayed out of the coffee shop and I exhaled with relief. *Thank God, now I can get down to business. Real business.*

"I got the drinks to go, but do you want to sit down?" I suggested to Pearl. She nodded.

Why I was so taken with this New Yorker, apart from her obvious good looks, I wasn't quite sure—she had a quirky kind of charm. I liked her. And I decided right there and then—I didn't just want to fuck Pearl, I wanted to get to know her, too.

She eased her way into an armchair but was unsure whether to cross or uncross her legs. Like a schoolboy, I found my eyes wandering to her crotch and imagining what lay beneath, but she was too demure for that. Her legs crossed closed, and she smoothed that sexy pencil skirt over her thighs. I thought about fucking her again—I couldn't stop myself. I wondered if what Sophie said was true: that Pearl would put out on a first date. I'd have to find out....

We were interrupted by a phone call from my assistant, Jim, telling me to snap up the Austin Healy I'd had my eye on—they'd accepted my offer. So the conversation with Pearl swung around to cars. I felt like a jerk. I knew what women were like; feigning interest about bits of machinery when they really couldn't give a damn. Pearl was no different. Still, she did a good job of pretending. She nodded and smiled and widened her pretty eyes. Meanwhile, I had one thing on my mind: to get her into the sack ASAP.

But then she took me off guard. She started talking about re-runs of old sitcoms, classic novels, and old songs and I began to think we had something in common besides physical attraction. Then, when I mentioned my black Labrador, Rex, that was it. I began to mentally tuck my tackle back into my pants, so to speak, because she admitted that she was crazy for dogs, too. She loved the fact that I could take Rex to restaurants in Paris and a flash of our future ran before my eyes. I swear. I had a vision of us together eating something delicious, Rex at our side, and something told me that Pearl and I would make the grade. It does sound crazy, that. Call it a premonition—I think it was.

She was telling me about her childhood Husky.

"My dog was called Zelda," she said, her liquid eyes flashing with happy memories.

"Like Zelda Fitzgerald?" I asked. "Scott Fitzgerald's wife?"

She looked up at me, surprised. "Yeah, you know about her?"

"Of course I do. She was a little bit crazy, wasn't she? *The Great Gatsby* was partly inspired by her."

"Well, like Zelda Fitzgerald, our Zelda was a little out to lunch. I mean, literally. She loved chickens. Went on several murderous escapades."

"The way you say that with a little smile on your face makes me believe you didn't have much sympathy for the innocent, victimized chickens," I teased.

"They were going to be slaughtered anyway, poor things." She put her hand on her mouth as if she'd put her foot in it. "Sorry, Alexandre, are you a vegetarian?"

I loved the way she said *Alexandre* with her cute American accent, trying to accentuate the *re*. "No, you?"

"No red meat. Only organic chicken. I know…kind of ironic considering what Zelda did. I do have a conscience— I'm against intensive farming, you know, animals spending their lives in tiny cages, so small they can't even turn around. Cows being forced to eat grain, not grass—being pumped full of antibiotics. People don't like inviting me to dinner. I'm a tricky customer."

"Not for me, you're not," I found myself saying. "I'd be delighted if you came for dinner. I'll cook you something wonderful." I narrowed my eyes at her. Fuck she was sexy.

Her eyes, in return, widened and her lips clamped around her straw, as she sipped her iced cappuccino, seductively. Jesus, I felt my cock harden watching her mouth. I shifted in my seat and leaned forward to hide my bulge. As I leaned down, I let my hand brush against her golden calf. Smooth, soft legs. *Nice.* This unexpected coffee date was getting too hot to handle so I tried to turn the conversation around to stop myself from mentally undressing her. She got there first, asking me why I chose to live in New York.

"France is a great country," I began. "Beautiful. Just beautiful. Fine wine, great cuisine, incredible landscape—we really do have a rich culture. But when it comes to opportunity, especially for small businesses, it's not so easy there."

"You own a small company? What do you do?"

Interesting. This woman has no idea who I am. Refreshing. She won't be after my money—she doesn't have an agenda. Good.

"That's why I was at that conference," I explained.

I expanded a bit, gave her the usual blab about 'giving back,' and how I liked to share a few tricks of the trade with others.

"And you?" I asked, wondering what the hell this unlikely sexpot was doing at an I.T. conference. She so didn't look the type. "What were *you* doing there?"

She flushed a little, slid down into her chair as if she wanted to disappear and shifted her gaze to her feet. She looked acutely embarrassed. Maybe she had a very boring job, I reasoned, and didn't want to spoil the mood. I dropped the subject. So we brought the conversation back to me again, and she *had* heard of HookedUp, after all. Of course she had. Who hadn't? Everyone and his cousin hooked up with HookedUp, even married couples. But Pearl didn't seem particularly impressed by me, even when I let it slip that I was the CEO.

"So when you're not working or zipping about in your beautiful classic cars, or hanging out with Rex, what do you do to relax?"

"I rock-climb," I replied, already having planned in my head that rock climbing would be the perfect first date for us. Not too 'date-like,' not typical—she'd go for it.

"Oh yeah? I swim. Nearly every day. It's what keeps me sane."

Ah, so that accounts for her tight peachy ass and sculpted legs. We discussed the benefit of sports—how it was good for one's mental state of mind as well as keeping your body fit. This woman had me intrigued. I was getting more than a hard-on talking to her. She made me laugh. She was bright, opinionated. Had read the classics, loved dogs and sure, I couldn't deny it, she had a body like a pin-up and the face of an angel. Besides, with all her straw-sucking, I knew what was going through her mind. She wanted to see me with my shirt off. Yes, damn it, I could tell. She couldn't take her eyes off my chest. She even licked her luscious lips while she was ogling me, and then said—her eyes all baby-doll...all come-and-fuck-me-now:

"I tried rock climbing once. I was terrified but I could really understand the attraction to the sport."

On the word, *attraction,* I swear to God, she looked at my chest, then my groin, and back again to my chest before she finally fastened her gaze on my face. Oh yeah, believe me, I knew what was going on in Pearl's mind. Her smart attire, educated voice and expensive handbag didn't fool me. Still, her come-on would have been imperceptible to an un-trained eye—not slutty, not over-flirtatious...just a split second of wanton lust on her part, which I bet she thought I hadn't clocked onto.

But...Miss Pearl Robinson, daughter of hippies, lover of dogs, quasi-vegetarian temptress....I had your number.

I knew everything there was to know—instinctively.

I wanted her quirky ass and I was going to have it. And everything that went with it, too. All of it. I was going to put my mark on that peachy butt.

I presumed I had her all worked out. Clever me.

Little did I know that I was dead wrong.

Things weren't going to be quite so simple.

If you would like to continue with books four and five of The Pearl Series, the paperback of the pair of books together, **Pearl & Belle Pearl** is especially designed as a match for *The Pearl Trilogy* and comes in the same size (6 x 9). It is also more economical to buy **Pearl & Belle Pearl** as one paperback than the two books individually.